LUCIE CHIHANDAE

The World Is Ours

A Novel

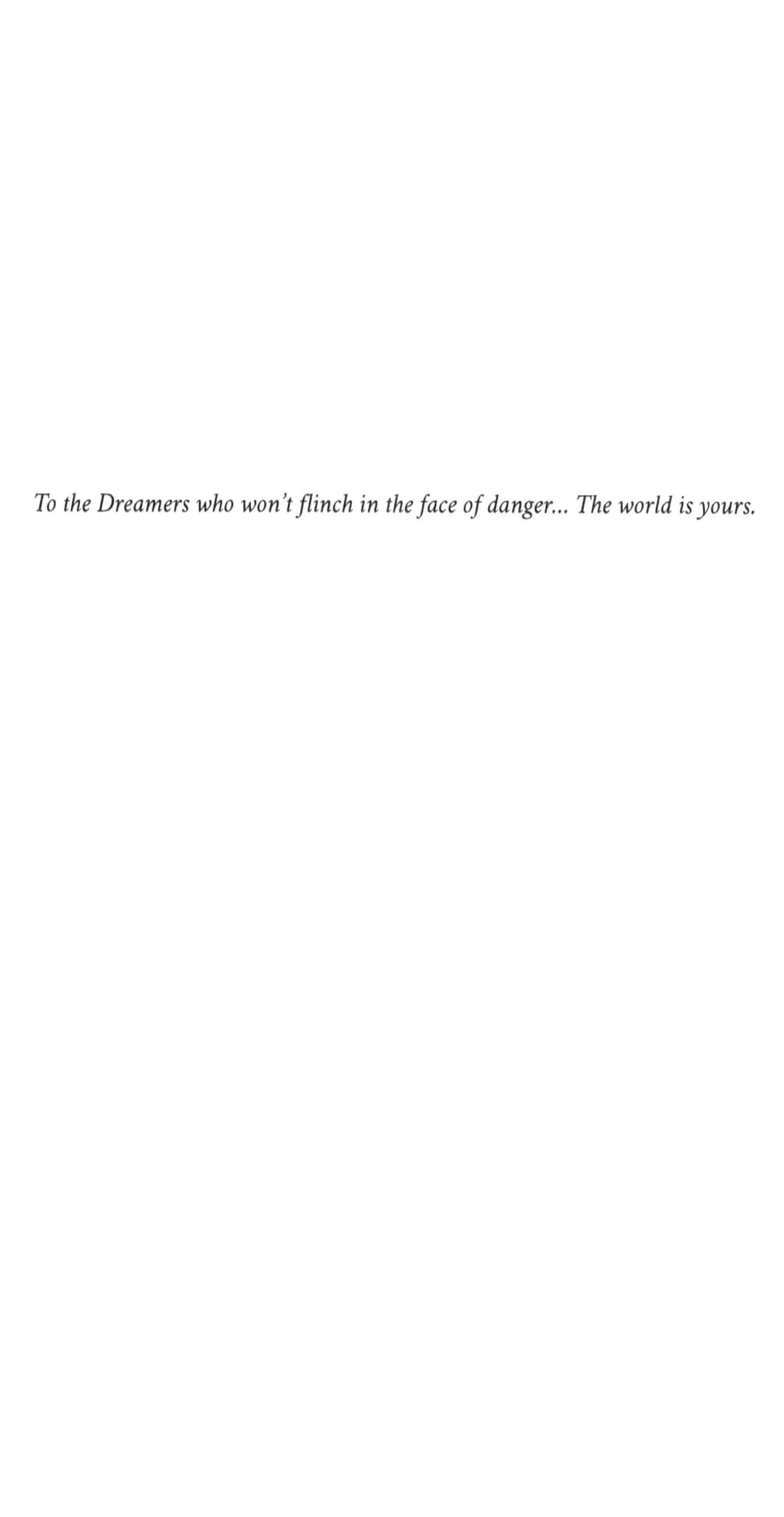

To the Dreamers who won't flinch in the face of danger... The world is yours.

Acknowledgement

I would like to thank every single person who has been with me on this journey to writing The World Is Ours.

My sisters, Dorothie and Flavia, got this ball rolling by unlocking my brain to pen the several pages and chapters you are about to indulge in.

Dorothie Ayebazibwe; Without your guidance, meticulousness in editing this manuscript, The World is Ours would not be as compelling.

Musa Noor, who would have helped me out with naughty Somali phrases, but you?

When I needed information on mineral trade, that information came to me miraculously from my dear friend Nancy Mugimba, her husband Chris, and business partner Pamela who sent me tons of information on the gruelling process of mining to buying to selling (phew!)

I am completely indebted to my Kenyan connections for the morsels of information you provided; For simply taking the time to talk about Kenya in the eighties and early nineties, your contribution was so so valuable!

My advanced Review Readers , real MVP's !

The folks with the pompoms; Usher Komugisha with invaluable linguistic skill, Peter Musaye, Daudi Kibalama, Charlotte Bossa (bestie!) and several high school friends who made my writing popular back then.

Above all, God, who has given me the gift to tell stories. I'm humbled. It has been an exciting journey. I hope you enjoy the results.

PROLOGUE

October 2016
Sheraton Hotel, Kampala

The cell phone rang twice before the caramel beauty at the corner of the luminous café picked it up.

"*Sasa*, is she here?" she demanded into the mouthpiece, her voice a sultry, deep symphony; a thumb running across each glittery acrylic nail on her free hand.

"Not yet, but she is close." The other voice, male and layered thick with pork lard and beer, wheezed into her ear.

"You need to exercise, *macaan*," she drawled and heard him grunt in response. Her thumb continued its mindless caress over the nail beds, occasionally lingering over the gritty texture of fresh manicure. She raised her delicate chin and shook her well-coiffed head, a thick mane braided and intertwined, then piled on top of her head with cascading ringlets of ombre enhancing the fine lines of her lean oval face. Her thick, long lashes fanned her eyes in deliberate grace as they surveyed the café seating, catching the eye of another diner—male, foreign, *probably Middle Eastern*—and she smiled faintly, then looked away.

Don't be too forward, she cautioned herself. Men, from her experience, are drawn to a woman who seems uninterested in them; it excites them.

"How close?" She returned to the conversation she was having, as if from sheer boredom.

"Tomorrow close," the fat man replied nervously.

Her rich, burgundy-painted lips parted in a jubilant smile.

"I told you *it* would work." She was suddenly alert.

"Hmm." The man fell silent on the other end of the line. This was awkward for him, and his guilt crept up over the airwaves to her ears. She shrugged it off. He needed to toughen up, she thought in irritation.

"*Asante, macaan,*" she cooed a mix of Swahili and Somali into the mouthpiece like the wind gently straightening out a folded piece of garment on the washing line. Her voice was as bewitching as she was, the fat man thought nervously. Only the effect was fleeting this time, lingering just to comfort him but not enough to erase the guilt.

"Okay, bye," he snapped.

She sensed his haste to get off the phone. She could not blame him but did not care.

Her gaze glided over the familiar off-white and espresso furnishings in the restaurant again, aware of the male diner's dark, wanton eyes on her. She dropped her eyes seductively and sipped from her cup of African tea; a slight sweep of her loose curls here, her hand lingering on the side of her neck there, aware of her effect, keeping him fixated on parts of her she wanted him to see. She counted to ten slowly under her breath, "*kow...laba...saddex...afar...shan....lix...toddoba...siddeed...sagaal... toban...*" and, from the corner of her eye, saw him get up hesitantly, possibly deciding how best to approach her. A ghost of a jubilant smile quickly flashed across her lips.

Works every time, she mused.

The caramel vixen observed him, calculatedly, and when he made the move toward her, her inner goddess gyrated.

I still got it! Her fingers brushed up the bridge of her neck absently where the creases of age showed.

About time I did something about these, she muttered to herself. *I'm too beautiful to grow old.*

Lately, she had been obsessing over the idea of plastic surgery and Botox. Just the night before, she had cringed in dismay at how many varicose veins snaked across her thighs. Cocoa butter was not doing much to erase the stretch marks around her breasts either. Instead, it tanned the caramel-soft flesh to a mocha brown she detested. The only solution to that glowing youth rested in the expensive hands of technology. Surgery!

Maybe then she would not have to count to ten in anticipation of male attention. They would simply fall at her feet and worship her as they did so many years ago. The urgency for this magical alteration clawed at her year after year. But she could not just keep dreaming about it. She had to do it *now*.

She cleared her throat and swiped a pampered finger over the screen of her phone, unlocking it. It opened to her Instagram app, where, for the umpteenth time that week, she scrolled through the pictures of the young ebony-skinned model with arresting aquamarine eyes.

BOOK 1

Ameena
1985–1992

The Somali have told the fascinating tale of a beautiful brave queen, Elba Awad, known famously as Araweelo. They have recounted her adventures to their daughters and whispered it in song in their secret chambers as they strengthened each other, woman to woman. They mutter it in prayer over their little girls, that they would rise, tough and bold, like the courageous queen who defied tradition to liberate women and give them a voice and purpose.

"We are more accommodating, more peaceful, and more practical than men."
—Queen Araweelo

Chapter 1

August 1985

Sex.

It was all Ameena could think of from the first time she experienced the unfamiliar but delicious waves of arousal. Urgent strokes of exciting pleasure knit seamlessly together as she lay in the lean cocoa arms of Hassan, her father's turnboy. There was nothing more indulgently addictive than it, and from her first experience, she was hooked.

She lay on her back, closed her eyes, and fantasized about Hassan, his warm touch, the feral grunts he emitted as he plunged into her again and again. Ameena pressed her knees together. A wildfire, which shocked and thrilled her, spread between her thighs.

A magazine lay open by her bed.

A secret stash she shared with the girls at school. They enjoyed ogling at the women dressed in low-cut, revealing clothing. They fancied the white and brown men with well-defined bodies that disorganized the hormones of thirteen-year-old schoolgirls.

Things were different in her community that revered modesty and privacy above all else. She envied her classmates, who freely talked about sex with one another and never wore a hijab.

She wanted to be those Muslim girls who wore colorful *baatis* her father would frown upon.

Most of all, she longed to see the outside world, the one in the forbidden magazines and newspapers she browsed through behind the school art room during break time.

School taught her a lot but not about sex, like Hassan did. Her favorite pastime was indulging in endless surreptitious conversations with her friends during the school break time at the far end of the school playground.

They talked about boys -as they cast glances at the half-naked teenage boys competitively playing a ruleless game of soccer- about sex and about *firaun:*

"Is it painful?"

"Hooyo does not remember..."

"Every girl must do it. Or we don't get husbands..."

"It's our sign of purity..."

"We won't be cursed..."

"But why? Aren't we born pure?" She would ask and the girls would look at her blankly. No one knew the answer, but they knew firaun was the ticket to being a respectable wife in the small tight-knit community composed of Somalis who fled their own country.

Firaun, the rite of passage to womanhood, fascinated her. It was six months since her first menstrual flow, and she had still not undergone the knife as her friends had. She was abashedly aware of the gossip that rippled through the little Somali community that her mother, Bushra, had strongly dismissed the idea.

"Ameena!" the sharp voice of her mother called to her as she yanked her bedroom door open. *"Kaalay!* The food won't get cooked by itself. Tonight is a big night!"

"Coming, *hooyo,"* she answered as she hastily stashed the magazine under her thin mattress and scrambled from the bed.

"Dhaqso! Araweelo was not lazy!" Her mother's voice carried to her as she retreated to the kitchen.

Ameena smiled to herself; she loved it when her mother referred to her as Araweelo. It also meant she was not *that* furious with her.

Brave, strong Queen Araweelo.

Ameena brushed her hair back and, with practiced skill, replaced her hijab over her head. She wondered what the fuss was. Her father had returned from Dodoma only two days ago.

Two days after her forbidden indulgence with Hassan.

Annoyed at being roused from her daydream, she shuffled to the kitchen that extended to the outdoor compound.

"Come, come!" Her mother was summoning her to help stir an enormous pot.

"Who is coming?" she asked, laboring to keep the irritation in her voice to a minimum.

"Faraax." The name trembled out of her mother.

Ameena groaned. "That old frog?"

She wrinkled her nose, recalling the pungent smell of spice and coffee on him, his willowy frame and high-pitched voice. How his spaced teeth lent him a comical look when he roared in contented laughter during dinner. A man so old and bent, he looked like he had no life left in his limbs. And yet she was uncomfortably aware of how his sharp eyes blazed with a bright light, stalking her movements when he visited.

Being as wealthy and as revered as he was in the little Somali communities clustered in northeast Kenya and eastern Uganda, there was always fanfare when he visited. Faraax, who was as generous with his wealth as he was ugly, was among the Somalis that escaped the unstable Ogaden region in the 1970s. He was her father's oldest and closest friend. Their friendship had weathered the times. Faraax had watched her grow up. She knew this because he mentioned it often when she served him on these occasional visits.

"*That old frog* is the man your *aabe* has decided will make a good husband for you...after you undergo the knife." Bushra did not look at her daughter.

Ameena's eyes widened. The shock of her mother's words jolted her violently.

* * *

Ameena was still shrouded in shock as their compound slowly filled with guests. Women came from the neighborhood with food for the feast. Everyone had heard that Faraax Sabunduur Mohammed was coming. Their compound was the biggest and could take up to thirty men comfortably. The women would sit indoors with the children stretching from their kitchen to the living room. It always got stuffy inside, and lighting fragrant incense never dispelled the powerful body odor and aromatic food flavors that clogged the atmosphere. It just amplified them.

Ameena waited for her father at the front entrance of the veranda. She was certain to see him in the company of several men as they milled to the courtyard. She wanted to look him in the face and ask, *Why?* or at least let her eyes speak for her if courage failed.

Questioning her father was something she would never dare to do outright. The thought of being Faraax's wife after her sumptuous affair with Hassan sounded like a nightmare. She *could not* do it. She *would not* do it!

Ameena did not need to be told her father had arrived. It was in the way her mother fussed, telling her to hurry with the *sabaayad.* Was the *surbiyaan hilib adhi* still warm? And Aabe's *maraq digaag* was lacking in carrots. Hadn't she asked her to add more? Could she help Zahir with the pan of *suugo suqaar;* it was specially made for Faraax…and on and on it went, from main dishes to desserts to snacks. Ameena snacked on a banana silently as the procession of men filed into the compound with accompanying jesting and conversation.

She picked up the enormous platter laden with *kac kac,* sweet bananas, and *samosas* and proceeded to the center of the compound, where the men assembled in a semicircle, leaving enough passageway for the women to ferry food from the kitchen. In the center of the semicircle was a makeshift table, only two inches away from the ground, overlaid with brightly colored tablecloths, *festive colors.*

Ameena felt sick looking at them.

"Ameena!" It was her father. He sat cross-legged on the cushion opposite her. His hoarse "godfather" voice bellowed with such authority that the platter in her hand shook as she laid it on the table. Her eyes flew to meet his, and she caught the glint in them, a light that registered triumph.

He sat among the men like a chief, his back straight as a rod, his slender frame never slouching. There was no day she had ever seen her father age. Not a wrinkle on his brow or around his eyes, not even a laugh line. He was slim with quick footsteps, a sharp mind, and a strong, assertive voice. The gods had spared him the devastating pains of a bent back and falling teeth and instead piled the years on his head, silver-gray at the sharply receding hairline and temples; his once thick curly hair was a countable mound atop his head. To her, he was still the most handsome man she had ever seen…that was, until Hassan.

Ameena lowered her eyes.

The courage she had mastered to ask her *"Why?"* faltered and fled from her.

"Saaxiibkay hore Faraax is our special guest tonight." There were murmurs of agreement. His voice summoned her. "I would like you to especially attend to him."

"Haa aabo," she replied, hating herself for saying so, hating her father for instructing her thus and her mother for letting her know the impending doom awaiting her.

She gritted her teeth as Faraax cackled like a dying cock and replied for all to hear, "You flatter me, *Saaxiib.*" He jested about how being attended to by one as young and beautiful as his friend's daughter was an honor for kings.

"In my home, you are always a king. For saving my life and my family."

Ameena sighed miserably on hearing her father's response.

The dinner feast stretched into the night, her mother nudging her constantly to go check on Faraax discreetly, to refill the teapot…to ferry out the *xalwo* and more sweet bananas. With every trip she made, her heart faltered. When they ate inside, their own conversations frequently interrupted by the loud debating of the men outside, she locked eyes with her mother several times.

"Why, *hooyo*?" she asked finally when her mother loaded a tray for her with more food.

Bushra worked mechanically for a second more before handing her the tray. She rested tired eyes on her daughter. "I'm doing my best…to delay this union."

Ameena frowned. "What?"

Her mother ushered her out. "Go, go…. They are waiting."

When she returned, she sought her mother, who was serving the children in the kitchen.

"Ameena…" she started.

Ameena could not hold it. "*Hooyo,* please," she pleaded. Anxiety ate at her.

Bushra looked at her daughter, and her eyes softened. "Tomorrow."

Chapter 2

Ameena first heard of *firaun* when she eavesdropped on the sharp exchanges between her parents. It was one of those nights they lingered in conversation after long days and weeks apart.

She often wondered why she was so special, why she had not undergone the knife much earlier. Abdi, a severely traditional man with few words to spare, a man who commanded with his aura, could not have accepted this.

"I told your *aabe* we needed to wait. When we left Mogadishu, you were three. It was the wrong time. Somalia was under fire from Ethiopia and Russia. They came together to fight us. We fled; many of us died; but me, your father, and Faraax made it out. Faraax had connections even then; that's how we left. When we came here, Faraax was by your father's side, helping him establish himself. Your *aabo* feels he owes him for those acts of kindness," her mother was telling her as they ate leftover *xalwo* with tea that morning. "It was a confusing time for us, and he understood. So he waited."

Ameena could not remember a time when this little community that sat between Kenya and Uganda was not home. It was all she knew. She had learned some Lusoga and Luhya, and Swahili was almost second nature as her own mother tongue. But she longed to know of home and the mystery behind her own existence.

Her father held on to the customs, clutching to the only things he had left of a country he still dreamed about when he slept, the traditions and beliefs. Busia town was a melting pot of peoples from Uganda and Kenya, a fragrant, seductive mix of cultures easily permeating the very fabric of rigid foreign customs.

"Forgive me. I did not tell you everything. He promised you to Faraax. It is a favor of friends, a very heavy one," her mother told her, her gaze far away. "I can only delay the inevitable. I told your father you would do it after your first bleed." Her mother looked at her, their eyes communicating. "That's why you must tell no one you have bled. Not yet."

Her mother breathed out. "Not until I think of something."

Ameena recalled the first time she menstruated. It happened almost as if God wanted to prove her father wrong.

She had tossed and turned as her parents argued in the next room.

"She is a disgrace!" Her father's sharp hoarse tone tore through the thin walls that partitioned their rooms.

Bushra's dulcet voice smoothed over his words.

"I look like a fool! *Me*, Abdi Abdullahi Mukhtar! The most prosperous businessman in this community! *Me! Doqon?*"

Ameena felt a knot tighten in her belly; her heart thumped rapidly.

She conflicted between frustration with her mother and dread of her father's anger.

"I tell you she is a disgrace to my name!" He piped out again amid Bushra's soothing mutterings. He lamented that at thirteen, the girls had bled and were being prepared for marriage, yet Ameena had turned thirteen only a few months ago, and she was not prepared as per tradition. She kept going to school, mingling with *kafir* and other cultures who would influence her. Time was running out, and he was getting impatient.

Some nights, the arguments were soft. Her father sighed in dismay, like he was losing his very life. Those nights, Ameena felt her mother won. Other nights like tonight, they were sharp and harsh, and Bushra received the heavy-handed punishment for being defiant, but she held her ground. "No! Let her first bleed."

"She should be prepared by then! They circumcised my mother and sisters when they were six years old! You prevented that from happening when we were in Mogadishu…" Abdi started.

"She was only three! Anyway, we are *not* in Mogadishu anymore…" Bushra responded with venomous iciness. "Look around you! This is our new home now! Who knows how long we shall be here?"

"That does not mean our traditions die! That's how we have survived!"

"Tradition can be delayed, considering the circumstances."

Ameena heard long stretches of silence before her father retired. It was not a defeated silence but rather a postponement of the inevitable. This was not over. It was *never* over. The shuddering sigh as he pulled himself together never escaped her itchy ears. Then he calmly said, "It is late, I must make it to Malindi tomorrow, or we won't eat."

* * *

The day her period started, Ameena was troubled. Her mother had told her she would be a woman soon. She had hoped it would be firaun, but Bushra laughed. "There is a more natural way. One ordained by Allah."

What could be more feminine than firaun, which had not happened yet and seemed unlikely? Ameena had wondered. Bushra had been impatient with her pleading for it and snapped, "We are not in Mogadishu anymore. We have to be different now." And that was that.

Now she understood what her mother had meant.

It was as if fate had another plan for her. The day she bled was the day her burden of womanhood materialized. The day she carried three secrets upon her heart that would utterly change the course of her life as it was.

First, she encountered her father's devilishly handsome turnboy. Before that day, Hassan was just another hired hand, just the help for her father's bustling transportation business aboard his lorries marked in navy blue italicized print *Aadan Express*. She had overheard the women talking about his heritage, "Kenyan Somali." The debate was whether he was Somali enough to be accepted into the community.

Hassan walked around with a carefree attitude, joking and playing with both adults and children alike. When Abdi insisted he join them for dinner, he enthralled them with hearty stories told with the precision and flair of a talented storyteller. He had never seen the white sands of Mogadishu or somersaulted at Lido beach, but when a lazy boyish smile tugged at his lips and he said, "Someday, someday," he charmed even the flies at the refugee camps to belief.

Hassan found her at the far end of their compound, seated on a mat under the mango tree, her thoughts emotional and charged: angry at her mother, dreading the conversations she had heard the previous night when her parents discussed her like an object needing to be priced and packaged for a suitable mate according to *them* and not *her*.

"It's time for *asr*." His calm voice sliced through the commotion of her battle within. It was startling.

"Huh?" she mumbled, confused. She glanced at him and felt caged and shy before promptly dropping her gaze.

"I want to pray," he restated, almost amused. As she scrambled to her feet, keeping her eyes averted, he took her hand and asked with concern, "Why are you sad?"

His touch was new. It warmed her heart and dispelled her confusion, only to be replaced by a new one. No man had touched her, not even her father, because it was against custom.

She panicked, suddenly conscious of his proximity to her. What if someone saw them? She quickly snatched her hand away and bolted toward the house. Her mother had not returned from the market, so she sat huddled in the kitchen on the only three-legged stool and waited. Her mind reeled, her lower belly throbbed and pulsated like a million fingers were clawing away at her soul...but something else clawed at her. The warm imprint of the touch, the concern of his voice. It did not linger and dance over her head like a mirage; it slid into her soul, merged with her convoluting emotions, forcing the fingers in her belly to claw harder and faster…a melodic dance of pleasure and pain.

"I did not pray," she blabbered repentantly, her eyes cloaked in guilt when her mother returned. Bushra sighed, unwrapped the extra scarf she had carried to keep her *baati* from getting soiled with produce from the market.

"Don't tell your *aabe*," she said wearily. "I prayed for both of us."

She started to put away the cassava chunks she had brought and paused. "Aren't you going to help me?"

Ameena did not move.

"Eh," her mother expressed surprise, "maybe your father is right…."

"*Hooyo*, I am…bleeding."

Her mother's expression shifted, the tired creases disappeared, and her attractive round face lit up. She laughed. "You are a woman now." She went over to her daughter and took her chin between thumb and forefinger. Ameena relaxed at the gentleness in her touch. "That is good." She dropped her voice in secrecy. "Who else knows?"

Ameena shook her head.

Her mother nodded thoughtfully. "Don't tell anyone. Your *aabo* must never know. This is a thing for women only. Come, I will show you how to take care of yourself."

And for the next four days, Ameena did not go to school, and her mother barely left her side, claiming Ameena was not well and needed attention while she taught her daughter about menstruation. Ameena also found out her mother's own secret: "I don't want you to undergo firaun; you are perfect enough without it. You need to enjoy the pleasures of life. You must enjoy your union with a man. That's why I delay it."

All this time, she had thought her mother was holding something against her. Embarrassment clouded her after listening to Bushra. "I'm sorry, *hooyo*…." Bushra's own painful secret then became Ameena's burden. Ameena held her mother, her eyes moist with tears. "*Mahadsanid*."

Her mother chuckled. "It is my duty; don't thank me, *gabadha macaan*."

The end of her first period felt like a rebirth, like the child died and the woman was born, vulnerable but sensual and full of wide-eyed curiosity. Her breasts were sprouting like little flower buds, and yet her mother lied to Abdi that she had not "bled" yet.

"I remember my sister, *Allah yerhamha*. May she rest in *Jannatul firdaus*. She did not bleed until she was sixteen, hmm. Maybe it's the curse of my family that Ameena has inherited," she would tell him with a touch of melodrama, a forlorn look in her eyes as she recounted the tale of scorn her sister bore for coming of age so late in life. Even though he grunted in response, Abdi seemed to believe her.

* * *

With the *xalwo* finished between them, Ameena sighed. It all made sense now, the late-night discussions, the visits from Faraax, her father throwing lavish dinners for him, her secrets. *Their* secrets.

"Now you know why, my *Araweelo*." Her mother gave her a knowing look.

She nodded. Then after a pause asked, "But…for how long?"

Her mother shrugged. "An answer will come, *inshallah*." It felt good to have hope that she would not end up with Faraax. Her heart pulsated with her own delicate secret: her budding love for Hassan. It sang a hopeful tune that fate truly required her to be happy with a man of her own choosing. She had already chosen, thanks to her mother. Her heart and body yearned for him.

Chapter 3

The evening meal was Ameena's favorite time of day, especially when her father returned from his long trips with Hassan. She eagerly waited on the men, catching wisps of their charged conversation. She savored the knowledge that dripped from their lips, passed back and forth between platefuls of food and *chai*.

They spoke of their history and their country, a place she had no memory of…Mogadishu? Mudug? It made her long to be there. To see this foreign place that was home.

Sometimes they bantered back and forth about their new lives, money, business, and traditions. They also spoke of war and losing family. They debated about Mohamed Siad Barre, Somalia's current leader; no one seemed to like him, not her parents, not any of the kin who sought refuge in Busia either. They called him *keli-taliye*: dictator, tyrant, a burden to Somalia. It was as if each leader delivered Somalia from one enemy in the '60s to another in the unfolding decade. New refugees and travelers always meant new information…*Waxa hada dhacaya?* "What is going on now?"

"We are friends with Libya again."

"It's not good, not good *xun*…the red berets are a menace."

"There is more war coming, *wallahi*, there is. *La samah Allah!*"

There were nights when the very air felt turgid and thick, weighed down by the emotion in the exchanges—with it, a draft of dread that made her shiver. She regarded the faces of the visitors as she served them in silent contemplation, enthralled and saddened by the rich and tragic history of her people. She lingered by the door to catch banter that carried to the main house. The ones that stirred pride within her breast were those in which the men argued about their clans and who was more royal, *Irir Samaale* or *Dir,* or any of the other three noble clans.

As much as she loved these nights because of the unpredictable nature of them—who would be a guest or what news they would bring?—she particularly enjoyed the nights when it was just her and her mother. They would cook their favorite meal, *iskudheh karis,* the aroma-filled rice and meat combo, and down it with *chai* laden with spices and goat's milk. Bushra would then probe and stretch her imagination with myths and legends of *Biriir ina barqo,* the heroic giant who was just and kind and brought unity and peace to all of Somaliland. She could tell the mood of her mother by the stories she told.

When Bushra was light and carefree, she indulged her in tales of the heroic coward *Egal Shidad,* and Ameena would always beg for a retelling. But there were those nights when she was in exceptionally high spirits, when she even called her *Araweelo,* indulging her in tales of the beautiful, daring queen who subjugated all men in her kingdom, positioning women as breadwinners at the peak of the Buraan droughts.

Ameena found it hilarious when her mother told her of how men were subdued to the point of taking up domestic roles in the home. "Eh?" She would gaze at her mother in wonder because she could never imagine such a scenario.

"Yes, *macaan* and Queen Araweelo went as far as castrating male prisoners." She would then mumble in Ameena's ear as she parted her hair with a wooden-toothed comb, readying the chunks of glossy home-conditioned hair for thick plaits. "My Araweelo, my Ameena. You are brave and strong and a queen. No one has the power over your destiny but yourself." She would say this with passionate resolve laced with a flicker of pain.

Whether Bushra was light, high-spirited, or sad, the sense that her mother longed for *something* hovered over them in those intimate moments. Maybe it was the longing for home…maybe the news of increasing unrest, the not knowing who survived, if home will be a place they could go back to. Maybe it was none of these things.

* * *

As more and more refugees trickled out of Somalia to a place she only heard of as Garissa, whispers of a persistent drought sweeping through Somaliland became the dominant point of conversation in their pseudo-Mogadishu.

It had started within the government, spreading like a cancer to the Gulf of Aden. She overheard the passionate debates her father engaged in one evening at the tail end of dinner. The radio was placed in the center of the compound, new batteries installed; you could hear a pin drop as they waited for the news to begin. As much as she hated the somber news reports, she listened anyway. There were talks of a meeting between Libya and Somalia to end its diplomatic isolation.

Wars. Droughts, growing instability.

Soon Ameena started to wonder if her mother wasn't right. Maybe they would never go back and it was time to bend traditions. Here in their little haven of Somalia, every one of her kinsmen seemed to cling to hope as they followed the discontent and happenings in the newly independent African state bursting at the seams with its need for liberation and not grappling well with the results of colonialism.

Uganda was no better; the country was riddled with a harsh economic drought brought on by their policies incited by their temperamental former leader, Idi Amin. With the recent overthrow of Milton Obote, it did not seem to be getting any better.

The world was depressing, and yet it called to her.

Her father started most of the conversations concerning Somalia.

When he did, she listened with pride. The knot of apprehension she felt around him loosened, and she loved him.

He had made it in Busia. He often said war was good. It gave a man work to do, and he was ready to do that work. With a soft loan from Faraax, he started an informal trade, learning Swahili and Luo early on to aid him around the border of Kenya and Uganda as he launched a barter system. Kenyans needed agricultural goods they could convert into consumable goods; Ugandans needed these goods; sugar, flour, the necessities, and he was the convenient middleman brokering the deal aboard his half-dozen lorries with Aadan Express. His business was flourishing, and he hired Somali and Kenyan drivers and turnboys while he himself drove one lorry. Hassan basked in the privilege of being so closely associated with the boss himself.

After Ameena's brief encounter with Hassan, she kept a lookout for him. When he made long trips to Kenya with her father and they were gone for more than a day, the tiny fingers that clawed at her womb and heart wrested her of peace and she became forlorn, making excuses for her lack of appetite.

She spent the days outside by the mango tree recalling his touch like a tape on repeat. When he returned, her excitement was tangible, no matter how much she tried to hide it. It poured from her pores and painted her skin with a warm glow. She looked forward to the evening meals, jumping to help on any occasion.

"I can serve and clear the dishes after, *hooyo*," she told her mother.

Bushra laughed. "Is that so?" She was pleased her mother was pleased.

"Where is my Araweelo that complains about her back hurting from bending too much?"

Ameena batted her eyelids. "The *dhegdheer* ate her."

They both laughed. When Ameena was younger, Bushra scared her into returning home before sunset by telling her *dhegdheer*, the female cannibalistic demon, would eat her if it found her lost and wandering alone.

Bushra joked, "My Araweelo *has* become submissive."

Ameena clicked her tongue and smiled back at her mother.

She enjoyed the nights Hassan joined them for dinner. His eyes danced with mischief, and he mesmerized the men, entertaining them with stories, proverbs, and songs. His exaggerated sense of adventure, recounting the trips they made as far as the northeastern corridor of Kenya, as if Abdi had not been present. Stories crafted with extra theatrics kept the men laughing, her enchanted and her father puffed with pride.

"Not only do you have an effective turnboy, but he is a superb storyteller," the guests would say.

"*Nin aan dhul marin dhaayo maleh* (A man who has not traveled does not have eyes)," Abdi would respond often.

On those nights, she loved them both.

While she lay in the darkness of her room and deeply inhaled the fragrant scent of *luubaan* stealthily invading every room long after it burned out on the *dabqaad* that her mother lit after dinner each night, Ameena listened to the men chatter, laugh, and drink copious amounts of tea. She ached to be out there. Why did the men have all the fun? Why couldn't they all sit down together? Whose idea was this, anyway? Queen Araweelo would have changed that, she often thought, setting her jaw. She would tell herself, "I will change *that* in my time."

Chapter 4

A month passed, then another, and Hassan did not approach her. The ache in her heart grew and scorched her soul, robbing her of gainful sleep. One day, on her way home from school with her school friends, she spied the familiar navy-blue scribblings of her father's business splashed on the front of a cream-colored lorry approaching the dusty road they took. Hassan sat behind the wheel, his arm hanging out the window frame. He honked when he saw them and slowed to a stop.

The girls giggled shyly, for Hassan was a guilty pleasure discussion when they were not looking at magazines, inquisitively asking Ameena about him.

"*Sasa*! So, which of you girls wants to ride in this truck today? It is your lucky day," he bellowed through the window. A smile illuminated his handsome dark features, his teeth as white as fresh camel milk.

The girls giggled again. Ameena's heart leapt. This was her chance. "Me!"

The other girls looked uncomfortable.

The older of them, Husna, glared at Ameena. "*We* are walking home, Hassan, it is okay."

Ameena's eyes twinkled. Husna asked the most about Hassan. With her hands on her hips, Ameena replied, "Who is walking home? *Si mimi.*

Ah-ah! This is my father's truck after all."

The girls hushed.

Hassan, amused, replied, "And who taught you to speak like that? Definitely not your father."

His eyes lit up, and she was glad. He *approved!* The fingers in her heart tightened their hold.

"Can I ride in that so you can tell my father of my insolent ways?"

Hassan whistled, shaking his head. "Is that so? Oh my! You have the spirit of Araweelo, I see. Well, if the daughter of my boss asks, how can I say no?" He got out of the truck and circled to the passenger side to help her up the step into the seat. Ameena beamed triumphantly at the girls and waved like a queen bidding adieu to her subjects.

"See you tomorrow!" She relished in their envious gazes.

Now that they were finally together, Ameena was not sure she could trust her tongue, so she waited, prayed he would speak up first. They rode along at a comfortable pace for a few minutes before he asked, "Have you been in any of the trucks before?"

Ameena shook her head.

They rumbled down the road for a mile, and then Hassan suddenly made a left turn.

Ameena spoke up: "That's not the way home."

"I know. I thought I should show you around."

Ameena, thrilled, acted nonchalant. "*Aabe* won't be pleased."

"He is out of town for a few days. He asked me to come back for some supplies while he negotiated a deal with the Ankara family group of companies." His voice dropped, forcing her to tear her resolute gaze from the road and put it on him. Their eyes locked briefly before she shyly looked away. It was something in his eyes. That something seemed compatible with the fingers in her heart, like his eyes knew her heart intimately.

"Are you shy now?" He chuckled. "The girl who refused to walk home with her friends. 'This is my father's truck, after all,'" he mimicked her. She relaxed, laughing, and shrugged, not sure what to say. Her earlier boldness melted like butter and congealed around her feet in the glowing presence of Hassan.

They rode in silence into Busia town. She saw for the first time the holding offices for the business her father ran, realizing it was not as small as he modestly liked to tell his guests. From the side-view mirror, she watched Hassan, aided by two other men, haul sacks into the back of the lorry. "You stay here," he had told her. He did not want anyone causing trouble for them both.

He brought her a mini box of the bright red "Big G" chewing gum and a handful of toffees covered in mustard yellow and brown wrappings. "Just in case you sulk that I kept you hungry," he teased when he returned to the truck.

She smiled, grateful, touched by his kindness. "Gifts for Araweelo?"

He tipped his head comically. "I need to preserve my balls from your wrath, your highness."

Ameena made a face. "I am still not fully impressed."

He faced her, his expression suddenly serious. "Really? Is it my balls you *really* want?" Her eyes widened; she was taken aback by his forwardness. Then he dished out his most winning smile.

"I was joking with you!" He slid behind the wheel, and the truck groaned and chortled to life. She strangely liked the way the veins in his hands popped as he moved the gear stick with admirable ease, and soon they were chugging down the road at a comfortable pace.

"Is it true you have not done firaun?" he asked, piercing through the silence.

It caught her off guard. *Again.* Ameena felt the fingers that had held her heart slide down to her belly and a little lower. It was a very sensitive question, but she held her head up and replied, "What if I haven't?"

He whistled.

"How did you not? No Somali woman survives it. Your mother must have some magic over your father. No wonder they call her *Araweelo!*"

Ameena did not respond. Her mother's secret burned heavy in her breast. *It hurt so much I passed out. I was only six. But my family was proud even though I cried for days.* Bushra's words haunted her. She told her of the healing that took ages to come, how her legs were bound close together for a month, how it hurt to go to the bathroom, the nightmares, the fever following a horrible infection, being sewn up again after the stitches had come undone. Bushra did not wish it for Ameena. *You shall not see the knife, not while I live, macaan.*

"When you marry and have children, you decide yourself," she told Ameena.

And Ameena had wondered out loud, "What would Araweelo do?"

Her mother's serious face had softened into a triumphant smile as if all the years of storytelling had finally washed up results.

"*Ahaaa,* I see that restless fire in you. I wish for you to see the world. Don't stay cooped up in one place and one society. The world is enormous."

"But a woman's place is in her home, isn't it, *hooyo*?" Ameena had sought confirmation of the war in her soul, the battle between traditional expectations of her and her own desire for independence.

"Where is home, Ameena, heh? We are far from home, but we make home where our hearts are. Follow your heart. Be strong, be brave, my Araweelo," her mother had assured her.

* * *

"I am glad you did not," Hassan was saying, tearing her away from that monumental moment with her mother, and her heart raced.

"Why?" she demanded

"Because you will understand pleasure, and I am not a man who follows tradition, anyway."

She scoffed, "*Aabe* says you are not really one of us."

He laughed. "Is that so?"

She nodded, then probed, "Why?"

"You ask many questions, Araweelo." He sighed. "If my father had been Somali and not my mother, then I would be Somali."

Ameena frowned. "How does *that* even matter? You *still* have Somali blood."

"Eh-eh *wewe*, it's the way of tribes and people." He seemed amused.

"Does it bother you?"

He shrugged. "Should it?"

Her heart skipped another beat as he flashed her a heart-melting smile. Ameena looked away.

"It does not bother me. I like being Kikuyu too."

She adored him. He seemed like a dream, so carefree and brave. She loved him.

"Where have you and my father been?"

"Ooh," he exclaimed, "many places…in Kenya and parts of Tanzania. Uganda, too, especially Kampala, Jinja, Masaka…You should come with me one day…."

"*Aabe* won't let me." She shook her head.

He dismissed her words with a wave of his hand. "Araweelo needs to see the world." His eyes danced mischievously. "I will take you one day. We will drive to Mombasa and Kilifi, and Nairobi. If you want, we will even go to Dar-es Salaam. The sands are beautiful. It's the place where the sun sleeps and white sands clothe your naked feet. You shall *want* to only walk barefoot." Ameena was watching him, enthralled by his poetic, dreamy description.

Her jaw dropped in admiration, and he laughed. "You will see."

She noticed she was staring, her heart open to him. She looked away.

"What?" he asked.

She urgently wanted to know if he had a woman, but she did not know how to ask, so she thought and carefully responded, "The girls in school think you will marry one of them one day."

He laughed. "What do you think?"

She shrugged. "I don't know."

He was silent for a minute or two, a smile on his face. "I want to marry Araweelo,"

"My mother?" Ameena asked naughtily; she was excited, flattered, a warm rush of sensation flooding her whole body.

He chuckled, his long lashes framing eyes that had gotten intensely dark as he glanced at her. "No. You."

Her inner thighs burned and tingled, her belly knotted, and the fingers within kneaded at her womanhood, stroking, urging, and begging. She struggled to breathe, flustered by these feelings. They seemed to overwhelm her, and being near Hassan was making it worse.

"Are you okay?" he was asking.

Ameena choked on her words, "I…Yes."

And then Hassan undid her; he reached out and touched her hand, applying pressure ever so slightly. "Are you sure?"

Tired of keeping her emotions in check, Ameena let out a heated breath slowly then said,

"You said I would understand pleasure."

He paused and jerked his head in recollection. "Yes, you will."

She smiled. "When I am yours?" she asked boldly. She adored this man more and more, and her need for him consumed her every minute of the ride home.

He laughed. "Araweelo…"

"Show *me* that pleasure," she burst out impatiently. Her mind was swimming, her body shaking. Ameena squared her jaw and looked at Hassan. "Please."

Hassan's eyes glinted in surprise. He slowed down and pulled on the gear. The truck groaned to a halt, hissing and trembling. He sat so still for a minute that Ameena thought he was going to lecture her. To her surprise and excitement, he took her chin in his hand, his fingers caressing the silky young skin, his eyes fixed on her full lips, and huskily responded, "Been waiting for this moment for a long, long time."

The sun was making its way to the west when Hassan pulled the truck to an enclosure, he knew, off the road.

"Are you sure?" he asked as he took her hand in his and both their eyes burned with an unbridled passion, a need that surpassed reason.

She nodded without hesitating.

Hassan smiled. When he took her to the back of the truck and undid her *direh,* she hesitated.

"It's okay," he told her, and she smiled, afraid her nakedness would not be good enough for him. But when his hands slid between her legs to the folds of her womanhood and stroked the heart of her with gentle urgency, Ameena sighed and purred. A strange sensation that enveloped her and exploded within and around her made her moan. This…*this* was the pleasure that had tortured her for days.

"No woman who has experienced firaun or *sunna* can enjoy this, the way you are," he whispered in her ear. He was watching her, and even though she tried to stifle her writhing, he urged her on. "Enjoy it." His voice, warm and buttery, peeled her inhibitions away along with his shirt and her underclothes, while his other hand played with her budding breasts, stroking and massaging them. The various sensations coursing through her in waves left her confused. A sense of drowning gripped her.

A good type of drowning.

A drowning that was satisfying. She gulped when, without warning, he gently inserted a finger inside her creating a mixed sensation of pleasure and invasion as his fingers probed. She gasped involuntarily, and when he stopped, his eyes searching hers, she shook her head. "Don't stop."

Outside, the *adhān* serenaded their act. With his fingers dripping with her essence, he undid his trousers and ever so gently penetrated her. Ameena moaned in pleasure and pain. The probe of his phallus between the tightly laced crevices of her vagina felt like an invasion of not only her body but her mind. She gagged as he, unable to control the wave of passion washing over him, thrust deeper into her. It hurt…She felt full of him…so full. She clung to him; and he thrust in slow, then fast, then slow, then fast; then his fingers reached down to stroke her clitoris gently as he moved inside her.

Ameena felt the rush of many fingers: jabbing, clawing, touching, soothing all at once and enveloping her in a warm rush. Then she was screaming, writhing, and convulsing. Hassan's groans accompanied her own cry of ecstasy as he exploded inside her.

He rolled off her, panting. Ameena felt numb, still convulsing slightly. The dainty fingers of pleasure stroked a thousand nerves.

They lay there in silence for a while.

"My mother said firaun would kill my joy," Ameena finally said, laughing. "*This* is my joy!"

When their eyes locked, her heart tightened, and she knew she did not want to look at anyone again. She did not want to make love to anyone else but Hassan.

She let him make love to her again, his touch romantic, not as intense as before, tender...deliberate. It was like a conversation she did not want to end. One about unfamiliar things, and she was a willing listener and learner. When he guided her to touch his rock-hard penis, she squealed in surprise. "This was making me happy?" she asked innocently and loved him when he both laughed and consumed her with his eyes.

"Do you like it, *mrembo*?" he asked, and she nodded eagerly.

He peeled the gauze of shyness off her with each garment of clothing he removed and tossed aside until he was completely naked before her. She gazed at his lean, dark body in awe, the dusting of hair on his chest. It was the mound below his waist that surprised her. She had never seen a naked grown man.

"Then let me make you happy again." His hands traced each curve, embraced, cupped, and gently squeezed parts of her she never imagined would experience touch by anyone but her.

Chapter 5

Hassan and Ameena stole behind houses, sneaked into forested places, and hid in the back of her father's lorry, behind the mosque or empty classrooms, to make love.

"Teach me," she said. She was insatiable, eager to learn how to please him, and he indulged her. He brought her little gifts from his trips and slipped them to her when she served the men in the compound for the evening meal. Ameena felt different.

"I find the other girls so childish," she told Hassan after a torrid session of lovemaking. He had returned from Uganda, delivering goods at her father's behest.

"Do you?" He had laughed and snuggled beside her in the truck in the same hideout spot he had picked. Ameena had told her mother she was going to see Husna in town.

Ameena sighed. The conversation in school about boys bored her now.

"I missed you," she told him.

He smiled. "I heard your father had an important guest at dinner when I was away."

She nodded. "Faraax. My father's best friend." Then she told him everything, studying his expression. He never once flinched, and she worried. "Aren't you worried?"

He lay back with his hands behind his head. "Why?"

"Don't you want to marry me? If I am married to Faraax, I can't be yours."

"But your mother won't let that happen," he reminded her.

She worried still. "What if she won't let me marry you?"

He shook his head. "Don't think about that, not today. I just got back." His eyes were hungry for her, and she balked underneath his stare. All her worries vanished. He was right. *Not today.*

She felt the change as the days wore on. She walked differently. There was a sensual spring in her step. She was aware of her beauty, the budding sensuality of femininity. She was so captivated by Hassan; she struggled to suppress it. When the men ate in the compound, she got clumsy around him; when he looked at her, she got tongue-tied. It surprised her how calm he remained.

When he joked with other women in her presence, she burned with jealousy, sulking until he cajoled her out of it.

"My Araweelo is jealous?" he would hum into her ear, and she would push him away, hating him for making her feel so vulnerable.

She loved him intoxicatingly. She wondered if it would get to that point where she would have to tell her mother. What would she say? She noticed her mother watched her with a different glint in her eyes, especially when she served the men at supper. She was apprehensive. Did she suspect?

One day she came home to find her mother seated outside on the veranda, chewing on sugarcane, spitting the chewed flesh drained of its sweet juicy moisture in a little shattered plastic bucket located strategically at her feet.

Ameena smiled uneasily and came to her knees by her mother's side. *"See tahay, hooyo, macaan,"* she whispered, her eyes downcast. Her mother seated outside the house was always a sign they needed to talk. It had happened when she brought home bad grades one term, when she had been late for school another time, when she had been sluggish with house duties, yet another time. *Now...what?*

Bushra did not respond immediately. She yanked at the firm white flesh with her teeth and tore it with a *tyck* sound, then chewed, occasionally sucking in the sugarcane juice as it collected in her mouth with every grinding pressure from her teeth. She chomped on the chunk of sugarcane she had just torn off the stem, spat it out, then said, "So, now you are running around with that *waxaa tahay wiil noloshisa add uhooseeyaso*, Hassan?" then scoffed, "Who would have thought this beautiful daughter of mine would fall in love with a lowlife shamba boy?" She spat the words *lowlife shamba boy* like the husks emptied of their sweet cane juice into the bucket.

An uncomfortable silence reigned between them.

"So, did you think I would not notice?" Bushra asked as she bit into the cane stem and yanked hard. It split with a *tyck* sound.

Ameena did not know what to say.

"*Ii jawaab!*" Answer me!

Ameena started at the firmness in her mother's tone. She let out her breath and tried to appease her mother. "What, *hooyo macaan?*"

Bushra laughed sardonically. "You can't play those games with me. I see how he looks at you and how you fidget and fumble near him during evening meals."

Ameena felt her stomach lurch. Fear was an ugly thing. "W-We are just friends."

"Eh? Friends? What sort of friendship is that? Hurry and tell me before I tell all to your father and have you sewn up and married off tomorrow!" her mother replied with a severity Ameena had never seen.

Ameena cowered. "N-not friends. He just greets me—sometimes." The truth clung to the tip of her tongue, fastened with fear so thick, responding was an effort.

Bushra did not respond immediately; instead, she bit into the sugarcane stem again, *tyck*. Ameena could hear the hum of the flies in the late afternoon heat as they settled on bits of food debris scattered on the compound. Her head swam.

She waited.

Her mother had a habit of punishing her with relentless silence when she was angry.

Finally, Bushra spoke. "Go inside and prepare yourself for the evening meal. We shall prepare *muufo* together. Check if those bananas *aabe* brought two days ago are ripe. Also, see if your father's favorite *surbiyaan hilib adhi* is ready." Then she added while letting her eyes sweep over Ameena slowly, painfully for effect, "In case he needs appeasing."

But Abdi did not need appeasing. The men gathered as they usually did, and the women and children sat inside as one big family. They all brought their different dishes and ate together. Ameena's appetite was low, and the smell of food had been bothering her for some weeks.

She craved Hassan more than she did food. The thought of making love to him sent a warm rush down her belly, farther down, settling in her womb before staining her underwear. She worried too about that discharge, which was as frequent as her urination. She did not bleed the last month, yet her mother had told her it happens every month.

She noticed her mother watching her across the room and smiled foolishly, picked up a banana and bit into it, chewing slowly.

The night dragged on for too long. A feeling of premonition weighed upon Ameena. Something did not feel right. She helped clear out the men's dishes and refused to look at Hassan.

The next day, Hassan met her on her way home and chased after her on the lonely dirt road. "Araweelo *weh!*" He whistled.

She ignored him. The feeling of premonition hit her again. "Go away, Hassan," she told him, her heart a tangled web of indecision. One part of her was afraid of what her father would do to her; the other wanted Hassan.

Hassan caught up with her. "Why are you walking home alone?" he asked, puzzled.

"Because I wanted to. What do you want, Hassan?" she asked, agitated.

He stood back and looked at her from an angle, then laughed. "Is this the same girl that begged me to go faster?" He imitated her moans and groans.

Ameena shoved him. "Stop it! My mother knows, and now I am in trouble!"

Her lips quivered. From around the corner, a man balancing a sack strapped vertically on the back seat of his bicycle rode by, waving to Hassan, who waved back with an animated display of pleasantry.

When the bicycle was out of sight, Hassan motioned to her to walk with him off the road, closer to the shrubbery that went on for a mile to her house.

His lips curled. "So? I shall ask for your hand in marriage."

Ameena shook her head. "They won't let us be together. There is Faraax! My not being circumcised! You! Oh, my world is falling apart!"

He reached for her and joggled her. "Calm down…So? We will run away together, go to Lamu or Dar-es-Salaam and live by the ocean."

Ameena lightened up a bit. "You would?"

Hassan smiled and his confidence boosted her. "Of course I would. I have money. I can start my business, and we can live happily there."

Ameena hesitated. "But they will find us."

"They won't know where to look," he added with a grin, "if we don't tell them."

She feigned a sulk. "I won't tell them."

"Is that all?"

She pursed her lips and nodded, unsure she wanted him to know what was really going on with her. But then again, she also did not know. "Yes, that's all," she said as her eyelashes framed the lie.

"What do you want me to bring you? Your father and I are leaving tonight for Meru. I won't see you till…" He stopped and counted on his fingers. "Friday night!" He held three fingers up like it was an astounding sign.

She made a sound deep in her throat. Their secret affair intensified what they shared. "What? That is too long!"

He smiled lazily. "I will miss you."

Her heart stopped, and she looked away. "Can we meet later? Like the last time?" she asked, quickly pushing her apprehension aside.

"Eh? I taught you well." He laughed. He inched closer. His hand brushed up against her blouse. Her nipples hardened in response, and she slapped his hand away. "Not here!"

"No one can see us." His reply was urgent and labored.

The bush was thick, and the light wasn't strong, but there were definitely no demons…maybe snakes. They had been to this forest countless times in the past several weeks, and no one had found them. The only problem was the dallis grass that stuck to her clothes. She had made excuses for it; however, she was not sure she wanted to risk that. Her gut told her something bad would happen.

But she feverishly burned for him. He seduced her again, lightly letting a hand run up and down her full-sleeved arm. "Mmm…"

"Don't you want to wish me well for this long, long trip?" he asked her, his voice low and laden with desire.

"Hassan…" she started; the inner voice that warned her became increasingly faint.

"Yes, my Araweelo?" He took her hands, placing them in his and drawing her into the woodland, through a haphazard path to an obscure spot.

The last strands of reason completely dissolved when he took her more passionately than he ever had.

Chapter 6

The next morning, she threw up and almost fainted as she prepared for school. Her mother stood in the bathroom's doorway, arms akimbo. "What is it?"

Ameena stood back, shaken. "I don't know." Her voice faltered. Her heart burned with regret. She should not have made love with Hassan the day before, was all she could think. *Allah* had struck her.

Her mother did not budge.

"Come here," she said, and when Ameena edged toward her, she took her by the arm to her room.

"Lie down," her mother told her.

Ameena looked confused.

"I said, lie down!"

Ameena obeyed and lay down.

"On your back!" her mother instructed. Ameena did, feeling the wave of nausea return.

"*Hooyo...*" she retched. Her mother was fast rolling her to her side, enabling her to throw up on the side of the bed. The yellow-brown and green mash of bile and dinner spilled and flowed down the side of the hardwood of the bed.

Bushra held her, urging her to throw up as much as possible. When the wave passed, she rolled her back onto her back and, in swift movements, pressed hard against her lower belly in the cradle of her womb.

Ameena yelped in shock and pain, "*Hooyo*!" and doubled to her side, curling up.

Bushra took in a deep breath and edged away from her daughter.

"How long, Ameena, how long?" Her mother's voice seemed to come from a hollow place.

"I don't understand, *hooyo*, 'how long' what?" Ameena hurled the question at her angrily.

Ameena gasped in shock when, without warning, her mother's firm hand flew across her face, jerking it to the side with a heavy, stinging slap. Ameena gaped in horror, her hand flying to her smarting cheek, then burst into tears.

"How long!" Bushra's elevated voice burned with a fury that made her wince. "How long have you been screwing that man?"

"What…?" She choked on sobs she was failing to suppress.

Another slap jerked her head to the opposite side. She panicked. "Only yesterday!" Ameena lied.

She yelped as her mother slapped her again.

"Don't lie to me! You cannot be pregnant from yesterday's sex! When? Tell me!" Bushra thundered.

Pregnant?

Her justified humiliation dissolved into fear that lodged deep in a dark unknown guarded by dread, a dread so powerful it numbed her.

"I think four…maybe six weeks."

Bushra staggered back and heaved deeply. The only sound reverberating through the room was Ameena's sobbing.

"You are *pregnant*, Ameena!" The terror in her mother's voice was tangible. "How could you do this to me?"

Ameena, shaking and sobbing, her face hot and throbbing from the slaps, responded despite herself, "I love him. We will get married, and you won't experience shame."

Bushra let out a hollow, dispassionate laugh. "And who will let that happen? Not *aabo*! Faraax is preparing your bride price at this very moment! Soon they will call you *suchuna;* outcast, oversexed, unclean, unmarriageable…and your father will blame me…"

"I will save you the trouble and run away!" Her tears stung her face; hot, liquid anger.

Bushra did not respond. When Ameena met her gaze, her eyes were as dry as the *Ogo.*

"You are not afraid, are you, my Araweelo?" Bushra's voice was shallow and spent.

Ameena felt sick with fear and confusion. But in her mother's dry, faraway look, she saw more fear and pain than she had imagined anyone would have. So she shook her head.

"No, I am not afraid."

She watched as the shadow of pain lifted off her mother, a weary smile touching her full lips. There was hope, and Ameena exhaled in relief.

"Did you like it?" she asked after a long silence between them.

It surprised her Bushra would ask and hesitated, then nodded, a bashful smile coating her lips. When her mother sighed in response, she could sense the weight in it, the burden she carried. She hated that she had done this to her mother, but her love for Hassan would not let her wallow.

"Let's clean up this place. I made *shahie* milk tea, *canjeelo,* and *maraqe. Aabe* finished the liver you like so much." As an afterthought, she added, "You are not going to school today."

When her mother touched her again, it was a gentle embrace. When their foreheads touched in warm congeniality and feminine solidarity, eyes closed, Ameena once more brimmed over with courage. Her sins were forgiven, and her mother was here with her. She was not alone in this.

The two women sat there for a long time, summoning courage and love from each other wordlessly. "I have a plan," Bushra spoke quietly, her eyes squeezed shut. "Nothing will happen to you, *wallahi.*"

* * *

Later in the day, as her mother massaged a mixture of henna with lemon juice and sesame in her hair, both their faces covered in a *huruud* and *qasil* mask, she told Ameena her plan like she was telling her one of the folktales she loved so much.

"*Gabadha la jecel yahay.*" She sighed wearily. "The *soo maal* have a saying, '*gabar guri ha kaa gasho ama god.*' Only a timely marriage or death can keep your daughter from disgrace. I have seen the rise of our women, *macaan.*" She slicked the henna mixture generously from the roots of her dark curls that stretched and clumped together as Bushra combed through them with her fingers, down to the healthy tips. "There was a time we could not vote, and then freedom came on the wings of unity, and Somali lands were one for a time. I was there. We chatted hopefully about new referendums, the power to vote, our significance in society, but *aah*...Abdirashid Ali Shermarke was killed, and Siad Barre took over, and peace has become a song on our lips...elusive and dying."

She could hear the twinge of sadness in her mother's voice. "So, home. Home is where we can pitch our tents and lay our heads. Where the camels can roam and we can sit together welcoming our own into our community with *shaah, sheeko,* and incense. *Hmm,* things change and I accept them."

Ameena wondered where her mother was going with this lengthy introduction.

"You know Faraax...Faraax's last visit was to make a final claim for you. He said, 'One more year and Ameena goes back with me to Zanzibar, whether she has seen the knife or not. Whether or not she has bled.'"

Ameena jolted in shock. "One year!"

Bushra smoothed over her hair gently.

"He has been bargaining and waiting for a long time...now..." Bushra faltered.

Ameena's reaction was sudden; she moaned, "*Hooyo....*" Her mother tugged at her hair to keep her still.

"*Aamus*! Be quiet!" she hissed.

Ameena let the silent tears fill her eyes and escape in single streams down her cheeks. She set her jaw stubbornly. Faraax was as ancient as she was young. There had to be a plan for her to get out of this, she had thought.

"Yes, I am still fighting for you. Do you know why? Because I want you to go to school. At least learn to read and write. Be better than me. Pregnancy is a different thing. I was angry because I wanted you to decide when you are much, much older..." Her mother scoffed. Ameena could sense her disappointment. "I was married young, about your age, and it was very difficult for me, but I have learned to be a wife, to steer my husband's desires and thoughts, to respect him and serve him but also to guard my children. It is my duty to be a wife and mother."

Ameena waited with dread; why were they having this conversation... *again?*

"But I am a woman who has lost a lot of things, cried a lot of tears. I wanted just one thing; to have my daughters be more than me. I don't want your life to be a bleak cycle of living...like mine. Even though we got some rights, culture dictates we are only meant to be traded like cattle to the highest bidder, our hearts denied their beating truth, and our loins denied pleasure. When we left Mogadishu, my heart grew new wings of hope because then I knew I could change certain things, if not for me, for you."

Her mother stopped, got up and went to the house from where, minutes later, she emerged with a deep basin filled with lukewarm water.

"Let me wash your face. We will give your hair some more time. It will be a rich color." She smiled, but the sadness in her voice reflected in her light brown irises. When she had washed her face and wiped it clean, Ameena sat back on the mat and waited, her tummy turned into knots. The hesitation was gnawing at her.

Bushra settled back down on the stool and continued to smooth over her daughter's hair, "So I want more for you. I have told you that before. I admire your strength, even though it breaks my heart. But maybe it is good for my heart to be broken so you can live a life I never lived. You love Hassan, I can see. He is different...young and excitable. May he make you happy. Our community may not accept him, but you love him, and that is important."

The hens clucked and plucked at the dirt in the compound. A tethered goat waiting to be turned into a feast in a few months chewed on grass it pulled from the bushes fenced out of the compound.

Ameena bit her lower lip, almost guiltily.

"I don't want my sacrifice to be in vain, Ameena," her mother finally said, a sharpness in her tone.

"What do you…mean?" she finally asked.

"It seems your father's vow to Faraax is stronger than my stalling tactics. He mentioned making it final with him by the end of this year. You are to marry Faraax in the middle of next year, whether you are cut or not. He is running out of patience."

Ameena felt her world crumble in a cloud of dust.

"But I won't let that happen. If he finds out you are pregnant, he will kill us both. So I am going to tell him, when he returns tomorrow from Eldoret, that…you are preparing to visit Leylo…for a month…maybe two at least. *Dhaqan celis.*"

"Leylo?" Ameena scrunched her nose, trying hard to place the name to a face.

"The woman whose third daughter got cut last year…and she suffered critically, then died…*Inna lillahi wa inna ilayhi raji'un.* She is a silent advocate and my friend. I will plan with her."

"But…"

"But I am *not* sending you there, you see. I just need to buy some time while you and Hassan leave, go far, far away—anywhere, somewhere. It will take your father months, even years, to comb the whole of Kenya or Tanzania to find you."

Ameena turned around on her knees, unable to believe what her mother was saying. "*Hooyo!*" she exclaimed, a mixture of happiness and sadness tearing at her. "*Aabo* will find us. He will kill us!"

"No, he will kill me…first," she assured her daughter gravely. "He will not forgive me for it. But I shall think of that later."

There were tears of disbelief. Just when she had thought her mother hated her and lived in fear that she would tell her father, here she was planning a way for her to leave.

"I shall speak to Hassan when he comes. Your father is going away when he returns to check on farming in the Elgon region. That should give me time to plan things out. *Macaan*, he cannot know you are pregnant!"

Ameena had thought it a last-straw attempt, but she trusted her mother. As soon as Abdi returned from the Elgon area, Hassan sought permission to leave immediately; *family matters*, he told Abdi. He promised to return as soon as they dealt with the situation, possibly in a week. Hassan had been Abdi's best worker so far, never taking time off or going off for long periods. He had grown fond of him like a father would, and he sent him off with a delicious farewell dinner.

Hassan returned to his home and waited two days. In that time Abdi took a trip into Kisenyi, a growing hub for many Somali clansmen fleeing Mogadishu. He always told Bushra, a "little Mogadishu" was growing from the roots planted by the refugees trickling into the small landlocked country, and maybe they could consider moving from Busia farther inward. He had heard of the small-scale trade of camel milk and sugar going on. He was hoping to partner with traders within and hopefully interest them to go further to Kisumu, maybe reach Dar-es-Salaam if the movement across borders permitted. His eyes lit up as he told Bushra that at least they still had areas where their people upheld their values and culture, and he wanted to see how he could be a part of them, creating wealth with and for them.

He told her of another growing community in the heart of Kenya: "Eastleigh is going to be home for our people...I believe. We shall have a home again with family far and near."

Bushra would nod and smile, although she had not neglected to highlight the tight-knit community they had at the border and how central it was to his business.

"Let's build here, *macanto*. Let Kisenyi and Eastleigh come to us."

She was aware there were pockets of havens for many refugees like them mushrooming around Kenya and Uganda. Those who were not holed up in the camps in *Dadaab*, the northeastern province of Kenya, were hustling underground, further inland, creating businesses and a life loosely held by traditions they left behind.

Two days later, Hassan was in their compound in the dead of night. Bushra handed Ameena a bag with treats and food, her clothing and henna, and they kissed and hugged affectionately.

"Don't say goodbye, *gabadh macaan*," her mother told her. "But whatever happens, don't come back either. Time will forgive us."

With that, she had charged Hassan with Ameena's safety, and they had stealthily gone out into the night, walking a long distance into town where they got the bus to Nairobi. Hassan told her when they got to his place, he would map out his next plan. Possibly to the coastal area where one of his cousins lived or return to Nairobi, where he shared a house with another cousin, and they could stay there until she gave birth.

Chapter 7

January 1986

"**N**obody should take that what is happening today or what has been happening in the last few days as a mere change of guards. This is not a mere change of guards. I think this is a fundamental change in the politics of our country."

Loud applause accompanied by celebratory ululation embraced the confident speaker's introductory address, the newly sworn in President of Uganda, Yoweri Museveni, leader of the rebel National Resistance Army whose fierce takeover battle for Kampala from Tito Okello had seen much bloodshed and carnage in the landlocked country.

The neighbors whispered of rumored destruction heading their way and stayed close to their radios, nervously imagining the worst. They wondered if this newly installed government meant anything for them at all. Trade along the border between Uganda and Kenya was suffering because of the political relations between the two countries. Traveling back and forth had become a nightmare, with passports and identification papers being placed under the strictest of scrutiny. There were roadblocks every three miles, and unruly soldiers who patrolled the spaces of border crossing were a menace, taking portions of goods and beating sojourners at whim.

Ameena huddled close to Hassan, listening to the speech like everyone else in the canteen.

"In Africa we have seen so much change that change has become meaningless...It is no longer change; it's merely turmoil," Museveni's voice rose as the applause died down.

The news reporter cut in, speaking about the numbers present at the inauguration and how Kampala, although bearing the marks of war, seemed to be calm, and life was progressing normally.

"Macanto, you need to eat." Hassan nudged Ameena. "Hmm?" He held up a balled lump of rice with fish and urged her to open her mouth. "Little Hassan needs to be fed." He smiled at her. Ameena opened her mouth.

He watched her as she chewed, brushing away food debris that clung to the corner of her mouth.

"I think we will be here for a few hours. With the politics across the border, we are being delayed everywhere."

"I am scared, Hassan. What are we going to do if things don't work out?" She finally voiced her concern.

"What? Not work? We will be fine. Your mother gave her blessing. I told you I would take you all the way to Dar-Es-Salaam if we must. It's okay. We will be safe once we get to Nairobi." He put his arm around her reassuringly and fed her again.

The travelers who had stepped out of the bus in Kisumu rest area to freshen up, eat, and get onto the next bus toward Nairobi chatted away noisily about recent developments in Uganda. There was talk of rebel groups being recruited in Kenya and rumors that there might be more war. Speculation filled the air, and fear ate at the souls uncertain of their lives and businesses. Amid these uncertainties, the little radio transmitted ululations punctuating the victory speech filled with promises of progress from the charismatic new leader…everything was going to be all right.

"We live in hard times? *Tsk tsk.*" They overheard a worried voice pipe over the drone of voices.

It was hot and steamy in the little makeshift restaurant, with hard benches and long farmhouse tables that sunk and rose with every shifting of weight. A man left the table they were seated at and shouted to one of the serving women in Kiswahili that he needed water. The women who ran the restaurant were all Somali, or at least looked Somali. They did not wear their hijabs but adorned long kaftans they kept out of the way by doubling a *kanga* around their waists and bottoms. Travelers packed the little rustic restaurant, either eating or craning their ears to the radio that sat on the counter, leaning against the wall with peeling paint.

Someone shouted for whoever was close to the radio to turn the volume up a notch. A toddler threw a short-lived tantrum, instantly quashed by the severe warning of a feminine voice, possibly the mother. The constant rise and fall of voices, clinking of cutlery and dishes, and the general bustle of a suffocating eatery made Ameena dizzy and nauseated.

"I need to go outside, Hassan. It's too hot here. I feel sick," she said after she forced down the second handful of food he had fed her.

His handsome cocoa face softened with concern. "My Araweelo." He stroked her face and nodded. "Let's go."

He helped her up, and they stepped out of the way of a handful of people coming into the restaurant.

"*Njia yangu, mwanamke haipo vizuri!*" *Make way, my woman is not well,* he was announcing loudly in Kiswahili as he shoved aside people with his hand so Ameena could get through.

Outside, the sound of men cleaning out the buses merged with the spirited cry of crickets.

Hassan leaned back against the old peeling wall and pulled Ameena to him.

"*Soo dhawow, macanto,*" he told her soothingly, and she relaxed, allowing herself to feel protected in his arms. He caressed her gently, asking her from time to time if she felt better. Ameena played with the patterns on his shirt, tracing their design with the tips of her fingers, her head nested against his chest where his heart pulsated loudly against her ear.

They looked up at the sky. It was an inky night, but the stars were bright and flickering. She stared dreamily.

"Dar is like that at night. You can hear the ocean water lapping up to the shore and the sound of the night, crickets, small animals, night crawlers…aah, it's beautiful. I will take you there, and we can lie on the white sands. They are warm even at night, and we can make love there. Hmm?"

She smiled bashfully.

"That sounds so beautiful," she agreed, fantasizing about it. The nausea passed and soon they were being called to get back on the bus for another twelve-hour trip to Nairobi.

He caressed her cheek. *"Wanku jeclahey."* His voice dropped, drooping with the honeyed weight of his words.

She smiled, her heart and belly stirring. "I love you, too," she replied in Somali.

A bumpy twelve-hour ride is a tedious affair for anyone when stops for leg stretches and bathroom breaks are minimal. Ameena believed she bore that journey only because Hassan was with her. The debilitating fear that her father would have found out the lie her mother had conceived gnawed at her. From time to time, when the bus came breast to breast with a truck, Ameena's heart stopped, terrified it would be her father peering into the bus and seeing her and Hassan. She stopped herself from imagining what would happen.

Hassan teased her. His infectious, carefree, and confident attitude was what she needed to cover them both. She was afraid—too young to be away from home on her own. She was nervous and yet excited. She had only seen a few Somali girls in their community married off to much older men once they bled. She had often wondered if they were happy. Were they scared? She longed for her mother. Did they long for their mothers too?

Ameena dozed off thinking of her *hooyo* sitting on the three-legged wooden stool outside their medium-sized house dwarfed by a large compound that was the soul of their neighbors—the little Somaliland. Ameena's last moments with her mother had been intimate and rushed— her mother, both determined and fearful, loving and angry, firm and vulnerable. Ameena admired her for the decision she had made.

As she lay back against Hassan, she dreamed of a new life, a happy one. Each bumpy jolt on the crumpled express bus brought her closer and closer to it. It was going to be all right—her unborn baby and Hassan were her world, her joy.

Chapter 8

May 1986

Ameena lay on her side, motionless, her eyes still shut. She allowed the *pita pata* of rain on the corrugated rooftop to lull her back to a troubled sleep. Every time sleep beckoned to her, the dreams returned, rudely nudging her awake. So she lay there as still as she could, eyes shut tight, cloaked with memories and tears she held back behind the lids. She counted to ten slowly, "*kow...laaba...saddex... afar...shan...lix...toddoba...siddeed...sagaal...toban.*"

And she was back there, with the midwife, the smell of blood and excreta filling her nostrils, and she was screaming as the woman urged her to push...keep pushing, *riix*! And then...she was tired, but the bundle of life bursting forth from between her legs would not let her rest. So she pushed one more time and then again, and again...She was not sure whether she heard the midwife exclaim approval or she heard the baby announce its existence with a wail because after Ameena pushed and gave birth to her premature son, she passed out in exhaustion.

When she came to, the midwife Hassan had taken her to was dry-bathing her, humming a sad little tune. She was an older Somali woman referred to as Garissa Lodge's *Hooyoo, hooyow* Fadoosa, and everyone in the community in Eastleigh swore by her. Ameena stirred and *hooyow* Fadoosa looked up at her. A small smile touched her lips but not her eyes. "*Siddee baad dareen?*" she was asking. *How are you feeling?*

Ameena smiled. "Weak. Where is my baby?" she asked.

Hooyow Fadoosa averted her old gaze, and Ameena knew instantly something was wrong. *"Hooyow Fadoosa,* please…."

The older woman put the cloth into a small green basin with a contemplative slowness that alarmed Ameena. Her eyes were downcast, and she pursed her lower lip. Her lips moved sinuously in an answer that sounded like a prayer. "May you find peace *inshallah.* May Allah Bless his soul, make his grave a garden, and grant him the highest level of paradise…."

A deep hollow wail of sadness emanated from Ameena's lips before Hooyow Fadoosa could complete her sentence. "…your son…he is in *jannah ameen…pole, pole.*"

Ameena could not be comforted.

She stayed with the midwife for a week to gather her strength and heal. The midwives tutored the younger mothers on basic childcare and self-care for forty days after they had given birth. Soon after, the mothers returned to their homes, often welcomed with fanfare from family and a huge celebration. There was no need for a forty-day wait for Ameena; Hassan had been impatient and defied tradition…and now there was no baby to present.

Today was Ameena's last day at the midwife's, and her heart sat heavy in the pit of her stomach. She was terrified of Hassan's reaction to her somber news, even more that she had asked for the child to be buried without either of them present. It was customary for Muslims to bury their dead immediately.

"*Mama,* I brought you food." Someone was talking to her. The same someone who had brought her food all week as she lay in bed, but she only rolled from her left-to-right side. A heavy cloud camped over her, and it rained incessantly.

The girl did the same thing she always did, laid the food beside her bed and left, usually returning at lunch to an untouched bowl. If Ameena did not eat by the evening *ṣalāt,* the *Hooyow,* came in and forced her to eat. When she wasn't lying in bed, drifting in and out from one bad dream to another—where a child cried to be held only for her to find it dead, moist soil and weeds invading its little body as it sunk deeper into the earth that swallowed it whole—she was crying. Sometimes she whimpered; other times she wailed. But most times she sobbed softly, continuously, muttering a prayer of supplication for forgiveness from God and Hassan.

The week finally ended, and the unease in her belly remained. She had rationalized it to blame; she was the reason the baby had died. The weight of her guilt would not allow her to look into Hassan's eyes when he came to pick her up in the old battered Volkswagen his cousin had let him borrow.

"Araweelo," he was saying, breathing in excitement, "our son! Where is he?" Hassan had run toward her when he came to the estates. He had been calling the unborn child a boy long before it was to be born. Ameena sat outside the house she had been living in for a week now, her travel bag crouched by her sandaled feet, and she had worn the black hijab and *baati* Hoyoow Fadoosa had given her. She had never prayed so earnestly as she did that week. All her prayer time had been lip service before because they required it of her as a good Muslim woman, but tragedy does something to one, makes one vulnerable and in need of saving grace.

Devoid of strength for much talk, she grimly replied, "He is dead. Our son died." And then the tears flowed, a river of shame and pain, and all strength gleaned from a week of mutterings to a higher power crumbled like the historical British Cemetery in Berbera.

Hassan stopped dead in his tracks, only inches from her; his mouth opened and closed of its own accord; his almond-shaped brown eyes widened over his handsome, dark, smooth face. Ameena's silent sobs morphed into audible whimpers. He walked past her into the nursing house, calling for Hoyoow Fadoosa, as if he needed confirmation.

Ameena groaned and moaned as she waited by the door, seated on a three-legged stool. Hassan returned and tapped her shoulder. "Let's go," was all he said with a strange tightness.

Amid tears, she hoped he would hold her, comfort her, and when he did not, her belief that it truly was her fault nested deeper into her soul as if in finality.

They drove back in silence. From the corner of her eyes, she could see his jaws clench and unclench. She sniffed, wiping her nose against the edges of the veil.

"Stop crying!" he told her, almost ten minutes into their journey back to his place.

"*Macaan*, he was born dead." She tried to explain like she was exonerating herself from blame. "I don't know…"

"*Essh*," he silenced her. She recoiled. And that was all that was said till they got home.

In the months that followed, Hassan did not touch her. He sat for hours alone outside the house that they shared with one of Hassan's cousins, Liban, chewing *qaad*. He talked less and less with her and went out most evenings with his loud group of friends. Guilt ate at her like a cancer until one evening, tired of the empty, loud spaces that had become their life, she decided it was time to speak about it.

She lay awake listening to the wind; it had been raining for days. That rainfall that is not a heavy downpour or a drizzle, an in-between steady flow that appears deceptively light but creates rivulets in potholes and soaks one wet to the underwear. She could hear a stray dog bark, and she tossed and turned, waiting, her heart growing heavier with anxiety. She wondered if talking about it would be a good idea. Tonight? Maybe not. Maybe tomorrow. She was not sure. She ached for him, for the wild romance they'd had. She wanted him to forgive her for the death of their child. She wondered how the light in her life had suddenly turned bleak in only a moment. She missed her *hooyo*. If only she could see her, ask her to help. There was no one she knew in Kenya. Their lives were excluded from the community she knew because they were still hiding from her father.

Maybe returning home, if even for a night, for the warmth of her mother, the smell of incense and breakfast in the compound, their fortnightly beauty routine…just the two of them. School. She missed *school*. Life was easier then, and she had taken it for granted.

She wondered if it would have been different if she had accepted marrying Faraax. Would she be less sad? She would never know now.

Then she heard the key turn in the lock, the voices of men rise and fall in laughter. Hassan and Liban were back, joking in Kiswahili like it was noon, loud and boisterous. Ameena sat up waiting; her chest heaved in anticipation. Hassan finally walked into their room, unbuttoning his shirt as he did and not turning on the light. The pale light from the security bulb outside cast shadows within and illuminated him.

"Araweelo!" he rasped, "waiting for me?"

Her heart leaped within her. "Yes," she replied quickly.

He chuckled, "Good…good."

She readied herself to speak.

"How was your night?"

He smirked. "Like always."

He removed his trousers and tossed them to the side. In the light that spilled through the light draping over their window, she could see him swollen, pulsating. Her heart quickened.

He walked to her, staggering slightly, and threw the covers off. She inched away, making room for him as he dropped beside her like a sack of potatoes that had fallen off a speeding truck. The smell of alcohol spread upon her and the sheets. She had learned to tolerate his drinking. He had dismissed her protests against it, telling her most people were hypocrites, even Muslims.

"I can take you to a club and count out for you how many are Muslims… all the ones with alcohol in their hands," he had told her dismissively, and they dropped the topic.

He turned to look at her. "Hmm, why are you awake?" The strong pungent smell of *qaad* and alcohol on his breath clouded her face, and it broke her heart. He had never drunk this much until after the loss.

"I am sorry," was all she could say, even though she had carefully rehearsed this conversation several days before.

"Hmm? Sorry?" he asked.

His touch burned her skin. It felt alien yet familiar. It had been too long.

Her body exploded with need, melting her tension. She nodded. "The baby..."

He sighed. "Come here, Araweelo." He coaxed her to him.

She inched closer, her head on his chest. His heartbeat, loud and fast, raged through her ears. It felt like coming home. The familiarity of it threw her back to many places they went to together, from Lamu, as he promised, to Dar-es-Salaam. Places that bore the hallmarks of their unadulterated love.

"Show me how much you love me," he whispered to her.

Tormented by guilt and fear that his love for her had waned, coupled with the ache of loneliness from being estranged from his touch for months, Ameena eagerly discarded her night dress and showed her man how much she wanted him.

The next morning, and for the next few days, it was as if their lovemaking had not happened. Hassan was further from her.

"Why are you doing this?" she had asked him tearfully when she finally gathered the courage. It was a warm afternoon after lunch. Liban was not around eavesdropping on their conversation, and Hassan was sober.

"Doing what?" he asked her, raising his brows.

"You...you treat me like I am not here," she sobbed.

He shook his head. "You are a child, Ameena. A real woman cooks for her man, cleans, gives him her body, and does not complain."

It took Ameena aback, for he had called her by her name for the first time in a very long time, "You said I should not..."

"That was before the baby..." he interrupted.

Ameena felt her body go numb. Since the loss, she had walked around with a dark cloud hovering over her. When she thought finally the sun was coming out, it wasn't. Hassan blamed her still. "I said I was sorry." She sank helplessly to her knees before him. His lean body occupied a three-legged stool on the veranda of Liban's house.

"I…we can do it again and get another one."

Hassan looked at her. His eyes flickered with amusement and something else she had never seen—something that shook her.

"Our firstborn son died!" he barked. "You are useless!"

The words reverberated through her like a cannonball shot out of a cannon with mega force.

She begged in vain for a second chance. The drinking did not stop; it increased, then the beating began…It was a shove here and there, a slap now and again, administered with hefty measures of insults. Then the women…fanning her jealousy and fury. When he took another woman and announced it to her, she cried for days, and he laughed at her, calling her a stupid child. She was not woman enough; she did not understand the world; he had made a mistake taking her away from her home.

"Faraax should pay me. I will hand you to him gladly," he would chortle, much to her annoyance and hurt. When he did not have a woman, he woke her up in the night and demanded she sleep with him. Refusal was tantamount to rape. She grew increasingly afraid of his friends whom he had, in a moment of drunkenness, offered her to, "if they were interested."

Ameena had shrieked in horror, quickly retreating to the safe confines of their room and locking the door.

She cried more than she ate, and she hurt more than she slept. Her mother came to her mind often, but fear numbed her when she thought of returning home. How could she go? She didn't even know the way home.

* * *

Hassan only let her go to the store to buy milk, bread, and eggs once a week. Sometimes she hid the milk or poured salt in it to buy her another day to leave the house and buy more. The grocery store was a mile away, and she left early, before Hassan was awake and right after Liban had gone to work. It was the only store within a mile of their neighborhood, and it sat alone in the four-block building that housed offices and a barbershop.

She covered herself up with her *abaya* and carried a strong shopping bag made of thick plastic, then slowly ambled to the store. Most days, she was lost in thought, thankful to be outside. Some mornings were as biting cold as Nairobi could get, but other mornings like that morning were warm, and she savored the walk like an inmate taking a routine stroll in the prison yard. The line at the store was relatively long, which was strange for morning runs on a weekday, till she found out fresh loaves of bread had just arrived and, as one customer in line put it, "The early bird catches the worm."

Ameena wasn't in a hurry to leave. She scoured the aisles of items that were piled neatly on three shelves; two faced each other and one was far off, vertically placed behind the other two. The rows allowed the lines to snake as far back as they could.

She bought OMO detergent in their blue and white packets, a tin of Blueband margarine, bread sliced in a plastic bag, and milk. As she proceeded to the line, she recalled Hassan yelling at her not to forget his *imperial lather* soap. He was struggling with the last paper-thin portion, the size of a communion wafer. Ameena quickly double-tracked her steps to the soap aisle and picked two pieces, looking longingly at the different soaps on the shelf but dared not pick any. As she backed away, her eyes on the shelf, she bumped into someone, dropping the soaps. Ameena bent over, quickly picking them up, then turned to apologize to the person she had bumped into: "*Pole, pole.* I am sorry…" she was saying to the woman, who was picking up a loaf of bread that had fallen off her overloaded left arm.

The woman laughed raucously. "Ah-ah, it's nothing. Just bread." She slid it back on her arm and looked at Ameena. Ameena stared back at her. The woman she had bumped into was no doubt coastal. Her skin was the color of pure refined honey, glowing and silky. Bright red lipstick coated her luscious lips. Her eyes were smoky and sensual, and she looked like she had just left an expensive outing with the outfit she had on. She had seen these types of women only in the magazines she had browsed through and the foreign soap operas on television that she spent so many idle evenings watching.

"Sorry…" she said again, dropping her gaze, relishing in the strong floral scent that wafted off this beautiful creature.

The woman laughed again. "What is it? Do I look funny?" She was appraising herself in the sparkly minidress she wore.

"No." Ameena shook her head, embarrassed. "Sorry. I have…just… never seen…"

"What? A *malaya*?" The woman stood with arms akimbo, daring Ameena to say something.

Ameena felt too embarrassed to pursue that line of conversation. Hassan liked his women dressed like this, and here she was wrapped up like a mummy. Instead, she said, "You are smart. I want to dress like you."

The woman laughed again, that raucous laugh. "I can teach you if you want…teach you about this and a lot more."

They stood in the aisle, appraising each other. Ameena contemplated lessons from a prostitute. Maybe if she became more daring like them, then she would not have to compete with the ones Hassan brought home. She would win him back to her. He would call her Araweelo again and more often, and rightly so. Araweelo was strong and wild and bold and, she imagined, oozed lots of sex appeal.

"I want to learn," she said.

The woman scoffed, looked Ameena over. "You are young, *nice young*. And you are beautiful. But so, so naïve."

Ameena held her gaze stubbornly. No one called her young and naïve without her proving them wrong. "Then teach me and I shall prove to you I am more than that."

The woman smiled. Pleased. She nodded. "You have some fire. Do you know Klub Malta, its *club* with a *K*?"

Ameena thought fast. She had never heard of the place before. With her eyes fixed on the honey-colored woman, she lied: "Yes."

The woman grinned, impressed. "Come tonight then. When you come, ask for Soonam. I am Hayira. Soonam is the one you shall meet. I will tell her you are our new sister."

A wave of anxiety seized Ameena. Leaving home at night was unthinkable, but she felt a need to please this woman. Her energy was magnetic, intoxicating, and wild. She seemed so free and sensual. In the aisle that morning she felt lost and small, a young, naïve girl in love with a man she was trying to please. Desperately.

Instead, she nodded. "Okay."

The woman smiled at her and walked off, sashaying seductively. Her heavy behind swayed from side to side in hypnotic motion. Ameena passed her hand over her backside, wondering if it was as big as Hayira's.

She did not go that night or the next or the next, but every day she bided her time, planned it out, and in the weeks that followed, she imagined bumping into Hayira again. She would throw herself into curated dialogues in her mind, how she would explain her reason for not coming, and every excuse she conjured up seemed as dry and as lifeless as her existence. Every trip to the store brought a nervousness, but she never saw Hayira again.

Three days before New Year's Day, as she placed a loaf of bread and eggs on the countertop, she mustered the courage to ask the shop seller if he knew about *club* Malta with a *K*.

The man tittered. "What do you want with Klub Malta? *Sio mahali pa wasichana wazuri.*" *It's no place for good girls.*

Ameena had loathed herself for the way the lies rolled off her tongue as though they were second nature. "My sister isn't...*msichana mzuri.* She ran away from home, and someone said girls who run away end up in Klub Malta. I want to find her, *Inshallah.*"

The man smiled, "They do," he agreed. "She must be long gone now, if she was a good Muslim girl like you."

He rang her order, and she gave him the money. As he counted it and gave her back her change, he leaned over and whispered, "On Koinange Street." He looked at her conspiratorially. "Be careful." He winked and moved on to the next customer.

"I shall." She gave him the biggest, most earnest, innocent look.

In her isolated world with no friends, no family, Ameena desperately sought counsel in the scattered *Drum* magazines that Liban left lying around the house. The art of seduction was a mystery to her, and everything she read was something she knew was unclean. Her circumstances dictated it was necessary.

She craved to go out with Hassan, away from the life that existed behind four peeling walls, television soaps, and *Drum* magazines, but Hassan would not hear of her going anywhere or talking to anyone either. "I am not your prisoner," she had protested once.

"*Wewe.*" He had wagged a warning finger in her face, and that was it.

The magazines became her refuge; she read short stories, of apartheid in South Africa and life in the shantytowns, browsed through pictures of beautiful looking people she longed to be like, and escaped into the pages for hours until Hassan returned and reality slapped her in the face like a harsh gust of wind.

The more she read, the more she decided, as her mother had said, *to see the world*; she planned her escape carefully, watching the pattern of the men—when they left to go to the bar and when they returned. She no longer cried, and she did as she was told—cleaning, cooking, and watching another consummate their relationship whenever Hassan pleased. Her longing to leave consumed her, and she blocked out the bleakness of her life.

* * *

On the night of New Year's Eve 1987, as everyone was out in the streets celebrating the birth of 1988 with music, food, and dancing and while Ameena was asleep, Hassan stumbled into their bedroom dragging with him a slim, dark-skinned woman in a tight miniskirt and revealing blouse.

"Araweelo," he slurred, "Araweelo, get up. Get out…get out…now!" He had gone to the bed and roughly shaken her. Ameena had woken up with a start and, upon seeing the woman, had instantly asked him what was going on.

"Get out!" he ordered her.

Pent-up anger blazed through her soul from months of torment. "No! This is my bed." Hassan had jeered and dragged her out bodily, raining slaps and blows to her face and her body. She fought back, lunging at him and scratching him, but he overpowered her and threw her off the bed. Shocked and surprised, she screamed for Liban.

"No one can save you…" Hassan slurred, half-laughing. "You can't go anywhere!" He roughly shoved her out of the room in her nightdress. "Get out, you childless whore!"

Ameena threw her weight against the door, frantically banging and scratching. It would not budge. It was pointless. Eventually she sank to the floor, leaning on the door, and sobbed noiselessly throughout the shamelessly loud, vulgar sex Hassan and the woman were having inside. No matter how many times she heard him in the night with different women, every time it stabbed at her like it was the first time. *What would Araweelo do?* she thought through the tears.

The night pulsated with music and life, with promises of new beginnings, forgiveness of old wrongs, and plans for a better future. Tonight seemed like the opportune time for her to go to Klub Malta to meet Hayira.

She changed out of the night clothes she was wearing and slipped on the only burqa and hijab Fadoosa had given her, then changed her mind, recalling what Hayira had worn when they had met. Ameena scanned through her modest clothing piled in a basket ready for ironing; nothing seemed able to provide that image she envisioned, so she settled for her best dress; a calf-length A-line dress fitted with a belt and a sweater to ward off the cold night.

What would Araweelo do?

She scanned the drawers in the kitchen where Hassan stashed change.

She emptied pockets of unwashed trousers that were piled in a wicker basket in an empty room they used to store things. After a good ten minutes, she had collected enough shillings for two bus fares.

As her fingers worked through her hair, fastening it behind her head, she wrapped a scarf over it; she prayed Hassan would not leave the room or Liban return from his reveling.

No one did, and in the dead of night as the world swayed in excitement at the turn of a new year, Ameena slunk away and walked purposefully down a narrow street she did not know or care to; all she knew was she needed to get away quickly and see the world, as her mother had advised her to. She needed to get to Koinange Street.

Chapter 9

New Year's Day, 1988

Ameena took a lift a mile from Liban's place, lying that she was going to visit her sister and did not have enough money. The little Beetle she was squashed into with two other drunks, friends of the driver, offered a scary ride. Her heart leaped when they swayed, and the woman and two men in the back would roar with laughter and then sing "Happy New Year" out of tune. Eventually, unsure of her safety, she pleaded with the driver to stop at any point. "I can walk from here," she told him.

"To Koinange? *Hapana!* It will be shorter if we take you," he insisted.

The passenger in the back with her laughed. "Stay, baby." The woman leaned into her drunkenly. "You can't leave me here with these two…" her speech slurred.

"We have another party! Come, come!" the man beside her said much too loudly.

They urged her to stay. Ameena refused until they eventually let her off.

"Bye, baby, see you soon." The woman waved at her, swaying in the seat like an understuffed doll.

"You are missing out! But Happy New Year!" The driver was grinning at her as she stepped out of the car.

"Happy New Year!" the drunks chorused and whooped in half-hearted gaiety as the car sped off, zigzagging perilously. Ameena hurried off, watching her back to check she wasn't being followed. She could not tell where she was and kept peering at the street signs and names.

Her mind raced: *What if Hassan found her? Did she really know or want to know these people? What if they killed her? Could she find a way home instead?* She brushed her doubts aside and walked on. If she was going around in circles, she would ask someone soon enough. The vague directions given her by the driver of the Beetle were not helping, but she scraped bits of what he had said in slurred verbiage and walked on.

With the daybreak, she could see better. The lone lanes led to different corridors and paths with bigger buildings, more clusters of buildings and better-looking streets. The city always took her breath away. When Hassan had taken her on a tour of Nairobi and then Dar-Es-Salaam, she had been struck with awe by the buildings and the way the roads snaked in and out of one another. The sketchy explanations and directions were finally making sense, and she trudged on until she came to the tall building stacked with blocks of buildings. Sitting at the corner of the traffic lights, a gigantic neon sign flickered on and off with the words "Klub Malta."

"*Club* with a *K*," she said to herself triumphantly. She was here! Her heart leaped with relief.

Just below the words "Klub Malta" was a silhouetted feminine figure, well-rounded hips jutting to one side, hands up in the air above swirls of hair as if the painter captured her in motion and paused at that precise moment.

There were empty cartons and bottles strewn along the pavement, the evidence of the previous night's reveling. She stood outside, staring at the partially open door with a charcoal-gray padding over it. She waited, uncertain whether to knock or call out. She bet on someone passing by or emerging from within.

The streets were empty. Revelers had slunk to their homes after a wild New Year's Eve, possibly nursing hangovers or shamefully walking home from a stranger's bed. One or two people stumbled drunkenly toward an unknown destination. Nothing moved in the club for a minute, then two. Eventually, a young man humming a tune she was not familiar with came out, broom and bucket in hand.

He was the embodiment of *bournvita* chocolate in a tall, lean glass... frothing at the top. He wore a black T-shirt with the image of Bob Marley on it, dreadlocks arrayed around his head, caught in ecstatic motion, a very lifelike black-and-white picture. The sleeves had been ripped off unevenly to shorten them, exposing the young man's well-toned arms.

When he saw her, his eyes—clear white with dark brown irises— sparkled with a smile that traveled down his narrow nose to his firm lips and stayed there. It was a smile that she longed for. A warm familiarity clung to it as if they had known each other for a very long time. She marveled at his teeth, stark white beautifully lined pearlies set in dark gums, and his arresting eyes beckoned to her—it made his smile priceless. She did not want him to stop smiling. There was a sexiness about him, an ease about him that reminded her of Hassan. She suddenly became self-conscious standing before him and smoothed over her dress absently. She took in a gulp of air and let it out slowly. That sensation of suffocation consumed her. It was as if whatever he exuded sought to smother her.

"Sasa?" he greeted, as he propped chiseled, lean arms over the broom and placed his chin on them, watching her.

Ameena hesitated, surprised. *"Poa."*

She hated how his eyes glided over her in a very languid and curious way. She felt trapped, like a bird in a cage. When she glanced at him again, she noticed the smile was not fading. If anything, it now carried a playful tinge to it.

"What is a good church girl doing here?" he asked in Kiswahili, his brows furrowing.

Ameena glanced away, realizing everything she was battling with was her sudden attraction to him. It *had* to be the arms and the uncanny raw masculine energy, she told herself...like Hassan's...*more* than Hassan's. *No!* The smile...the *warm* smile.

"Hayira…said I come here…" She spoke haltingly. "…to see Soonam."

"Aah." He nodded like a mystery had been solved, then asked, "Are you Christian?"

Ameena scoffed at his teasing. She smiled and looked up at him, focusing on their banter to keep herself composed.

"Does it matter?"

He raised an eyebrow. "Fine. You would not be here if you were."

"Maybe you are assuming too much." She narrowed her eyes, amazed at how she was leveling with him. He ran his thumb over his lower lip, looked her over one more time, and shrugged.

"Let's go then. Soonam, it is." He placed the bucket and pail by the door.

He wiped his hands on a wet rug and threw it in the bucket, then disappeared inside briefly and reemerged wearing a stonewashed denim jacket over the Bob Marley T-shirt.

"It's not far where we are going. Madam Soonam lives near her club."

"This is her club?" Ameena asked, her eyes widening. She had never known a woman to own anything.

He snorted. "What do you know?"

She frowned at his condescending tone. "I know you are the man who cleans up after everyone," she shot back.

"Manga, my name is Manga, and I am not the cleaner. Watch your mouth, Christian girl!"

Ameena pressed her lips together, more out of irritation than fear.

True to his word, they arrived at Soonam's place in less than ten minutes. She lived right by the University of Nairobi in an apartment complex. The apartments were colonial stone and brown. They looked like they had dropped out of time into the very heart of K- Street, as people liked to refer to Koinange Street. Two flights of stairs brought them in front of a cream-colored door. Manga knocked on it as loud as he could.

Ameena could hear muffled voices within, and then someone jiggled with the locks, and the door flew open. In front of them stood a woman in a see-through negligee. Ameena gasped, visibly shocked, the woman's nakedness boldly staring back at her. The woman looked Manga over, hardly acknowledging Ameena, and called back, "*Uko,* Manga!" Her toenails were a bright blue in pink bathroom sandals. She left the door open and walked off like her nakedness was nothing to hide.

Ameena hesitated. The only times she had been boldly naked were with Hassan and in front of the mirror. For a split second, she wondered if she was in the right place. Manga did not seem to mind the nakedness. He motioned to her with his head, urging her to enter. He followed behind her. The doorway opened into an expensively decorated lounge area, spacious with the most beautiful furniture she had ever seen. It smelled of a perfume she could not place. The carpet was rich, thick, and multicolored…definitely not from Kenya. The couches and seats were things she saw only in magazines.

Ameena gaped. *This,* she knew, was how she wanted to live. She did not know how long she stood there gawking at the décor, the paintings on the wall, the scents, the colors. Now and again, a woman passed by half-naked or in something sheer, but she was enchanted by the opulence of the living room.

"Who?" she heard someone ask, and then a mix of voices. She thought she recognized one of the female voices.

"That's our new sister!" came the exclamation from a voice she knew she had heard before. Ameena wheeled around on her heels and smiled, relieved to see the familiar face of Hayira.

Hayira hurried to her and hugged her. "You came! I thought you would not."

Ameena smiled. "I could not…but now I am here."

"It's okay; you are here." Hayira did the dismissive wave gesture with her hand like she had done when she'd met Ameena at the store.

"Who is this?" another voice rose from behind them. Hayira stepped aside, and Ameena looked at the woman who had spoken. She was Somali, tall, exquisite, and smelled of otherworldliness and wealth. Ameena knew then she wanted to be like her.

"Ameena," she introduced herself.

The tall, exquisite beauty whose hair was flat-ironed and coiled, falling to one side of her face to her bare shoulders, smiled. *"Iska warran."* *How are you?*

Ameena swelled with pride. The connection she longed for seemed to find its place here, *"Alhamdulillah, waan iska fiicanahay,"* she replied. *I am well by God's grace.*

Manga, who was standing nearby, looked at them, bored. He mumbled under his breath.

The taller woman smiled, took Ameena's hands, and leaned in, kissing her cheeks lightly. An acknowledgment of kinship. "I am Soonam, and yes, Hayira is right; we *are* sisters." Soonam's lips spread into a warm smile that touched her eyes, and they sparkled. She spoke in a very polished English accent Ameena had never heard before. It was so beautiful, so out of this world, she did not want her to stop speaking.

"Manga says you are a good *Christian* girl." She let out a little laugh.

Ameena smiled. "He assumes so."

"Oooh, I like her," Soonam said, a small smile played at the corner of her lips, her eyes sweeping over Ameena with curious interest. Hayira gave a proud nod in agreement, for her instincts had been approved of.

"Here, let's help you out of that."

Soonam reached for Ameena's veil, and Ameena recoiled from her. "But..." She hesitated, torn between her convictions and offending Soonam.

Soonam's smile widened reassuringly. "It is all right. Feel free. I'm sure hell has worse criminals than Muslim girls who don't cover their hair."

Hearing Soonam say it that way, trivializing a religious practice she had believed in all her life, astounded her, so she boldly asked, "Don't you believe in God?"

Soonam shrugged delicately and rolled her eyes like she was entertaining a child. "Let me tell you, all those rules handed by imams, sheikhs—those men who think they alone hear God—are stupid!" She took Ameena's hand as she spoke.

Ameena could not help feeling there was a lesson they had immersed her in, and it was important she paid attention. *She is the perfect Queen Araweelo*, Ameena thought.

"God…Is God real? Is he the wind? A she? A he?" Soonam looked at Ameena and shook her head. "I don't believe in a God who will send me to hell because I did not wear a veil. That sounds man-made. No female god would pass such a ridiculous law."

Ameena did not know how to respond. She mulled over Soonam's words.

Maybe Soonam was right, Ameena concluded, besides where else could she go?

Soonam squeezed her hand. "It's all right."

Ameena glanced around and nodded, allowing Soonam to lower her veil. "There," the older woman said as she unfastened it from her head. "Lovely hair. This is your crowning beauty. Why hide it? Don't worry…I will teach you many things."

Ameena nodded, feeling suddenly exposed and conscious of Manga more than Hayira or Soonam.

Manga watched them briefly before mumbling something about going to the kitchen. As Ameena stared at his retreating broad back, she thought of Hassan. Would he find her? Would he even look for her? She doubted it, and it made her ache inside. Perhaps she would go back to him after learning how to please him, and he would never leave. Then together, they would see the world, have lovely children, and maybe even live in South Africa, where she would dress like the women in the *Drum* magazines.

Soonam was observing her. "That man, he is a beast. Never look at him." She waved a delicate, manicured finger toward Manga's retreating back. "Come, let's sit. Tell me about you, *macaanto*. You look so tired, though."

"I'm okay," she replied, eager to please.

Soonam requested Hayira bring them tea. Music played from another part of the apartment, and Ameena saw the girl in the sheer negligee walk past the living room, her hair in large blue and pink rollers.

Ameena sat down. It had been a long night and the relief of finally being away from Hassan, the warmth of her reception, left her aware of how drained she was. She needlessly put on a brave face.

Soonam was watching her keenly. "You have not seen this, have you?"

Ameena could not help thinking how keen this woman was, noticing her every movement and gesture. Ameena shook her head. All the women she had seen so far were in light, silky clothing. Hayira had on a gold wrap gown held together by a matching belt. The wrap was so short it barely covered her huge jiggly behind.

She learned later it was a *chemise*...sexy nightwear. After all, it was still quite early. Out of the corner of her eye, she saw Manga grab the buttocks of the sheer-dressed girl, and she shrieked and slapped him.

"He is trouble," Soonam said almost fondly.

"Is he the help?"

Soonam laughed. "Oh no, he is my nephew. My half-brother's son. My brother died while I was in England, and I returned often to see Manga. Smart lad," she said.

England. Ameena thought.

She stared at Soonam in awe. It all made sense. No wonder she was so polished.

"Why did you come back? Weren't you happy?"

Soonam scoffed. "Happy is relative. I have lived in England for over twenty years. My parents left Mogadishu, came here to Nairobi for a while, and then went to England. My father returned soon after, or maybe before—that part of the story is never clear, depending on whose angle you get it from—had an affair, had my half-brother with a Kenyan woman, came back to England as if nothing had happened. My mother lived in the UK until she died. She and my father divorced, but he was always supportive. I traveled with him, met my half-brother, and, well, like they say, the rest is history."

Ameena searched for the why and looked at Soonam. "You could have stayed in England."

Hayira came in with a tray filled with little cups on saucers and a huge thermos flask in the middle.

"Yes, I could, love, but I did not. I could not have children, you see, so I took care of Manga and started this business. It does well here, the club, too. Pleasure is big business."

Ameena waited. Soonam poured hot *chai,* steaming milk tea with spices, into the little teacups. Ameena stared at the cups in disappointment, imagining how in one gulp, teatime would be all over. Soonam opened a little glass jar on the side that contained cubed sugar, and with small metal tongs, she popped a cube into each of their cups.

"Too much sugar isn't good for you," she told Ameena as she picked up the teaspoon beside the saucer and daintily stirred her tea. Ameena could hardly hear the clinking sound as she did it. She tried to imitate Soonam.

"The trick is to not let the spoon touch the bottom of the cup as you stir," Soonam gently told her.

"But the cup is so small, *habo,*" Ameena complained as her attempt failed miserably and tea splashed onto her fingers.

Soonam smiled kindly. "Give it time," she responded in Somali.

Hayira returned with a plate full of slices of bread, boiled eggs, and shortcake biscuits on the side.

"You are a darling, Hayira. Sit with us." Soonam motioned to Hayira.

Ameena watched enthralled as Soonam chatted with grace and finesse. Even as she sipped her tea, her lipstick never smeared on the edge of the teacup. It stayed perfectly coated on her lips. She seemed to exist in this elegant bubble that was only hers, effortlessly. She sat up straight with her chest slightly arched, giving off a false impression of ampleness, never sipping her tea noisily or chomping on her bread and biscuits. Her knees pressed close, and they leaned to one side. There was an air of decorum that wafted off her. She noticed Hayira sat in the same polished way she later learned was how proper young women sat.

Before tea was over, she was telling them an edited version of her life story. One that did not involve Hassan. *What would they think of her? Could she trust them?* But the other reason was it made her feel inferior to them. They looked like they had it good. Much, much better than she ever had. Speaking of the mistreatment under Hassan or losing a baby would dent her newfound relationship with the sisterhood. She instead indulged them in half-truths about an arranged marriage she could not go through with. About escaping to Nairobi, about a friend she lived with, and finally bumping into Hayira that morning at the grocery store.

Soonam's keen attention unnerved her. Ameena constantly dropped her gaze, praying the lie would sell.

The older woman appraised her, and, with a slow smile spreading on her unsmudged lips, she asked blankly, "Are you then still a virgin? Did you undergo the knife?"

The knot in Ameena's belly tightened briefly. She shook her head at both questions.

"No knife? That is rare," Soonam replied, then called out to Manga, "I know you heard everything. There you have it. Is she still a good Christian girl to you?"

Manga emerged at the doorframe of the kitchen, leisurely stirring tea in a mug. He shrugged. "There is still something fresh about her."

Soonam laughed. "That one…" She pointed at him. "Stay away from him."

Ameena averted her gaze to Manga. Their eyes locked, and she saw in them that familiar fire she had seen in Hassan the first time he looked at her in her father's truck. It thrilled her broken heart and destabilized her starved body. She was not sure she wanted to stay away. He seemed to summon her with just a glance. She wanted him and was ashamed of the intensity of her feelings.

A flicker of a smile played on Soonam's shiny bronze-colored lips, her gaze drifting from Ameena to Manga. "Don't say I did not warn you." Ameena dropped her gaze, self-conscious.

After tea, Soonam introduced her to the establishment. She owned three of the flats and all of them were home to her society of girls, known as "Soonam Sisters," sixteen girls in total.

"You want quality, not quantity," she told Ameena. "I pick them myself, the highest-quality type of girls who are teachable, young, and preferably not been around too much. I can tell you have fire, but it's still dormant. I will train you to be *kulul*...hot, to burn these men with just a glance, to play with them, to amuse them, to excite them...Would you like that?"

Ameena nodded eagerly.

At the end of the tour, Soonam asked Hayira to take her to her room. "I want her in this house. This is a *special* one," she told Hayira.

"You must be tired, *macaanto*," Soonam told her gently, and Ameena felt that stinging throb for her mother rise like a tidal wave in her throat. She nodded, looking away so Soonam would not see the tears that brimmed in her eyes, dancing on the edge of her lids. Soonam gave her a room in the house, which she shared with another girl she had not met yet.

"Edith sleeps here. She is no trouble. She is working this week," Hayira told her. She found out Edith, her roommate, was in Tanzania escorting a rich businessman.

"Escorting?" Ameena said it more to herself. She did not understand what that meant but figured she would find out, eventually. The room was more beautiful than any room she had ever slept in. The beds were wide and covered with pretty, colorful duvets. Everything in the house looked foreign and exquisite, and the more Ameena saw, the more she was certain this was her destiny. This was what her mother wanted for her. She plopped on the bed, bouncing as she did, feeling its sleekness beneath her. She ran her fingers over the fluffy material in wonderment.

Hayira laughed. "Soft, eh?"

"Yes. How does Soonam have such beautiful things?" she asked, bewildered.

Hayira shrugged. "I don't know. I heard her mother left her a lot of wealth...her father, too. She was an only child. Some say she is friends with the Queen of England. Who knows?"

Ameena gasped in awe. "Oooh," was all she could say.

Hayira smiled importantly, like her being close to Soonam made her just as close an associate to the English queen. "*Unaonekana umechoka,* sweetie. There is a shower outside this door for you, and I shall put some clothes here that fit you. Rest. Yesterday was wild for us, so we are all tired."

Ameena nodded happily. For the first time in her life, she felt she belonged.

As she got ready to go, Hayira turned and winked at her. "You will like it here. Soonam likes you. That's always good. When Soonam *likes* you."

Chapter 10

In the days that followed, she learned basic table manners and the use of cutlery.

"We are not in the village. This is the city," Soonam told her.

Ameena recalled how well she would make a ball out of fried rice and stick goat meat pieces in it before she scooped it into her mouth. Cutlery felt like the interference of a natural process of eating. It was frustrating before it got easier. There were more lessons: how to read body language, how to speak like a lady, how to chew one's food, and how to sit. All components of the making of a proper lady.

"Before you become an escort, your value and worth is in your training to be the perfect lady. Hot in public and *hotter* in private." Soonam winked at her wickedly. Speaking many languages was one of Soonam's top skill requirements, and she squirmed in pleasure when Ameena told her she could speak five languages fluently. Her English was a little lacking. "We will work on that. Read more and watch more television in English."

The hardest part was reading. She hated books, so she settled for magazines, and Soonam did not push her. "Better to read something than nothing at all, *macaanto*." When the news came on at 8 p.m., Soonam called her to sit by her side so they could watch it together.

With Soonam, it was like having an elder *abaayo*, a sister, and Ameena inadvertently tried to please her by learning fast. More than that, Ameena made it a point to imitate Soonam's mannerisms. At bedtime, after she showered and changed, she would stand before the mirror brushing her hair and stare at her reflection, push her chest out like Soonam, lift her chin, and try to speak like Soonam: slow, sensual, and deliberate.

"Your voice is huskier and deeper." Her roommate caught her one night when Ameena thought she was asleep. Ameena jumped. The other girl snickered, pulling the covers from over her head. She sat up in bed. A fairly buxom chocolate-skin girl with a face as round as a saucer. "It's nice. I like it." Edith encouraged her.

Soonam told her the same thing. "It's a lovely sexy-sounding voice, *macaan*. Use it well. It can spellbind any of these *ragga*. That is what *you* want."

"How?" Ameena asked her.

Soonam sighed. "It will come to you eventually as you become more aware of yourself."

She wanted to ask how that was possible but decided against it. She had asked too many questions already. In the two weeks she had been there, she had watched girls come and go. Sometimes they were gone for a night, sometimes days. Every morning she had breakfast with Soonam and brushed up on her culinary skills.

"Sometimes the clients are very exposed. Learn to use various spoons and knives and forks, *macanto.* Don't worry; I will teach you. You are doing so well already." Soonam encouraged her. Ameena could not imagine escorting a rich investor or someone highly placed in society.

"Are they old?" she asked Soonam, who laughed at the query. She imagined with alarm seeing someone like Faraax there. Did he even visit such places? she wondered. Her mother told her he'd had over six wives already. Surely, he needed no more pleasing.

"Some are old. Some are young. Don't worry about that now. By the time you experience them, you will be my crème de la crème."

One morning, Ameena woke up to find a sheer bright yellow dress placed at the foot of her bed. She showered and sat on her bed, wondering what to do with it. She recalled the girl who had opened the door when she'd first arrived with Manga almost three weeks earlier in a similar pale blue chemise. After several minutes, there was a knock on the door, and Soonam came in. "Tea is getting cold, *qalbi*," she said, just like a big sister. "Get dressed."

Ameena stared at the short see-through gown, and Soonam laughed. "What is wrong?"

Ameena could not bring herself to wear it. "I c-can't do it," she stammered, hating to let Soonam down.

"Let me help you," the older woman said, and thus began the lessons of the beauty of the nude body. Soonam made Ameena stand and stare at her reflection in the mirror and appraise her slender curves, the faint flair of stretch marks on her thighs and stomach, her breasts that she felt were much bigger than they should be on her body, her little flaws and bumps. Soonam had her pay attention to the tiniest things. "Things women don't pay attention to, but men do. The neck. The shoulders, collarbones, the back of her knees, her heels, insignificant but very erotic." Soonam had drooled the words out.

Mesmerized, Ameena stared at her reflection while listening to Soonam, paying attention to those areas. She pondered the meaning of beauty and where it dwelled in some of these places on her body and on the other girls. She was glad to realize they all had things they were not comfortable with. Her stretch marks after the pregnancy were a stubborn reminder of the tragic loss of little Hassan and her life afterward. She hated those. Letting Soonam see them scared her, but the older woman said nothing.

The older girls in the sisterhood oozed a different level of confidence. They were not shy about their imperfections, and to her that made them even more beautiful. "Men see your confidence, and it draws them to you like flies to honey. If you are not yet confident about some things, focus only on those things you are confident about," Soonam concluded her lesson in self-confidence. She held Ameena's face in her hands and said, "*Waad quruxsan tahay, qalbi*," *You are beautiful, heart.* And Ameena believed her.

It was over two months now since she had left Hassan. Some nights, she dreamed of him and missed him. Other days, she hated him. It was a torturous experience. Hayira took her to the Klub on weekends, along with a few other girls. "Mix and mingle. Understand the nightlife in Nairobi." Soonam encouraged her. She had spied Manga often but never spoke with him. He was always busy in a little back office, only showing his tall frame to clear a dispute. His eyes would smile at her in acknowledgment, and her heart would race, praying he would speak to her. He hardly did.

She woke up one morning to an empty house and a brief note scribbled on a colored notepad. Soonam had signed the message. "It's Manga's birthday" said the cursive scribble, an open suggestion that required her action. Soonam had let her know she was going to be out of Nairobi for a couple of days on business. Hayira would be her best contact if she needed anything and, "Oh, Manga will be at Klub Malta, if you want to stop by to study how things work."

Ameena gasped upon reading that. *Manga's birthday!* She ran back to her room, conscious of herself in the sheer, short gown she was now used to wearing around the house full of women. She was even more carefree with wearing nothing underneath the sheer material, like the other girls. Her confidence was further boosted by the compliments that followed, not just from the girls but from a handful of clients who were intimate with Soonam. They called for tea and spent a considerable amount of time in her office. Usually, when they emerged, a girl or two were selected to accompany them.

"Who are those?" she asked Hayira one morning

"Soonam's special friends." Hayira winked at her.

After trying on several outfits, Ameena settled for a tank top and a wide floral skirt that buttoned to her knees, a part of a set of new clothes that Soonam had given her. "I got them from England last year, and none of the girls could fit in them, but I think they are your size. You have fine, delicate curves," she told her. Ameena relished the new outfits. Soonam discouraged her from covering her hair again, "You need to be free. It's bloody bullshit to have a woman covered up like a mummy. *Macaanto*, look at you, gorgeous as can be."

She taught her about makeup: "A woman is a flower, meant to bloom and be looked upon."

She was beginning to feel it, her femininity. She flaunted it and felt the effects. She learned to giggle like a naïve virgin, especially when Soonam had company, but she had no clients calling yet. Soonam used her as bait, allowing the men to see her flutter by in the house and decline with lightness. "You will be her first, love," she would chide each client who asked after Ameena when they saw her.

"Special Client" visit days were a bustling affair. Hayira spent the better part of the morning flat-ironing her thick hair that fell luxuriously to her back. Hayira would darken her eyes with thick pencil, a dusting of glitter and color. Soonam insisted her lips only needed a little color or shine. Ameena could never get enough of the different looks on client days. Some days she was a vamp, others a blossoming teenager, and other days a regular working woman. Each effect lured in different men, and she relished in their lingering gazes that undressed her long after she left their presence.

She impatiently longed for the day she could start putting into practice all the lessons she was learning.

"When it's time, my best clients will come themselves…I am baiting them…" Soonam promised her. "We are not *kahaba* on the street like those in Mathare or Majengo. Our business has elegance and class, and so we are 'food for the gods.'"

Soonam's words resounded in her mind that day as she retraced her steps to the kitchen to make herself tea. But Manga had beaten her to it. He was in the kitchen filtering the tea through a strainer into the flask.

"I did not hear you," she said accusingly, suddenly aware of her braless top and how her nipples strained against the thin material. He smiled, hardly sparing her a glance. "I come and go as I please." His cockiness enthralled her.

"It's a big day for you today." She smoothly cooed out the words just as Soonam did.

Manga paused and looked at her with a frown. A ghost of amusement flashed his face. "Is that how we say happy birthday? *Asante.*"

*It's Manga's birthday...*The words played a tune in her mind.

She floated to his side, and her arm brushed against his slightly. The hairs on the back of her neck stood on end.

"Let me make the tea. You sit," she told him. Suddenly, every art of seduction escaped, reducing her mind to a muddle of lessons. Maybe she could only play the seduction game with those she wasn't attracted to, she thought with a short scoff, hating how undone she felt. He grinned lazily, sparkling eyes and that bright flash of teeth against a smooth chocolate masculine face. Ameena stifled a groan. He made her insides turn to butter.

"Didn't my aunty say 'Stay away'?" He leaned back against the counter but did not move, as if deliberately to torture her with his presence.

"She let me know it was your birthday…I wonder why," she quickly responded, her eyes on the tea strainer still sitting atop the mouth of the flask.

"Did she now?" He picked up the strainer, placing it on the sink top. He handed her the flask. "Okay." He moved out of her way.

She poured the tea into two huge mugs and carried the tray to the living room.

"*Ei, pole pole,*" he was telling her. He stretched out on the sofa, watching her, and she wished he would look away. Her palms sweating, she finally made it to the coffee table with a minor spill and heaved a sigh of relief.

"Your balancing skills are top-notch." He flashed his mesmerizing smile at her, then said, "Come here." She obediently sat next to him, her appetite fading rapidly.

"Why didn't you use those little cups, or are they only meant for beautiful people?" he teased her.

Ameena shook her head. "I cannot stand them. There is never enough tea in them."

He laughed. "My aunty is too British."

He steered the conversation on to her. "So I never got to ask where you were coming from that day."

She sipped her tea and munched on her bread, savoring the salty, buttery texture of the thickly spread blueband on bread.

"From far. A friend's house."

"Why did you leave?" he asked, eyes fixed on her.

She kept her eyes on her tea, watching the little specks of tea leaves swim in and out of focus in the peach-colored liquid.

"Why do you ask so many questions?"

"It's my birthday," he chided.

"So?" she shot back.

He raised a brow in amusement.

And just as she braced herself for more of his probing, he disarmed her. "Have you been to see a film down at the theater?"

She shook her head.

"*That* would be a birthday well spent," he told her.

Ameena raised her brow in surprise and simply nodded. Their conversation was casual and mundane, as if they were carefully edging around a huge elephant in the room. She was lost in the aura he exuded: pure, raw sexual masculinity.

On his way out, he turned back to her as if an afterthought and said, "Let me take you to the theater tonight."

She said yes.

Ameena spent the rest of the day reviewing the conversation she half-remembered, his smile, his hands, and his aura imprinted in the place of words exchanged. She went on another round of trying on clothes that did not seem good enough for their evening rendezvous. Hayira laughed at her.

"Soonam said it was his birthday..." Ameena hastily defended her actions.

"You like him," Hayira said, her eyes dancing mischievously.

"Is it bad?" Ameena did not deny it. Every time she saw him, she got wet, her soul melted. She had never felt so violently attracted to anyone before. With Hassan it was different, a slow smoldering fire that burned steadily. This one hit her like the first flow of ice-cold bathwater in the morning, and she could not help thinking about him.

"What do I do?"

Hayira shrugged. "Enjoy it," she said, then added conspiratorially, "You are the first girl in the sisterhood he has approached. He always says he can't mess with us. We are too much for him."

Ameena smiled, not sure of Hayira's sincerity. She helped her pick out a simple polka dot dress. "Relax. He isn't a client."

"But I want to look fantastic for him."

Hayira waved her hand. "He likes you too. There is no need for all that. Even if you wore a sack, he would still be smitten."

"How do you know?" Ameena's mind swam, hearing he liked her too.

Hayira laughed, long and hard. "You are such a child." Then a serious expression came over her. "Be careful. Manga is…crazy."

Ameena looked at her curiously, catching a faint look of dread that crossed Hayira's features. Then it vanished. "Crazy?"

Hayira laughed, shaking her head. "Yes, crazy *crazy*. But…" Hayira let her hand caress the dress. "He will behave with you. He likes you."

Ameena shrugged. *He likes me.*

Hayira stared at her for a moment, then shook her head as if dispelling a memory. "He will take care of you. He takes care of us." Ameena thought she had misheard the tremor in Hayira's tone, but a shadow came over her honey face, confirming Ameena had heard right.

Maybe she likes him too, Ameena thought.

Manga returned for her at six in the evening. Hayira sternly warned him to bring her back before midnight or she would report him to his aunty. She was going to be watching the club while they were away. Although there would be an ongoing special night event since it was his birthday, he could attend after the birthday movie. But Manga shook his head. He had his hands full, he said, his gaze sweeping over Ameena.

"Before midnight!" Hayira hurled the words at him.

"My goodness, she is not glass," he rapped out in Swahili.

"But she is young. She is the youngest we have ever had. And Soonam likes her," Hayira responded protectively. "When Soonam is away, I am in charge of the girls."

Manga grinned that cocky grin. "And she is the only one I have ever liked of all of you."

Hayira jeered at him dismissively, abusing him in Kiswahili—a torrential volley of words that sent Manga rushing out the door, Ameena in tow.

"That woman says the most vulgar things I've ever heard." He laughed.

They were out in the streets, a lively fanfare of people leaving work. The express bus stopped by, and they hopped on it. Manga was easy to be around. He made jokes and treated her like *his* lady. She compared him to Hassan. Maybe they were similar, but if it was love, she admitted to herself, she loved them both. Just differently.

They watched *Born Free,* the movie of his choice at an outdoor cinema, under the moon, and he bought her strawberry ice cream, which she loved. Ameena had never seen a film on a big screen and jumped a little when the lions roared and almost leaped right off the projector screen. Manga laughed at her. "Relax." He would throw his arms around her and pull her close as if to protect her from the man-eaters on screen.

When the final credits had run out, they rode back, and he asked if she was hungry so they could stop to eat. Ameena would have stopped time, if she could, to stay in his presence.

When they got to Soonam's place, he hesitated at the door.

"Is that all? How about the party at the club?" she asked him desperately. She could not stand him leaving yet.

He smiled. "Did you want that?"

"Hayira said…and it's your birthday…are you happy?" She dared him with her eyes.

He raised a brow, baiting her. "A little."

"A little is not good enough," she told him. She had to keep him longer, or she would die.

"So, what are you going to do? I am at the club all the time. So, no," he told her.

Their eyes locked, relaying a mysterious message to each other. She could feel her own feverish need overflow, and, without tearing her eyes from his, she took his hand. "Come," she told him huskily.

He hesitated. "I don't think you are ready for me."

She shrugged. "Let's find out."

"Hmm, let's see what surprise you have for me," he challenged her.

She opened the door and dragged him to her room. She did not hesitate as she removed the dress, afraid he would change his mind. The polka dot dress slid to the floor in a little heap, and she stepped out of it. Her hands clasped over her breasts self-consciously, and she trembled visibly when their eyes met. He dared her to go on. Encouraged and emboldened, she slid out of the silky underwear. Manga watched her till she stood naked before him.

"You are beautiful!" He whistled.

Their eyes met again, each baiting the other. She smiled triumphantly, relieved the moment of shyness had passed.

"So…let me make your birthday one you won't forget." Suddenly, everything she had learned seemed to be clear. In that instant, she realized she had the power, the control, and she could do anything with it.

Manga scoffed, slowly undoing his shirt. "Soonam warned you…I am dangerous…but you like that, eh?"

"Why?" She ignored the teasing edge at the end of his statement; instead, she focused on helping him with his belt, steadying her fingers and remembering: deliberation is key. *Delay the pleasure*, but her fingers shook, betraying her need.

"Because…I like to do things…most women cannot handle." Before she knew what was happening, he had scooped her off the ground and pinned her against the wall. She gasped faintly, a shiver running through her.

"Like that?"

"Oh, I am just getting started."

He licked her, sending waves of tremors over her body. She curled her toes. "Soonam's flower," he drawled and tugged seductively at the loose curls that cupped her face. "I will *try* to be nice."

"No." It was the last thing she wanted. Her body was a war zone of raging hormones. "You will show me." She bit her lip, realizing she was rapidly losing the control she had mastered only seconds ago.

He growled and nipped at her bare shoulder, unleashing desire like a torrential rain from within her.

Ameena yelped.

"Are you sure?" he asked. When the shock of it passed, she nodded. "Yes!" She was determined to know the extent of his intensity, determined to learn, eager to please.

Manga grabbed her buttocks, crushing her to him, and carried her to the bed. The sudden weightless sensation of being lifted and unceremoniously dropped onto the bed made her heave. The mattress dipped and bounced back, steadying her. It excited and terrified her.

"It is your room, so…." He was towering over her, and her eyes were glued to the bulge in his trousers.

"What are you going to do?" she dared him, propping herself on an elbow.

He hummed as he undid his trousers. He kicked them aside, completely naked before her. She marveled at the size and length of him, more curious and excited than afraid.

Their eyes met; a sizzling spark passed between them, hot and intense. Manga slid beneath her, grabbing her legs and propping them over his firm thighs, licking her. Ameena cried out as he sucked, licked, and fingered her simultaneously. Pleasure erupted upon her in waves. It was more passion than she had ever experienced. He did not stop till she came. When he penetrated her, he held her down, grazing her with his teeth and nails. He choked her as she convulsed in ecstasy. He pinched her breasts, and when he flipped her over, he slapped her butt cheeks raw, grazing her back with his nails and teeth. He penetrated her from behind, her hair in his fists. He tugged her head back, biting and licking her neck, cheeks, and back. The mixture of pleasure and pain brought her to the apex of utmost desire, an unfamiliar experience, not even with Hassan.

Manga did things to her and with her that night that she had never experienced. He took her against the wall, on the thick Persian carpet, against the dresser, and on the bed. He whipped her body raw with his savagery, and she relished in it, excitement mounting with every stroke, every nip, and every growl. They rode the waves of ecstasy over and over until, finally spent, they clung to each other and fell asleep. Ameena did not wake until the next morning. When she reached for him, he was gone, her sheets still covered in his scent, a faint masculine perfume she had never smelled on anyone but him. But he was gone like he had never been there at all.

Soonam did not seem surprised when she caught a glimpse of the discoloration on the exposed skin on her neck and shoulders at their ritual breakfast. "Hmm, a good birthday, eh?" Ameena rubbed the tender spots where Manga had nipped at her, placing tiny love bites in his lovemaking.

Ameena smiled. Her body was sore and raw, as if she had run a thousand miles in under a minute. She was glad Soonam was not upset. "A suitable present."

The older woman shook her head. "I go away for a short while, and you two waste no time in hanky-panky?"

Ameena giggled. The word "hanky-panky" sounded funny. When their eyes met, there was a graveness about her that stifled the momentary humor. Something was coming.

"Don't fall in love with him."

Ameena was taken aback by the rather short warning.

"Why?" She was tired of hearing all these cryptic nuances about Manga. He had been nothing but passionate and charming with her.

"I wish for you to see more. Manga is a good start. He is not *conventional.* Maybe you can be with him a little more."

"So, like training?" Her eyes widened. This was ridiculous.

"For you, it should be. *Qalbi,* in this business you cannot have a heart. You pleasure people; you give them their wildest dreams. Sometimes it's your body; sometimes it's your time. This is an art, a skill you learn with every single client. You remain a mystery to them, something they always want but can never have, and they pay you for it. That's your strength." She chewed on a piece of biscuit. "Manga is…wild and young. Too wild. Today he likes you. A lot. Tomorrow…" She shrugged.

Ameena shook her head. "He likes me. I know it."

Soonam looked at her blankly. After breakfast, she said, "Do you want him?"

Ameena nodded. She had never known she could want someone so much.

When Soonam let out a tremendous sigh, Ameena held her breath. It might be good news after all. She spread her fingers onto the coffee table, studying her pearly silver nail polish. She was silent for what seemed to Ameena almost a lifetime before her gaze finally rested on her, a troubled look in her eyes…then it vanished. "You're young too. Be with him, learn what you can, and soon, you shall be ready."

The months flew by like a long, beautiful dream. It was no secret Manga and Ameena were inexorably attracted to each other. She went to the club more to see him than to observe the other girls, and he came to Soonam's for breakfast and dinner to see her. They made love every minute they were together, each time more intense than the last time, each time more uninhibited than the last time.

"You like my kind of danger?" he whispered to her one night as he removed the blindfolds he had added to their foreplay.

Ameena nodded, helplessly accepting his domination over her as he seduced her deeper into his erotic role-play.

"Be careful, Ameena." He tagged lightly at her chin.

"Everyone tells me that…Why?" she asked him another night as they cuddled, gently lulled by the crisp, clear sound of Miriam Makeba's "Malaika" playing off a classic radio with an attached vintage record player he said Soonam got for him from England. It took up a hallowed space opposite the oak dressing table where Ameena liked to sit and brush her hair when she slept at his home.

Manga smiled, caressing her bare arms. "Because I am dangerous."

Ameena smirked and turned away from him.

She never imagined this blissful existence would change until three months later, just like Soonam had said. It was over. Manga suddenly pulled back; his conversations dwindled to a halt as did his visits to Soonam's. He had just moved on. She spent a week in bed crying after he stopped talking to her.

Soonam walked into her room one Sunday morning and drew the curtains back. The warm sun rays spilled into the room and remnants of it scampered onto her bed. Ameena flinched from them like a vampire.

"*Qalbi*, how long will this go on?" Soonam gave her a few days and then told her it was time to lock her heart and get him out of her mind.

The weeks after Manga were slow and arduous, but she took Soonam's advice and fought her way out of the hurt. She mulled over the reasons he could have just pulled back…was it her skill? Was she not as experienced and exciting as the women he had been with? Or did he want just one thing from her? she wondered. No matter which way she analyzed their torrid affair, some things did not add up. Even though it hurt, she intended to ascertain for sure that he did not want her anymore.

She discovered Soonam had sent him to England on business, but Hayira let her know it was Soonam's way of enabling her to heal.

"She loves you like a daughter," Hayira reassured her, "Besides there were things to be done." While Manga was away, Hayira ran Klub Malta. In that time, Hayira encouraged Ameena to stay with her at the club, learn about it and the regular customers most of the girls were leased to.

"How come I am not doing this?" she asked Hayira.

Hayira had swirled her drink. "Because Soonam has bigger plans for you. Most girls start here…not you."

Ameena was glad for it, for healing happened faster than she expected, not wavering from seeking the truth from Manga. He must have liked her, at least? Surely, it was not some sort of target practice, their wild three months.

It was a week before Christmas when she saw Manga again. It was a slow Sunday morning, and, bored with being at Soonam's, she went to the club along with five of the sisters. He sat hunched over at the lonely bar in conversation with the barman. She occupied the stool next to him and stared ahead at the drinks lined on the bar shelf.

"We thought you had died."

"You and who?"

She caught the tightness in his response.

"And all the alcohol. We still have a lot from your absence."

He cackled at the joke.

"Eh!" He called to the barman, "Make Soonam's flower a drink."

Ameena settled back on her stool, slowly turned, and looked at him. His eyes were blank, but she was not letting that deter her. *There must have been something between us.* She lured him into conversation as if the past year had not happened, and he eventually relaxed enough for her to seduce him, and she triumphantly rejoiced when, an hour later, his eyes reflected the same raw hunger she had grown to relish. But this time, it was different. She had learned control, and she had learned how to please as much as she was pleased.

When they spent the night together, she knew she had conquered his heart and had him dazed with her skill, her intuitive ability to give him erotic satisfaction that left him hungry for her even when they were spent.

"Did I do this to you?" he asked her, enthralled, and she squirmed with pleasure seeing that she had brought him to his knees. His eyes pleaded for more, and she held back with glee.

She laughed and untied the bands of cloth around her wrists that he had used to tie her up.

"You are not that special." She downplayed it, but somewhere in the sentimental part of her, the dark room where her heart throbbed for two men, she knew it was a lie. For now, it was safe, and she did not want to hurt again. This time, she crept out of his bed in the wee hours of the morning and went back to Soonam's singing a victory tune.

It became easier to walk away, easier to charm and flirt and say all the right things, do all the right things and have men eat out of her palm. The newfound power in her femininity excited her, and she maximized it, enjoying the attention she drew with a smile, a glance, or a flick of her wrist…Soonam watched her with pride, and if they missed their ritual breakfasts, they had dinner. Soonam was adamant about them eating together.

By the dawn of 1990, at seventeen, Ameena was a household name in Soonam's sisterhood. So much, the price on her was tripled and the class of men changed rapidly, from lawyers and accountants to Parliamentarians and CEOs to even a higher and more clandestine list of clients: visiting Diplomats and important foreign billionaires who were clients of the sisterhood registered in a black book that Soonam kept locked away in a safe with three doors. To be an escort to the one percent of society was a coveted position very few of the girls ever achieved. Hayira and four others had achieved it. Now Ameena joined that list. Soonam prided herself on maintaining the privacy of her clients and the class of her girls: well trained, clean, and open-minded.

It had shocked Ameena to have clients who simply needed someone to go to dinner with. Others needed someone to hold them through the night. Some had fetishes that Soonam said *If it does not kill you, do it.* There were the private high-end pool parties, where she witnessed the rich and famous indulge in orgies, drugs, and hedonistic feats she had never imagined possible in her life.

"Stay focused," Soonam told her sternly. "That lifestyle is a waste. I have seen it in England. Work for the money. Be the best you can be, but don't forget yourself."

Ameena had done as she was told, being both pleasant and amiable when offered drugs and alcohol and yet subtly denying indulgence. On two occasions Hayira accompanied her, being her point of reference for when to stop drinking, what to consume and what not to, with a secret code they all had to learn.

"We have to take care of each other. These are spoiled, entitled people who think they can buy anyone with money. Not me. I have integrity and I take care of my girls," Soonam had lectured, "so take care of each other. That's the code of the sisterhood."

Ameena learned then just why a lot of Soonam's faithful high-end clients trusted her and paid any amount she asked for. The integrity of the code. Soonam's girls were the most sophisticated in Nairobi; it was well known. The secret as to why they had no scandals or deaths was precisely that.

She got comfortable in the 1 percent crowd, enjoying the gifts, the indulgences, the sweet pain of self-control. It was a fast life…little sleep sometimes and superficial smiles. She loved it. This was what she wanted. This is how she wanted to live, she told herself. It did not matter who loved or hated you as long as you were comfortable.

"You are a natural at this. None of my girls have developed this fast," Soonam told her in February 1990. Ameena had spent Christmas and New Year's in Rwanda with a visiting Belgian diplomat. She had enjoyed the perks of the trip more than the boring nights under him as he grunted and came in two seconds, then rolled off her and fell asleep. She would slide the condom off him and wipe him down, then go to sleep, her thoughts heavily loaded with Hassan, sometimes Manga, but always the love she longed for with Hassan, a steady constant her heart refused to lock out. She met a few other incredibly exciting clients she was attracted to, but it faded after their time together because she had learned she only played a part.

Two years of being a high-end escort, wearing the best clothes and jewelry money could buy, dining in places one only dreamed of, and being on the arm of the who's who seemed like a larger-than-life achievement, but loneliness ate at her. She wanted to go back there, to those first beautiful moments with *Hassan*—waking up with him, going to places with him, watching *The Bold and the Beautiful* or *Another Life* with him. She enjoyed Soonam's plush existence, but the emptiness was disconcerting.

Then it happened.

She was in the grocery store buying her favorite Fa soap when she heard Hassan's voice call her name. Ameena wheeled around looking across the aisles, and behind her in the line, a hand tapped her shoulder. He had not aged a bit and looked well. His eyes seemed empty, not the Hassan eyes full of youthful adventure as she had known.

"Ameena," he was saying.

Her mouth ran dry, her eyes widened.

"Hassan." She did not know what to say. He waited for her to buy her soap and get out of line. He was looking at her, appraising her. "You look good, Araweelo," he muttered. Charming. Never hurrying, never assuming.

A familiar flame stroked her heart. Here he was! Her first love.

"You too," she replied coolly, despite her feelings.

He smiled, ruffling his curly hair. "I have missed you. And…"

"Hassan…"

He stopped her. "Please…I am sorry, *mrembo*, I am sorry. I pushed you away. I was young and stupid and…and…. chewing *qaad*. I did not treat you well."

"No, you did not," she agreed.

He continued explaining himself, and she listened, even though she knew she shouldn't. When he extended a lunch invitation to her, she accepted; *no harm in a free meal*, she thought.

They dined in an expensive restaurant in South B. He told her about his plans for their future. He promised to marry her. Told her they needed to think about the future and children. Ameena listened to his glowing promises. It made her feel as special as he had made her feel back then, but she had learned a thing or two. He would need to prove himself to her. She held back and let him woo her again, an exciting and familiar pleasure dance that took him half the year.

Late September 1990, Ameena decided Hassan had proved himself, and she needed to leave.

"I am in love," she finally confessed to Soonam.

The older woman's face had fallen. "Is this Manga again?"

Ameena shook her head and looked away. "*Ma.* Someone I have always known. Before you. Before Manga."

They were having dinner in the living room, sitting side by side, like mother and daughter.

"You never told me about him."

She could hear the disappointment in the older woman's voice.

"I am telling you now," she replied, ashamed that she had not found the courage to tell her the truth in the previous two years.

"*Qalbi,* why?" Ameena did not have to decipher her words to know why she had asked.

She shook her head. "I cannot stop loving him. He is my heart."

"What if he is not good for you? It is why you came to me, isn't it?"

She nodded. There was no use hiding the truth; she told Soonam everything.

"Only a fool would go back," Soonam told her at the end of her tale. "You disappoint me."

Ameena sighed. "I just made you a lot of money." She murmured, "You don't care for me…"

"*Joogso!* I opened my house to you, introduced you to a wonderful life. You could meet anyone and have anything you want, and you are choosing love, *love* over all that? What has love brought you but pain? What has it done for you, eh? *Waxba!*" Soonam was irate.

Ameena looked at the older woman whose full, bright cherry lips quivered and squared her shoulders.

"Thank you for everything but…I love him and that's it. He has changed."

Soonam laughed bitterly. "Men don't change, *qalbi.*"

"No, he has!" she protested stubbornly.

The women stared at each other wordlessly for a few minutes. The determination on Ameena's face was palpable.

"Then go," the older woman finally consented and got up to leave their dinner. "I lost my appetite."

Ameena hated to hurt Soonam and was grateful for the two years, but there was a part of her that had wanted to learn everything she had learned so she could go back and woo Hassan, make him want to be hers forever. And now that he was back, it was time to leave. She did not waste another minute. She cleared their dishes and packed her suitcase, leaving behind a lot of the things she had gotten, only carrying a few clothes and jewelry and shoes, the money she had kept from her most recent clients, and without a word of goodbye, she guiltily crept out of Soonam's sisterhood, got a taxi, and rode across town to Githurai, where Hassan had moved after a falling out with his cousin.

Ameena was certain this time she would please Hassan, restore their relationship, and finally give him a child, the child they both yearned for.

Chapter 11

December 1990

Hassan took her to the coast, and she walked on the scorching sands barefoot. They visited Stone Town in Zanzibar and stayed at an old colonial hotel that had the history of the charming island engraved on its walls.

"Where do you want to go, *Macanto*? Egypt? Sudan? Zambia? Malawi? I will take you anywhere."

"Let's see the world together," she responded happily.

They made love inexhaustibly, and he marveled at how she brought him to his knees. She used the full force of her lessons to control him, to have him forever eating out of her hand, to never look at any other woman ever again.

When she found out she was pregnant, she told him in excitement. Hassan wasted no time in preparing a feast in her honor and invited all his friends, even Liban.

He went out of his way, making preparations for her to see his parents, who had moved to Tanzania and had been there for a year. She became Araweelo again, special and beautiful to him. He constantly talked about their unborn child, "my son," he would say.

Ameena laughed. "What if it's a girl?"

He would shake his head. "No, this one is a boy."

She registered his desire, maintaining the hope that it would be nothing less than that. *A boy.* She prayed every day it would be a boy until the morning she woke up in jarring pain. Hassan was not home. He was away for two days, working with another long-distance delivery business, driving farther south to Zambia, Mozambique, and Zimbabwe. He made better money.

"You won't need to work to spoil your looks," he had bragged to her.

She shuffled to the bathroom early in the morning, groaning with each step as the pressure on her bladder mounted and screamed to see the red clot-like drops that sat in the toilet bowl.

The hospital confirmed her worst fears. She had miscarried.

"When can I try again?" she had desperately cried while at the doctor's office.

"Wait until you are better, and your uterus is strong again. Relax. You are still young," the doctor told her comfortingly, oblivious to her actual distress.

It terrified her that Hassan would return, blame her again, and morph into the monster she had once encountered. She wept all day, praying for a miracle.

Hassan returned the next day, but she did not tell him. She kept the facade up until he insisted they go for her regular checkup together. Ameena tried to brush it off, claiming she was fine, and they could go the next day, but he was adamant. He wanted to be sure their son was strong and healthy.

Ameena looked at him and burst into tears.

"I am not pregnant anymore. I lost him," she sobbed.

Hassan stood and stared at her blankly for a full minute, unmoving. Ameena backed away, to the wall of the living room.

"Please Hassan, I am sorry," she begged, seeing the pain in his eyes. Something was wrong with her. There had to be. She wanted him to share his sorrow with her, but Hassan walked out of the house and did not return for a week. When he came back, he was drunk, and he beat her senseless, called her a whore, a cursed woman with a womb that buried children. He rained his anguish and anger on her in blows, kicks, slaps, and words that hurt deeper than his fists. When he exhausted himself with raving and ranting, he slumped on the floor, crying. Ameena blacked out on the bathroom floor, where she had crawled to get away from him, and there she lay for hours.

She recalled Soonam's words: "Men don't change, *qalbi*."

She shivered and sobbed, her broken heart irreparable this time, her pain slowly calcifying over her love for him. A part of her knew she did not deserve this. She had left everything for a man who only loved her when she was pregnant. A man who beat her, who treated her worse than she had seen some pimps treat their women. As she lay on the ground swollen and bleeding, Ameena closed her eyes. When she next woke up, she knew she was not who she had been. It was time to leave again. Love was a myth.

She accepted her true vocation; it was with the sisterhood.

She limped out of the house to a pay phone, dialing the only number she knew, the sisterhood's.

"Hayira," she breathed, knowing Hayira always picked up all the calls. "Please...I need you."

Hayira gasped. "Ameena?"

"Yes. Please tell Soonam...I...I am so sorry."

There was silence, and a few seconds later, Soonam's assertive voice carried to her on the phone.

"Where are you?" she was asking urgently.

Ameena told them where she was. "I can't, I can't go back. He-He will kill me." She sobbed.

"Oh, my God! I will send Manga to get you." The older woman was sharp. "Stay right there, love."

Ameena calmed down. She owed Soonam an apology for her foolishness and she was grateful the older woman still cared for her.

The old Peugeot that often sat outside Klub Malta picked her up in thirty minutes.

"Who did this to you?" Manga demanded when he saw her.

Ameena swayed dizzily; Hayira's face was a welcome sight, and she smiled gratefully. "Hayira," she mouthed. Her lips felt thick, her tongue too heavy.

Hayira shushed her and nudged Manga hastily.

"Not now Manga; Soonam said we get her back to the sisterhood… now!"

"We are not going till we get that bastard…" Manga growled. His fists clenched and unclenched. Hayira had her body against him, shoving him back to the car. Manga took another step, and Hayira leaped at him, doing the best she could to restrain him.

"No! Manga!" Hayira was sharp. "We. Go. Now!" she barked at him.

Ameena faded in and out, a wan smile on her face, their altercation a feeble drone in her mind. "Thank you," she kept whispering. "Thank you."

They were finally driving away, with Hayira speaking comfortingly to her and Manga cursing loudly, saying something about fixing the son of a dog who had beaten her up.

"If you do not shut up and drive well, you will not make it to beat that son of a dog! *Mschenzi!*" Hayira at one point shouted at him when the car lunged into a pothole.

When Ameena woke up, it took her a minute to register that she was in her old room at Soonam's.

Soonam sat by her bedside, looking as radiant as ever, delicate, and well kept. She had a thick scarlet headband holding her luscious, straightened hair away from her face. Her eyes looked pained as she stared at Ameena.

"*Gabadh,*" she whispered. Ameena felt her soft hands over her own.

"*Waan ka xumahay, Habo, waan ka xumahay,*" Ameena replied penitently. *I am sorry, aunty.*

"It's okay, *jacayl,*" the older woman replied comfortingly. "The heart wants what it wants."

* * *

Depression is a cancer; it eats away at any traces of light and turns a multicolored painting to sepia and gray. Ameena turned lifting her depression into a goal; she worked harder at being as adept as the other girls and as polished as Soonam. Christmas came and went. They ushered in the New Year jubilantly, and Ameena celebrated her rebirth and evolution. In a time when it was taboo for a woman to smoke, Ameena did it anyway, and if men looked at her disapprovingly, she dared them to say something. She drank more regularly, and Soonam let her be, just like a mother abetting a spoiled child.

Hayira would shake her head. "Those things will kill you."

Ameena would scoff and flick the ash off the long, slim cigarette caught between her fingers. "I died already."

In February, the smoking dwindled to three a day, and by April she did not want it anymore. A new hunger replaced it: sex, not for pleasure but for control. It was the only way she imagined hurting anyone. It was the only way she wanted to hurt Hassan. Through the months of deep depression, she had planned secretly. She swore upon her miscarried child. She would hurt Hassan as much as he had hurt her, and if any man dared to hurt her again, they would face the full brunt of her wrath.

"Men are dogs," she told Soonam bitterly, as if her mouth was filled with chloroquine tablets squashed and liquefied, as they had coffee after dinner.

Soonam sighed. "*Mmm*, pain will make you say that *qalbi*."

"No, they really are."

Ameena opted for a glass of scotch. It was an expensive imported bottle from England that Soonam only pulled out for special occasions, and Ameena did not know why it was out today.

"Men are like children," Soonam told her. "They eat, sleep, and fuck…"

Ameena raised her brows, amazed the woman had used the word "fuck." She was the only one in the sisterhood who was proper; all the other girls used vulgarities Ameena had been initially too shy to repeat. She giggled.

"It's true. So you treat them like babies; only babies don't fuck, but you know what I mean."

Ameena smiled, then thought of Hassan. "But they hurt you too."

Soonam heaved and picked up her coffee mug, a medium-size piece with the UK flag draping its cylindrical frame. "Everyone hurts everyone. Some more than others."

Ameena let out a low, cynical sound between a laugh and an exclamation.

"Let me tell you a story…" Soonam drew her legs underneath her on the sofa and took Ameena's hand. "It is not a secret that I favor you."

Ameena nodded. "No girl could return as you did. My policy is, once you leave, you never return…"

Ameena lowered her gaze. "So why me?"

"Because to me, you are the daughter I lost. You are also the young version of me, strong-headed, heart full of love for a foolish man, wild, full of ambition."

Ameena adored Soonam already and felt glad that she considered her a replica of herself.

"When I was young, in England, my father arranged for me to marry at sixteen into a good Somali family. They had lived in England longer, but they stuck to tradition and expressed disapproval because I had not undergone circumcision. They said I was cursed and a whore." Soonam shrugged. "But their son, Aden, loved me, so we eloped, fled to a small village in North Yorkshire. Only my mother knew. I got pregnant, lost the baby. Aden stopped loving me, returned home, repented, and his family welcomed him with open arms. He got married a year later to a circumcised Somali girl. I returned ashamed and broken to my mother. My father never forgave me. It shocked me that he left me anything at all in his will. I guess he forgave me after all." Soonam sipped her coffee.

"But…when I was pregnant, I knew she was a girl. A mother just knows these things. I knew she would be strong and independent. I knew she would be a fighter. So, I called her…Ameena."

Ameena swallowed, tears welling up in her eyes. She was seeing a part of Soonam she had never seen before.

"That's why you." Soonam smiled at her and patted the hand she held.

"Now you know why you leaving broke my heart. I knew you would be back because you and I are not meant to live beneath men, Ameena. We rule them; we own them. No man should ever make you feel like a slave, like you are dirt. They don't deserve us."

Ameena lapped up the words, nodding, allowing herself to be vulnerable. They were the salve that healed her soul. Soonam wiped the tears that trickled down Ameena's cheeks with her hand.

"Don't cry, little one. You are a queen. Like the brave, strong Somali queen, Araweelo…"

They said it together and laughed.

Ameena beamed through her misty eyes. "My mother always called me that."

Soonam smiled and kissed Ameena's cheek, and the gesture made her ache for her mother. "Your mother saw your fierce strength and independence. I see it too. Live free. And if you marry, marry rich. Extraordinarily rich. But even then, be independent. If you want children, have them. If you don't, don't. No tradition or religion should hold you. You are your own woman. A strong, beautiful one. I will always be here for you," Soonam said as she dabbed her tear-streaked cheek, "I promise you."

Ameena believed her.

"I know you plan to hurt him like he has you. Don't worry about that. Just get better. He is not worth you." Soonam looked at her knowingly. "Now, let's get your nails done." Her eyes had fallen on Ameena's fingernails, the bright pink nail polish chipped on most of them.

Between breaks from boring clients, most of them much older, Ameena would wind down at the Klub Malta, where Manga managed the staff. He was ruthless, and she enjoyed watching him bossing everyone around, firing and hiring at will, but despite his almost erratic managerial methods, Klub Malta thrived. The attraction between them resurfaced.

"If I had never met Hassan, I would be baking bread in your house."

She would laugh as they clicked their never-ending glasses of whiskey.

"*Hapana*, you would be here sitting on my lap, doing things to me."

She had flirted and suggestively smirked. "I still do."

"Yes." He smiled. "My office still smells of you. I want to take you there again."

She grinned at him mischievously. "The thrill of anyone walking in, eh?"

"That's why we leave the door unlocked."

She beamed at him; he was her sexual haven. With him, she abandoned herself, experimented and opened herself to every wild imagining she had watched, learned, or that he had taught her.

"I have a few new tricks to share," she whispered in his ear.

"Mmm, I like the sound of that. My tricks might outlive yours." He downed his glass of whiskey.

Ameena slid her hand suggestively over his thigh. "Do you want to test me?"

His eyes brimmed with an unbridled lust. "I want to taste you."

It became a competition between them, who would come up with the newest sex antics. Ameena outwitted him by learning quickly how to stroke the male ego. She praised him, flattered him, and assured him he was the master of the game.

* * *

By the middle of 1992, Ameena was the textbook from which Soonam referred to the newest girls. She had mastered manipulation and erotica to her advantage and taught the girls how to "express themselves and make a man want them without so much as touching them."

"You must use everything you have, your hands, your smile, and your eyes. Everything. Use it all. You are not like the regular street hookers; you don't dress up like them outside the sisterhood. You dress classy; you look your best. You *must* look like 'food for gods,' all the time," she had told them, fully aware of Soonam's proud eyes resting on her.

Ameena settled in. This was her life. She began to enjoy her clients. The variety was astronomical. The younger ones were exciting and reminded her of her youth. Some older ones were gross and outright obscene, even for her. There were shy first-timers urged by their friends, usually children of wealthy parents who needed discretion in their dealings. The entrepreneurs who needed escorts were her favorite. They always knew exactly what they wanted and got down to it. The one she particularly liked was impotent but needed a woman who would make him feel desirable. Apart from performing to a "dead" man, he was generous and kind, and she could sense he was falling for the persona she had created for him.

"Soonam, the client, the Bank man."

"Who?" Soonam had asked.

"Deedan. I think he is falling for me."

Soonam nodded. "Okay."

Every time a client got too attached, Soonam switched them up. No matter how much they paid. They all gave a report on their clients. Did they treat them well? Were they generous? They used each report as a marker for what tier to place the clients. Everyone knew the rules, both clients and escorts.

The last time they spent a night together, he gave Ameena a gold ring.

"Have it," he told her. "I know you are aware of my feelings for you, and it is against the contract. I might not see you again, but…take this…it's a twenty-two-carat gold ring. That little diamond is worth five hundred thousand shillings," he told her when he opened the little velvet box and offered it to her at their last dinner.

"Why are you giving it to me?" She had been both overwhelmed by it and guarded.

He reached for her hand, and she could see in his eyes a lonely man who was terrified of a life outside the illusions he had been creating with her.

"Because you are beautiful, and it is mine to give."

She had received gifts but none as expensive as this. Her mouth still hanging open in surprise, she thanked him.

He smiled. "You have been good to me. You deserve it and more," he added.

She did not see Deedan again after that evening but kept the ring along with her other valuables and money clients had given her. Every day, she counted, estimating how much she made from tips. She wanted enough to move and buy a house. Maybe start her own business, a high-end escort service. Maybe in Uganda. She had always wanted to live there. Kenya was full of memories she wanted to forget. She did not know how Soonam would take it; she did not want to let her down again. However, she still had unfinished business with Hassan.

Ever since she had left, she had not seen him. Sometimes when she went shopping, she deliberately went as far as Ziima, hoping to see him in the sprawling bars with Liban.

At a bazaar in Uhuru Park, she lost track of Hayira and the other girls, and while scanning clothes and jewelry made with the intricate beauty of the Masai heritage, she spied Hassan seated at a stall that sold *mutura* and *nyama choma*, the aroma of roasting meat filling the air, deliciously beckoning to her. He had a girl with long box braids by his side, a thick big-bosomed girl. The girl laughed and leaned against him as he gave her his glass of beer.

Without a thought, Ameena walked up to him, "*Wewe.*" She sneered and spat to the side.

Hassan looked at her, his eyes glazed, tipsy. He pushed the girl off him, and she stumbled, trying to steady herself with a yelp, shouting at him simultaneously. He stood up, swaying slightly. "Araweelo, is that you?" He peered at her. "Or am I seeing things? I thought you were dead."

Ameena laughed a bitter laugh. "You remember."

He dropped his gaze. "I am sorry. I am so sorry." He hung his head like a child caught stealing sugar.

Ameena made a face. "Save it." She was sharp, but she could not help feeling sorry for him. Somewhere in her heart, she wanted to hope, but she held back. "You are so drunk, pathetic." She turned her mouth downward; her eyes rolled at him.

"But you love me, heh?" He grinned that smile that used to make her heart stop. Her heart stirred but not as much.

She scoffed. "Used to. Pick up your *malaya* and enjoy yourself. Don't stop on my behalf." She pointed at the furious girl who was watching them on the side, and on hearing of herself being referred to as a prostitute, she shouted again. Hassan hurled insults at her, telling her to shut up and not to disrespect Ameena.

"Who is she to you?" the woman demanded angrily.

"That's *my* woman!"

Ameena was walking away, the scab over her heart so taut it hurt. She counted her steps as she walked like a drug addict walking away from a pusher who was yelling the cheapest price for a hit to her.

She trudged on, trying to drown his voice, him calling to her, "Araweelo! come back...I am sorry. Let's try again...I did not mean it...I love you...*Ni kupenda sana!*"

That night, she drank half a bottle of whiskey at Klub Malta. Manga watched her. "Ameena," he warned.

And she told him all, hysterically: "I saw him again. I saw him again. I am not strong enough. I am not...."

"You are. You left twice. Don't do it again."

"I don't know what it is. But I want to show him he was wrong about me. I can be..." She stopped short before the words formed on her lips. Was that it? Was it why she could not let him go? Her ego was caught in a tussle with his?

She shook her head.

"You are right," she said instead. But a week later she was in Githurai looking for him.

Soonam had traveled again to England, as she did every six months. Being a citizen, she stayed as long as she wanted. Before she left, she made Ameena swear to her: "Swear it, you will not be restless."

"I will try." Ameena looked away.

Soonam shook her head. "Oh. You are so stubborn."

Ameena smiled. "Maybe you understand?"

Soonam replied, "I do, but…it can cost you. Swear I shall find you here."

Ameena swore.

The day she left, Ameena told Hayira she was going visiting friends, and even though Hayira was suspicious, she let Ameena be, secretly asking Manga to follow her.

Ameena alighted from the taxi at noon. The house she had lived in with Hassan still stood at the end of a row of houses with its half-gate slightly off the hinges and its lawns mowed. A little car sat in the dusty driveway. Ameena let herself in and knocked on the door. Hassan was in and, without a second hesitation, the door opened. The noon sun washed over his handsome face, his shirt partially open, revealing the sparse sprouts of hair on his chest.

He grinned. "You came."

Ameena walked past him into the living room, surveying it like a police officer searching for an elusive criminal. "Who else is here?"

"The drapes, the dishes, the walls…" he waved his hand languidly around the modestly furnished room.

Ameena scoffed.

"You should hate me," he told her as he shut the door and leaned against it. The rosewood scent in the air, nonexistent, had been replaced by the choking smell of tobacco.

"Since when do you smoke?" she asked instead.

"When I found you gone that day…" He shook his head. "…It was unfair. I cannot blame you for all the losses…I was ignorant." He made his way to the couch and dropped onto it. An ashtray sat on the coffee table, a freshly lit cigarette rested over its wide mouth.

She sat next to him and picked up the cigarette clasped between his fingers and dragged on it, inhaled, then let it out slowly.

"When did *you* start smoking?" He looked at her in shock and surprise.

"After you killed me. But…I stopped." She handed it back to him. Its effect was not there anymore.

"Do you still pray?" He sighed, took another drag, and squashed it in the wooden circular ashtray packed with several cigarette butts fighting for a spot on the blackened surface.

"Hmm, I don't think God is happy with me, neither me with…him or her, whatever God is." She waved her hands to disperse the smoke billowing from the cigarette, making indeterminate shapes.

They sat in silence for a while. It was not a tense silence but a more familiar existence, and he spoke first: "So what now?"

Ameena shrugged. "I don't know." She missed old Hassan, and she felt she owed him a debt. Two miscarriages made her feel there was something she had yet to complete before she moved on to the next chapter of her life.

"Have you…seen my people?" she asked instead.

"Who? Your father?" He jeered, "How? I steer clear. Especially now. With everything."

"I miss you, Hassan. I miss what we could have been. I miss us."

He grunted in agreement. "Me too. I think I am possessed. I do not know what comes over me. I dunno…" He was hitting his head with one hand, his legs stretched out lazily. "I always think about us, back at the border. In Zanzibar. The time we did it in the truck…. I don't know…."

She was quiet, reminiscing as he spoke. "You are just…*mchenzi*, and you chewed too much *qaad*," she said underneath her breath and was surprised he agreed.

"*Mrembo*, let's not think about children at all. No children. Just you and me, like before?" he was pleading. His eyes betrayed him, his soul was bare, and he was in torment.

Ameena was not sure she wanted that anymore. They *must* have a child for her to redeem herself and prove it to him. She did not trust Hassan anymore. The sisterhood was a haven for now. She had many plans. Would Hassan fit into them? Would a baby? Confusion plagued her. Her ego battled with her sensibilities.

"I shall come back to see you." She treaded lightly on the matter.

"No, no, let me take you out. Let me chase you again and prove myself to you, *mrembo*."

Ameena cocked her head to the side, thrilled by the prospect. It was the one thing she missed about Hassan now, that familiar courtship she enjoyed with him…"Westlands?"

"Anywhere." He made a sweeping motion with his hand.

She smiled from the corner of her mouth, appraising him.

"Okay. *Kesho?*"

"*Wapi?*" he asked.

She paused, thinking of an appropriate location for him to pick her up. She had lied to him and told him she worked for a boutique shop owner on K Street. "By KCB, on Koinange Street."

"You live there, too?"

She smiled. "Just pick me up there. I see you have a car."

He grinned. "It is Liban's, but he is in Dar."

"Okay, you patched your differences?"

"It's like this and that, but…blood is blood," he told her with a shrug. He appraised her, his gaze sweeping over her delightedly. "You look *mzuri* these days. Maybe you can tell me what else you are doing other than being a shop assistant on K Street or…who you are doing?"

She smiled, baiting him, enjoying the fact that she was a mystery to him. "Maybe."

* * *

The next day at seven, he picked her up by KCB. She looked dazzling, and Hassan could not help ogling at her. "My Araweelo." He breathed. "You were always beautiful, but these days, *tsk tsk tsk.*"

She jeered lightheartedly, "Will we eat beauty? Drive. I am hungry."

He wined and dined her; he chased her as he had promised, and she allowed herself to be seduced. When they made love again, it felt like the first time in the back of her father's truck, lulled by the imam's call to prayer, spied upon by the setting sun.

She stole away in the wee hours, hurriedly returning to Soonam's. If Hayira noticed, she said nothing, but for those two weeks, Ameena glowed. Hassan did everything to make her happy. He made promises, and they made love like starved lovers, casting caution to the wind. They talked about the younger days, skipping the gory details, the pain, and the trauma, only strengthening the parts that needed to be strengthened.

Ameena nurtured this secret reunion; its discretion kept it exciting. This was her chance to prove her childbearing worth to him. Her decision tittered between leading him on long enough and leaving him when he was convinced she would never leave or having a child and convincing him they could be parents.

Hassan was the thin connection to the home she had once known, and she jealously guarded that. In him she saw her mother, her youth, her father, her home, and tasted the sumptuous dishes they feasted on when her *aabo* returned from long trips, the stories of Mogadishu, the stories of monsters and Araweelo that spilled from her mother's lips. A treasured archive she could unlock only with him.

With Manga, she felt safe, but it *was not* home. She was not supposed to plant roots there. She had already done that with Hassan.

They whispered promises and sweet nothings to each other, and she talked dismissively about the idea of another child. "No, it makes me a monster," he told her.

A week after Soonam returned, Ameena stole away to see Hassan. He was leaving for Kampala.

Ameena had planned it expertly; today she would get pregnant. She seduced him with her words, her gestures, her charm; she played by the sisterhood's playbook; and he gave in to her with reckless abandon. When he left, he was more in love with her than she could imagine him to be. This time she would have the baby, she decided. This time, he would want her.

The months dragged, but Ameena's heart sang a merry tune in anticipation. Soonam asked her why she was so happy. "You got over the Hassan blues?"

She shrugged. "You were right; I need to embrace life and live it."

Soonam observed her as they had dinner, trying to figure out if her words were true. "*Wewe ni* sly," she said instead, and Ameena smiled. There was no fooling Soonam.

It was Manga who confronted her. "What are you doing?" he barked at her, while he ushered her into his back office at the club.

She feigned innocence. "What do you mean?"

He grabbed her by the shoulders. "I know you have been seeing Hassan. What's wrong with you?" His face was close to hers, and his voice carried a steel fury.

Ameena tried to break away, but his grip was viselike, and she flinched. "Did you tell Soonam?"

He loosened his grip. "No, I couldn't. But why are you doing it? After all he did!"

Ameena looked away from him, and he forced her to look at him, with his forefinger and thumb guiding her chin. "Why?"

Ameena swallowed. "I wanted to get back at him."

"By screwing him? Going out for dinners with him, heh?" Manga shook his head; his look withered her.

"How do you know all this, anyway?" she demanded. "Are you spying on me?"

Manga leaned against the door, trapping her between him and it. She could smell the whiskey on his breath. The strong, crisp scent of deodorant and aftershave lent it a new flavor. It played with her mind...their steamy sex.

He leaned his head on the door. "I have been following you. I know you love him enough to fuck him!" he said between gritted teeth, slamming his fist above her head. Ameena let out a shriek. "That man will kill you. Haven't you had enough?"

"He already did!" She raised her voice as well, trying to be brave. "But I am like an addict. I go back!" She drummed her fist against the door, her shoulders slumping helplessly. The music outside boomed and vibrated against the door like a muffled giant.

Manga drew back, his eyes danced with a different light; shaking his head, he cursed. "That's why I don't fall in love," he told her, suddenly calm. "You act like a rabid dog. Look at you. Look at you..."

"So you never loved me." She pouted, suddenly needing to hear she'd had some effect on him.

He stared at the ceiling, hands on his hips, and for a lengthy second, he said nothing. The music outside boomed and vibrated, a loud throbbing that concealed the emotions in the little black-and-white-painted office, then nickered mirthlessly. "Would it make you stay away from him?"

Ameena was not sure what to say to that.

He was watching her, and the glint in his eyes vanished, replaced for a millisecond with a dash of solemnness. "I would not be so mad if I did not."

He arrested her with his gaze, and his heart lay naked before her, encapsulated in the dark brown irises that had glistened often in the throes of ecstasy. She lowered her gaze. The effect was tangible. Her soul pulsated with the pleasure of that knowledge.

"How long?" she insisted curiously. The unquenchable need within her to have him want her consumed her. It had consumed her from the day she had first laid eyes on him, a pail and broom in his hand outside Klub Malta.

He leaned back, his brawny arms folded over his chest. "Do you think I left you because I was bored...like I had said? No, I left because...You should not get close...any closer than you have."

Ameena let the words sink in. "Why?"

Manga shook his head slowly and scoffed. "I can't be trusted with love." Then a hardness enveloped his features. His eyes flickered intensely.

"I don't want to see you hurt. I saw it and it scared the hell out of me."

He was intense; everything about him emanated an intense protective masculinity. It swallowed her, and the sensation of drowning engulfed her.

"I...love him, Manga. I always have," she managed weakly. "I am ashamed."

Manga scoffed again. A flicker of emotion crossed his eyes for a moment.

"Hmm. Insanity is what it is! If he hurts you again, I will kill him. I swear it."

Ameena knew he meant it, and it both scared and excited her.

"Let me go." She backed away from him, and he inched back, pointing to the door, indicating she was free to go.

* * *

Soonam planned for her to escort a Ugandan businessman named Matthias Kahinde.

"He is vying for a parliamentary seat. That is always a good one to escort. But this one, be careful. He is married with two children and seeks a discreet delivery of services. He will send a car to pick you and drop you. He will meet you where he chooses to meet with you, okay?"

Ameena nodded.

She had missed her period. She called Hassan from the call box outside Klub Malta twice a week and swooned to hear his voice but did not tell him anything more than that she loved him and she was very busy, but she would come to see him.

As she dressed up to meet Matthias Kahinde that evening, a man prominent and savvy in real estate and farming, a prospective member of Parliament, Ameena carefully picked out her attire, a beautiful figure-hugging evening gown.

He wanted to go watch a play, an acclaimed piece by a famous Kenyan playwright who was in exile, and then they would have dinner and spend the night together. Hayira helped her get ready, coiffing her hair and applying her makeup for her.

"*Wooh,* you look like a princess!" Hayira told her when they appraised her finished look in the black gown, sporting a deep dip that exposed her fine back.

Soonam smiled, satisfied. "You look like a model on the catwalk. I knew that dress would look simply gorgeous on you," she said with a big grin. She had handed her that dress, one of many presents she had brought Ameena from England.

Ameena batted her eyelids, thickly lined with mascara. "Thank you."

The evening was mesmerizing. Meeting high-class businessmen always awed her, and she paid attention to their business or political talk, never saying a word. A smile here or there. She was supposed to look pretty and not be a nuisance, and that's what she did. She responded pleasantly to compliments and sipped on her drinks slowly. She declined all the alcohol, opting for soda and water.

"Please drink," her companion urged her. His rough palms brushed her exposed back frequently. When their eyes met, she could tell he was more interested in removing the gown she wore than all the business chatter. He glowed when she was complimented, like she was the crown jewel he needed to bait potential investors.

"I want to be fully awake when we go back to the hotel," she whispered to him seductively, and he nodded, flattered and glad she was saving herself for a night of pleasure.

She spent three days with him until his business in Kenya was concluded. When she returned, Soonam was pleased. "He paid well for you. I have your tip. He could not stop raving about you."

Ameena smiled faintly. "I aim to please." She recalled he lay like a dead dog as she worked hard to please him, and on the third night, he refused to wear the condom, promising her double pay. Ameena had thought about it and decided this one time would not hurt.

But the night was longer than she had hoped. He wanted her again and again.

Soonam smiled. "You know, one day soon enough, I shall get you married to one of these rich men. You deserve to be happy. After all you have been through, *qalbi*."

* * *

The nausea started soon after, and when she spent the night with Manga, he commented on her body: "Your body has changed, your breasts...your thighs..." he had told her as he watched her climb into bed beside him.

"*Wacha!* What are you talking about?" she had sneered, pulling away from him on to her side, but it was true. She was glowing and filling up. In the mirror, she could tell her breasts were fuller, her thighs thicker. She loved the look. Her dresses hugged better, and her clientele rose. Her libido soared, as well.

Before the end of two months, she knew she was pregnant and prepared to tell Hassan.

He was leaving again for Zambia, and they planned to meet since she was not working that day.

She allowed herself to enjoy the afternoon with him, and when they got back to his place, cuddling on the couch watching *The Terminator*, she broke the news to him: "I am pregnant."

His reaction was instant. "Ameena, no. Why! I said no more!" he groaned.

"We can start again, that's why. We...we can..."

She did not see the slap coming; she did not see his hand raised and the back of it whip her hard across her face. He morphed before her, his eyes angry; his face darkened like a man possessed. "Get out! Get out!" Saliva spewed from the corners of his mouth.

"I said leave now!" He was picking her up and shoving her toward the door. "You don't listen!" He raised his hand to slap her again. Ameena screamed, shocked and terrified.

He pushed her out the door, slamming it shut and turning the lock. Ameena, on her knees outside his door, burst into angry, hot tears laced with pain. She had done it to herself again. Soonam's words played hauntingly: *Men don't change.*

"Ameena..." The voice that called to her was familiar. Manga.

She did not care that he had followed her.

"Ameena!" his hands gently clasped around her shoulders, helping her to her feet. "Ameena..." She buried her head in his chest, and he held her.

"He doesn't want me…" she sobbed. "I gave him what he wanted… but…he…doesn't want me…" she cried.

She felt his chest heave. "The bastard," he whispered. "Let's go."

He picked her up and cradled her, carrying her to the car he had parked outside the gate. Manga did not take her to the sisterhood. He drove straight to his apartment and called Soonam, saying he was with Ameena and they were planning to go out. The weekend was coming up too. Could she stay a few days?

She could hear Soonam sigh. "If it wasn't you and her, I would say no. What are you planning? Don't sweep her away, *macaan.*"

He chuckled. "We are like birds in your nest, aunty; where will we go?" he pacified her.

Ameena could hear her suppressed laugh in response on the other end.

When he took her inside his apartment, he set her on the couch, noticing the swelling on her cheek where Hassan had slapped her. An imprint of the ring he wore had wedged itself like a stamp on her smooth skin.

"Soonam won't like this," he was mumbling as he stroked the strands of hair away from her face. Ameena lay on the couch like a delicate porcelain doll.

"Want to watch something? I borrowed some movies from TV Land on Moi Avenue," he told her.

She did not respond.

"*Chakula?*" he asked as he headed to the kitchen.

He went ahead anyway and warmed up a pack of chicken and chips he had kept in the fridge, placing it all in the oven and turning it up.

"He doesn't want me," Ameena finally croaked from the sofa.

Manga popped open two bottles of Pepsi and brought her one.

"Ameena, forget him. He is a bastard."

Ameena kept talking like she had not heard him. "I gave him everything he wanted…everything. He took everything."

Manga sat and listened as she rambled on and on.

He got up again and picked up a few ice cubes, wrapped them up in a kitchen cloth, and held it to her cheek, which was red and darkening from the slap.

Then finally he asked, "What happened?"

Ameena drew her legs in and sighed, "I told him…I was pregnant."

Manga paused. "Are you?"

Ameena nodded.

"Oh shit," he cursed. "Whose is it?"

"His."

"Why, Ameena? How could you be so stupid?"

"I thought it was what he wanted, and we could try again. I lost two children. Maybe…" She broke down, sobbing again.

Manga gathered her up in his arms and held her, rocking her back and forth. When she calmed down, he asked her, "What do you want to do?"

"I don't know," she told him honestly. "I don't know what to do. Soonam will kill me."

Manga was silent. "Maybe she won't."

Ameena said nothing more. She finally sat up, placed the cloth on the coffee table and picked up the bottle of Pepsi. "I will think of something. I have three days here with you."

He smiled. "You do. What do you want? Supper, anything?"

She put the bottle down and faced him, her eyes sad and pained. "Fuck me," she told him. "I want you to fuck my brains out."

"Are you…?"

She was unzipping the dress she had on. "Please, Manga. And don't be gentle."

Manga shook his head and held her. "Tonight I will hold you." She resisted, pleading with him to make love to her till, wearied out, he relented.

* * *

Ameena decided she would hide the pregnancy until it showed, but by

115

then she would have gone. She was not sure where yet. She only knew she needed to leave Kenya. The thought of an abortion scared her, and the horror stories she had heard the girls at Soonam's retell constantly terrified her, not after two losses. She would keep this one and maybe give it away. A part of her wanted to prove to herself that her womb was not a graveyard.

Manga played with her fingers as they lay side-by-side Sunday morning. She had told him everything about her relationship with Hassan, the reason she could not go back home, the losses, her reason for joining the sisterhood.

"Let's go away together, maybe…South Africa…" he told her.

Ameena put a finger over his lips. "I did that already. Look where it got me. How can I trust you won't do the same thing to me?"

Manga smiled. "I would not. I would hurt anyone who hurt you."

She smiled sadly. "You did not touch Hassan."

He lay back and pulled her to him. "How sure are you I did not?"

Ameena raised her head from his shoulder, leveling with him. She demanded, "What did you do?"

"Nothing…yet."

Manga confessed he had returned to Hassan's house when she was asleep with a bouncer from the club, but Hassan had already left.

"*Aad tahay waalan!*" she screamed at him.

He frowned. "What's that?"

She shook her head. "Are you crazy? Don't hurt him!"

Manga threw his head back and laughed sardonically. "Pathetic that you can protect a man who has done nothing but rob you of everything you have. I am only trying to help!"

"Don't help!" she shot back at him.

"That's *juju* talk." He snickered in disbelief at her outburst and swung his long legs from underneath the covers, his back to her.

Ameena paused. She needed to pacify him. "Manga, it's not that. That is my business. And I don't want you in trouble for anything."

Manga had inched away from her touch. "I take care of those I should take care of…Soonam, you. The sisterhood. *You*, mostly."

Ameena reached out again, touching his back. This time he let her, and her fingers traced the fine muscle on them. "I am sorry," she half-whispered. Her fingers gently kneaded into his back, traveling up to his neck…He relaxed.

Ameena worked her fingers down his spine, then up again. "Come back to bed," she said seductively.

She needed him if any of her plans were to work. She needed him to keep loving her.

He turned to look at her, his eyes displaying a rejuvenated need. "You are so complicated, you know?"

She smiled innocently, coaxing him. "But you know me."

"*Hapana*." All traces of anger had been erased by her touch, her voice.

"Oh? Now how will you protect me?" she egged him on; he lay beside her now.

His eyes flickered, a mad glint that both scared and fascinated her. "I will do anything for you…anything."

She smiled triumphantly, "Then fuck me."

* * *

She ate less and craved boiled eggs with sliced tomatoes only. Still, she glowed. Sometimes she slept a little longer and complained she had had a long night.

Matthias came back and requested her. This time it was a pleasure trip, and he needed her to go with him to Amboseli National Park.

Soonam was beaming when she brought Ameena the message. "The Ugandan soon-to-be member of Parliament wants you again. It's been two months, no?"

Ameena smiled. "I guess I made a good impression."

"You always do." Soonam winked at her.

Ameena tried to enjoy the trip, her mind on the fact that her stomach was going to show soon. She watched Matthias as he laughed and clapped, enjoying his game drive in the evenings. He was chatty at dinner and endeavored to be a little more participatory between the sheets.

"I think we should establish an arrangement," he told her one night as they sat outside the balcony of their hotel sipping wine as she sipped tea.

"What type of arrangement?" she asked.

She had mastered the art of enjoying a cup of tea like a proper Victorian lady, relishing how he stared at her in fascination each time she daintily sipped from the little China teacup and set it down on the table, her lipstick intact.

"I will pay an extra amount for an exclusive engagement with you for a year," he told her.

Ameena sat back, horrified at the idea, then realized the advantage it gave her. She let her answer hang in midair. A pungent scent of suspense swirled between them as she toyed with her tea. Then, to Matthias's visible relief, she said, "Yes, I would like that."

When they returned, the negotiations were heady since Soonam knew exclusivity of her best always meant she would have to lose a little on profit, especially from clients that would require Ameena by name, and there were regulars who paid good money for her. The negotiation came to triple payment for six months.

This was her escape plan, she decided, since Matthias resisted the use of condoms. In another month, he visited for a conference, and while she pretended to be asleep, she overheard him speaking to an irate woman on the phone. From the conversation, it was clear it was his wife. He was begging her to relax, that the rumors were false. That he was not lying, he had a lot of business in Kenya....

Ameena played her sisterhood cards right, and after their lovemaking, when he was tipsy, she drew out the truth about his life and marriage from his ravished soul. He told all; he was not happy. However, an aspiring member of Parliament must be married and properly positioned in society.

He liked Ameena's company. She was young and exciting in bed. He had never met anybody like her. Ameena had heard that so often it was becoming like a broken record in her ear, but she purred and cooed in response like a teenager in love: soothing his ego, stroking his battered heart, and loving his flabby body.

"You treat me better than my wife," he murmured before falling asleep. He made the mistake of giving her his personal information, something that was not permitted, but, totally disarmed and charmed by Ameena, he gave it to her.

"Call me anytime you need me. This is our secret. Soonam does not need to know."

She kissed him passionately. "Yes, of course."

Two weeks later, she called him to say she was not feeling well. She wanted to see him. He panicked and came to Nairobi the very next day.

"I don't want Soonam to know," she told him with urgency. "Maybe you can go with me to the hospital?"

Matthias, a man smitten and not suspecting any foul play, agreed readily and paid for her full-body examination.

An hour later, the doctor came back with the test results. Ameena was pregnant, three months pregnant, placing conception around the first time she had slept with Matthias when he had insisted on not using a condom.

Ameena had stared at the results in feigned shock and burst into tears. "Soonam is going to kill me," she had wailed dramatically, and Matthias, to avoid public attention, quickly whisked her to the waiting car and comforted her.

"No, no, no, she won't," he told her, and even as he comforted her, his expression conveyed his worry.

She calmed down halfway through the journey back to his hotel, where he ordered her a meal. The silence between them fell heavily. Ameena watched him, wondering what his mind was brewing, playing her own guessing game, placing herself in his shoes in her mind; what would she do if she were him, with a wife and children and a prospective future? He would not want that botched.

"How long have you been with Soonam?" he asked her finally.

Ameena shrugged. "Three years…"

"Is she good to you?"

Ameena smiled as she chewed on her *ugali*. "She is good to all of us."

He watched her eat, and from the corner of her eye she saw how conflicted he was.

"Ameena, you know…" He hesitated. "I am an important man…"

She waited.

"This pregnancy…" He looked away from her. "…Puts me in a very precarious situation."

"But you…"

He waved her words off before she could finish.

"I know, I know…but it just seems too…. I don't know…"

"So you think I am lying?" she demanded, her voice raised, an added touch to her feigned indignation.

He touched her arm in a gesture to calm her down. "I don't know what to believe. You are a call girl." He looked at her matter-of-factly.

"Oh?" She was angry this time. "So when you put your child in me, I am just a call girl? We shall see about that." She dragged the chair back noisily, and he stopped her.

"Wait!"

She sat down, pushing the plate of food away.

"Okay, that was uncalled for. How about…an abortion?"

Ameena raised her brows and laughed. "That is the only solution you can come up with?"

"I will pay for it; tell me how much, and I shall pay for it," he told her, and now she could see the desperation in his eyes.

Here was a blank check placed before her, and she needed to use it well.

She shook her head. "I could die. I…"

His eyes hardened. "I will not be the father of that child!"

"I will not die trying to get rid of a twelve-week-old baby!" she responded just as sharply. "You think you are the only one affected?

How about Soonam? What about *my* life?"

"I shall cancel the exclusive agreement I made with...."

"Because I am pregnant?" She glared at him and watched him shift uncomfortably. Her voice dropped emotionally. "And I thought you were different."

He sighed. "I am married, Ameena. This was a mistake. I shall take you back and let Soonam know I changed my mind."

Her gaze never wavered, willing him to look at her. "And *my* life?"

He took a deep breath. "I am sorry. I can give you money to get rid of it. Think about it. Let me know. You have my contact," he said with finality.

"If you cancel the contract," Ameena started slowly after they had sat in silence for what felt like eternity, "Soonam will be suspicious."

Matthias rubbed his hands, his head bowed. "So, what do we do?"

Ameena let his question linger between them. "I am not getting an abortion. It could kill me."

She kept her eyes on him. He was shaking his head.

"Get me out of here." She finally dropped her price.

He frowned. "What do you mean?"

"I mean, my life with a baby is already over. Soonam will not keep me. So, get me a house and some money to start a new life...and in exchange, you can forget about me."

Matthias laughed. "You must be out of your mind! A house?"

Ameena knew she had placed a tall order, but she was not backing away from it; her mind worked ahead of his answers to her responses to the possibilities of their conversation, arriving at different outcomes, some favoring her, others not, and she quickly tied the loose ends so that unfavorable variables dropped off the probability list.

Their eyes locked, and he saw the severity in them. He shook his head. "Over my dead body. You chose not to have an abortion."

She cussed him in her soul, finally lowering her gaze. "Take me back," she said simply.

"That's it?"

She pushed the hair out of her face and straightened her blouse. "I would not cancel the agreement with Soonam yet."

In the end, Matthias could not bring himself to cancel the exclusive arrangement. On the way to K Street, the once light and giddy atmosphere between them was stifling and uncomfortable. Matthias rubbed his face, distracted, juggling the problem. She knew he was not a wicked man, and he was terrified of the prospects a baby born to a prostitute would cost his campaign. It was the perfect scenario. Ameena shuffled her cards mentally. It was her ticket.

When she got out of the car, he took her hand. "I...I am not a bad person but...this is at a *bad* time..." he told her. "I hope you can understand."

For the first time in a long time, Ameena felt tired, tired of giving and receiving the short end of the stick. She was worn out from being the underdog, and since nothing she had ever done had helped her get what she wanted, she decided she would get it herself, no matter what it cost.

She turned to him, smiling sweetly. "I understand." He sighed with relief.

"You...do? You will get an abortion?" he asked.

She placed a hand over his. "I'm sorry for all the trouble. I think I was just distressed. But, let me first settle down, even find a good clinic, and I shall call you back. Give me a few days."

Matthias cleared his throat uncomfortably and reached to give her a clumsy hug. "Thank you, *Asante, Asante.*" He immediately fished out a wad of money from his pocket and clasped it in her hand. "If you need anything in these few days. Anything. If it is not enough, call me."

Ameena smiled coolly. A lump rose and settled in her throat. The more he babbled like a clumsy teenager, the angrier she got, the more she loathed him. She clenched the money and shoved it in her bag when the car pulled away, leaving her before the ancient-looking building that she called home.

* * *

Two weeks of calling to negotiate with a resistant Matthias was becoming tiring.

"Here we go again; I thought we agreed." Matthias groaned.

"I won't say anything, as long as I can get far away from Soonam. Even you will not know where I am," she reiterated to Matthias the nth time she called him, proposing her terms. "A house. Money to start over. You will never hear from me again…or I will tell Soonam and your wife."

"Let me think about it." A man typically tormented by his "sin" hesitates in these moments, and Matthias did. He did not realize how much this would cost him.

Ameena waited twenty-four hours before calling his home phone, when she was sure he would not be home. A cheery female voice answered it.

"Mrs. Kahinde?" She spoke haltingly into the phone, and the other woman responded suspiciously: "Who are you?"

Between deep forlorn sighs, Ameena told her everything and even promised her proof if she met with her to show her the pregnancy results, medical reports, and a copy of her exclusive contract agreement.

Even as she heard the woman on the other end swing from angry and defensive to a helpless sobbing mess, she remained cool, nonchalant, and even bored.

They arranged a private meeting, time and place picked, and Ameena took a bus to Kampala. The dejected and humiliated-looking Matthias sat next to a stony, aloof woman. Whenever he tried to protest, his wife yelled at him for embarrassing them. The evidence Ameena presented was indisputable, Matthias's signature was on one of the contracts. With his wife as a witness, Matthias signed over a title deed to one of his flats in Bugolobi that he had been hoping to sell and handed Ameena an envelope with two million Uganda shillings.

"We are done here. I never want to see you again." Mrs. Kahinde had threateningly hurled the words in Ameena's face on their way out of the Fairway Hotel lobby, where the meeting had taken place.

Ameena had shrugged. "You won't, co-wife."

Chapter 12

December 28, 1992

Ameena lay back, panting. Her body felt the drain of the past twelve hours. The surrounding voices swam in and out of focus. Somewhere she could hear Boney M's "Mary's Boy Child" playing, and then she heard the nurse, chirping joyously, "A girl!"

At first, she could not place it, her mind as exhausted as her body, then someone came to her, placing the squirming, screaming bundle in her arms.

"You have a beautiful big baby girl! Five kilograms!" the woman said, an edge of excitement in her voice.

Ameena tried to speak, tried to protest, wanted to tell them it could not be right…it was not possible…she was expecting a boy…but she was too tired…so so exhausted…the last she heard was the nurse saying, "She is tired…"

She was in Nsambya Hospital for three days. Nobody came to see her, and she ate from the cafeteria. Ameena had never felt so alone. It was just her and the baby in the crib next to her bed. Since the day she had given birth, she had not wanted to carry the child or look at her. She instead grieved deeply, much to the surprise of the nurses who could not understand her behavior. The nurses had to force her to breastfeed the child. They sympathized with her, imagining her reaction was because she was alone. One of them offered to give her hand-me-downs from her own collection. Her child was two years old now. Ameena thanked her but declined, too proud to take anyone else's used clothes. But after much insistence from the nurse, she obliged.

On New Year's Eve, Ameena, armed with her bag of hand-me-downs and her new bundle of life, sat in the doctor's office, faintly listening to the hum of the standing fan that whirled to the left and right, blowing her unruly curls into her face while she gave details for the birth certificate.

For father's name, she scoffed, and then said, "He is dead."

The doctor glanced at her. "I am sorry for your loss, but we need the name for records." She had bitten down hard on her lower lip and given Hassan's name, reluctantly wishing it had been anyone else's but his.

Even Manga's.

Manga.

She thought fondly of him. She had let him in on her plan to leave the sisterhood, and despite him being against it, which led to multiple rows between them, he had watched as she executed it instead of confessing to Soonam.

She remembered the worried expression he wore the day he went with her to the bus station bound for Kampala.

"Call me when the time comes; I want to be there," Manga had told her with urgency, as if he was the father of the child. "If you need anything, anything…" He had scribbled the club number on a piece of paper, even though she knew it by heart from frequently calling him.

She regretted not telling anyone else in the sisterhood.

"Ameena…" Manga had held her as they stood at the bus station in the wee hours of the morning. "You were always a wild one. You always had something up your sleeve. Soonam knew you would want to leave. She loves you. Apart from me, she has loved nobody as much as she has you. Please…tell her at least."

Ameena had buried her head in his chest. "I will miss her very much. But it's time for me to go. I don't want her to know about the baby. I am too ashamed. I have been…only trouble for her…she deserves…better.

Please don't tell her."

"They will know I know; you know that," he told her.

Ameena had sighed. *"Fadlan* just don't tell them now, *macaan.* Please."

Manga had smoothed back her curls and held her for a long time before saying, *"Ayaaa...*I'm pathetic. Look at me." He jeered almost casually although she could sense the battle between his heart and his head. It was good for her, she convinced herself.

He was somber; the fate he ran from had caught up with him, yet he still fought it. "Choosing you over my aunty."

She smiled faintly, sincerely grateful for him and yet ashamed too that she had to let him do this. "I am sorry it had to be you. You are the only one I can trust."

"Promise me you will keep in touch. I want to see the baby. I want to help." His eyes were firm, holding her up to a promise she barely wanted to keep.

As they stood there holding memories fondly in an embrace Ameena felt she would miss dearly, she nodded. He released her as the bus she was to board called.

"Call me when the baby is born," he told her again. There were no goodbyes said, no *I love you*s. Simply a lingering, meaningful look that said more than the words between them could.

* * *

At the reception desk, the nurse who had given Ameena the baby clothes met her and asked her cheerily what name she had given her daughter.

Ameena took out the birth certificate issued by the hospital from her bag and read it back to her like she had a hard time remembering it: "Shenzi."

BOOK 2

Shenzi & Kevin
1999–2000

Your soul and my soul
Once sat together in the Beloved's womb
Playing footsie.

Your heart and my heart
are very, very old
Friends.
—Hafiz

Chapter 1

August 1999
Bugolobi, Uganda

"Five...six...seven...eight..." Marjorie's loud voice drawled to a low before she stopped counting completely and then yelled out, "You better not let me find you!"

Shenzi sat on a broken concrete slab on Block 4 veranda, one of the many eroded slabs that were once steps and elevated pavement mini guardrails worn from age. A slow smile crept upon her oval face, the color of night, smooth and pale, framed with shabby shoulder-length braids. The outgrowth at the base made her head look like a mass of untidy dreadlocks in need of a retwist. She rested her slim left arm on her knee, and her other hand held on to the walking cane that she went nowhere without.

She had her knees pressed close together, her head upturned, while her unseeing blank gaze searched for something *or* someone. It was a warm Saturday late afternoon, when all the children in the flats came out to play. It was always a lot of fun, even for her, to sit and listen and try to identify each of the players by the sounds of their voices and the echo in their footsteps as they sauntered about in play.

Shenzi tapped at the ground below her lightly to feel for the little bag of goodies she was guarding. While the games were afoot, she was the keeper of all the treasures of the players: an assortment of pencils, marbles, broken toys, gum, pebbles, snacks, and other knickknacks that they had pinched from home, school, and God knows where else.

Since she was the only one unable to take part in their many activities, they had chosen her to be custodian of all their goods, for a small fee, of course. She was a faithful keeper of things. Her rewards varied; most times she got away with more than she bargained for because her best friend Kevin was a shrewd negotiator, bullying the rest out of all their loot. Amid tears, groans, and bitter complaints, they handed goods over, one-way transactions made, and unhappy children walked away in defeat, hoping to scavenge for more treasures elsewhere.

Shenzi wondered what she would get this time. The smile settled like a single beam of light on her striking dark features. The game of hide-and-seek dragged on and on, and soon she grew weary, her buttocks getting numb from sitting for so long. She stood up to stretch.

"Thirty minutes…swear upon God!" was the emphatic promise made to her by the overly energetic children.

"If longer, you pay double, okay?" Kevin had smoothly inserted that clause, and there was hesitation…then low mumbles of agreement that became choruses of affirmation.

"Yes, okay!"

So far, there had been three hide-and-seek games played, each longer than the last because the children hid farther and farther from their block to keep the seeker on their toes.

Kevin turned up first every time they played, announcing his presence by slapping the counting pole, a sign he had gotten there before the counter, Marjorie.

"I am first!" he screamed out, much to Shenzi's amusement. Marjorie's voice sailed back to her: a deep disgruntled voice hurling threats and accusations.

"I will find you! You cheats!"

Then Kevin's breathless laughter followed, every time, as if it was curated. Heaving as he gasped for breath and laughed simultaneously, he yelled back, "Shut up, Marja! It doesn't work!" He had his hands on his hips, one leg protruding out front before him in a slouched sort of pose as he watched Marjorie's plump shape waddle farther away to Block 3 and burst into fresh peals of laughter.

"That girl can't run to save her life." He wagged a finger in her direction and backed up slowly toward the slab where Shenzi sat.

"Leave her alone; you already won!" Shenzi called out, but the grin on her face betrayed her. It was hard to be mad at Kevin.

Being first to come out of hiding was of advantage; they got to sit in between games and tease and laugh at the others as they were smoked out. She looked forward to it because Kevin described the goings-on in hilarious detail.

"You know it's true, Shenz," he called back.

Suddenly there was a *whoosh,* and Shenzi sat still, poised to attack, when a hand reached out and grabbed at her braids. Shenzi was faster. She swerved into her position and seized the shirt of whoever it was.

"You got faster!" Kevin sang out naughtily, his hands flying over hers, which clenched his Sonic the Hedgehog T-shirt.

Shenzi's smile widened.

"I knew it was you."

"Not Bosco?" he asked, settling on the slab next to her.

"Bosco smells like shoe polish..."

Kevin burst into laughter. Shenzi laughed with him. "It's true."

"What about me?" Kevin asked. His hand reached for the braids closest to him, and she slapped his hand away. "Ow!"

"I told you, I can feel it," she huffed.

Kevin raised a brow, impressed. Touching her hair was a pet peeve. When they were younger, her long curly locks had fascinated him and Bosco, his best friend, and two other boys, and they spent hours devising schemes on how to touch it. He had ogled in amazement as Teopista plaited Shenzi's hair. He had seen no one on Block 4 with hair as long as Shenzi's or her mother's or as loosely curled and lush, just like white people's hair on television. What puzzled them was that her complexion did not go with her hair; even her mother was several shades lighter than her.

Sometimes, Shenzi, tiring of their pestering, burst into tears. Boys could never understand the hellish perils little girls went through dealing with freshly plaited hair. After several attempts that ended in tears, the mothers on Block 4 made the boys apologize to Shenzi. Each of them got a whack on their behinds by Teopista. Kevin recalled his mother approving of it, to his dismay.

To add salt to the smarting wound of his battered ego, Aunty Dina, his mother, started having Shenzi over for lunch, sometimes dinner.

"You will treat her well," was his mother's instruction, and that was it.

After a few weeks of her having supper at their home, Kevin decided it wouldn't kill to ask.

"I'm not your friend because you got me beaten." He had watched her spoon her rice slowly, chew it carefully, lips pressed together most delicately. It was impressive to watch. "But why don't you want anyone to touch your hair?"

It was just them at the table. Shenzi was a slow eater, and his mother would not let him leave until she had finished her meal. Shenzi put down her spoon, felt for the glass of water, and drank ever so delicately, Kevin wanted to kick her shin from under the table. He let out a low growl. She averted her glassy gaze toward him and made a face. "Because it hurts!"

It surprised him how tame her voice was, even when she hissed at him.

"Oh," he said, then watched her eat another spoonful of rice soaked in beef stew. "But how can it hurt?" he asked.

She did not reply, not then and not again for the rest of the night.

However, it was the beginning of their friendship. Kevin figured if he was to get to know the *why*s he and his friends mused upon about her, he needed to talk to her a little more, even attempt to be nicer.

"So?"

"What do I smell like? It better not be shoe polish!"

Shenzi grinned. "I won't tell you."

"What?" He feigned shock, and she laughed.

"Never, ever, ever." Shenzi shook her head viciously.

"Hmm, if I smelled bad, you would say it, so I think that's my answer. I smell like a prince," he bragged, and she made a noise between a laugh and an indignant exclamation.

"But," Kevin added, "I have made you more alert; that's good." Shenzi never stopped grinning. Kevin could be such a braggart.

"No."

"Yes, I have."

"No, you haven't."

"Should we ask shoe polish boy?"

Shenzi shook her head. "Poor Bosco. Why is he your best friend if you tease him like this?"

"Because when you two get married, I shall be the best man."

"*Urgh!*" She made a face. "I will marry no one."

Kevin laughed. "You will make Bosco sad."

Shenzi pushed him off the slab. "Go away!"

He stumbled off it, chuckling. "Okay, okay, you won't marry him…." He steadied himself and threw a hand around her shoulder then whispered, "He will marry you."

"Kevin!" Shenzi yelled, breaking away from him and swinging her cane at him. Kevin jumped off the slab, laughing.

"Go! Go!" she called out to him, still waving the cane.

"But the game is not over. Marja hasn't even returned yet!" He was enjoying the moment; she could tell.

"Go help her then; I think you said you would marry her." Her weak attempt at teasing him always fell flat because he laughed it off like it was nothing.

"Marjorie can't even dodge a ball during *kwepena*. How can I marry her!" Kevin exclaimed, and she giggled.

"But if I stay here, I will make sure she does not slap you by mistake thinking you are the counting pole." Shenzi's giggles morphed into laughter as Kevin made a *pah* sound with his lips and swept his hand in front of her, a motion of a slap. She caught the cool jut of air released from the sweeping motion.

Kevin beamed, enjoying the effect his words were having on her, his big toe pressing on the hot, rugged cement.

"Since we won't marry Bosco or Marjorie, I think we should become brother and sister forever," he added with his brows creased like he had been thinking about that for a long time.

Sometimes Kevin said things she never expected. Touched, she spun her gaze to him, "Really? Yes!" she chirped. "But you have to stop trying to touch my hair until I tell you to."

"Eh! Okay, okay…so when do I touch it?"

"When I say you should."

Then she added with a pout, "Aunty Dina's right; you are so, so stubborn. *You* get into trouble because of it." She felt very grown-up as she said that.

"If I wasn't stubborn, how would I protect you, heh?" He smiled then sat up. "Now…today we are taking half that loot." He squinted at the little plastic bag cradled in a misshapen heap at Shenzi's feet.

Shenzi made a humming sound as she positioned her chin into her open palm, leaning her elbow on her lap. "One day everyone will gang up on us and beat us…"

"None of them can. I beat the hardest and run the fastest." He puffed his chest out.

"Even Marjorie?" Shenzi attempted to tease him again.

"Huh! Are you joking? I won't ever be the seeker if I keep hitting the pole before her; don't you think?" he asked playfully, trying to give off the impression her view was a by the way to him. Shenzi cocked her head to the side knowingly, glad he asked and then dillydallied with the answer in a silence that weighted heavily on Kevin.

"Hm…" She tapped her chin dramatically.

Kevin chuckled.

"I think so."

"Of course," he hollered.

"It's because I have no choice, big head. You are a bully, but you are my best friend, too." She shrugged, her voice caressing and warm.

She could sense his eyes on her, and a smile crept up her lips. He glowed like a firefly in the dark, leaned into her shoulder, and gave it a brief shove, a satisfied smile never leaving his face.

"*Hmm.* At least you enjoy the benefits of my bullying."

"Hmm, maybe."

His face softened; his ego boosted. Someone appreciated the effort, even indirectly. A comfortable silence fell between them, while the scrambled noisy voices of children at play gradually rose to peak screams as they all rushed in from their hiding places to hit the pole. Marjorie's loud, deep voice overrode the symphony of jubilant screams.

"You cheaters! All of you! You planned it!" she was gasping for breath, waddling as fast as she could to the hide-and-seek pole.

Some children snickered. Others, tired from running around and switching hiding places, flopped onto the grassy lawns of Block 4 and dared to stare into the sun, trying to find its middle. Marjorie huffed and puffed, frustrated. It was the third time she was the seeker. Being the youngest and chubbiest, weight and age left her at a disadvantage. And it was so every other Saturday. Usually, after a third game, Marjorie gave up trying to be a hider in a pool of tears. The children waited like they did every time they played with Marjorie and before anyone could mention the spoils and token of thanks to Shenzi, Marjorie's pouted lower lip quivered, her eyes turned downward, her round cheeks stretched, her eyebrows furrowed, and her nose twitched in that all too familiar I'm-about-to-cry face.

The children scattered. They dared not hang around when Marjorie cried. Her voice was deeper than two of the older boys in their prepubescent stages. When she cried, it echoed right down to Block 3, past it to the main road. She never let off until her mother showed up, screaming, and yelling at the children who remained behind to watch her cry for making her last-born miserable. Marjorie's crying was a sight to behold.

Kevin always stayed and snickered into his hand, trying hard not to belt out his laughter. When Marjorie's mother showed up, a skinny wee woman with a *kanga* always tied around her waist, he wore a poker face, so tight, it was hard to believe a second ago he had been close to tears in a laughing fit.

After the brief drama, yelling at the rest of the children, even threatening to beat or tell their parents, a few words of comfort were lavished on Marjorie, and she was taken back to the safety of her house, usually with her constantly casting glances over her shoulder at the rest of the children.

The other children would then return, knowing the coast was clear. Kevin and the few brave ones had taken the fall for them all.

"She will be back, you know." It was Bosco telling them what they already knew.

They all agreed. No one wanted to stay indoors when the outdoors beckoned enticingly.

"So now we take our things." One of the older boys—a year older than Kevin—stepped forward to pick up the bag that was nicely tucked behind Shenzi's legs.

Kevin barred his way, stepping in front of Shenzi.

"Not so fast." Kevin stood poised with his arms crossed over his chest.

The older boy sighed and looked back at the rest of the children behind him. "So?" he asked.

Shenzi spoke up from behind Kevin: "You said thirty minutes, but the games were too long."

The boy frowned. "What did she say?"

Kevin was about to respond when he felt Shenzi's cane knock against his calf, and she spoke up. Louder. "I said you took longer than you said you would. My bums are hard from sitting here."

The older boy glared at Kevin. Kevin arched his brow daringly. The older boy did not budge. The kids suddenly went quiet.

Everyone on Block 4 knew Kevin's middle name was "fight."

The older boy sneered and, without warning, Kevin shoved him hard while flicking his leg around the bigger opponent's calf, catching him off guard. He staggered backwards, trying to steady his footing, and Kevin charged at his unguarded midriff. The older boy landed on his back, arms flailing helplessly.

"What did you say?" Kevin sat on his opponent's chest, pressing his fist down hard into his neck.

The older boy gasped: "Get off me! Guys! Get. him. off. me!" But the other children simply watched, mumbling. No one wanted to be caught up in the ensuing tussle.

Kevin pressed his knee into the boy's side and he whimpered in pain, "what did you say?" he threatened

The older boy panted. "Okay. Okay. How much?"

Satisfied, Kevin got off the boy, dusted his hands and went to consult with Shenzi, and after a long negotiation, they walked away with more than half in coins, guavas, mangoes, dolls' heads, broken cars, and pancakes in payment. They then retreated to their secret place and munched on a little mountain of peppered pancakes until their throats and tongues were numb.

Their secret place was a six-story climb to the roof of their flat. Up here, the view of the city was breathtaking. Kevin had brought Shenzi when they became friends, as an act of contrition and acceptance that he would see her a lot anyway since his mother made it so. He had also heard the rumors. He saw how alone she was, how her own mother seemed to live her own life like Shenzi did not exist. It tugged at his heart.

* * *

"This sort of business suites us." Kevin laughed, his cheeks swollen with pancakes.

Shenzi guffawed. "You mean stealing from the rest?"

Kevin nodded vigorously. "It's not stealing. They broke the rules.

Yeah! We make a good team, don't we?"

He put his arm around her and squeezed. "I see us in the future...the terrible two...triple T." He nodded dramatically. "Very scary...triple T. What do you think, Shenzi?"

"Err, it's funny-sounding..."

"No, it's not. I steal while you play the damsel of distraction." Shenzi threw her head back and laughed.

"Sometimes I wonder if your head is full of hot porridge or maggots... like Mama Rose would say, 'a wicked mind indeed'!"

They both laughed at that. Mama Rose was the light-skinned woman on Block 4 who bragged about being more enlightened and well bred than anyone because she grew up in a seminary surrounded by white fathers that her mother kept house for.

"Where do you get such things, Kevin?" Although she tried to scold him, she admired his ingenuity. "God will surely punish you for such wicked thoughts."

The spell suddenly seemed to break as Kevin heaved. "I think he has punished me already."

Shenzi's face grew long and stony, every trace of laughter and bemusement obliterated. A gloomy silence hung over them like a dark cloud, their minds on the same thing...*Taata Bob*. Shenzi was aware his sentiments toward his father were far from civil. Sometimes she feared what he would do. She had been at his house on occasions when Taata Bob returned in his usual drunken stupor and hurled insults at them all.

Kevin looked at Shenzi. "It's okay, Taata Bob won't hurt you or Mom when I'm there." Fighting came as easy as breathing, so when Taata Bob was in a fit, Kevin learned to throw some punches back, sometimes verbal, sometimes physical...or both while quickly ushering Shenzi to the door to shield her from the toxicity. His fear was having Shenzi caught in the middle of his father's drunken artillery. He could not protect both her and his mother at the same time. Anxiety settled like the previous night's leftover *katogo* in the pit of his stomach every time he heard the old Suzuki cough to a halt below their two-bedroom accommodation.

"Sorry…" Shenzi started apologetically.

"I know." He cut her off brusquely.

It would not help to dwell on it; lately, he was wrestling with darker thoughts because the abuse and beatings were more frequent. He had resigned to brooding, away from Shenzi.

"Do you want to go back and play?" She asked as lightly as she could manage. "It seems like everyone is going for round two." The voices of their playmates rose in a distorted muddle of laughter, screams, and name-calling; they were regrouping to play before the chill escorted with the blanket of night settled over what was a lovely, warm Saturday.

Shenzi felt Kevin rouse beneath his covers of gloom. "No…" He dragged the words out as he unrolled the invisible quilt of melancholy from his face. "There is nothing more to steal, anyway. We took all the good stuff!"

She smiled, feeling the life seep through the darkness. "But I think they are going to play something else?"

Kevin shrugged. "We have money to get chips and liver if you want… and watching them from here is fun…like we are gods watching little people play."

"What does it look like?" She loved this part when he described the scenery below, as far as the eye can see…

"Marjorie is back!" he exclaimed at one point, and they lapsed into choked fits of laughter. Kevin leaned against the low raised guard slab and shouted out encouragement for another game of hide-and-seek.

She could only imagine what the view was like from this height. When Kevin described it, he made it feel like they were gods looking down on the little people and their lives, willing them to do their bidding. For those moments on the roof, she felt transcendent, craning her ears for sounds, her nose for scents familiar and new. Her fingers traced the corrugated rough edges of the slabs on the rooftop, and in her mind, she created a little paradise; she could forget life in her own apartment even for a moment.

Then he hesitated. Shenzi cocked her ears. It was the sound of an engine, smooth and unfamiliar; it came to a stop. She frowned.

"Who is that, Kevin?"

Kevin hesitated, and she tugged at his sleeve. He took in a deep breath and replied, "Nobody from the flat…but it spoiled the game of *kwepena*."

Shenzi groaned.

"I think the ball is under the car…"

He bobbed his head up and down, peering at the car curiously, then his eyes spied the head of curls that crossed the veranda gracefully; a beautiful caramel colored woman, holding an expensive-looking clutch bag, dressed in a sky blue off-the-shoulder minidress.

A man in a charcoal black suit got out of the driver's seat, nodded briefly at her, and opened the backseat door for her. Kevin watched in awe; he only saw that in movies when important people were entering their cars. But why her?

Kevin realized he was hunched over silently, watching like most of the people down below. They gawked shamelessly at the surrounding scene with curious interest…knowing disdain even.

"Oh…" He sat up. "I think the car is going away. Okay! They found the ball!"

Shenzi clapped.

"Now tell me everything before we go get chips and liver!" She settled back as if they were about to watch an exciting football match.

Kevin looked at her. The golden afternoon sun sent cascading shimmering light on her coal dark skin, and she looked like a beautiful statue seated still listening for sound, in harmony with the universe. His heart dropped, saddened that his young companion was not aware she would be home alone tonight…again. It made his blood boil, but he was sadder to think of how he bore the weight of knowing he had witnessed *her* leave and still not had the heart to tell Shenzi. So he asked, "Will you come for supper tonight? Mummy said it's chicken."

"But my mummy…" she protested, and he quickly cut in.

"I think you should come. Maybe your mother doesn't mind? What if she is not home?"

He sensed her read into his words and waited; his eyes following the tail of the black Mercedes as it eased away from Block 4 back onto the narrow, somewhat tarmacked path that led to the main road.

"I like chicken," Shenzi said after what felt like forever.

He looked away. She knew.

Chapter 2

Ameena rocked back and forth, perched on the toilet seat.

The gnawing urgency in the pit of her tummy, a reminder that the Mercedes would come in less than an hour, made her both nervous and numb. The Prime Minister's best friend was seeking company for a few days—a vile man with outlandish sexual requests and a formidable brat. *But he is rich*, she comforted herself.

"If it doesn't kill you, do it." Soonam's words echoed in her ears. Her fingers fumbled with the full pack of Sportsman cigarettes she smuggled to smoke in the bathroom's solitude. The basin of water was getting cold. *Maybe boil another kettle?* She toyed with the idea, but the numbness kept her glued to the toilet seat. She lit the cigarette and inhaled deeply.

"You have started smoking again." Manga's voice sipped through the nervous haze of her thoughts.

Manga! She breathed in deeply.

"It keeps me sane," she said aloud just like she had told him in stark defiance, blowing out the smoke in measured puffs, concentrating on how they fogged her view of the off-white sink with a pink toilet bag spilling over with makeup stacked at its corner.

She took another long drag on the cigarette…

Soonam was kissing her forehead, calling her *Mrembo, qalbi, macaan*. Ameena groaned. She was relieved Shenzi was out with Kevin. Today was not the day to be a parent. Hell, she wanted her own mother!

"Mothers need mothers too," she pep-talked to herself absently.

Ghosts of the past played in the singular smoke swirl. She ached for them. Every deep drag on the cigarette unfolded snippets of Koinange Street, and she smiled. She had become a pleasure adjective inserted into every man's dictionary: *desire, fresh, seductive*…perfect. And oh, the men that took her. Old, young, distinguished, foreign, respectable, rich…*oh, so rich*!

Then the baby. *Damn* Hassan and his bastard!

Her head dropped; her heart still throbbed for him, even after everything he had put her through. She whimpered. Maybe Manga was right. Maybe Hassan had bewitched her.

She wondered often about Soonam. Soonam never came looking for her, even when Manga had visited after Shenzi was born.

The cigarette had run its course, and she dropped the butt onto the clear-tiled bathroom floor, then absently stared at her freshly manicured nails.

The prime minister let her know that his oil-mining Nigerian philanthropist friend Ayinke had a particular taste in his women's looks, *oyinbo-looking black women* and she fit the description. That was four months ago when she'd first met him. He would not see her unless she wore what he gave her to wear. Her makeup and hair had to be done precisely as he wished, something that Ameena thought was annoying. In public, her place was always beside him with her mouth shut except to eat and smile.

He hated the smell of cigarettes, too. Ameena sighed. *These men can be exhausting, especially those with money.* Painfully exhausting, but she had mastered this part a long time ago. How then was it she mixed the crème with the mud? Some months it was the best of this exhausting lot, and other times it was a budget package but easy to be around. That was how she met Silver Mulenzi.

In a cheap little club in Kisementi, during her downtime listening to middle-class workers gossip about their nasty bosses, their husbands, and their friend's husbands, she nursed a Nile Special quietly surrounded by her ghosts when he manifested.

"If you won't finish that, I am glad to relieve you of it."

She took an immediate liking to him. He was easy to talk to, and he was funny, with that edge of danger all the men that stuck around her possessed.

He reminded her of Manga, a milder, less polished version. Silver had no morals, and every vagina was fair game, even female animals, if he could.

She would have disposed of him easily if only it wasn't that he supplied her with the best marijuana she had ever had and tolerated her stress smoking. He knew how to keep her hooked on him sexually, just like Manga? Hassan? She raised her brows, *both*.

The first time he slapped her during sex, she thought he was playing rough, then he half-strangled her another day, and she realized she had called out Manga's name, Hassan on another occasion. "It's my special way of saying I'm coming," she mocked him.

And even with that, he stubbornly clung to her. "I will be the only name that matters."

She let him stay because he was useful, carrying back armfuls of groceries: bread, milk, eggs, the little things she was glad not to buy, just so she could save up for her own extra frivolities.

Her body hurt today because he had slapped her hard across the face for calling out Manga. She had been so shocked; she had lost her balance and fallen right off the bed on her back.

"So why don't you just go?"

She sneered, recalling his answer: "Please, baby, I can't live without you."

It became a routine, the fights midway through sex that only led to more sex. She was exciting, mysterious. He always said that...and beautiful. She was his femme fatale, a dream he could escape into but never fully own, and that thrilled him. But for those moments together, he imagined he owned her...until she screamed the wrong names.

Manga...nobody could be as good as Manga. She toasted to that thought.

Most of the men were boring now, so she set her sights higher than she had in Nairobi. She looked for more than wealth…that dangerous edge excited her, and she was determined to find it. She cast her net for a wide catch: more foreign, more exposed. The best catch was those with both the money and the danger. She flirted with these flames, fanned them, and made them lick at her, even scorch her, wanting more of her attention, her presence, her performance. It was this game that sent her home to Silver for a finale. When they were done, they would lie back and smoke weed.

"Maybe when your blind daughter is older, I can have her," he told her once as he allowed the calming delusional effect of weed to take over his faculties. She recalled laughing and cussing at him in Somali, and he laughed with her…like a fool.

But for the next couple of nights, she was stuck with the suffocating, dominant Ayinke, a man she would have passed in a sea of clients. She had not picked him; he had picked her. He reminded her so much of the black-book clients Soonam had. No wonder the ghosts from K Street visited.

They had lunch on the patio at the Nile Hotel, and the small man consumed her with his wanton eyes…irritating. But she smiled and laughed girlishly, allowing her feminine aura to pervade and engulf him. However, she found her charms had their limits with him. Before she left, he made sure she had gotten her nails and hair done and picked out her dress for the next evening.

"Be ready at four. My driver will pick you up. We have dinner and a night out with some associates."

That was how it had been four months ago and how it was now.

Ameena willed herself off the toilet seat and stood before the half mirror. She examined her breasts. Motherhood had been kind to her; except for a few stretch marks on her belly and hips, she had only filled out where it mattered.

She stepped into the bathtub. There was no time to boil more water. Lukewarm would do.

* * *

The eyes followed her. They did not bother to hide it. She tossed the curls to the side gently and stretched her long neck decked out with pearls… her hips swayed gently with every step she took down the flight of steps, across the porch, toward the waiting Mercedes. A small smile played at the corner of her lips, touched up with a baby pink lipstick. Her eyes, subtly made up (just as her date liked it), swept over the women seated by the sides of the entranceway plaiting each other's hair, the children quarreling over a plastic bag converted into a ball, others engaged in another game. Their chatter rose and fell around her like praise. The handful of men who sat farther away on the grass, pulling up bottles of beer from a black crate, laughing rowdily at a game of cards, paused momentarily to cast admiring glances.

Their eyes ravished, despised, and envied her all at once, and she glowed in that knowledge. She was a mystery. There had been queries, "Where are you from?" She would smile and respond in Kiswahili, leaving them puzzled. Kenyan? Coastal? Ethiopian?

She enjoyed them guessing, snickered at their discomfiture with her brazen lifestyle.

Aunty Dina had once asked indirectly, "Does Shenzi see her father?"

She smiled. "He is dead."

At first, they hoped it was Manga.

He came shortly after the baby was born, and, for the first time, the flat dwellers felt they could give Ameena some sort of history. The tall, dark, mysterious stranger with conspicuous bright eyes and an arresting smile was all that the Block women whispered about.

When they walked out together, Shenzi in his arms, the women smiled and looked away. The children stopped and gazed.

She recalled the day he knocked on her door, the relief and joy she felt at seeing him. Shenzi took to him, and for once, she felt she might even like her daughter. The two of them looked good together, and he carried her often, spoiled her with his presence, with gifts. Maybe a future with him would have been perfect, for Shenzi's sake. When he held Shenzi, she gurgled and laughed like his arms were where she belonged. When he made love to Ameena, it was familiar, uninhibited, and passionate.

Manga! She sighed regretfully.

When he left, he never returned.

She tried to date; there were many willing, but they only lasted a few weeks, nothing past three months. Ameena bored easily with the stable, sensible man, so two years later, her chambers were open for business and the more than willing customers flocked to her door in droves.

She eased into this position; it was an exhilarating familiar territory.

Someone shouted, *"Mukyotara!"*

She ignored them. Another whistled. The door to the back of the Mercedes opened. Ameena beamed, and, as gracefully as a queen, she nodded to the driver in thanks and slid into the plush leather seats. They welcome her like she always belonged. As if they missed her.

"Ready?" the driver asked from the front as he stirred the engine to life.

"Yes," she replied. She had pulled out her little powder case with an accompanying mirror. Ayinke's words sailed back to her: "I can't wait to see you, *bebi*. I know you will look perfect, *oo*."

Perfect.

It is that word that kept her straying back to the mirror repeatedly, to ensure her makeup was in place, not a stain on the dress he had picked out, her hair a radiant haven of curls.

Perfect.

High-maintenance clients were a pain but a profitable pain.

Chapter 3

On the flats, you knew everything.

It was a small community; residents borrowed salt, sugar, and even money from one another, so it was no surprise that Shenzi became an almost permanent guest in the Byamukama household. The children played together, went to the same schools, and whatever gossip raged among the older people often trickled down to them.

The teenage girls found out first and started the talk, but it was an open secret, and Kevin was curious.

She is a prostitute, *Malaya.*

Even at his age, he thought she was beautiful. If only she were kinder to Shenzi, he would try to like her. However, prostitute seemed a harsh judgment.

The boys on the Block would gather in groups to watch her leave and return in an unfamiliar car each time. Sometimes she called to them and gave them five-hundred-shilling coins. "Buy some sweets," she would say, her voice soothing like the evening breeze on a sweaty brow.

Ameena was like no one's mother on the Block. She was young and feisty, bursting with life and a sensuousness that bothered his young mind. Half the boys had a crush on her. Kevin nursed a grudge against her, balling his hands into a fist every time she waltzed in and out of a car onto the flat's veranda.

"Kevin," she would call him now and again, press two one-thousand-shilling notes in his hand (she often gave him more than the other children), and tell him, "Please buy Shenzi anything she likes. I won't be home."

He would stare at her stonily. Somewhere in him, he knew they had a secret pact, one Ameena involuntarily forced him into based on their shared interest...Shenzi. Her eyes said it all. "You are like a brother to her. She trusts you."

He would say nothing but would take the money. *For Shenzi*, was how he managed not to hurl his grudge at her.

She was never home. When she was, she was too busy for Shenzi or too impatient with her.

At eleven, now accustomed to naughty pre-teenage conversation, he paid more attention to Ameena's activities. The men who came to pick her up, a handful who stayed over...way too many, and they changed more than Mama Rose's hairstyles. He spied her flirting with one, one evening, watched how he touched her and how she giggled, arching herself into him. He was mesmerized. The rumors, he eventually accepted, were true.

For weeks, he watched the different men come and go. Then he heard it, the screams of ecstasy. She was shameless and shook the Block's floors with her passion-fanned moans. *"macaan...waye boqor ayadh...igu wodh...macaan!" Darling. This is good! You are king!*

Children talked more than adults. When he wasn't with Shenzi, he found the cluster of older children by Kopa's; a famous shop they all frequented because it had the best pancakes. They ran out quickly so it was important to be there early in order to get some. By two in the afternoon, the shopkeeper they called Kopa would be yelling at them to "make a line and only two—two for each of you," which would be received with groans.

"Eh, you want to eat me out of my shop?" he would exclaim, much to their amusement.

It was the older girls who started talking...something had been happening for weeks. He did not see Shenzi much then, except in school or occasionally for dinner, before his mother hurriedly took her home.

"What?" he asked absentmindedly, realizing he had missed all the gossip being dished out liberally by one of the oldest girls, Stella, who had pimples and sprouting breasts.

She jeered, casting him daggers, "Ah! Are you deaf? Your friend's mother is *a malaya,* and my mother was saying they want her to leave because she is evil."

Stella's mother was Teopista, the oldest tenant on Block 4, who made the Pulitzer Prize-winning *mandazis.*

Kevin cast his eyes downward. "Leave?"

He wondered if that meant Shenzi would have to go too.

"Yeah." Stella rolled her eyes at him impatiently and continued to entertain the little crowd of children as they munched on their pancakes.

"So, my mother is going to…" Kevin circled the group; most of the boys pretended not to listen, but they leaned closer. "…Call a meeting for Block 4. She said she will talk to the local council chairman Mr. Chris Kyangera and the landlords."

Someone piped up sharply, "But why? Aunty Ameena is pretty!"

The children's voices rose in discourse.

"Shut up," Stella commanded, then paused, not sure how to say it. She looked at the inquiring faces. "She has *bad manners.* She is not your aunty!"

Kevin grinned and tapped her. "So you also have heard?" he asked naughtily.

Stella glared at him, put her finger over her lips and said, "Shh."

The other children looked confused. However, Kevin noticed that those who had heard the moans and screams were smiling knowingly.

It was all true. A meeting was going to be called. He walked in on his mother and a few ladies visiting talking about it. When he crossed the living room to the dining room, the conversation fizzled to a stop. "Kevin, do you want to go outside and play?"

He shrugged. "Can I have a mango?" he asked, and just before he left the house, mango bitten into, he gathered that the ladies were concerned for their children and husbands.

Ameena had to leave!

* * *

It was a Friday night when the Block 4 dwellers awoke to sharp bickering and a dramatic exchange outside. Kevin threw his window open and stared out onto the veranda overlooking his bedroom window. He had the perfect view.

Voices rose and died out; Mrs. Lubega was wailing, a couple of women held her, and about three or four men stood far back talking among themselves and then…

Ameena happened.

At first, Kevin did not see her. His attention was drawn to the figure when the men stepped back.

She waltzed into the middle of the melee with nomadic grace as if walking was a deliberate, choreographed skill meant to be harnessed with calculated finesse, her nightgown flowing behind her, revealing a short negligee that clung to her gorgeous body. She swayed gently from side to side, oozing sensuality in a dazzling hypnotic motion that left a sultry trail of arousal in its wake.

She was a geisha, a natural courtesan.

The cooling breeze of the evening brushed up on Kevin, and he shivered slightly, his eyes never leaving the scene not too far from his window.

The men on the Block stood around, more mesmerized by her, unbothered that this was putting their wives and girlfriends on edge.

Ameena stood in front of Mrs. Lubega and exclaimed as if addressing an audience at a theatrical performance, "What's this?"

Someone jeered.

Another person said, "Leave her alone; her husband is the devil."

To which Ameena laughed, much to the surprise of the bystanders. Kevin leaned even closer, his little body almost halfway out the window.

"Tears don't appease the devil," she said. "You will have only a headache tomorrow and a bigger devil."

Everyone froze. Mrs. Lubega peered up at her. Kevin could not tell if she was angry or sad.

"Let me help you," was the surprising thing that Ameena said after a minute's beat.

Someone protested, but Ameena was reaching for the woman's arm, gently cooing words of encouragement.

Soon, Mrs. Lubega was walking back to the flat with Ameena by her side, much to the surprise of most people—Kevin, too.

The next day, the Block could speak of nothing but that incident; Mrs. Lubega had discovered her husband was having an affair with his secretary at that hour. While the men tried to restrain an incensed Mr. Lubega and the women tried to calm a broken-hearted Mrs. Lubega, Ameena had showed up.

Weeks later, the women were still talking excitedly about the "*ssenga* session" Ameena had had with Mrs. Lubega.

"Hmm, let's see if a *malaya* can help a mother of three. That will be a miracle!" exclaimed Teopista, who was still vehemently pushing for the meeting with the agenda dubbed "oust Ameena from the estates."

However, weeks turned into a month, then two and three, and a lot of the women had to eat up their own doubt. Mrs. Lubega looked happier than they had ever seen her, and Mr. Lubega was home by six every evening after work…seven, if traffic was heavy.

"What did she tell her?" Kevin eavesdropped on his mother with Aunty Rose.

"Hmm." The light-skinned woman clapped her hands together…. "I don't know, but whatever it is…it has saved the couple. Tomorrow I will ask her."

The other women made up their minds to try some "Ameena advice" for themselves and consulted as often as they had problems, discreetly, too.

Kevin saw how they poured into her door with gifts. Sometimes, he and Shenzi found them outside her door after school.

"I will help you carry those." He would volunteer to help her carry the gifts into the house.

"Why are people giving us things?" Shenzi had asked him, and Kevin shrugged, mumbling ignorance, although he had an idea.

His other friends told him how their mothers were constantly talking about Ameena but now in a good way. His own mother kept insisting Shenzi come for meals and even sleep over…it was more enthusiastic than before. She had won them over. No one complained about her train of men and late-night moans. In fact, they pretended they did not see or hear.

Even Teopista dropped the subject of ousting her. Everyone seemed to deny she had been a problem for the past years.

When one time Ameena loudly proclaimed she would not look after a stupid dark-skinned child like Shenzi, she became the Block's child because whenever she cried, the whole Block could hear Ameena scream, "*Doqon ayadh tahay!*" in that language they did not understand and Swahili, including the word *Shenzi*. At least he knew it was a Swahili word that became attached to the child as a name. *Savage, stupid.* He had found out from Kopa, the kiosk man who sold pancakes.

How a woman could spew both venom and honey from her mouth was always a puzzle to Kevin.

* * *

Kevin stirred, remembering where he was. Shenzi was speaking. "Can you describe my mother to me again? I wonder if I look like her."

Kevin stiffened, wondering if she had heard the car drive off and had somehow sensed it. "Err…" he paused. A part of him thought her beautiful and enchanting, but the other part loyal to Shenzi resented her for treating her like a reject.

"Why?" he asked.

"Because everyone says she is beautiful. When the uncles come home…

"

"Shenzi, those are not your uncles," he said heatedly. He had a special dislike for Silver Mulenzi, who occasionally called Shenzi his future wife and looked at her in a way that made him feel uncomfortable, immediately arousing his protective instincts.

Shenzi paused, then continued, "They say nice things to her and call her beautiful, princess…I even get gifts sometimes because she is beautiful. And when she speaks to them, she sounds so…" Shenzi could not describe the spell her mother's husky voice cast when it dropped seductively, light and gushing. It made her feel inadequate, like she was in the presence of royalty.

These uncles would casually tell her mother she had a lovely daughter, her own spitting image. Then she would scoff and respond deprecatingly in English spoken carefully by one whose first language was typically something else, the damning words, "Shenzi looks like her father." The words were often spoken with a hint of cold regret—that made Shenzi recoil within—accompanied by a girlish giggle like it was a silly joke. She grew to hate the man she never knew.

If he was good-looking, her mother would have stayed with him, she reasoned with Kevin. "Mummy would stay with me and do homework with me and all those nice things if I looked like her…"

Kevin felt a pang of anger jab at his chest. Shenzi looked just like her mother, only several shades darker. It infuriated him she did not think her daughter was worth anything.

"No, Shenzi, you look better than her!" he said. Then, to diffuse the awkwardness, he added, "That's why I have to keep you away from Bosco and the other boys."

Shenzi looked up and laughed. Charmed.

The somberness did not dissipate. "Kevin, what does *propaganda* mean?" she asked.

"Dunno. Who wants to know?"

Shenzi was silent, then shrugged. "Nobody. I just heard it. I will find out."

It was one of those rare occasions when her mother was home with her, watching the news while she worked on her homework.

"*Wewe* Shenzi, what is...*propa-gan-da*?" Ameena called out sharply to her, and Shenzi tensed up as she traced her homework with her fingers on Braille.

Shenzi thought for a second, and nothing came to mind. She did not know the meaning of it and wished she did, just to make her mother proud for once. Finally giving up, she whimpered in defeat, "I...don't know."

There was a momentary silence before her mother's voice, loud and angry, rained insults that assaulted her little body, seeping through her soft dark skin into the crevice of her even softer heart.

The end of the torrential abuse was "Urgh! *Doqon ayadh tahay!* You are so stupid...and ugly!" she jeered.

Shenzi had familiarized herself with the sound of some words, and she knew when her mother called her stupid in Somali. Her ugly words chipped at her esteem daily. *Is it because I am ugly like Papa?* She wondered. *Is it my eyes?*

Kevin.

Only Kevin told her she was pretty. Kevin treated her like a princess. If she ever met God and wished for a brother, it would be Kevin.

* * *

Shenzi could hear him mouth the word to himself, roll it between his lips and tongue, as if it would help him find the meaning of it. He intoned it, then fast, then thoughtfully, and stopped. "It's such a big word! I will look in the dictionary and tell you," he said, and she smiled.

Suddenly, she longed to hear him read to her, for them to stay up on the roof a little longer. "Kevin, can you read me a book? Please," she pleaded.

Kevin smiled, in his heart a light spark of pity and affection caused him to reach for her small dark hand gently and ask, "Which one?"

Her face lit up. *"Jack and the Beanstalk."*

He smiled too. Something passed between them, a phantom of a dream they both shared, which *Jack and the Beanstalk* brought to life every time Kevin mouthed it off page by page to her. Every word was like a golden egg with the promise of better, just like from the goose in the story.

"I will be back," he said and got up to exit the rooftop and swiftly down the fire escape stairway to his house, where he had the book in tatters from overuse, hidden under his mattress.

They both felt that one day, they would have to sacrifice a cow for those beans that would make all their dreams come true, and they would never have to live the life they had now.

Chapter 4

September 1999

"Hurry or you will be late for school!" Dina Byamukama, Kevin's mother, called sharply from the kitchen, where she fanned a charcoal stove between the balcony and the kitchen. It was pouring outside, and she worried her little boy would not get a ride with his father if he dallied a moment longer.

Mr. Robert Byamukama, known as Taata Bob by everyone on Block 4, was a tall man with long slender fingers who grunted as he heaved fistfuls of his *katogo* of offals into his mouth, chomping noisily, a sound produced because he was chewing with his mouth open and whizzing simultaneously.

Mr. Byamukama drank so much that each meal was a convoluted sight of haphazard chomping-whizzing and sweating by the gallons. Dina, who was affectionately known as Aunty Dina (pronounced *Dee-nah*)—a deliberate sing-song drawl adjusted the *i* to two *e*'s—hid her nervousness by fanning the charcoal coals faster while blowing into the stove, where the flames peeked out from beneath the black coals.

"Kevin!" she called out again, "Your breakfast is getting cold!'

Mr. Byamukama grunted again, this time in disapproval. Kevin finally appeared at the kitchen doorway, where his father sat at the table, jabbing his slender fingers into his *katogo*. Aunty Dina had heard his shuffling footsteps and sighed. "Sit. Eat," she instructed. "Taata is going to leave you."

"Uh-hmm," Taata Bob responded in the affirmative, casting his son an irritated look. His eyes widened and rolled in their sockets like a gecko as he appraised his son in his oversize school uniform.

Kevin hated the look and the uniform: a pair of khaki shorts that rode down to his calves and an oversize white shirt with the Bugolobi Primary School badge embroidered into the pocket. Even after two terms, he seemed not to be "growing into it," as was the initial plan.

Mr. Byamukama shifted his attention to his *katogo*, elbows propped on the table, his long bulldog-like face complete with beady eyes and thick, wide lips lolled slightly from the hangover he was nursing. Sweat beads formed on his brow and forehead.

Kevin relaxed a fraction, keeping his guard up in case he moved abruptly, and that motion connected with his head. He could see the clear marks of a sweat buildup spreading underneath his armpit where his blue shirt was a darker hue than the rest of it. The irritating smirking and chomping noises he made while he ate made Kevin cringe. *He needs Mama Rose to teach him table manners*, Kevin thought, wishing he could tell him out loud, but breakfasts lately had been less violent. He was determined to maintain the peace for a while, for his mother's sake. He did not want to start the beating trend he had been relieved off for a month now.

"Sit, sit!" His mother ushered him to a chair impatiently. "Did you oversleep on your first day of school?'

He nodded, his eyes never leaving his father. His mother noticed and rubbed his back slightly. Kevin slid into the seat opposite his father, and his mother urged gently, "Well, eat up before Taata is done, and I will go see if Shenzi is ready and can join us."

Kevin brightened. "Shenzi is coming with me to school?"

"Yes, Aunty Ameena asked Taata last night if he could drop her off because she was busy." Aunty Dina hurried to the door, exiting quickly.

"Hmm that *malaya*." Taata Bob said. "That Shenzi will die before the age of ten, if not from starvation, probably AIDS, when one of those men her mother brings home rapes her." He cackled like he had cracked the joke of the century.

Kevin felt a heatwave of anger smart in his brows and stub into his scalp. "She won't die!" he hissed, eyeing his father from beneath his downcast face, his entire face tightened with rage. He did not understand why his father would say something so hateful.

Taata Bob looked at him in mock surprise. "Oh? But it's true. How many times does she sleep and eat here because her mother couldn't care less?" He shook his head and cackled, unaffected.

"No!" he hissed. "I will protect her!"

Taata Bob laughed. "You? How? with what army? How? Eat your food before I get up and leave you. I am in a good mood today, so don't start being hopeless," he jeered in mock amusement. "I will protect her," sneering between mouthfuls.

Kevin felt his stomach knot, his appetite gone. He hated to admit he felt bitterly helpless to protect Shenzi or his mother. He hated to think his father was right. However, he poked at his food and scooped a forkful, for his mother's sake. She would not like that he did not eat at all.

His mother returned almost instantly, leading Shenzi behind her. She was dressed in her school uniform, a maroon pinafore, a heavily starched cotton material that seemed to fit stiffly and a cream shirt underneath. Maroon socks ran up right over her knees. They disappeared at the hem of her pinafore and black *Bata* back-to-school shoes. "Bugolobi Special Primary School" was printed all around the collar. The rumor was that a certain minister Ameena slept with was paying for Shenzi's primary education. The school for children with special needs was a little steeper in price than the regular schools.

"Sit, Shenzi. Let me get you *katogo* and milk tea. Kevin, eat your food, and don't play with it."

Shenzi shuffled to the dining table, her nose sniffing the air. "Umm, it smells good Aunty Dina," she complimented her.

"*Bambi,* thank you. Are you hungry?"

"Very," she replied enthusiastically.

"That is what I like to hear." Aunty Dina replied.

"How are you, Shenzi?" Taata Bob bellowed out. "Did you sleep well?" He seemed to be suggesting something.

"Yes, I did, thank you," Shenzi replied politely.

Bob got up and helped Shenzi to the chair and drew it in next to Kevin. Instinctively, she reached for Kevin and laid a small hand on his thigh.

Kevin reached out from under the table and squeezed her hand.

"Weren't you afraid? You could have come and slept here," Taata Bob continued. "At least you slept well, in peace, not so?"

Kevin looked at his father in disbelief.

"Taata, some milk tea?" Dina quickly interjected as she watched her son's expression from the corner of her eye.

Taata Bob was grinning, enjoying his moment of sadism. "Of course, make it very sweet and put more *bitangawizi* and *budalasini.*" He sighed and pushed his empty plate away from him. "Shenzi, you know you are always welcome to sleep here. Kevin is your brother, so feel free when you cannot sleep in that house with your harlot of a mother!" He slammed a heavy fist on the table.

Both children jumped.

"Taata!" Aunty Dina was sharp. "Please...on their first day of school?"

Kevin squeezed Shenzi's hand from under the table, embarrassed. Shenzi's head remained bowed; it was hard to tell what she felt or what was going through her mind.

"I said she is welcome here. Is it bad to say that?" Taata Bob feigned innocence and leaned back in his chair. He looked at Shenzi. "Don't mind me. If you keep on going to school, get to the university, you will be a better person than your mother. Do that to prove it, okay?" He touched Shenzi's head full of hair that was held back in one thick plait but was untidy from not being plaited again for a week.

Shenzi nodded slowly.

"Eat." Aunty Dina brought her an aromatic plate of *katogo* and a huge coffee mug steaming with fresh milk tea, browned, spiced, and sweetened for Taata Bob. "Don't be late for school. *Taata,* your polished shoes are in the bathroom, and your coat is on the bed." She was exhausted and angry from trying to be diplomatic.

When everyone had been served, Aunty Dina sat by the stove, lost in thought. There was a hollow silence until Taata Bob rose and left the table, letting them know loudly that they should be done by the time he was finished putting on his coat and shoes and visiting the bathroom.

The children relaxed, and Kevin side-eyed his table companion. "Are you okay?"

Shenzi nodded and took her cup of tea.

"I am sorry..." He apologized for his father's behavior.

She shook her head; it was better to dismiss than acknowledge the exchange of moments ago. From his gentle squeeze of her hand, it was assurance; he understood. She was aware that what her mother did was highly unacceptable. It made her the joke of the Block, but she comforted herself in her imagination that it was not worse than certain things people were put in prison for. It could not be that bad.

When Taata Bob came out, they were done with their breakfast.

"It looks like it will rain all day," he announced confidently as if he had had an interaction with the weatherman. "I suggest you all keep warm."

"My sweater is in my bag," Shenzi announced softly, sliding out of the chair and feeling for her stick. Kevin helped her reach for her stick and bag.

"Kevin, go get yours," his mother spoke up. He did not respond but went to do as told.

They left the house, minutes later, bundled behind the old Suzuki with worn beige leather seats, and amid a medley of the roaring engine, the scratchy sound of Radio One blazing oldies from the rusty speakers, Taata Bob humming along tunelessly, and pelting rain, Kevin and Shenzi whispered to each other.

"Did he win a Coca-Cola Honda prize draw?" Shenzi asked Kevin, who grinned, and replied, "Does he know what Coca-Cola is?"

She giggled.

"I think it was a Uganda waragi lottery draw," he added. Shenzi had to cover her mouth with her hands to choke back the laughter.

"Are you okay?" she asked him when the laughter had died out.

He nodded. "Yeah. It's still a good morning. Can't wait to see my classmates."

A smile spread across her face and lit her lips. "Will you come to the fence?"

"I will."

Then she held out her hand. "Look, my mother put henna on my nails. Do you like it? Wish I could see what it looks like."

Kevin picked up her fingers and nodded. "Yes it's nice." Her fingers spread out into his palm, and he smiled. The reddish-brown color dark against her own dark skin did not enhance the smooth ebony glow she possessed. "Although I think silver Cutex would be nice on you."

"You don't like it, do you?" She snatched her fingers away, pouting.

"I didn't say that; I just said silver would look so much better on your fingernails."

"Hmm." She scoffed.

He quickly asserted, "But I like it; I just like other colors better."

"I don't care about the colors. My *mother* did it for me!" She emphasized "mother." "Kevin, she did it for hours and even asked me about school."

The half-sob in her voice when she said it broke his heart. Every rebuttal he had prepared completely vanished.

"They are nice. Let me see again?" he whispered, reaching for her hand to express his apology.

She resisted slightly, then let him take it. He cupped her small palm in his all the way on the ten-minute drive to their schools, which were right next to each other, a fence providing the partition between them. One school was for the regular able-bodied pupils, and the other, smaller one was for special needs pupils like Shenzi. Both schools were under one principal.

At break time, before he saw his friends, he spent a few minutes with Shenzi. Sitting by the fence, he made sure she had enough to eat, offering her treats he had gotten from the canteen to top off her meals, sitting in congenial silence mostly before Kevin bid her farewell to catch a game with his friends. It was a ritual now between them, his way of looking out for her.

Chapter 5

"Ah!" Shenzi sat up with a start as her mother slapped the table she sat at with a flour-covered hand, sending flurries of flour particles in the air between them.

"*Wahan kudahe bananka ubax!*" "I said get out!" she screamed at her daughter.

Shenzi scrambled to her feet. She caught the tangy whiff of *waragi* punched with lemon on her mother's breath. Her heart lurched and dropped into the anxious pit of her belly.

"Take your stick! *Bah!*" Her mother shouted out again, "How can I cook with you in here? Go and read with that boyfriend of yours!" She muttered angry cuss words under her breath. "And don't come back here till I am done!"

She wanted to protest that Kevin wasn't her boyfriend, but that would hand her another mouthful from her mother. As it was, she had no energy for it, so instead, she meekly responded, "Yes, *hooyo*."

Fear and shame mingled into a ball that rose to her throat, forcing its way up to her eyes. She wiped the single tear that slid down her cheeks as she pulled her books to her chest. One of them slipped and fell. She cursed sharply like her mother and bit her lip guiltily for doing so. The inconvenience of searching for the book with her foot was something she dreaded. She felt around with her foot till finally her big toe nudged into a folded page, and slowly, carefully, she reached down for it, feeling her way to the ground, then up again with the book clasped tightly in her hand. She tucked it under her arm and positioned her walking cane before her.

She easily made it to the wide-open doorway that led into the kitchen from the living room. She had counted the steps it took her to get to every part of the house. If she was in a hurry to get away, it took her two fewer steps whichever way she was going.

As she headed for the main door, she counted twenty steps as a norm; only this time, it was eighteen. Her hand reached for the door handle and felt it turn of its own volition. Shenzi stepped back quickly to allow the door to swing to the inside without throwing her.

"Hellos, hey *mumbejja!*" She heard the familiar voice of Silver Mulenzi. Her mother insisted she call him *Uncle*.

"Don't be stupid; everything you have in this house is because some nice uncles like your Uncle Mulenzi provide for us!" Her mother stressed the point one morning.

"But you said I don't have any uncles…"

Before she could finish her claim, Shenzi had felt the stinging stab of a slap meet her lower cheek and lips. "*Shenzi!* Idiot! He is your uncle, and you will call him Uncle Mulenzi. All of them are your uncles, or you won't have liver for breakfast!"

Shenzi stood still, stunned, like a bucket of ice-cold water had been emptied over her head.

Now he stood before her, and it immediately dawned on her why her mother was making a fuss. When her clientele called, she always shushed her out of the house for a couple of hours or more, sometimes all night, unless she let herself in the house. It almost felt like Ameena forgot about her on most occasions.

"Mummy, it's…u…Uncle Mulenzi." Her voice cracked as she announced his presence, ignoring him.

"Thank you, *macanto,*" her mother called to her, all sweetness in her tone. It was hard to believe a few seconds before she had been snapping and cussing at Shenzi. The switch in her mother's reaction always threw her into a state of convoluted emotional turmoil. Just when she was determined to hate her, Ameena threw a curveball and her poisoned tongue dripped sweet nothings, a drug Shenzi lapped up hungrily for lack of its daily dosage in her life.

"Shenzi, *qalbi*," she cooed from the kitchen. "I will call you for dinner. Okay, let me talk to your uncle."

Her mother called her heart *qalbi* in Somali whenever she wanted her way, at times *macanto*, "sweetheart." Shenzi believed her even now because she sounded so warm and loving, just like she always felt her mother was supposed to be to her. It elevated her from her habitual dark place, and she happily skipped out of Mulenzi's way to exit their apartment.

"See you then, black beauty." Uncle Mulenzi let his hand stray over the top of her head in a careless motion over her matted hair. Shenzi recoiled from his touch and jerked her head to the side.

"Be nice to me," he roared. The pungent smell of sweat and waragi left its tinge on her, and she wanted to scream. When the door closed behind her, she could faintly hear Mulenzi's roaring voice merge and mix in a sultry, tantalizing dance with her mother's own smooth, husky voice. Her mother laughing at something he said, Mulenzi blabbering like a love-struck seventeen-year-old.

The voices rose and fell together in a torrid wave, mostly incoherent, but the nuances of seduction carried in the tones were not lost on Shenzi. She had grown accustomed to hearing her mother flirt and quickly learned to differentiate this type of communication from those she heard on the Block between men and women.

She also learned to pick up on flirtation directed at her and shied away from it vehemently. A part of her felt it was dirty, and yet another part of her admired her mother for being able to speak so soothingly with not just men but with everyone, even her. She seduced them all.

Shenzi was conflicted again. She wanted to hate her mother but also wanted to be like her, able to enthrall and enchant everyone with her two-sided personality. She sighed. How could she when she was blind as a bat? she thought sadly. Her mother was beautiful and tall and mesmerizing.

The few times her mother was gentle to her was when she fixed her hair and nails. In those few scattered moments, Shenzi abandoned herself to the seductive lure of her voice by coyly asking her mother to tell her stories. Her husky, smooth drawl would rise and fall like a steady wave at sea, bringing stories filled with rich lands and harsh kings, young girls sold into marriage, and camels with double humps riding for days into unknown deserts. Shenzi always dreamed that one day the handsome desert Tuaregs would rescue her from this place. In her mind's eye, the only Tuareg who came to rescue her was Kevin. There were two things her mother impressed upon her, "Be beautiful always; do your hair and nails, and you will get anything you want in the world."

"And school?" Shenzi had asked.

Ameena sighed. "Hmm. At least learn how to read and write, so you are not a very dumb beautiful girl." And her husky voice rose in peals of laughter.

Shenzi did not find it funny, but she laughed nonetheless to please her mother. She knew her mother did not mean the "beautiful" part. Hearing her say it, though, however impersonally it was directed, made her feel ever so slightly beautiful.

"Shenzi?" She heard her name being called. "What are you doing outside; it's 7 p.m.; shouldn't you be doing homework? Taking a bath?" It was Teopista.

"Mummy is busy now; she said she will call me for dinner; I was going to Kevin's house." She felt Teopista's hand brush up on her head.

"Eh! When did you last plait this hair?"

Shenzi felt her heart lurch. She must look hideous. *Beautiful girls always have neat hair*, she thought guiltily.

Teopista did not wait for her to reply. "It needs to be worked on, Shenzi; maybe I can do something with it till your mother is ready."

"No…" Shenzi protested. "I have homework."

Teopista was already leading her up the stairs to her own apartment. "Don't worry; I will finish quickly. In fact, let me call Kevin…Kevin!

Then he can help you while I do this hair, because *Bambi,* it is too messy! Kevin!" She punctuated her every statement with his name. "Where is this boy? KEEVIIIIN!"

"Teopista, what do you want from my son!" It was Kevin's mother. She had come out of her apartment, a mingling stick in her hand, and Kevin peeked through the door.

"He isn't in trouble this time." Teopista laughed and slapped her hips dramatically.

Aunty Dina's eyes fell on Shenzi sympathetically. "Ah, I see." She looked back at Teopista knowingly.

Teopista nodded. "I want to plait her hair, *ko,* and she has homework. She cannot do it in there now, you know." Her eyes accused Ameena in absentia, and she pointed to the "there" with her mouth toward Shenzi's home. Speaking in gestures around Shenzi was pretty much what most of the adults did, except Taata Bob.

Aunty Dina drawled out her knowing, then went back in, and Shenzi could hear her talk to Kevin.

In a few seconds, Kevin peeked out the door again and spoke: "Shenzi?"

Relieved at hearing his voice, Shenzi smiled. "Kevin, Teopista is going to do my hair, and I need some help with my homework. Can you help me?"

Kevin hesitated. "Hmm."

"If you are not busy," Shenzi almost pleaded.

There was a shuffling of feet, and Kevin was taking her hand. "Okay."

While her hair got braided and oiled in Teopista's noisy apartment that smelled of frying dough all the time, Kevin tried to read to Shenzi and help her with her spelling homework. Between spurts of Teopista yelling at her own litter of five to shut up and watch television and the hum of dinner cooking, the house was so lively, Kevin needed to literally scream above the noise until he gave up. "Shenzi, it's too loud here. Teopista has almost finished. Maybe we can do it in my house."

Shenzi tried to nod, only to have her head held down in a brief tight grip, a sign that Teopista needed her still.

"Mommy, can we have the cassava in the fridge?" Shem, Teopista's skinny, long-legged ten-year-old, asked. He was leaning against the living room door, watching his mother braid with expert speed.

"No," was his mother's brief response.

"But..." he protested and stomped his foot.

"*Ei!*" Teopista's voice rose abruptly in matriarchal warning. She cast him a dark glance to go with it, and Kevin watched the tall boy shrink and slink away, his face sullen and drawn back. There was nothing more said. In less than a minute, Teopista's youngest, a chubby five-year-old with a smear of dried peas around her mouth, washed clumsily, carefully inched up to her mother. She stood silently watching Shenzi, her eyes never leaving the shoulder-length braids.

"What is it?" Teopista asked impatiently.

"I want cassava," she barely whispered, her fingers jammed in her mouth and her eyes pitifully rolling from her mother to Shenzi.

Teopista sighed. "Can't you see I am doing something? Dinner is almost ready. You wait."

The little girl did not budge. She stood there toeing the rough edges of the crisscross designs on the living room floor, sucking on her thumb, her eyes downcast.

"Shem, get Stella to take this girl away. Tell her to wash her mouth," she called to her son, who reluctantly walked out of the room calling for Stella.

Teopista returned to the task at hand and then decided it would be best to serve the children and finish unhindered.

"Shenzi, can you wait a little? Let me put some food out for these children. Can I put some out for you and Kevin?"

Kevin shook his head. "Mummy will kill me if I don't eat at home tonight. It is Taata's birthday."

"Oh? Aunty Dina did not mention it," Teopista piped as she walked off.

"It is?" Shenzi asked when Teopista was out of earshot.

Kevin nodded. "Yes, but he is not home yet."

"Oh." Shenzi did not have to guess where he was. "Maybe he will be home by 9 p.m.,"

"Maybe," he replied dryly.

"Well, at least tomorrow is Friday, and we leave school at lunchtime." She tried to be cheery.

"Yes! I am going with the boys to the other flat. Bosco has a new bike," Kevin told Shenzi, suddenly animated.

"Okay."

"What will you do after school?"

Shenzi shrugged. "I don't know yet. I might sleep after lunch."

"Okay. Bosco might want you to come feel his new bike, maybe take you for a ride," he teased.

"Kevin! Stop teasing me." She laughed despite herself.

He sighed. "He won't mind if you come."

Shenzi shook her head. "I want to take a nap," she said stubbornly. It was true the week had been emotionally draining, and she had had a hard time falling asleep. On Fridays through the weekends, she had the house to herself, and she spent the afternoons alone falling asleep in the living room with the television on. Supper was always at the Byamukamas right before she and Kevin took a trip to the roof as the sun set.

"We will go to the roof, I promise," he told her in a whisper amid clinking plates and cutlery, discordant children's voices, and Teopista's rising and falling voice scolding and encouraging.

"I know." She beamed. "I can't wait."

"Do you want to come to Taata Bob's birthday?"

"I don't know. Mummy is cooking. Maybe..." Shenzi strayed off, feeling her head for where the hair lay loosely tangled in a comb Teopista had stuck in it. "I can only stay till my mother calls me. Do I have a lot left?" she asked.

"No, not much, just the left side. It looks okay."

"Okay?" Shenzi gasped, horrified. It had to look good. Her mother's words haunted her.

"Okay, it's good...for a girl."

She could sense his discomfort saying it and laughed. "You boys are no fun."

"Girls waste so much time on hair and all that. I am glad I am a boy." He always said that, and she shook her head; boys were really no fun.

"What would you do if you woke up tomorrow, and you were a girl?" Shenzi teased.

"Oh, no!" Kevin almost howled. "No way! How would I go to school, and my friends! That is a nightmare."

Shenzi laughed.

"And the girls in primary six and seven say all these things about being a girl." He shuddered.

"Really? What?" Shenzi whispered back. No one ever told her anything unless she heard it whispered at play. Now curiosity ate at her, and she nudged him.

"I can't tell you, Shenzi; you are still too young, but when you are in primary six, I will tell you," Kevin replied importantly, like he was the keeper of a big secret.

"Kevin!" She nudged him again sharply. "I'm your friend!"

"But I can't tell you this. It's a *big-girl secret.*"

"Then how come you know it?" she asked accusingly.

"Because…" He shrugged.

"Teacher Opolot says that you cannot start a sentence with *because.* That's not an answer."

"Oh my God." Kevin groaned. "Are you a lawyer too?"

Shenzi wasn't having it. "Kevin, tell me…"

"Okay, okay…but not now."

"When? When I am thirteen?" She kept pressing. He hated it when she pressed for information.

"It's a secret for older girls; that's all."

"What's a secret for older girls?"

Teopista walked in on their back-and-forth.

Kevin jumped. "Nothing."

And Shenzi took her moment of glory to sing him the "they have caught you" song. He pinched her slightly, and she yelped.

"Kevin Atwooki Byamukama, don't you see Shenzi is much younger than you!" Teopista glowered at him, her voice sharp.

Kevin shook his head. Sometimes Shenzi was really a baby.

Teopista threw him a dark glance and sat down, urging Shenzi to lean back between her thighs, tilting her head to the right as she reached for her hair.

"Hmm!" she exclaimed, and they dropped the subject till Shenzi's hair sat atop her head in perfectly lined rows, and they politely thanked Teopista and left.

"Kevin!" Shenzi nudged him once they began their slow descent, two sets of stairs down to Kevin's apartment.

"I was going to, but you got me in trouble." Kevin was still angry she had hummed the famous "trouble song" and would not take her hand.

"Okay sorry, but I was angry too," she conceded.

"Okay, but now you have to wait till you are thirteen," he told her.

Shenzi groaned. A sob rose from deep within her.

"And if you cry, I won't tell you at all," Kevin assured her. After a momentary pause, he sighed. "Okay, on your birthday."

"Too far," she whined.

"Patience is a virtue," he added, slightly enjoying the fact that he was keeping her on edge and punishing her for getting him snapped at.

To pacify her, he added, "Your hair looks *really* nice. Can I touch it?"

Teopista had made several braids and held their ends with colored rubber bands.

Shenzi said no but figured this would be the best bargain. "They are a little tight, makes my head feel funny. First tell me, then you can touch," she told him.

Kevin shook his head, simpering.

They dropped the subject.

They passed by her house and hesitated only so slightly. "She knows where I am," she told Kevin.

"Who is it today?" he asked as he guided her. "Uncle Mulenzi? He is the only one who gets VIP treatment,"

"Yeah, him," Shenzi replied.

In Kevin's house, the smell of deep-frying chicken and curry powder filled the air. The television had a farmer talking to a journalist about his sweet potato patches on the show *This Farming World* on UTV. The volume was moderately low enough for Kevin to hear his mother humming along to an Afrigo Band song playing off a miniature Philips radio that had made its home, leaning back on the window seat by the sink in the kitchen. It was a scratchy, unstable sound that erratically increased and decreased when one passed by the sink, as if in response to body energy. His mother kept sashaying from the sink to the stove and the counter, distorting the frequency with every motion.

Kevin liked to see his mother humming and cooking chicken. It was always a sign that she was in a good mood.

"Mummy, that chicken smells good!" he called out as he walked in. "I am going to help Shenzi with her homework, and…if her mother doesn't come for her, can she eat here?"

"Of course! Shenzi is always welcome," Aunty Dina called out. "Come and get her some tea and bread. Food might take some time to be ready."

Kevin did as he was told, and when they were settled at the table, Shenzi eating her mini snack, they went through her spellings one more time, and finally, math homework.

"You're so smart, Shenzi. Why do you even ask me to help you? Help me. I bet you could do my homework for me."

Shenzi grinned. "Maybe." She basked in his praise of her. "So, what did you get Taata Bob for his birthday?"

"Nothing," he replied. There was nothing he could think of that Taata Bob loved more than booze, not even him or his mother. Sometimes he felt that his mother enabled his father to be as he was. She was afraid of him. She couldn't help it. Kevin knew that fear.

"Maybe we should watch TV," Shenzi said.

Kevin made a face. "It's all boring. Let's play a game."

"What games?"

"You know our wish games?"

Shenzi nodded with a smile.

Kevin grinned. "You go first."

Shenzi breathed in deeply and stretched her skinny legs out over the couch, her feet barely touching the floor. "Um…I wish we could be friends forever and live together forever," she blurted out shyly.

She sensed him smile. "Just us? The other boys would be jealous."

She laughed and nudged him. "What do you wish for?"

"I wish to live in a big house when I grow up, huge, so big I can live there with Mummy and you and…"

She waited while he paused. "And?"

She could hear him breathe in deeply, then slowly let it out.

"I will have many cars…so many they won't all fit in the garage. I will need a whole parking lot to park all my cars, and you can have one…"

Shenzi laughed. "Just one? That's selfish!"

"I shall drive you in any car you want."

"What if I want to drive my own?"

"Okay, okay. How many do you want?"

"Um…I want ten!" She spread out all her ten fingers before him, grinning widely.

"Only?" Kevin teased her, and she laughed so loud that Kevin's mother called out to find out what it was they were laughing about.

"Nothing!" Kevin called back.

"Girls!" He sighed playfully. "Okay, you will have ten. I will have one hundred."

"Yes! With different colors! And where will we stay?"

"*Aaah*, Muyenga, Kololo, or Nakasero, and I will also build us a home in Jamaica and in America and Paris and Spain," Kevin drawled on dreamily, imagining himself as the character he watched in the films he saw on television.

"Can we have a house everywhere in Uganda?" Shenzi suggested.

"We can do that!" He smiled. "That's a wonderful idea. We will live everywhere like the world is ours, right?" he said, the dreamy look still in his eyes.

"Yes, we shall." It sounded exciting and wonderful.

It was almost ten o'clock and still no sign of Taata Bob. Kevin watched his mother's radiant glow wane. She turned the radio off, and they all sat in the living room, staring at the television. The news ended and a music show was coming up next. Neither Taata Bob nor Shenzi's mother appeared.

"Do you want to take a bath? It's late, Shenzi." It was Aunty Dina's customary remark signifying that further waiting was futile, and they all felt the same way, silently acquiescing to their lives. It was a habit Kevin abhorred; they waited constantly on people who did not seem to care about them.

At 10:30 p.m., Aunty Dina fed the children. No one spoke of the birthday or the special meal. A heavy silence hung over them until the knock on the door.

Aunty Dina sat up, a hint of expectation in her posture, which was quickly dispelled. It had to be Ameena. Why would her husband knock at his own house?

"*Sasa*, Aunty Dina." The warm, husky, seductive drawl of Shenzi's mother floated through to the dining room when Aunty Dina opened the door.

"*Poa*, Ameena, would you like to come in?" She asked Ameena, opening the door wide, a gesture of invitation.

Ameena peered into the house and exclaimed, "Hmm, that smells good! Chicken?"

"Yes, you can have some," Aunty Dina invited. "You are welcome to supper."

Ameena stepped in and smiled at the children. "Oh, I see my *macanto* is eating," she gushed. Aunty Dina was never sure if she meant it or spoke for formality's sake, as was expected of a mother.

Shenzi felt her throat constrict. She couldn't swallow and her heart banged rapidly against her chest. She had hoped to sleep over at Kevin's, but hearing her mother call her *macanto* made her want to hug her and bury her face in her amla-coconut-scented hair and tell her how much she missed her.

"Yes, she is. A plate?" she heard Aunty Dina say and prayed her mother would sit with them, if only for a moment to eat, so she could show off her hair, eat up all her food, and declare how full she was, tell her mother about their wish game with Kevin...

"Oh no Dina, I ate. Thank you for feeding her. I will wait till she is finished, and we shall go home."

Shenzi heard her mother decline dinner, and her heart sank.

"How are you, Kevin?" she heard her ask instead and held her breath. Kevin could be mean to her mother, and she prayed he would not be tonight.

"Fine, Aunty Ameena."

"You did your homework with Shenzi?"

"Yes, Aunty."

Shenzi could tell he was fighting hard to be polite and tapped him gently under the table in acknowledgment.

"A glass of juice?" Aunty Dina asked again politely. The comfortable air of familiarity had shifted since Ameena had walked in.

Ameena shook her head. "No, my dear, it is fine. I am *mzuri*. I thought I would see Taata Bob."

Aunty Dina smiled, maintaining her calm, passive tone. "He is not home yet."

Ameena smiled, knowingly. Everyone knew Taata Bob and his drunken ways. "He has missed a good meal," she said. "You should teach me how to cook chicken like that. I bet my *macanto* will eat it all up."

Shenzi immediately sprang to life. "Mummy, I eat everything you cook." She did not know why she suddenly felt guilty and ashamed.

"Oh, I didn't say you don't..." her mother started and trailed off. "Look at you! Your hair looks wonderful. Sorry I have been busy. Did you do it?" she asked Dina, her voice rising in false surprise, and Kevin made a face, discreetly tapping Shenzi under the table.

"No, Teopista," Aunty Dina replied in the same practiced fashion of politeness. Ameena grinned and clasped her long, well-manicured fingers together. "It seems that my child cannot die in this place. Someone will always take care of her."

She shook her head and reached over to Shenzi, running her hand over her head. "This is lovely. Did you thank Teopista?"

Kevin tapped Shenzi, annoyed at Ameena's exaggerated gestures.

"Yes," Shenzi replied quietly. Her heart swelled.

They were finished in a few minutes, saying their goodnights. Kevin helped his mother clean up and save the remains in the fridge. Taata Bob's Suzuki coughed and grumbled as he pulled up to his customary spot that overlooked his apartment window just as Kevin got ready to retire to bed.

Chapter 6

October 1999

Kevin found Shenzi on the rooftop the next day as he raced up and away from the crowd below. He had told Bosco he would see his bike on Saturday, but the morning brought with it new emotions. His body, battered and assaulted, ached. All excitement about the bike fizzled out, blow after blow from the hands of a drunken maniac.

As he raced up the stairs, he stopped by Teopista's door. Her huge frying pan bobbed precariously with bubbling oil and browning swollen dough...*mandazis*! Beside the frying pan was another pan layered with old newspapers and filled halfway with hot browned *mandazis*. Kevin peered quickly into Teopista's hallway. Her sharp scolding carried amid young whining voices, letting him know she wasn't far from the doorway. Hastily, he grabbed the biggest *mandazi* and skipped off in time to hear Teopista's heavy footsteps announce her arrival at the front door.

Every evening at three o'clock the smell of frying *mandazis* swept through the whole flat and with it the accompanying yells from Teopista's children. As if held by a pied piper's spell, children bolted out of their houses to Teopista's door to snatch one or two *mandazis*.

They were the most delicious *mandazis*. He always wondered why she never sold them for money to pay school fees for her five children. The children on the Block would buy them, with him first in line.

Shenzi sat with her back to him, in the usual spot they occupied…close to the edge where the view of town was mesmerizing and even more so as the sun sank over the horizon and darkness blanketed its path. She straightened from a slouching position.

"Kevin?" Shenzi called out faintly, without turning. She had an uncanny sense of knowing it was him from several feet away.

"How do you know?" he had asked her once.

"You walk fast, and I can smell you, too." She could hear the way the soles of his feet hit the ground. Not just his but most of the people who lived on Block 4. "Everyone is different, so I just know." She shrugged.

Kevin breathed in sharply to calm his raw nerves and hopefully loosen the knot in his belly. His left hand cupped the *mandazi* still. He settled next to his best friend, tucking his legs beneath his thighs.

"Here, have some." He cleared his throat as he said the words and steeled himself against the fading heat of the day, trapped within the rough concrete surface of the rooftop of the flat he loved to escape to when he needed to get away from life's madness. He handed her his loot, the prized *mandazi* of Block 4.

Shenzi averted her face from the scenery before her and felt for his hand. "Smells like *mandazi*. Is it?"

"Teopista's *mandazi*," Kevin agreed and placed it in her hand.

"Oh, thank you!" She took a hasty bite.

From the way her little fingers cupped the warm fried brown dough, he figured she was hungry. *Starving.* He could hear her chew delicately, gently, like Mama Rose had taught them to.

She would slap their lips lightly with her pointer finger when they chewed sloppily, throw her heavy arms on her ample hips, and heave out, "*Ah-ah!* Not like that. You will not see the Queen if you eat like that!"

Despite the gossip about her very fair complexion in connection to her mother's probable wild days with the Italian fathers, she never ceased to boast of her "privileged" childhood. The white missionaries who run the mission schools had taught them how to eat the Queen's way. She would laugh out loud, dance a little jig, and tell them the rules she remembered:

elbows off the table, chew slowly, savor every bite, mouth closed, no chomping noises, and on and on it went.

She would now and again relapse into some Catholic hymn, her light brown eyes brimming over with tears. When the humming ceased, she reemerged into the present and continued with a few more stories of the foods she ate: Italian noodles, chocolate éclairs, and various sweet treats she received as presents from her mother when she returned from the White Father's abode... Thinking of Mama Rose made him smile; it dispersed the unpleasant heaviness that loomed over him on days like this.

"Thanks. Where is yours?" Shenzi asked him.

Kevin shrugged. "Not hungry."

"And quiet." She spoke between morsels.

Kevin sighed.

"You told Bosco you hit a door," Shenzi prodded with concern, as always, keeping her voice low. It rose like she had summoned it from an abyss of sacredness. Maybe it was the reverence he had for her that lent her voice a superior lilt to it. Something about it always calmed him. He picked at the dirt beneath him and sighed.

"Who told you?" He felt exposed and needed to guard his scars.

Shenzi was silent for a while as she chewed the last of the *mandazi*. Eventually, she shrugged and breathed out a response, an honest response. She never lied to him or hid anything from him; he could trust her.

"Bosco did, at home time today. You did not come at break time as well. I thought you were in the sick bay, and he said so too...but...for the entire morning? Was it...?" she trailed off. Kevin did not want to talk about it, but she went on, "Last night, I heard some screaming..." she added haltingly.

Kevin smiled bitterly. He raised his hand to his battered face, gently feeling his perforated lip. It ached. Then he traced the bump on his left temple that throbbed mildly. The temperatures on the sides of his face were unequal. His heart surged with anger, frustration, and hurt.

"I am tired, Shenzi," he replied piteously.

After a minute, he felt her small hand trace the area that hurt, and he wanted to shove it away, wanted to be a man, be firm, not cry. But he let her anyway, even though he steeled himself against her touch; he did not want her sympathy. He knew she knew because he told her everything. He could feel the cool breeze from the noisy night air trapped between her fingers and his throbbing, sore, and cracked skin caress him with no respite. He bit his lower lip, so as not to cry as she whispered, "Sorry."

"It's okay."

He tried to sound casual, but the morning argument was still as fresh as her touch.

He frothed with rage as he told Shenzi how ungrateful his father could be. Taata Bob kept drinking all night, making every excuse possible to assault him and his mother. The reasons grew as long as his bottles lasted:

"Why did you eat without me?"

"The food is cold,"

"Chicken? I want pork!"

Then he simply got irrational and beat his mother. So, Kevin, with his fingers clenched in a tight fist, a knot of fear in the pit of his stomach, his teeth grinding hard into his jaw drawing spittle on the side of his lips, huffed and puffed like a bull about to charge and faced Taata Bob. Taata Bob laughed in mock disgust at his scrawny four-foot form and rained on Kevin his full measure of hell: brimstone and fire with an extra poison-laced tongue lashing.

"Scrawny fool! Stupid! Do you think you can stand up to me, *mtscheeeew*! You will never amount to anything! Maggot! Stay out of this! Your mother is as foolish as you! What hopeless idiots!"

The words fell heavily like acid rain, cutting deep into his soul, where his little frightened, angry heart lay and seared it a little at a time. His father slapped and hurled him aside. Kevin shuddered, recounting it: the slaps, the blows, his own fight back, shouting and abusing his father as his father pounded on him and kicked his mother off when she came to his defense.

He died more and more each day. Fear gradually turned to hate—an intense hatred that only being with Shenzi pacified. He often wondered why Taata Bob had become the beast that he was.

Was it the war? Was it his job? The business that failed. It was too overwhelming to make sense of. The night had passed on in neo-violence, and in the morning, still drunk, Taata Bob had slammed him against the front door and refused to take him to school.

Kevin walked to school, avoiding everyone he knew. His temple, right eye, and lips were swollen, and he made a beeline for the sick bay, telling the school nurse he had hurt himself on the way to school. He hardly attended class that day. Thankfully, it was half-day, so by two o'clock in the afternoon, he was heading home with his homework. Only Bosco had seen him and asked him if he was still coming to see the new bike.

"I can't. I don't feel well."

"Whoa…what happened to you?" Bosco exclaimed wide-eyed when he saw his face. "Eh!"

"Nothing!" he snapped. "I just hit myself on the door. I will come tomorrow." He was brusque and short. Truthfully, he only wanted to be with Shenzi—for two reasons: she calmed him, and she would not feel sorry for him. She understood. It was all right for her to "see" him like this.

As he deliberately took the long route home, the spring in his steps faltered increasingly, while the butterflies in his tummy turned themselves inside out so frequently, he was sure he was going to throw up. When Block 4 loomed into view, Kevin was a terrified bag of nerves. He could not make himself enter the little two-bedroom flat he lived in. Events of the last so many hours played afresh in his tortured mind. He shivered involuntarily when he thought of the morning beatings. He stealthily peered in the doorway and sighed with relief when he realized he was alone. No one was home.

But his joy was short-lived when in less than five minutes that old familiar loud coughing sound of a tired Suzuki engine— as the car slowed to a halt outside the flat two-story below—shattered his peaceful moment.

Panic seized him like a thief caught in the act. His broken heart hammered frantically in his chest, and he ground his jaws, nervously wincing as pain reverberated against his slight frame.

He was sure the whole flat had heard him scream and hurl insults at Taata Bob with every lash of his thick leather belt. Even though he hated Taata Bob, he loathed the fact that fear gnawed at him so much he could not summon appetite for the delicious *mandazi* he had picked from Teopista's pan.

"I knew it was Taata Bob," Shenzi spoke, and he spied the strain of helpless anger and frustration lace her usually mild tone.

Kevin let it out.

He told her, bravely at first, like he did not care, like it was someone else's story, but soon he choked, and he cleared his throat more often than he should have. Midway through telling, he wiped the hot, angry tears that coursed down his face and sniffed, wiping his runny nose on the collar of his school shirt. He then stopped, blinked, and tried to laugh, and she let him be, lest he got mad that she was feeling sorry for him. She pretended not to hear him cry and tried to sound off dry, nonchalant remarks like she did not care, but inside, her heart broke for her best friend.

When he was done venting, they stared out silently into the night as darkness deepened its course over the horizon.

"How long do you want to stay up here today?" she asked him after a while.

"Till the mosquitoes start to bite," he said.

"We often stay here later, you know," she told him.

He nodded. "We do, and it is the best part now."

The red embers of daylight faded…bright highlights meshing with the streetlights and lights from the city beyond. It was a most beautiful sight. It felt like being on top of the world.

"Tell me again," she whispered, longing to see what he saw.

He often launched into it with a prelude: "It's beautiful, Shenzi. It feels like…like we own all of this… Like the world is ours."

And she believed it, too.

In these moments, as they escorted the sun to bed, it dispelled pain and misery.

Kevin allowed his mind to unravel the beauty of the scenery below, describing the sunset, the cars, the sky, the far-off hills and trees, the crisscrossing roads and the tall buildings that were the telltale signs of a busy town. He wished she could see it as clearly as he did.

Satisfied by her entranced *oohs* and *aahs*, he added a twist in the tale, weaving Kampala out to be only a city in storybooks. It delighted him to see the hope in her face when he described this new and improved Kampala.

Even though she caught him in his improvisation of the facts and pointed it out, "You said there was a bridge last time," he would feign animated amnesia. Her laughter would ring through the night, encouraging him to weave further. That was all that mattered. Telling her what he saw and more strengthened their resolve for a better life.

"One day, Shenzi, we will own the world."

Up here next to Shenzi, he could be his own man. No fear. He needed no one, least of all Taata Bob. He could not recall when he last called him *Daddy*. Kevin took a deep breath. It momentarily washed away the pain, and when he released it, it came out hot through his nostrils. It felt good. He touched his companion's hand. Shenzi felt the question weigh between them before he asked it: "Did you eat? Is your mother home?"

Shenzi shook her head. "She left with Uncle Mulenzi in the morning when they dropped me at school."

"He is *not* your uncle!" Kevin let out an exasperated sigh. "I wish I had come up with more *mandazis*. You must be starving."

Shenzi smiled, a tiny nervous giggle caught in her throat, and she shrugged. "No, this was okay. Thank you."

"You say that all the time, Shenzi. You are such a…such…" His voice broke, shaking his head in wonder at how composed she always was.

"We can get some more if we ask Teopista." She turned her blind gaze to him. Every time she did that, he was almost sure she could see him—in fact, see right through him. It was the strangest thing.

Kevin felt sad for his best friend, saddened because he had been too frightened to bring her more *mandazis* in his haste to get out of the house. And now she was starving. A fresh wave of anger, capped with hopelessness, built up on the inside of him. How could she? How could she leave her daughter starving all day!

He sighed. "How can you stand *her!*" He spat the *her* with renewed anger.

Shenzi winced slightly, then her voice, rising from that deep abyss, floated in the prickly space between them, melting the ice.

"Kevin, Mummy *has* to work. It's okay. I will wait till she is back." He did not realize his fists were clenched till she reached out, searching for his hand, and placed hers over them.

"But she could have left the key!" he insisted.

"She forgot…she was in a hurry this morning…I was late."

"No, Shenzi." He hit the callous ground with his fist, ignoring the stinging pain.

"Kevin! She was in a hurry, you know. She is so forgetful these days. She is so, so busy!"

Kevin looked at Shenzi in disbelief, listening to her defend her mother, a woman who outright showed she did not care for her.

If Ameena had known what illness Shenzi had gotten when she was three in the first place, it could have saved Shenzi's eyes. If she had treated her in time, Shenzi would not have had to be blind.

He hated that some men who came to see Shenzi's mother were harmful to Shenzi, especially the so-called Uncle Mulenzi. He had witnessed this once when he was helping Shenzi with homework at her house: Mulenzi's leering, greedy face as he ogled Shenzi. *She is only eight!* It was a scream that died down in his throat, failing to make its escape past his lips.

He doubted Ameena worked as hard as Shenzi had put it, but he did not say it out loud.

"If she had taken better care of you, you would not be blind!" he instead blurted out angrily.

Shenzi recoiled from him like she had been burned, hugging her arms.

He quickly realized what he had said and shifted to her, throwing a skinny arm around her shoulders.

"Sorry, Shenzi. I am so sorry!" he mumbled quickly. "Please forgive me. I did not mean to...I am sorry. Forgive me."

Shenzi sat there stolid like a beautiful ebony statue, turned to stone by the evil eye of Medusa. She neither rejected his embrace nor accepted it. They sat there in silence until Kevin felt her breathing normalize. Then the old Shenzi was back.

"It's okay, Kevin. She got me a new school bag and new crayons. She was happy today when I left for school, but the work is too much. She is so tired, and next Sunday she will braid my hair."

It dawned on Kevin that it was how she coped. She made excuses for her mother because she longed to be loved by her. His heart broke for his friend, and he hated Ameena for it.

"Shenzi, you know what? When we are older, I will buy you twenty cars. You wanted ten last night, but I think you deserve twenty," he said thoughtfully.

Shenzi replied expectantly. "You promise?"

"Uh-huh." He grinned. "I know you will haunt me for that till we die."

She laughed. "Yes I will, and we won't die!"

"Oh no, we won't die!" he blurted. "And anything you want, I will make sure you have it...big, beautiful houses, and you won't have to stay here with..."

"Can my mother come?" Shenzi asked. "Maybe she will have more time for me then."

Kevin gritted his teeth. "But I thought we don't want any grownups, just us."

"But you keep saying you will bring your mother," she challenged him.

Kevin sighed. "Okay, just us, you and me."

Shenzi smiled, satisfied. "Nice houses, big…on top of the hill, Muyenga or Kololo."

"Yeah, we can even go to another country that's far away from all this." He motioned with his hand, waving it around.

"Maybe even Bosco and the others can visit us?" she asked.

"Yeah, and we will be among rich people over those hills where they live, and we will have many friends and lots to eat and people that love us…and we will always be friends, and we won't have to cry or…get beaten…or go hungry."

He could hear her sigh at his passionate outburst.

"You know what else?"

"What?" she liked it when he dreamed.

"We will have enough money to fix your eyes, too, and you will see again. I promise you that."

"You say that all the time, Kevin. Is it possible?"

"Anything is possible when you have money," he told her in a matter-of-fact way, and she believed him. It had to be true. When her mother told her folklore of brave men and women, the men were all like Kevin, rescuing her from life itself. Her heart leaped blissfully. The wind blew lightly around them, healing on its tranquil trails. Shenzi basked in the lull of his voice and the weight of their dreams, unremitting in their "top of the world" location. She imagined their future just like that, uninterrupted, exciting, and magical: Kevin bringing her platefuls of chips and liver, sometimes *mandazis*. In her dreams, she ate till she burst and felt not an ounce of pain.

Some nights, Kevin added a little more to their dream list: "Oh, and we will also have so much money, we can go to any country in the world for the rest of our lives!"

"Hmm, which is your favorite, Kevin? You know mine." It made her giddy speaking about countries she did not know of.

Kevin laughed. "Umm, America or Jamaica, where all the best musicians come from."

Shenzi nodded in agreement. "We will go to Germany and Spain and England, too, to watch the Olympics and World Cup?"

Kevin beamed. "Yes, of course. The world will be ours, Shenzi. I swear it will be!"

"Most important is we will always be friends, right?" she asked. In the back of her mind, she did not feel worthy of his friendship. He had more lively friends who could see. Who wanted to be friends with a blind, ugly, and stupid girl?

He put an arm around her clumsily and shook her. "Of course, you are my best friend. I told you, you are like my sister, and that means you are the only one who has permission to see me cry."

She gloated with pride and giggled. "Permission?"

"Uh-hmm." Kevin sat up, his chest puffed out, feeling alive again.

She shook her head. "But…I did not *see* you cry." Her oval face softened, and she looked younger than eight.

"Yes, you did."

"No, I didn't."

"*Urggh*, of course you did. Hearing me is just the same as seeing me," he said lovingly.

"You cry like a baby!"

"I might take away that permission if you say that again." He warned warmly, slightly embarrassed.

"You won't," she replied gleefully, and her laughter rang out into the night air, and, for a while, all was forgotten. It was just them, on top of the world, against the world.

Chapter 7

December 27, 1999

"It's almost your birthday, Shenzi! Is your mother back yet?"

Kevin and Shenzi were sitting on the rooftop again after a long afternoon of hide-and-seek. It had rained in the morning, but the sun sprung up hard after lunch, and despite all caution, all the children were out in the wet grass slipping and sliding and preparing for a game of hide-and-seek. Block 4 was almost empty since most people had traveled to the village to celebrate Christmas and the New Year.

Taata Bob had declined to go to the village, and Ameena had asked Aunty Dina if she could look after Shenzi for a few days over Christmas because she was going away for a "business" trip. Only two days earlier, she had captured the attention of a Belgian expatriate who was taking the last two weeks of his year-end vacation traveling to Western Uganda. She had flirted with him enough for him to pay for her drink, seek a second date, and, consequently, take her with him to Queen Elizabeth National Park.

"I will bring you presents, *qalbi*," she cooed to Shenzi and kissed her cheek. "I will be back before your birthday, okay?"

Shenzi nodded, her heart sinking. She could not recall a time she had spent the holidays with her mother, and yet she never stopped hoping.

"Will you?" she asked Ameena, her head bowed.

Her mother laughed that deep, husky, raucous laugh. "Eh? You are a big girl now. Come on."

It wasn't an answer.

Her heart sank further. Her mother was not coming back for her birthday.

"I will miss you," she simply said, too saddened to protest, knowing full well how this played out. Ameena would return and complain about fatigue. If Shenzi brought up the promises Ameena had made about plaiting her hair or painting her nails, Ameena would guilt her for being ungrateful and spoiled. Then a week later, she would be nice, as if the evil spell had lifted. Ameena would buy her pretty dresses and shoes and even wash and condition her hair. The best part would be when she would braid her hair, tell her stories, and paint her nails any color she wanted. That week would be blissful and short-lived. Sooner than later, Ameena would hurl insults and keep her hungry for long hours again. She tried to smile. "Don't work too hard," Shenzi said.

* * *

"No, Mummy is not back yet," Shenzi heaved sadly, rousing from the memory.

They both got silent for a moment. Kevin was holding back, and she did not want to hear it, anyway. She was sad enough. "Maybe we can do something nice, buy chips and liver?" He was saying instead.

Shenzi brightened. "Yes! Chips and liver!"

"I know. Should we get it now, or you want it tomorrow? I can get some from Middle East market."

"Yes! Let's do it tomorrow in the afternoon." Shenzi swayed in delight.

Kevin laughed. Anything to keep her occupied and not thinking about her mother. "Don't worry; maybe she will come tomorrow, but today you have me."

She beamed shyly in his direction. She adored him almost as much as she adored her mother.

"Girls." He sighed in mock exasperation, and her grin widened.

"I did not forget either, that thing you were supposed to tell me about big girls."

"I will tell you when you are nine, I promise. It's tomorrow."

"Boys!" She shook her head.

Kevin puffed his chest. "Don't worry, big brother will tell you everything."

"Really?" She feigned seriousness, her brow furrowed, and her chin set, even though within, her heart swelled with both pride and love; it was sacred he called her his sister, but it was more sacred the warm rush that filled her with hearing him say it.

"I swear upon the living God," Kevin told her dramatically taking his pointer finger and dipping it in his mouth for a brief tap on his tongue then sending that same finger in a Nike sweeping motion across his neck, as a swearing sign. It was the undoubted expression of "my bond is my word. "I even did it with my fingers!" he assured her naughtily.

"Put saliva on it?" she asked.

"Uh-huh. I can do it again and put it on you if you don't believe me."

Shenzi made a face. "*Urgh*, you did not brush your teeth this morning; it will smell!"

Kevin laughed.

"I know you," Shenzi told him and shook her head. "Boys cannot take care of themselves."

He shrugged. "We don't care like you girls." He put his hand over his mouth, cupping it and breathing into it to smell his breath himself and scrunched his nose. It was stale.

"You just smelled it, didn't you?" Shenzi asked.

"You heard me? Shenzi, it's not fair! You can't see, but I could swear you have eyes everywhere."

Shenzi laughed. "You breathed very loudly, big head!"

They lapsed into a comfortable silence, listening to the distant traffic and everyday familiar sounds of their home. Shenzi thought about her birthday and the promise that would be unlocked. She could not wait to harness a deep secret of maturity. It made her feel almost grown up. As the sun made its slow exit over the Kampala skyline, Shenzi felt a queasiness rise from the pit of her tummy: the bitter sensation of joy and dread that enveloped her every December around her birthday. She unconsciously, out of habit, started to count down the minutes and hours to another birthday without her mother.

December 28, 1999

"Happy birthday to you! Happy birthday to you..."

A loud off-tune singing of the birthday chorus echoed around the Byamukama living room.

Kevin, Shenzi, and Aunty Dina sat on the worn brown leather couch, a coffee table spread before them with a small round birthday cake, iced in pinks and greens with writing in green icing on top: "Happy Birthday Shenz," the "I" missing because it could not fit on the circumference of the cake. Around the cake were colorful plastic bowls of potato crisps spread out in a medley of the crunchy, doughy snack bites *bagiya*. Bottles of soda stood neatly arrayed in semicircles around the cake; a transparent bowl filled with homemade popcorn, sat opposite the bowl with crisps and *bagiya*, and a large flat plate in front of the cake was decked out with a mixture of shortcake biscuits, Nice biscuits, sandwich crème biscuits and Marie tea biscuits. It was the complete feast.

Teopista, who was knocking on the door that instant and breaking up the celebratory singing, had baked a little fruit cake.

"The door, Kevin," Aunty Dina chimed. Her mood was light, and her heart softened as she looked at Shenzi seated meekly on the couch between her and Kevin.

Teopista burst in with a loud, *"Ahaaa!* Started without me? *Iyiii?"* She had a packet of serviettes in one hand and her littlest girl balanced on her hip.

"Of course not, Teopista! Thank you for the cake, by the way." She turned to Shenzi, who looked so passive and beautiful, she almost seemed unreal. "Did you thank Aunty Toppie?" Dina asked Shenzi soothingly.

Shenzi gasped, shook her head, and blurted out, "Thank you for the cake, Aunty Teopista."

"Ah-ah, it's not a problem. Aunty Dina, it's her birthday!" Teopista scolded mildly although obviously pleased.

Aunty Dina smiled at Shenzi. The conversation she had had with her mother only a few days before Christmas played back sharply in her mind.

"Dina!" Ameena had hissed her name from above the stairs. She was doing her weekly washing that morning and had an enormous basketful of wrung clothes ready to be hung out on the wire. She looked up. Ameena was a stunning vision of beauty, clad in a shimmering black halter-neck blouse and cream capri pants; her hair was curled carefully and fell around her thin face graciously. Her eyes were kohl darkened and lips a dark red sheen; a single silver bracelet went around her slim wrist. She looked like a model, and Aunty Dina often wondered why she did not do television commercials for makeup, maybe sign up with Sylvia Owori and not be an escort anymore.

"Yes, Ameena."

Her eyes spied the travel bag with a huge Adidas logo on it. She could almost guess what was coming. It came every year. Ameena hurriedly clip-clopped down the stairs in her five-inch stiletto heels, lugging her bag behind her. "I need a favor," she blurted out, her strange accent capping over the words.

"Yes, how can I help?"

A guilty smile played on Ameena's lips. "I need you to help me...please throw Shenzi a birthday party."

Dina started to protest: "I..."

They did this back-and-forth every year.

"Please, *qalbi*." She was persuasive. She held a balled-out fist and reached for Dina's free hand, hurriedly stuffing a wad of shillings in Dina's palm. "Please, I have to go. I won't be back till next year!"

"But…"

Ameena kissed Dina's hand. "Thank you, my friend. You are a better mother to Shenzi, please. Get her anything with this. But don't tell her it was from me." Their eyes met and Dina could see the steel determination in them. Feeling as if the guilt was being transferred to her, she tried to protest, but Ameena held her gaze. "Promise me."

Dina sighed. "Ameena…okay." She finally obliged.

"*Asante*! May God bless you." She hurriedly hugged her and proceeded down the next two flights of stairs, clutching the big bag in tow. When Dina could hear the clicking heels no more, she opened her palm and sighed at the wad of rolled-up notes of money in her hand. It was enough for the goodies, some presents, and, above all, a little stash for Shenzi on days she had no food.

It was not good for a child her age to go hungry for days.

"I hope you like the cake, birthday girl," Teopista was saying, her hand smoothing over Shenzi's hair. "I wish you could see your hair; it's beautiful…Kevin! Come! Isn't this hair nice?"

Teopista had bought some braid extensions and expertly braided Shenzi's hair in cornrows decked out with colorful beads. Teopista seemed to be the only one on the Block who had mastered how to plait Shenzi's fine-textured hair without it loosening so fast. She insisted on using extensions because she claimed it held the hair firmer for a longer time, and she was hoping these would hold for a month.

She also gave Shenzi an old hair net to sleep with to keep her hair in place while muttering that her mother should have taught her these female tricks. Shenzi had patiently sat for the two hours that morning grimacing when Teopista pulled and combed out the matted coils. She sighed with relief when it was all done and Teopista's callused hands massaged amla oil into the exposed tight scalp.

"It is lovely!" Aunty Dina responded amid Kevin's groans. "A true princess."

Shenzi grinned and winced slightly, for the tight grasp of her hair came with pain. She proudly swished her head from side to side and the ends rustled the back of her blouse falling this way and that, the beads colliding and emitting a sound.

"Thank you!" she told Teopista enthusiastically. She tried to squash the feeling of sadness at her mother's absence. If only she had been the one who had thrown her a party, plaited her hair, and bought her a new dress. It would have been the perfect birthday. Other mothers were not like her own. Aunty Dina was closer to her than her own mother. Ameena felt like a special ornamental piece only brought out to be exhibited on special occasions, then gently returned to its safe, never to endure the wear and tear of her mundane sightless life.

Did she love her at all, or was she really busy? Shenzi wondered. Aunty Dina hugged her more than Ameena did. Ameena's love was like morsels of cake rolling off a king's table, and when those morsels fell, she leaped at them for fear they would disappear with a change of mood or an uncle's sudden appearance.

While she sat on the couch, enveloped in the safety and uncertainty of her darkness, the celebratory calls and greetings dispelled her optical blindness and the gnawing emptiness that permanently sat in the pit of her tummy. The little apartment lit up almost instantly with the vibrant chaos of love and warmth.

"Did we miss anything?" Teopista was asking. "I had to get this *ka* girl ready, children!" she scolded loudly and even underneath the cudgeling, there was a lot of warmth, like she enjoyed getting her littlest daughter ready.

Dina laughed. "I know! Come, come, you missed nothing. We were just singing 'Happy Birthday.'"

"I asked Bosco to come," she heard Kevin say—not particularly to her.

And then his mother responded: "Did you ask the birthday girl?"

"That's okay," Shenzi interrupted, enjoying the fact that it was her day and that honor was being given to her.

She could hear him saunter to the door. A warm draft indicated he had opened it again. "I think I hear him on the stairs," Kevin replied.

Shenzi smiled, knowing whether she had said yes or no, Kevin would have gone right ahead anyway to invite Bosco. He was their friend, so it did not matter.

Sure enough, Bosco's "Happy Birthday" came sailing into the living space.

"You came!" It was Kevin feigning surprise.

"Of course, but I can only stay till seven o'clock. Mummy wants me to help my cousins, you know, the ones who came from the UK."

"Oh okay," Kevin replied. "We end at seven, anyway."

"Is your father in?" Bosco whispered, and Shenzi caught the half-whispered question.

"Do you see him?" She heard Kevin's sardonic response.

And then she sensed Bosco right in front of her. His footsteps were careless and heavy, not light and quick like Kevin's.

"Birthday girl!" he quipped. "You look very nice."

She knew he was smiling from the way he had said it and that Kevin was pointedly making a face as he groaned and embarrassed his friend.

"By the way, I told her what you said the last time!"

Bosco's eyes widened, and he clasped a hand over his mouth, gasping. Kevin threw his friend a devilish grin, and before Bosco could say a thing, Aunty Dina interrupted their banter. "Can you two sit? It's not your birthdays."

The birthday chorus started again once everyone had comfortably found a sitting place. Shenzi grinned throughout, colors playing in her mind's eye, imagining what the room looked like, just like the way she felt it: warm. She welcomed it hungrily and even laughed when they all burst into the "you look like a monkey" chorus; it was hilarious that some sang, "angel," others "monkey," so it all came out confusing and silly.

"Monkey Angel sounds right." Kevin tapped his friend on the shoulder.

She shoved him with hers. "You are the monkey. I heard you tell Bosco." He shoved her back. They went at it for a few seconds more before she laughed, clasping her hand over her mouth.

The cake was cut, soda poured, and soon the children were noisily chattering and giving Shenzi hugs.

Kevin held back till everyone had given their birthday salutations, then went ahead to declare himself loudly and auspiciously the best gift Shenzi could ever have, doubling both as her brother and best friend. Everyone laughed at his comical pose, left foot stuck out toeing the carpet, chest puffed out for his small stature.

As the final hour approached, Kevin noticed his mother glance out the window now and again, and he knew she was half hoping, just like him, that his father would not show up too soon. Taata Bob was negativity about to happen everywhere he went.

Teopista helped Aunty Dina clean up while the children played with Shenzi and her new toys.

"Hmm! But Ameena is shameless. I cannot believe she ran off to Queen Elizabeth and left her daughter over the Christmas season, hmm!" Her lower lip drooped in judgment.

Aunty Dina sighed. "It's not new, you know."

"I know, but, eh!" Teopista wiped the dishes and put them in the cupboard. "No mother should do that to her daughter."

Aunty Dina shook her head. "It's not our place, and you know the story…"

Teopista slapped her hands together before dropping them dramatically on her hips. "Ah! Who knows the true story: rape, boyfriend trouble, whatever…that child doesn't deserve to be treated like a rag."

"*Shhh.*" Aunty Dina hushed her, watching the children in the distance from the corner of her eye, then shook her head. "I guess the best we can do is take care of Shenzi."

Teopista heaved, her face screwed then shook her head. "Hmm, I think so, but…"

"No 'buts,' Toppie; we do what we can. Ameena has been good to us, too. It's the best we can do for them both."

Teopista did not look convinced but dropped the subject. As she got the last dishes put away, she looked over at Shenzi, who was seated between Kevin and Bosco. "At least she has someone who really loves her." She motioned to Kevin with her mouth.

Aunty Dina smiled proudly. "My son will protect her with his life; I see it."

Teopista agreed. "Hmm, that is his sister, really!" They watched the children as they loudly disagreed about a game they played.

Seven o'clock rolled by fast, and the happy, playful chattering, TV sounds, and music dwindled to a single humming sound as Aunty Dina arranged the dining room, placing the four chairs around the dining table. Everyone got ready to leave and filed out of the house almost at once, leaving Kevin, his mother, and Shenzi in the empty space filled with the ghostly memory of a birthday party. The essence of it lingered in the air still, a light, shimmery, celebratory magic dust.

"What time is Daddy coming home?" Kevin suddenly asked his mother, dissolving the celebratory mood instantly. A tense chill seeped through the light, open spaces of the house. Kevin dreaded that moment more than he let show, the moment his father walked in the door.

It being the holidays, it was hard to tell. Still, Kevin felt uneasy. It had become a constant state he lived in, unaware of how much he wore it as a personality.

Shenzi always felt it, his nervousness, his jittery motions, or his curtness. At times, he overcompensated with broody silence. This time around, he swayed between moody silence and jitteriness.

They often lay awake in Kevin's room when she stayed over, and she would tell him he was too jumpy. Sometimes she would ask him if he wanted to hold her hand while they slept to help him sleep. Maybe it would bring him a little comfort in his conflicted soul.

"I don't know." Aunty Dina avoided his quizzical gaze. "Go help Shenzi," she said instead.

"Aunty Dina, Kevin does not have to help me," Shenzi protested. "Thank you for the party; it was very nice."

Aunty Dina smiled and squeezed her shoulders. "You liked it? You are special, Shenzi; may you enjoy your ninth year."

"I did. Thank you, Aunty Dina."

Aunty Dina nodded to Kevin resolutely. He took Shenzi's hand and led her down the short corridor to the room they shared. He knew when a topic was not to be broached, and he let it alone.

"Thank you for my gift, Kevin," Shenzi finally piped. Her voice quivered with emotion.

"Mummy wanted it to be special. Me too," he replied, giving her a little shake on her shoulder. "And she said I must see you to the bathroom."

"Okay," Shenzi replied resignedly. How could she say no to Dina Byamukama? "She is coming to help me?"

"Uh-hm," Kevin replied as he took her hand in one hand and her towel in the other hand and led her to the bathroom.

He had to agree this had been a very extravagant birthday party. For the last few years, it had been just them; Taata Bob had been around for her sixth and fifth birthdays. They always had food, but this year they had all the snacks they never ever had. Kevin wondered how his mother could have afforded it all, including the queen cakes from Hot Loaf that they always looked forward to having on special days like Sundays.

"This was so special. I always want to have a special birthday when we grow up; can I?"

"Uh-huh," he replied absently, carefully guiding her out of the way of any stray object or an open door. His father's absence preoccupied his thoughts. It bothered him. He had watched his father become increasingly unbearable this year, especially to his mother, and it seemed to depend on the amount of time he spent out drinking.

"Don't think about it," he heard Shenzi almost whisper.

Kevin smiled. "The way you read my mind scares me."

Shenzi shrugged. "It's actually your hand. You are squeezing my arm a little too hard. You do that when something is bothering you."

Kevin sighed. "Sorry. I Just…"

"Just what?"

He stopped and hung his head. "I feel like something bad is going to happen."

"Maybe not," Shenzi chipped in hopefully. "Taata Bob has not been drinking since Christmas Eve."

Kevin was quiet. "I know, but he has also been worse than last year."

Shenzi felt for his arm that held her and patted it. "Don't worry."

"Thank you, Kevin. Now go sweep up the kitchen and then take your bath, okay?" Aunty Dina was coming through the corridor toward them, her rubber slippers making a squelching sound on the smooth cemented floor. "You two should be in bed soon too."

"But it's holiday time." Kevin groaned.

"Did you forget tomorrow is market day and I need you to come with me? We will be back quickly, and you can catch up on sleep."

Kevin made a face. "Okay."

Aunty Dina liked to go to Nakawa Market very early in the morning. She claimed the food was fresh and cheapest then. There were always truckloads of fresh fruits, vegetables, meats, and tubers ferried long distances from the countryside. Most of the stall owners at the market got the choicest foods for cheap as they offloaded them from the trucks. Aunty Dina had discovered that secret, and she went twice a week for a fix of fresh food. When Taata Bob was around, he usually drove her to the market.

Despite Shenzi's protests that she was a big girl and could take her own baths and get dressed without help, Aunty Dina insisted on helping her.

"I am not a baby!" Her weak protests fell on Dina's deaf ears. "I do it by myself when I am at home." Shenzi had learned how to take care of herself earlier than most children. She had locked the bathroom door behind her frequently after the time Uncle Mulenzi deliberately refused to leave the bathroom—only once she was undressed did she realize he was still there—when she insisted she needed to use it to shower. She had gotten wary of the different men that came through the door of her house, so locking the bathroom door for hours while she showered had become a routine.

"Do you realize you are not home now? So in my house, I will do what I feel is right. Besides, it's your birthday," Dina scolded her gently.

Shenzi smiled and nodded. "Okay." It was different at Kevin's.

Aunty Dina's hardworking fingers, firm to the touch and yet gentle on her skin, lathered a loofah and scrubbed her down, exclaiming about how much dirt washed off her body, turning the soapy foam a light brown from all the dust collected from play.

She would then take out a tin of the Night Rose–scented petroleum jelly that Shenzi loved and would apply it to every inch of her body before helping her into her nightclothes. But tonight was special, so Aunty Dina oiled her down with her Solea lotion, and Shenzi savored the strong floral scent as it enveloped every inch of her and stuffed her nose.

Even though a part of her felt she was too old for this treatment, she succumbed to it because it made her feel special and loved.

"Good girl," Dina was saying, and Shenzi could sense her smile. Dina massaged the lotion into her face and pulled on her cheeks lightly. "You are all fresh and beautiful now."

Shenzi grinned, her heart as warm and as full as the spa treatment she had just been given.

"I have a gift for you by the way."

"Another one?"

"But I haven't given you anything yet."

"You cooked, you bathed me…those are all gifts."

Dina smiled. "You are a brave, clever, beautiful, and kind girl, Shenzi," she told her, sympathy lacing her voice as she thought of Ameena. "Your mother should know how lucky she is to have you."

Shenzi swayed, a warm, gooey feeling of love that she rarely felt, except at Kevin's home with Kevin and his mother, began to rise from her tiny toes—making her wiggle them—and work its way upward to her belly, filling her and proceeding to her heart, where it settled in a gooey, warm puddle. She shook slightly with emotion, reached both her hands out, held whatever part of Aunty Dina she felt, and blurted out, "I love you, Aunty Dina!"

Aunty Dina squeezed the arms that enclosed themselves about her.

"Oh, Shenzi, my dear, I love you, too."

She pulled away. Shenzi heard a ruffling of something, and then Dina placed something wrapped tight in her hands. "So...here is..." She hesitated. "Here is my gift to you..."

"This is...thirty thousand shillings, Shenzi. Keep it well. I know you will do well with it because you are very young but also very old. You will take care of yourself with it." There was a sad note in Dina's voice as she closed her hand over Shenzi's with the money.

"Money?" Shenzi asked, closing her fist over the notes tightly rolled in a rubber band.

"Yes, you can ask Kevin to keep it for you."

She nodded, not understanding why Dina would give her so much money. The most Ameena had ever given her was a thousand shillings.

Shenzi thought of all the chips and liver she could eat with it.

She heard Dina sigh, and the magic of the moment fizzled. "Now, did you enjoy your birthday?" she was asking again, as if to ascertain.

"Yes, Aunty Dina, very much. Thank you so much."

She brushed the ghost of guilt away and ushered Shenzi into the living room. "Stay here; I can put the TV on, and you listen. When Kevin is ready, you can eat supper together and go to bed."

"Okay." Shenzi tucked the money into the pocket of her light cotton nightdress that hung to her ankles. Aunty Dina handed her the stick and guided her to the living room. Even though Shenzi could maneuver her way through the Byamukama household, she let Dina lead her.

The heavy splashing sounds of water possibly flowing from a higher plane than the bathtub (Kevin lifting the basin to pour the last bits of water in it over his body) indicated the end of bath time for Kevin.

Chapter 8

"Do you know what time it is?" Shenzi was asking for the nth time that night. She rolled onto her side, facing the direction Kevin slept. They positioned their beds against the walls opposite each other. Kevin slept close to the door, claiming since he was the stronger of the two, it was his duty to fight off anything that came in before it got to Shenzi.

"I think it's ten; it feels like ten," Kevin replied, sleep weighing heavily on his eyelids, and as he tried to drift off to sleep again, Shenzi's soft, husky, buttery voice floated to him.

"Aunty Dina makes the best chicken and matooke." She did not want to sleep yet because that would mean the new light of day would roll away today. She wanted to hold on to it a moment longer.

"Hmm." He smiled proudly, his eyes closed. "Mummy is the best." He grinned, partially revealing a gap where he had lost a molar only a week ago.

"Hmm," Shenzi agreed.

"And when I grow up, I will build her a house and buy her a restaurant so that everyone can taste her good food."

"Uh-mm," Shenzi agreed wholeheartedly. "Me first!" she shot her thin arm in the air. "I will come every single day. For lunch, for supper, for breakfast…"

Kevin agreed. "We will go together. Aaaah, you know what? We would eat for free. You and me!"

Shenzi beamed with pride, honored to be associated with Kevin.

A comfortable silence fell between them, and Kevin welcomed sleep as it lazily beckoned to him.

"Today has been the best day of my life!" Shenzi exclaimed, stirring Kevin up again.

Shenzi could hardly contain her excitement and her gratefulness, so much so that she had forgotten about her mother and the fact that she had not even been there for her birthday.

"Shenzi, I'm happy you enjoyed your birthday," Kevin drawled.

"By the way, you're the best present I have had today," Shenzi added.

Kevin swelled with pride. "Of course I am! And you always will have that, especially when we grow up; every birthday you will have me there, and I will make your dreams come true." He saw their future as he spoke with stark confidence, never wavering from the vision.

Shenzi wished she could be as consistently hopeful as Kevin was. Deep down, she feared the worst had not yet come. Her thoughts frightened her: what if it did not happen?

What if they never stayed together or got rich?

What if she remained stuck with her mother and became like her when she grew up?

What if Kevin got beaten to death by his father?

"Shenzi?" Kevin was calling her name sharply, dragging her back from her gloomy thoughts.

"Huh?" She gasped.

"Are you OK?" he asked.

"Kevin, mother didn't come back like she promised," she said quickly.

A heavy sigh emanated from the opposite side of the room as Kevin slapped the blanket in frustration. "She never comes! Shenzi! Never!" He was speaking between clenched teeth.

Shenzi curled up, hugging her knees. Silence fell between them.

He calmed himself. Sleep was fading away. "Shenzi, I don't like that she never comes! I hate it."

"I know," Shenzi piped, "but…"

"No!" He interrupted her, knowing the excuse she was going to give, then added even more exasperatedly, "Maybe I should ask Mummy if you can stay with us forever. I can be your big brother, and you won't have to be near any of those uncles. They are bad, Shenzi!" He was loud and angry.

"Kevin, please stop!" Shenzi cried out.

He dragged in a trembling breath, then paused. "You know what, Shenzi, let's run away. Let's go away from here! I HATE Taata Bob; I hate your mother. I am sorry but I do because she hurts you. And…and we go away, and I will take care of you."

Shenzi stilled herself against the urgency of his words and calmly asked, "Where will we go?"

"Anywhere! Just go away!" He was waving his arms in the air, gesticulating. "And Aunty Dina?"

Kevin paused. "I dunno. Maybe…maybe she will come with us." The spring bed groaned with every move he made. Shenzi sat up abruptly, her mind mulling over Kevin's outburst. He sounded more serious than the many times they had talked of running away. "But…but we can't run away. What about school?"

"Ah! Who needs school? We will make money and be rich. We can go to the city center and tell the rich *mzungus* we find there to take us with them, and then they can make your eyes and…" He was rambling on and on, swaying and gesticulating so wildly that the springs of his bed cried out, begging him to calm down and go to sleep. Shenzi listened, pensive.

The brilliant outpouring of Kevin's mind was cut short by the front door being flung open so hard it hit the wall with a thud.

"Dina! Dina! Eh, Dina! I need food!" Taata Bob roared drunkenly.

They both froze, listening as his drunken feet shuffle to the sitting room.

They heard the bedroom door a few feet away from them open, and Aunty Dina called back almost timidly, "I am coming, *Taata*. Let me put on my nightdress!"

"Eh?" Taata Bob's voice boomed loud enough for the two children to hear him through the partially closed door to their bedroom.

"What were you doing there? You mean…you were naked!" He slurred.

Kevin clenched his teeth, and his eyes shut tight. A nervous groan escaped his lips. The huge tight knot that had exploded in his belly grew again and rose like bile up his throat.

Shenzi called out to him in hushed whispers, "Kevin, can I sleep with you?"

Kevin did not respond, his mind racing, fear and anger boiling in a cauldron in his soul and about to spew out like an active volcano.

"Kevin!" Shenzi hissed, unable to stop the quiver in her voice. When he did not respond and Taata Bob's voice got louder as he left the bedroom heading to the bathroom, Shenzi threw the covers aside and felt for the edge of the bed.

"Kevin." Her voice carried a frantic plea. Something told her tonight would not end well if Kevin got involved.

Taata Bob's slurring, drunken voice was obnoxious and loud. His powerful fist pounded on the bathroom door. Aunty Dina half-pleaded with him, half-sweet-talked him. Shenzi heard the bathroom door open and feet going back and forth. There was a jumble of voices.

Aunty Dina and her husband's dialogue got sharper and louder, and their voices rose and fell as they moved from one room to the next.

"There is food over there on the stove…"

Her sentence ended in a sharp, short scream as a loud slap resounded to their room.

"Don't talk back, woman!" Taata Bob hurled the words with all the drunken effort he could manage. *"Kumanyoko!"*

The muffled cry of Aunty Dina crept into their room and settled like a dark cloud over them, followed by another slap that made Shenzi flinch at its intensity. Her little body shook with fear. She grasped Kevin's hand tight, feeling for him on the bed. Kevin groaned in anger, jumping out of bed, wriggling his hand out of hers.

Shenzi felt him sweep past her, opening the door.

"No, Kevin, please…"

"Stay here!" The firmness in his tone made her shrink back. It was not good. "This. Has. To. Stop!" Then he was gone. She sat on his bed, unsure of what to do.

Kevin bolted for the living room and the nauseous bile in his chest rose at the scene that greeted him. Aunty Dina was curled up by the sofa, her nightdress torn at the shoulder. She shrieked and shouted at her husband, then pleaded simultaneously.

As her husband brought down a heavy foot to her side, her hands flew instinctively to her face, shielding it from the assaults raining mercilessly on her body. She doubled over and cried out when his foot connected with her left rib cage.

"Taata, the children…" She was begging hoarsely now, her fight gone.

Kevin froze for a second, pain filling his heart, and a fresh wave of anger washed over him. He looked at his mother sprawled on the floor against the sofa that was now broken, leaning onto one side, sobbing.

Kevin let out a loud yell and flung himself at his father. "You are going to kill her, you filthy pig!"

He spat the words and accompanied them with blows on his father. Taata Bob swayed against the weight of the blows, stunned at the outburst from his son. He recovered quickly, and, growling, picked up Kevin by the wrists and shoved him away.

Kevin tumbled backward, his balance compromised as he landed on his backside and right elbow. He winced as his body hit the cold concrete, and an electric shock wave vaulted through his arm and spread instantly throughout his body. He let out a half-sob. Overwhelmed with both numbing pain, fear, and anger, he rolled to his side. His father was hurling insults now, and his mother was pleading for him

"He is only a boy. That's your son, Taata!" She wept.

Kevin recharged, limped onto his feet, and with a growl, he charged like a bull toward his father, fists aimed at Taata Bob's massive belly, distended and drooping. This time Taata Bob was prepared. "Oh-oh, now he thinks he can fight me," he sneered and laughed like a madman, slapping his charging son with the full force of his backhand. Kevin staggered unintentionally into his mother, who was still struggling to get up.

"Who is the man now? Stupid boy! *Malaya* of a mother!" he slurred, coughing and laughing simultaneously, producing a curious sound akin to choking.

"From today, both of you…are…are no longer Byamukamas! You go to Opio, that neighbor who you have been sleeping with…" He wagged a finger at Aunty Dina exaggeratedly, leaning back against the table side.

Kevin fought back the tears of anger that cradled his eyeballs. He ground his jaw hard to keep them in, but his whole being was awash in unquenchable fury. He felt both helpless and terrified for his mother.

"If you were here, you would know she was here with us because it's Shenzi's birthday!" Kevin shouted. It was all he could say to deter the madness of his father. The pain of holding back the tears was crushing, so he let them flow.

His father waved a dismissive hand at him and steadied himself on his feet. "*Wewe*, don't speak back to me, stupid boy!" He made as if to reach for him and Kevin flinched back. His father laughed like a madman. Where is that *malaya*'s daughter. Where?"

Kevin did not wait for his father to make another move. Shenzi's face, ebony smooth, tilted back in laughter, flashed before him momentarily. Not only had Taata Bob hurt his mother, but he had also ruined Shenzi's day.

Growling with redoubled anger and a strength he fathomed came from a dark place inside of him, he charged at his father again. "Don't. Call. Her. That!" he yelled and with all the strength in him, Kevin shoved his father backward, punching him with all the anger that bubbled inside him, an unstoppable volcano burst through the layers of years of provocation; a red-hot lava tinged with a volatile heat exploded to the surface, unhinged.

Kevin later could not quite reconcile his actions with the effect of them; it was as if he had momentarily escaped the confines of his body and was watching the scene in slow motion like a nonchalant spectator.

He heard his mother scream. It was a different sort of scream, one that he would never forget. Kevin saw his father lose his balance and struggle to hold on to the side of the table. His eyes bulged; his mouth opened wide and twisted in what seemed like a torrent of abuse he could not remember even later. Kevin watched him stagger wildly and tumble back over an overturned, broken chair, lose balance completely, and sink onto a pointed end of an upturned coffee table leg.

In that spectator state, Kevin stood still as Taata Bob landed heavily, like a sack of potatoes, onto the wooden leg. The oblong splintered wood went through him with a sickening squelch.

Aunty Dina gave a short shocked scream of horror again as her husband's body convulsed. Kevin stood frozen, staring at the wood that had surfaced at the top of his father's body; dark red blood stained it to the hilt.

Taata Bob made a guttural sound akin to a laugh, then his voice rasped and caught in the throes of death. He hissed, "You did it, son…you…killed me."

Kevin stood frozen.

The twitching stopped, and Taata Bob's body relaxed like one who had given up the fight, a sick smirk plastered on his dead face.

Aunty Dina moaned, crawling to the body of her husband. She stared in shock at the heavy, lifeless body that had, only minutes earlier, threatened their very lives.

Shenzi was moaning in the other room, scared. And someone was knocking on their door.

"*Kuku*, is everything okay?" It was the frantic voice of Teopista. For several minutes, time stood still. Aunty Dina caressed her dead husband's face and lay on his chest, lost in a place Kevin could not reach.

The banging on the door got more urgent. "*Kuku!*"

Kevin was not sure he was awake or whether the scene before him was real. His mother's sharp, urgent call to him stirred him.

"Kevin!" she hissed out.

He gasped, confused. "Mummy, mummy…" He mumbled, "I…I did

not mean…" He choked on his words.

His mother shook her head, her eyes blank, a strange calmness about her. "Go to Shenzi. Both of you. Get out of here. Now. Go. Let me take care of this. Go. Now!"

"But Mummy…"

"Kevin, bad things have happened tonight. This is not your life. Get Shenzi and go…go…go for now. I need to think."

Kevin felt weak. "Mommy, I don't want to leave…it's my fault…I… killed him."

The realization that there was a dead body and not anyone else's but his father's shook him to his core. He did not want to believe it or see it.

The look in his mother's eyes revived a strength that the paralyzing fear that gripped him had dissolved. "Kevin, I am in some pain. But let me handle this. Take care of Shenzi. I promised Ameena. Please go. Everything will be okay."

"But Daddy…" he half-whispered. Somewhere there was still the frantic knocking on the door…was it voices he was hearing?

Aunty Dina took her son's face in her hands and gazed into his eyes.

"You did not kill him. He was too drunk to stand and fell. Now… promise me you will look after Shenzi. You are a man now. You cannot be afraid."

He nodded, tears rolling freely down his cheeks. His universe had fallen apart, crumbling in a messy void of confusion. All he felt was loss.

The voices outside the door persisted…the banging was less frantic. No one came when they fought. Why tonight?

Kevin sobbed like a baby for the last time in his life. The weight of the world was tangible. He knew something had changed, and it depended on him. Shenzi depended on him.

When his sobbing ceased, and he locked eyes with his mother, he saw she had been crying too. She embraced him one more time, and they both seemed uncertain of the next time they would hold each other again. There was something final in this touch.

"Go, Kevin." She sniffed and wiped her cheek with the back of her hand. "Get some money out of my bag. Pack some clothes and things for you and Shenzi. Go get a taxi from the stage; go to Bwaise, where Uncle Benson lives, and wait there for me."

Kevin nodded mechanically. He got up, wiped his face, and walked to the bedroom where Shenzi was leaning against the bedroom door, shaking like a leaf, making whimpering sounds.

She heard him come and jerked up. "I am scared, Kevin. What's going on?"

Even in the darkness that had enveloped them, seeing her comforted him, a ray of hope in a bleak situation.

It was that hope that got him to take her hand silently.

"We have to go now." He did not know how to be a man, but he knew he had to be the big brother.

"Where? Why?" Shenzi's voice sounded frail. She sensed something terrible had happened. "Where is Taata Bob?" she asked.

Kevin hung his head, unable to respond, but instantly she knew— the urgency of their conspicuous departure and Kevin's mood. The conversation she had half heard with his mother confirmed what she did not want to believe.

"Sit," he told her abruptly. "Wait for me."

She did so obediently. The voices outside the door were dying out, and there was no movement in the living room. In the bedroom, she could pick up a rustling sound and Kevin's swift, silent back-and-forth movements.

Kevin emptied his school bag and rammed a couple of shirts and shorts into it. He grabbed a few of Shenzi's clothes and underwear and shoved them in the bag, then proceeded to the kitchen to rummage through the cupboard for a few leftover snacks from the party: a pack of family biscuits and two bags of potato crisps, which he stuffed in the bag as well.

When he returned to the room, Shenzi had not moved. "Change into other clothes," he whispered to Shenzi. She did not resist.

Kevin made for his parents' room to retrieve the money his mother had told him to get. It was for their shopping rendezvous that would never happen. A part of him longed to reverse the events of the night so they could go shopping the next day.

Why did he have to come home drunk! Kevin agonized.

When he swept past the living room, his mother sat hunched over by the body of her husband. The blood flowed freely onto a rag, soaking into it. His mouth in that twisted posture dripped crimson. His mother cradled the limp head, rocking back and forth in mourning. Kevin looked away quickly, his heart beating wildly in his chest as he made for his bedroom.

Chapter 9

December 1999

The night breeze was cool as the two children, a skinny boy about four feet tall and a little girl, a little shorter and just as skinny, walked through the scattered Lego-like blocks of flats. They trudged through a rare untrodden path overgrown with tufts of grass to the major shopping center in the Bugolobi suburb. A taxi stage loomed into view on the right-hand side. People crowded the stage in clusters, ready to climb into the next taxi that pulled up. The conductor would fling the rickety old minivan doors open as he simultaneously announced the next destination.

A few vendors selling roasted chunks of meat on skewers lingered, hoping revelers or late-night riders would buy their final stock. The lady who sold airtime cards on the corner by the taxi stop was counting her day's wages and closing shop. She spoke animatedly to another man, who chewed leisurely on a roasted maize cob.

The crowds thinned as the night shadows lengthened, and the blanket of darkness engulfed everything in its embrace. Kevin held on to Shenzi's hand tightly as though if he relaxed his hold, she would slip away in the folds of darkness that shrouded them. They spoke very little, each lost in thoughts they were afraid to voice. Shenzi gently nudged at the ground before her with her stick, her nose upturned, sniffing the air for familiar scents that draped Bugolobi trading center: the dizzying smells of exhaust, charred meats, frying dough, and roasting maize.

She sighed. "We are here." She spoke more to reassure herself.

Kevin squeezed her hand. "We are."

An empty taxi pulled up, the conductor hanging on the sliding back door of the minivan serenaded waiting passengers with his customary call, *"Old park! Old Park! Old Park!"* he shouted. *"Kampala Road! Old Park!"*

Kevin tugged at Shenzi's arm and hurried her along. "Let's get the front seat!" He slipped through the crowds at the door and yanked the co-driver's seat door open. Shenzi rapidly swept her guiding stick from side to side in a semicircular motion, clearing the path before her. A woman that attempted to get in sneered and abused Kevin, drawing the attention of the conductor.

"Ei, ei...wassup!" the conductor asked in an exaggerated English accent.

The woman pointed at Kevin, who was now doing his best to lift Shenzi into the front seat, urging her to grab onto the leather strap and hoist herself in.

The conductor watched in amusement and laughed. *"Kale, singa oli muuto, you would have beaten him to it."*

Kevin's gaze swept the scene from conductor to driver. The lean man had an amused glint in his eyes as his jaws ground onto something, then he averted his head to the open window and spat over his arm that rested against the window frame. When he locked eyes with Kevin, he was laughing along with the conductor.

"Madam, just sit anywhere...anywhere." He waved his hand to indicate the back area. The lady, prim in a pale blue suit, glared at Kevin, muttered under her breath, and proceeded to the back with everyone else.

Kevin made sure Shenzi was comfortably hoisted and seated, then swung up to sit next to her. He pulled the door closed, leaning back against it. The conductor's loud calls were strangely comforting.

"Kampala Road! Old Park! Kampala Road...madam! Kampala Road...

.eh, Manager…Old Park!" The taxi filled up slowly.

Gradually, he became aware of the driver's eyes sweeping over him and Shenzi. Shenzi did not sit back…she was upright, stoic like a little statue. He was reminded of their evenings sitting on the roof. He started, *their* roof!

"Yanga, ogenda wa?" where are you going, young boy?

Kevin looked back at him blankly, his mind racing at fifty kilometers per second, adrenaline pumped hot in his blood. "Town," was all he could manage. The instinct to run was imminent.

He could feel the man eye them curiously, chewing in that annoying way that made Kevin want to give him a lesson or two in chewing manners from Mama Rose. The man shifted a little when he leaned in to take a better look at Shenzi. *"Eno muganda wo?" This your sister?*

Kevin nodded.

The driver grunted, leaned his head out the window over his arm, and spat. "You have money?"

Kevin nodded.

The man chuckled, then turned to Shenzi. *"Harro."*

"Hello," Shenzi whispered a response.

Kevin's eyes shot up, sweeping from Shenzi to the driver. He reached for her hand. It was then that the man saw the stick. "Eh *bambi*, she is blind?" He indicated with his hands pointing to his eyes.

"Yes." He wished the questions would stop.

"Where are you going at this time? It's late!"

Kevin felt beads of sweat form, desperation crowded his thoughts, and then his mouth opened, and everything he said surprised him. "We got lost. We came to visit our uncle, but he was not home. We waited, but he did not come, so now we are going to Kampala Road to meet our mother. She is waiting for us there."

"Iyii, at this time?" The driver's half-lit face registered concern.

"She works in a take-away there, and it closes late."

"Oh. Is it Best Take Away? There is a woman there who looks like your sister here." He was peering at them. Kevin clutched Shenzi's hand protectively, then shook his head.

Think, *think*, he told himself, as his mind rummaged through the Kampala Road stretch like a traveler laying out his destination markers on his route. Then he recalled the big, fancy take-away right next to the big, big Pentecostal church. They had the best chips he had ever had. He had only been there once, but he could still taste the salty grease on those fat chips. "No, Diamond Take Away," he said, still surprised at how he was easily making up these stories.

The driver clapped and whooped with energy Kevin envied at that moment. "Huh! Best chicken on Kampala Road! Ayayaya!"

Kevin wished he would stop speaking and they would leave already. Sitting there was making him anxious.

When his attention turned to the conductor, Kevin sighed with relief to see him shutting the door; the taxi was full. Kevin relaxed. He focused his attention on the gear stick, the way the driver moved the rounded knob of the gear stick back and forth. The mini taxi van jolted to life in response. In no time, they were gliding away from the stage onto the dark road spread out before them, lightly illuminated by the headlights of the taxi. He closed his eyes, his hand never letting go of Shenzi, who, huddled between him and the driver, finally leaned back onto Kevin.

The overwhelming feeling of aloneness coupled with a numbing fear engulfed him. There was an entire world out there, and all he had was Shenzi. As they rode silently into the city, Kevin felt tears force their way out of his tightly shut eyes.

For the first time since they had left the place he knew was home, he was aware of three things: he did not know where they were going, they were never going back home, and they were not going to his uncle in Bwaise. He was thankful for the music that blared through the badly tuned speakers, drowning his silent, frightened sobs. Only Shenzi could tell he was crying, for her head rested on his shoulder and her hand on his chest, which rose and fell as he sobbed.

* * *

215

When the taxi dropped them off on Kampala Road, they found a spot along a corridor after the enormous church that stood like a forgiving God. At a significantly conspicuous intersection, a couple of beggars lay sprawled in their corners covered with plastic bags, torn and tattered garments, and old bedding thrown in the dump. Kevin scolded himself for not packing sheets or a blanket for them. The night was warm, so he made a headrest with the bag for Shenzi and lay by her side, holding her hand.

"Kevin, where are we?" she asked for the fifth time.

Kevin swallowed. "We are safe."

"Okay." Her steady breathing moments later indicated she had fallen asleep with her hand tightly entwined in his.

Soon, Kevin followed suit as sleep overpowered him. He dreamed of his father was chasing him down Block 4, a stick in hand and a sharp plank jutting through his body. Blood freely flowed from the wound, but he ran like an experienced hundred-meter sprinter shouting, "I will kill you, too! I will kill you, too," and Kevin ran down the stairs, leaped over them two at a time screaming, "Go away!"

His father laughed a madman's laugh. Kevin could feel him gaining on him, and then he fell. Kevin panicked. The menacing large shape of his father hovered over him. Blood splattered on him. Kevin screamed.

"Get up!" his father shouted.

"Get up! Get up!" The voice melded from a deep growl into a girlish cry.

Kevin sat up, heaving and wheezing. "No, no, no, no." He shook his head.

Shenzi was shaking him.

"You were having a bad dream." Her soft, husky voice bore the strain of a tremor.

"No, no, no," he whispered to himself. The dream lingered and hung over them. He absently rehearsed the dialogue in it when he heard a snicker.

"Kevin," Shenzi whispered. She coiled her arm around his and shifted closer to him. "I don't think we are safe."

Kevin looked up. There were shadowy figures around them, four, maybe five. They looked like children but a lot bigger than them, maybe thirteen or fourteen years old?

"You took our spot," the tallest of them, a tall, lanky, dark-skinned boy, said, stepping forward.

Kevin pulled Shenzi close and moved back. "Says who? I saw no marks," he responded, telling himself these children did not differ from the kids on Block 4. He drew courage from that.

The tall boy roared. "*Oli* funny. Everyone here knows this is *our* spot. Unless you are new and don't know the rules."

"Rules?" Kevin thought about it, his mind going blank. Beggars had rules?

"*Kale*. Leave now." The tall boy inched closer.

Kevin felt his heart leap with panic but held back, telling himself fear was the last thing he would show these people. He got up slowly, picking up the bag and urging Shenzi to stand up. "We are leaving. Let me help my sister. She is blind."

The tall boy cocked his head to one side. "Blind?" The others snickered, a hum of chaotic mischief.

He pointed toward the bag. "What's in there?"

"None of your business!" Kevin hurled the words at him, unsure whether he was underestimating them. His body begged for rest, at least for a few hours. The night was proving to be longer than expected.

The tall boy lunged for him and, in a swift grab, yanked the bag from his hands. Kevin's quick sense was jump-started. He pushed back at the teenager's chest and seized the bag in one swift yank while kicking wildly at the taller boy.

The rest cheered and as fast as the fight had started; it ended with a loud, angry grunt from a man who staggered recklessly toward them. "Wasswa! You again? I am going to kill you and your friends this time! I am…"

"Uh-oh." The taller boy dropped his clutch on the bag and ran, his friends at his heels. They stumbled over other beggars who woke up cursing them.

The boy who they called Wasswa shouted back, "We are not finished, bag boy. I will find you!" They laughed like a pack of hyenas as they disappeared around the corridor.

The man who had called out slumped like a sack of potatoes right where Kevin and Shenzi had slept. In no time, he was snoring loudly enough to wake up the remaining sleeping beggars. Kevin stood there hanging his head, not sure what his next move would be.

"Are we safe? Kevin?" Shenzi was tugging at his shirt hem.

Kevin sighed. He could not disappoint her. He promised to protect her. "Yeah. We shall stay here. Tomorrow, we will find another place." He settled back down next to the snoring man and held Shenzi.

"No one can take this bag," he told her, then thought better of it and removed the money they had in it.

"This money will buy us breakfast tomorrow."

Shenzi nodded, then said, "I have some money too; it's in my nightdress."

Kevin sighed with relief,

"Oh, good!" he whispered back. "Now we will have food for some days."

When he lay back down, the pungent smell of old sweat and alcohol choked the air in their little space. The image of his father, drunk, slurring, beating him and his mother, flashed repeatedly in his mind, and immediately he was sitting upright.

"Shenzi, we have to go," he muttered urgently.

"Why?" She groaned. "I'm tired."

Kevin did not reply. He got up and helped her up, handed her the walking stick, and stared out into the night. It was hard to tell what time it was. He stared out at the alleyway, which opened to two exits. Left or right? Kevin scrunched his nose as he pondered it. Right led them back to the busyness of Kampala Road, and he was wary of anyone who knew them finding them sleeping out in broad daylight. So, *left.* Positioning the backpack on his shoulder, Shenzi's hand in his other hand, he led them out determinedly into the unknown, his heart beating wildly in his chest.

219

Chapter 10

He was uncertain as to whether it was the sunlight streaming through the rafters of the little half-built shack they had stumbled into that woke him up or the droplets of lukewarm water that trickled onto his face.

Shenzi was still asleep. He adjusted the bag under her head and rolled out of their little hiding place to get a better look. He had seen beggars on the street sleeping in wide-open spaces. Their little haven under a mango tree in the middle of the city was much more private than downtown. He became aware of casual chatter not too far from where they had spent the night. On swerving to follow the voices, he spied a man seated at a wooden, cardboard display on stilts that housed samosas and *mandazis.* He was familiar with this setup. They always covered the boxlike wooden display with a glass casing over the top and the side that faced the buyer.

The seller was eating a piece of boiled yam and spoke in rapid Luganda with his companion, a buxom woman who had her braided hair held up in a tight coif. She wore red bathroom slippers and had a *lesu* wrapped around her waist.

The town appeared deserted, and there was still a festive mood in the air. It was obvious most people had not yet returned from the villages where they had gone to celebrate Christmas. Once the fireworks of the New Year died out, Kevin was pretty sure they would be bombarded by human traffic and not enough space for runaways in the city.

He wondered if maybe he should proceed to Bwaise to see if Uncle Benson was around. Then the weight of the previous night's occurrences came crushing down on him, and a horrid dread engulfed him. He panicked. Shenzi! What would he do with her? It wasn't her fault. But then it was too late to go home. He wondered what was happening. Would anyone look for them? Where was his mother?

"Eh!" the man sitting at the stall called out to him, jolting him away from the throng of questions that assaulted his mind.

"Are you lost?" the man asked in Luganda. Kevin stood rooted, not sure what to say.

The woman beside him stirred. "He looks hungry, don't you see?"

The man spat and scoffed. "These beggar children…"

But the woman was peering at Kevin.

"Come!" she called to him. Kevin obeyed. Maybe they would be of some help. She smiled. Her face was a glowing golden brown, her lips as dark as the hands she held out to him.

"How are you? Merry Christmas. Where is your mother? Are you lost?" she enquired with maternal concern.

The man ignored them. With his yam finished, he was gnawing on a cob of roasted maize.

"No, I am not lost," Kevin finally responded. Something about her reminded him of his mother, and he missed her terribly.

The man sneered. "But of course he is not; he must be part of that Big Boy Gang that steals from us!" He waved a hand dismissively then slumped into a torrential vent. "If I see that *ki-boy* Wasswa again, I will cut off his testicles and feed them to those dogs in Kisenyi."

Kevin lit up, seizing the opportunity.

"I know Wasswa. He tried to steal from us last night." He figured if he had an ally for another night or two, he could buy time enough to strategize their next moves.

The man then turned and looked at him curiously. "Hm! And I am supposed to believe you?"

The woman cocked her head to one side. "You and who?" she asked.

Kevin nodded desperately, "My sister and I. We…" *Think* Kevin, *think!*

"We ran away from home. My father drinks and beats us. He does not give us food. So…we ran away." He dropped his gaze piteously, his eyes on his shoes as they dug into the loose earth on the pedestrian walkway.

"*Bambi*," the woman exclaimed sympathetically, then in Luganda continued, "I knew he wasn't a street boy. This one has manners," she was telling the man beside her.

The man was adamant. "These kids are smart. I can't trust him."

Kevin lunged once more. "It's true; my sister is there… and she *is blind*." He emphasized Shenzi's condition, hoping it would sway their hearts.

"*Wanji?*" The woman looked shocked. "Iyyyiiii, what sort of man is that! And your mother?"

Kevin dropped his gaze again. "She died when my sister was four." It amazed him again at how quickly his mind churned out these lies.

The woman *tsk-tsk*ed and asked Kevin to show her his sister. She then helped them freshen up, handing them warm water to wash their faces and rinse their mouths. Upon hard insistence, the man finally gave them samosas and *mandazis*. She brought them each cups of spiced milk tea. Tiny black specks of tea leaves that had escaped the plastic sieve she used to strain it sat on top of the light brown tea.

Kevin weaved a piteous tale of their home situation: a negligent drunken father who abused them regularly until it was too much. He labored to show the bruises he had sustained from his father shoving him, his elbow scars, and even a few on his back.

He could see the man was slowly laying down his guard, even grunting in disapproval at the scars and swellings on Kevin. "Hmm, what about your other relatives?"

Kevin shrugged. "We don't know them." He did not know what else to say. Everyone knew their cousins or uncles and aunts. It sounded ludicrous, but it was the best he could come up with to stop the questions.

The man kept staring at them, frowning. "Your sister? She looks different from you. Sudani *oba* Somali?"

Kevin stared at Shenzi, her head bowed in her cup of tea. Her hair was still held back in the plaits that Teopista had done the night before, medium-size braids that fell to her back with beads at the ends of them.

The woman cajoled the man. "*Nawe, tsk,* they could be steps, not so?"

Kevin nodded in relief.

"Where will you stay now?" the woman continued, asking Kevin.

Kevin sighed, "I don't know. We will stay on the streets for a little while."

The man clapped his hands dramatically. "Ha! You must be tough for these streets, especially if you meet people like Wasswa! Do you know how these streets work? *Oyoyoyoyo!*"

The woman nudged the man. "*Naaweee….* Stop scaring them. *Wama…*"

"Ah-ah, you must tell them the truth," the man interjected. "Boy, *eno* streets *si* easy. If you want to live here, you must pay tax. You pay as you earn…heh!…it's what I heard." He folded his arms across his chest, looking away dramatically. "Big Boy Gang own this whole area." He swept his arms around him indicating from the left to the right. Kevin stared into his cup. His tea was cool enough now, and he sipped silently.

"How do I take his territory?"

"Eh?" The man's eyes widened as if Kevin had asked how far it was to Paris. The woman guffawed.

"How do I take it?" Kevin asked again, surprising himself more and more.

The man sucked his teeth.

"Just drink your tea." The woman hooted with laughter. "My dear don't think about it; do you think you can fight those boys? Look at you."

"He can do anything!" Shenzi cut in, her voice, soft and soothing, held a steely determination, an unshakable faith in Kevin, and he smiled at her with pride. Even if the world did not believe in him, as long as Shenzi did, it was all right.

The man stood akimbo. "*Eeh*? Okay, how? You are small and thin…"

He pointed at Kevin.

"He can beat big boys," Shenzi continued. "Where we used to stay, he would beat them. All of them!"

The man sucked his teeth again. "This is the street. Those boys can kill you. It's not a joke."

The woman sighed. "Hmm. Maybe he can fight, but everyone fears Wasswa. You see, you have to beat him thoroughly in a fight to take his territory…isn't that what they say?" The man nodded, affirming her claim.

"Yeah, you see." She shrugged.

He thought about it long and hard, then glanced at Shenzi.

"I have to protect my sister," he told the man determinedly. "I can work for you. If you give us a place to sleep."

The man laughed and shook his head. "I like this boy. He has guts."

The woman laughed too. "If I did not have children of my own, I would have taken you in, but…I can offer you food and some bedding and clothes. I live there." She pointed to a flat across the road, the marks of time scribbled all over it.

Kevin nodded; it was something. "Thank you." They finished their breakfast in silence and got up to leave.

"Where are you going?" the man asked them.

Kevin shrugged. "To see the city."

"Take care of your sister. I hear the blind people get more money from begging. You should consider putting her to work," he told him. "Also stay away from the Big Boy Gang. They will take her." He was wagging his finger at Kevin.

Kevin nodded, and, taking Shenzi's hand, he led her to the roadside. "Come on, let's explore. Maybe we can find another place for the night, far from the Big Boy Gang."

Her small hand pressed into his. It was comforting. "Those people were kind."

Kevin shrugged. "Yeah, but we don't need anyone else ruling us. It's you and me, and we will make it."

Shenzi nodded.

For the next few days, they took the taxi up and down every route possible from old Kampala to Mengo, from Old Park to Mukono, from New Park to Entebbe, and on a Sunday they went all the way to Jinja, stopped in the town, and ate chips and liver at a little take-away, which took almost an hour to serve them, then hopped in the next taxi back to Kampala. They stopped by the stalls that sold mangoes in plastic bags with pepper and salt, purchasing enough for the day. They also stocked up on pancakes and roasted maize.

At night they slept at the bus park or sometimes returned to the street corner they slept on. Other times, they met the lady who allowed them to take a bath and fed them in her house. Sometimes, Ssuna, the man who sold samosas and mandazis, would give them some of his fresh goods.

While they sipped watery sweet tea, Kevin would indulge them in stories of the places they had gone to: Ggaba beach on a quiet weekday or Entebbe resort, which was hard to get to without transport, so he always begged the men who transported people on bicycles and taxis to help take him and his sister there. He usually bargained down hard. This amused the woman whose name he learned was Grace.

Ssuna would laugh and simply say, "Ahaaa…the street life."

Gradually, Kevin began to enjoy their new life more. Adults were so gullible, Kevin mused, and Shenzi's condition made them even more believable; poster children of abuse. Their story became more dire with each adult they encountered. For as long as he thought about the night of Taata Bob's death, he could pull it off.

Days rolled into weeks, and he was careful to avoid the territory considered the Big Boy Gang grounds. He observed from a distance, asking questions and always watching. Every so often, his mind strayed to his mother and Ameena. No one had come looking for them. Too soon, maybe?

Usually Ssuna bought *The New Vision*. He would hand Kevin leaflets he had finished scouring through. There was nothing about his mother or the death of his father.

"Do you think something wrong happened?" Shenzi asked him. That night they spent on the rooftop of the flat where Grace lived. She brought them old blankets she claimed had become too small for her children and some hand-me-down warm clothes since Shenzi was battling a cold.

Shenzi had huddled close to him, her nose runny. She wiped it on her sleeve.

Kevin mused over her question. "I don't know. I want to find out too. Do you want to go back?" He realized he had never asked her, always making the decisions, and she seemed content going along with it.

After a long silence and a little sniffing, she said, "No, I don't want to see Uncle Mulenzi. Maybe *hooyo* is looking for me?"

"I can find out," Kevin promised her.

The next day, he convinced Grace to keep Shenzi and gave her two thousand shillings for food, promising to return later. He had to do an errand by himself. Grace shook her head. "You…" She wagged a long finger at him. "Okay. Better come back for her. She is not very well."

Kevin promised.

He boarded a taxi for Bugolobi at noon and sat in the very back of the fourteen-seater commuter van right by the window, watching everyone who came in and out at every stop. He recognized a few from his Block and sank in his seat or kept his posture turned toward the window.

When the MTN sign loomed into view at the taxi stage, Kevin sat up gingerly, peering out the window. The passengers filed out, and he merged with them, allowing himself to get lost in the crowd.

He walked through Middle East market and hastened down a winding road that he had discovered with his friends up to the flats. Block 4 came into view: a tall old building of brown and terra-cotta brick, a place he had called home all his life. As he approached the Block, his heartbeat quickened.

What would he find? Was it safe? Did he want to see his mother? The image of his father flashed before his eyes again. Kevin stood rooted on the spot. Huddled beside a limp, slender tree that leaned out onto the dusty road was the famous pancake stall all the children had loved to go to. It stood there, a lone, neglected structure. He frowned. *What happened?*

He shifted his gaze toward Block 4, scanning the parking area for familiar cars. There were none. Not even his father's Suzuki.

Then he saw a silver Toyota amble up to the front entrance of the flats. He crouched low and watched. A tall, well-dressed man got out of the driver's side and went around quickly to open the co-driver's door. He watched as a woman alighted from the seat. Ameena! She was smiling at the man and said something to him before hugging him. The man reached for a kiss, which she responded to in lewd exuberance. Kevin grimaced as he watched the man hungrily grab her behind and clumsily draw her close. Ameena playfully shoved him. This was a man he had never seen before. He let her go and dug into the side pockets of his suit jacket, handing her something. Kevin assumed it was money. He watched the man get back into the car. Ameena waved at him as he backed out of the entrance of Block 4.

Ameena watched the car leave, then proceeded to the brown granule-like stairway. She wore a beautiful pink dress held together by a huge black belt. Kevin watched until she was out of view. It suddenly dawned on him: she had gone on with her life, like nothing was wrong. No one was *missing them,* and his heart sank.

Feeling drained, confused, and angry, Kevin returned to Shenzi and let her know what he had seen, confirming his worst fears: that they only had each other now.

Chapter 11

January 2000

I n the weeks that followed, their excitement mounted as they explored, once daring to go as far as Soroti. They slept between towns wherever they could find a place to: once or twice in a classroom, by secluded houses with empty boys' quarters, and scrambling out before dawn when the owners would awaken. Sometimes, they huddled with other street dwellers. They found the homeless community out of Kampala a lot more welcoming, and when their clothes got too old, Kevin stole a few off washing lines for them both. They mastered walking through the wide-open market, Owino, and stealthily grabbing clothing items from different perimeters as the vendors haggled prices with potential customers. Sometimes they walked off with unimportant items of clothing, which they resold.

To save on the money they had, they dined on fresh mangoes, jackfruit, avocados, and guavas Kevin had plucked from trees wherever they wandered.

Sometimes people came after them with sticks, warding them off like pests. Most times, they stopped upon seeing that Shenzi was blind.

The first time Shenzi begged was in Jinja town. They had passed by a stall with sizzling *muchomo* and their mouths watered, their stomachs rumbled and grumbled, tired of their staple diet of mangoes, guavas, and avocados. Kevin took Shenzi aside and whispered his plan to her.

She nodded in agreement. He then placed her a few feet away from the stall, and Shenzi, with her stick guiding her, walked gingerly toward the stall, piteously asking for a few shillings. Kevin stood by the sidewalk watching the nonexistent traffic in the sleepy town, the old colonial shopping buildings baked in the midday sun like the people that walked from one store to another. He squinted against the sun as he darted glances toward her, then away. Shenzi inched toward the wooden stall, tall and stacked with a barbecue charcoal stove covered with a wrought-iron wire mesh. Shenzi felt her stick hit an obstacle, and her nose told her she was right in front of the stall. She put on her practiced begging pose. "Please…" she said sadly. Kevin watched as the man glanced at her and back at his roasting meat. Shenzi did not move. She stood there tapping her cane against the stall's wooden leg.

"*Eish!*" the man finally responded, irritated. Shenzi was adamant. The man shooed her away with words and his hands, shoving at her shoulder. Kevin watched from the corner of his eye, waiting for the signal.

Then it came.

Shenzi let out a shrill wail as the meat seller tried to shove her one more time. She sucked in a belly full of air and wailed as loud as she could, attracting the attention of passersby and tenants in shops along the street. The stall owner's irritation morphed into surprise, then back to anger.

Kevin made a sprint to the stall and dropped his hands to his knees, bending over, breathing heavily like he had run a relay. "Shenz" He touched her shoulder slightly. Shenzi shook it off, wailing louder. A few onlookers trickled by the stall.

Kevin looked at the stall owner apologetically. "Sorry, my sister is blind."

The stall owner *harrumph*ed. "Go away. Take her away. She is bad for business."

Kevin sucked in air and stretched his hand. "She wants meat. If she doesn't get any, she will not stop screaming. I think you should give her some." He had to shout above Shenzi's wailing.

"Eeeh *Ssebo*, don't you see the child is blind!" scolded a woman who had come out of her store to see what the commotion was about. "One *ka* stick of meat won't kill your business, and God will reward you," continued the woman.

"The man looked torn. "Her brother should take her away!"

Kevin shook Shenzi, and she raised her stick, waving it. The stall owner ducked, so did Kevin.

"Please give her some meat!" Kevin pleaded.

Three more people, then four, six…they pooled and gathered, trickling to the stall, all of them pressuring the man to give the child meat.

Shenzi's wailing did not cease, and Kevin looked on, hanging his head, admiring her act. As the crowd thickened, more people throwing insults at the stall owner and urging him to stop her wailing by giving her meat, Kevin slipped out quietly and rounded the less crowded corner where the meat seller hung sticks of roasted meat dripping with fat straight from the fire.

Kevin glanced at the adults heatedly insulting the stall owner, whose protests were drowned by their voices in competition with Shenzi's own wailing. The distraction was good. He expertly unhooked two of the sticks and rolled them in his oversize T-shirt, then tried his luck for a third. He almost made it, but the stall owner was reaching for two of the sticks hurriedly, acquiescing to the demands of the people. Kevin pulled his hand back quickly.

The tormented seller rolled two sticks of *muchomo* into a newspaper and gave the package to Shenzi, who on raising it to her nose instantly stopped wailing, a smile lighting up her face. The spectators paused, then roared with amused laughter. Kevin took advantage of the moment to gather Shenzi away, hoping the man would not see the awkward way he held his shirt. As they walked away, they could hear someone say, "You see, that did not hurt. The poor children are probably homeless."

The man grumbled and muttered something. When they were far enough away, Kevin and Shenzi scrambled to the back of a building and sat down to eat their spoils.

"That was perfect!"

Kevin clapped Shenzi on the back. She smiled between mouthfuls of meat. "I need water; my throat is dry."

Kevin laughed. "I will get you water."

Begging and stealing became easier. It almost came naturally to Kevin. He was quick-witted and sharp, but even as he masterminded their plans, he was careful Shenzi did not get hurt. If it got too chancy, he promised himself, he would have to figure out a way to make money for them both so she could be safe. He still secretly harbored the idea of going home to find his mother.

He missed his warm bed, and his heart ached for Shenzi, usually leaving her up on the roof of Grace's apartment building while he went out by himself. They had more escapades as they begged for food and money throughout Jinja, and when they tired of Jinja, they took the next taxi back to Kampala.

"Where do you want to go?" he asked Shenzi.

"Wandegeya! I feel like chicken tonight!" Shenzi threw her arms in the air in excitement.

"Again?" She chuckled when Kevin groaned. "We had chicken yesterday and the other day..."

"I want chicken or I will scream."

That sent them both into peals of laughter.

They made their way to Wandegeya's busy center and purchased two brown bags filled with piping-hot chips and chicken.

As they tucked into their meal on the steps of a restaurant long closed, they did not notice the youthful, masculine figures of five boys walking along the pedestrian strip until they were standing in front of them. One of them dropped to his haunches and laughed. "Look what we have here!" He whooped at the four behind him.

Kevin had completely forgotten to keep watch and now stared back into the eyes of his nemesis, Wasswa. He made no immediate move, his mind working faster than his limbs, scrambling for ideas and a plan to get out of this situation. Not for his sake, but for Shenzi's.

"What do you want?" he asked, needing to stall them. In the months they had been out in the streets, he had heard the terrible stories of Wasswa of the Big Boy Gang. He had avoided them for Shenzi's sake.

Wasswa unfolded his arms, put one on his hip, and pointed toward the rucksack they had, which had all their little knickknacks and clothes.

"That," Wasswa said, his voice tittering on the edge of manhood, yet his boyhood peeked through when he spoke.

Kevin caught a whiff of his sweaty odor, armpits so pungent, he wrinkled his nose. He raised his brows, pretending not to know what he was pointing at. "What?" he asked stupidly.

The other boys grumbled. Wasswa smiled, his teeth a shocking white in the dim light. He tilted his head to one side and motioned. "That one thinks he is strong," he said to the boy next to him, slightly shorter. When the boy next to him laughed, Kevin was astonished at the bass in his voice.

One of the other boys jeered, "Let's teach him a lesson!"

Wasswa raised his arm to silence his boys. "Small boy," he sneered at Kevin, "we want *that* bag…. *And* that girl."

Kevin was on his feet faster than they could back up. With his fists balled, he stepped closer to the boys. "Okay. But you will have to fight me for both." He spat out the words.

The boys all laughed.

"He thinks he can fight us all." Wasswa was laughing. He bent over, his head level with Kevin's. The smile on his lips registered amusement, and his odor filled Kevin's nostrils, tinged with something familiar that danced around his mind fleetingly refusing to register. "Okay, step aside, and let us have what we want."

Kevin did not move. "You will have to fight me for *my* sister and *our* bag."

Wasswa made an *oooh* sound, and the rest laughed.

That odor…

"I like him; he has balls." One boy spoke up.

"Shut up, anus!" Wasswa dismissed the boy who had spoken. "This one here will eat his own shit soon."

"You will eat yours first!" Kevin sneered.

Kevin and Wasswa stared each other down. Then Wasswa spoke: "Your sister, she is blind."

"So?"

Wasswa and the others burst out laughing, "This is the streets. It's our business to know what happens and who comes into it."

Wasswa continued, "Now…we have been watching you, you two make a good team, but…I think you can survive alone without her. She will make our gang rich."

"She goes everywhere I go, so if you want her, you must fight me to get to her."

From the corner of his eye, Kevin could tell Shenzi was nervous by the way she sat bolt upright, like a little statue.

"It's okay." His voice dropped comfortingly in her direction.

"Indeed, we will fight." Wasswa's voice took on a serious and threatening tone.

And Kevin instantly recalled why the musky smell on him was so familiar. Uncle Silver Mulenzi!

He laughed. "All I see is you standing. What are you waiting for, son of a whore!" He mocked.

The older boy reacted like an ignited engine. He swung a fist with all his might but missed. Adrenaline raced through his veins, pumping into his limbs and blocking his ears and eyes to everything but the boy before him. Kevin ducked and threw a quick punch into Wasswa's belly, then jumped back, poised for a second round.

Wasswa let out a strangled laugh. "For a shorty…" he started.

Kevin puffed. A good fight did not involve dialogue, and already he could tell the older boy was a bigger bully for saying so much and doing so little. He cut him mid-sentence by kicking his left knee in, propelling him forward as he struggled to gain composure. The boys cheered.

He faintly heard Shenzi call him, but he watched the boys edging toward Wasswa. As Wasswa stumbled, Kevin jumped onto his back and bit into his neck. Wasswa howled in pain and thrashed violently, trying to throw Kevin off his back. Kevin leaped off as agilely as he had leaped on and in swift movements punched Waswa in the ribs, then kicked the back of his knees in.

The other boys did nothing but cheer. At first, they called out Wasswa's name, but as Kevin rained down punch after punch, the cheer code name became "Shorty! Shorty!" Wasswa, being at the disadvantage of height, missed a good number of times, and now that he was hurt, his swings were slower, and he was not as focused. Kevin pranced around him like a cat concentrating on its prey, making sure he kept it defeated, played with it.

"Assholes!" Wasswa called painfully, and the cheering stopped. By this time, bystanders had gathered.

"Let's go!" One of the Big Boy Gang members called out as attention drawn to them was raising numbers and infuriated voices. "The police will come for us!" They grabbed Wasswa, who was groaning and rubbing his neck. He glared at Kevin as he limped off. "This is not over!"

"I will be waiting!" Kevin shouted back at the boys as they retreated to the traffic lights and rounded the corner.

The crowd slowly dissipated, and Kevin was left alone with Shenzi on the step they were seated on. Shenzi reached out her hand to him, and he took it.

"Are you hurt?" she asked

"No," Kevin lied. One of Wasswa's random blows had caught the side of his head. It throbbed and was swollen to the touch.

"Kevin, those boys are dangerous. They could…they could…"

"No one touches you unless I say so. No one takes you away from me unless I say so!" he replied passionately, and Shenzi knew from the angry tremor in his tone, it was final. "I will protect you," he added more calmly.

He had not taken Wasswa's words lightly. A wounded bully always retaliated with a malicious vengeance.

* * *

Kevin was vigilant for weeks, calculating their moves, watchful, careful. He often gave Grace a little money they made from begging off the steps of KPC, the church building that sat right in the center overlooking the roundabout on Kampala Road. When they had enough money, they treated themselves to ice cream from Chippers, always selecting the same flavors: strawberry for Shenzi, vanilla for himself.

At the end of each week, they made a trip to Tipsy Takeaway and had their fill of chips and liver, sometimes chicken. Once or twice Kevin ducked from someone he knew from Block 4, and once or twice someone came up to him asking him what he was doing on the street. He often slipped away. When Shenzi begged on the steps of the church or around the back entrance, he hung around watching for any member of the Big Boy Gang, making sure she was safe.

He thought more and more of his mother but less of the trip he would have to make to see her, so he postponed it for better days, when he did not feel the pangs of guilt anymore. It would be better then, he told himself. But for now, they would survive until something happened.

Chapter 12

August 2000

The rains started in late August, and everyone said it was a surprise for rain to fall in August; the seasons were changing, and people puzzled over it. He heard someone say "global warming" and another speak of the "devastating deforestation that was happening in their natural forests like Mabira."

The pesky rains were not good for street dwellers; they fell sicker more from long exposure to the cold temperature that accompanied the rains. Their bodies became enticing meals for relentless mosquitoes, which sang merry tunes in their ears each evening and latched onto their bare bodies, sucking the life out of them.

Kevin would spend half the nights waving his hands wildly in the air to chase mosquitoes or slapping against his bare legs to kill any that had locked on. He grinned in triumph when he raised his palm to the streetlight, revealing a splatter of blood and smashed black insect body, mangled beyond recognition. Other times, he missed and waited until he felt another stinging itch. He sacrificed his plastic covers and half-torn blanket for Shenzi; she was ill more often than him, causing him to worry.

One night, the drizzle started just as he was falling asleep. Kevin quickly woke Shenzi up, and when she resisted with a whimper, he carried her to a veranda on the backside of a house. They had moved farther from the city center to avoid a run-in with the Big Boy Gang. Kevin had not minded a confrontation, but Shenzi's growing agitation was rubbing off on him, so they took a taxi toward Mengo and alighted at the first stop. It was not as lucrative a begging area as the town center was, but they found better sleeping options, from verandas to tool sheds and empty garages, often stealing away before the first rays of sunlight kissed the earth.

The drizzle quickly evolved into heavy drops, falling fast and furious, lashing against their bodies. Shenzi gasped awake, calling Kevin.

"I am here," he told her as he drag-carried her toward a house whose front porch was infested with white ants flying rapidly around the single bulb. Kevin had always wondered what seduced ants and grasshoppers from their havens on rainy days, the lights or the rain? The front porch proved too conspicuous because of the security light, so he made for the back of the house, his shoes squelching as the rainwater soaked him. Shenzi held on tightly to his neck, her legs wrapped around his waist, her head buried in his shoulder. She could hear him breathe with a little effort as his skinny frame carried them both to a drier place to rest.

Thankfully, the back of the house had an extended slab for the backdoor, wide enough for them to snuggle up. He held Shenzi close to provide body warmth.

"Are you cold?" he asked, worried she would fall sick; she had only just recovered from a bout of cough.

She shook her head, but Kevin knew she did this so he would not worry. That night, he hardly slept. It rained till morning and the sky was gloomy and gray, the light of the sun smothered by threatening dark clouds. When he jolted awake, his eyes felt grainy and his head hurt. Shenzi had slumbered on his lap, stretching her little body over his legs. Kevin groaned, pins and needles coursed down his limbs, and he cursed the rain. They needed to find a better place to sleep so he could sleep a little longer, he was thinking, when the back door suddenly opened, hitting his elbow. He yelped and the person who opened it suppressed a scream, instantly shutting the door.

Kevin tried to gather up Shenzi, but the sensation of pins and needles and a peculiar numbness slowed his progress. His body begged for rest, but his mind insisted on flight.

"Shenzi, Shenzi." He shook her lightly. "Wake up."

She stirred and stretched. "Hmm?"

"We have to go; these people are awake."

As much as she protested in her sleep in the night, she almost always obediently responded to "we need to go" instructions.

But this time, she took her time sitting up. He could see her shiver and reached out to rub her arms. "We will get dry clothes soon."

The door opened as they scrambled to their feet. "Hey, boy!" It was a woman; her voice sounded stuffy like she had a cold.

Kevin ignored her, grabbing Shenzi's hand.

"Boy!" the woman said louder and grabbed his shirt collar from behind.

Kevin tried to wriggle free from her. "Leave me! We are leaving!" He felt grumpy and moody for lack of sleep.

The woman did not leave him alone. "Where are your parents?" she demanded.

"We don't have any." He wriggled out of her hold and turned to look at her. He held Shenzi's hand tightly.

She was a large woman with kind eyes. Her hair was still covered in a hairnet, and she had a shawl thrown over her long white nightdress. She looked around and then at the sky and back at them, then she said something Kevin did not expect: "You are both wet; come in."

Kevin had gotten used to people kicking them off their verandas, street corners, and garages with anything they could. The only people who had been kind were Grace and Ssuna.

Kevin hesitated and the woman said again, "This rain is bad. Come in or you will be sick like me." She stood back against the narrow back door and Kevin gingerly guided Shenzi in, comfortingly letting her know they were entering a house and he would protect her.

The woman laughed, amused. "I don't eat children." Then she led them through her dining room, past the living room, to another corridor that held what looked like a bedroom to one side and a door that was closed on the opposite side. The corridor dipped into a bathroom.

"You need to wash up," she said, then asked him, "Your sister?"

Kevin nodded. Since they had been on the street, Shenzi's nakedness and hair were no longer a mystery. When she had diarrhea, he cleaned her up. When she vomited and stained her clothes, he undressed and washed her.

The woman told him to wait, went to the second room with a closed door and came back with two towels.

"Wash yourself and your sister. I don't have small clothes for children but…." She was tapping her lower lip in thought. "I think…" she trailed off, "I have some things for the orphanage." She was speaking to herself and went off again.

"Where are we?" Shenzi was asking Kevin as he lathered soap into her thick, messy hair. He was sure they would have to visit a barber soon before lice migrated to the matted forest on her head. He shuddered to think of them having to deal with lice again or for her hair to look like the madman's that shouted profanities with his junk hanging out of his torn trousers outside Bat Valley Primary School. The other street people called him *Rasta*, often laughing at him for his theatrical antics. He was quite the spectacle, flailing his arms and shouting at anyone who passed by him or running after women while he grabbed at his exposed phallus.

"A kind woman's house. Now, we will smell good for a while," he told her as he scooped water in his hands from the basin beside which Shenzi squatted and let the warm water drip through his hands over her hair, then rubbed it in, repeating it over and over until there were no more soap suds forming or running down her face.

"We need to cut your hair again; it grows so fast."

Shenzi sighed. "I hate cutting it," she protested.

"But we have to. I hate it when we get lice."

They were done and toweled down, and the lady, now wearing a white nightgown over her nightdress, handed them clothes. "Here. These are donations I got for the orphanage on my church runs. I am sure they won't miss these items of clothing."

Kevin looked at the pair of jeans and T-shirt with a Spiderman picture. He helped Shenzi into her own pair of snug pants that were a little long for her and a floral dress top that fit her perfectly. All scrubbed and clean, Kevin smiled, thinking of how pretty she looked.

When they were all dressed, the lady ushered them to the dining table, where bowls of porridge sat steaming. She had some milk tea and bread laid beside the porridge.

"Eat." She motioned for them to sit.

Kevin ate but watched her suspiciously. The woman looked up repeatedly, approvingly from a book she was reading. Kevin peered at the cover.

"*Good Morning, Holy Spirit?*" he read out aloud.

The woman sniffed and rubbed her nose with a wrinkled pale blue handkerchief. "Yes, it's a story about Pastor Benny Hinn. Have you heard of him?"

Kevin shook his head and ate his porridge.

"Why did you help us?" he asked instead.

"Let's start with names. I am Charity." She was smiling. "What are your names?"

Kevin hesitated, looking over at Shenzi, who was picking at her porridge. "I'm Kevin and she's Shenzi."

"Hmm, Shenzi? Interesting."

"So?" Kevin cut in impatiently. "Why help us?"

"Because you are outside in the rain. Because colds are nasty and because it's what Jesus would do."

Kevin raised an eyebrow, not sure how to respond to that, so he ate his bread.

A pregnant silence reigned as spoons clinked the sides of bowls. Then she spoke. "I work at Kampala Pentecostal Church with the Watoto Children's Choir, and we also run an orphanage. I am an assistant director at one of the homes. That is also why I invited you in. You see, as a Christian, if I see anyone in need, God would be happy if I helped them. That's why I helped you. I think God brought you here for a reason."

She was smiling like she had found a long-lost relative. Even though he kept himself guarded, Kevin could not help sensing a genuineness about her.

"What reason?"

She seemed to be waiting for that question because she put down the book and turned to face them both. A little light danced in her eyes. "Would you want to have a proper home?"

Kevin averted his gaze to Shenzi. She was taking a little bite of the buttered bread and chewing delicately, lips pressed together, her little jaws and cheeks moving silently as she ate. He sighed. Maybe this Charity was right. He was worrying more and more for Shenzi, sickness, the Big Boy Gang.

"A home?" He bit into his bread again.

"Yes, you will be with other children, learn about God's love, have new friends, go to school, and also you might get adopted."

The last part caught his interest. "Adopted by who?"

The woman shrugged. "So many people don't have children, some from Uganda and most from outside the country...so..."

"Wait, people come from other countries to adopt children?" he asked with a frown.

She nodded. "Yes."

A slow smile crept up Kevin's face. "I think you are right. God brought us here for a reason."

Chapter 13

September 2000
Kampala, Uganda

Hardly a month had gone by, and Kevin already hated the orphanage.

The rules were so linear, and he longed for freedom. They had breakfast at eight, did chores at ten, and then had classes from eleven till one when they ate lunch, then classes till four, evening tea and the after-class activities were not exciting: pottery or dancing or singing. Sometimes they played football, and that was when he was excited about being in the orphanage. The only thing he was grateful for was they had a shower every day, comfortable beds and food.

He saw Shenzi during lunch and after classes, when they could be in the compound of their homestead. Since they were of different ages and sexes, they had been placed in different quarters, and they only mingled during Sunday school time, after classes, and at breakfast. Those stolen moments were precious. Even so, he wanted to be sure she was fine. They had given her a new stick to guide her.

"Are you happy?" was his constant question.

"I miss you," was her constant response.

"Me too. At least you won't fall sick a lot, and, like Charity said, maybe we will get adopted by a rich family from America or England, and we will get out of here, eh?" He tried to be animated.

Shenzi smiled and said nothing.

With less time to think of survival, Kevin thought more about his mother. There had been no news from her or any of his family since he left.

The tail end of August found him restless, thinking of his mother. He decided to see her. So, on a Saturday after chores, when they had the afternoon to themselves, Kevin stole out from a wide tear in the wire fence on the far end of the playground they all converged on and made for the road. He hopped into a taxi that took him three stops to another taxi bound for Bugolobi.

The ride to his home was like walking down memory lane. Dread and fear imploded on the inside of him like a sudden heavy downpour. The sheer force of these emotions ripped open the scars; he bled afresh: the anger, the pain, the humiliation. His eyes clouded and he blinked back the tears.

His chest heaved with the uncanny weight that ground against his ribs and lungs, forcing him to gasp for breath. He clutched the tartan shirt he wore and swallowed, wincing. What would he tell his mother? The image of his father lying with the wooden leg jutting through his body, his eyes wide open, his mouth twisted in an unnatural death-grin was an imprinted logo etched somewhere in his mind as if with a hot branding rod. He did not realize he was already at the Bugolobi stage until the conductor called out Kampala Road once again and the taxi emptied. Kevin jumped out and stood by the airtime stall hesitantly. It was a warm early afternoon, just like the afternoons when all the Block 4 children lingered out to play till late. He thought of Bosco, Marjorie, and all the other children. He wondered what life was like now.

Kevin hesitantly took his first steps toward the dusty road leading up to the light brown flats that loomed ahead. He darted his eyes left and right, praying he would remain invisible to those who knew him.

"Kevin?" It was a voice he recognized. He wheeled around. "Kevin!" Teopista ambled to him. She carried an enormous shopping bag in one hand, and her free hand swung wildly at her side. Kevin froze.

"Kevin Byamukama? Oh my goodness, where have you been?" She approached him, dropping her bag and holding him in a half-hug. She smelled faintly of fried dough and a floral aqua perfume. He choked down a sob as he thought of her mandazis and the rooftop. The gnawing ache in his heart grew. He just wanted to be home. "I am so sorry." Her face dropped a look of pained sympathy.

Kevin nodded, not sure what to say.

"Where have you been?"

"Where is my mother?" he asked instead.

Teopista sighed deeply. "Hm, those are things we don't talk about on the wayside. Come." She beckoned to him and waddled away toward a bench. "Eh, this bag is heavy," she complained as she placed it down and sat on the bench propped against a makeshift take-away. She motioned for him to sit, wiping her brow and forehead with the sleeve of her blouse.

"Kevin, hmm I don't know what happened that night but…" She was shaking her head like a woman about to break the worst news ever. "They took your mother to prison, for *Mwami* Byamukama's death."

Kevin felt his head spin; his throat closed and he choked. "No!"

Teopista looked at him surprised. "Eh?"

He did not realize he had balled his hands into fists.

"I am so sorry; I don't…"

Kevin could not help heaving. "Where did they take her?"

"Luzira…I can take you…"

Kevin shook his head. He got up mechanically, walking back to the stage. He wanted to run and hide. Guilt ate at him more rapidly than it did earlier, threatening to consume him completely.

"Kevin!" Teopista was calling. "I have your things at my house…. Kevin!"

He was running now, running away from it all. He did not want to hear or see anyone from Block 4. The weight of his guilt bowed his head and back. He got into the taxi, without looking back, and was glad when it left the stage toward Kampala Road as soon as he sat.

"I am not ready," he told himself. "I am not ready."

He got back to the orphanage and complained he had a tummy ache. "Can I see my sister?" He curled up in the infirmary bed, glad to be away from the others. Here he could mull over things without interruption.

"They said you were not well." Shenzi's soft voice roused him from his dark thoughts, and he turned on his side to face her, his hands behind his head as he looked up at the blue ceiling of the infirmary.

"My mother is in prison," he blurted out to Shenzi.

"Aunty Dina?" Shenzi hissed out in shock as she plopped onto the bed.

"I did it, Shenzi. It's my fault." He cleared his throat as his voice broke. He let out a shaky breath.

Kevin was inconsolable, and all Shenzi could do was sit by his bed silently. Her presence was all the company he needed, the silence between them comforting, just like on Block 4.

"I can't stay here anymore." She heard the strain in his voice and was saddened. Since coming to the orphanage, she could sense his restlessness. She liked it there. It was better than home. There were friends to play with. Aunty Charity (she insisted they call her Aunty) always brought her something at the end of her classes and spoke with her. She did not want anyone touching her hair, so it was trimmed short. She liked to wake up to breakfast; she longed for the lunch bell and hardly kept still for evening tea when she could be with Kevin.

Why would he want to leave?

"Where will we go?" she asked instead.

"Maybe get adopted soon. But I cannot stay here. I can't." His words were heavy, laden with sorrow that broke her heart. Shenzi reached out and hugged him.

Kevin hugged her back. She felt skinnier, and her hair was a tuft of soft curls plastered on her scalp. He was glad he had her. "I have no one," he mourned.

"But I am here. And now you want to leave?" Shenzi said quickly. She did not want him to think she had abandoned him, ever.

"But, I…I have hurt people."

"Not me; you are still my only friend and brother."

She shrugged, and he marveled at her strength and held her tighter, convinced that without her he might have done something irrational. But her calm peacefulness pervaded his troubled soul and soothed him.

"We have to be together," she told him. He agreed. It was the only thing that made sense.

***

It was a nice sunny afternoon when the Matthews spied the little dark-skinned skinny girl in a denim pinafore and plastic pink shoes leaning against the railings of the church building; her medium curly afro glistened with that fresh-oiled look, and she smiled at something the boy seated by her side was saying.

Kevin was describing the streets and the people to Shenzi. In his comical way, he exaggerated it, and she laughed loudly, then clasped a hand over her mouth. Kevin noticed them first as they lingered and smiled at them both.

"Shenzi, there are two *bazungu* looking at us," he whispered to her conspiratorially.

"Really?"

"Hmm-mm, they are now coming toward us," he whispered to her.

Shenzi felt for his shoulder and gingerly sat herself down next to him on the steps.

"Wait and see," he told her between closed lips like a ventriloquist and reached out his hand in begging fashion, a forlorn look in his eyes. "Please give us some money; we are hungry."

The couple looked at each other and smiled. They were not buying it.

"Where are your parents?"

Kevin remained relentless in his begging stance. "We have no parents; they died…it's…just me and my sister."

The couple exchanged glances again.

"And my sister is blind; it's hard for us to…survive," he added, his voice falling with dramatic effect, a begging style he had mastered effortlessly from watching the other beggars.

The man seemed unconvinced. "Hmm. You don't look poor to me."

"It's because we live in an orphanage. But we are hungry." Shenzi breathed out the words delicately. Kevin resisted the urge to nudge her.

The white lady was staring at Shenzi sympathetically. "What's your name?"

Kevin replied for them both: "She is Shenzi and I am Kevin."

The woman smiled, glanced at him, and crouched low to be level with Shenzi. "Aren't you adorable? Tell you what. We will take you to the restaurant over there, and you can have anything you want."

Kevin's eyes widened. Finally! Something that was not orphanage food.

"Shenzi, you hear?" He nudged her. She nodded.

"Do you want to…?" he asked her when they heard a familiar voice… Charity.

"Shenzi, Kevin, we need to get back." They both groaned.

"But…" Kevin protested. They were so close to a delightful meal.

"No *buts*; let's go. The van is already running. You know how Paul gets when he has to wait too long," she was telling them, urging them up on their feet. It was then she noticed the white couple. "Sorry, I hope they did not bother you."

The blond, petite woman shook her head. "No, it was no bother, and we were hoping to treat them to an early dinner." She smiled at Charity, who smiled back. Kevin lingered, listening and watching. There seemed hope. He nudged Shenzi discreetly.

"Thank you, but the orphanage does not allow…"

The man beside her interjected, "Oh that's all right; we did not know the protocol; we saw them and they asked for money…"

Kevin's eyes widened. Why did he have to tell her!

"Kevin! Shenzi!" Charity fixed Kevin with a stern look; embarrassment crossed her face. "I…I'm sorry…"

"It's no problem, really. I am Richard and this is my wife, Maxine. Would it be possible to seek permission to take the children for lunch sometime?" He waved away the awkwardness as if he was used to this. Kevin found this interesting. Maybe they traveled a lot and saw many begging people; this could explain why they were not easily convinced.

He wished Charity would let them linger, but she was ushering them into the wide doors of the church. "Take Shenzi to the van." He took Shenzi's hand and made hesitant steps into the building. He was glad the couple wanted to see them again. He had prayed every night for someone to adopt them. This could be it.

While he led Shenzi through the hallway with people crisscrossing their path, he dropped to her pace. From time to time, he looked over his shoulder to see the white couple intently listening to something Charity was saying. When he glanced over one more time, Charity was handing the White man a brochure. He knew it; it was one for the orphanages, and he beamed.

Two days later, the white couple took them to lunch, asking them many questions about their lives and their background. Kevin responded to all of them, while Shenzi stuffed herself with chaps and chips, nodding in agreement to everything Kevin said.

When they met after classes, they dreamed about their marvelous future.

"How many cars, Shenzi?"

"Now I want twenty." She grinned.

"Twenty cars? Oh my God, Shenzi...okay! In America, they must have nice cars!"

They had more lunches with the Matthews for the next two weeks as they waited for something to happen. Kevin worried again. What if they were simply buying them lunch just because they wanted them to eat better? That was until Charity called them in one afternoon to let them know there was an American couple interested in adopting them. Then he relaxed.

"There is only one thing," she added, and he held his breath. "They cannot adopt you both at once."

Kevin frowned. "Why?"

Charity scrunched her nose. "They say the paperwork for both of you will be different. Shenzi is a blind girl…younger. You are older, with no disabilities and a boy." She leaned forward in her chair so her arms rested on the old hard desk.

"They feel Shenzi needs more help and care urgently. They want to see if they can help her get medical care for her eyes. It all costs money. Then they will file for you. If you can wait…maybe six months or eight?"

Charity clasped her hands together. Then she added, "I am telling you because you are very close, and you don't want to be separated, but it will be for a short time."

It took a moment for both the delight and disappointment to sink in. On one hand, Shenzi would be okay; on the other hand, they would be apart.

He had been gazing at the gray carpet while she spoke. He almost missed it when she called his name: "Kevin?"

He looked up at her, then at Shenzi by his side, who had not said a word, and nodded. "You say only six months?"

"Six to eight, that's what they proposed."

"Shenzi?" He turned to her. There was silence as Charity and Kevin waited.

"It is okay, I will talk to her," he assured Charity, who nodded compassionately.

Later that day, he brought up the subject of her adoption.

"I don't want to," Shenzi told him pointedly. They were alone at the playground, seated on the swings.

"Shenzi, we prayed for this, remember? Well, you prayed more…that we get adopted. These *bazungu* seem like nice people. They will come for me. You need it more than me for now." He pleaded with her. Since he had heard his mother was in prison, he had battled thoughts of leaving the orphanage, going back on the streets to make enough money so they could leave. The more he thought about it, the more impossible a feat it became. He wondered how grown-ups managed life with children and jobs. His job prospects were as slim as any other ventures he dreamed of getting into. There was clearly no way an eleven-year-old could save anyone. The option of waiting some months seemed nothing compared to waiting their whole life on the street or at an orphanage.

Shenzi sulked. "I won't see you for a long time."

"No, it's not, only six months, eight months."

"What if it's longer?" she insisted.

"Aunty Charity did not say it would be longer than eight months," he told her, trying to convince her. "Please, Shenzi, go with them. We will be together after a short time. You will see; time will fly."

It took two more days and a tad bit more convincing before Shenzi agreed to the adoption.

Mid-September 2000 found Kevin seated next to Shenzi in the director's office, listening to the low buzz of the fan as its head swiveled left and right, blowing whiffs of golden hair off Maxine Matthews' face. The couple had their eyes glued to the slim paperwork in front of them. They double checked with each other, nodded, put pen to paper, and in less than ten minutes were smiling in what Kevin saw as accomplished demeanors on their faces. "Right! We should celebrate!" Mr. Matthews was saying, his eyes sweeping from one child to the other.

They had dinner with the Matthews at Nile Hotel. Shenzi's mood had been fluctuating since morning; she swayed between excitement and fear, adamant refusal and acceptance but mostly uncertainty. "Will we be together? Promise?"

Kevin hugged her. "I promise. I swear. We will always be together, and we will do everything together, and we will take over the world together." And he meant it.

Shenzi smiled, comforted in that promise.

"Okay," she responded, reassured.

The day Shenzi left, Kevin spent every moment with her. He helped her pack a little bag that they gave her at the orphanage.

"Don't forget the other slippers," she kept telling him, and he scoffed.

"You are going to America! They have better slippers!"

Charity took Kevin to Entebbe airport the afternoon the Matthews boarded British Airways back to Washington, DC, where they lived.

"I can't wait for you to come, " Shenzi was telling him as he hugged her one last time.

Kevin nodded. "We will always be together," he told her hopefully.

With Shenzi between them, the Matthews waved to Charity and Kevin and turned as they entered to check in at Entebbe International Airport.

"How far is America?" Kevin asked Charity as they drove out of the airport.

"Oh," she exclaimed, "so far that when it is daytime here, it is nighttime there." Kevin frowned, not fully comprehending the phenomenon of time zones.

She smiled. "It's okay; you will go there, and you will see."

Kevin turned back to stare at the airport, pressing his nose against the vehicle's window. "I will go there. I will." He spoke resolutely.

BOOK 3

Kevin and Shenzi/Kenzi

2000–2015

"And one by one the nights between our separated cities are joined to the night that unites us."
—Pablo Neruda

Chapter 1

September 2000
Dulles International Airport, Virginia

The plane grumbled and ambled along the runway like a fat woman in heels trying to steady her steps on a pedestrian sidewalk filled with potholes and loose gravel. Shenzi jumped and gasped, gripping her seat arms with both hands.

Maxine Matthews, slim and golden-haired with puckered lips filled out with pale lip gloss, reached out, placing a reassuring hand over Shenzi's dark smooth little ones.

"You are okay, honey," she whispered.

"It's the takeoff thing. Used to make me jumpy as a kid too," Shenzi heard Mrs. Matthews say.

"It's okay, kiddo. Nothing will happen to you. We are here." Mr. Matthews was gently patting her shoulder.

Shenzi was not sure about it. It was her first time aboard a plane, and all sentiments of excitement fizzled. Her heart bounced from excitement to anxiety and a deep sadness.

"Kevin?" she whispered.

"Oh darling, Kevin will come join us someday, won't he, honey?"

Richard Matthews nodded and reached for Shenzi's hand.

"Uh-huh. He will be here soon; you will see. You like that?"

Shenzi did not know if they expected her to thank them or to smile.

So she focused on calming her breathing and shut her eyes as she waited for the moment to pass.

"It will be all right soon; you will see. Promise. Can't wait to introduce you to your brother and sister." The woman sounded excited.

"You have the earplugs?" her husband was asking.

"Oh, yes…" Shenzi could hear the shuffling movements of someone searching for something in a bag, then it stopped. "Got them!"

"Now hold still. I am going to put these in your ears. It should help with the pressure when the plane lifts off, okay?" the man spoke.

Shenzi swallowed, taking in a deep breath, and nodded. He nuzzled soft, rubbery objects into her ears.

"Is that comfortable enough?" Mr. Matthews asked again.

Shenzi nodded.

He patted her hand and sat back. Maxine checked her safety belt to make certain they had strapped her in right.

"Now relax; we will be home soon," she said.

Shenzi could tell she was smiling from the tone of her voice. Picking up on human nuances was as breezy as a fish breathing through gills. Being blind came in handy, especially on the streets; her heightened senses became their getaway ticket when Kevin and she raided goods from the other street children on their turf.

The plane lifted off the ground, and despite the buds, Shenzi felt the queasiness in her belly and the faint lightheadedness. With every height level they mounted, the sensation of being in a box that was falling gripped her. She held on to the seat and muffled a groan. She badly wished Kevin was with her. She regretted coming without him, but he had told her, "Go with them; they will come for me, and we will be together again."

"But I won't see you for a long time," she had whined. He had hugged her and smoothed back her hair clumsily. "No! They told me before this year ends."

Shenzi had held on to him like she would never let go. "What if I don't see you again?"

"You will. I promise."

"And you will get me new eyes?" she whimpered.

"Yes!" he replied, enthused.

"And a house and a car, and we will live in Jamaica? Go to Germany to watch football and…"

"Yes," he had interrupted. "We will always be together. It's you and me. Always."

After a moment's silence, she sighed with an edge of reluctance. "But I don't want to go; I don't know them."

"But they are nice. They bring us food, toys, and books. They like us. You won't have to starve anymore Shenzi."

"But you are taking care of me." She was adamant.

Kevin had sighed impatiently, and she knew he was trying, and it was hard for him, for both of them.

"I will always take care of you. But we need a new home. We can't go home. These *bazungu* are nice. I can see it. Please, Shenzi, promise me you will go with them."

And now, here she was, two days later, on her way to a country she and Kevin had only talked about when they dreamed together, idling the hours away on Block 4 rooftop while the sun made its mundane trip to hibernate.

She kept her eyes closed for a long time, long after the plane steadied in the air. The voice of the air hostess announcing drinks to be served and Maxine asking her what she wanted got her attention.

"Fanta," she replied.

The twenty-hour trip should have been exciting. Shenzi realized that when they stopped for a layover in Amsterdam and all her adopted parents could say to her was, "Aren't you excited, honey? We will take more plane trips once in the United States. We will go to Disney; will you like that?"

Shenzi did not know what Disney was, and this plane trip was already getting on her nerves. She just wanted to sleep and wake up when it was all over. She missed Kevin even more. The fear of losing him terrified her, and the feeling mounted steadily.

When her new parents weren't being excitedly chatty about the trip or their home and how she would enjoy it, she would quip, "Will Kevin come and live with us too?" or, "Will Kevin come soon?"

They always replied with enthusiastic yeses.

The atmosphere about her smelled unfamiliar; there were buzzing sounds, chattering in different-crescendo tones, rising and falling. Somewhere a baby would cry, or children would giggle. The languages were unfamiliar too; some were English, and others sounded fascinatingly alien. For a little while, she curiously listened, tuning in to everything around her at the airport terminal. Richard brought her something to eat. When she bit into it, she made a face at the savory, creamy, and doughy taste of a hotdog. She spat it out.

"Oh, it's a hotdog, honey; you don't like it?" the woman was saying.

"A dog!" she exclaimed, alarmed.

"No, no, no, not a real dog. It's the name of the meat…err…like a sausage…and you put it in a bun with mustard and ketchup…"

But Shenzi was already shaking her head, her lips twisted; besides the texture made her nauseous.

"What do you want to eat? Err…chicken then?" Richard was asking, amped to please her.

Shenzi nodded. "Chicken."

Richard brought her chicken nuggets, breaded and oily. After one bite, she was not sure she would like any of the food. So she opted for another Fanta.

Thirteen hours later, the flight captain announced they were landing at Dulles airport in Virginia.

"Well, here we are," Richard was saying. Shenzi was only glad they were going to be grounded finally, and as much as she thought of Kevin, wondering what he was doing now, she also curiously wondered about the new life awaiting her outside the walls of the plane.

She was aware of the shuffle of passengers as they filed out of the plane to the customs and immigration station, staying closely sandwiched between Maxine and Richard, who took turns holding her hand until they were past the checkpoint.

She could hear voices over loudspeakers making announcements she did not understand, and again, the rise and fall and sharp voices of many people, men, women, and children. Unfamiliar accents all meshed and jumbled in swirls around her, making her head spin.

Nothing prepared Shenzi for the DC September heat and humidity that engulfed her when they stepped outside the airport sliding doors onto the sidewalk and hailed a taxi. She gasped in surprise. She had never experienced weather so uncomfortably sticky. Beads of sweat quickly formed at the back of her neck where her hair gathered in a neat plait of corn rows and trickled down her back.

"Oh, it's hot," Richard was muttering apologetically, like he could control the weather somehow. "It's not like the weather in Uganda. But you will get used to it."

"In a few months you will see some snow too."

"That's right!"

Shenzi frowned. "I can't see," she reminded them.

Richard squeezed her hand. She felt his breath fan her face lightly, with the smell of stale coffee wafting past her nose, and she knew he was level with her. "You will see snow, I *promise*."

Something in the way he said, "I promise," reminded her of Kevin's "I promise." She could trust him, too.

She lit up inside. "Will Kevin be here when I see?" she entreated.

There was a slight hesitation before the adults both replied in unison, "Yes!"

Chapter 2

Bethesda, Maryland, USA
December 2001–2003

They patiently waited for her to come out of her shell when they brought her to America. Her first night was overwhelming, and she could sense them tiptoeing around her, not wanting to agitate her. She was aware of the whispering and shushing as the familiar small hands of Mrs. Matthews clasped hers, guiding her through an unfamiliar terrain: the front door. Her cane, clasped in her other free hand, slid on the smooth marble tiles. Her nose caught the faint whiff of an unfamiliar sweet smell in the air. It smelled different and *rich*. Even though she was curious about the people she was going to be living with till Kevin joined them, she missed him even more. With every second of their journey from the airport to her new home widening the distance between them still, Shenzi felt the tangible emptiness in her chest grow and grow.

Now feeling her way across an unfamiliar vast marble landing, she could not help feeling lost, swallowed by the emptiness that had grown in the last twenty hours of her trip.

Then the voices of two young people shattered her gloom.

"Mom! Dad!" It was a young boy's voice. He did not sound older than Kevin, she mused. Maybe Kevin's age, even.

She could hear the joyous reunion as parents and children hugged one another. How much they had missed each other, how big they had grown, and had they done their homework? Were they giving *Consuela* any trouble?

Shenzi did not know what she was to do, so she stood and waited.

"Shenzi…we want you to meet your new brother and sister!" Maxine Matthews, who always sounded chirpy and excited, like a high school girl around a boy she had a crush on, chimed in sweetly.

Shenzi wondered if all American female grownups were that animated, in contrast to her mother, whose intensity had often overwhelmed her. She did not have time to ponder a probable response to her thoughts, for Maxine's soft hands had found hers again and clasped them, urging her forward.

"I want you to know Shenzi is incredibly special to us. She was in an orphanage in Uganda, and we want her to have a better life with a loving family here."

There was a moment's silence after Maxine's moving speech.

"Oh," she heard one child reply. From her voice, she thought she might be a big girl like Teopista's eldest daughter.

"Hi, Shenzi, I am Heather, and I am the oldest. Brent is the annoying little brother. I will protect you from him."

"What's wrong with her eyes?" the boy Heather referred to as Brent was saying.

"Buddy," Mr. Matthew interjected kindly, "Shenzi is blind, but you know Daddy can help fix her eyes, right?"

There was a silence where words seemed to hang in the air unspoken, questions unasked, and Shenzi waited, irritation and discomfort gradually spreading over her. Was it necessary to be a specimen of study for the younger Matthews?

"But where are her parents?" Brent was insisting.

"We *are* her new family now. She does not have any, and we want you children to love her and treat her like your own sister. You got that?" It was Mrs. Matthews gently impressing Shenzi as the new family member.

Another bout of silence, and she felt a presence, then the smell of mint from freshly brushed teeth fanned her face. Brent was looking at her curiously. "Do you have any brothers and sisters?"

Shenzi frowned, a little startled by his voice suddenly so close, and yet she was irritated by his inquisitions.

"Brent…" Heather retorted exasperatedly. "Oh my goodness, didn't you hear what Mom said?"

"But…"

"Oh, stop!" She harrumphed at him impatiently, much to Shenzi's relief. Suddenly slim, unfamiliar fingers enclosed over hers making her start in surprise, then the voice she recognized as Heather's said ever so gently, "Come, Shenzi, I will take you to your room."

She nodded but stood her ground. Brent had asked a question she needed to answer. Puffing her little chest out, she replied, "Yes, I have a brother."

She heard rapid running feet and then Brent's far away voice loudly exclaiming, "Mom, Shenzi has a brother! Are you bringing him to live with us too…?"

She could not make out the muffled response from the adult Matthews in the distance as she walked off with Heather, who gently guided her in a different direction.

"We need another boy *urrrggh!*" she heard Brent respond exasperatedly.

Heather was kind, but Shenzi dared not get close to them yet, and for the first three years of her life with the Matthews, she slept downstairs, in the room close to Mr. Matthews' study. He made it a point to read her a story and chat with her. It took her the longest time to get close to the adults, and they did not pressure her.

Her first months in America were painfully lonely. She missed Kevin terribly, affecting her mood. Some days she leaned on hope; other days fear and uncertainty got the better of her, dashing hopes of a reunion. When she was hopeful, she had happy dreams about her and Kevin, a boy whose face she could never see but whose presence strongly stayed implanted in every portion of her dreams.

On the days she dreamed about her mother, she woke up crying and retreated within herself and stayed in her room for days, refusing to eat and play.

Mrs. Matthews worried so much she took Shenzi for counseling after several visits to get her to open up, to no avail. The therapist suggested kindness and love. "Look into finding a nanny for her…of similar descent. That should help Shenzi adjust." She recalled eavesdropping on the conversation between the therapist and Maxine.

Mrs. Matthews, strongheaded and desperate, decided kindness and love would be what she would administer but excluded the nanny bit. She vowed to do it all by herself.

After the last visit from the therapist, stuck in traffic on the I-270 that warm spring afternoon, Mrs. Matthews begged her: "The therapist thinks you might need a nanny from…Africa."

Shenzi did not reply. She was not sure how that would help. They would be strangers, no less.

"What can I give you to make you happy?" Mrs. Matthews asked. "I don't think a nanny will solve anything. We love you and treat you well, don't we? Shenzi, you are not playing; the therapist says you are depressed; now I am depressed because you are depressed."

"Kevin, I want Kevin," Shenzi found the opportunity to respond. It was the truth.

"Oh, honey…." It was both relief and concern in Mrs. Matthews' voice. "Okay, we will work something out."

A week later, the letters started coming.

"Letters from Kevin!" Mrs. Matthews shrieked in excitement, letting her feel the paper.

Shenzi's heart skipped a beat. At last!

When they read the letters to her, they sounded just like Kevin, and the wide smile on her face stayed long after the last full stop. She asked for rereadings at bedtime as well and insisted on responding.

"Kevin knows braille; he will read it," she told them confidently when they worried about him reading her letters.

She told him she missed him, she could not wait to see him. Spring and summer were as warm and vibrant as her little soul when she waited eagerly for the letters to come.

The letters trickled in less and less and eventually came to a halt by the end of the summer, and life mounted, demanding her attention. There was school. Maxine found a special ed tutor and homeschooling curriculum. Shenzi still battled with the novelty of her American life. She struggled to eat and cringed at all the cuisines Mrs. Matthews attempted to fix for her. Nothing tasted as good as Aunty Dina's cooking.

Consuela, their Peruvian housekeeper, changed that by talking Maxine into letting her fix her meals.

"Let me make her *buena comida*," she told her boss one day and carried on preparing a plate of rice and beans with *pollo*. Shenzi immediately loved it, and it relieved Maxine that Peruvian chicken had saved Shenzi from malnutrition.

Shenzi's first time Christmas shopping with the Matthews introduced her to the extravagance and time put into the holidays. They made a splash of it as early as mid-November.

"It's better to stock up on most of the decorations early. Besides, we have Thanksgiving, Halloween, and birthdays," Heather explained to her regarding why they were shopping so early for the holidays.

They strolled around the Westfield Montgomery Mall, sidling in and out of different stores Shenzi could only identify by smell. "Keep close to Heather," Maxine constantly reminded her, even though she had a walking stick (she had been awfully afraid of the service dog they wanted to get her).

Mrs. Matthews was in the toys and children's aisle at the Target and called out to them, "Heather, bring Shenzi here," then added, "Shenzi, I want you to tell me if you want a teddy bear or a Barbie doll for our Thanksgiving party or…" and then they all heard the laughter, a low-pitched giggle.

Mrs. Matthews immediately jumped to her defense. "Excuse me, what's so funny?"

Heather and Shenzi both held their breath as the woman who laughed responded. Judging from the accent, she was not American. "I am sorry, madam, but is that child there *Shenzi*?" she asked.

Mrs. Matthews, still irritated, responded curtly, "*My* daughter? Yes. Why?"

"Oh. Sorry, forgive me, madam. I am Kenyan. *Shenzi* is a Swahili word that means…stupid, savage. I just thought it was ridiculous. Is she Kenyan?" The woman sounded apologetic.

Mrs. Matthews stumbled over her words, "I…*err*…no…she is Ugandan." Shenzi had felt Maxine pull her close, as if there was a potential threat.

The woman made a *tsk-tsk* sound. "Whoever called her such a word is a bad, bad person. Forgive me, madam, but…"

"Thanks," Maxine said stiffly, then added, "Girls, let's go." And that was the end of shopping.

As they weaved through the parking lot, Mrs. Matthews spoke comfortingly to her. "Don't worry about that, honey. You are certainly none of those horrid words. We must do something about it. I'm so sorry, honey…" Shenzi was numb, Maxine's words rolled over her, hardly comforting. Why hadn't she known this all her life on Block 4? was all she could think.

One thing was certain to her, though; her mother had not wanted her. That thought was too hard to endure, so as quickly as it came to her, she dismissed it, buried it deep down inside her, along with her longing for Kevin.

Later, Shenzi overheard Maxine in the study with her husband. She sounded distraught. "*That* poor little girl has had a hard life, Richard; someone named her 'stupid,' and I did not even look up her name, honey; oh God, I feel like such a bad mother. I let her hear that woman in the store. How will she ever unhear what she heard? Oh Rob, we must change that name…" She was rambling on and on. Mr. Matthews was soothing her.

Shenzi lay awake that night fighting the dark thoughts that resurfaced, her little heart breaking. She cradled a little stuffed rabbit Heather had given her on her first night. She called him "Mr. Pink" because his ears were baby pink.

Her dreams were dark, echoing her mother's laughter, her abuse muddled in with her singing, a bittersweet nightmare she wrestled with. She called for Kevin much of the night in her sleep. Mrs. Matthews woke her up twice with a warm glass of milk, then held her till she slept again.

Her mood deflated again after the Target incident. She imagined Kevin would come soon, as the Matthews had promised, but there seemed to be no empty bag to bad news.

Fall billowed in on the back of dead leaves and gorgeous sunsets she did not care to want to see, no matter how much they described them to her. Mr. Matthews announced then that the research center had given him authorization to oversee her operation. "You will see again, honey, you will!" he sounded so hopeful that day he broke the news, she reverberated with renewed hope.

She was in and out of the research center's clinic, and it forever created an aversion within her toward hospitals: the sanitized smells, the echoey sounds of footsteps in the never-ending hallways she walked through, the tasteless food and the nurses' usual sympathetic gestures.

Sometimes she did not go home for nights. Other times, upon request by Mrs. Matthews, she stayed home, away from the beeping monitors and smells of disinfectant and bleach.

They promised her she would see by December 2001 and they were working hard to bring Kevin.

"Honey, America is going through a lot right now. We are doing our best for Kevin, but it might take a little longer."

In September that year, she heard about the terrorist attacks on the twin towers in New York. It was all the Matthews talked about. It seemed a forlorn spirit had gripped not just her but the entire country. The fear was tangible, and Mrs. Matthews was more protective of her than before.

As Christmas approached, she hoped for news that Kevin would come, terrorist attacks or not.

She imagined scenarios in which they would meet. She could hear his voice in her head, laughing, teasing, and always angry but always protective.

Christmas came and went, and on her birthday, as she spooned the last of her banana pudding, she asked, "When will Kevin come?"

"Let's open the presents first, darling, right?" Maxine said quickly.

She shook her head; there was always something to do first before she was told anything. "No, I want to know."

The silence that seeped through the dining room was like the chill that crusted the pavement and trees in ice outside.

Mr. Matthews spoke up as gently as he could: "Kenzi, all we want is the best for you and Kevin."

"Well, honey, we love you a lot; you know that," Maxine chirped in supportively.

She did not know what to say; the past year had been so overwhelming with therapy, clinics, and getting used to new food, new schedules, a new brother and sister, not forgetting the back-and-forth visits to immigration offices to change her name from Shenzi to Mackenzie (Kenzi), filing for her citizenship, certificates, and a million requirements from the DC office; she had not had time to process whether they loved her. All she had felt was pain, loss, and bewilderment. The only way she had held on was thoughts of Kevin, the letters in the initial months, and the promise he would be here in a few days. Now, the few days had run out, and she demanded to know.

"We love you, hon," Mr. Matthews was saying. "We want you to be happy, always; that's why we are doing the best we can to make you comfortable."

"We know it's hard, and it takes a little getting used to, but soon you will see..."

"Kevin?" She had cut in their little speech. The couple hesitated, and a sense of dread settled in her belly.

"Honey, we…found out that…Kevin ran away from the orphanage. We had already gotten the papers ready. The orphanage…" They broke it to her as gently as they could, as if she would break into a million pieces if they said it any other way.

"No! He promised!" She balled her fists and thumped the plush carpeted floor beneath her. Why would he lie to her? He never had. He always said they would be together no matter what. He said he would come for her.

On the morning after her birthday, her heart could not be put together, no amount of hot chocolate and marshmallows or crackers or muffins or toys could appease her. The only reason she had come was because Kevin had made her a promise. The Matthews smothered her with attention, fussed over her like she was an only child, bent over backward to lift her spirits.

It was a dreadfully cold midmorning in February 2002. School was canceled because of a winter storm warning. Kenzi lay in bed, holding Mr. Pink tight, telling him the Jack and the Beanstalk story from memory, when Brent walked into her room.

"I know that story," he interrupted. "I'm bored with playing video games. I can read it to you."

She felt him hesitate when her silence encamped between them. It would not hurt. She had been moody since her birthday, not to mention lonely, and winter was not pleasant to her.

"Or I can go…" he said after a minute.

Kenzi sighed reluctantly. "Okay."

"I can read it to you?"

He did not wait for a response. With renewed energy, he replied, "Hold on, let me get it!"

Ten minutes later, Brent shut the book. "The end." She tried not to cry. While Brent read, Kevin's voice echoed in her ear. *It was* our *story*, she thought sadly, *but you broke your promise.*

There was an awkward silence before Brent said, "You liked it? I betcha

I can read you a whole lot more stories!"

She hesitated. The connection they had when Kevin used to read her *Jack and the Beanstalk* was significantly theirs. It was a window for them to dream of a better future, like Jack. She desperately wanted to hold on to that magic.

Two days later, she asked Brent to read to her. Kevin was not coming, and maybe Brent could become her new brother. Her very own brother.

Brent started to read her stories every time he could. At first, as she wrestled with feelings of disloyalty to Kevin, she simply listened and turned away when it was done. But gradually, she started to ask him questions and then ask him to read them again and again like she had done with Kevin.

Like a delicate strand of strings woven together slowly over time over stories, Kenzi started to let him in. She laughed when he made funny voices and imitated characters he had watched on television. And when Mrs. Matthews refused to let them have any more cookies, he snuck her some at bedtime. "Here. For you. Don't tell Heather." He would place the huge round chocolate chip cookies in her hand, and she would hide them underneath her sweater.

"They are yummy!" she would say while biting into the chewy warm cookies that melted in her mouth.

"Chocolate chip cookies," he would respond enthusiastically, like he had discovered the cure for cancer.

She would frown and say, "Why chip?"

"I dunno, I dunno who called them that, but they are chocolate. Chip. Cookies." Soon a brilliant idea hatched in his young mind, and Kenzi became Chip or Chippy to him.

"Why?" she asked him once.

"Because you're like chocolate, and you like chocolate *chip* cookies so, 'Chip,'" Even though she did not fully understand how that married together, Kenzi took it anyway because he said it with so much warmth.

By the end of spring 2002, they were thick as thieves, much to the relief of the Matthews, who were wondering what would take her out of the doldrums she had fallen into. When Mr. Matthews told her he was going to take her in for another eye treatment, Kenzi had protested, tired and appalled at the thought.

Mrs. Matthews had felt the strain too, and the contention had brought her husband to promise if this last stage of treatment did not work, they would have to leave it alone and let her be. Mr. Matthews, strongly believing in his novel scientific research in medical correction of damaged corneas through the replacement of the corneas, worked all summer, one of the longest, dullest summers for Kenzi, who remained holed up at the research facility for three months with Brent and Heather visiting regularly to keep her company.

After a six-hour operation and then another twelve-hour wait for her swollen eyes to deflate, Kenzi woke up…eyesight restored. Mr. Matthews had finally cracked the code and changed the face of ophthalmology research by repairing the cornea through corneal replacement using high-tech laser technology.

Kenzi became the first trial patient to receive new eyes. Science journals were awash with the news that seeped into the *Washington Post,* making headlines in the local press, peer reviews, and science magazines and blogs.

The Matthews kept the press away as best as they could, with Mr. Matthews doing brief interviews for weeks after and strongly suggesting no cameras or pictures as yet, until Kenzi was out of the hospital. A week after the operation, as she adjusted to vision, her brown eyes slowly changed. Mr. Matthews admitted her for more tests, and the only conclusive evidence being her DNA was reacting to the new eyes, and the adjustment process was not as smooth as they originally hoped.

She would have to use eye drops for a couple more years until she did not feel as much discomfort. However, her vision steadily settled to the perfect 20/20. By the end of another two weeks at the research center, Kenzi's iris color was a blue green, a stark contrast to her smooth ebony skin.

The first time her adoptive father brought her a mirror, he made a long speech, telling her how beautiful she was, a rare gem, before letting her see herself.

Kenzi had been curious about her reflection. She had asked Mr. Matthews, whose eyes were light brown, why hers were not like his… didn't everyone have light brown eyes? *No, Kenzi, we all have different color eyes; some people have green, blue, brown, and like yours too.* He explained to her comfortingly.

Even then, the sight of her new eyes against her dark skin frightened her. Something about them felt misplaced. "Can you make them like yours, please? This color is weird!" she cried "I look scary!"

On her first night home, Maxine fixed a delicious meal and invited their neighbors. Kenzi walked in through the door blindfolded and Mr. Matthews removed the blinds and shouted, "Home sweet home!"

She gazed about her with curiosity. She marveled at the expanse and exquisiteness of her home. The doorway led to a big archway that led to another room. "I can see?" she sighed, whispering under her breath.

No matter how much she looked around herself in awe, she could not get over the fact that she had restored sight.

When she saw Heather and Brent, the brown-haired girl, tall and skinny, and the handsome boy with dark hair and a rueful smile, somewhere in her, she missed Kevin but was glad she could see the children who had visited her often, talked with her, fought around her, read her stories, or fed her her favorite cookies. Brent had rushed to her first, hugging her. "Chippy! You are home!" he said as he squeezed her.

Kenzi beamed. Heather hugged her too, much calmer and more collected. She grinned. "Welcome home, sis. I love your eyes."

"You look like Storm!" Brent told her. "And she is my favorite X-man…X-woman…who cares; she is my favorite."

Heather gave him a withering look. "*Urgh!*" And took Kenzi's hand. "Let's go; let me show you your room for real—and Mr. Pink."

Brent followed. "Wait for me!"

*　*　*

The attention she got at the mall or when she went to the playground close to their home distressed her. People openly stopped and stared at her, others commenting to her mother how lovely or *how surprising her eyes were for a black girl.*

Kenzi recalled three children at the playground who she thought looked like her tell her she had funny-looking eyes. She told them her father said different people have different color eyes. At that, the older of the three children told her dark-skinned people did not have eyes like hers. Kenzi left the playground in tears. "Mom, is it true?" she had bawled to Maxine.

Yes. Maxine replied and then added, *but honey, there are a few who have different color eyes, and they are beautiful. You are unique and beautiful.* She showed her pictures on the internet of different black people who had blue eyes.

"But they don't live here." She pouted. "I hate being different," she moaned. From then on, Kenzi refused to go anywhere without sunglasses, and no amount of reassurance would make her take them off.

Chapter 3

Kampala, April 2001

In the beginning, he had written every week, telling Shenzi about the new children in the orphanage, how he beat everyone at a relay race and was still the champion "hider," at the hide-and-seek games. He told her about Sunday school and how he crammed Psalm 23 for a church performance. He told her of the chicken meal the orphanage was now giving them every Saturday and Sunday and how it never could beat his mother's chicken stew. Did she miss it like he did?

As he wrote, he skipped tiny details like the graver news he came to discover after the death of his father. He did not tell her he attempted to go see his mother, but always retraced his steps back to the orphanage, overridden with guilt. He did not tell her about the nightmares that robbed him of sleep still and that he counted to one thousand or almost one million some nights, afraid his father would kill him in his sleep. He did not tell her he got into fights, that he got moody and kept away from everyone frequently. He did not want her to know Aunty Charity was taking him "for prayers" and to see a counselor to help him with his anger issues and nightmares.

He did not want to shatter her happy world. He did not tell her he had gone back to the Flats and though he had not talked to her; he had seen Ameena, and he had hated her even more. She had moved on with life as if nothing had happened.

But he told her he had their picture, the one she had not wanted to take, their *one* picture together and in the last letter he had written to her, finally signing off on the tenth neatest draft, that he was tiring of waiting—waiting for her to respond, waiting for the Matthews to come back for him.

Waiting.

So, he was going to take matters into his own hands and come look for her. *I promised we will be together, always. Your loving brother, Kevin* he had signed the letter as easily as breathing. He then sealed it carefully…twice into a rectangular shape and slipped it into the blue and white envelope Aunty Charity had given him, already stamped with four stamps bearing the image of the Uganda national bird, the crested crane, balancing stoically on its one leg. He had crammed the Matthews' address by heart from writing so often. Much easier than Psalm 23. He pondered over the addresses in America that did not start with "P.O. Box…." He liked it: *2346 Shadowfall Road, Bethesda, Maryland 20876, USA.*

He wondered if maybe the lack of a P.O. Box caused the letters to go missing. It was not like Shenzi not to reply. He expressed his concern to the director, and she laughed and told him the American system differed from the Ugandan system, and if it had bounced, then the letters would have been returned. "See, I put two addresses? Theirs and ours?" she told him.

At first, the *maybe* responses had been hopeful. Then they got tiring:

"*Maybe* she is still in the hospital. *Maybe* they are too busy helping her get well. Mr. Matthews is an important man in the medical world. *Maybe* she is getting settled. Those things take time. *Maybe*…" she would tell him, her eyes warm and glassy. She would lean forward in her chair behind her desk, and he would believe her; after all, she had taken them in on a rainy morning and brought them here.

"Be patient…" Her final words. *Always.*

One Sunday, he feigned sickness and while he lay in the infirmary listening for the minivans to drive off packed with the children heading to prayer, he stewed on his plan.

He stole into Charity's office, looking for one thing; any other form of contact, a phone number maybe, so he could hear her voice and know she was well. He figured talking to her might help answer the millions of questions that mounted each day since Shenzi had left.

He rummaged through the drawers, making sure he left minimal evidence of intrusion, his eyes continually darting to the plain circular-faced clock, the only ornament on the wall opposite the director's desk.

At the bottom of the lowest drawer, he spied a pink manila file, one he almost passed up till he saw the name printed on it: *Shenzi.* Hope surged in his chest. Curious, he flipped through the loose leaflets. Most of it was standard paperwork: the day they registered with the orphanage, their school reports, her medical reports in ragged handwriting that he could not read. Underneath that were the adoption papers, and he slowed down, trying to gather as much information as he could comprehend from those leaflets. There was nothing new, at least not something he had not been privy to. Her new parents, their address, the two children who were to be her new siblings. He thumbed through it and more paperwork he cared not to read, for the print was tiny with signatures at the bottom. There was an envelope tucked away in those pages, and he shifted his attention to it. It was torn open, the stamps on it were unfamiliar, a head of a green female statue with a crown that reminded him of Jesus with a crown of thorns. About six of them were pasted on the white back of the envelope. Inside was a letter... It was a typed letter dated only two months earlier.

The last part read,

We can only adopt one child, especially because of her condition. We picked Shenzi, (now Mackenzie Zawadi Matthews). We apologize for any inconvenience this must be for you. But we will send you some upkeep for Kevin. Whatever he needs while in your care, we hope we can provide it. We hope he can understand. In time we shall bring Kenzi to see him with his new family (if he is placed in one), and they shall always have each other.

Best regards, Richard and Maxine Matthews

The letter slipped from his hand, lightly brushing his sneakers before settling on the floor at his feet. He had completely forgotten about the time, nor did he care when he heard the van come in or even when the caretaker walked into the office and found him still standing by the great wooden desk.

Then the difficult conversation began, a conversation, he realized with deep disappointment she had been buying time to have. Time had run out.

"Why didn't you tell me?" he yelled at her, and when he could not restrain himself any longer, he picked up the large gaudy vase on the desk filled with a warm arrangement of roses, hydrangea, and delicate green foliage and smashed it in emphasis.

Everything was a blur; he could hear her raise her voice above his, and then strong arms grabbed him, steadying him, their grasp so tight he could not move.

As the sun sunk low in the sky, carrying the heaviness of the day on its flaming tails, he lay in the infirmary exhausted from raging, spent from fighting off two strong men. Charity instructed him to be placed there until he was calm. He lay on the bed, his face to the wall. Then she told him everything.

"I am sorry. The plan was always to take you, too, but things change. They got your letters. She has read some... She has not written back. But..."

She gave him an envelope with money. "They sent you this. They shall send you more until you are older or get adopted. Even pay for your school. I can keep it for you until you need it."

"Why? Shenzi would write. Why hasn't she?" Angry tears slid down his face onto the impersonal, flat pillow of the infirmary. There was nothing else to say. They had lied to them both. He had trusted them.

Finally, she mumbled, "I am so, *so* sorry. But Kenzi is fine, and with time, you will be able to see her again." And with a heavy sigh and a slight hesitation, she got up and walked out of the infirmary.

He had believed them, and when the excuses came, he still wanted to believe them. Every time he asked Aunty Charity, she told him all was well. "Be patient; everything will work out soon; don't worry," she assured him.

But nothing had worked out. It was time for plan B. He knew what he must do.

A long while later, Kevin picked up the envelope with the money, cradled it, and fell asleep. In his dreams, Shenzi was there, fading from him. When he woke up, it was late.

With the picture safely nestled in his pocket, he wrapped the envelope with the thick wads of notes tightly and stuffed it in his socks, then pulled the jeans he had worn that day over it, neatly laced his sneakers, and walked out of the infirmary.

* * *

The lone, tiny figure of a skinny, short boy ambled purposely with measured speed from one street corner to another. Oblivious to the irregular lighting from the light posts, his frame emerged and vanished at intervals along a ghostly pavement.

A moist thickness that dared to lend the night breeze personality skulked in the shadows after the boy like a somber god whose aura lingered stubbornly. Stray dogs howled and barked in discordant tones, and somewhere, a stray cat shrieked and hissed at an unknown assailant. The collaged street pavement stretched before him. The boy wiped his eyes furiously and sniffed wetly as he dragged back a trail of translucent phlegm that threatened to pool lower to his upper lip, then swallowed.

Every so often he looked over his shoulder, peered into the silent gray darkness behind him, half expecting someone to jump from the shadows and grab him, never changing pace. His purposeful gait did not betray him, for he did not have a clue where he was to go. *Just keep going* he told himself on beat. Safely tucked in his brand-new socks was the envelope tightly wrapped and wound around his ankles with a thick rubber band. Even as he walked, he could smell the crisp notes.

He forced his mind to accept his situation; he was here again, but the scrapping heavy bundle trapped between his stocking and left leg promised things would be better. Different. He would find her, whatever it took. He would find her starting tomorrow. *What if she did not want to be found? What if she had forgotten him?* A voice taunted him, and he brushed it away. Not Shenzi, she would never forget him.

Instead, he mulled over ways he would make it to America; he hatched a daring rescue plan in which he would go to the airport and board a plane. Was it that simple? He would need a passport. He had never possessed one. How would he get one? He shook his head. There were ways. He had money now.

You are only eleven, that same voice told him. He stubbornly brushed it off. "Twelve!" he spat out to the heavy fog god, kicking at an empty black plastic bag. There was nowhere to go. It was a ghost town, but he walked anyway. It helped clear his mind, spent the anger and torment his soul wrestled with.

After a brisk two-mile walk, he found an empty familiar corner, a spot he had slept in once before with Shenzi, and curled up on the ground, knees pulled up to his chin, and fell into a deep, troubled sleep.

Chapter 4

It wasn't the hum and sound of traffic that roused him from his sleep but the terrifying dream that always recurred, his father mocking him, chasing him, then falling and dying, his mother crying.

The demons he wrestled with were more alert in his sleep, and he could not rest. The street sounds merged and meshed with the combined aura of city smells, exhaust fumes from cars stuck in a never-ending line of traffic…*ahh,* then…food; the mouthwatering smell of frying *chapatti* and *katogo* filled his nostrils. His body felt stiff, and he winced as he picked himself up, dusting off his backside and quickly wiggling his feet to feel the weight of the money stashed within his socks. The freedom from the orphanage was a relief. The meals had become mundane and boring. He was glad he could decide what he wanted to eat.

He sat inside a hole-in-the-wall take-away, waiting on his order of chips and liver. That combination made him feel closer to Shenzi. He remembered how they would eat through three plates of liver and chips in one sitting, fighting over the last pieces. Most times, he sacrificed the last pieces of liver for her and watched her chew them delicately.

She ate so slowly. He was never sure she got full since he wolfed down most of the food in record speed. The memories sat like a heavy stone in his chest, forcing him to stoop over. The familiar embers of a rage built again, slowly smoldering his heart on its trip to his mind.

He was helpless against the memories, even miserable. He jabbed himself for letting her go. He had not believed the *bazungu* would lie. In the orphanage, every child dreamed of being adopted by a white person because they believed they were nice and wealthy and never told a lie. His heart bled afresh at the realization that they had lied to him.

When the waitress brought his glass of passion fruit juice, thick and yellow like it had not a drop of water, he fished the picture of him and Shenzi out of his pocket

Now as he stared at it, the wheels in his mind turning and churning out plans that made little sense even to him, he thought about sneaking onto a plane to America. Or he could go back to the orphanage and get adopted. But that was a plan he did not want to go with anymore. Grown-ups were a disappointment. Finally, he decided he would find a way, make it to America soon.

By the time he swallowed his last drop of juice, he was not sure what he would do except find a place to stay, shower, and sleep. His body felt crumpled from sleeping upright, and somewhere in the back of his mind was a growing uneasiness that one day he would meet the Big Boy Gang.

* * *

Kevin did not flinch. He ground his teeth. He kept his knees apart, poised to pounce. His eyes flitted from Wasswa to Boda to Livingstone and the other two boys whose twin names he had not grasped, even though they were not identical.

Wasswa crowed. "So you are here again. Where have you been?" He circled Kevin slowly like a lioness playing with its prey. Kevin watched him from the corner of his eye. The hairs on his skin bristled, and he kept his fists balled.

"Heh?" Wasswa lunged at him as if to hit him, and the rest laughed as Kevin lashed out and missed.

"He looks healthy!" one twin shouted.

"I think he has money," another boy was saying in Luganda.

Wasswa kept his eyes locked with Kevin's in a dance of wills. Kevin held his gaze. He had fought bigger boys than Wasswa, and he told himself he was not afraid of anyone; if anything, he was spoiling for a fight.

Wasswa watched him long and hard, then asked, "Where is your sister? Lost her? Heh?" He smirked, and the boys laughed in unison.

Kevin kept his gaze watchful, consequently resting on the lanky opponent circling him. He anticipated hitting out and wondered how long it would take before the rest of the boys reacted. Being smaller and shorter than them, he would outpace them, he calculated. One twin was heavy, but the horror stories of his body slamming smaller children on the streets, almost suffocating them if they did not hand over their spoils, were legendary. The thinner twin was fast with his arms and could swing widely, but his legs were clumsy, so Kevin imagined swinging at him from below. It was Boda and Livingstone he knew he would have to make a lot more effort for, even though they were both a few inches shorter than Wasswa, who had become group leader because he was the tallest and most threatening bully. The streets ran wild with stories of their fighting antics. Kevin knew he would only beat them mentally, distract them in order to win a fight with them. But taking all five boys down, he had not done that…yet. He was up for the challenge. He dedicated the looming fight to Shenzi, glad she was not around to see it. He would have worried about her and been unable to focus on it with her there.

Since he had left the orphanage, he had shadowed the Big Boy Gang to master their routine and movements. He knew one day they would find him, and he did not want to be caught unawares. The stories he heard pouring from every corner of the streets from the industrial area to Kamwokya were rich, even to him. They terrorized other gangs and fought for their territory. So far they had pushed their territorial influence from City Square, right where Crane Bank sat, to Wandegeya, a little before the lower gate to Makerere University. Kevin knew that area well, for he and Shenzi would take a taxi there to indulge in a pork feast at a little makeshift pork joint where no one asked questions as long as the meal was paid for.

While they roamed the streets, he learned about territories and told Shenzi that for as long as they were on the streets, they would have their territory one day.

This was the perfect time to get one, he told himself.

"Search him!" Wasswa suddenly shouted to the boys, who immediately closed in on Kevin. Kevin decided his only option now would be to run. He dove into the fat twin with all his might, shoving him aside to make his escape, but someone grabbed his shirt from behind.

The fight had begun, and he immediately shifted his mindset. Today was not the day to escape. With a growl, Kevin lashed out, hitting whoever grabbed him with his elbow. A blow shook his lower jaw and another his belly.

"I told you I would get you!" Wasswa was screaming over him. Kevin felt the spray of stale saliva on his face. He was on the ground, a knee pushed up on his chest. "Search him!"

They peeled his socks back, took off his sneakers, tore his Tom & Jerry T-shirt amid loud laughter, and pulled his jeans down, only coming up with a thousand shillings.

Kevin grinned through a swollen upper lip. His nose was bloody, but his heart sang a victory song.

Wasswa glared at him. "I will find your money. We are watching you." He got up from his chest and kicked the side of Kevin's head.

Kevin stifled a wince, a grin frozen on his lips. The boys gave him one last look and walked away. Kevin got up, dabbed his hand against the jaw that hurt, and shouted, "I am coming for your territory!" Wasswa stopped in his tracks and wheeled around. The other boys snickered.

"What did he say?" Wasswa had a smug grin on his face.

The fat twin replied amid sneers, "*Mbu*, he is coming for our territory."

Wasswa cocked his head again. "Sorry, *your* territory," fat twin corrected himself quickly. Kevin watched a slow smile of pride spread across the tall, lanky boy's face.

"Then, I will fight you for it." Kevin glared at him; pain shot through every part of his body, but he balled his fists tight to steel himself against it. He would not let them see his pain.

Wasswa dropped his head with a chuckle. "You? Will fight me?"

Kevin did not say anything.

"What do you think?" Wasswa asked the group.

They all yelled approval.

"I know the rules," Kevin assured Wasswa. "If I win, then I take over and you move out of town."

Wasswa's eyes danced wickedly. "Aaah, *oli mu street kilassi.*"

The boys snickered. Kevin found it annoying.

"Okay, let's fight. We meet at Freedom Square at noon, next Thursday. Everyone will be there." Then he turned and walked away, the boys sneering at Kevin.

Kevin watched them leave, and when they were out of sight, he limped away slowly toward Grace's flat, where he had kept his bag with his money. The smoldering anger at being humiliated burned his soul and spurred his determination further. He would win this street war for Shenzi. She would be proud of him. Drained from limping, he leaned against a little boutique store glass window and stifled a groan. He pushed his head back against the glass and closed his eyes. His lips pulsated painfully, and he could feel them, perforated and heavy. After what seemed like forever, he got up and walked on to Grace's. He needed to get money to buy himself another shirt, pairs of socks, and shoes and plan a permanent abode.

Somewhere dogs howled, one to the other, and the almost full moon glowed amid a cloudless sky. It made him think of nights he and Shenzi curled up on that same rooftop, and stared out at the moon, with him conjuring up faces and animal shapes from it and telling her about it. Then he would recite to her the story of Jack and the Beanstalk.

They talked about the places they would go to, changing often with their mood. Sometimes they came across new information. Some nights it was Canada or Jamaica, other nights it was Sweden and Germany and

South Africa, but the constant was they would see all these places; they would live everywhere and have everything they needed. "And we will always be together. You and me. On top of the world," Kevin would assure her, and Shenzi would grin; her white teeth would gleam against the light of the moon, and inspiration would filter through his soul. He would do anything for this dream to unfold.

When he finally got to the top of the stairs, his feet treading heavily on the rough rooftop concrete, Kevin mulled over the coming fight. He knew he could beat Wasswa as he had done before, but knowing that a fight for territory would be riskier, he added a knife to his list of things to buy.

"Learn to survive in these streets. You die, or they die. Sometimes the police can't help you. You must protect yourself." Ssuna's words resounded somewhere in his memory. Kevin realized what this fight meant. He had just put a price on his own head. With that thought, his shopping list lengthened.

* * *

"Are you mad? *Wolololo!*" Grace was looking at Kevin bewildered as he ate the porridge she had handed him. "Why are you doing this?"

"For Shenzi," Kevin replied unbothered, then carefully scooped up a spoonful of porridge into his mouth. He let out a muffled gasp of pain, stiffened as his jaw closed over the hot white mush, and relaxed. It was going to be a long breakfast session.

"*Hmm!*" Grace looked him up and down. "She is in America enjoying life, and you want to kill yourself?"

Kevin cast her a stony glance and kept eating. After scolding him for a few minutes more, she shook her head, retreating to her kitchen. From the way she bustled and banged the pots and pans, Kevin knew it upset her, but he was not backing down from a challenge he had put up. He would see it through.

He took the bowl to the sink and rinsed it off. Grace was watching him. "You miss her."

Kevin nodded. "We will see each other again."

"When? Will she remember you?"

Kevin looked at her like she had asked the most stupid question. "Of course. We will be together. I promised."

He spoke with as little facial movement as he could muster. Every motion shattered his face with pain, but his eyes blazed with a new flame, renewed hope that every step, every single day, drew him closer to the day he would see Shenzi again. "One day."

Grace looked bored. "*Hmm*. Okay." She shrugged. "But today you can't be out there on the streets. Those boys will kill you before the fight."

Kevin nodded. "I know. But I need clothes."

Grace held a hand out. "I am going downtown."

Kevin fished out some wads of money and handed it to her. Grace counted it. "Ten thousand; I need at least twenty more."

Kevin counted out twenty thousand shillings, then added an extra ten. "Thank you," he told her. His soulful eyes met hers in gratitude.

"Ah! It's okay," she brushed him off, then went off to her room, grumbling, "The things I do for you. If my husband and children knew you were not who I say you are, *simanyi*."

He smiled. "Thank you, Aunty Grace." And as he said that, he thought about his mother. He had not been to see her yet. Even though he desired to go then, he thought it better to wait till after he had taken over the streets. *A little more time, a little more time,* he told himself. Patience still was a hard concept.

He also told Grace he would not be living on the street much longer. "If I am going to own the world and be very rich and take care of Shenzi, I cannot live here anymore."

"Hmm, so you will fight for the street for what?"

Kevin shook his head. "Because when I win, everyone will fear me. I will own the street, and I can live anywhere I want."

She looked at him with admiration. "My children should think more like you. But where will you live?"

He shrugged. "I shall find a place but no more sleeping on the street."

Chapter 5

Threstaurants stood in a curve, dotted with butcher shops and a wide
opening at the far center to Wandegeya market. The light turned green,
and Kevin shuffled along with the crowd, avoiding a taxi packed to the
brim still calling for more passengers, and deftly made it to the other
side, breakfast on his mind. He straightened his gray T-shirt, hoping it
would have uncreased itself by noon.

A sign, "Room to Let," scratched on with a bold black marker, screamed
out from haphazard cardboard that was stuck to the corner of a little
Celtel Kiosk right by Friecca pharmacy at the taxi stage. Scribbled on it
was a phone number, which he promptly called after paying the kiosk
vendor a fee for the service.

In less than thirty minutes, the owner was showing Kevin the room.
"If you like it…fifty thousand a month," he told Kevin.

"I shall take it," Kevin told the man and paid him for three months
in advance in cash. The man grinned, satisfied, and Kevin noticed that
every question the owner might have wanted to ask vanished at the sight
of the money.

It was a small room with a single small mattress on a wooden frame covered with a thin colored blanket, which Kevin rejected and instead bought his own blanket and sheets. The room sat on the third floor of the apartment block. The corridors smelled of urine, and two floors below him were commercial buildings. The lowest was a restaurant, and the middle floor had a constant stream of people moving in and out.

Kevin made his way to Tipsy Take-away and ordered liver and chips and a bottle of Coca-Cola. He imagined Shenzi was there with him. The memories flashed at breakneck speed: how he always left her the last morsels of liver and last sips of soda, how he would get all the napkins to wipe her hands and lips and she would complain she wasn't a child but still let him do it anyway, how he would ask her if she wanted more and he would buy half a bag of chips and liver and they would descend upon it with less haste, savoring the taste like satiated royalty.

He smiled to himself, imagining the smile on her face when he would see her again. When he had washed the food down with his last drops of the dark, fizzy drink, Kevin set out for the stage. He would take a taxi to Kampala Road and from Fido Dido Icecream parlor, walk toward City Square. He had time.

Kevin went prepared, a knife tucked in his back pocket, hidden from view by the T-shirt he wore. He figured Wasswa would not come empty-handed either.

The grassy lawn was populated with street children he came to learn were from different groups. They were there to witness the fight. Word had gone around, and it had been a while before they had been entertained with a territorial fight. It was several days later that he would only come to realize how epic "territorial challenges" were. Anyone who challenged a territory leader had two choices: win or die.

Kevin strolled slowly, counting every footstep he made to the fated battlefield. He imagined every outcome possible, not leaving anything to chance. The look in Wasswa's eyes told him he needed to guarantee he beat him. In his pocket was the monumental picture. He jammed his hands into his pocket and felt for it. It comforted him, made him feel even the slightest bit closer to Shenzi.

"Ooh! He is there!" a voice called out, alerting most of the children on the lawns. Kevin looked up in time to catch the eyes that were riveted to him. Some of the street children stood up, others pointed at him, none moved from their position, but they watched him make his way to them.

Kevin kept his eyes screwed ahead, looking over their heads at the *kaloli* birds that languidly strolled in the park. One or two stood still like statues on one leg, as if in anticipation of the fight. He was acutely aware of the hum of city noise at noon, the smell of lunch wafting from every corner, the stream of pedestrians who, oblivious to the pending war, strolled by, glanced at the crowd on the park lawn and walked on, lost in amiable chatter one to another or casually strolling singularly captured by the goings-on in their own world.

The taxi touts cried out their route destinations in the background, drowning the noise of the city and the activity in the foreground. Kevin stepped onto the lawn.

Finally, he let his gaze sweep through the crowd: not more than fifty street dwellers, not older than twenty, not younger than five. They all looked enthusiastic, hungry to witness a fight. He wondered how long it had been since the last territorial war.

As he inched closer, the children lying on the grass rolled away. Those who squatted or stood stupidly gawking stepped aside, letting him stride through. Kevin stood in what seemed like the center and waited, his eyes surveying his surroundings.

A hush fell on the city square lawn for a second; the only sounds that swirled and swelled around them were noonday busyness.

"Hey!" a voice called from behind him. Kevin waited, hunched and ready.

"Bag boy, short boy…whatever your name is." The sneers came again. He did not have to turn to know it was Wasswa; neither did he respond.

There was a chuckle, but no one else spoke.

"Are you ready…" Wasswa spoke, then paused for effect. "…to die?"

The children roared with laughter and chatter, blood-thirsty and entertained.

Kevin turned around slowly. A slow smile spread on his face. "I am ready to kill you," he said. The crowd of children were stunned for a second and then a few booed; some laughed.

"Go on then!" one of the children shouted.

"Yes!" another shouted.

The children all together picked up the roar. Wasswa raised his hand to silence them. "This fight should take a minute because...he..." He pointed at Kevin. "...is...dead!"

Kevin decided it was time to launch. He charged toward Wasswa making as if to crush into his belly and, in that quick assessment, saw him take a defensive position, grinning madly from ear to ear. Kevin smiled and slid on the slippery grass, jutted his foot out, and with all his might swung, knocking Wasswa down, an unexpected move for even the children who watched. There was a moment's silence, then a cheer.

Kevin wasted no time with his opponent's back on the ground. He leaped to his feet and jumped onto his belly, pounding with all his might. Wasswa roared, shoving him off. Kevin sprawled back and immediately gained composure, the noise of blood-thirsty cheer faded as Kevin zeroed in on his opponent. Wasswa was up on his feet, and Kevin noticed something else, the knife that he carefully concealed in his balled left hand. Kevin glanced around him. The rest of the Big Boy Gang stared...leering.

Wasswa charged at Kevin, the fist with the subtle knife angled for effect. Kevin dove for his leg and, with the speed he had practiced, pulled out his own knife and sliced at Wasswa's lower leg. The taller boy yelped and flailed.

Kevin somersaulted backward and watched wide-eyed as the cut gushed blood. A memory of blood seared through his mind, and he froze. He saw his father again, the wooden leg jutting through him, the blood that pooled around him, thick and dark like an invading fluid monster.

He backed away as Wasswa hobbled toward him in pain and surprise.

Suddenly he was aware of his surroundings, the voices of children yelling distortedly. They wanted the fight to go on. Wasswa roared. Kevin could see his nostrils flare, his mouth quiver and spit stain his chin.

Quickly dragging himself back to the present, Kevin dodged the punches that came at him. He circled Wasswa and charged at him from behind before he could turn around. Wasswa was slowing down but not giving up. He successfully swung a few times, cutting Kevin on the shoulder, his jaw, and ribcage. Like a wounded lion, Kevin charged, impairing Wasswa with another cut on his thigh and then on his side. He kicked and lashed and punched; he lost himself in the frenzy. In his need to win, Kevin was unstoppable, almost possessed. When the other members of the Big Boy Gang dragged him off the surrendered body of their clearly defeated leader, Kevin was screaming and crying at the same time.

He did not recall how he got to his room. His body and fists ached. When he shifted his weight on the thin mattress, he yelped. His ribs seemed to touch the wooden boards beneath the foam, and he bit his lower lip to prevent himself from crying out.

The overwhelming pressure to pee antagonized his lower belly, and he panted. Shifting again to his side and with effort, lifting his battered body off the bed, he fought the tears that came to his eyes. He felt miserable; he wasn't sure if he had won the fight or not because a lot became hazy.

Right when they dragged him away screaming and crying, there was a scramble, voices of children screaming…panicking, then the loud shouts of another voice. Older. He felt himself lifted, weightless, and someone asked him where he lived…. He recalled mumbling something. He gave in to the exhaustion, fading out. But how was he here?

Kevin finally managed a sitting position, and it was then that he noticed the shadows by the door, crouching low. Adrenaline jolted his nerves. He could not scream; his voice seemed to catch in his throat.

Then light flooded the room, and his shock melted momentarily. "W…

what are you doing here?" he asked, looking from the first boy to the next.

"We brought you here. We had to leave because the police came."

Kevin was not sure he trusted them. "Why? You are with Wasswa?"

One boy shrugged. "He lost. So, we need a new leader."

Kevin looked at them for a moment, frowning. Wasswa lost? The events on the lawn in City Square tumbled from his memory, clearer now. "Is he…" he asked, then trailed off, dreading the answer. "*Dead?*"

"He will be fine," the other boy said and then added, "Me Boda, him Livingstone." He pointed to the boy, who was taller than him, seated next to him in a corner, knees drawn up to his chin.

Kevin looked from one to the other suspiciously, but even if they were lying and they were plotting a way to harm him, he had no fighting strength.

"Are you here to kill me?" he asked, and though it sounded stupid in his own ear, he wanted to be sure.

The one called Livingstone hooted. "*Waa, oli wakabi, gwe bossi!*" he assured Kevin.

Boda nodded. "Wasswa should not have fought you!" he said in Luganda.

Kevin was silent, trying to digest all the information. "And the twins?"

The two boys shrugged. Kevin realized then what had happened. The Big Boy Gang was no more. His thoughts strayed to Wasswa, his wounds, the cuts, the blood, his battered body on the ground.

"Will Wasswa come for me?" he asked again, knowing he sounded stupid. All he wanted was to know he could rest a few days.

Boda shrugged. Livingstone shook his head. "He is not supposed to. That's the rules."

"He has no one now. If he tries, when you have your boys…us," he indicated with his thumb to the two of them, "he will have trouble."

Kevin looked at them, unconvinced. He had made a mortal enemy, and now he would have to be on his guard.

"But where is he?" Kevin insisted.

The two boys looked at each other. "Hiding. He is hurt badly."

Kevin stared at them suspiciously. "How can I trust you?"

The boys grinned. "We have been sitting here waiting for you to wake up. We could have killed you."

Kevin raised an eyebrow, looked away briefly, then said, "Help me up."

Boda stepped forward and helped Kevin to his feet. Kevin groaned as sharp shards of pain shot through his body.

He hobbled to the little full bathroom in his room. When Boda shut the door behind him, Kevin stared at his face in the mirror, dried blood crusted the ridge between his nose and upper lip. His lower lip had a crack, and when he stretched his face, his head throbbed. He raised his hands and winced as he tried to ball his fingers into fists, marks of his anger imprinted on the knuckles in traces of blood and exposed broken skin.

He took his time, peed, and then examined the rest of his body. He spied cuts in different places: his left shoulder, his right side where his shirt bore the telltale signs of a knife job slicing through to the skin. The cuts were flesh wounds, lucky for him, but he hurt all over excruciatingly.

When he got out of the bathroom, he half expected to find the boys gone with all his meager property. But Boda and Livingstone sat where he had seen them, talking in low tones to each other.

"I think I need Panadol," he told them, imagining that now that he was their new boss, he could tell them what to do for him. Besides, he needed them out of his way so he could think.

"*Sawa*," Livingstone responded first.

Then Kevin added, "Tomorrow, I want to see Wasswa."

The boys looked at each other, bewildered. "Why?"

Kevin heaved onto his bed with a flinch. "Because he won't leave this alone."

The boys *tsk-tsk*ed. "But he has to. Those are the rules. Daudi, who he beat, left. He now runs Kawempe side."

Kevin was quiet. "What if he won't leave it alone?"

Boda sighed. "Hmm, it's not good. No one disobeys. Rules are rules," he explained in Luganda.

The sound of traffic and the woman in the upstairs apartment squealing with laughter shattered the silence that reigned.

"What will you do?" Livingstone asked.

Kevin had not thought that far.

He looked at his bloodied fists, hating who he was becoming. This wasn't him. The rage and pain he pummeled into Wasswa in that fight frightened him. He wondered if he had always been like this, but because he had Shenzi, he could not let the beast out.

Shenzi…he thought about her and his mother. He needed them now more than he ever thought possible. He thought about his mom's chicken when he was ill, about Shenzi nagging him for a story, telling him it would make him feel better, her soft voice, her laugh. Her little hands nestled in his. Her silence.

"Find out for me where he is, Boda." He paused, then reached under his thin, overused pillow and pulled out a few notes. He handed both boys five thousand shillings. "And bring food," he said. His eyes searched them.

The boys looked at each other, nodded, and left.

Kevin lay back on the bed and took in a deep breath. He counted to ten and then started back to one. If they were telling the truth, they would return, he told himself. He dribbled the possibilities in his mind. He could only wait, he decided. Wait and see.

He fished out the photo that was still in his pocket, a little folded at the corners, and stared at it. The memory of that Saturday afternoon hit him like ice cream on a hot day. He could still hear the ice cream van, see Abdu the photographer, hear Shenzi's devil-may-care laugh, smell Teopista's *mandazis* frying…

And from an abyss inside, he mourned; a tearless grief overwhelmed him. He inhaled sharply. His mind strayed to his mother. He was still mustering the courage to visit her. He had tried several times and walked the one-kilometer stretch of road through the dusty corrugated roofed dwellings, past the St. John's Church Luzira, to where the road turned right toward the prison. And then he froze and turned around.

He felt himself change, as if the fight had initiated him into a man. He had to be *that man*.

Chapter 6

"Crown supermarket! Stage *seveni, eno!*" the conductor cried out, sliding the door of the taxi open; it was a fourteen-seater minibus with blue and white vertical markings on its sides all round, the branding of all the taxis in the city and around the country. The conductor swung to the side of the open door like an agile monkey.

He jumped off the landing, high-fived a few taxi touts at the stage who munched ferociously on salted, boiled peanuts in their shells that they passed around in a black plastic bag. They laughed loudly at something, and the conductor joined them, cupping his palm to receive peanuts. He shelled and popped all the purplish-pink nuts in his mouth at one go and threw thumbs-up to the driver, who motioned he wanted some as well.

It was a warm early afternoon; Kevin had finally worked up the courage to go see his mother at Luzira Maximum Prison. He hesitated in the taxi, even though this was the stop he needed to get off at. He was not sure he was ready to embark on this journey. As the last person filed out, Kevin thought again. Was it the right time?

The conductor walked back to the taxi and swung into the seat handing the driver a package of boiled peanuts wrapped in old newspaper, telling him in Luganda how good they were, "Mmm *Hajjati alina binyebwa biwooma!*" oblivious to Kevin seated only two rows away from him.

They parked the taxi for more customers. Being hardly a rush hour this far out, it was slow.

Could he do it? he wondered.

A voice told him he had put a bigger boy, a ferociously feared head of a gang in the hospital; surely, he was not that cowardly. Kevin sighed and reluctantly made his way out of the taxi.

The conductor hardly noticed him. Kevin looked around the looming supermarket and the dusty road that stretched out. He knew the direction to the prison.

He thought about Wasswa, his face swollen, his left eye so perforated, he could not see through it. Boda had brought him to his hideout, a slum in Kitintale. A part of Kevin wanted to be certain Wasswa would not come after him; another part wanted to see how much damage he had done to his rival.

Wasswa had smiled through his battered features. "So…you found me."

Kevin had looked at him. "I own your city," he told him. A part of him surged with pride.

Wasswa had scoffed. "And my traitor boys."

Kevin had stared at him for a long time. Then turned and walked out, but just in time to catch Wasswa labor painfully. "Watch your back."

Kevin smirked. "You watch yours."

Even as he walked down this dusty path for the nth time, Kevin felt for his knife. He would have to put it somewhere safe before he got to the prisons. Right where the path snaked to a right turn after St. John's Church, Kevin squatted by the side of the road and plunged the knife into the grassy sidewalk, patted the ground beside it, and walked on slowly. Boda and Livingstone had been curious, wanting to go with him earlier. He had told them to watch the place and scout their territory for any uprisings. "I will be back," was all he said.

Now only a few yards off from the prison gate, Kevin felt like a little boy again, filled with uncertainty and panic, needing assurance from his mother, needing her to protect and love him…forgive him.

He paused at the right turn. The sun beat down on him mercilessly. He reached into his pocket, felt the photograph there nestled safely on his thigh, imagined Shenzi's hand in his, urging him on, believing in him, and he took that step. And another. And yet another, each mounting step leading him closer to a fate he dreaded but to the closure he so badly needed to have.

He was at the gate sooner than he expected, even though the guard appraised him suspiciously, from his sandaled feet to his dark-washed jeans and graphic T-shirt. He hoped he did not look like he hailed from the streets, having washed up as best as he could and wearing the newer clothes in his collection. He had bought the African sandals cheaply from a Masai street hawker.

After going through the first gate, he was led to the women's maximum section, into the inspection room, where security patted him down while questioning him.

"Why are you here by yourself?" The warden, whose name tag read "Nakalya" stood akimbo.

Kevin stared her straight in the eye and said, "My aunty could not make it; she is sick."

The woman looked at him for a second, said a low, "Hmm," then led him to the visitors' room.

"You have fifteen minutes."

"But…"

"It's fifteen minutes."

Kevin sighed. The room had only three other prisoners dressed in their yellow uniforms, seated on mats on the concrete floor, speaking to their visitors. One lady carried a child another woman had brought her, and she held on to it lovingly. In another corner, a man in a suit spoke in a low tone to the woman whose hand held her crestfallen cheek. In yet another corner, there were three children about his age, all seated on the floor with a woman. They held one another, and he noticed the youngest was wiping her eyes while the man sat on a bench. He could have sworn the woman was innocent.

He wondered what his perception of prison had been. The women he saw in here looked as normal as any he saw on the streets every day, going about their daily business. Their hair coiffed, they looked ordinary and smart.

What if he turned himself in and his mother got out?

"Kevin?"

The voice behind him made him wheel around on the hard bench he was perched on.

"Kevin!" His mother grabbed him and held him tight. "Oh Kevin, Kevin!" Her voice quivered. Kevin returned her embrace, holding on tight.

"Mummy…" he whispered. The weight of guilt suddenly felt like a boulder sitting on his chest. He could not breathe. "Mummy…" he choked.

He could feel his mother shake, and then he heard her sob silently. Kevin was sure they embraced for the whole fifteen minutes on that first visit because just after they sat, with her laying a *lesu* on the ground, the warden who had brought him returned to inform them it was time up.

"Kevin." Dina touched him, his arms, his face. "Turn around; let me see you."

She looked him up and down. Tears rushed down her smooth cheeks like light rain on a bare marram road.

"I thought you were dead!" she whispered, pulling him back in for an embrace.

Kevin choked, fighting the urge to cry. "I have nine lives, Mummy," he tried to joke.

Finally, she asked, "Where is Shenzi?"

Kevin looked away. "Mummy it's a long story…"

"Is she okay? I told you to…" Her hand flew to her mouth.

Kevin quickly assured her. "She is better than okay. She is in America."

His mother frowned.

Kevin sighed. "I will tell you the story later."

His mother looked at him one more time. "Where are you? How are you living? Who is making your meals?"

He shook his head and lowered his gaze. "Mummy, I am sorry. I cannot keep on living with this guilt…." His mother shushed him and hissed, "Don't say anything stupid in here. I will protect my son to the death; you hear?"

Kevin felt his eyes fill with tears and blinked them back quickly. "Mama, but I…"

"*Shh!*" she told him quickly. "I am okay. They treat me *well* here. I even cook great food that you used to like…not chicken, but I have my little cooking tricks. I am in the kitchen department," she told him, trying to ease the mood, her hand caressing his arm, soothingly.

"So…?" she inquired, and he could see it in her eyes. She wanted to know how he was.

"Mummy, I am fine."

"Your uncle said he never saw you. It's been over a year, Kevin!" she hissed again. He could sense her exasperation and relief. "I have been so worried."

Kevin shook his head. "I am sorry, Mummy. I was afraid to go to Uncle's place. So…we stayed on the street, and then Shenzi got adopted… but they did not come for me…" he choked. "I miss her," he said, the boy in him peeking through. His mother placed a hand on his cheek. "You did well, my son. She would not survive without you if she went home. You did well. God has a reason…"

"God?" he asked. "All this mess…"

His mother shook her head. "No, we cannot blame God. We are responsible for our mistakes and decisions. But God will help us. I want you to go to church. Okay, don't run around with street boys. Go to church."

Kevin shook his head. "God is punishing me for what happened."

"Ah, Kevin." His mother reacted like he had blasphemed the Holy Spirit. "God is not like that. No one is punishing you. I am here because I chose to be here. No mother would want her child in a prison, if she could help it."

"But, Mummy…" he pleaded.

She shook her head. "Do I look unhealthy?" she asked him. He looked at her and agreed she looked fine.

"Okay then…You saved me. Let me save you."

Kevin said nothing.

"Teopista told me she saw you. That relieved me, but when I did not see you, I worried even more."

"Mummy, I killed…" She glowered at him, and he shut up.

"I told you to *stop* that nonsense. Your father was drunk. Stop it, Kevin, stop it! "

He pressed his lips together. For her, he would. He did not know if he would shake off the guilt. She was here because of him.

"What do you do here all day?" He finally dragged the conversation away from the grim topic of his father.

She turned her lips downward; her eyes rolled slightly. "Oh, many things. We even have classes. I am learning how to plait and treat hair. I now read a lot as well. Maybe I shall get you a book."

Kevin shook his head, smiling, marveling at how his mother never ceased to take care of him, even behind bars.

"What's the sentence?" he finally asked.

His mother sighed and looked away from him, then back at him. "Life…"

Kevin frowned, not sure he understood.

"I am here for a long, long time. I am not getting out," she said, reaching for his hand.

Kevin pulled away from her abruptly, suddenly angry. "Mummy!" he yelled, oblivious to how the other visitors turned to look at them.

His mother reached for him again. "Kevin…" She tried to hold him down, lest his outburst blow the lead off her secret.

She held his arms down between them and hissed at him: "Look at me, Kevin Atwooki Byamukama!"

Kevin shook his head from side to side. "Mummy no…" he whimpered.

"I said. Look. At. Me!" she hissed.

Kevin could not bring himself to.

The voice of Warden Nakalya interrupted them. "It's almost time. One minute."

Dina nodded and responded politely that they were almost finished. "You must behave like a big boy. The world is cruel. All you have is God and Shenzi; don't forget that. Promise me that."

How could he? So instead, he kept his eyes averted. He felt the pressure on his arms relax.

"Come back and see me," she told him, the firmness replaced by the warmth he had known on Block 4. "I miss you."

She stood up. He felt her briefly touch his fingers, and then she was gone.

Kevin sat there for a few more minutes before following the warden out.

At the door he asked, "Can I come back tomorrow?"

She looked at him, perceptively this time, almost as if she could sense the anguish between mother and son. "Visiting days are Tuesdays, Wednesdays, and Thursdays. You can come then. Any time in the afternoon is good since your mother is on kitchen duty earlier in the day."

Kevin nodded. His eyes scanned the huge prison facility, bone-colored walls, prisoners in yellow and orange, seated under trees, reading, chatting in groups. They had a different life behind these walls, yet it was their life now.

"Thank you," he said and turned to leave.

The following day was Wednesday, and he was back to see his mother. It got easier every time. In the weeks that followed, he told her everything in a miniseries, like a story that wasn't his own.

"No fights. I don't want to hear it." He kept his eyes averted when she said that. Then the list grew. Every visit.

"You carry a knife? Ah-ah! No!"

"But, Mummy, I have to protect myself. " He avoided her eyes; the worry in them would reduce his resolve.

After a couple of visits with a fresh scar or swelling, she changed the tune of her warning. He told her about the fights, the refined versions, and she cringed, but when their eyes met, he saw that blanketed beneath the fear was pride. He was glad she stopped urging him to go to his uncle.

I will go, not now, he told her.

Those fifteen minutes every Tuesday through Thursday to see his mother became the pivotal point of his existence. He walked with a fresh spring in his step. His dreams flourished in the light of new hope. Most days, he brought her money.

None of his colleagues knew about this part of his life. He shared almost everything with them, but he wanted his mother to be just his. His own secret.

The months flew by as quickly as the allowance the Matthews had sent. Even as his mind occasionally revisited their living situation, Kevin did not worry. He surprised himself. Only a year ago with Shenzi, he constantly worried, but a year later, with Boda and Livingstone…and his mother, worry was the furthest thing from his mind.

The boys had taken up space on the floor by the door in their room. After a day of productive policing of their territory, they sat back against the wall, devouring a dinner of chips and chicken. On tougher days, they had chapatti, washing it down with ice cold water encased in thin plastic bags. Satiated, they launched into lessons of the streets. They told Kevin about the people to avoid, those to befriend, those to appease, and those to ignore.

"I have been on the street from *yanga yanga* age." Boda spoke minimal English and Kevin delighted in learning street Luganda slang from him. "It's not easy, boss. You learn, learn, properly…slowly…uh! You be top top!" He enunciated with hand gestures.

"*Wama*, boss, we have the best area. The best!" Livingstone chimed in impatiently. Boda's slow drawl with accompanying dramatic effects always seemed to irritate Livingstone, Kevin noticed, and from the fluent way in which Livingstone spoke, Kevin felt he must have studied for a little longer before coming to the streets. He never talked about his life before the streets.

Both boys had seen leaders come and go, and by far the stretch of Kampala Road to Wandegeya was most coveted by the street leaders, and the protection provided for a leader was immutable. They considered it the "rich stretch." *Stretcher* was the slang. It opened anyone controlling it to underground dealings with prominent wealthy people who did not appear so, resourceful members of society who understood how effective a relationship, with what everyone saw as street bums, was to their businesses and operations.

Kevin soon learned that there were eyes and ears everywhere. Commands given were whispered from corridor to rooftop to street, and everyone in the territory was aware of goings on, reporting it to the leader's gang. It was a chain of information.

A notice had been passed around to watch for the twins and Wasswa. So far, Kevin was the youngest leader of the most lucrative part of the streets, and the other street section leaders were curious to meet him.

Under the guidance of Boda and Livingstone, Kevin quickly learned about the streets and all its sections. He went out of his way to meet other gangs and their leaders. Even at his age, he figured this information would be useful. As much as his boys told him there were people he needed to ignore or avoid, Kevin welcomed the challenge, mulling over ways to create ties with even the worst of the leaders.

"I will do small favors for them, invite them for pork…so they will have no choice but to owe me," he told the boys, and from their sighs, he knew they disapproved.

"We might need them," he assured them.

He settled into the leadership role. He enjoyed its perks, especially of the busiest and most lucrative part of the streets. Any of the street children who wanted to beg in their section had to pay a "tax" on their earnings. Kevin thought of how the children on Block 4 had to part with their trinkets and goods when they let Shenzi watch over their property as they played hide-and-seek.

He not only gave Boda and Livingstone the responsibility of collecting the "street tax" bringing in money they could survive on for a month or more. He gave them managerial positions in the Wandegeya area to Kampala Road, knowing that the distribution of power would keep them loyal and vigilant and give him an opportunity to see his mother regularly.

They kept an eye out for the twins, whose allegiance still wasn't clear, and for Wasswa, who had suddenly disappeared. After six months, it almost seemed he would not show up, until one night after seeing his mother, Kevin took a leisurely tour of Kampala city making note of all the different territorial positions of the different gangs and groups. As the sun sank low behind the thick blanket of night, he alighted at the Wandegeya stage and made for a *chapatti* stand he regularly purchased from.

Both Boda and Livingstone had started their daily run of tax collection and had left under Kevin's instruction to go easy on the newer children.

"But you know how everyone will complain..."

Kevin shrugged. "Tell them I said so, and if they don't like it, they can move to another place, or I will come myself...they don't want me to come myself." The boys meekly agreed.

Kevin scanned the chapattis on the stand, chatting amiably with the man who knew the streets well and the stories that run amok about it.

"Now you are big boss?" Ssuna asked, wiping the sweat off his brow, his grin revealing long, spaced teeth. He had long since upgraded his stand with an a la carte menu comprising chapatti and roasted meat in the evening hours.

Kevin shrugged. "Something like that. I told you I would take over."

"Heh, *ki* boss." The man chuckled like he was tasting the words on his tongue...how it rolled...if Kevin deserved the title. He patted out dough, slapped it on the narrow wooden table, and pulled out the rolling pin. "*Kale,* you should just go to school. These streets ah-ah."

Kevin watched him roll the pin and flatten the dough, keeping the shape perfectly round. He kept at it for a while and then flipped the flattened, round dough over, sprinkled a little flour over it, then rolled it out some more. Kevin kept his eyes on the dough, zoning out as Ssuna told long animated tales of the streets. Sometimes, he repeated them, like now.

"Do you make good money with this business?" he finally asked.

The chapatti seller quickly switched topics like it was nothing. "Oh, good, good money. You see, campusers like chapatti very, very much." He spoke emphatically. "Cheaper than take-away," he told Kevin.

Kevin agreed, smiling, and made his orders to go. "Make me hot, hot, fresh ones, ten of them." He told Ssuna.

Ssuna smiled.

"Do you want meat? I have meat, too." He indicated the charcoal grill where pieces of beef clung to skewer sticks over the mesh on the stove.

Kevin smiled. Shenzi would have insisted they buy them. "Okay, five sticks," he told the man, whose grin widened.

"Three hundred each."

Kevin was feeling gracious tonight, so he did not haggle prices with Ssuna; besides, he had grown to trust his products. When he had said his goodbyes, a paper bag of piping hot chapatti and meat in one hand, Kevin made his way to his place, ambling along leisurely. He passed by a barely lit corridor—the death corridor—that was wrought with horror stories of kidnappings and murders, but he had shrugged them off as ghost stories to keep beggars from hovering.

Suddenly, he felt a sharp jab against his shoulder. He swiftly turned around in time to sidestep the sharp-edged object that was making its descent on him again. His eyes darted quickly around him, and he jogged backward, away from his assailant and the object. The lanky figure lunged forward, lashing out again. Kevin tossed his bag of food aside and, yanking his knife from his back pocket, stepped into the sliver of light cast by a lone streetlamp.

"I told you to watch your back!" the voice in the shadows spoke.

Kevin shook his head, recognizing Wasswa. "And I told you to watch *yours* instead," he replied. He could hardly feel a thing. Adrenaline pumped through his veins; warm, moist, sticky blood trickled from the wound on his shoulder.

Wasswa laughed and then lunged for him. Kevin dodged the lanky figure. "I won. Let it go," he told Wasswa.

Wasswa laughed, a bitter laugh. "You humiliated me. One of us dies."

"You should go. I am leader now!" Kevin hurled the words with all the authority he could muster, but the taller boy angled for another slash. Kevin had learned how the streets worked, the secret calls and codes, and the privileges of leaders. He wondered how Wasswa could bravely come out of hiding to challenge a leader without due process. It was a death wish. Kevin had vowed he would not kill another man, not like his father, so he put his fingers in his mouth and whistled. Wasswa froze for a minute. Kevin could see his mouth hanging, and then the tall, lanky boy turned and fled into the "death corridor," followed by accompanying calls and yelps from a block away, approaching him.

Three boys sprinted toward Kevin, hesitated for instruction, which Kevin gave with a simple signal toward the retreating fallen leader as he limped away. He watched as three figures bounded through the tunnel at breakneck speed, catching up with the fourth runner faster than he could get away.

He felt around for the bag of chapatti and found it soon enough, the paper bag torn. Thankfully, his chapattis stayed intact, neatly wrapped in *kavera* before being inserted into the paper bag. He lost a meat skewer in a soaked pothole but decided one gone was better than all gone.

The next morning, they found Wasswa's body in a swamp in Kisenyi. Nobody talked about it. The knife wounds were an indicator this was no drowning. Some of the street people decided it was best he was dead. Others thought it was unfortunate he had not conceded defeat.

The police closed the case almost immediately. No one talked, no one was going to say anything, and Wasswa had been in and out of prison one too many times.

Kevin wrestled nightmares for a week, until he stopped sleeping at night altogether. He woke up in a cold sweat at the end of a torturous dream, breathing heavily, his arm and shoulder still bandaged from the wound sustained. He pulled the picture from under his pillow again and looked at it long and hard. He could hear the taxi touts call for taxis to the old taxi park, new taxi park, all the way to Bugolobi and Kitintale.

He swung his legs to the side of the bed and picked up the T-shirt he had taken off before he slept. He needed to do one thing.

* * *

His mother was smiling as usual when she approached their meeting corner. Kevin smiled back wearily.

"You look tired." She leaned into her open palm. "Is everything okay?"

Kevin nodded. He wanted to tell her another boy had died because of him, that he hated his life, that the dreams would not let him sleep. He wanted to tell her so much, but he could not. He did not know how, so he simply said, "I am going to start a chapatti business."

His mother sat back, folding her arms over her chest. She looked at her son. Kevin spied a mixture of emotion in her eyes.

"I knew you would be a businessman. I wanted you to go to business school, do your degree, even a master's, and start something. *Hmm*, you are not even thirteen, and you are thinking of business?"

Kevin smiled, hoping at least it made her proud.

"Do what you can do to get away from street survival, my son. Please call your uncle…"

Kevin shook his head. "No, Mummy, let me do this. I am a man now," he told her determinedly.

She sighed but said nothing.

"I will make a lot of money and get a good lawyer to get you out. Then we will find Shenzi, and everything will be fine."

Kevin loved to see his mother smile, and it gave him hope.

"Do you think I can get out?" she had asked him rhetorically.

"Anything is possible. It's what I learned at the orphanage, at the church. They said anything is possible. And it's true."

* * *

Kevin brought the good news home to Boda and Livingstone: "A chapatti business."

Both boys looked at each other, then at Kevin like he had gone mad, then snickered, trying their hardest to hide their bemusement.

"Boss, how?" Boda said, shaking his head. "Customer, from where? *Atte* stoves?" He shook his head.

Kevin did not respond. For two days he stayed in his room, so accustomed to the ecstatic moans and groans coming from the upstairs apartment, they did not even faze him anymore. His mind conceived a plan.

Chapter 7

December 2002

Livingstone and Boda convinced him to attend the party. It was happening in a little room in a tall building by New Park. The landlord rented it out to Festo every so often and turned a blind eye to whatever happened there.

"What happens at the party?"

The older boys exchanged grins. "It's a hot party. Even the landlord cannot disturb us. Festo gives him money." Livingstone enlightened Kevin, who learned later that all the drugs pushed on the streets had their origin of exchange at the parties Festo threw.

"What if he gets caught?" Kevin dreaded being in the hands of the authorities, especially after his visits to the prison.

The boys rubbished his apprehension. "*Polisi* want *da* money. Dey come we pay. Game over!" Boda assured him. Festo knew all the drug deals and pushers in their area.

"But how?" Kevin remained unconvinced.

Livingstone guffawed. "We own *Stretcher*. Festo owns park. He is friends with many businesspeople. They also give him these drugs to sell. Hmm! So now we have our own bodyguards for the party. Police cannot touch us." Too many important players in the drug businesses needing to protect their profits agreed with Festo and the other gang leaders to protect those party nights. It was a mixed crowd of little groups of different street gangs from the city center to as far as Jinja.

"These people here here, they are not simple. We on the street we know because we deal with them," Boda assured Kevin. Later Kevin would learn that business in the city was not as it seemed, nor the so-called businesspeople.

"Come! You will like it," Livingstone told him.

"Also, because the gangs want you to come. Remember how you say, 'we might need them'?"

Kevin craved rest and time to complete his mental notes on the different scenarios of starting a chapatti business, but the boys would not let him.

He reluctantly agreed, and they set out at ten at night. When they got to the building, the music was all they needed as their compass to point them to the venue. It was a little room on the second floor, manned by a bulky man with a mean face at the door who, on seeing them, nodded and opened the door. Kevin gulped a lungful of air as they stepped into the room that reeked of sweat, booze, and cigarettes. The intoxicating smell of *ganja* choked Kevin, and he coughed.

He had stayed away from drugs and booze for Shenzi's sake and because alcohol reminded him of his father. The benefits of sobriety seemed to outweigh intoxication from his perspective after witnessing all the people on the street who got inebriated, tipping over the edge of sobriety in the most baffling way imaginable. He exuded mixed reactions to drunkenness: the impossible dread of danger looming, which, yes, led to fights, mild to violent depending on the crowds; then he found some funny, when the intoxicated crew sang off tune, wept, or laughed nonstop. But the memory of his drunken father dissolved any traces of humor, and he clung to the conviction that nothing good would come of it.

A thin-as-a-reed boy approached him, clad in baggy jeans, a red bandanna, and a baggy tartan shirt; his left arm jingled with multiple chains and wrist bands of various colors. Above the din of Ginuwine's *pony*, he stuck out his thin arm in greeting to Boda and Livingstone.

"*Ki Rasta.*"

They clapped arms and then he turned to Kevin. The toothpick that stuck out from the corner of his mouth was spat out to the floor. The reedy youth grinned, revealing yellowing teeth.

"*Ki boss, bad man!*"

Kevin smiled back and took the hand offered to him. Festo's reputation preceded him. Many stories of his pickpocketing exploits blazed from Kampala Road to Masaka. There was no one like him. He could escape a Houdini magic trick if given the challenge or pick your teeth right out of your mouth as he smiled to say good morning to you…those were the stories Kevin heard. His forte, the small and compact Old and New taxi park area, was notorious for high rates of pickpocketing. Still, the perpetrators remained elusive; no one reported it either. And so Festo's kingdom thrived.

Festo then led him away. "I have a gift for you. From our side to your side. *Ya gwan!*"

Kevin glanced once at his boys who looked on encouragingly. "Okay," he shouted above the music.

Young people filled the room, some he had seen on the street, others he had not, but he observed they were all young, a few younger than him, but most older than him. Festo had a hand on his back as he ushered him through the crowd of young intoxicated dancing men and women who whooped and swayed against each other. They got to the other end of the room, where a few plastic chairs leaned against the wall. A girl in a white minidress sat on one. Her hot water braids were an array of colors: blue, pink, yellow and black. Her make-up was so heavy Kevin could not tell if she was beautiful or not. She sipped on her beer casually, swaying her head to the music, not trying to get up to dance. When she saw Kevin and the king of downtown, her face lit up with a smile. She waved.

Kevin waved back, unsure who she had waved to. The girl got up as they approached her and hugged Festo. Kevin watched how his hands slid to her backside, how he squeezed her ample behind and then languidly let his hands travel up to her back, to her slim waist and pull her close as he leaned in, their lips almost touching, and spoke to her. Kevin watched them; the lack of privacy on the streets had taught him a lot more than a biology class in his former school would have. Here, the lessons were free and a lot more graphic. He could indulge, he told himself, but there were far too many important things on his mind: making money, getting his mother out of jail, and then finding Shenzi. He was still curious, though. Still slightly fascinated at these carefree interactions. He gave the girl in the white dress a once-over and instantly decided she was not his type, anyway.

Festo was leaning toward him and whispering in his ear, "Here is my gift. Shamsa." He told Kevin.

Kevin frowned. Festo nodded, urging him on with his facial expression. Then he pushed something in his pocket and left Kevin with the heavily made-up girl.

Kevin stared at her stupidly, for once at a loss about what to do. Shamsa smiled at him, sipped her beer, and swayed her hips. Kevin looked around, still unsure what to do with her. This was not what he had expected.

Suddenly, she laughed and edged closer. *"Ki boss!"* she said in his ear.

Kevin nodded and held his breath. The smell of beer on her flooded his nose. She was leaning close, urging him to dance with her, but all he could smell was the alcohol. She held on to him, and he was sure he was going to throw up. Quickly excusing himself, he mumbled his need to use the restrooms and bolted in the direction she pointed him to.

He threw the door open, panting. The alcohol had zapped him back to a place of trauma, and he choked on memories. Leaning over the sink, trying to steady his breathing, Kevin was oblivious to the door opening until the music rushed in, and then it was closed and Shamsa was behind him. She smiled at him through the mirror. "You need help?" she asked.

Kevin stared back at her stunned; she was reaching for his belt. He hastily pushed her hand away. "No, go away!" he shrieked, almost panicked, feeling silly at the same time. When he saw her face transform into one of confusion, he realized he would have to make it up to Festo. Gifts had to be accepted. It was a pact.

"Give me a minute," he told her.

Shamsa was looking at him in the mirror blankly. "Don't you like me?"

Kevin stared back at her face. Her eyes were heavily lined with dark pencil, her lips bright red, and the powder on her face created a mismatch of color with her neck. The one woman he had thought wore makeup to perfection was Shenzi's mother. Even though he could not stand Ameena, he hated to admit that Shamsa could not compare. She probably should not have worn the makeup at all. His gaze dropped to the sink.

"I am tired," he told her finally, looking up in the mirror and smiling weakly at her.

She seemed reassured and moved closer, "I can help you feel better."

Kevin cursed under his breath. A pact was a pact.

* * *

As they headed home past two in the morning, Boda and Livingstone pestered Kevin about Shamsa, who had hung on his arm almost all night.

Boda nudged Livingstone. "I think she gave him good, good time."

Kevin shrugged. If Festo found out that he had paid Shamsa not to touch him, there would be one of two reactions, disappointment for a rejected proposition or admiration for his ingenious solution. Kevin discovered the roughrider condom Festo had planted in his pocket and tore it open, then left the wrapper on the bathroom floor, in case there was a need for evidence. Shamsa incidentally, seemed happier with money than sleeping with him, anyway; so was he.

The boys snickered like children. Kevin shook his head and bid them goodnight.

He drifted off almost instantly into a surreal dream where Ameena came to him naked, telling him she could make him feel better and he protested, saying Shenzi would find them, but she proceeded anyway.

Kevin started awake, and instantly touched his manhood that was pulsating with a rush of blood, hard and stiff, and his shorts wet.

$$* * *$$

Kevin declined to go downtown to celebrate the New Year with the other boys, who would spend the night hopping from one celebration spot to the next. Theft was on a high tide during the festive season, as well as wary police eyes. He counted their earnings from street tax and marveled at how much they had made since the 21st of December.

He strolled along the Wandegeya stretch, up to the main Makerere University gate, and then back down.

He stood by Tipsy take-away, observing the crowd as they surged and moved in either direction, then made his move. The stall that was busiest stood a little apart from the other sellers, close to a butchery that was closed for the evening. Kevin, hunched and scurried like a cat, gliding toward the stall. While the seller, a tall, fat man who sweated profusely as he rolled out the dough, handed over a little plastic bag stuffed with fresh hot chapattis to a customer, Kevin dove in for the kill, grabbing a chunk of freshly fried chapattis off the griddle they were stacked upon.

Someone screamed out, alerting the seller, who immediately lunged at Kevin. Kevin was quick sidestepping his heavy hand. He made a run but tumbled over, falling forward. A passerby tripped him, then grabbed him, shouting, "*Wuuyo, boss!*"

Kevin struggled under the tight grip of the passerby. Two other pairs of arms, amid angry shouts, clamped on to him, one arm across his neck in a chokehold. They shuffled him bodily to the seller, who had abandoned his stall in anger, charging at Kevin.

Kevin braced himself for the worst. The tall man slapped his bare arms and grabbed him by the collar.

"*Muleke,*" he ordered and then thanked the two men profusely. "I will deal with him," he added in Luganda, and the men left Kevin to his demise, even though they each got a kick in, a slap there, and nudged his head, pulling at his ear. Kevin slapped them off. The man dragged him by his collar to the stand.

"In my culture a thief loses his fingers for stealing." Kevin tried to shrug out of his grip to no avail. The chapattis still in his hands, the big man yanked them away from him and hurled them to the ground.

Kevin kept his eyes glued on him, defiant. "Those were fresh chapattis. Each would cost me three hundred shillings. You are going to make that money back for me. And then when I think you have made my profit, I shall let you go."

Kevin kept his eyes on the man, then spat on the side. "Do you know who I am?" he smirked. Their little scuffle had drawn a crowd of fellow vendors and customers that started to bay for blood.

"*Ssebo, mukuube* beat him!"

"Stupid street children!"

"*Muuwe engolo!*"

More people pooled in their direction, drawn as if by a magnet to the chaos.

Another chapatti seller helped disperse the small audience while keeping an eye out for his partner-in-trade's stall. The robbed chapatti seller, whose name was Ssalongo Bwanika, immediately put Kevin to work.

"Don't touch my chapattis with your filthy hands," he barked at Kevin, then instructed him to wash his hands from a jerrican of water that was pushed under the stall. A little soap dish with yellowish bar soap sat by the old yellow jerrican. Kevin scowled as he squatted and washed.

When he was done, he stood up, glowered at Ssalongo, and said, "I own this street."

Ssalongo laughed. "*Mtscheeew*, just pass that dough here before I slap you to the next stall, where they will kill you. You street vermin own nothing."

Kevin pushed it. "I will call my boys, and they will…"

Ssalongo dismissed him with a loud, "Aah! You will call no one because I own three stalls, and we will keep you here forever. Don't play with me! And don't try to run." The man wagged a fat finger in his face. It was almost midnight, and Kevin knew they would be closing soon. He waited as Ssalongo finished selling the last of his chapattis, then obediently started passing him the dough he needed to make more. He watched the big man slap the dough on the board, knead and stretch it, then pour oil over it and let it sit.

Finally, he took a break, sat back on an old pile of beer crates, wiping his brow with his inner upper arm, then looked at Kevin squarely, almost curiously. Kevin looked away.

"What's your name?" the bulky man asked.

Kevin stared ahead stonily.

"Heh!" The man nudged him roughly.

Kevin swayed and turned to him. "Kevin."

He could feel the man appraise him. "You don't look very street," Ssalongo said finally.

"And you look like a nightclub bouncer, not a chapatti seller," Kevin responded, then winced in surprise when a sharp slap landed on his cheek.

The man sucked his teeth, then laughed. "Ah-ha, no wonder you are here, talking back to elders! I am going to keep an eye on you."

Kevin spat. Ssalongo Bwanika slapped his ear.

They had a second round of selling more chapattis. This time, Kevin kneaded and Ssalongo shouted instructions at him. When he felt Kevin was slow, he would shove him aside and impatiently take over while yelling at him to do it right.

"Press, press it in!" the man told him. "*Gwe musai muto;* you should be able to press this dough."

Two hours later, with sweaty brows, burned fingers, and aching shoulders, Kevin was famished.

Ssalongo handed him a chapatti and a cup of black tea. "You earned it. Good job," he told Kevin, like a father looking out for his son. He proceeded to pack up his equipment in a bag and fastened it securely with sisal rope.

"Tomorrow we start at four in the afternoon."

Kevin hesitated. "What if I don't come?"

The man looked at him. "You will."

Kevin started. "No, I won't."

The man shrugged and smiled faintly. "You owe me. Or it's the police and Luzira."

Kevin slowly leveled with the man, their eyes meeting.

Ssalongo Bwanika looked him over suspiciously, then nodded briefly. "Now help me carry these."

Kevin obediently did as he was told.

When Kevin told the boys what he had done, his long-winded plan to get them off the streets, Boda hung his head, and Livingstone whistled.

"That was dangerous. Do you know they killed a boy for stealing chapattis in Bweyogerere?"

Kevin shook his head. "I am not stupid. I had been watching Ssalongo. He is not an evil man. If he was, I would be dead. Trust me. We will learn this trade and start our own."

"Hmm, okay." The boys guffawed, unconvinced.

The next day, Kevin was at the stall earlier than expected, which pleased Ssalongo. Boda and Livingstone continued to carry on their routine, reporting to Kevin at the end of the night when he returned smelling of fried dough and grease.

In a month, Kevin could man the stall by himself, from quickly rolling out the kneaded dough to frying it on the flat plate, rotating it with a piece of folded cardboard paper with a flat base, then flipping it over and doing the same. Ssalongo watched him like a mother who approves of her daughter's first meal as she prepares it.

"You are even better than me." He could sense the wonder in Ssalongo's tone.

Kevin shrugged. "I am *musaai muto*," he replied and dodged the fat hand that swept up, missing his ear by an inch.

For three months, Kevin worked for Ssalongo for free, much to the chagrin of the boys, who felt he should earn something.

"Patience," he told them as they wolfed down take-away Livingstone had gotten that evening for them all. He had visited his mother, telling her of his prowess at chapatti making, how much of a chapatti maestro he had become, and she laughed, her eyes brimming with pride. "Are you making money?"

He lowered his gaze, shaking his head. "Not yet."

To his surprise, she did not cajole him. Instead, she told him, "Good things come to those who wait. Be patient."

He wanted to tell her their lives had been unfortunate, and it seemed like no good thing had come to her; she was going to die in prison because of him, but he held his tongue. Moments with his mother three days a week were precious, too precious to spend fighting over events past or events uncertain, so he basked in the now.

If his mother said good things came to those who were patient, then he figured in time he would get her out and they would find Shenzi, and everything would be all right.

"Ssalongo will pay you," his mother said with a smile, then with a finger pointed in his face she added, "You don't belong to the street, my son. You are going to be very great, okay?"

Kevin hang on the words of his mother every visit, mulling over them and letting them invade every sore part of his soul. He scarfed them up: her encouragement, her scolding, her correction, all wrapped in a package of love he felt he was receiving even more now that they were away from his father. Her presence gave him strength in his soul and spring in his step. He missed her greatly when he did not see her and always returned on those three visiting days to indulge her in more news of his chapatti-making prowess.

Kevin not only helped Ssalongo with the chapattis, but he also watched the other stalls keenly: their customer base and their hours of operation.

One day, he suggested to Ssalongo, "Why don't we open in the morning for breakfast, then close and open for lunch, then close and open at six?"

Ssalongo grunted. "Too much work."

Kevin made a note of it and mused over it. He figured if they opened all day, then they would make more money in the long run. "Okay, how about we do morning and night only?"

Ssalongo glanced at him darkly as he flipped over a chapatti. "You talk too much. Do you know how long I have done this?"

Kevin watched him. "No."

"Okay, don't school a master then."

Kevin realized waiting to start his own would be far better than trying to convince an old expert to try new things.

Competition was growing as younger, more aggressive chapatti sellers mushroomed all over the street, lining up to the back and front gates of Makerere University.

With the newer stock of chapatti sellers came the added fascination: "rolled eggs." He saw one of the stall owners make it, frying the eggs on his flat pan and spreading it over a fried chapatti, then roll it up.

Kevin asked him, "What is that?"

"*Eno rolexi,*" the man said with a toothy grin. He told him the story of Sula, the man everyone claimed had invented this all-in-one wholesome dish.

"Rolex?" he frowned.

"*Yeh,*" the man said with emphasis. "Rolled eggs," he added, and Kevin made the connection.

Kevin tried to convince Ssalongo to start making *rolex*. "These new chapatti sellers are making a lot of money with rolex!"

Ssalongo did not respond immediately but six months later announced to Kevin that they needed to open in the morning as well since competition was robbing them of profits.

"But I can't come in the morning, so you will come and set up and start, " said the older man. "And you can add some rolexi, but don't waste too much money on eggs. They are expensive."

Kevin took the equipment to his place, promising Ssalongo he would take good care of it. Every morning with the help of Boda and Livingstone, he hurled it out across the street, and while the sun figured out its path from its eastern bed, lulled by the Imam's call to prayer, Kevin took those few minutes to teach Boda and Livingstone. In a few weeks, Ssalongo's profits climbed once more. Working two shifts with the help of the boys in the morning, Kevin's hope grew wings. He saw his future much clearer. In between the breaks when Ssalongo would take over, Kevin would stroll along the pavement, browsing through magazines and newspapers. He usually looked at the pictures of well-placed people in society, and read all their stories. Some had come from the streets; others had had their ugly share of life, but in the end, it had not defined them, and they were there staring back at him with even teeth peeking through a lustrous smile, smooth, shiny skin, and clothes he saw in the windows of boutiques. He lived for the pages of these magazines and newspapers, telling himself if they could do it, so could he. Then he would sit back with the photo of him and Shenzi and dream, like he had in Block 4. In his daydreams, they drove the poshest cars, they went to many cities around the world, and when she smiled and laughed, her eyes were large and brown. Some days they were watching soccer together; other days they were in another country; other days they had so much money they were just giving it away.

"Patience," his mother's voice would sound in his head.

"Patience," he told himself.

Chapter 8

Late July rode in on the coattails of dust and heat. It rained unceremoniously, then stopped. Business dragged both on the streets and at the chapatti stands.

"Why don't you rent a little *kafunda* near the market...?" Kevin proposed to Ssalongo, who brushed him away impatiently. "Don't tell me what to do."

Kevin always made mental notes of all the gestures of progress that *Ssalongo* rejected, planning his own exit. It had been almost seven months of routine. His only moment of freedom was in the mornings, when he seized the opportunity with Boda and Livingstone to explore how best to market the chapattis and rolexes. He suggested they make them bigger and thicker, and *Ssalongo* rejected the idea until a newcomer took almost half his clientele with bigger chapattis. He insisted they increase their rolex volume, but Ssalongo was hesitant, grunting his disapproval and leaving instructions for more chapattis to be made in the morning, to which Kevin said he would need more help. With proof of the growing profit, *Ssalongo* agreed to have Boda and Livingstone help Kevin in the morning. "But if you steal from me, I will cut off your balls and give them to the witchdoctor in Mabira."

Kevin stifled a low chuckle and nodded solemnly.

"How long will you work with this *ki-man?*" the boys inquired of Kevin.

Kevin smiled and simply said, "Be patient." He was saving whatever money Ssalongo had given him of the profits, and he had sternly instructed both boys not to waste the money they collected. They faithfully brought in the money in the evening, and Kevin stashed away huge chunks, giving them enough for the week. "The agreement was 'We must start our own business.'"

His opportunity came one afternoon when Ssalongo had taken his children to school.

"You know how boarding school can be. I shall be back. Take care of things." He had given him a stern look.

Kevin nodded.

It was relentlessly hot, and Kampalans walked around sluggishly, stopping by stalls surveying the different chapattis in their variety. Kevin was hungry and faint. He had not eaten in four hours, and liver and chips beckoned to him. He hesitated, not wanting to leave the stand since Boda and Livingstone were doing their street rounds. He thought about making himself a rolex from the eggs Ssalongo always stashed at the stall for breakfast. But his mouth pooled with saliva as the savory smell of meat clinging to skewer sticks slowly browning wafted to him. His stomach grumbled. He asked the vendor at the next stall to watch his goods as he made a quick stop at the take-away only a few steps from them for liver. Suddenly, he had a bright idea.

He got his order of liver and chips and returning to his stall, unrolled a chapatti and warmed it on the flat pan, he broke an egg into the bowl, diced a few onions and tomatoes, and fried it on the flat-based wrought-iron pan they made chapattis with; he laid it over the chapatti, poured some of the liver in its thick sauce with chips in the mix, then rolled it carefully so nothing spilled. He sat back and munched greedily on his newest creation.

Just as he bit into his combination a third time, three white tourists—two ladies and a man—crossed the road from a taxi they had alighted from. They looked young and fresh, sunburned but oblivious. Their awe-struck gazes at the scene of Wandegeya that greeted them was not lost on Kevin or the other sellers. One whistled, *"Mzungu wooyoo!"*

Kevin watched them as they made their way toward a take-away. They stopped and seemed to disagree on something. Suddenly, one girl walked right up to his stall. Kevin smiled cordially, "Hello, madam, a chapatti… omelet…rolex?" he asked, turning up the customer-care charm.

The girl smiled back, her eyes a clear blue, dancing in anticipation. Laid in a pale freckled face, her lips, a little thin and red, widened in an earnest smile. Her blond hair was thin and held back in a band. Kevin decided that apart from her eyes, she was not pretty enough or fleshy enough. He was noticing the girls a little more these days and was stirred by the curvier ones. With his ever-growing attention to women, he discerned how his insides stirred at the sight of a full woman, with ample breasts and a healthy backside; the more it jiggled, the more it fascinated him.

He had seen the prostitute who lived above him a couple of times and fantasized about her, dreaming about her occasionally. To him, she was perfect; her chest carried breasts that sat firmly, and on days he brushed by her on the stairway to his room, he would notice the huge nipples peeping through her see-through blouses. Sometimes he pretended to have forgotten something, only to turn around and walk slowly behind her watching her buttocks jiggle up and down. Her name was Desire. He liked it…it truly fitted her.

Boda and Livingstone urged him to approach her, but Kevin always said he was too busy trying to get them off the streets. He hated to admit he was just shy. Her aura scared him; she was so experienced. The most he had gotten was Shamsa, who touched his penis while in the bathroom in an erotic attempt to "help him pee," and he had freaked out. He told himself one day he would overcome the fear and step up to Desire.

"Holly, I thought you wanted…" the man with brown curly hair and a bleached goatee stood by the girl at his stall; the other girl with him jogged along slightly. She was plumper, and in her tie-dye romper, her body filled out better, although to Kevin's disappointment her breasts were pea-size small.

The girl called Holly glanced at the man standing beside her. "Changed my mind; I want these…" she was pointing at his meal.

Kevin could feel the eyes of everyone in the vicinity on him. Watching. "This?" he asked eagerly.

"What is it called?" the girl grinned back.

The man beside her started almost apologetically, "Er…Holly…" but she interrupted him, her eyes trained on Kevin. "What's that?"

Kevin smiled, following her finger. "My food?" he said, and she giggled.

"Yeah, but what is it? Can you make it for me? It looks delish."

Kevin shrugged. An opportunity to please had come. He still had a pack of the chips and the liver, hoping to make another one for dinner. "Yes, I can."

Brown-eyed girl chimed in at that point, "But what is it?"

The young man looked at Kevin like he needed to apologize. His face flushed, and his lips thinned almost in exasperation. Kevin had never seen a white person turn pink. A part of him was enjoying the scene. "It's okay…"

"No…" Holly's determination made the others flush in embarrassment, and the chubby girl waited, her brown eyes never wavering from him. Kevin blinked, trying to absorb the situation as they all haggled about what to have and how Holly was embarrassing Kevin, and what did it matter; *it's roadside food. We are hungry; let's get whatever and go.*

Kevin sighed and, like an umpire determining the fate of a player on a football pitch, he blared, "It's like er…rolexi, but with liver and chips. That's all." The squabbling stopped.

"Doesn't that sound nice?" the chubby girl said, probing the tall man, who pursed his thin lips and shrugged.

"Okay, I will try it. Do you make it often?" he asked Kevin eventually, then glanced at his watch. "We need to hurry; we will be late."

"Yes, I do," he lied, for fear they would reject it if he said it was the first he ever made one. Conscious of the eyes that appraised him, Kevin retrieved their stash of eggs and broke six. He chopped the onions and tomatoes, splurged on the green pepper, and whipped the mixture with a fork. He then rolled out the biggest chapattis he could, fried them, set them aside, and poured a portion of the slimy, colorful egg mixture on the flat pan in a circular motion. He placed them in the chapattis, apportioned the remaining liver and chips on each of the three rolex bases, and folded them extra neatly and tightly to avoid any filling escaping, then he wrapped each in a thin, translucent plastic wrap and handed them to the three eager white people, who *oohed* and *aahed* at the speed at which he had fixed their meals.

Kevin watched with satisfaction as they eagerly bit into them. Holly reacted first. Her blue eyes rounded and danced with a different light. "Yum! This is better than a burrito!"

The man nodded. He chewed delicately, as if he was a judge on a cooking show critically accessing the ingredients in the dish presented to him. "Oh, these are good. African burritos?"

The brown-eyed girl waited expectantly for Kevin to validate that rhetorical statement. "What are they called?"

Kevin paused briefly. "In Uganda we call them *barito*."

"What?" Holly's blue eyes, which Kevin enjoyed looking at for the way they darkened or lightened, widened.

"He said *bah-ree-toe*," brown-eyed girl raised her brows, her tongue digging into her cheek.

"I know, just like *burrito*." The man was grinning. "It really is a unique one, I tell you that. Love it!" They all laughed.

"How much, sorry?" Holly was asking.

Kevin had not thought about the price. They often sold their chapattis for three hundred shillings, their rolex for five hundred, but with liver and chips? He made a quick mental calculation: if he split the amount of liver and chips he had bought between them and added the rolex price... "One thousand," he chimed out.

The man fished out a crisp five-thousand-shilling note with its pink and blue watermark colors.

After Kevin gave them their change, they let him keep an extra one thousand, which they called "a tip," promising to return for more as they headed to the university.

When they left, Kevin noticed the small crowd that had gathered as if Ssalongo's stall had become the venue of a thrilling crime scene. The curious horde had leaned in, listening to the dialogue and inquisitively watching what had transpired. Eventually three people from that crowd stepped up to the stall ordering the same, *"Eh kyi? Barito?"* asked a clueless-looking girl who Kevin perceived instantly was a campus student; her braids were tight and smelled of olive oil hair spray, fresh from the salon.

Kevin made them all barito*s*. When he ran out of ingredients, he asked his neighbor to watch the stall as he made a quick dash to the market to purchase more eggs, onions, tomatoes, and green peppers and to Mama Nanka's for fried liver.

In less than two hours, the word spread like wildfire, and Ssalongo's stall burgeoned with curious onlookers and interested buyers of the famed barito*s*. By the time the sun had set and the moon, the size of a fingernail, took over the skies, Kevin had sold more barito*s* than chapattis and rolex*es* and made more money in four hours than the twelve hours they had worked between the morning and afternoon-to-evening shift.

The next day, when Ssalongo came in, Kevin excitedly introduced him to the world of barito*s*. They even wrote out a placard announcing the introduction of their barito product on a large cardboard paper in black and red markers and stationed it at the foot of the tall charcoal stove. Kevin had half expected objection from the older man, but on seeing the profit made in a day, he grudgingly watched and learned from him. Before August ended, their profits had risen ten times higher than when he had first started working for Ssalongo.

Despite their growth, Ssalongo would not think of opening a restaurant. One night, after a frustrating conversation about a *kafunda* for barito and chapatti, Kevin told Ssalongo, he felt it was time for him to move on, do his own thing. Ssalongo laughed. "Do what?"

Kevin looked him squarely in the face and said, "My restaurant."

Ssalongo gaped at Kevin. For once, he was at a loss for words. Then he drawled, "Okay. Go."

* * *

Kevin saw Desire again on his way up the stairs to his house. This time she wore jeans, with a fitted crop top that exposed her midriff, in the dimly lit light of the stairway. Desire's arms glimmered, and like a spell it cast on him, it chased the fatigue and irritation that crowded his mind. The sight of her was as relaxing as cold water on a hot day flipping chapattis. She turned around to see him and smiled, then hesitated on his landing and opened her huge handbag, searching for something. Her shiny black braids streaked with brown fell into her face, and Kevin stood there foolishly transfixed, staring at her.

She looked up momentarily and smiled. "*Oli otya,* neighbor."

Kevin swallowed, his mouth dry. "*Gyendi…*" he responded, not sure what to call her. Whatever she was frantically searching for caused her to tip her bag, and the contents tumbled out. She sucked her teeth in annoyance.

Kevin wasted no time in busying himself collecting her valuables off the rough landing. "Sorry," he half-whispered and picked up the items one by one. Desire was cursing under her breath. "These *bu* big bags… things just disappear in them!" she *tsk-tsk*ed.

Kevin's eyes widened at the contents; makeup, useless papers, a wallet, condoms, hairbrush, tooth brush, even fork and spoon, carefully wrapped soap, and what looked like miniature bottles with Sheraton marked on them. She thanked him and hurriedly put them in her bag. Her house keys were what she was seeking frantically, and they found the bunch within the folds of the middle compartment of the big brown bag.

"*Bambi,* thank you," she said cheerfully and walked away, then turned and appraised him slowly, a slow smile on her sensual red lips. "You should bring me some rolex, and the other thing…*eh kyi? Bari…*what? I hear they are famous at Ssalongo's."

"Baritos," Kevin enunciated. For days on end Kevin, could not stop thinking about what Desire had said, her baby face, smooth and round, red full lips smiling at him, her eyes roving over his lanky frame that had scaled inches. Even his mother had commented, "Eh! You are getting tall!"

She loved the idea of the baritos. "You know you can do more with this barito idea?"

He was eager to learn. "I want to start my own restaurant and sell *chapattis* and baritos. If Sula started rolex, I am the one who started barito."

His mother smiled approvingly. "Yes! Now, maybe you can even do one with chicken, fish, peas, or beans? Maybe grasshoppers?"

Kevin's eyes lit up. "Mummy, that's a good idea! But they should be so, so good. I can't cook like you…"

Dina shooed him. "Next week when you come, I shall give you some recipes, my *secret* recipes that you can use. Find a good cook for the restaurant who can work on these recipes. You can have liver barito, chicken barito, pork barito…"

"Yes! I like the idea!" Kevin bounced in his seat excitedly. His dream would come true after all. If he worked hard, his mother could get out and be the cook for his barito restaurant.

* * *

He brought barito for Desire every day for three days, but she did not sleep at home all those nights. When he went to see his mother again, he was distracted as she showed him the recipes she had written down in an exercise book, and she thought he was sick.

"No, I am okay. Just thinking," he lied to her. How could he tell his mother he liked a prostitute? A woman like Ameena.

Weeks later, when he brought home enough baritos for him and his team, he carefully took out two for Desire and waited in his room, listening for any sound. It wasn't long before he heard the familiar high heels shuffle up the stairs slowly. They paused at his landing, then continued. He heard the keys jiggle in the lock, and with a groan the door was swung open.

Kevin counted to fifty, then picked up the plastic bag and took the single flight of stairs to her section of the apartment block. Kevin knocked on her door and waited. It was silent for a second, then light footsteps approached the door. He heard the lock jiggle, and a tired voice within asked, "*Ani ono?*"

Kevin hesitated, his palms suddenly sweaty. "K…Kevin, from downstairs," he spoke through the keyhole.

There was a pause, then the door swung open. Kevin gasped. Desire stood in the doorway with nothing on but a sheer nightdress. He stared, stricken and suddenly shy. She was beautiful. He quickly looked away and handed her the plastic bag. "I brought you *liver* barito."

She snickered, taking it from him and smoothly said, "Thank you, *mukwano*." Kevin nodded and quickly bounded for the stairs. Once in his room, he kicked himself for being so childish. He could not forget what he had seen; her full body, the mound of hair that covered her femininity…he longed to see her again, even more than he did before.

On his day off, he told his boys the plan he had in mind. They occupied a little table in a small cafeteria near their residence, a little restaurant that was a hole in the wall where countless young people from the neighborhood and university came for cheap homemade food and alcohol and, at night, roasted meats and beer with a deejay who challenged them to dancing competitions or karaoke all weekend.

"We have some money; we can start our own chapatti stall."

The boys nodded. "Yes, we have a lot of money; we can buy a house."

Kevin shook his head. "It's not enough for that, but it's enough for a stove. And all the things we need to make barito."

"How about other food?" Livingstone asked.

Kevin shook his head. "We have to find a cook who can make the recipes my mother wrote for the barito fillings first."

The boys agreed. So far, Kevin's plans, bizarre as they might have been, had taken them far. They comfortably trusted him now as their brilliant leader, even though he was younger than they were. While they deliberated on a plan, Kevin spied Desire, a wide smile on her baby face. Behind her was a man he wasn't familiar with. He was lean, wore a white suit with a multicolored tropical shirt inside, his upper chest bare except for a vulgar silver chain. He was the color of dark chocolate against her smooth latte complexion. She leaned into him and laughed at something he said, and when her eyes caught Kevin's, she waved at him with just her fingertips flailing delicately like one would wave at a beauty contest.

Kevin felt his breath catch. The man with Desire slid a hand around her waist possessively, steering her in the opposite direction to an empty table.

Boda whistled. "*Kyakabi!*" he said.

"*Ba Jamaica*, that one," Livingstone added.

"Boss." He looked at Kevin, and he and Boda smiled. "You talked to her?"

Kevin composed himself and shrugged. "Yes"

Boda whistled again. "Eh, *oli wakabi!*"

He made a vulgar gesture suggesting intercourse with his hands, and Livingstone laughed. Kevin smiled. "That's neighbor *naawe*," he told them, almost embarrassed on their behalf, hoping Desire had not seen it.

The room became small, and he fought off his unrest, the flutter in his belly, the wind in his lungs.

"That one, who cries at night," Livingstone added.

"We should also give it to her," he slapped his thigh continuously, and Boda laughed

"Boss, what do you say?"

Kevin turned and swept his eyes over her location. She was still laughing at something the man was saying. He looked back at his boys, fronted a bored expression, and said, "If you want."

The boys tee-heed naughtily. "And you?" they asked. Kevin glanced at her again and felt as if his heart would burst, then looked away.

"Huh," he said with effort, and they dropped the topic.

Rumors ran along the street, circling territory after territory, that Kevin did not like street girls. The gossip that often reached his ears was that his only girlfriend broke his heart and ran away. He always corrected the story, telling Boda and Livingstone that Shenzi is his sister *technically,* and she did not run anywhere, she got adopted; he would find her someday.

The boys left to make the last collections of the day, and Kevin finished his freshly ordered *katogo.* He kept his eyes trained on his plate, but Desire's laughter drowned every other sound around him. Thirty minutes later, congratulating himself for not turning around, he felt a hand on his shoulder. "*Ki,* neighbor?" It was the smooth, silky voice of Desire.

Kevin started and shifted back in his chair; he looked up at her leaning against the table. The smell of alcohol washed over him, and he grimaced. "*Ki,*" he responded and glanced around for her companion.

"*A li mu toilet.*" She indicated the restrooms. Kevin watched her carefully plant herself in the seat Boda had previously occupied. "How old are you, *mukwano?*" Her eyes widened, lazy with intoxication.

Kevin sighed, feeling young before her. "Fourteen," he said and cleared his throat.

She sighed. "*Mhhm.*" Her left hand supported her cheek. "*Gwo li younga,*" she drawled.

He did not know what to say to that. Then the man who was with her emerged from the bathroom.

Desire stood up and whispered, "Come to me when you are eighteen." She smiled and touched his cheek lightly, then walked off to her waiting companion.

Kevin wished he had told her he was older, but he knew she would see through him. Later that night as he lay in bed (Boda and Livingstone had gone out to find women), Kevin had felt his heart shatter as he listened to the moans and groans from upstairs against a bed that creaked and cried. When sleep finally caught up with him, he dreamed of her, her full breasts with their huge nipples, the tuft of hair between her legs, her lips whispering to him sweet nothings, moaning, giggling. They were entwined in each other rolling on the floor of her apartment, and she would not stop or let him stop. When he woke up, the creamy, sticky marks of ejaculation smeared his shorts, and he groaned with exasperation. His wet dreams, which seemed to have become more frequent, troubled him. He vowed to go to the internet café. Maybe the answers lay in the search engine somewhere. He could not imagine asking his mother.

However, when he went to visit his mother again, her questions were strange. "Kevin, I know the streets can be...very open. No one to guide you, but...do you have a girlfriend?" She was watching him.

He scoffed. "Why are you asking, Mummy?"

"Because I am your mother," she replied. "I want you to be safe. You are growing up fast, your voice is changing, you are almost a man, and your body will go through changes."

Kevin shook his head.

He had not expected to find his mother armed and ready to take him through the class of biology he had missed, and he shifted uncomfortably as she briefed him on his hormonal changes and how he will see girls. He grimaced. "Mummy, I only came to see you, not have a science class."

She shook her head, amused.

"I want you to be safe. If you feel you need a woman, even if I don't want you to at this age...please use a condom." She looked away. "There is AIDS. Those people out there are not all safe."

Kevin nodded.

When he left his mother, he heaved a sigh of relief. The lessons had thrown more light on his sleep condition, and he knew where to start from. He was less worried about it, realizing it was normal, but he was more determined to sweep Desire off her feet.

Patience.

Chapter 9

Wandegeya
April 2003

Since the invention and popularity of the barito, every street vendor had flipped over their chapatti business by trying their hand at making them. However, Kevin beat the competition because his recipes for the fillings, be it meat or vegetables, stood above the rest.

He started his own *kafunda,* which he called The Original Barito Restaurant. With his own haven in place, he constantly changed the menu or added to the recipes every other month. Being the original inventor, his customer base grew robustly. After all, who wanted to buy *kiwani* barito when the original had a slew of revolving choices with an incredibly delicious taste.

"We need another cook, Kevin." Shakira, the chef, came to him at the end of another successful evening. "We have too many people, and I can't cook alone." The demand for this new delicious food was fascinating diners, and their menu was expanding to accommodate the different tastes and preferences.

"Do you know a superb cook like you?" Kevin asked her.

She nodded. "Give me two days."

In two days, she was introducing the boys to a younger woman, "Her name is Adong; I will teach her."

Adong was creative and contributed to the new menus.

Kevin updated his mother at every visit. "Mummy, your recipes are working!" he told her excitedly.

"I am so proud of you." Dina looked at her son with pride. "You have grown so fast."

Kevin took notes from her in the exercise book he carried with him everywhere now.

Without the suffocating instructions from Ssalongo anymore, Kevin breathed new life into the barito place, and it flourished. He woke up each day thinking of all the ingredients a barito could hold, sought approval from his mother, and then discussed them with his team, and they tried them out for a month. The highest-selling remained on the menu, and they changed the rest. His bestselling so far were the onions, shredded carrots, chaps, liver, chicken, pork, spinach, and peas.

Everyone now knew the barito story. The chapatti sellers who were eyewitnesses to the ordeal told the story so much that it became an urban legend that even Ssalongo could not refute or claim fame for.

On one occasion Kevin decided to stuff sauteed vegetables, beef *pilau* rice, and eggs in a chapatti as a special for Muslims on Friday, then he made a medley of pork with chips and veggies for Sundays.

"What shall we call them?" Shakira asked him.

He thought about it: "Super Friday and Sunday Best." When they became a hit with the Muslim community on Fridays, he excitedly told his mother.

"I told you it would work. People like to feel acknowledged," she told him.

Kevin took a leaf from his mother on fixing the ultimate African tea with ginger root, cloves, and cinnamon, and in their dimly lit restaurant with a slanted roof, they created a homey touch. He bought a dozen flasks, and Shakira and Adong prepared huge saucepans of *chai masala* and *plain chai* to fill them.

They carved six table settings in their restaurant and for space placed chairs against the wall. Their grandest setup was an old couch that had once glimmered audaciously, complete with colorful floral cushions, a relic from the famous hole-in-the-wall club *Kyamex disco* below their residence. Kevin cleaned it up and, with the help of the boys, they had turned the rejected sofa into a prime seating item in their restaurant. They bought two rattan chairs and a coffee table wide enough to hold at least four cups of tea and two flasks and still have space for plates of *baritos*. At first, he had worried no one would find his place since it was in the back of the least exposed lucrative part of Wandegeya. He had wanted a location closer to the street intersection, where passengers alighted from the taxis, but the money required was steep.

His mother told him, "When you have a good thing, no matter how hidden it is, people will come looking for it. Patience."

So he took the back beaten-up space that was given to him for cheap.

They celebrated profits in December 2002, only three months into the business, and Kevin made it a point to celebrate Shenzi's birthday, in her absence, with his mother.

"You are sure you will find her?" his mother asked.

"I promised," he told her.

She reached out and touched his hands. "You make me so so proud."

He beamed with pride. "You help me, Mummy. I would not do it without you." He wished she knew how much seeing her and hearing her affirmations meant to him.

"I want you to promise me something," she told him on one of his visits.

"What?" he asked.

"I want you to go back to school at some point..."

"Mummy..." He groaned.

"Or...or at least read. I want you to read and read about the world. Please." She told him. "And every week bring what you are reading and tell me what you have learned."

His mother was relentless, so he made her this solemn promise. He knew a place downtown where a man sold schoolbooks, novels, and nonfiction books cheaply. He would make the purchases his mother told him to get, especially English, math, and science books.

"Be smart. If you dream big like you do, Kevin, then you need to know more than Kampala to get there," she would tell him.

He read through English comprehension and did a few math calculations only when he was about to see his mother, and science bored him. Then he came across an old worn copy of *Rich Dad, Poor Dad* by Robert Kiyosaki hidden among a pile of *Mills and Boon* romance novels spread out for sale by the seller he regularly went to. The man sold it to him for one thousand shillings, claiming the romance novels were more lucrative. The word *rich* stuck out for Kevin, and he held on to the book all the way home, thumbing through the cockroach-eaten corners carefully so as not to damage it any further. Something in him connected with this book of all the books he had gotten, and he immersed himself in its pages, and, in a week, he had finished it, then read it again and again.

He told his mother about it, and she scolded him for veering off the curriculum structure they had set but listened with rapt attention as her son spoke of money, and how his eyes lit up. His whole soul seemed to brim over as he thumbed through the pages and told his mother, "Rich dad says I should study to have my own company; poor dad says I should study to work at a company."

Kevin knew which dad he liked. "Rich dad is right. And he says they do not teach people about money; I will go to school to learn about money," he told his mother.

"These dads who live in America, what do they know of the Ugandan struggle?" Dina said, amused, but Kevin could sense the pride in her voice.

"I don't care what they say, as long as you stay hopeful and focused. Let nothing confuse you…especially women. Not until you are older." He heard her plea, and her voice was stronger than his thoughts of Desire.

He nodded,

"Be patient, okay?"

Kevin had never felt more hopeful than he did that year. His business grew, as did his influence on the street. He stole time to read the papers and magazines he found and even bought the *Monitor* and *New Vision* daily, placing them in his restaurant. He cringed to see them being used to wrap up *chapattis* and placed a rule that none of the newspapers should wrap any food despite protests from his team.

He listened to his mother and focused all day on working and meeting the different street leaders and expanding his relations. His idea was to have as many of the sections agree to him opening more chapatti stands on their turf and make chapattis to help them get off the street by earning decent money.

Festo and another leader called Mulumba in the Makindye area agreed to the idea.

In the evening, he battled his dreams and his growing lust for Desire. He made it a habit to bring her a special barito at the end of his day, and when she opened the door, his heart leaped with joy, but when she did not sleep at home, he was moody and gloomy, like a rainy day.

Boda and Livingstone teased him when they noticed his mood swings. "Desire has taken you!" Boda would intimate in Luganda, laughing as they wolfed down food Shakira had left them.

"Shut up!" He would be sharp, and the boys would stifle their laughter and glance at him mischievously.

"*Naawe bossi*, you like her."

Kevin was silent. But later in the night, he finally spoke to Livingstone. "What do I do?"

Livingstone's eyes raised in surprise, and then he composed himself, suddenly feeling important. "Heh? But you know what to do."

Kevin shook his head. He told him what had happened between him and Shamsa. He told him he had never been with a girl before and about the dreams. Livingstone wasted no time in educating him about his body and how he should "vibe" a girl.

The weeks that followed got too busy for him to focus on his crush, working with Festo and Mulumba to set up their own chapatti stands.

He took Shakira to teach their cooks how to create a few barito dishes. Kevin limited them to about three for a start. That took an extra month. When he returned to his own location, Boda and Livingstone encouraged him to rest for a couple of days while they managed the running of the restaurant, inspection of taxes, and following up with Festo and Mulumba.

He dragged his body up the flight of stairs to his little room, his eyes barely open, then the silky-smooth voice jerked him awake,

"*Mukwano,*" he heard behind him. "Hi, dear," she said sweetly.

Kevin wheeled around and all the fatigue faded. She was in an all-black hi-low velvety dress, her slim feet enclosed in a pair of strappy red heels, her toes manicured perfectly in coal-black nail polish. Her skin glistened like always, and he often wondered what lotion she wore to give her that glow. Her face was a vision of perfection.

"Hi…" He choked on his words and cleared his throat. "Hi Desire. You are…very smart."

She twirled in delight. "Thank you, and thank you for all the food you bring me. Your business is popular, I hear."

His eyes slid from her perfectly made-up face resting on the cleavage that accentuated her full chest. "You should come and visit."

She smiled, thrusting her chest forward as she swayed, arms akimbo. Kevin was glued to the spot by a powerful enchantment. The sparks of it traveled all over his body, setting it ablaze with an unfamiliar fire.

Her full cherry red lips parted slightly, and she rolled her eyes. "I don't know…" she started, and his shoulders drooped. "Maybe." She noticed his crestfallen face, "But…if you bring me more, we can eat together. *Tsk, naye…*I am trying to maintain a *ka* figure." She smiled, batting her lashes with girlish prudence, her hands smoothing over her waistline and resting on her hips.

Kevin watched the movement of her hands and quickly added, "No, no, you look…nice."

She giggled, lapping up his adoration. "Thank you."

Kevin smiled again. The thought of being alone with her was very enticing.

"When?" he asked too quickly and ground his jaw in embarrassment. Her eyebrows raised, and the smile teased him.

"*Hmmm*, tomorrow?"

He hated the out-of-control sensation. A myriad of unbridled feelings whizzed through him in a frenzied roller-coaster ride within the minutes and seconds he stood talking to her. When she finally bid her farewell, Kevin pushed his door open with such force, he almost destroyed the lock.

The next day, he waited for her after picking up baritos at noon, hoping they would have lunch together. He walked up to her floor and paused at the door, not sure if knocking would be appropriate. He leaned against the door with his ear to the hardwood and thought he heard some movement. After counting to ten, he knocked and waited.

Her silky voice, laced heavily with sleep, drawled back to him: "Who is it?"

Kevin sighed. "Neighbor…Kevin."

There was a pause, then shuffling of feet and the door swung open. Kevin braced himself for what he would see. This time, a multicolored *kanga* embraced her fine curves. She squinted against the light from the corridor.

He smiled at her. Even in her drowsy, disheveled state, she was beautiful…in fact, *sexier*.

"S-Sorry for waking you up, Sleeping Beauty." He tried to be charming. She frowned. "What time is it?"

"Almost one. I brought lunch," he told her. She was swaying against the door, and the smell of alcohol wafted to his nose.

"Thank you, *mukwano*." She stuck her hand out to him. Kevin hesitated, then handed it to her. "Do you want to eat now? With me?"

Her face registered fatigue. "Not today. I need to sleep…but thank you." She forced a smile.

Of course, she is still sleepy, he rationalized. He had stayed awake, expecting her to return the night before. He heard her door open in the wee hours of the morning as he drifted in and out of sleep.

So, he stepped back mumbling his goodbyes.

He would try again.

The Original Barito Restaurant was growing in popularity. More and more campus students milled in on their period breaks, on their way to and from a lecture, to buy a doughy delight. Sometimes they bought dozens for a group study session. Then he started special sales for the university students, a discount on large quantities to keep them coming back, and it worked. It was affordable and generously portioned, not to mention the many choices.

One Tuesday afternoon, Desire walked in, dressed like she had a wedding to go to, in a figure-hugging ruched purple dress and high-heeled shoes. Kevin presented her the barito himself and stirred when she smiled and hugged him, the lingering scent of fresh hair oil and spray stayed on his collar all day.

"Thank you, *mukwano*." She smiled, batting her eyes at him as she picked up the grand barito from her plate. "Hmm this is so big; I need to keep an appetite for my event."

Kevin grinned foolishly. "Take a little and I can pack for you the rest for later…"

He hardly finished his sentence when Desire shrieked and slid back in her chair. Kevin's eyes widened. It was too late. While she bit into the barito, the end of the rolled *chapatti* loosened, and a blob of thick gravy and meat plopped onto the front of her dress, smearing on the neckline, slipping into her cleavage. It was a mess. She dropped the barito onto the plate aghast.

Kevin leaped up instantly to help, grabbing napkins to wipe the mess. "So…so sorry, Desire!" He panicked and only made it worse, spreading the smear along the neckline. Desire shrieked again.

"No, no, leave it!" She was sharp. "*Urgh*! Now I have to go back and change," she lamented, taking the napkins from him and scooping out the chunks of liver buried in her cleavage with it. She glanced at him accusingly, and Kevin felt horrible. He stood there staring at her, inanely.

"I am sorry," he repeated as she got up.

She forced a smile. "It's okay. Thank you but I need to go." She quickly sashayed out of the restaurant.

Kevin watched her go with a sinking feeling in his chest; he did not care that the eyes of the clients were on him. The one time she had made the effort to come to his restaurant, he had messed up. He was kicking himself.

All day from that moment, he thought about ways to improve the barito. "I need to make baritos that people who are smartly dressed can eat," he told Shakira after they were closed, and Livingstone counted their day's earnings.

"Hmm, these *bu campusers* also say, it's too big sometimes, their hands get dirty, their lipstick…eh *banange!*" She leaned her elbows on the table rolling her eyes in exasperation.

"But they still buy," Adong quipped in, serving them all from the last flask of milk tea.

"They do," Kevin said thoughtfully. "But we don't want them to stop buying because it messes up their lipstick or clothes."

"But…" Shakira started to protest.

Kevin stopped her. "Let us make a new type of barito that they can eat. We'll add to our menu."

"A smaller one?"

"Hmm, no…one that does not leak. They can have all the gravy in it, but…"

"Huh! Oba, how will we do it when it is rolled?"

Kevin's eyes suddenly lit up. "We don't roll it then!"

The others looked at him confused. "Now how will they eat it?"

"With…with a fork, no! A spoon. No-mess barito! Listen…we make the chapatti, put all the ingredients inside, whether it is eggs or offals or peas or…" Kevin bounced up from his chair excited. "We call it a flat barito!" he explained to Shakira and Adong. "We make our baritos the same, but this time we don't roll it. We keep it flat and even cut the chapatti in pieces so they can eat with a spoon. A fork?" He shrugged.

"Their clothes will not get dirty!" he concluded on a triumphant note.

"I like that," said Livingstone, who now stood by the cashier listening intently.

Shakira was lost in thought, and Adong stared at Kevin. "Will it work?" Shakira was doubtful.

"Let us try it tomorrow. A flat barito," Kevin said.

"A flat?" Adong asked absently, and Kevin gasped as if a new epiphany just hit him.

"Yes…yes! A flat…I like that."

Livingstone laughed. "Ahaaa, a *fulatti*…"

By the end of the evening, the name of the newest barito on the menu was coined, the *fula,* loosely pronounced *fuuu-laah*, a barito that comprised a flat chapatti chopped with flat slices of meat, a dash of thick gravy, and sautéed veggies. For the next weeks, they made fulas with a variety of fillings already part of the barito menu, and it was graciously received by female customers who praised Kevin for the invention.

"Looks like the ladies like it a lot. We have more sitting customers," Kevin told Shakira.

"Yes, boss. I did not think it would work, but the campus girls really like it." Shakira grinned.

Businessmen thronged Kevin's restaurant to hold meetings in anonymity away from the conspicuous rendezvous spots. They occupied the rescued couch, where they downed massive quantities of baritos and fulas chased with multiple cups of hot spiced chai, with or without milk. Kevin considered them his customers of stellar choice, often greeting them with light banter and listening piously as they advised him on their tastes and preferences. They often marveled at him being so young and yet already so ambitious. "Do you want to go to school?" one had asked. "I can arrange for a scholarship for you."

"This business is good; I can invest…"

"Have you thought about partnership?"

"What are your future plans?"

They bombarded him with questions, carefully wrapped in subtle self-interest not lost on Kevin. He kept his responses short and sweet: "I will think about it." Then, "How about another barito? Try this fula; you won't regret it. We have a new one on the menu, and I would like you to sample it…first." He flattered them, and they basked in it.

When he told his mother, she scolded him and told him he should consider these offers, especially the ones concerning school.

"I can't leave this now; I will study later," he told her.

Just when he thought he was making progress in every aspect of his life, including Desire, he was devastated to see her leaning on the arms of a tall man as he crossed the road late one evening from his barito place. They were leaving her apartment. Her body suggestively brushed against her beau, and when they crossed paths, their eyes locked briefly before she looked away, ignoring him. Her scent lingered long after she was out of sight, and anger rose like bile from the pit of his stomach. When he got to his room, taking the stairs in quick, livid strides, he decided he would stop playing the agreeable neighbor who greeted her and brought her food.

It wasn't long before his indifferent attitude brought her back to him… as he had hoped. Desire had a way of getting under his skin. On the stairway, she would purr a greeting and even lightly touch his shoulder. A day later, she was urging him to come up to her apartment. He was reluctant at first, but the practiced skill of a bewitching *fille de joie* broke his barricades.

He assured himself he would be there a minute and leave with his dignity intact. But she sat him down, offered him soda? tea? beer? and continued her motherly inquisition. Was he well? How was business? What was left of his barricade crumbled to the floor about him when she bared her soul about why she pedaled flesh for a living, why she had ignored him that morning, and who the man she was with really was. Kevin was swayed to pity.

"He is a crazy asshole, but he owns me. I did not want you to get into trouble, *mukwano*." She was sweet; her puppy-dog eyes implored him for forgiveness and understanding.

He struggled to hold on to fragments of his barricade to no avail, indignation and sympathy smothered every trace of anger and indifference he had mastered, but…then his undoing happened, Desire edged closer and touched his face. "I am sorry, dear." She was smooth, whispering in his ear as her breasts heaved against him.

Kevin felt his breath quicken. His mother's words surged forward from a place of reason in him. *No distractions.* But the intoxicating floral scent on her, the way her fingers caressed his earlobe and her breast jutted against his arm dispelled reason.

"Okay," he said and took in a gulp of air. "It's okay."

He could feel her breath in his ear. "You are so kind to me, *hmm.*" In a moment he barely had time to calculate, Desire was on her feet unzipping her dress and in one swift movement stepped out of it. She angled herself in a way that he could see nothing but her. She dominated his field of vision with her luscious curves encased in a blue lace bra and underwear set. His struggling barricades became unreclaimable debris.

"How old are you now?" She was standing close. *Too* close.

Kevin swallowed, the space between them gone. "…fifteen."

A small moan escaped her lips, and his body responded shamelessly like a dog in heat. "Young blood," she said soothingly, urging him to his feet, then peeled the final layers of the barricade that kept them apart. She took her time. Kevin stood there stupidly, emotions and thoughts colliding in a jumbled mess inside him. He did not resist as she planted little kisses on his face, his hands, and his pubescent chest while she stripped him.

His blood boiled when she licked him, her hands leaving a trail of heat in its wake upon his skin. When she dropped his jeans and boxers, his instinct was to cover his genitals, but her voice nudged lovingly while her hands awakened a sensation deeper than what he felt in his dreams. His body shook, and he had to spread his legs to hold his ground. His eyes widened in astonishment, and a gasp of satisfaction escaped his lips when her fingers encircled his cock. When her lips replaced them, he bit down on his lips to crush the groan that raced in his chest upward to his open mouth. Involuntary tremors rocked him from his toes to his head. He could barely hear her when she instructed him to touch her, groping for her breasts, and she giggled, guiding him. "Like this," she whispered.

He was clumsy and awkward, but she brushed off his nervousness as she continued guiding him, and when he thought he would explode with the tension, she rolled a condom up the length of his shaft, sighing agreeably. When she had him on the couch, she straddled him and guided him gently into her, her eyes never leaving his face, her voice coaxing, gentle, and encouraging while she lowered herself onto him. Kevin let out a deep groan as the unfamiliar yet extremely pleasurable sensation washed over him. He was in unfamiliar territory, gripped in place by another body, being possessed by it. It sucked on him and caressed him fondly, releasing and grabbing, releasing and grabbing as she moved up and down on him.

In two minutes, he was exploding in the condom and his breath coming out in short bursts. The release washed over him with a new relief he had never felt before. A sweet relief. However, he did not want to leave the comfort of her warmth. He heard Desire laugh as if from a faraway place. When she cleared her throat to stifle her laughter, she smiled. "You were a virgin?"

A faint smile of embarrassment played on his face. "Something like that."

When he opened his eyes and gazed upon the woman he had coveted for months, his body exploded with a fresh fire of desire. She was smiling, relishing in his naivety. He did not care. "Young blood," she mumbled.

She was rolling the condom off and cleaning him. Her touch lit his body like an ignited light switch. "Ooh." Her eyes met his, a teasing glint in them. "*Mukwano.*"

Kevin licked his lips. There was no way he was going to his room tonight. He needed to try one more time. "Can we...?"

He did not have to ask.

It was a long night of orgasms and lessons in sex. Halfway through, he was putting into practice the lessons she had given him. His heart sang a merry tune when she groaned and cried out his name, enjoying the fact that he was the man above, not the one in his bed listening to the groans, grunts, and complaints of bed springs.

Kevin crept out of her apartment just as morning tore through the sky, making a dash for his shower as soon as he entered his apartment. As he rushed out of his apartment, he prayed he would stay alert the rest of the day. It was pouring, and traffic was impossible. He hoisted the jacket he had on over his head and dashed across the street, groaning at the squelching sounds in his sneakers that accompanied wetness. Drenched through, the memories of the night before gave him wings. His heart shuddered tenderly. He was sure he was in love, and he would make her his only, buy her gifts, and take care of her.

In his mind, rosy fantasies of their life together materialized and rested in an intimate part of him. How would his mother react? A small voice of reason inquired, but he brushed it off. He would keep it a secret until she was ready to know. He instead focused on his daydream, lying in her arms and telling her about Shenzi and how they would meet eventually. His mind toyed over varying fantasies that only stirred his heart further.

The rain had crammed the original barito restaurant with customers by the time he got there: enthusiastic clientele escaping the rain and hankering for a cup of African tea served together with a scrumptious barito.

His team was in a state of flurry; Boda and Livingstone were between tables and the cash register. Adong was churning out breakfast baritos and fulas, while Shakira was using a giant plastic mug to scoop the strained milk into flasks.

Kevin dove in to serve and only managed to catch his breath at noon. When their menu flipped to cater for lunch, the clientele dipped for thirty minutes and picked up again till 3 p.m. It helped that the pelting rain had tapered off to slight drizzle falling from an overcast sky. It was going to be one of those gray days. At any moment, the sky would burst open with fresh showers.

As he slumped back against the rescued colored couch, two men walked in, one heavy-set with exaggerated features, thick brows, thick lips, and huge eyes set in a big face. His companion was shorter than him with clothes that fit too tight, but he walked with the boisterous swagger of a man who had known money through hard hustle and now was a self-proclaimed master of the hustle game.

Kevin observed them both, amused; the stark contrast between them was staggering. Drowsiness and fatigue promptly evaporated, and instead, he pasted on his best smile, motioning the newcomers to the couch, "You won't find better seating." He made a sweeping gesture to the couch. "Than this!" The bigger man paused momentarily, taken aback. "*Ba boss*, hello. Please feel at home," Kevin added as the men made their way to the couch.

The bigger man relished in the libations of Kevin's welcome; a bright smile breaking the poker exterior he had worn when he walked in. Kevin kept it up, appraising them discreetly as he buttered them up. He made note of the gold-plated premolar that lent the man with an enormous face a mysterious air. When he placed his hand on his thigh, the gold ring that straddled the last finger of his left hand gave off a smidgen of appeal to his big unimpressionable hands.

"*Asante*," the big man said, shifting to the corner of the couch and leaning back. The other man occupied the center.

Kevin switched up his tone to a light banter as if they were colleagues selling different merchandise, making sure he did not come across as too haughty or overeager. Businessmen in Kampala were easy to spot. There were three types he was aware of; those who had no secondary or university education but sharp business acumen, multiplied wealth under the radar, and owned businesses downtown. He met those often because they used plenty of their street network to get things done when they needed to have their way. There were the more educated ones; the 'new money' group who had airs, some class, and were a lot showier about their wealth accumulation. They seemed to consider themselves the saviors of their peers' children and started business training events to do so.

Kevin smirked. He often thought them showoffs; they, too, used the underground networks he and most of the street leaders ran to square off loose ends. Negotiations with them were always a headache. And then there were the foreign investors and the old-money farts who had very little need of them. He could decipher them, but he gleaned from Festo's tutorial that they were the ones with real money.

The men in front of him were the first-category businessmen. The bigger man was Bampa. The smaller man in ill fitting clothes preferred to be called Zake. Kevin brought them two flasks of hot ginger milk tea and three different baritos they were trying out that week.

"This is the manager's special." He conjured up the name, making a mental note to change it on their menu.

"Hmm." Bampa leaned forward, inspecting the huge, rolled chapattis on the plates. "Which, which, and which?" he asked.

"The original liver barito, liver, chips and avocado; the champion's chaps barito with veggies, eggs, and chaps; and the grand barito with offal and vegetables. That's just a sample. We have fulas..."

Bampa moved to the edge of the couch and reached for the grand barito. "Offals, eh? I like that. I will take it."

The man in the tight clothes asked for a knife so he could take half of each of the remaining two. He smiled at Kevin. Kevin returned with a knife and found the two men engrossed in conversation, what sounded like a friendly debate. He placed the knife slowly by the plate of barito, and Bampa, smirking, motioned to Kevin to sit. "Heh, I have a question. Maybe you can help clear something up for me and this young man here."

"Young? *Namuna gani!*" Zake made a clicking sound with his tongue as he sat back, crossing his legs.

Bampa ignored him. He beckoned to Kevin to come closer. Kevin moved cautiously, and when he was in front of Bampa, the big man motioned to his ring and watch. "I told this *jamaa* here that this is pure gold."

Zake clicked his tongue again. "I know gold. *Wewe.*"

Bampa chuckled. The action made him bob up and down. "He does not believe me," he continued conspiratorially. "What d'you think?"

Kevin looked at the huge plain band that suffocated Bampa's little finger again. He did not know what real or fake gold looked like, but his instincts told him if he was on the street, he would have stolen it and pawned it for a hefty amount, claiming it to be real gold. He shrugged. "I don't know."

The big man made a sound of disapproval. "Aaah, also you!" he barked, then slid it off his finger effortlessly and passed it on to Kevin to hold and examine. "Is it heavy?"

Kevin hesitated. If this was a test that opened some doors, he needed to be careful to pass it.

He dribbled it through his fingers, feeling the eyes of both men on him. It was hopeless. "Yes, but I don't know about gold…"

"Bampa, how do you involve this man in this…?" Zake was waving his hand indignantly. "Sorry, boss, leave this man alone." He turned to Kevin apologetically.

Bampa was laughing as Kevin handed the ring to him, their debate resuming. Kevin cleared off nonexistent debris as he caught whiffs of their discussion. "Congo is a hot zone…"

He wiped the corner of the table and asked if they needed anything, to which they waved a "no."

"The mines are still open in Kivu."

"But the soldiers, I don't know…"

"Ah, it's easy to get by if you know people…I know people…"

Gold.

Kevin returned frequently, pausing by their seat or close by.

"Where there is risk, there is great gain," Bampa was saying convincingly as Kevin passed by their seat with tea for another customer.

Gold! What he wouldn't do if he could get some gold. He thought of his mother and Shenzi. His hands trembled with excitement just thinking of the freedom gold would offer him.

He agreed with Bampa. Much risk equals much gain.

The two men were not in a hurry to leave. Kevin pondered his approach. He wanted to know where and how they got gold if it was true.

At half past two o'clock, as the restaurant cleared out again for a slow phase, Zake finally left, thanking Kevin for the barito.

"This place is...really different." He told Kevin, pumping his hands as he paid.

Kevin thanked him and stashed the money in the cash register box they had recently acquired. He quickly set about clearing Zake's portion of the meal, his mind working doubly fast when the big man's sharp voice called to him, "Heh!" He motioned for Kevin to sit. Kevin sat, trying not to seem eager.

"I like this place," Bampa told him. The man appraised him, just like most people did when they found out he owned the best street food joint in town. "They say you own it?"

Kevin leaned back. "Who are *they*?"

Bampa laughed his raucous laugh. "You know these things. Word goes around; they said a youngster runs it..."

Kevin allowed a ghost of a smile to play on his lips. The aura about him was mixed, and Kevin felt wary of him. Bampa wasted no time and dove into it. "I told that man there to work with me...gold. It's big in Congo."

Kevin waited, not wanting to seem too eager.

"So, this is big money, er...name?"

"Kevin," he introduced himself.

"Yes, Kevin, this is good. And for your business, you can give this place a facelift, renovate, buy it out, open more branches across Kampala. Imagine how much you can make downtown near the park, or even Kamwokya, Nasser Road, Jinja Road. Nakawa is a great place for business by the taxi park. You could expand all the way to Mukono."

Kevin thought for a second. The idea of expansion was already on his mind, but capital was the issue.

"Why not Zake?" he asked.

"Ah, he thinks Dubai gold is better than Congo gold."

Kevin frowned. "Is it? It's all gold."

"It's easy to get Congo gold to Uganda and make money for yourself from it, but Dubai gold." He flipped his fingers in a gesture that showed it was more difficult. "So most people get it from Congo and sell it to Dubai. Those Arabs love gold."

Kevin nodded contemplatively. He could already envision the impossibilities in his life fading, but he had reservations. The streets had taught him to be cautious, and he did not know Bampa. "Let me think about it."

Bampa shrugged, his thick fingers clapping Kevin on the back. "It's up to you; by this time next year you could be a *capo*."

Kevin agreed but stood his ground. "I will let you know."

"Don't take too long. I want to leave in a month, and if you agree, we can discuss. Let's keep talking. I shall come back. I like this place."

He stood up, gauging the modestly decorated restaurant, with a fan that struggled to dispel the smell of freshly fried chapatti and his mother's medley recipe that coated most of the dishes from the room while doing its best to keep the ever-growing crowd of customers cool, to no avail, especially when the space was full.

Nobody complained; if they did, it was that they had not gotten their order when they needed it.

The big man pumped his hand in an emphatic handshake and handed him two ten-thousand-shilling notes. Kevin signaled for him to wait for his change, but Bampa waved him off. "That's my tip. It's fine," he motioned and grinned, revealing his gleaming gold tooth.

Kevin smiled; the idea of tipping was interesting to him. It was an appealing gesture of gratitude he did not see often. It seemed people who had traveled liked to tip. He put that on his list of things to research on the internet next time he stopped by the café around the corner.

As he stashed the money away, he couldn't help thinking how his day had turned out better than he had hoped. His thoughts strayed to Desire. He imagined her still curled up naked in her bed, sheets thrown to the side revealing her smooth bare arms, thighs, and buttocks, just as he had left her. The thought of her stirred his loins.

Life was getting better and better. He beamed.

When he told his mother about the gold discussion he'd had with Bampa, Dina clasped her hands in joy. "Oh that sounds wonderful!" Her eyes brightened with delight even though Kevin had noticed she looked a little thinner and her skin looked paler.

"Yeah…are you okay, Mummy?" he instead asked when he could not hold off any longer.

She looked at him, frowning. "I am fine. Why?"

Kevin met her gaze. "Is it me or have you lost weight?"

"You are seeing things," she chided him. "I am fine."

Even though she brushed it off, Kevin's sense of apprehension increased. He studied her more than listened to what she said. Her eyes were sunken in like she had not slept, and when he pointed that out, she dismissed him as being paranoid.

"Just listen," she scolded him.

"Okay, I'm listening," he said. Maybe he was overthinking it, he thought. But he was troubled nonetheless.

"Are you really okay, Mummy?" he asked again, slightly intense, needing to be sure he was not walking away only to hear she was not well. Aunty Dina shook her head and smiled, "I am the mother. I ask those questions. Now go, go, go." She shooed him away.

That night, he was in Desire's arms again. He had let the boys know, and they clapped him on the back like he had run up Mount Everest in two hours and planted the Ugandan flag at the peak.

"*Kyekyo*, now you are a man!" was the jubilant chorus.

He could not take his mind off his mother. It made him somber and as he and Desire drifted off to sleep. He told her his life story: about Shenzi, her mother, his mother, life on the streets, the business, and wound it up with the gold deal. He only realized that she had fallen asleep amid his heart-wrenching tale when he called out to her softly and she stirred in response and burrowed into him. He made a mental note of it; women did not want to hear sob stories. The next morning, she was chirpy and apologetic, claiming fatigue.

"Maybe you won't be so tired if I take care of you. Only me." He emphasized the last bit as she slid out of bed to head to the bathroom. She was the most beautiful woman he had ever seen, naked and clothed. She had laughed, a hint of disbelief. "How can you take care of me?"

Kevin felt a quickening in his heart. "I make good money. I can get a better place for both of us, and you don't have to do this…" He meant her trade. "I will take care of you. I work hard. You can have anything… I love you." He wore his heart on his sleeve and did not care. Her lovemaking intoxicated him, and her smile bewitched him. He was hooked, constantly baited by her inconsistency, the games she played, flirting away from him and back. It drove him insane, grounding his determination to have her all to himself.

She giggled. "Hmm, I don't know…"

"I will prove it…" He almost pleaded. She held his face in her hands and shushed him. "Let's enjoy each other for now, okay?"

She cast a spell on him with her words, and they whipped him to silence. He nodded, "Okay." Then he touched her arm where a scar ran against the satiny flesh. It looked fresh. "What happened?"

Desire's eyes met his and flickered. "Nothing. I think that nail downstairs at the entrance scratched me." She pulled away from him.

Something was wrong, and he sensed her reluctance to speak about it.

"Someone hurt you?" he probed. It killed him to think anyone had touched her.

She scoffed. "I think you should go to work. Bring me *ko* a grand barito."

She was dismissive and it hurt. His eyes narrowed, but he let it go. Picking up his clothes and dressing, he walked out silently. When he left, he vowed not to return, but as the day ended, he wrapped her a grand barito and, fighting the urge to see her, clambered up the stairs to his room. The overpowering need to be with her pulled at his heart and loins, and he took the next flight of stairs to the top like a puppet on strings. He knocked once, twice, then lingered for ten minutes more before finally giving up and heading back to his room.

In the night he was awakened by the thumping upstairs, the moaning and groaning, Desire's high-pitched shrieks of pleasure, and his insides felt like a giant hand had scooped all of him and crushed him mercilessly. He gasped at the pain and the hollowness that spread throughout his soul. Sleep escaped him like a forgotten word that dries on the lips.

"A *malaya* will always be a *malaya*," Livingstone sympathetically told him. "It's just her job."

Sore inside, he worked hardest that day and avoided seeing his mother. He decided it was best to focus on making money and finding Shenzi. The two weeks of pleasure had ended. He was not as special as she had claimed. Memories of their passionate nights stayed etched in his soul, and he fought the urge to go to her every evening as he trudged the steps to his room. He avoided her as much as he could, and when she came to his door, he refused to open it. He needed to forget her.

Festo had been his contact, providing background details on Bampa. "He is a businessman here, has taxis, and owns that tall gray and black building on Kampala Road, Bampa Plaza…yes. My boys said they see him in *Kikuubo* as well."

The next day, Bampa came by the restaurant for a grand barito and tea. Kevin served him personally and sat with him cordially with the disposition of old acquaintances.

"So?" Bampa wasted no time.

"I accept. Tell me what I must do."

"Ho!" Bampa clapped his hands together. "Good, good. You are a busy man, I know, but if you have a moment to spare, I will fill you in."

Kevin nodded. They deliberated on the details: Bampa and he would travel by road to the Congo mines where Kevin, posing as his young and nimble assistant, would do the mining along with the other miners. Bampa would take care of the middlemen. They would be there for three months at most and return. When their cash came in, they would split it thirty/seventy. Kevin drew his legs in and sat upright.

"Fifty-fifty. I am sure that mining is difficult."

Bampa shrugged. "Okay forty-sixty. Yes, it's not so easy, but the mine is newer, so it will be faster. I will do the other stuff, which is a lot of work too. Forty/sixty."

Kevin scrunched his nose. He weighed it then shook on it. "Okay, forty/sixty."

"*Sawa boss,* you are on your way to making a barito empire." He laughed and Kevin laughed with him, genuinely excited at the prospect of so much money in such a short time. Suddenly the pain in his soul over Desire dissipated as the most important things in his life regained their topmost position: he could see Shenzi sooner; he could get his mother a good lawyer and get her out of jail.

Desire met him at the entrance of their building and stopped him. "You are lost." She was as smooth and intoxicating as ever. Kevin felt the swirl of her effect, but the hope of money gave him strength over his feelings. "I have been busy."

She closed the gap between them. "Too busy for…this?" Her hand strayed to his crotch, her gaze fixed on him. Kevin gasped; his resolve was being tested, and he hated to feel himself lose.

"No, Desire," he tried weakly, but his body betrayed him, and in less than ten minutes, her bed groaned and screeched along with her shouts of ecstasy, instigated by him and not a stranger who he would hear while he tried to fall asleep.

She seduced him and he reiterated his terms; she had to be his alone. He could not stand her with anyone else. His heart opened to her again, and he told her his plans and how he would be in position to get her the best of everything by the following year.

"Trust me, by March next year, you will shine like a star." He dazzled her and melted when she giggled. She listened to him more. She even made him breakfast, and Kevin quickly acclimatized himself to her reaction when he spoke of wealth, so he fed her his dream and pleasured in the result of it. The money talk ingratiated her to him. Somewhere in him, he justified it.

For two weeks, it was bliss: dreaming about a bigger place, cars that would need an extra garage, a swimming pool, and travel to see Shenzi. After work, he would go to the park and pick up *Cosmopolitan* and *Vogue* from the man who sold stationery just outside the old taxi park. Together, Desire and he would browse through them. She told him the little things: how she would like him to dress when they were richer, what she loved and how she loved them. Kevin would lean back, spellbound by her. He wanted to provide anything she needed, dinner at the Sheraton, the best clothes from Wina Classic…nothing secondhand for her, trips to the national park without counting a coin.

They admired the models in suits and casual wear he longed to see himself in, and she nurtured the dream, whispering in his ear about how fancy he would look. She filled his head with dreams, and going to Congo became a fixation in his mind.

He told his mother a week before they left that he was leaving for Congo. He had been alarmed on walking into the meeting room and she was pale, her eyes sunken in, and she coughed like her chest was collapsing.

"Mummy!" He had been very shaken, but she had firmly told him. "It's okay, it's okay. I got medicine for it, just pneumonia, but they caught it in time. I am okay."

Kevin agonized over not seeing her on the previous days, which he had spent with Desire. "I am sorry I did not come sooner."

She waved him off. "My son is going to be a millionaire; how can I stop you from working?"

He had told her about the gold deal and how he would be a millionaire sooner than later. "I can come and take you to a proper doctor for a checkup." He gave her the money he had on him and begged the warden to let his mother get better care.

Dina had smiled at him. "You take good care of me, Kevin. These people can only do what they can. But I am fine. Don't worry about me. Go on and be brave and strong and make us all proud."

When his visit ended, Kevin hesitated, wondering if it would be appropriate to tell his mother about Desire. Instead, he looked into her warm brown eyes, smiled, and said, "Please take care until I return." His mother hugged him tight.

"Hmm, I will take care of myself. You are such a good son. Shenzi would be so, so proud," she told him.

He watched her leave the room, out through an opposite door before he turned and left as well. He lingered for a moment longer, wondering if there were things he should have told her but had not; three months was a long time.

He met briefly with the entire crew after they had locked up for the night and told them he would be traveling for business.

"Take care of things here and keep watching the street. When I return, we will do bigger things with more money." He asked Livingstone to visit his mother every week. They had agreed and wished him all the best of luck.

"When are you come *backa*?" Boda asked.

Kevin thought. "Maybe end of this year. Maybe earlier. Just make sure you keep things running smoothly, okay? You are both managers now. Keep putting money away for emergencies." He took them through the drill again like he did every morning when they ran the streets to collect their tax.

"Okay, boss," they both replied.

Kevin bid a passionate farewell to Desire two days before he left, telling her he would miss her. He gave her fifty thousand shillings as a parting gift and told her Boda or Livingstone could get her a barito any time she wanted. She cooed and purred and sucked up to him, telling him she would wait for him to return so they could start a better life. She took his breath away, but inside he faltered and worried she would not wait, she would find someone else; she was way older than him, almost thirty, and lived a life different from his, but he held on to the hope they would defy all odds.

His heart surged with anger when, on his last day as he waited for Bampa to pick him up in the wee hours of the morning, Desire alighted from a taxi with a man holding her. They walked past him and she did not notice him, laughing heartily at everything the gentleman who held her possessively said.

Luckily for Kevin, almost immediately, Bampa's Land Rover pulled up to where he stood.

"*Ay,* my man!" Bampa called from the driver's seat. Kevin mechanically walked to the passenger side and hurled his bag in the back.

"How are you? *Banange,* it's so cold. You know…" he rambled on as he shifted the gears, then paused. "What's eating you?"

Kevin sighed. "What do women want?"

Bampa laughed. "Ah! You can never understand them. Give them money, that cock, and they are happy, but only for a day or two." He *tsk-tsk*ed. "If you find the answer, tell me because I also want to know."

Kevin shook his head, anger unabated.

"Take it easy, man. There are good women; there are wicked women… for now forget about it; we have money to make." He patted Kevin on the back as they drove away from Wandegeya, heading for the Northern Bypass to Fort Portal.

"How long is this journey?" Kevin tried to focus on the trip ahead. Bampa was right; the faster they got the gold, the better things would be for him and Desire.

"About six hundred kilometers. Relax. I drive there a lot."

Kevin sank back in the car seat and dozed off; in his dream, he was fighting the man who held Desire.

Chapter 10

Congo, 2003

Bampa proposed a couple of different route choices for caution. Part of the plan was to head to Kasese, where they would trade the Land Rover for a truck crammed with bags of charcoal going over the border. On reaching the border of Uganda and Congo, they would take a slight detour to a little village that hosted an inconspicuous handful of Bampa's trusted network to gather supplies.

They spent the night in Fort Portal with an amiable family of six who wasted no time in making them as comfortable as they could. It was clearly a task they performed often, Kevin observed.

The following morning, well rested and fed, they embarked on their trip, heading toward and past Kibale National Park to Kasese. In Kasese, they stopped by a roadside restaurant. It was midday, and the sun pummeled them mercilessly. Its rays were harsh against the simple restaurant structure, and the countable customers slurping away at their food, were sweating profusely. It reminded Kevin of his barito restaurant.

"We are waiting for someone else," Bampa informed him when the menu, a decorated paper encased in laminated plastic and worn at the corners, was brought to them.

"*Eh!* Bring passion fruit juice, very, very cold. It's too hot!" Bampa motioned to the waitress with a poker face. She mumbled something and walked away.

As soon as their food arrived, Bampa, whose eyes constantly surveyed the entrance, suddenly stood up and yelled, "Heh!"

Kevin saw the man Bampa had called. He could not have been taller than him. His jeans were stonewashed and old. He gathered them at the waist with a thick belt that stuck out from underneath his half-tucked-in T-shirt. His small frame adorned an old leather jacket, the type worn by bounty hunters in western movies. His steps were swift and springlike, and when he saw Bampa, his small ratlike eyes lit up, and his smile widened, revealing protruding front teeth, and his nose twitched in that rodent style when they smelled food. Kevin choked a chuckle and sipped his overly sweet passion fruit juice. He ordered for *obundu* (cassava bread) and fried tilapia stew, a combination that the *Bakonzo* of Kasese were most famous for.

The man pulled a chair from another table and slipped into it once he joined Bampa and Kevin at their table. The waitress came back with a steaming bowl of fish stew and a plate of obundu with steamed *nakati* on the side. Kevin nodded his thanks. As he dug into his sticky, gluey mound of *obundu,* he watched the rodent of a man. He was a curious sight.

"*Mbote* bwana," he squeaked to Bampa who boomed back, "*Mbote* Donga, how are things?"

The man brushed unseen crumbs off the table, and Kevin noticed his left hand had an ugly knobby deformity where his pinky used to be. "Ah-ah" he switched to Luganda effortlessly, "It's been good. You came at the right time. I thought you would be here last week."

Bampa pointed at Kevin with a grin. "I was waiting on this *Kadogo* to decide. Kevin, this is Dongawe." It was then that he noticed the ratlike man paying him attention. His eyes were unreadable, small and slightly rheumy. He had the look of experience, harsh experience. Whatever his story was, Kevin was more than impatient to find out.

The man smiled from the corner of his mouth and still his protruding front teeth bared themselves. "So, this is your *kadogo*?"

Bampa nodded. Dongawe folded his arms over the table, staring at Kevin full in the face. "Where did you find him?"

Kevin wondered if this was a sort of interview to access his competency in this endeavor. Bampa waved his hand, plonked a toothpick between his teeth and sucked air through them to clear it of any meat debris, then tossed it and picked up his fork slicing through the *matooke* in front of him.

"A young enterprising gentleman, I found him in Wandegeya. Has his own business."

"Eh? You lie!" Donga's voice sounded smaller and more singsong when surprised.

"Ask him," Bampa said, his eyes on his food.

Kevin raised an eyebrow, waiting.

"So, it's true?"

"Yes." Kevin was short. The man appraised him again. This time, there was a different look in his eyes. *Respect?*

The smell of fresh fried fish overpowered the other dishes at the table, and Kevin experienced a momentary regret for his choice of lunch. Dongawe did not make a move, still appraising Kevin.

"Did this giant here tell you about Congo? Do you think you can manage?" His accent was unfamiliar, but Kevin had long since figured out he was not from Uganda.

"A little." He shrugged. "I can manage."

The man paused as if he was being remotely controlled, then burst out laughing and clapped his hands. Bampa smiled, enjoying the exchange.

"Do you know me?"

Kevin hated it when adults said that as if to assert their superiority based on their age difference. *All* adults did it. "I think you are going to tell me." He challenged him quietly. The man's little beady eyes widened, then he shriek-squeak-laughed. He looked like he was being electrocuted.

"Aha, *nasepeli na oyo*," he rattled out in an unfamiliar tongue Kevin later found out was Lingala. Kevin frowned, his eyes racing from one man to the next.

"He approves." Bampa was biting down on his chicken thigh.

"Do you fear guns?" Dongawe asked after a full minute of scooping a fistful of millet bread, kneading it slowly in his hand and dipping it in roasted beef stew, its descent aimed at the miniature hole his mouth made.

Kevin shrugged. "I don't fear many things." He kept his cards close to his chest, not sure where Donga was leading with his questions.

The man dabbed at his lips with a serviette and belched. "Ooh Congo is a wild animal. Untamed. Guns, disease, struggle…and *wólo*…gold! Wealth. Only the fittest survive." He spoke like a storyteller about to launch into a riveting tale comprising many twists and climaxes, which he did. "You know how I got this?"

He raised his left hand to Kevin, where the knobby skin, shrunken and tight against his ring finger twitched. Kevin stared, waiting.

"Heh," he muttered in another language and then launched into the tale: "I met that terrible rebel Laurent Nkunda. Worse than Kony, eh Bampa? Maybe the same…" Laurent had him tortured and had his finger brutally sawn off. They then held him prisoner for a month before an escape window opened.

"No one escapes these guerillas. But I did, with only a pair of shorts to cover my buttocks." Bampa beside him grunted in agreement.

It was a narrow escape, enabled by a slip-up. After a heavy meal of wild boar and beer usually taken off ambushed trucks passing that way, his captors fell asleep, forgetting to shackle him up. It was then or never, so he took his chances.

"Let me tell you, I *ran!*" He made the motion of a runner with his hands rapidly moving in the air and a *bububububu* sound.

"So *bwana* Kevin, to survive out there, you cannot fear anything, even death." He raised his stub of a finger again and waved it. "You must always live like you will die the next day. That's how you live longer, *n'est-ce pas le cas monsieur* Bampa?"

He had an interesting habit of bouncing from language to language: a phrase here, an exclamation there. It colored his vermin features, lending him an aura of adventurism.

Bampa nodded. "*Oui*, but can you not confuse our young man here? Speak one language. He doesn't know if you are conspiring against him or not," Bampa joked.

Dongawe laughed, "*Pole sana*. Sometimes I speak a thousand different words in my head in different languages at once."

"What languages do you speak?" Kevin probed, curious, for so far Donga had spoken Lingala, French, English, Swahili, and some Luganda.

Dongawe sat up straight. "Lingala, English, French, Kinyarwanda, Luganda, Rutooro, Ruyankole, Rukiga, Swahili, and some Kikongo… those are seven?"

Kevin had been counting. "Eight…ten…ish." He was impressed.

Dongawe beamed, revealing a surprisingly full denture. "*Ish?*"

Kevin played with him, "Ish."

The man grinned, then challenged him. "And you?" he asked in Runyankole.

Kevin shrugged. It was a familiar tongue he could understand.

"In my head? About one hundred."

Both men laughed, producing a shocking mishmash medley that Kevin found insanely hilarious.

The novelty of the introductions wore off, and the gold seekers indulged in more complex matters. Kevin eavesdropped silently. Between Bampa's bass and Dongawe's multilingual squeaks, Kevin concluded there was more to the man than met the eye indeed. No wonder Bampa insisted they make the stop. From what Kevin could siphon off their conversation (when Dongawe spoke English and Luganda), Dongawe proved to be an encyclopedia into the history, politics, and economy of the gold region.

A vital middleman.

He had brokered more deals than Kony had killed Acholi and Langi in the north of Uganda. He was more than a middleman; he was the daily tribune, the local news, the FBI of the gold territory.

"He knows a lot, eh?" Bampa bragged to Kevin. Kevin nodded and Dongawe shrugged.

Kevin entertained himself as the men deliberated. Their conversation was more fascinating than the latest action movie he had praised.

"I'm not as knowledgeable as the king of the jungle. Have you told him about that man?" he asked Bampa.

Bampa frowned. "We won't meet him. That's a one-in-a-million probability."

"Who is that?" Kevin's curiosity was piqued.

Dongawe fixed him with a serious look. "He knows this gold jungle better than anyone I know. No one really meets him. He is elusive. And powerful."

"Supposedly, he is the only thing keeping these gold regions from erupting into World War 3."

"How?" Kevin was enthralled. What sort of person or thing was this?

Dongawe grinned and Bampa shrugged. "Damned if I know."

"Have you seen him?"

Both men looked at each other. "Maybe we have, maybe not. We only hear of him and see the effects of his presence, but it's hard to tell who he is."

"He is a legend in these parts," Dongawe said. His eyes registered a faraway look. Bampa agreed.

"We just don't want to cross his path or his camps," Bampa added, and the topic was closed, leaving Kevin more curious and with more questions than answers.

The two men speculated on the possibility of a surge in military presence and deeper clashes in the Kivu region. Kevin did not move a muscle, absorbing this information in awe. They loosely related detailed and almost personal horrifying accounts of the soldiers' and rebels' tensions over gold mines. Gorumbwe mine kept surfacing in their conversation, and Kevin guessed that would be a stopping point once they got to the Congo.

As a waitress cleared their empty plates and brought them more drinks, Dongawe told Kevin mini stories of the plight of the natives, the involvement of the UN and troops from Uganda to Rwanda joining the caucus.

Story after story was bathed in the ruthless risk that was gold mining. It thrilled Kevin, who considered death at the hand of a vicious rebel or soldier quicker and more merciful than dying of any disease. When Dongawe told of the Marburg virus outbreak in the late nineties, Kevin's eyes widened like saucers.

"It's over now." The man laughed and slapped Kevin lightly on the hand. "People will risk it all for gold, *bwana*. Now, if you have *any fear, any type*, in your heart, just leave it at this table," he told him jovially, like he had just indulged in a beautiful happily-ever-after tale.

"What do you think?" Bampa asked Kevin when the little man excused himself to the washroom.

"How many times do you come to get gold?" he asked Bampa finally.

Bampa stretched his thick legs. "Twice a year, sometimes thrice; the trick is to have enough insiders who keep you in the loop of what's going on. I have that. Even spies." He shrugged, "Don't worry about that; you just worry about your part."

Kevin stared at him. "I am not worried."

Bampa grinned. "Not afraid?"

Kevin knew he was not. The riskier the endeavor, the more determined he was. He pursed his lips. "No."

The man grinned, revealing his gold-capped tooth. "I like you. You are fearless. No worries because it won't be deadly. I don't mine in the popular mines: full of soldiers and backstabbers. I have other places. This *Lingala* man will show us." He pointed toward the bathroom where Dongawe had disappeared to.

They spoke about gold in code and hushed whispers. It was a topic discreetly handled by men who sat in clusters outside of restaurants out of earshot. Kevin learned that many "spies" occupied a lot of the lodges and restaurants along the routes simply to find out what was going on.

"You don't speak about *nani* just like that," Bampa told him.

In his downtime, he worried about his mother. Not knowing was both a blessing and a curse. When the sun hung low and the moon sashayed its way into the sky, Desire enveloped him. She teased his loins and broke his heart.

Shenzi…the photograph in his pocket was the balm to his heart of all the aches that it endured. And now a new light bloomed in his heart. Hope. With so much gold, he could do anything. He could not believe his luck.

They waited a day more for Dongawe to load up the charcoal on his truck. His turnboys worked all morning, and Bampa parked his car in Dongawe's compound, something they did often when Bampa traveled to mine gold.

As they filed into the back among the chunky sacks of charcoal, Dongawe clapped Kevin on the back and called out to Bampa, "This is a strong one. I am sure you will get more this time than the last."

Bampa roared with laughter like it was the funniest joke he had ever heard. They set off after an early lunch. The plan was to get in after dark to avoid a lot of hurdles along the way. Kevin's instruction was to stay hidden within the sacks of charcoal.

The ride to the border was mostly nonstop except for moments to use the bathroom in Kasese and over the border in Ishasha. The thick foliage overpowered the setting sun as it dipped low over the hills. Trees reared their heads for miles against untamed grass and a narrow two-lane murram road that meandered around the hilly curvature like the famous fifty-foot Congo snake.

Kevin peeped through the thick canvas that was thrown over the truck's backside, watching the brown road rise and fall like a well-fed reptile. The tarpaulin did nothing to keep the humid heat out, but it worked effectively as Dongawe promised it would when they needed it—at the border. There was no way Kevin would have gotten through without a passport or any paperwork.

Now and again, he peeked out through the bars that held the sides of the truck hatch together, and when the canvas flapped against the wind, he glimpsed a flicker of sunlight and a dash of breathtaking greenery smothering rolling hills. He had never been anywhere this far.

Kevin drifted in and out of sleep, usually awoken by either a nightmare or arousal. One had his father and death; the other had Desire, *beautiful* Desire, moaning in his ear while she made love to him with wild abandon. When he was not sleeping and pondering the trip, he thought of his mother. In between bouts of bad dreams and awakening, he would caress the glossy photo as if feeling for the essence of that Saturday afternoon, Shenzi's uncontrollable laughter and her reluctance at taking a picture.

Someone shook his shoulder a little too roughly, waking him up. "Heh!" the squeaky voice hissed. He could smell stale cigarettes from the breath that fanned his face and scrunched his nose.

"Get up, we are here." It was Dongawe.

Kevin stretched his limbs, which ached from the many uncomfortable positions his body was subjected to for the duration of the trip. He scrambled over the charcoal sacks trying to maintain his balance. Edging along the borders of the truck, he grasped the rails for support. When he got to its edge, he hoisted himself off and slid then leaped to the ground landing on all fours. He was able to calculate his steps aided by the light of an almost full moon set in the perfect canvas: a sky awash with a million stars. When he stared up at it, peering beneath the shadowy trees, Kevin marveled. He wondered whether it was that he never really paid attention to the sky or that Congo skies were a class apart. Stars clung delicately to the thick blanket of night for miles. He sighed; they were the brightest he had ever seen. He made a mental note to take a better look at the Ugandan night sky when he returned.

"Beautiful, eh?" It was Bampa. "I tell those fellows back home that the best skyline is in Kivu; nowhere else have I seen a sky so clear." He paused and Kevin glanced at the big man, who was also staring out at the night sky.

"Yes, it's beautiful," Kevin agreed.

The man sighed as if seized by nostalgia. "Wait till that moon is full. You will feel Kampala cheated you of the best night skies in the world."

Kevin inhaled deeply, a fresh, crisp air tinged with the smell of grass and soft mud…an earthy scent. It was a wild raw scent that excited his senses and his danger antennae pricked beneath his skin. It had been an enlightening three-day journey, and he had learned a lot from eavesdropping on discussions between the people he met with Bampa. He laughed at the pity in their eyes when they regarded him. "Mining is difficult work."

"I am sure," he often replied underneath his breath. How could he tell them his life story and why he remained undaunted in the face of mining gold? He thought *they would not understand.*

Dongawe led them to a corrugated tin roof house lit dully by a kerosene lamp sitting on the front porch. Later Kevin learned it was a signal of recognition between "gold miners" and their comrades, dog whistles.

Usually, someone sat outside smoking a tobacco pipe to ascertain hospitality. Other times, the lamp was simply hanging from a string attached to the slanting roof.

Dongawe knocked three times rhythmically before they heard dull footsteps, then a fumbling with the lock and the door swung open. The wide-set eyes of a young girl about Kevin's age darted from one man to the next; quick, furtive eyes trained to scan for danger. One half of her hair lay in flattened rows of crisscrossing plaits, while the other half stood on its kinky ends, a comb jutting through it. Her eyes lingered on Kevin. She cocked her head to one side, stepped aside to let them in.

Dongawe opened the conversation in a language Kevin had not heard him speak on their trip. Later he found out it was this *kikongo* he claimed he knew "a little of" from memory.

The girl motioned for them to sit in a barely lit living room, humbly furnished with a worn-out brown faux-leather sofa that peeled at the headrests. A little stool and a large rectangular coffee table dominated the center, the top of it covered with a knitted off-white tablecloth. Kevin and Bampa took their seats, while Dongawe and his turnboy remained standing.

Kevin watched, engrossed, as a man of medium build walked into the room to meet with them, nodded his greeting, and motioned for Dongawe, who went to another room with this man. Bampa called him *Monsieur* Kida. Then the girl with half-plaited hair served them juice and food, almost as if there was an unwritten schedule they followed.

Another woman Kevin suspected was related to the girl—she was much older and looked uncannily like her—kept them company in the living room, smiling occasionally while her knitting needles flew furious up and down, twisting the bright green yarn, in and out and over itself, possibly new chair backs for her worn-out sofas. The house was warm and oddly quiet, as if the walls were secret eaters and custodians of any dubious exchanges that occurred in the night.

Dongawe had not yet returned when the travelers received refreshments; generous portions of *makayabu:* salted codfish with sauteed vegetables served with boiled sweet potatoes. Kevin, being very picky about food, ate cautiously and sighed in appreciation when he realized he thoroughly enjoyed it. Bampa, who had been observing him, grinned widely, slapping him on the back. "You might like Congo after all," he said.

Dongawe finally emerged, a smile on his face, and when he had received his portion of dinner, he spoke with Bampa in Lingala. Kevin watched them all keenly, trying to decipher the facial expressions and communication. They slept in the living room on thin mattresses and blankets provided by the hosts.

The next morning, Bampa woke Kevin up and handed him a square laminated card that had an unfamiliar name neatly printed on it against texts in a language he could not understand.

"What is it?" Kevin asked, wondering how overnight they had created one for him.

Bampa had smirked. "This is your pass. Carry it everywhere you go, especially when we get to the mines. You can only be permitted if they see this. Let's say it's your passport here."

He had looked at the name on it again. "Francois Mukendi?" he read out carefully.

"You live in Itombwe with your grandmother, and you mine gold. That's it." Bampa told him. "Kevin does not exist *here*, only *this* guy," he pointed with a fat forefinger at the name printed in a black font on the card. "And I am Anatoli Musa."

Kevin nodded. He wasn't a stranger to shadow identity. Pseudonyms always meant what had to be done was near illegal, at least in his world.

"You understand?" Bampa was peering at him closely.

Kevin stared back into the big man's eyes. "I do."

Chapter 11

e quickly became Francois Mukendi.

Bampa called him *Franco* for short. Dongawe announced he had done his portion of work and would wait for the next wave, "when *wólo* came in." At this both he and Bampa sniggered like schoolboys ogling dirty magazines. He walked to Kevin, who was standing by the door they arrived through the previous day and leaned closer, whispering,

"Be careful," he told him, then tapped his chest lightly and smiled. "It would be a shame to lose someone so young," he added in Luganda. There was a soft light in his eyes for a second, and then it vanished, replaced by the cheeky, mousy demeanor Kevin had grown accustomed to seeing the whole trip.

Kevin found it particularly curious that Dongawe should whisper to him. He smiled back and pondered the warning as he watched the little man walk back to his truck, still full of charcoal.

"*Twende!*" he called out to his turnboy.

He and Bampa shook hands, and the cream-colored truck, scrapped and dusty, groaned away from the clearing of Monsieur Kida's front lawn. The gentleman whose family had taken them in, Kevin found out, was an even more vital inside man; he had actual locations of the less conspicuous mines, connections within the network that would ease their passage and got all the paperwork done ahead of time. He was most efficient and most loyal. He often got a percentage of any gold that was mined as a thanks for his role in the game.

Kevin made a keen note of this web of associates. Just when he thought he had it almost figured out and had met the most efficient person in the ring, a new one surfaced, throwing him deeper into the intricate spiral yarn of this dangerous game to find he was far from full disclosure. Every single one played a unique role in a timely manner. Anything amiss would throw the entire process off.

When he could respond to being Francois or Mukendi or Franco effortlessly, Bampa decided it was time to proceed to phase three. That was the next day. Monsieur Kida guided them through an obscure muddy path that stretched for an hour to a gated house with an old blue Datsun pickup truck perched in the driveway.

Monsieur Kida put two fingers in his mouth and whistled, then leaned against the gate. "People are moving south these days because there is more gold in *Ngweshe;* that is good for us here..." The man spoke to Bampa slowly. "But we have found *wólo* in Kobu; that's where this...will take you." He pointed to the front of the house they arrived at, a house with a bright blue door, and Kevin spotted a kerosene lamp placed at the corner of its front porch.

The door groaned as it opened, and a man motioned for them to go in. Monsieur Kida unlatched the gate and opened it, letting them all in. When they got to the front porch, the man who was waiting at the door got out. Kevin noticed he had a slight limp.

"This is Anatoli, remember? And...," he pointed to Kevin, "His worker, Mukendi."

The new man with a limp grunted, "First name?"

Kevin pulled out his identity card. "Francois," he said, keeping his eyes level with the new fellow. Confidence lay in holding the gaze of anyone. The man glanced at the identity card and nodded. "Let's go," he said and shut the door behind him, promptly shuffling them into his old pickup truck. Monsieur Kida declined a ride back, saying he would walk.

The newcomer, their driver, was silent, his English broken, and when he spoke, he addressed Bampa in French or Lingala. Bampa, not as fluent as Dongawe was, spoke slower, carefully. Kevin listened to the two men keenly. Names like *Kivu, Bukavu, Numbi* featured often. Sometimes words like *soldiers, military,* and *smugglers* escaped in English as both men juggled and swirled the foreign lingoes on their novice tongues to better understand and be understood.

Familiarity was their bond, Kevin realized. They spoke as if they had known each other for a long time. A tone of respect resonated between them, as if the symbiosis of their roles preceded them and fated their destiny. The ride was long, bumpy and hot; the air was humid, and Kevin slid in and out of an uncomfortable slumber catching himself when his head lolled to the side or gasping when the road snaked around a mountainous curve crushing him against the car door handle or when the car clambered over gravel and sank into potholes. They finally arrived late in the afternoon at a ghostly site, a vast expanse of mountain and adulterated red earth, where tunnels jutted from dug-out holes, ransacked and abandoned. A few yards away from the site was a broken-down signpost. Little mud huts dotted the shrubbery.

The three men got out of the car and stared out at them. "What happened?" Kevin asked.

Bampa chuckled. "They left. Soldiers came and raided this place, so most of the miners left."

Kevin waited for more, but Bampa said nothing else. Instead, the two men chatted, and Kevin zoned out, staring out ahead. A weird smell coated the air, and Kevin crinkled his nose.

The newcomer, whose name Kevin never grasped, led them to one of the huts where an old woman and two children lived. The rest looked deserted. The woman handed them cut-out gourd-like bowls filled with a creamy, frothy liquid.

"*Mandale,*" Bampa told Kevin. "It's like *malwa,*" he explained. Kevin wanted to resist; alcohol was one thing he had vowed not to take after his father...

"Take a sip. It's a sign you acknowledge your host." Bampa encouraged him when he noticed his hesitation. Kevin sighed and sipped, made a face, and shook his head. When he looked up, everyone was looking at him in amusement. Their driver said something to the older woman, who grinned, revealing wide gaps between long front teeth, and the children shy-snickered.

"He said you are an alcohol virgin," Bampa knocked Kevin with his elbow jovially. Kevin shook his head; at least no one was upset. He was later told Teresé, the old woman, and her children would take care of him, and Bampa would sleep in the next hut.

"I thought this place was deserted?" he asked Bampa later.

Bampa replied, "That's why we are here; the fewer miners, the easier for us to get more gold in a short time."

Kevin had not expected mining to be so hard; the adulterated earth and pits he had seen previously became his workplace every day. He was not alone either. There were approximately six or seven boys his age that filed in daily shoveling the earth; six or seven others formed a human chain armed with curved metallic basins that they used to scoop the soggy earth, sieve it, and pass it on to the next set—this time, men and women who sorted through the mash for any gold nuggets. He was taught how to tell if it was gold or not. Some men bit into it, washed it off, and held up the dull metal the size of a pea to the sun. When someone discovered some nuggets, jubilant shouts reverberated through the mine.

The first weeks were hard… Kevin scraped his fingers, and they ached formidably, especially in the morning. He winced as he stretched them out. Teresé was kind and very experienced in dealing with miners. They spoke to each other in a rudimentary form of sign language, and their coexistence in the hut was serene. In the evenings, She soaked his hands in warm water and massaged them with shea butter. Even though he had initially refused to drink *mandale,* she still offered it to him along with his food.

Days rolled into weeks, and his hands adjusted to the coarse nature of his work. His fingers callused just as his determination concretized, emboldened by the thought that when it was over, he would have enough to take home, make things right with his mother, please Desire, and find

Shenzi. Some days he was frustrated, but Bampa's casual encouragement thrust him right in the center of a mine the next day.

His first gold nuggets, three small irregular pea-size gold bits caked in mud, appeared after three weeks of clawing at dirt with his hands and pickaxes.

"Some people take months before they even come across any gold. Do not worry, this mine is still loaded. We must be patient—patience, I tell you," Bampa would tell him.

Every morning, after a chilling cold bath in a little makeshift structure of wood and leaves, right behind his hut, Kevin began the daily ritual of staring at the glossy photograph. It transported him through months of turmoil to better times with Shenzi. He allowed his daydream to capture the people he needed most in his life and the life he dreamed of for all of them. Recharged, he then folded it carefully before jamming it into the pocket of his jacket that he hung on a hook by the door.

Bampa discovered his secret and jested, "Eh, important people in your life, heh?"

Kevin shrugged, unwilling to divulge the details.

After his initial find, it was as if the gods smiled on him, and two days later, he found more nuggets. Then, for an entire week, the nuggets just rolled into his searching hands. Soon the other miners curiously thronged to his dig site. Kevin demarcated the areas he dug in so he could keep the other miners away from them. He realized he discovered more gold nuggets farther from the center where most of the diggers clustered. Soon enough, he figured that there might be more gold nuggets farther north of the mining pit, and he told Bampa, who paid a guard to keep everyone away from the northern crater of the pit. In another two weeks, he found more gold nuggets, then the finds stopped even though Kevin fervently dug farther north.

"Possibly we exhausted that area; let's try a new plot," Bampa said encouragingly as he handed him a plate of rice and chicken stew for lunch. Kevin wolfed down the food so fast, he did not realize how hot it was. His whole body was caked in dirt, most of his clothes were destroyed by the consistency of the red earth that stained and stubbornly clung to them no matter how much washing they received.

"Don't worry, we will buy you designer clothes when we return," Bampa assured Kevin, and he nodded, holding on to all the promises Bampa dished out. It would be fine; things would pan out well.

Some days were so long he wished to go home, while others were short and eventful, and it wasn't so bad. There were also those days when "mine watchers" brought news and it rippled through the camp like a powerful wave over the ocean. Soldiers *were coming*. On those days, they mined less or stayed away. However, soldiers never came, at least not in the months he toiled in the mines.

Before Kevin knew it, Bampa was announcing their scheduled return. "We leave in two weeks. You have done well so far."

It was not what Kevin wanted to hear. "Have we got enough?"

Bampa had tilted his head. "Not the goal I was expecting but close."

"Two weeks?" Kevin asked, his mind working through the kinks. The more gold they returned with, the bigger his share.

"Yup."

"Okay. I will certainly find more."

Bampa laughed. "I like that determination! In two weeks…who knows what can happen?"

The last week of the three months proved to be the most exciting. Kevin accidentally clawed into the ground and brought up a large stone that they found out was not a stone. When they cleaned it, they discovered it was a large quartz rock with gold veins lacing its jug-like body. The other miners stopped for a moment to gaze at it. "Oh, my god!" Bampa whooped. "Oh my god! This is the biggest find of all the gold we have gotten." He roared with laughter, clasping the rock to himself excitedly.

The other miners chattered animatedly and almost immediately swarmed Kevin's location and dug deep ferociously.

Their find was not as lucky, although a lot of little gold nuggets surfaced. Nothing was as big as the mother rock.

That evening, Bampa chattered nonstop, clapping Kevin on the back. "You have the luck of the gods with you," he told him as he drank his *mandale.* "I knew it when I saw you. I knew it!"

Kevin smiled. "It's my mother's prayers and my little sister's love that keeps me."

Bampa roared with laughter and winked. "Have you forgotten your woman, already?" Kevin realized the ache had subsided, and in place of mindless desire was a hunger, a different hunger.

He shrugged. "Maybe I am too busy."

Bampa guffawed. "Good fortune will make you forget *punani.*"

Kevin hummed, unconvinced. He still wanted her, but something was different, and he could not put his finger on it.

The next few days, Bampa let Kevin rest as he went to get the gold nuggets cleaned and weighed. Kevin knew they had struck a fortune when Bampa returned with his eyes a bright glow. "We are going to be so rich!" he told Kevin excitedly. They had mined two and a half pounds of gold.

"This is not even possible in three months, eh!" He opened a parcel he had with him, a brown cloth tied at the top, and showed Kevin the gold nuggets: dull irregular forms of stone.

"They don't look so worthy." Kevin peered at the several nuggets.

Bampa laughed. "They don't, but they are!"

It was time for them to leave. Bampa told Kevin he never came to the same mine twice since most times soldiers invaded them, and he preferred the smaller mines where you saw what you dug out.

"We need to leave soon; we cannot stay longer," he told Kevin urgently. Two days later, the familiar battered truck of their driver returned. The man thanked Teresé and her children. Bampa handed her an envelope. She smiled widely, her front spacious teeth gleaming in the sun.

Thunder roared through the sky, and Bampa blessed God that it had not rained in the time they had been at the mines. Three months had sailed by with muggy heat, a few drizzles here and there, but nothing catastrophic. The drive was slow and laborious. Their driver got off the beaten track and veered onto another road, claiming they would have to get closer to town or a place with better lodging.

The wind howled and lashed into the trees; the storm was heavy, and the car did its best not to slide on the path that quickly muddied with clay soil. They made it to a structure that looked like a set of houses in a row: a cheap boarding house and a well-known stopover for miners and gold traders seeking refuge from bad weather on their return journey to their homes. It also housed miners who had nowhere to stay as they worked the different mines, paying the owner a percentage of their gold for meals and boarding.

"Farther down is a little town called Itombwe," Bampa told Kevin when they got onto the front porch of the dorm-like accommodations. He spoke of the history of the town Itombwe, a haven for miners and traders, a peculiar sanctuary with unwritten rules everyone adhered to, even government officials, rebels, and soldiers. It was Switzerland.

They passed the night in silence. Kevin got the room and bed, while Bampa and the driver took the couch, telling him they were fine and he needed all the rest he could get for working so hard.

Bampa handed him the gold in a khaki pouch saying they would be safer with him in a room than with them on a couch.

Kevin, still exhausted from three months of rigorous mining, passed out into a deep sleep, lulled by the howling wind and storm. In his dreams, he held Shenzi's hands, and she whispered to him the Jack and the Beanstalk story.

Chapter 12

Kevin started.

It was not the loud, distorted noises from outside that woke him; it was the dream. Shenzi's storytelling had morphed into a frantic cry, and the crier was Desire telling him she needed him to come home soon. The distress on her face gnawed at him, and he tried to soothe her animatedly, letting her know he was heading home. He would see her soon, but she kept crying. It was as if she could not hear him.

He got frantic and the frustration jolted him from sleep, and for a moment he was not sure where he was, then the familiar surroundings and his senses swirled, merged, and became one.

"Bampa!" he called out, then remembered names here were different. "Anatoli!"

He scrambled off the thin mattress that was cradled on an overused bed with metal springs that groaned and grumbled as he leaped off it.

Kevin reached for the door and swung it open; the sun flooded into his eyes, and he blinked, blinded.

There was commotion outside, and Kevin started to panic, heading right into the melee, where throngs of men and a handful of women gathered, yelling and talking simultaneously. He scanned the small crowd rapidly, his eyes sweeping through women and men.

He touched a man beside him and asked him the time; the man shook his head and continued shouting back at another man on the opposite side. Several minutes passed, and he was none the wiser on the cause of the commotion. He withdrew and returned to his room. His bag was still on the floor beside the bed.

Kevin searched through his clothes and emptied his bag looking for the pouch of gold, but it wasn't there. He searched twice over to be sure. The noise outside finally died down, but his confusion mounted. He picked up the jacket he had worn when the storm started and ransacked the pockets, *maybe*…. His hands felt something. It was the photo of him and Shenzi, and in a tight roll next to it were a couple of loose Congolese francs, not enough for a day's meal and a scrap of paper with the words, *thank you* on it.

Kevin sat back, stunned. Not fully comprehending what was going on, he went out again and inquired of the few people sitting outside. Had they seen a big man with a big voice, and a lean man wearing blue jeans and a white shirt with a cap? He had a limp.

Everyone shook their heads as he labored to describe the men to them with signs. It was aggravating that no one could speak English or Luganda; they did not pay him any mind. Despair and rage gripped him. He slumped onto the grass, dejected. An absolute acceptance of the situation dawned on him; they had abandoned him and were not coming back.

The people in the boarding place came and went in shifts. A pickup truck came by early in the morning and later in the afternoon dropped some people off and then picked up others.

Kevin sat on the grass, still numb with horror. A million thoughts coursed through his mind as he pieced together what had happened. As much as he did not want to believe his predicament, there was nothing that could deter him from that reality. He watched glassily as people walked around him to their different destinations. No one spoke to him. He picked himself up mechanically and walked back to his room. His clothes still lay scattered across the hard, cemented floor. He picked them up slowly, then when he had put them back in his bag, he sat on the bed and felt it groan and sink beneath his weight. He clasped his face in his hands, and the shock of the betrayal rocked his nerves drawing from deep within angry sobs. Anger was always his strongest emotion.

Dongawe's warning came back to him. "Be careful," he had told Kevin.

Kevin balled his hands into fists and, even as he roared in rage, he hurt deeper for his mother. He promised he would be back in three months. He thought about his dreams. Was it all over? Where was he to go? Could he go back home? How? He lay on the floor heaving, groaning, grasping the reality of his circumstances. Panic melted into anguish, rage, then pain and, several hours later, into a deep-seated need for revenge.

Two days later, someone walked into his room, where he had lain on the floor since discovering the betrayal, and motioned that he needed to leave. From the impatient way in which they talked and waved their hands, gesturing to the door and tapping their wrists as if to specify time, Kevin knew he had overstayed his welcome.

Even though he had hardly slept from thinking, he still had not come up with a concrete plan. He did not know the way back to anywhere; he had thought about going to Teresé, but he did not know how. Going onward to the border was another option. He kept mulling options over in his mind, and when he picked his cold stiff body off the floor, shouldering his bag, he knew one thing: there was no way he was returning empty-handed.

He walked out of the room to the grassy lawn and stared out before him; all he could see was rolling hills and mountains and a narrow road he had come by only a few yards away from him. He sat on the lawn and waited, and then he saw the pickup truck he had heard from a distance when he had lain on the floor in the room. In a few minutes, it came into view, circled the lawn, and the people on it jumped off as another group started to get on. Kevin followed them, not sure where they were going, but he guessed they were heading to a mine. Everyone waved an ID in the driver's face, who chewed sloppily as he motioned for people to get into the truck. Kevin searched through his pockets for his fake ID, sure he had shoved it there, but his hands came out empty. The driver watched him for a while as he searched frantically, then shouted something in Swahili slapping against the body of the truck, and everyone sat down hurriedly. The truck sped away toward the horizon.

Chapter 13

Weeks after Bampa abandoned him, Kevin was surviving by the skin of his teeth, passing off as an artisanal miner and living from one gold deposit to another—if he found any in the crowded sinkholes the truck ferried him to, morning after morning.

Frequently he was thrown out for trying to pocket a tiny piece of quartz stone laced with gold in it, denied wages, and starved, then forced to work till his body gave way and his lungs burned with the dust and mercury that was their occupational hazard.

He fell deathly ill, and the truck dropped him off a few kilometers from the only hospital for miles around: Itombwe mission hospital. Even at this point of near-death, Kevin drew strength from the only memento he had of him and Shenzi. He cringed at the fact that the fold lines were eating away at the picture, but it spurred him on.

The hospital kept him only until they needed the bed for another patient who could pay. Emmeline, one of the junior nurses, took to him and nursed him to health at her house. With nowhere else to go, Kevin stayed with Emmeline and recovered. She had a two-year-old son, a runaway husband (as is the mine story), and a generous heart. When he first had a proper view of her, he thought her alluring and meek. She had the biggest eyes he had ever seen; her hips and bottom were heavy and sat like beautiful mound hills on either side of her. She was as kind as she was attractive, and he was drawn to her. His feelings for Desire had long since waned. He doubted she would even remember him if he returned. The fledgling emotions seemed to dissipate in the light of this cocoa-skinned beauty.

They filled their communication, or lack thereof, with hand gestures, smiles, and nods. Words fell to the floor around them because they could not understand each other. When he was stronger, he went out to mine again, even though concern creased her smooth face. But Kevin was unstoppable; in sign language, he told her he wanted to make it up to her for helping him. He also showed her Shenzi's picture, placed it on his chest, where his heart thumped steadily, and said, "My sister...sister." She had frowned, and to explain further, he had pointed to her son, and she had responded with an "Aah" in apprehension.

He came up with nothing that week and ventured off to an obscure mining area, a small and possibly private nook, for the unfamiliar faces in the small group that dug and sorted the stones, and that was when he turned around and looked up right into the barrel of Ssaka's gun.

Ssaka was a man who took no prisoners. He was ruthless and cunning, but something about Kevin made him hesitate, and Kevin unraveled the reason for it a month later, after a long day's hike to one of the gold deposits. They had found a hideout and set up camp. One of Ssaka's men had brought back a hog, which they hovered around as it slow-roasted and spat over an open fire.

"When I lowered the gun, and you looked up—fearless and determined—I saw myself, many, many years ago, at your age... standing with my hands raised in surrender, a barrel of a gun in my face, shuddering involuntarily from the cold and rain..." Ssaka told Kevin.

Ssaka.

His real name was Pierre Mbayo; he had been captured by rebel leader Pablo Tansi; his family home in North Kivu was ransacked, while he was tied up and whipped till he passed out, but not before being forced to watch his sister gang-raped repeatedly, then killed. He did not know where the rebels took his parents or if they even lived. They had other plans for him, manual labor in the mines for four and a half years, turning soil over, inhaling mercury to enrich the Freedom Movement of Tansi; they had pillaged villages to strike fear and create dissent between the governments of Rwanda and Congo.

He learned to eavesdrop with a deadpan expression and made himself an asset to Pablo in that time, scouting out mines ahead of his men and scoring big most times. When he did not, there were consequences. But he was relentless, decidedly becoming the most valuable prisoner they had taken.

He recognized his freedom would be in the gold and diamonds. If he could monopolize it, taking control away from the rebels, he would need an ally for amnesty.

"What did you do?" Kevin asked.

Ssaka laughed softly. "I decided to make myself valuable to governments. Give them what they need, dangle it in fact, so they can give me what I want. I needed to be indispensable to them like I was to Pablo."

At seventeen he planned his escape while out on a gold-mine-scouting expedition. This time he had been allowed just one guard; Pablo had started to relax his hold on him. Armed with a bag of gold nuggets worth thirty thousand dollars, he attempted to flee from his handler one rainy night, but his plan was not foolproof, and he was caught and threatened with torture and death.

"I raised my hands in surrender. Like this. I stared into that barrel and told him 'Do it.' I did not care. I had lost everything and everyone I cared for. Life was a war zone I could either take part in or tap out of. So, death was not scary anymore."

"What happened?" Kevin held the man's gaze.

A slow smile crept up the bushy face. "He hesitated. Big mistake."

Ssaka had calculated that move. He was an asset, and his death would be the death of his handler. The man uncocked the gun eventually, then said, "Give me the bag," and in that moment, as he reached for it, his feet gave way, and he slipped on the rain-soaked grassy bed beneath him. Ssaka saw his chance. He fell upon the man, knocking the gun aside in a vicious tussle for survival. The struggle did not take long. Ssaka, nimbler and slighter, stabbed him with a knife he carried and finished him with the barrel of the gun, crushing his skull with several blows of rage and unbridled hatred.

"I did not think it was worth living anymore, even with all I had…the gold, the intel, but God saved me for something."

He probed at the roasting hog, and it hissed as fat seeped out of its hind quarts into the fire, "I knew I had to live…life is a gift, and I was given it again…"

So, he made his way across the forest until he met with the military guards at the border towns and fearlessly made a trade deal; he would lead them to the rebel hideout in exchange for protection and the ability to keep mining without restrictions. "I did not realize what I had gotten myself into. I just wanted gold at the time to build a big house and see if I could find my parents."

"Did you ever figure out why you survived that night?"

Ssaka nodded. "Yes, recently actually…thirty years later…. On that night, I had my gun aimed at your forehead, the head of a fearless teenager…like me." He had looked at Kevin across the roasting hog suspended over the leaping flames. "I was to show mercy as God had shown me." Ssaka kissed the crucifix that never left his neck, a light, delicate chain that he had had made from the gold he had stolen. Hanging from it was a cross pendant that had belonged to his sister, Faustine.

She would have been thirty-nine that year.

"You and I, we share a kindred spirit. Family, violence, and ambition for wealth and power. It was as if fate said, "You shall live!" Ssaka said as he drank from a gourd of fresh mandale. "So, I named myself Ssaka. It was short, mysterious." He shrugged. "Unforgettable. Like the Great Shaka Zulu. Pierre Mbayo died a long time ago."

For Kevin, remembering the night he stood staring at the barrel of a gun, he felt that once again the God of the universe he prayed to at the orphanage and abandoned time and again never seemed to leave him alone; he seemed to constantly barter his life with death and spare him a few more lives to see his mother and Shenzi. *I wonder how many chances*

I have left, he thought. Maybe this God did respect promises after all and would keep him alive until he fulfilled them.

"Why do they call you King of the Jungle?" he asked Ssaka.

The older man shook his head. "The militia leader I met then gave me that nickname. It stuck. But I am sure you can imagine why." At five-foot-six, lean and muscular with attentive eyes, Ssaka was a paradox of nature, a nuclear warhead in a most ordinary-looking casing. No wonder he earned the nickname.

He could pass for a stern school principal in his occasional *kaunda* shirts fitted over denims. Sometimes it was the kente shirts he got from Kinshasa. "Buy African, wear African as often as you can."

Ssaka trained Kevin, pushed him hard for five months, got him to meet every key person in the gold trade that worked for him. "Unfortunately, you don't have the time I have, so you must be quick-witted. No mistakes," he told Kevin.

When he had started two decades earlier, he had worked anonymously with a team of miners, sellers, traders, and buyers from Congo to the Kenyan coastline. His contacts over the next twenty-six years had stretched to over twenty African countries, about six Arab nations, three Asian countries, and seven European countries, where he stashed gold bars, diamonds, jewelry, and enormous wealth in offshore accounts.

"When will you use it?" Kevin asked him once.

Ssaka shrugged, amusement lurking on his features. "When I launch my rebel war." When he trained his gaze on Kevin, the amusement was gone. "Telling you what I do with the gold I have amassed will make you an accomplice to very, very intricate conspiracies."

The conversation had ended there and Kevin had not understood what he meant, but as he watched him through the months, he started to make sense of what these conspiracies might be; it suddenly dawned on him that everything Ssaka had told him wasn't a fairy tale, that indeed Ssaka was not an ordinary man; he was one to be greatly feared and rightly so. To think he had spared his life humbled Kevin, and his respect for the man grew.

Ssaka did not just manage expeditions; he owned gold and diamond mines in Congo and ten other African countries. He negotiated with leaders in off-the-record meetings they held in the dead of night at the camping grounds he had set up; military squad leaders stopped by occasionally, and Kevin would watch as they deliberated, hardly understanding a word of their conversations. Ssaka spoke more languages than Dongawe.

"It was French, Lingala, and English growing up; the rest I learned in the jungle with the rebels and as I mingled with foreign diplomats. One must know many languages when dealing with different people; it goes a long way."

He even met with Ugandan military commanders and the president of Uganda himself. The other uniforms he saw were new to him. Ssaka bought their allegiance in gold and precious stones and ran the gold-lined coasts in his favor; nothing happened in the deep forests of South and North Kivu mining areas that Ssaka was not aware of. They whispered his name from the central to the far end of the eastern shores of Africa, and his influence was still gathering speed farther down as he had expressed interest in South African mineral wealth. Ssaka indulged him in stories of leaders he had only heard of in the news, men he never dreamed of ever meeting. He spoke of them like they were bosom buddies, calling them by their first name so often, Kevin had to inquire twice before Ssaka declared who they were.

Intricate goings-on and clandestine exchanges took place either in the tents occasionally pitched or in the little shack Ssaka inhabited in the deep Kivu forests. Kevin had been curious about the rebel leader and how he had not found him and killed him. Ssaka had laughed and rubbed his hands together. "In this abode of mine, gold is the language that soothes a wasp's tongue and gets you what you need. But to answer that question would include you in secrets of governments I don't think you are ready to hear…let's just say…Pablo is no more." Kevin waited for more, hoping, but the older man simply looked away and added, "For as long as I keep the balance of things, we are all happy."

He found it a strange statement then, and he probed on. "What if something goes wrong?"

Ssaka had shrugged. "And they have, but a few bullet wounds and some fights later, I still rose, undaunted. So, deals remain as they do; there are agreements and oaths and decrees in place; I hold the strings one way or another. And there have been other rebel groups rising. Laurent Nkunda, for example, is wreaking havoc between Rwanda and Congo again. A lot of mayhem is pulling these countries apart." He shook his head like he recalled something funny. "It is good for business."

Kevin waited, fascinated. "Why all these rebel groups?"

"One day I will tell you. Don't bother your young mind now with these things." He waved his hand. "Be aware, though, that everyone owes me…. I give them what they want."

"I want to be like you," he finally told Ssaka, who had stared at him, a cloud of sadness passing his eyes.

"You *are* like me…a better me. One who will do better than I have, *bwana*. Stick to your promise. Thirty years and this jungle has grown on me, and this is my throne; you have yours. You also have a path," he told Kevin.

"But…"

"You have things to live for…." Ssaka was brusque. That trademark scab that still throbbed now and again surfaced momentarily, then disappeared. "And I am always here. You will always have me, and me, you." There was a finality about that statement. Like a promise.

At first, his tough, quiet exterior had puzzled Kevin, but as they grew close, he secretly relished knowing that his mentor enjoyed his company. He was the father he wished he had had. "If you were my son…" Kevin liked those rare statements that featured like diamonds in their conversations. The older man would smile at him from the corner of his mouth. "You would rule the world easily." That, Kevin rationalized, was his stamp of approval.

"The world is a big place."

"Aah, you can handle it." Ssaka would brush it off.

And Kevin nodded. He believed that too.

Kevin returned to Emmeline's weeks after mining, with Ssaka in tow. Emmeline almost collapsed in fear when she learned she was looking at the elusive king of the Jungle Kevin had described to her before. But he assured her it was all right. It was helpful Ssaka spoke Lingala, and after several minutes of deliberating, Emmeline served Ssaka. It was Kevin's first time witnessing the reverence poured on his mentor. One miner let him know how lucky he was that Ssaka was close to him. "He is as elusive as Laurent. We don't see him much; we only receive orders," he explained. Kevin felt special, and Ssaka was a useful ally to have.

Kevin toiled at understanding the black market until Ssaka could send him to negotiate and make transactions by himself. Kevin threw himself into it, reciting code names, understanding the map of the jungle routes to avoid or detours to take, and procedures and patterns right before he fell asleep so he could interrupt his disturbing dreams with a gold transaction gone good or pick up the trade lingo because Ssaka told him it was important to interact with the traders as best as he could. The more familiar the jargon, the more relaxed they became, the sweeter the deal. In the first few transactions, Kevin used Ssaka's name, and that alone aided smooth transactions. Then Ssaka upped it to dealers who respected his name but not his messengers and middlemen. They would have to prove themselves. "That's when you use your smart mouth, wit, and some Lingala and Swahili."

Kevin embraced the challenge. He paid keen attention to their body language, and when he spotted weakness, he dove in and made a fantastic deal. Ssaka stomped with pride when, on the fifth transaction trip, Kevin roped in the best deal of all his henchmen.

Clapping him on the back, Ssaka told him, "You are a man now. You can fearlessly negotiate at any table…. Let us see how well you can negotiate between a woman's thighs." They traveled to Kinshasa for a week, where Ssaka had a meeting with the president as talks of a transitional government hung like heavy nimbus clouds, ready to disrupt the lives of the gold miners in an unforgiving downpour.

Meetings done, Ssaka introduced Kevin to a world of pleasure and extravagance. They dined with important people and attended private VIP gatherings where they were entertained by Africa's finest artists that he had only heard on radio and seen on TV. Kevin had never experienced lavishness as he did that week.

He had resisted alcohol at first, but Ssaka would not let him get away with it, brushing it off as a hang-up. "You are not your father; you're your own man. Prove to me you are better than him."

"I am!" Kevin was indignant, and Ssaka shoved him a glass with a colorless liquid in it that stung his nose when he inhaled.

"Try this. Neat. Top shelf."

"What?"

Ssaka indicated for him to drink, ignoring his questions. He hated the taste once it went down, charting a fiery pathway from his mouth through his chest. Every gin, whiskey, or vodka he tried tasted worse than the spirit before. It was settled; alcohol was not his thing at all.

"Acquired taste, this is the best stash," Ssaka told him, his eyes flashed in amusement.

They were out almost every night dancing in the company of some of the best-looking women he had ever seen. He was enchanted by the Kinshasa women; there were high-class beauties that would pass for Miss Universe, their skins a high yellow, glowing, and smooth, their hair in expensive wigs and hair assets he had not seen on women in Uganda, not even Desire. They were soft yet firm; they made love with an insatiable skill like it was an art grasped from an ancient rule book of intimacy.

"You love Congolese women, heh?" Ssaka had roared when Kevin came down to the hotel parlor for breakfast. It was an opulent private breakfast suite just for them.

"They are beautiful."

Ssaka laughed. "Don't be deceived by all that *waawaa* looks. They are not very clever, up here." He pointed to his head. "A man like you needs..."

Ssaka loved to talk with gestures. He had put down his fork clumsily and meshed his fingers together, forming a cage. "You need someone that fits. Not just body parts...but brains, passion, destiny." He kissed the crucifix on his neck again. "You will find that woman. But these...*tsk-tsk*, just toys; play with them, learn a lot."

"Emmeline..." Ssaka suddenly mentioned her in the middle of an unrelated topic. "She wants you, but she thinks you don't. Maybe she feels too old for you."

The observation took Kevin aback, and he shook his head in disbelief. "That's not possible. I want her, but I think she *thinks* I am too young."

Ssaka laughed. "Be a man; go prove it to her."

Kevin hesitated briefly. The only woman he had approached was Desire.

Ssaka was quick to spot it. "For all your talk...you're a virgin?" he challenged him, loudly spurring him on.

"I am not," Kevin shot back defensively.

"Then what? Been in love?"

Kevin smirked. "Have you?" he retorted, and Ssaka chuckled, "Tough man, eh? Okay, Ssaka will toughen you up a bit; these women need you to bait them..."

Their final night was a highlight. They had a live band with Tshala Muana, and Kevin was entranced by her live performance and enchanted by her when she came to their table afterwards, pecking Ssaka on the cheeks. Then they delved into a familiar conversation of two people that knew each other well. It was an interesting swirl of French and Lingala. He listened absently, not registering a word of their interaction. When Ssaka introduced him, he kept his poise well enough, containing his excitement as Ssaka had taught him. It won him a night with one of her queen dancers.

"Now you can show your Emmeline what you are made of," Ssaka teased as they drove back to the thick forests of northern Kivu.

Hours later, Kevin was putting into practice what he had learned...this time with someone he liked a lot.

When Ssaka bid him farewell as the first rays of light crept up on the undulating horizon, frocked in woodland and shrubbery, he was both saddened and excited to leave Congo.

"You don't get out of here until you are many kilometers after the border. Driver will signal for you to come out for bathroom breaks." Ssaka was hard as steel; his forefinger pointed into Kevin's face as if they were strangers.

Kevin was calm. Six months of being with him had taught him to be undaunted. Everyone was afraid of Ssaka. Not him. He was a big bully with an empathic heart, a man oozing with such charisma and charm even the wildlife stopped when they heard his sharp, brusque voice.

"Thank you," he breathed out the sincere words.

In his severe warning lurked the elusive whiffs of concern. Kevin nodded, and they clasped hands, their eyes meeting. Communication passed between them. "*Bwana*, it's nothing. I will see you when I am in Uganda, late October, early November. I will find you," Ssaka responded.

Kevin nodded, then broke eye contact. "Emmeline…"

Leaving Emmeline after he had charmed and wooed her left him feeling hollow. He caught the hurt registered in her eyes when their eyes met, but it did not deter her from working on his departure preparations as well as she could, and in the nights, they had made love more urgently, more fervently as the day drew closer for him to leave.

Kevin offered her almost a pound of gold, urging her to leave and start her life elsewhere. She smiled, shaking her head, declined the gold, and said in French, "*Je vais vous attendre.*"

He threw a glance at Ssaka, who raised a brow and said nothing. When they stole out to the clearing where the truck waited for him, Kevin asked, "What was that?"

Ssaka harrumphed. "She loves you…she said she will wait for you."

Kevin felt a small glimmer of warmth. Someone loved him and treated him like a king, yet he could not stay or guarantee a return.

Ssaka shook his mini afro crown that lent him a seventies hippie look.

"That chapter is closed; you know, she will be fine." He laid a hand on Kevin's shoulder, sensing his struggle. "Life goes on."

He grinned, and Kevin could see the white glow of his perfectly even teeth, against an earthy chocolate complexion framed with the bushiest beard he had ever seen on a man. Manly, Kevin thought. A *real* man.

Kevin nodded.

The older man ushered him on to the truck that hissed and grunted as it was loaded. "Now go."

Kevin adjusted his shoulder bag and hoisted himself up the side of the truck, then over the thick logs that two men hurled and pushed into position, stacking them neatly over each other.

Kevin made himself a haven of small comfort amid them and the sacks of charcoal heaped up in the truck's corner. The driver handed him a thick blanket to cover the knobby ends of the trunks and to even out the bumps on the sacks if he wanted to stretch out, an exercise that proved increasingly uncomfortable throughout the trip to Uganda.

He shifted cautiously, making sure not to rip a tear in the thickly lined seams of his jacket and shirt. He hugged his bag close—Emmeline had sewn the gold nuggets into the hems of his clothes, created different pouch pockets in his bags, and a thick cloth parcel that he jammed at the bottom of his backpack spreading out the twenty kilos of gold nuggets that he was to take to a dealer in Kampala to continue his transaction.

"One of mine, Haruna, will be there. He works covertly in a printing and design company. But in the back, he tests the minerals for purity and sells them on the international market. He has one of our customers in Switzerland, a few in Dubai, India, Turkey, and South Africa. He will ask you for a few things, but it's all set. He is expecting you. Don't be late under any circumstances."

"How much is this?" he had asked Ssaka.

The bushy man whistled. "You are a millionaire, *mon ami*. That one hundred fifty million shillings you could have gotten from dealing with Bampa is *taka-taka*....nothing compared to the thousands of dollars you have there!"

Kevin beamed. He had done it: Even when he thought he would die in Itombwe hospital; he did not, when death visited him in the mines, when it sneaked up on him stealing food, when it embodied the barrel of a gun, when on the street scavenging and fighting…he was still here.

He caressed the bag as it pressed against gold deposits sitting uncomfortably in the hem of his shirt and his mind filled with thoughts of the mines; he and Ssaka's men had traversed to collect so much, from Kamituga to Haut-Uele district to smaller mining towns near Itombwe, small priceless nooks that only a man with as much experience as Ssaka could unravel, places virgin and untouched.

"Only I know these places, *bwana.* No one else, not even Dongawe and Kida," Ssaka had responded to Kevin's question as they uncovered yet another gold deposit nine days earlier, and their last spot. Ssaka told him he would travel farther northeast but would not want him to go. "It's too volatile down there. Military forces from Uganda, Rwanda, and Congo are killing people. Not good for you. You go home, see your mother. Find your sister."

Kevin had nodded, obediently in awe of the man he would have called father in a heartbeat. Kevin smiled in recollection. He admired him. If any good had come out of the tough months in Congo, it was one thing… Ssaka.

Chapter 14

Wandegeya, Uganda
August 2004

The sunbaked streets cooled down; the pavements creaked from the effect of expansion caused by changing temperatures and the hundreds of feet that drummed up and down their granulated length. Kevin alighted from the "special" taxicab, his backside still sore from the long winding trip, aside from occasionally getting out for air. He longed for a hot meal and a bath. It had been a long fourteen hours of nibbling on bread and dry-roasted chunks of beef. He wanted a warm bed too, a beautiful view, clean cotton sheets, some comfort.

The thought of a barito or three was enticing as he fished out the notes of money he had exchanged at the border from his backpack. He looked forward to seeing the guys, Shakira, and Adong. He romanticized the look of shock they would have upon seeing him. My, it felt good to be back.

"*Webale* boss," the taxi driver thanked him, his hands cupped together to receive the wads of rolled banknotes Kevin did not bother counting.

He slid across the seat to the left side that opened onto the pavement of Wandegeya taxi stage. "Aaah," he groaned slightly, drawing in a deep breath as his body flared up with a cocktail of aches.

"Boss, change *yawe*." The cabdriver had flipped through the notes with the expertise of one who counts money often and handed him a small wad in return.

Kevin looked at the several one-thousand shilling notes and shook his head. "Keep it," he told the man whose seriously screwed-up face suddenly lit up, and he laughed shortly, whistling under his breath.

"Heh? *Tweyanziza,* manager!" He let Kevin know that whenever he needed a ride, he could call him and began to recite his number slowly.

Kevin smiled. "Boss, no need for that. Do you know Original Barito?"

"*Iyii? Tsk,* of course!"

"That is where I shall be. Come there tomorrow for lunch," he told him cordially.

The cabdriver looked taken aback. He leaned out the window, a surprised look on his face.

"*Iyyi, oli younga…*really?"

Kevin smiled tiredly. "Come tomorrow; ask for *boss wa* barito."

The older man grinned and thanked Kevin for the money again while promising to come in for a grand barito when he was in Wandegeya the next time—which would not be too far off—and drove away.

The street lights flickered on, and traffic eased up. Kevin glanced toward the intersection where the town clock stood and strolled through the Wandegeya market center, shouldering his bag. His mind raced, and he concentrated on quieting it down. His emotions were askew from the trip, his nerves raw, his heart expectant for seeing his mother and for Ssaka's trip to Uganda at the end of the year.

As he strolled through the busy mess that is Wandegeya, he took his time drinking in the familiar sights and sounds. He absorbed the sound of music that meshed across the center from different stores and motor vehicles, shops and restaurants, the throngs of young people, students, arm in arm or in groups gathered at a chapatti stand, others making a beeline for a take-away. He sighed with relief to see chicken rotating in a glass roaster, "TV chicken"; that's what everyone called it. He slowly walked past the stand that used to be Ssalongo's, and the person at the next stand instantly recognized him,

"*Ki gwe? Ayayaya, oliluda wa? Nga,* you are lost? *Mbadde nti,* we thought you went to outside countries, eh?"

Kevin laughed wearily adding that he had been away on business, then carried on. It was the woman who bumped into him that zapped him out of his reverie. She shrieked momentarily as the contents in her huge handbag fell to the muddied ground. She cursed. Kevin quickly dove to the ground and picked it up. "Sorry," he told her, wiping off the mud splashes as best he could with the body of his oversize shirt being careful not to press too hard against the gold nuggets sewn tightly into the hem.

He was so busy making sure her plastic bag containing hot, delicious-smelling food, possibly take-away, was intact that he did not realize she had stopped fussing and was staring at him till he heard a familiar voice breathe his name: "Kevin?"

Kevin looked up. He was staring into the light-skinned sparkly smooth face of Desire. She wore her hair in gold and blue extensions, her eyelids a dusting of blue, her lips a warm red, not freshly put on. Kevin liked the look, a lazy evening type of look. She was still stunning. "Desire?" he spoke uncertainly.

She smiled and breathed a sigh of relief. "When did you come back? I just came from your barito place; we all thought you had died…how are you, *mukwano?* You even got tall." She was seizing him up. Kevin reached out and hugged her. "I am okay. How have you been?"

She nodded, letting him hold her. "I missed you. We could take a shower together," she coaxed flirtatiously.

Kevin smiled, vividly recalling the last day he had seen her only a year ago, laughing gleefully in the arms of another man. But now he felt nothing for her, nothing except a desire to take her to bed. "I know I need one badly. We can do that." He marveled at how easily he had said that with detachment, then added, "I am going to get a barito. Do you want to come with me? I could use company." He again surprised himself with how smooth and calm that had come out and registered her look of surprise too, which she quickly recovered from.

The Original Barito place was slightly modified. What had been an old rickety door with peeling paint was touched up with a bright yellow; the interior was brighter owing to better lighting and a noticeable upgrade that offered it a larger appearance from what he remembered. There were more seats, and the old sofa was gone, a new one in its place. There were two fans mounted to the wall that buzzed lightly as their swirling heads moved from side to side. The sound of an anchor reading news on the television gave the semi-filled atmosphere ambience, and Kevin could not have been prouder.

It was Shakira who saw him first and screamed, her hand flying to her mouth. "*Banange* Kevin? Kevin!" she screamed, disrupting the news watchers and diners as well as the people lined up at the counter for their barito orders.

"What? Where!" The euphoria caused by his sudden appearance brought business to a momentary halt. Livingstone was behind the cashier alongside a girl he did not recognize. He left her to carry on with the orders and hurried to the entrance to see for himself. Shakira still had her hand to her mouth; Livingstone whooped and the two hugged.

"Where is Boda?"

"Street tax," Livingstone told him. "*Ki boss! Mama eh*! You are back? Eh! Eh! Hoo, what do you want to eat?" He quickly ushered him in, completely ignoring Desire, and motioned for him to sit on the couch.

Kevin stretched out on the sofa, dropping the rucksack at his feet, then smiled tiredly at Desire and patted the seat next to him, motioning for her to sit. She was in a floral mini fitted dress with a peplum hem that hugged her curves to perfection. Kevin draped a possessive arm around her hips and for a second ignored Livingstone's ramblings. "Shakira, bring Desire anything she wants." His eyes stayed fixed on her, and the effect he was looking for came; she shied away, smiling. His ego soared.

"Okay boss, eh! welcome back!" she sang excitedly as she scurried off screaming at someone to get a menu.

When the menu was brought and drinks served, Livingstone fell into catching up, giving information as asked. Kevin wasted no time. "How are things?"

Livingstone clasped his hands together. "Good, good. *Eh? We* thought you died!"

Kevin smiled, as he drank his tea. "Nine lives."

"Bampa told us…"

Kevin was suddenly alert. "Bampa was here?" He ground his jaw.

Livingstone nodded. "Boss, that man isn't good, ah-ah."

"What did he say?" Kevin interrupted, ignoring the comment.

"That you disappeared." Livingstone cast glances at Kevin and Desire, indicating he needed to fill Kevin in, in private.

Kevin sighed, his gaze dropping to the thin tartan-patterned plastic covering that embraced the coffee table.

"You like the place? We tried to do some work." It was Shakira, carrying a plateful of barito in one hand and steaming hot *katogo* with *e' byenda* and avocado slices on the side of the plate. The smell of the delicious hot cooking awakened his appetite, and Kevin shook thoughts of Bampa off. It was something they would discuss later in the night.

As he dug into his food, he listened as Livingstone spoke of the renovations and how business had picked up. "We knew you would come back," Livingstone concluded.

Kevin nodded, hardly paying attention. His mind had gradually lurched on to something else. "How is my mother?"

* * *

When he had heard the news, his appetite fled as fast as it had come. He quickly turned to Desire, fished out some money, not bothering to count, and placed it on the table by her barito plate.

"I will see you later," he told her. She tried to reach for him, but he flinched from her, getting up. He walked out of the restaurant, making his way mechanically to the place he had called home before he had traveled ten months earlier.

When he got to the third floor, he unlocked the door with his copy of keys Livingstone had held on to while he was away, dropped the bag on the floor, stripped, and stretched out, naked, on the thin mattress bathed in a dull fluorescent light from the street corner. He lay there for a while, drifting into a disturbing dream and was only roused awake by a knock on the door. Boda and Livingstone shuffled in. They stayed by the door as if the weight of grief on Kevin kept them at bay. Kevin glanced at them, reality hitting him again. The pain that had slumbered within stirred violently. He half managed a pained whisper. "What happened. *Please* tell me what happened?" He directed it at Livingstone.

Livingstone sighed sadly, sensing the need to bypass informalities. His voice low and sympathetic, he said, "Boss, *kitalo nyo.*"

There was a split-second silence, then he cleared his throat. "*Ban'gam-bye* tuberculosis."

He walked to the left corner foot of the bed, where a small shelf stood, flicked on the light of his *katorchi* phone, and rummaged through the few books Kevin had bought, pulling out *Rich Dad, Poor Dad* and from it retrieved a folded paper, torn from an exercise book.

He motioned to Boda to turn on the light and handed Kevin the paper. "Mama Dina wrote for you," Livingstone told him, a little taken aback by Kevin's nakedness. Kevin took the letter. The weight of grief was suffocating and, with whispered excuses, both boys left, mumbling something about a party at the bar downstairs they were going to attend. Did he want alcohol? They asked, even though they knew Kevin had decided never to drink. A grieving man would need something to numb the pain.

Kevin shook his head.

Barito?

No.

Marijuana?

A pause. *Later.*

They filed out, leaving him in the semidarkness, shrouded in grief. The letter he held slipped to the floor, pieces of it echoed in the familiar soothing voice that was Dina's. "*You make me so proud.... You are going to be such a success in life. God will reward you because you are a good boy.*

Please keep looking for Shenzi. When you find her, take care of her. Promise me..."

The words leaped off the dog-eared paper and anchored themselves in the core of his soul. She had prayed for him, wished him the best, assured him, encouraged him, and hoped, kept hoping he would return. He sat on the bed hunched over as a despairing numbness surged through him. Suddenly, his head hurt, and his soul warred and raged. His heart shattered as it crashed against his chest. He gasped for air; he fought the violent, angry tears that forced their way up his heavy chest, refusing to stay down like bile rising in his throat; they rocked his gullet, and Kevin let go. In the safe secrecy of darkness, he wept bitterly for his mother.

The boys did not return.

Daybreak crept slowly, like a sleeping giant shaking misty dew off its brow, sending ripples of atmospheric change with each movement. The sun was peeking through the covers of night. The streets were awakening languidly accompanied by familiar sounds, and Kevin stared out, letting the cool breeze that stole through the partially open window fan his fever-hot face, spent from grieving. A lone taxi conductor was calling out, "Old taxi park!"

He reflected on the last ten months, the things he had learned, the perilous misadventures, the pain, the backbreaking work. The ache within did not dissipate. Instead, it grew and engulfed him now. He gasped again as the ache in his chest, palpable and grinding, shook his body. While it did, his groins stirred. His body cried out for release.

His mind worked through the replay of his life, and the end was always where he was now. The only person who tangibly gave him hope, the other person he had slaved away at the mines for? Shenzi. Where was she? He still had her, but he did not know where to start.

"Start here," a voice within nudged him.

Kevin thought about his next moves calculatingly.

* * *

It was 11:30 a.m. when he got to Luzira Prison. Walking the same dusty path that led to the gate reminded him of his first trip there. This time he trudged the same path with a weightier emotion than all the ones he once had combined: grief. The lady warden, Nakalya, met him at the desk. A mixed expression of surprise and sadness framed her glowing Vaseline-shiny face. "Where have you been? We are so sorry about your mother," she said in one breath.

Kevin acknowledged her greeting. "She was such a godly woman. *Tsk-tsk.* She is in a better place." She touched his shoulder lightly. Kevin had taken in the information silently, almost mechanically. She let him know a man who signed off as her brother, his uncle, came and took the body. He thanked her for the information and, without requesting his uncle's number, left.

He was not sure his uncle would look upon him kindly. There were questions that plagued him and many steps he wasn't ready to take yet. He would see her grave soon. Maybe ask Teopista or Mama Rose at the flat.

His next stop was Nasser Road, where Ssaka had told him he would find a buyer for the gold.

Kevin found him exactly where Ssaka said he would be. At 12:30 every day, like clockwork, Haruna ate his lunch at a local restaurant only a block from his printing and design business location. A restaurant whose low ceiling fans did nothing to stave off the heat emanating from the open cooking center. Kevin walked in and sat at a center table at noon poised to watch the door, training his eyes to fish out a fat short man with a constant grin on his face and a high-pitched voice.

"Almost feminine," he recalled Ssaka saying with a short laugh. "Don't underestimate him; he is very alert."

Kevin ordered a Pepsi that was produced in a sweating bottle. It seemed to warm up as soon as it was in his hand. He sipped deliberately. At exactly 12:29, a man walked in, short and plump with a beer belly and thin, small arms that seemed misplaced on his body. He wore circular-rimmed spectacles, which he pushed up his nose constantly.

He was engrossed in conversation with a taller man who walked beside him, gesticulating emphatically. Kevin's eyes followed them with interest.

The two men sat two tables from him, still sparring emphatically in Lusoga. Five minutes later, the short man bid a friendly farewell to the other gentleman and walked to Kevin's table, pulled the chair across from him, and sat. "It would not hurt if you had a phone," was his opening remark, then he shrugged. "But you are easy to spot. Too young for a place like this." He winked at Kevin.

"How is my old friend, Ssaka?" Haruna folded his arms on the table. A waitress came in to take their order. The restaurant buzzed with the sound of inaudible conversation, the fans and cutlery.

Kevin smiled. "He is good. He is coming to Kampala soon."

Haruna chuckled. "Ah, that sly fox. He says that, then…just appears like a ghost." He raised an arm dramatically and brought it down on the table with a thud. Kevin eyed the man, amused.

"Eat with me." Haruna told him as soon as the menus were placed before them. The man he was meeting was as cautious as a soldier with PTSD. He studied everything and everyone. Nothing escaped his eyes.

"You have to be cautious in Kampala," he told him between bites.

He is sly, don't eat more than him. If anything, leave your food half-finished. Listen more than talk. But you must accept to eat with him. He takes offense at that.

Kevin thought it odd, but if it got him money, it was all right.

He likes to eat with clients...anyone I send him. He uses this time to study them. It's not just food. So... Kevin remembered Ssaka giving him these instructions deliberately and slowly, making sure Kevin remembered everything he told him about Haruna. *Again, don't eat too much. He is superstitious, thinks great eaters are greedy. And you teenagers are greedy!* Ssaka had teased.

Halfway through his steaming *matooke*, Kevin stifled a belch audibly enough to attract Haruna's attention and pushed the plate to the middle of the table. "Asante," he said with a tight smile and reached for the bottle of soda.

The man frowned. "Finish, finish! I am not even halfway," he grumbled.

Kevin politely declined. "I am full already, boss," he said instead.

Haruna sighed. "*Esh*, young people today; it's as if they were born without stomachs." His eyes stayed on his plate, and Kevin settled back in the plastic chair, his arms planted firmly on the armrests, and watched this man with sparse hair and outdated glasses sitting atop his nose eat his lunch, the steam from the hot matooke fogging the little lenses. Haruna cleared his plate except for one piece of chicken wing, which he left deliberately on his plate and called for toothpicks.

Superstition. Ssaka's voice reverberated through his memory.

Kevin was thinking twice about his lunch, but everything depended on this gesture.

A waitress cleared their plates, brought the receipt, and Haruna paid.

"Bring us juice," he told the waitress, then turned to Kevin raising his eyebrows, "Juice?"

Kevin shook his head and looked at his half-full bottle of Pepsi. Haruna shrugged. "One, please." He signaled to the waitress.

They left the little restaurant in exactly an hour, sweaty with the stench of boiled meat stuck to their clothes. Haruna's office was an obscure little hole in the wall, past a huge printing and design office and warehouse. Past the warehouse space, they went through another door to the back and a little corridor with fluorescent lighting. His office was at the end on the right of the corridor, a regular four-room with no windows.

Haruna pulled on the string attached to the fluorescent bulb, and the little room lit up. The white light washed over the lifeless, pale gray walls. An office table, heavy-looking, sat in the middle of the room. Two large cabinet drawers rested against two sides of the walls, each encased with shelves that were marked in numbers and serials he did not understand. Rows and rows of different box types sat on them.

"Sit, sit." Haruna indicated to the chair in front of the glass-topped desk. "Let's see what you have."

Kevin pulled his rucksack to his lap and drew the pouch he had with the nuggets from inside.

Haruna took the parcel. "Have you seen the gold test before?"

Kevin nodded.

Haruna grinned, looking over his glasses. "I don't doubt it's pure. Standard procedure," Kevin nodded. "We have machines here for testing large quantities, you know."

The bespectacled man got up and excused himself. "Give me a few minutes," he said as he exited the room, returning ten minutes later with a smile. "That was pure twenty-four-karat gold. Very good, and nuggets are rare. These will sell well with our buyers in Dubai, Europe, and America."

Haruna stood pondering, as if he was counting money. "*Haaa* Ssaka always knows where the quality stuff is." Kevin waited. Haruna took his seat and pulled out a notepad where he scribbled for a minute or two, then tinkered with his calculator and pushed both notepad and calculator to Kevin. Kevin leaned in and looked at the figures; his eyes widened. All that would be his!

"After I take out my fees and costs, that…" He pointed to the calculator. "…is yours."

Kevin nodded. He knew the process took a few weeks, including transportation of the gold to its destination point, but the buyer paid him almost instantly. "We have a regular buyer already waiting; in fact, we expected you two days ago."

Kevin looked at his lap. "I had some things to deal with," he told Haruna, who ignored him and continued to let him know what more was expected.

"You know what to do, eh?" The man's eyes narrowed.

Kevin met his gaze unflinchingly. "Yes."

"The accounts will be in Ssaka's name," he told him. Ssaka had already informed him that as a minor, he could not have an account. Unless he wanted to carry a load of cash in Kampala, it would be safer to stash it in a bank or a safe. They would wire the money to different offshore accounts as it was received from the buyers via escrow accounts that handle the amounts without the rigorous scrutiny of the conventional banking systems.

"So, I will do it for you," Ssaka had concluded the laborious explanation of how money and minerals moved.

"Why do you do this?" Kevin had asked him later, and Ssaka had patted him on the shoulder and smiled. "Your journey has just started. You need someone to guide you."

"You don't have to; I can find my way," Kevin had told him.

Ssaka nodded. "You could, but you would waste a lot of time. Consider it the easier path…. When you are eighteen, you can transfer to an account you open. Or you can put it under your bed. Your choice." Ssaka had teased at the last part. Kevin had resisted the urge to reach out and hug the older man. It was a relief to have Ssaka. He felt fortunate.

"Ssaka told you I don't carry cash?"

Kevin nodded. "He said you will work out those details for me."

The short man rubbed his belly. "Now, there are three accounts, two here, and one in Switzerland, both in care of Ssaka." He paused and twisted his lips. "Because you are with Ssaka, we have a special discount for you, so the total of all that work comes to twenty percent."

Kevin sighed. "Not fifteen?"

Haruna air-punched numbers… pursed his lips in thought, then shook his head. "Um no, eighteen… maybe."

Kevin let the number hang and then said, "Okay." It was what Ssaka told him he would settle on. *He likes to haggle prices. Go along with it.*

Haruna beamed. "Done!"

He signed the paperwork handed to him, stacked neatly in a beige folder, his name printed on its sleeve. With that out of the way, he only needed to wait for the money to be transferred into the accounts.

"Twenty-four hours," Haruna promised, handing him a package with the Union Bank logo on it. It was owned by another of Ssaka's close allies, safer than most banks, and since it was controlled by friends and members of the gold trade, the regulations of deposits were less stringent, and questions on amounts deposited were dissipated. They had a slew of escrow accounts and withdrawal accounts. "For you to use to withdraw."

How are they safe? He had asked Ssaka about their banking system, and he had powered on educating him. "Because we have established trustworthy connections directly with offshore accounts in Dubai, Switzerland, Singapore, the Virgin Islands, Panama…I shall explain further later, no worries."

As he walked out, he heard the man clear his throat. "One more question, *kadogo?*"

Kevin paused, partially turning to him.

"What is it about you that Ssaka likes? In such a short time? It's never his way."

Kevin shrugged. "Maybe you should ask him. It seems you are in touch."

A startling high-pitched laughter shattered the air, and for a second Kevin wasn't sure it was from the same man. He laughed with tears rolling down his cheeks, much to Kevin's amazement. "You are like him. I see." He wagged a short finger at him.

When he walked out of the little room through the narrow corridor that opened into the printing and design office, Kevin studied and mused over the cover up that it was. He pursed his lips. Clever…

Chapter 15

It was the day after he returned from Kibuli. He had taken flowers to his mother's grave, a simple mound of earth with a wooden cross erected at the top. Teopista had waited in the car while he venture onto the lone grounds where her grave lay. Kevin requested the caretaker have a slab of concrete replace the cross.

"Ha, you must go through Mr. Kaggwa," the man had told him. Kevin's heart raced, knowing a meeting with his uncle, Benson Kaggwa, was almost inevitable. He thanked the caretaker.

He met the boys at lunch at the restaurant, and Shakira, who still was not over her joy at seeing him, ordered the new waitress to bring him food.

"Serve your boss!" she told her with the urgency of a woman who tells her maids to serve her husband when he returns from a long journey. With Kevin away, she had inadvertently become head cook and host, complaining she needed extra hands with the service, so Livingstone had obliged and picked her two girls that Festo had recommended. Kevin could not help feeling gracious toward the team for their effort in keeping the business going while he was gone.

"Thank you, Shakira," he told her and stretched out on the couch. As she prepared to leave, he asked her, "The other night, you were telling me about Bampa…remember?" he started.

"*Iyyi,* how can I forget him? He came here to tell us *nti* you run away!" She slapped her hands together and twisted her lips in a downward loop.

Kevin nodded. "Yes…what else did he say?"

Shakira made her way to the couch and leaned in conspiratorially. "I thought these boys told you. He came here in March, I think…. Yes! He demanded to see you. We thought he was mad because we told him you were together, and he got angry. Then he said you ran away with his gold, and he was looking for you. He threatened us, told us we owe him now."

The older woman sat down, placed her elbows on her thigh, her left hand fingering her fading gold loops.

"*Ah ha*, we were confused. Why would the boss steal from him? Didn't they go together? That's what I told the boys. We thought and thought. Then we decided, this man is lying. He is not telling the truth. Something is not right here."

Kevin drew in a deep breath. Ever since he had been back, even though he was glad to be home, the smoldering flame of revenge was growing into a fiery furnace that was ready to consume everything and everyone who had not only hurt him but deprived him of his mother. He listened to Shakira tell of the numerous threats levied against them, threats to take a percentage of the business earnings, to take the business altogether or shut them down, his eyes widening, his brows furrowing deeper at the audacity of the man. "He has not closed us as you can see." Shakira guffawed. "Those boys brought all their friends here, ready to fight. So, he left us alone."

"And?"

Shakira shrugged. "We have not seen him now…five months," she said counting on her fingers and raising her palms up to Kevin. "But Boda and Livingstone, they know."

Kevin shook his head, when his eyes met hers, they were red. "He will pay," he told her.

Shakira sighed sadly. "*Banange*, I am so sorry about your mother, boss. *Kitaalo banange.*"

Kevin nodded, hardly hearing her, his mind working through the information, and as he processed it, he mulled over different plans.

Later he castigated the boys for not telling him about Bampa.

"Boss, you were sad; we were going to tell you…"

"You tell me everything that happens; it does not matter if I am sad or not."

He immediately backed down; he was being unfair. They had tried to tell him, but how could he process both shocking pieces of information at once?

"He took my mother from me. If he had not abandoned me in Congo, I would have seen her. She would not have died. He stole from me! And for that, he will pay. I swear upon my mother's grave and on Shenzi, he will pay double for everything he did! Double!"

The boys cowered in silence.

Finally, Livingstone spoke. "We know where he is and what he does. Festo helped us too." They gauged Kevin's reaction.

When he did not respond, Boda picked up the momentum of the intel. "We tell him da story. Festo *ali sharp,* he know this man well. He have a taxi business, ten taxi, and want buy more. He building da another mall, Madirisa Plaza…*ali mugaga nyo*! He is very rich."

Livingstone grunted. "*Wama,* no, he has borrowed much money for business." He emphasized it, slapping his hands together.

Kevin turned and looked at the boys. "Why didn't you just take over the business…didn't you think I was dead?"

"Esh? How? You own this whole part of Kampala streets. If our boss is dead, we are in trouble. So we said you were on important business so that no one would take our street. Also…we know you. We suspected he double-crossed you; that's what I told Boda. I said 'Let's wait; boss will come.'" Boda nodded.

Kevin felt the flicker of a smile cross his face. Amid everything he was going through, he truly could rely on his two henchmen.

He nodded. "That's good, that's good," he said instead.

A pregnant silence hung in the air between them, and he could almost read the curiosity permeating from the boys.

"So what happened?" Livingstone picked up the courage to ask.

Kevin shrugged. "After I worked for him, Bampa left me in Congo with nothing. I met someone else. You may see him. He helped me, taught me many things, and he helped me get back." He smiled, thinking of Ssaka with respect.

"Ay." Boda leaned in. "So, *kati*…no gold?"

Kevin assured them. "We are going to be very rich! And I am going to take down Bampa, make him pay for everything he has done to us…. all of us and my mother."

The boys looked at each other, not sure they followed his outburst. "Where is the gold?"

Kevin nodded. "Don't worry. First, we are going to expand this business, increase your payment, and rent a better place…no! *Buy*. Then we are getting a house in…"

"Muyenga? Kololo?" Livingstone jumped up, his eyes dancing in excitement.

"Later, we also need to live close to our business and within our area of influence. We will stay around here. Maybe the flats outside Makerere, maybe. But we don't want everyone to know we have a lot of money. Ssaka says you have to be discreet."

"*Disicreeti kyi?*" Boda frowned.

"We have to be simple for a while so that we can grow quietly. When we have all of Kampala, people will be shocked." He spoke conspiratorially.

The boys lightened up. "Aaah. Okay!"

"I will go back to Congo also, later. By the way, thank you for being loyal." He opened his bag and pulled out two thick envelopes with fresh notes from Haruna.

"Here." He gave them each an envelope. The boys oohed excitedly before they delved into plans for the big changes they hoped for.

Even though Kevin carried on checking on his friends on the street, partying with them, and smoking weed with them. He returned to his room and wept silent tears of anguish, regret, and pain. He replayed the episodes of moments he spent with his mother and then Shenzi. On nights it was unbearable, Festo supplied him with a bevy of gorgeous girls. He halfheartedly accepted the gesture. A part of him longed for Emmeline's earnestness, and when he did, he sought Desire. Weeks before they moved to a bigger house, Kevin spent a better part of that period between Desire's legs. He spent his sorrow on her, aggressively possessing her again and again. Anger and pain aided his virility, and she cheered him on, soothing his soul with her words and body. There was no pretense in her moans and orgasms. It egged him on.

When he dozed off exhausted, nightmares afflicted him, and Desire woke up shrieking with him. "What is it? What is it!" She would panic and Kevin would slump back against the pillow, breathing heavily.

"Nothing, just dreams," he would tell her, and when she drifted off to sleep snuggled up against him, Kevin lay awake staring at the dark ceiling. Pain that sleep numbed would find its way to the surface of his soul, and he would let the tears flow unhinged, the hollowness in him threatening to swallow him up. His mother remained a vivid memory in his mind; he replayed scenes from his childhood with her, to when his father died, to the visits in prison and the promises he made to her, the way she looked when he last saw her. He had worried, but Dina always rubbished his concerns.

"Heh? Are you my mother now?" She would thrust an arm akimbo at her waist and widen her eyes in mock melodrama. He would smile.

"I should not have gone," he whispered to himself over and over as tears rolled from the sockets of his eyes, gliding freely onto his cheeks and wetting the pillow; he sniffed. His emotions wavered erratically from grief to anger.

He had everyone on the streets spying on Bampa, giving him as much information as they could on his movements.

He lay awake late that morning watching Desire dry her hair; she was talking about going to the salon. His mind drifted.

"*Mukwano.*" She was on the bedside by him. "Did you hear what I said?" she was asking.

Kevin gazed into her brown eyes and shook his head. "No, what did you say?" He sat up.

She smiled. "You are too preoccupied these days. What's on your mind?" she asked.

A slow smile spread on his lips. "Business." Then he added, "I have something for you."

Her eyes widened, expectant. He swung out of bed and walked to the wicker chair that sat by the dressing table, his jeans and shirt draped over them. He pulled out a wad of money from the pocket of his jeans and handed it to her. "For you. Thank you," he said with a faint smile and watched in bemusement and satisfaction as her eyes lit up.

Desire reached for it. "Thank you, *Daddy!*" she squealed, and Kevin snatched it out of reach, wagging a finger in her face. "Ah-ah. You have to promise." Desire reached for him seductively. "*Iyii,* anything," she purred, stroking his ego with her voice and his manhood with her hands simultaneously until he throbbed and stiffened.

"Prove to a woman you can provide, and you have her." Ssaka's voice resounded in his head. "Real money will get you the women and everything else you want in life. Maintaining is another thing…but this is a start. Always remember…choices come easy with wealth."

Emmeline was different. All she wanted was him. Shenzi wanted a brother, and that was more important to him. He saw the effect of money on Desire and did not trust her; she had not wanted him in the beginning, but the tiny feeling of triumph that he had conquered her gave him a rush of excitement.

"You cannot sleep with anyone else anymore. Only me." He pointed to his gradually filling-out adolescent chest.

She was leaning back on the edge of the bed spreading her legs. "Of course, Daddy, anything!" She writhed seductively.

Kevin felt his heart race; his groin throbbed, a bittersweet pleasure sensation; he smiled. He had conquered her.

Ssaka was right. Money *indeed* solved everything.

He enjoyed the thought of the power and freedom it gave him, and as he drowned himself in her scent and warmth, Kevin thought of Bampa and the several ways he would inflict pain upon him. "Patience," he told himself.

"You want to do it when the time is right. That's when revenge is most effective," Ssaka had advised him.

Despite his rigorous scrutiny of Desire, Kevin allowed himself the pleasure of other women, older, more sophisticated women he dared himself to approach and was pleasantly surprised when they accepted. Despite some rejections, Kevin was further propelled by more acceptances. It became easy, and he studied women more, understanding their needs, learning to be what they wanted to get what he wanted.

Ssaka's visit only fueled his appetite. They spent weekends in his high-rise apartment in Kololo, and Kevin marveled at the exquisite wealth and plushness of it.

Ssaka smugly told him, "This is how kings live."

Kevin wholeheartedly agreed. Ssaka continued to introduce him to people he would never in a lifetime have dreamed of meeting, often calling him his nephew. No one asked questions. They attended dinners with people whose names made breaking news headlines and were the epitome of press coverage.

"How do you know all these people?" he asked Ssaka.

Ssaka laughed.

"Don't you know me yet?"

Kevin retorted. "I think I do, then you astonish with a new hat trick."

Ssaka grinned, satisfied.

"I want to be like you." Kevin told him again.

"Don't be like me. Be *more* than me." He raised his toast glass to Kevin.

They had retired from an official dinner with close, intimate friends and one of Kampala's top tycoons. Kevin had worn his first tuxedo, an expensive piece of clothing custom made and fitted for him. He had silently watched how the rich and sophisticated behave and even avoided the eyes of the daughter of a guest.

"Date upward, always," Ssaka had told him when dinner was over. "The Desires and Emmelines of the world are many, but as you climb the ladder of influence, your tastes change. Your pool of choices narrow down, become more patrician and intentional. And they should. Date like a king."

Kevin could never get used to seeing how well Ssaka blended in: speaking of stock markets, politics, and social conversation peppered with contained punch lines. He was larger than life inconspicuously, and everyone drew to him…respected him.

"What you miss out in school, you learn in the field. You travel, you dine with the rich and famous, you learn how to talk like them, think like them, *be* like them. They will never guess you never went to Harvard, because it does not matter. What is Harvard anyway? Or even that your lot was a wooden spoon…a barrel of a gun." Ssaka had turned to him with a death stare, one he gave him when an important epiphany was to be delivered. "In fact, they will want to be like you because your own life is different and romanticized. Don't forget where you came from or be ashamed of it. That is actual power. It's where your inspirations come from."

Kevin eventually studied the pattern of people Ssaka met with, not just the one percent of society across the globe, but those he called the middlemen, the helpers, usually people of the law, police officers, inspectors, high-ranking government officials, and even traffic police officers. There were doctors, too, men of influence in different spheres. "Don't despise the little fish; they come in handy in times of a drought," he told Kevin with a wink.

Kevin went to the internet café to look up "Harvard" and then a whole list of Ivy League schools the rich and well placed in society attended.

As they sat in the huge pearly-colored Jacuzzi on Ssaka's rooftop, drinking scotch and lemonade, they deliberated on the evening. "Soon I will take you to meet a longtime friend, Garang. He is going to be a political person in Sudan. Sudan needs some stability. I think that he is a good contact for you to know." Ssaka assured him.

Kevin listened eagerly, sipping his lemonade.

"And then we will travel to South Africa. I have established myself in the mineral business there, especially diamonds. I have my territories in Liberia and Sierra Leone ; big diamond hubs that place them on the world stage. I couldn't miss that platform. I think you are ready to meet more of my associates and see the vast empire of minerals I have, hmm?"

Kevin chuckled. "Why, I am not surprised? All this time you were working your way into the south ? So fast?"

The older man *tsked*. "Did you underestimate me?"

Kevin shook his head. "I am never sure what to expect."

"When I say things like, 'You should own the world,' I don't speak lightly. And you are ready. I have some friends in Kenya and Tanzania, very low-key traders…and an enthusiastic thought leader…. You know, these phrases people call themselves these days, in South Africa. I want you two to become friends." Ssaka wasn't suggesting it. He never did.

Kevin nodded, then asked, "Are we going to sell to them?"

Ssaka leaned his head back, lulled by the force of water massaging his back. "We are already doing that, merely getting you into the wider market. And now, history has caught up with Congo. My father used to say it would."

Kevin did not understand what he meant; the faraway look in his mentor's eyes was an indication he had spiraled out of time. There was something going on and possibly something out of his depth. Nonetheless he was curious.

Ssaka stirred the bubbling water with his forefinger in concentric circles and continued, "You see the troubles in North Kivu have always been, since colonial times, since the inhabitation of the Belgians, the Rwandese we like to call *Nyamulenge*, the Congolese…the land disputes, the minerals. One leader comes and says one thing; another comes and changes it." He shook his head. "I knew it would happen; I had a meeting with the acting president, Joseph Kabila. It was intense. I asked him if he saw a redo of the 1998 war…"

Kevin waited as Ssaka sipped from his glass, swirled the ice in it, and placed it on a tray by the Jacuzzi.

"Did he?"

"I think so…and it is here. He did well to keep the peace with the

Luanda peace agreement his government signed in 2002. It has not been easy for him, but I look forward to elections in another year or so. I think he will do well for us." He smiled at Kevin. "Enough politics. Congo is a bubbling pot of instability. It makes me essential. It's both good and bad, on one hand there is tension between Rwanda and Congo; Uganda is involved. General Laurent Nkunda has gone rogue in Masisi in North Kivu. As we speak, there is fresh fighting in the north. It's…." He made a motion with his hands to indicate it was shaky.

"What happened to all the agreements with the government?" Kevin asked.

"It's complicated. Very complicated. "

"How long will this conflict last?"

"This one?" Ssaka laughed. "I might be obliged to seek the oracles for that answer." His eyes strayed out in thought. "On one hand, war is good. Instability gives us an advantage. We simply need to be more vigilant in safeguarding our interests. It's a delicate dance of diplomacy and conspiracy…and suspense." His eyes returned to Kevin. "I need to tighten my hold on Congo. Everyone wants Congo. Especially the western superpowers."

Kevin had heard him speak like this before in brief spurts, but today he unraveled more. The pieces were slowly falling into place. Ssaka was one of two, a vital ally or deadly enemy. A most invincible and vital position he had not known anyone to hold.

"Anyway, I need you to see the bigger picture. Is it too much?" the older man asked him, and to Kevin it did not seem like a question of concern, more a challenge.

"No, it's not," he assured Ssaka. It excited him. It was a playground he wanted to master. He lived for these challenges.

"We survive a lot of inspection and investigation because of my position in this business. Besides…I hate paperwork. That's for Haruna and his team." He waved his hand in the darkness.

Kevin nodded.

Ssaka smiled. "We may call some illegal…mainstream corporate language, but…it isn't…we understand the laws and merely use the loopholes they provide. Not illegal, just not written." He laughed. "Especially industry minerals. But with airtight connections, efficient people that move things…money does the rest; we stay in business."

"The balance you speak of?"

Ssaka nodded. "Yes, maintain the balance. I want you to be wealthy and happy. Never succumbing to the mercy of anyone. Not anyone with a gun." His eyes twinkled as he added, "I hope one day I can meet your sister."

Kevin replied, "You will."

Ssaka nodded. "Life is strange."

Kevin wondered what he meant but brushed it off. The information was already as overwhelming as his awe for this man who owed him nothing and yet who, without question, was opening him up to a world of opportunities.

'Yes, it is," he said.

"We are in a good place," Ssaka told him calmly and raised his glass to Kevin.

"You are going to be great, and your sister will be proud. Losing a mother is always devastating. I did not forget."

Kevin dropped his gaze. The familiar ache he had carried around for months like a personal dark cloud hovered, projected itself, and he let out a shallow sigh. "Bampa will pay."

Ssaka agreed, "I would be disappointed if he did not. But don't be in a hurry. Take your time; plan it well so that when you execute it, it's a masterpiece that even Bampa will grant you an award for a stellar plot. Patience."

Kevin had not thought of revenge as a work of art. It slightly took the sting away. Ssaka was right. It had to be a grand plan. He resigned to the forces of the word *patience*.

"When pain and anger subside, the by-product is clarity…. When the time is right, clarity will show you," Ssaka drawled, suddenly lost in time. The bubbling warm water rushing between them swirled with the passion and conviction of both men lost in the hallways of their intricate pasts where they paid respect to unforgettable losses and made vows with the earth against their enemies.

Chapter 16

Kampala, August 2005

At the end of 2004, Kevin and Ssaka had again traveled to Congo, where Ssaka spent an enormous chunk of the time in meetings with the four vice presidents of the D.R.C on matters of trade and the North Kivu crisis, then to Ghana for two weeks. Kevin eagerly awaited the South Africa trip, which was pending.

"If I like it a lot, I might get me a South African woman," he told Ssaka. Ssaka made a face and said, "I don't touch South Africans."

"Why?"

"There is something wrong with them. They had too much blood shed with Apartheid; now up here…" He pointed to his head. "…It's *chakala*, and they are sicker than all of Africa. Ah-ah. You should marry a girl from Rwanda. They make good wives," Ssaka said like it was law, and Kevin mused over it.

"We will see," he told the older man.

When Kevin asked if he worried about the situation in Congo, Ssaka smiled. "Me? Worried? No! I never worry. I seek opportunity. I take advantage of the chaos. I study the weak links and weed them out," he replied, then told Kevin of his opportunities in Sudan. "Good time for business. Simply finding an angle that benefits us all. The Sudanese are ruthless."

Kevin hung on every word that spilled off the busy man's lips. He often indulged in a brief history lesson, then fast-tracked it to the current situation in Sudan and about his friend, a political revolutionary, John Garang.

"He is to be vice president, you know."

A smile lit up Ssaka's eyes as if in all the drama sweeping the eastern part of Africa, there was a sprouting hope.

"He will be good for the people. Things will be fine."

Kevin made it a point to read as much of the news as he could to keep up with Ssaka. His attention shifted from sports, politics, to the wider world business trends. His thirst for knowledge led him to the internet café daily as he scoured the World Wide Web for material from *Time* magazine, the *Telegraph*, the BBC, and any news agency he could find.

One morning, a news article about a plane crash caught his eyes and he started. Ssaka was yet to introduce him to Garang, and here before him was tragic news that he had died in a plane crash a couple of hours earlier.

Kevin called Haruna immediately. "Did you see?"

"I did. I am waiting for Ssaka to get in touch."

Kevin did not have to wait long, for no sooner had he hung up with Haruna than the call came through from an unknown number. *Ssaka.*

He stepped out of the internet café; his time had run out, and he did not bother to purchase anymore. Standing a few feet from the doorway to the bustling café, he answered the phone.

"Ah! I warned him!" Kevin could hear the grief in his voice.

"Sorry, Ssaka."

"I feel sorrier for the people of Sudan. This is not good. I had a bad feeling. I told him not to come to Uganda. But…politicians. They think they know everything. Ah!"

Ssaka ranted about Garang's death, how it was a planned attack, how Uganda played a part, how this hampered the plans he had for mineral business in Sudan. Garang was a most profitable ally. Kevin allowed the older man to vent. In the volley of angry cussing lay the sadness. But

Ssaka was not one to dwell. Eventually, he recovered and chartered an alternative path.

Kevin wandered away from the café into the busy pedestrian walkway on Kampala Road, his eyes scanning traffic, without really seeing it; the animated call of conductors to potential passengers mixed with altered sounds of music from vehicles to restaurants meshed in a familiar confused cacophony. Then he saw him.

It was the unforgettable Land Rover.

And the big man, with his arm hanging out of the driver's side, drummed lightly on the hard-bodied silver vehicle, gazing ahead into traffic. Kevin noticed his lips move, his head jut back in hearty laughter, and then something else moved into the periphery of his view: a girl, about fourteen or fifteen, her hair braided in golden-brown-colored braids held back with a headband from her oval face, her forehead stricken with adolescent pimples. She was smiling and animatedly indulging him.

The resemblance was striking. He froze momentarily and all the raw emotions that were airtight "for that doomsday" stirred violently in their contained banks. Traffic loosened and the silver Land Rover shot off toward Wandegeya.

"Kevin!" He realized he had faded out, and Ssaka was calling him. "Are you there?"

"Sorry. I...I..."

"Another woman?" Ssaka teased.

"No, not at all. It was Bampa, and I—I think his daughter."

"*Aaah.* The devil himself."

Kevin puffed out the pent-up energy that suddenly surged through him in powerful bolts. "I can't wait any longer..."

"Young blood, too much in a hurry to kill off their enemies. *Wait.*"

"For what?" Kevin snapped. His hands trembled, and he gripped the phone tighter.

"*Hmm.* You see how my man went down today? His enemies were waiting. They waited till now, right at this moment when Sudan was making peace with its past, and he was the man of the people. They waited until now. You must think like that. Don't think with your heart. It will let you down. You must plan with your head."

Another lecture, Kevin thought. He had heard it repeatedly before.

"Think, Kevin, think!" Ssaka was short. "Now let me prepare to bury my friend. Don't do anything stupid."

Kevin pocketed his Nokia 3330 gingerly, then clenched and un-clenched his hands to stop the tremors. His heart pounded so vociferously he was convinced everyone walking past him heard it. When he wiped his brow, it was moist. He walked into the nearest take-away and ordered a plate of chips and liver. It was after he had washed it down with a cold Coke that the calm flooded him. He had thought seeing Bampa again would have no effect on him. He was wrong.

The incident stayed with him like the pungent smell wafting out of a latrine after a series of impossibly long dump sessions. The nightmares returned viciously, and they would not let up to allow him a couple of hours of rest before the crack of dawn.

The Original Barito place was growing, much to his delight, and he figured it was time to move. They moved to a more conspicuous location on the opposite side of the road, where the Ntinda and Bwaise taxis made their stop and took up space in a new building next to a take-away. Kevin opened another branch along Kampala Road, right where Chippers Ice Cream used to be. It was the largest, most accessible space he'd found. He put both boys in charge of the businesses and oversaw the daily running, going between Wandegeya and Kampala Road, inspecting, looking at the numbers, and paying workers. He had become a household name on the streets, and he asked for more detailed data on Bampa.

Haruna, being his cryanoid and representative of his business and money, oversaw the signing of all agreements. Kevin spent plenty of time with the suspicious inside man, making sure they had lunch with him and his associates thrice a week. With them, he learned about business in Kampala, and as a gesture offered his street resources. He often sat silently in the presence of police officials, heads of security,

Park officials, and businessmen in Kikuubo who occasionally traded in gold and diamonds. He also got to meet a few Asian middlemen who knew a thing or two about government dealings within the Asian and Indian community.

"Every single person is important; we are like a chain link," he recalled Ssaka telling him of all the people he had introduced him to. He learned to invite them to the Original Barito restaurant, keeping them close as allies.

"What did you find out?" he was asking Livingstone at the end of a long day, when the last worker had retired, Livingstone was locking up on Kampala Road.

"The girl is his daughter. Mercy Mutesi. She is fourteen. Goes to Kibuli Secondary. He does not have other children. His wife, they say, got complications, so she is the only child they have."

"Anything else?"

Livingstone was piling the sturdy wooden-legged chairs atop one another as close to the wall as possible. "No, nothing yet. He is buying more taxis as usual, and his shops are thriving. The business complex is coming up slowly, though. He needs a lot of money. Oh! By the way, that new hostel, Clarion's near Makerere? It is his as well. *Eh,* I forgot to tell you that one."

Kevin nodded contemplatively. "Thank you."

Buying a car was next on his list of to-do's. He was told the best people to teach him to drive would be truck drivers; after all, they drove the biggest vehicles for long distances. He found one willing to show him the ropes for a small fee. After a tedious three months, he had the hang of it. His practical secondhand Corolla bore the marks of training, dented on its bumper and severely side-swiped with irregular scrape marks on its white paint to boot, but it still braved the rough, bumpy roads of the city. Kevin drove it for a few weeks before selling it to a garage for parts, then purchased the latest Benz 2005, a dark blue sleek Mercedes with beige leather seats.

Ssaka humored him. "Toys. It's just a toy."

"It's a good toy," he told Ssaka. "A damn good one!"

"Enjoy the sweat of your brow," the older man encouraged him.

Kevin then moved out of Makerere, into a four-bedroom house in the upscale suburban Muyenga neighborhood, but the boys opted to stay behind. Barricaded with an iron gate and high wall, the top of it lined with spiral barbed wire and shards of glass, the house's interior oozed luxury with a pool in its backyard opening to the wide living room.

He had watched enough music videos peppered with home pool parties to decide he wanted one. Maybe then he could have Shenzi here with him.

When he lay back in a deck chair by his pool, he marveled at the twists in life that had finally led him here.

* * *

December 2005 was a somber time for him, especially as Shenzi's birthday loomed closer.

At the beginning of the month, he found out Desire had betrayed him and spent a week at a businessman's flat in Kololo. He silently cut off all communication with her.

He thought about Block 4 and how his childhood festivities were a whirlwind of shopping and good food, so he gave his staff the rest of the season off.

"We open again on January second." His generous announcement was drowned out by the loud cheers of excitement.

He could not blame them; they had worked hard all year, and business was flourishing. Ever since he opened the second restaurant, his profits had been climbing just as steadily as his staff. Boda and Livingstone had proved more reliable than he had imagined. He pondered opening two more barito restaurants in Ggaba and Bugolobi.

With these turns of events, Kevin relinquished more authority of street leadership to Boda and Livingstone, who took it up gladly. In that way, he could focus on expansion and growth while keeping an influence on the streets. His name alone opened doors. While Boda solely managed the daily routine of the street, Livingstone saw to the restaurants with Shakira.

After almost three years on the street, Kevin imagined no one could possibly enjoy staying shackled to the harsh and perilous means of that existence. He wanted to improve their lives, and it became a passion just as big as his determination to see Shenzi again.

"You only just started. Take it easy. Expand with professional expert advice, and then…provide opportunities to those willing to work," Ssaka advised him when they spoke about it.

With the restaurants closed for Christmas and New Year's, Kevin became a recluse, shuffling aimlessly through the rooms of his house when he could not sleep, or spending hours on the internet educating himself about business ownership and the stock market. After dinner, he would sit by the pool smoking a blunt and reminiscing. It was his moment to mull over the past cherished moments he had shared with Shenzi and celebrate her by himself.

He declined every invitation to indulge from his street comrades, Haruna, and even Ssaka.

The streets were curiously empty, and he planned a couple of days in Jinja, a pilgrimage of sorts, scouting their old haunts and spending nights at the Source of the Nile Hotel, something he had promised Shenzi they would do.

The eve of her birthday found him at DV8, shooting pool and viciously playing to win. He had just won the second game amid cheers, instantly garnering him a teenage fan club.

He had gone out more, partied harder, always closing the clubs down as the soberest man standing. He mastered the art of holding girls' attention amid the revelry; he learned quickly that if he remained relaxed, humorous with a touch of unhinged spontaneity, he would be spoiled for choice on the girlfriend order card. At first, he hesitated, but as with all things, practice makes perfect; he was steadily keeping count of his scores, readjusting mistakes, and revising his steps with calculated moves customized for every woman he fancied. He studied them like an eagle hovering for an opportune moment to swoop in for the kill. Usually, they dismissed him as being too young, but after he ordered a few rounds of top-shelf drinks they had never heard of, they paid him more attention. Kevin charmed his way through the hearts of women he was sure would say no. Nothing was more thrilling.

Their resistance was all part of the game. Eventually, like moths to a flame, they drew to him…. It was intoxicating. His relaxed charm tested their guard, which they cast aside almost instantly. His wit and humor unlatched those who would not easily loosen up. He was an exciting enigma with tremendous virility both in and out of the bedroom.

Kevin wined and dined many; however, he dated only a few. It did not matter if it was a one-night stand or a longer engagement; he had learned one thing: treat a woman like she is special, and no matter how it ends, she will always come back when you need her.

He lavished them with gifts, trips, clothes, and anything he could give them…for him, it was a game, a process, the journey of the thrill. Each woman was unique, with different expectations and upbringing. He hungrily learned from them as well by watching and listening. He invested time and energy in understanding them and their world. *The older, the better*, he told himself. The younger ones fell too easily and had hang-ups he did not want to deal with. Their naivety gave him an edge over them. He loved to groom a girl, but he knew when he had spent himself pampering and spoiling, boredom reined in, then whatever exchange had been thrilling, even scintillating, paled rapidly, and a new hunger gripped him: an insatiable need for someone older, more experienced, more worldly-wise.

He was picking up his winnings worth two bottles of beer, which he concluded he could trade for a cup of tea at the Grand Imperial Hotel. There was a band playing that evening and he could not imagine a better way to wind down before Shenzi's birthday the next day, when he heard someone say, "Hey!"

Kevin wheeled around on his heels and leveled with the chunky boy, who wore a low french-cut, a checkered shirt, and jeans. Kevin narrowed his eyes, a slow grin spreading all over his face. "No!" he exclaimed.

The chunky boy whooped and reached out, crushing Kevin in a hug. The boys laughed as they clapped each other on the back.

"What?" they both said in unison.

"Man! Long time!" they said again and laughed.

"Too long!" Kevin replied, genuinely glad to see someone from his past. The familiar sensation of childhood groped at his soul, and his longing for Shenzi deepened. "Bosco! How are you?"

"Easy, man, easy." Bosco laughed, appraising his friend in his khaki shorts, sneakers, and D&G T-shirt agreeably. "And you? Where are you? I don't even know your school; I would have kept in touch!"

Kevin smiled. "School of hard knocks!" He grinned. Their conversation was interrupted by Bosco reaching back for a girl whom Kevin recalled catching a glimpse of from the corner of his eye, pretty but too young.

She played with the ends of her long black twist braids that fell past her bare shoulders, over the strapless tank top she wore. She covered a portion of her revealed midriff with the multi-patterned long-sleeved shirt she had wrapped around her over a short denim skirt. He snickered to think how she must have tried to cover the silver chain that draped her waist, to no avail. She was chewing deliberately, and her big innocent-looking eyes widened further when they rested on Kevin.

Kevin caught her eye and held it as Bosco made introductions. "*My* girlfriend," Bosco was saying, throwing an arm around her waist almost possessively. "Michele, this is Kevin, the guy I told you about…"

"Hi." She dropped her gaze shyly when Kevin did not drop his.

Kevin smiled. "Hi Michele. Whatever he told you is possibly fabricated. Lies!"

The boys chuckled. Kevin shook her hand. "Nice to meet you." She smiled.

"We do go way back, Bosco and I." He dawdled his hold on her hand, for the sheer enjoyment of watching her squirm, and the desired effect was as he expected. She smiled and uncomfortably looked at Bosco, mumbling she was hungry.

"We should go eat. I am hungry too. What do you think, Kevin?"

Kevin shrugged. "Was thinking the same thing."

Bosco looked over his shoulder and frowned. "I could have sworn you were with Shenzi."

Kevin smiled. "That's a story over a meal."

Bosco's face dropped. "Oh, where is she?"

Kevin raised his brows. "Are we going to keep Michele waiting?"

Bosco hugged Michele briefly, his face registering a sincere apology. "Sorry, my bad; let's get out of here."

They slipped out of the club packed with revelers not older than twenty-one and strolled to a nearby take-away, another famous holiday hangout spot, but it was almost empty since most parents had shuffled their children upcountry to spend the holidays with family in the village.

They conversed about the old days on the short trek to the restaurant, and when they sat and ordered their food, Bosco impatiently asked, "Okay, so, where is Shenzi? I never imagined a day would come when I would see the two of you unglued from each other."

Kevin wanted to tease him about his crush on Shenzi. "She is Kenzi now. Mackenzie Matthews. Got adopted after we left, you know, my father dying and all…"

"Yeah…. That was so…Sorry, man."

Kevin nodded, trying to be dispassionate. "Yeah. It's all a long story."

"She was all right, right?" Bosco probed.

And his girlfriend piped in, "Who's that?"

"Er…Shenzi…she is Kenzi now, the girl I told you about whose mom was…anyway, she got adopted."

While they ate, Kevin briefly told the story of their street life and the adoption, leaving out a lot of details. "We ended up in an orphanage," he told Bosco as a final note.

Bosco shook his head, chewing on his chaps. "Man, how did we go from a birthday party to the tragic loss of your dad to…" Then he paused, shaking his head. "I am sorry about everything. I heard about your mom."

Kevin nodded and silence draped them for a minute before Bosco asked again, "So where exactly is Shenzi...I mean, Kenzi..."

"America. I am going to find her, eventually."

"Does she write? How is she?"

Kevin dug his fork into his fried liver and shrugged. "I haven't heard from her since she left Uganda."

"That's cold. Why?"

Kevin sighed. "Probably not her fault. She was blind, remember?"

Bosco nodded. "Yeah, of course I remember..."

"And tomorrow is her birthday."

Bosco held his fork midair, his face lighting up. "Wait...yeah! The twenty-eighth!"

Michele leaned into the table. "What's it about this girl?" she asked.

Kevin made a humming sound, eyeing Bosco. The need to tease him was an itch he did not want to contain.

"Kevin and she were inseparable; she was...different," Bosco said, and Kevin spied the flash of warm memory in his eyes before it faded. "Kevin hoarded her from us like she was gold."

Kevin shook his head. "She was blind, and I...became her brother."

"They stole from us..."

"Stole? We negotiated really well, and everyone was *happy*."

The boys went back and forth on the unfairness meted out against the rest of the children on Block 4.

"He and Kenzi would take all our goodies after a game of hide-and-seek, *mbu* keeper's fee. All our pancakes, all our money and toys. Then they would go up to the rooftop of the flat, sit there by themselves, and indulge in our goodies. All. The. Time! Kevin's excuse was she was blind and needed protection. Self-appointed bodyguard blah-blah-blah..."

Kevin could not contain his laughter. "You are not over that?"

Bosco grinned. "I am not over a lot of things. I need therapy."

Kevin grinned at him mischievously. "Ooh don't tell me..."

"Oh, shut up, man!" Bosco flung at him, embarrassed, not wanting him to bring up the crush topic.

Michele watched them, enjoying their banter.

"Truth, Michele, these two were the snobbiest friends anyone ever knew, especially when they were together. Kevin here would beat anyone and everyone if they so much as looked at Kenzi sideways,"

Kevin gulped his Coke, amused. "It was us against the world, Michele," he told her. "I would protect her with my life if I had to."

"See?" Bosco interjected.

Michele giggled. "Wow, I think you should protect me like that Bosco…" She play pouted, her eyes never leaving Kevin.

"See what you are doing?" Bosco complained to Kevin, who laughed.

"So, was she *like* your girlfriend?" Michele was looking from one boy to the other. Kevin frowned.

"Nah, it's Bosco who had a crush on her…"

"I was ten," Bosco protested; an embarrassed look crossed his face, and Kevin tried to suppress his laughter.

"We were children, and no, she is like my sister. Bosco just…"

"Oh, stop, man!" Bosco shoved Kevin.

"He has you now," Kevin added, basking in his friend's embarrassment.

Amid the low chatter of a few young holiday makers and the high falsetto tones of Mariah Carey's "All I Want for Christmas" in the background, Kevin asked Michele about herself. She engaged enthusiastically, and Kevin listened before the conversation steered back to their childhood.

"I miss her, Bosco. But I am going to find her."

Bosco nodded. "If you are still who you used to be, I don't doubt it. At least where Kenzi is concerned. I like her new name…Kenzi… Mackenzie."

"When you find her, I think I want to meet her too, this girl that got my Bosco all gaga over her." Michele rolled her eyes as she said this and grinned.

"I have a picture," Kevin said promptly. "Maybe you can see your man's crush."

Bosco groaned. "No, Kevin!"

Kevin was enjoying the moment. He pulled out his wallet and carefully fished out the old photo, worn from being moved around so much. "It's probably not as clear…but…" He held it out to Michele, who peered at it, her mouth making an "ooh" shape.

"Was that you?" She glanced from Kevin to the picture.

"In the flesh." Kevin nodded.

She stared at the picture long and hard. "Wow, she is so dark-skinned," was her final comment.

Kevin smiled to himself, folding the picture and tucking it into his wallet. "Black beauty," he concluded.

Bosco nodded in agreement.

"Bosco should tell you how hard I teased him…"

Bosco groaned again. "Kev, man! Just finish your Coke!"

Michele was enjoying their childhood escapades, and having Kevin tell it sent them all doubling over with laughter.

In another hour they were sorry to see her go. "I have curfew. It's almost eight," she told the boys. "It was nice meeting you," she told Kevin.

Kevin replied, "If you are okay with it, I can drop you home." Then to Bosco, "Maybe you can come back to my place after that?"

A look of surprise crossed Bosco's baby face. "You drive?"

Kevin shrugged like it was nothing.

"Okay then."

Bosco could not hide his surprise when they got into Kevin's Mercedes. "This? Is yours?"

"Nope, I borrowed it from the president…of course it's mine," he joked, punching Bosco lightly. "Who's giving directions?"

Bosco volunteered, giving Kevin directions to Michele's house. It was only five minutes away from DV8 in Nakasero, past Akii Bua Road.

When Bosco said his farewells to her at her gate, he probed Kevin impatiently. "Okay, you need to start talking! Where have you been, what have you been up to? You. Drive. A friggin' Benz!" Bosco's jaw dropped. "Which mafia are you tied in with, or which sugar mommy? I saw how you spoke to that waitress!"

Kevin grinned. "A lot! Too much to tell. Let's go to my place and talk, cool?"

"Hell yeah!" Bosco sat back like he was not going anywhere, even if wild horses dragged him, then paused. "Wait, what? You have your own pad?"

"You could say that."

Bosco harrumphed in disbelief. "I need to see this *muzigo*."

In less than thirty minutes, they were pulling up to Kevin's house.

Bosco glared at Kevin. "This is yours?"

Kevin nodded.

When he got the gate opened and drove in, Bosco hooted, "Eh!"

Kevin pulled up to the driveway, and the two boys got out.

"Welcome to my *muzigo*."

Bosco leaned back with his arms over his chest and whistled. "So what's the secret to your…" One hand swept up and down Kevin's house then toward Kevin.

Kevin stood akimbo. "If I told you everything, I might have to hold you hostage."

"I knew it! Mafia shit."

"Um, not really, say, fortune favors the brave?" Kevin walked up to the front door, turning the key in the lock. "But now that we have connected, we should hang out more. You might learn a thing or two."

"Like 'how I got rich at sixteen'? I am all ears, *compadre*."

Kevin showed Bosco around his four-bedroom house, minimally decorated but exquisite in hues of beige and dark brown. Kevin was a minimalist, his furniture chocolate, gold, and dark wood. "And who did the interior décor because this is fab-u-lous!"

The last surprise of the tour was the unveiling of the pool. Sliding doors from the living room led out back. A few garden chairs were scattered on the sides of the pool, along with low side tables.

Bosco let out a low whistle. "Seriously, who owns this pad?"

Kevin doubled back on a lounge chair and stretched out. "Me."

"Wow," Bosco mouthed. The chubby boy sat down across from Kevin; a silence permeated with questions hanging between them. The low hum of traffic from far off carried on the night breeze. "Now I know where to go when I need to run away from Aunty and Uncle. I live with them now; my parents are abroad."

Kevin said. "Uh-huh. *Karibu.* I am glad to have someone from way back with me."

"So?" He waited. "What's the story?"

Kevin told him about Bampa and Ssaka and the gold and the people he had met…he was careful to keep out as much of the intricate details of Ssaka's function on the broad scale. By the time he was done, Bosco was looking at him like he was an alien.

"I can get you a drink to loosen your tongue."

Bosco was shaking his head. "Whoa. Okay…"

"What are you drinking?"

Bosco let his breath out slowly. "I need a beer for this."

Kevin grinned. "Or ten." He brought him back a Nile special and a 7Up for himself.

"No beer?"

Kevin shook his head. "I can't do alcohol. I think my dad drank for the both of us."

"Right," Bosco agreed.

"To Kenzi then," he toasted, and Kevin toasted with him.

"So, what's the plan?"

Kevin shrugged, "I am waiting it out with Bampa. With Kenzi, it's a wait too. I am not there yet. I need to get myself together…so I can take care of her."

"How sure are you she isn't already being taken care of?"

"We promised each other. That's why I did Congo; that's why I am here today. I don't want her to think I *snaked* her."

"I hear you." Bosco paused. "How about *shule*? It's not too late."

Kevin sighed. "I do what I can to keep up. I don't think I have time now."

"You have all the money; you can sign up to any school and start over."

"For how many years?"

Bosco made a face. "Hmm, yeah, it will be a long time of studying. I see what you are getting at. So next year I am joining the university in the UK. I might be there three…maybe four years, who knows?"

"Oh." Kevin's face dropped.

"Yeah, remember I said my *paros* are abroad? Moved to the UK recently. Dad got this economic analyst job with the United Nations. That's how I got the scholarship. They want me to study and stay but…I kind of like living with my cousins," Bosco explained.

"Didn't you already have cousins abroad?"

"Yup, on my mom's side. These…on my dad's side. Cool chaps."

Kevin mulled over this revelation. "What are you going to study?"

Bosco took a swig of his beer. "Business. You and I talked about doing business together…"

"Yeah, I know, but I already am doing business." He tried to brush it off.

Bosco smiled. "My application got accepted, and it's on a scholarship. I start in February. Leaving for the UK end of January."

The sky was a dark inky blue, a reminder that daylight had only been around the corner an hour earlier. "You are leaving too," Kevin finally said. "We just reconnected."

Bosco looked up, surprised. He had never heard vulnerability in his friend's voice like he did then. "At least it's not an unknown like Kenzi's. I will keep in touch. "

Kevin agreed, recovering, and for an instant, Bosco felt he had dreamed it. "I could visit, too, since I have money."

They both laughed. "Don't rub it in, fool. I will catch up."

Bosco had a second beer, and they watched a match together before Kevin dropped him off. They had moved to Luzira after the unfortunate incident with Kevin's family, and Kevin told him about the frequent visits he made to see his mother in jail.

In one night, a lost connection was reignited, and as they spoke and jested, it was as if time paused had restarted, bridging the distance between them until it seemed like they had never been apart at all.

"Maybe you will meet Kenzi out there, in the UK."

Bosco shrugged. "Possibly." Then added mischievously, "You have money now...you could go."

Kevin jeered, "Asshole!"

Bosco grinned, said his farewell as he got to his gate, then turned to Kevin. "What's the plan for the absent birthday girl?"

Kevin shook his head, melancholic.

"How about a pool party?" Bosco suggested wickedly.

Kevin spent a large amount of time with Bosco in the last month before he traveled, taking him to his barito restaurants, their communication more about the future and a business partnership.

On his last day, Kevin threw him a pool party, and for the first time since he'd left home, he relished in being a teenager with not a care or the weight of the world on his shoulders. He never knew he could feel so free.

The day after Bosco left, Kevin signed up for computer and business classes. In the morning, he carried out his responsibilities as a CEO, and in the afternoon, he attended classes.

"Putting your money to good use, I see," Ssaka remarked when they basked in a steam bath at the Sheraton. "Be better than those young men who go to Harvard and Sandhurst."

Kevin nodded. "I intend to be."

Six months later, the computer classes finally ended with Kevin scoring highly on his final exams. Ssaka whisked him off to the Seychelles for a beauty pageant he was attending at the behest of one of his important friends, a fashion designer showcasing at the pageant.

"We have one more stopover," Ssaka announced on the night of their trip out of Seychelles.

"Where?"

"The place called Egoli..."

Kevin frowned, not yet grasping the content of his announcement. "Is that supposed to be out of space?"

Ssaka smiled. "Johannesburg. South Africa. It's called the city of gold. You will see why."

After a five-hour flight, they landed at Oliver Tambo International Airport, where a sturdy, light-skinned, bald-headed young man met them. His face lit up when he saw Ssaka.

"Bigz!" Ssaka greeted the younger fellow like a long-lost uncle.

"Welcome, *Oom*." The younger man clapped Ssaka on the back.

"You make me sound old, just Ssaka…" Ssaka grumbled cordially, and the handsome young man tittered. "You have made me an imposter to myself already with this 'Bigz' business."

The two men shared an affable exchange before Ssaka introduced Kevin. "Kevin, meet Bo. To me he is Bigz because look at him…robust and tall, a proper son of Shaka Zulu!" Bo shook his head.

"Don't mind this old man, eh? Kevin, right? I'm Bo Chauke, and if you follow in his footsteps, then…Bigz is fine too."

Kevin smiled and took his outstretched hand. "Kevin. Byamukama."

"No pet names?" The young man had a mischievous glint in his eyes and turned to Ssaka. "What happened; did you lose your edge already?"

"Aaah, long trip," came the excuse, and the two younger men exchanged roguish glances.

They had dinner at the rooftop of a fancy restaurant, lulled by the sound of trickling water from a statue waterfall fountain. As the water cascaded and pooled around a cherubic marble angel on a skateboard, giving it a shimmery glaze, Kevin made proper acquaintance with Bo.

"How do you know Ssaka?" Kevin was curious.

"We met at a business symposium on minerals a few years ago. A breakfast table shared between two strangers…and here we are."

"I liked him." Ssaka said with a nod. He had found Bo enterprising, agile, and witty with knowledge of both the black market and the legal gold trade. Bo was an investment trader dealing with financing small-scale businesses and had recently formed a hedge fund.

"At the time he was biting off more than he could chew, tussling it out with the Chinese in Namibia for diamonds," Ssaka added. "So, I promised I would help him out with his Namibia problem, if he helped me out with my own South Africa problem."

Bigz nodded. "Put me to the test. That's what he did. Handed me mines to manage and…to follow up on a stalling deal with the government to secure a diamond mine."

Kevin listened intently.

"A very treacherous business, smaller mines were being dwarfed by the De Beers. They just wanted to hoard the diamonds for themselves."

Bigz proved resourceful in this transaction, securing a mine in the northern Cape by Kimberly, which was a second choice from the Limpopo region Ssaka had set his mark on. In only two months of managing Ssaka's gold and diamond mines, he had proved to be more instrumental than ten middlemen. His contacts were versatile, he spoke eight languages, and nothing escaped his scrutiny.

"And Namibia was his in a month." Ssaka snapped his fingers. "We sort of partner with that too."

Their connection was instant. Kevin admired the robust South African. He wanted to know what made him tick.

"I grew up in the shantytowns. My dad was a taxi driver before he started working the mines. We scrambled to put food in our bellies. Poverty was richer than us," he told Kevin. "I got out and swore I would not return."

A kindred spirit, Kevin felt. Bo was a package that did not disappoint. He impressed Kevin more and more into the night as he outlined his resume casually. A self-made young man in his late twenties. A compassionate and vigilant businessman who had created youth business mentorship programs under one branch of his corporations spotting Johannesburg.

"I am glad you like him," Ssaka told him on their way back to Uganda. "Because you are going to be going to South Africa and Namibia more often, then Sierra Leone, and when I solve the issues here in Congo, you will come with me to meet President Kabila."

Kevin was elated. "I am ready!"

"Not so fast…. There is a lot to be done." Ssaka scowled, and Kevin stifled a smile with a poorly pasted poker face.

Chapter 17

May 2007

Kevin's relentless ambition urged him on.   His quest for knowledge and influence kept him doggedly disciplined. He resorted to weed and women for bad dreams and relaxation. The frequent trips he was making to the cape of Africa by this time provided a new perspective on dating. The beautiful southern women were a lot more open to a younger man's proposal.

The constant interaction with dignitaries and business partners twice his age was gradually polishing his communication with an edge of finesse. He commanded and held their attention while quickly analyzing their psyche.

"It's so exhausting," he told Ssaka one evening after a heady discussion brokering a gold deal with the government of Mali.

"It becomes second nature," Ssaka assured him. "You are street smart, charismatic. You are sharp-witted and alert. Life is like a game of chess, especially with this crowd. Their guard is up. You must be able to bring it down. Win their trust." Ssaka taught him to watch, study, and be patient.

"Your own shadow could betray you." He told Kevin layers of stories of betrayal in his life. He often repeated them like reruns of a daytime drama soap; Kevin could relay them word for word.

Kevin expressed optimism. "Livingstone and Boda and now Bosco…

those cannot betray me. Never."

Ssaka shrugged. "Never say never."

It was a wet morning in May when a call came in from Boda. Kevin squinted and sleepily answered the phone. "Is everything all right?" he asked, for a call at 6 a.m. was rare unless something had happened at the restaurant.

Boda launched into rapid Luganda. "Yes, Festo called. Bampa is losing business. His debt has grown so much, and he cannot pay. It looks bad; business is not working. Two taxis were stolen upcountry last week. His hostel caught fire this morning; no one knows why, *oba*...bad wiring, and his building in Madirisa, *hmmm* there was a *gu* padlock."

Kevin sat up, instantly alert; he pondered Boda's words. Then, when he spoke, he said, "Do you know his lenders?"

Boda sighed. "They are dropping him."

Kevin smiled. "Get me the information of all his lenders."

In two hours, Kevin, dressed in a pair of dark-washed jeans and a neatly tucked-in dress shirt, pored through the information in his notebook as he ate breakfast at a new upscale café that recently opened in the chic Nakasero neighborhood. It belonged to a friend of Ssaka's. He made notes and, when he was satisfied, dialed Haruna.

"I need that Harvard lawyer you told me about," he told him. Haruna let him know he had the privilege of accessing a list of law firms that dealt with Ssaka and his associates. Their fee was only mineral deposits.

"Eh, *kadogo*!" Haruna chuckled in response. "How are you these days?"

Kevin scoffed. "Fine."

"Mike? Let me talk to him. He will meet you; don't worry...where can he find you?" Haruna was saying before he could repeat his request.

"At the Bluebird Restaurant."

"Aah, send my greetings to the madam of the house," Haruna replied and promptly hung up. It took a while getting used to Haruna's brusque manner.

In another half-hour, a man Kevin placed in his mid-thirties, average height and build in a slim-fit navy blue suit, walked right up to Kevin's table, the scent of his musky perfume filling the air. He took a seat, and when he removed his shades, his eyes bore into Kevin almost arrogantly. "Haruna told me to find you here."

A small smile played on his lips. "Mike Bangirana of Ochola and Bangirana Advocates. You one of Ssaka's?" He put his massive diary on the table along with his BlackBerry, then pulled out a matte business card with rounded edges, a black-and-white ensemble splashed in neat Calibri font.

Kevin squared his shoulders. Dealing with high-nosed lawyers was becoming an easier and less daunting experience. "Yes, and I require your services for say... as long as possible?"

Mike crossed his legs, signaled to the waitress, and cocked his head to one side, his eyes never leaving Kevin. "What can I do you for?"

* * *

In another hour, all of Bampa's assets and debt accumulated to the moneylenders were signed over to a shell company managed by Ochola and Bangirana Advocates on behalf of their client. Kevin watched the money-lenders' eyes widen as they opened the envelope and thumbed through the clean currency notes, licking their counting fingers from time to time and breathing out the count simultaneously.

Later, he perused a report from Mike. In his possession now were some of the most essential assets of the man who had taken everything from him.

Within months, Kevin had selected which of Bampa's businesses would be an initial target amid his struggling ones; he had a car import business with an office in Portbell. They transported his cars through the Kisumu port. It was the one promising lucrative venture. He specialized in rare luxury cars from Italy and America, selling to the crème de la crème of Uganda. He had sold to tycoons in Rwanda, Kenya, and Tanzania. It was a monopoly he held, and his demand and supply chain were reputable. Kevin imagined how much that would explode in his own hands. He sought Haruna for information. The inconspicuous small man knew every businessman's business in Kampala. He had a relationship with the dealers at the port and set Kevin up to meet with them.

Days later, the news of the vandalism of goods at the border spread like wildfire in the business community. All two dozen luxury cars under Bampa's company were reported stolen, while those left behind, severely damaged. However, there was no clear report on the vandalism, and investigations dragged on for days. The border patrol spoke of looting and a fire in the night at the container center. The prime-time news cautioned businessmen about robberies at the border, and trade stalled for a few weeks.

Shortly after the unfortunate incident, information of fraud and tax evasion crept and crawled to the surface of Bampa's otherwise perfect score card, held together by the copious amounts of bribes he dished out as a reward for silence. However, he was struggling, and blackmailers were greedy; Bampa was not altogether straight in his dealings, and the tax men were clamoring for their cut while the different business fraternities he belonged to bayed for accountability. It did not look good for his customers.

"His loyal customers are not so loyal after all," Haruna told him when they had lunch at the little local restaurant the odd bespectacled man loved to go to.

Kevin raised his eyebrows. "Oh?"

The other man nodded as he wiped his face and took a gulp from his beer glass, topped with passion fruit juice. He grunted. "They are a superficial bunch. They don't want to be associated with scandal." The papers showed they were denying any involvement with Bampa and dropping him.

Kevin put down the newspaper and marked that business off his list. Bampa had lost close to two hundred and fifty thousand dollars with the destruction of his cars and even more with the withdrawal of his customers.

The market was open, and Kevin decided to wait till the scandal was not a news item anymore, then he would step in and fill the gap.

Through Ochola and Bangirana Advocates, he registered another business venture providing capital to small startups with the aim of helping the street community; the focal interest was to buy Bampa out. With the money he channeled from the mineral trade, Kevin inched his way in, bought a dozen taxis, and placed job vacancy advertisements around the city with the help of Festo and his boys. Kevin raised the bar in remuneration for drivers and conductors including bonuses for Christmas and Eid.

He had become acquainted with the city council transport association boss during one of his lunches with Haruna, and he requested him for a "simple favor." Kevin was given leeway to veto seasoned taxi drivers that eagerly showed up to the interview held at their offices, overseen and carried out by the head of public transport associations. As expected, the offer attracted more taxi drivers than he needed. Kevin made the final vetting when the names were given to him. He picked Bampa's drivers.

"He is in a rage, found his taxi minivans parked in the park. No one there." Kevin was feasting on a plateful of roasted groundnuts and hard corn with black tea at Festo's place. He smirked.

"Good. But he will get other drivers," he said more to himself.

"We can arrange for him to not be able to function here at all." Festo grinned.

Kevin arched his brows. "I have just thought of something. Get me a few men who have no licenses but can drive. "

As Kevin had predicted, Bampa, desperate to get his taxis back on the road, hired anyone willing and available, with or without a license. He figured he would deal with those technicalities later, but right now with his finances taking a downward spiral fast, he needed a source of income. Six of the men without licenses had been procured by Festo. Bampa was back in business. But hardly were the taxis back on the road before they were impounded and the drivers arrested by different traffic police officers in different locations for driving without a license.

A week later the Public Transportation Authority let Bampa know his license had been revoked; he was required to cease all business at once and remove his minivans in thirty-six hours, the reason being some of the new drivers he hired were not registered or licensed as taxi drivers in their database. Thus, license suspended till further notice.

"He needs to wait out the probation period and let the authorities decide how best to proceed. He will have to pay a fine as well," Haruna reported.

Kevin basked in the mini victory he had acquired; the plan had worked.

Kevin swooped in and finally set up meetings with two luxury car buyers in the city. Mike Bangirana and Haruna had gone in his stead and brought back news. They would get into business with the new person in the market. Kevin was pleased.

"The name, Ssaka, even whispered to the right people, goes a long way." Haruna grinned.

Mike drew out the legal paperwork.

"Although…Ali of Delight Motors is a bit of a big mouth; he might talk to Bampa."

Kevin shrugged. "That will play to my advantage. I am sure Bampa is going crazy wondering who is pulling the strings."

Haruna agreed. "That, he is."

Kevin never worked front office. Haruna had people run around for them, so Kevin's name barely featured anywhere. Ochola and Bangirana Advocates handled Kevin's business dealings and saw to it that his identity was discrete unless Kevin requested otherwise. Under his business venture, Kevin placed all the land and property titles he got from the lenders as surety and had notices of eviction placed on them.

In September, he received a phone call from an irate caller. *Bampa.*

"Who the fuck are you!" he boomed into the phone.

But Kevin could sense the panic in his voice.

"A close friend," Kevin told him calmly, and for a second Bampa hesitated.

"Do I know you?"

"Let us meet and talk," Kevin told him. All the cards were looking good. He had allowed for his number to slip up right where Bampa would access it.

"Where?"

Kevin had only one location in mind. "Original Barito place on Kampala Road, 3 p.m."

Bampa hesitated, then agreed

At 2:59 p.m., Kevin was waiting. The big man emerged through the doors, his shoulders stooped, his face lined with stress. The misfortunes he faced weighed upon his shoulders so profoundly they drooped, making him look shorter than his actual height.

Kevin signaled to him, then watched the big man's reaction skid through a labyrinth of emotions, from a momentary freeze, shock, fear, incredulity replaced by a tiny smile that started from the curl of his lower lip and touched the rest of his face in slow progression although never reaching his eyes. He straightened as he approached the table. ·

"Ah, old friend. I haven't seen you in donkey years."

Kevin shrugged dispassionately.

"Possibly because you left rather hurriedly? Have a seat."

He motioned to the man, who looked at Kevin stupidly, wondering how a boy half his age could instruct him and, worse still, that he was going to obey.

He sat.

"Now, please order anything you want. It is on me. I am generous like that."

Bampa chuckled bitterly. "Generous enough to bring my progress to a standstill?"

Kevin raised his brows.

"I think you should eat. We have a lot of catching up to do."

The man was nervous, but he ordered anyway, and the two of them appraised each other like gunslingers at a duel.

"I heard you were around. I wasn't sure. I thought it was a street rumor. Then I saw this…" He motioned to the barito place. "And I was suspicious, but…"

"What did you think?"

"You were supposed to get arrested and die in some jail in Kivu or…meet your end through rebel fire." The man scrunched his nose arrogantly.

"No one told you about my nine lives?" Kevin grinned suddenly. It amazed him how easily it came to him; it scared him even. His cool disposition, the way his mind made no assumptions, was as clear as day, his soul singularly set on one thing, to destroy the man who betrayed him and stole from him the one thing not all the gold and diamonds in Congo or South Africa could buy: his mother.

Bampa looked at him idiotically, then furrowed his brows.

"What do you want? An apology? Okay, I am sorry. I needed the money for business. It's all just business."

Kevin folded his arms on the table, enjoying the hole Bampa was digging himself into.

"It is all just business. You are right. But…you cheated me."

Bampa shrugged and guffawed. "So?"

"So now you owe me…." Kevin pulled out the messenger bag—that doubled as a laptop bag—he carried with him. From it he retrieved a file, Bampa's name printed neatly on it and then asked sardonically, "Should I wait till you have eaten? This might not be pleasant table talk."

"Nothing comes between me and my food." The big man tried to act unfazed.

Kevin spied the beads of sweat forming on his brow. No one could disguise the effect brought on by a file laid out on a table by a seeming enemy.

"If you insist," Kevin said calmly and opened the file. In it were spreadsheets and receipts attached to different spreadsheets and different receipts along with what looked like a well-prepared legal contract.

"What is this?" Bampa asked, the barito in his hand midway to his mouth, slowly finding its way back to his plate.

"All the money you have borrowed from local lenders. This amount is almost one hundred million Uganda shillings."

Kevin pulled out a pen, circling each amount on each paper receipt, then added, "I paid it all and the interest, so let's say about one hundred and fifty million…. Does that number ring a bell?"

Bampa paused. He pushed the plate away.

"Kevin…" he spoke, eventually licking his lips. He sipped his tea.

"So, according to this record here, you now owe me all this money. I have the license to operate your taxis as surety, your land titles, the hostel, your two commercial buildings in the city, the luxury cars business…oh, even your house. Is it that bad, Bampa? Where will your family live if you cannot pay? The lenders were glad to be rid of them since you have not paid in…a year now?"

Bampa looked like he had seen the ghost in his worst nightmare.

Kevin continued, "When we finished with Congo, I was to have one hundred and fifty million shillings, which you never gave me. I have added that to this. Including interest accrued over the last four years. Oh, my mother died in that time as well, and you harassed my people in Wandegeya…the interest is…"

Kevin pulled out another spreadsheet neatly charting out interest on the one hundred fifty million by the year.

Bampa's breathing became strenuous. "What is this!"

Kevin shrugged, gathering up the papers. "It is business. Honest business. I am collecting. So now you owe me three hundred and seventy-five million shillings…and that is me being nice. Just. Sign. Here."

He indicated the document splashed with legal lingo.

Kevin was prepared for any eventuality of the meeting; he had expected him to rage and try to lash out at him. True to script, Bampa roared, raining insults on Kevin; he slammed his fists on the table, drawing the attention of the diners and servers in the restaurant. Kevin watched him calmly.

"I won't pay, you shit! I will not! You thief!"

Kevin shrugged. "No one can help you. Your lawyer won't help. You must wonder why they have been stalling your issue for weeks now. I have all the paperwork. So…you pay, or I will keep operating your businesses. And you will keep losing everything. I am making plans to…"

He had hardly finished his statement when Bampa grabbed him by the collar, dragging him to his feet. Kevin glared back at Bampa, his fists curled.

"I don't fear you, and I will gladly beat you on my turf. *You are in my restaurant.* Don't forget that," he hissed at the man.

A girl shrieked and Livingstone called out, coming to their table. Kevin raised his hand, in signal that everything was fine.

"You want to fight here?" Kevin dared him; he could feel the old rage tear through the scabs the years had carefully covered.

Bampa was breathing down his face, his nostrils flaring. "You stealing…"

"You stole from me. Everything! My mother died because of you!" Kevin shot back, his voice as cold as steel, his eyes flashing angrily. "So hit me here and now, and I swear upon my mother's grave your misery now will seem like paradise."

Their eyes locked for several seconds. Everyone in the restaurant froze, watching. The silence was palpable. With a grunt, Bampa pushed back at Kevin, releasing him. Kevin steadied himself.

"When you are calm, I have papers for you to sign…"

"Fuck you!" The big man stomped out of the restaurant. "Fuck you and your whole clan!" he bellowed, and a torrent of other words Kevin did not catch.

Kevin sat down and Livingstone was at his table. "Eh?"

Kevin had a faraway look in his eyes. "He will pay. Or his whole life is mine."

"But boss, that man may kill you."

Kevin straightened the collar of his shirt like nothing had happened.

"He will try, I know that, but nothing is going to happen to us. Let Festo and his boys know I want a meeting."

Livingstone nodded.

"Also, where did you say Mercy hangs out?" he asked as Livingstone turned to leave.

Chapter 18

December 2007

Kevin found out about the boat cruise a day earlier. He had not heard a squeak from Bampa in forty-eight hours. He would entice him out of hiding with the new twists in his plans. Maybe that would get the older man's attention. Kevin needed him to understand he could destroy him.

He found Mercy at the exclusive only members' club; Kampala Club, where she regularly met with friends for a swim, and he positioned himself a table away from them as they basked in the sun and chatted loudly. She excitedly convinced her friends to attend a boat cruise party that Capital Radio was throwing for holidaymakers; she was going. The small group of teenagers prattled excitedly about it as they lazily hung on the edges of the pool, splashing the cool, chlorinated water at one another. Kevin immediately purchased his ticket. Lucky for him, it was the last one they had.

Capital Radio fans filed onto the huge party boat on the boat cruise day, music blaring from the deck, punched with the capital radio jingles, and station ID. Kevin kept his shades on for most of the trip staying close to the stern of the boat. Drinks were aplenty, and the crowd was a young adult group, university students mostly; it was obvious Mercy and her friends had struck gold with this one; three girls dressed a little older than they looked sat on one side of the boat whispering animatedly to one another and giggling. Now and again when a song played, they got up whooping and dancing and the deejay had to keep reminding people to keep the boat balanced.

"Not too many on one side! Balance the boat, yo!"

They were headed to Bulago Island, where the party would continue until six, when they would return to the mainland by sundown.

Kevin sipped his punched nonalcoholic drink slowly, occasionally glancing at the girls. He rehearsed all the information he had on Mercy, daddy's angel, spoiled rich girl, generous with a wild streak. Kevin observed her; from the girl he had seen three years earlier, she had grown some, still wearing her braids in that oh-so-familiar brown hue. They fell past her shoulders to her waist, those straight hot-water-type braids. The pimples were nonexistent; she was not a stunner, but when she smiled, her face was something you wanted to carve and frame, displayed on a conspicuous wall. On the occasions she danced, Kevin kept his gaze trained on her. She was a superb dancer, her slim curves nimbly vibrating with every beat she applied them to amid wild cheers from her companions. Not completely his type, he thought. This would be easy.

He forgot to be discreet, his mind mulling over his little plan, tweaking it, upsetting it only to begin all over. It was an exciting process then… their eyes locked unexpectedly. It took him by surprise. Kevin pushed his shades away from his eyes, letting them rest just above his forehead, squinted in her direction, and smiled. Her friends glanced at him with suspicious frowns and eye rolls, then at her and giggled. Kevin glanced back and, with practiced poise, turned his back to them, letting his eyes glide over the revelers and rest on the spray of lake water as the boat raced toward the island.

"My friends think you're cute," a jovial girlish voice said behind him, three songs later. Kevin did not turn toward her, keeping his gaze on the water.

"Do they?"

"Yeah, they dared me to talk to you. We saw you stare."

Kevin finally gave her a sidelong glance. It was Mercy. He decided he liked the sound of her voice, the light spirit it carried.

He smiled and turned at an angle, pushing his shades over his head again. He squinted at her.

"Did you talk to me because they dared you or because you were curious?"

She smiled, and he noticed the dimples then, deep indents in her cheeks; her whole face lit up. She shrugged. "You're by yourself, so yes, it's easy to approach you. Both," she replied, carefully accessing him; her light brown eyes danced over him delightfully like he was a meal she was pondering devouring.

Kevin was impressed. She was not as dumb as he had hoped she would be.

"I like people watching," he said.

And she let out a short laugh, that "you are so cheesy" laugh.

"That's for losers. Everyone is having fun!" She leaned close enough to whisper in his ear.

Kevin leaned in and replied, "Touché! So, what are you drinking?"

She mouthed, "Spiked punch."

Kevin smiled faintly. "Because you called me a loser, I will oblige and join."

When they got to the island, he spent a bigger part of the afternoon with Mercy; they bonded over light banter and teasing, forgetting about her girlfriends for a moment.

"I haven't seen you around." She was curious. "We know almost everyone in the schools we go to; it's a thing," she told him.

Kevin shrugged. "I don't study here."

She raised a brow, suddenly interested. "Where then?"

Kevin scrunched his nose, responding as fast as he could, aware that hesitation would give him away. "South Africa. I am here for a program… six months."

Her face fell. "Oh." Then she smiled again, the dimples imprinted, and he observed her. "I am going to South Africa for the Christmas holidays next year. My dad thinks I need a treat before finals. Maybe we can meet then?"

Kevin shrugged. "Maybe. Who knows?"

She frowned as one who was so used to being lavished attention on. "You don't want us to meet again?"

Kevin baited her. "Life is weird. You meet someone fascinating on a boat cruise, share drinks, spend a whole afternoon in each other's company and...you might never see them again." He shrugged, studying her reactions to his elusive verbosity; confusion embraced her pubescent face; her eyes flashed with *something*.

He reeled her in. She had taken an interest in him. He read her like a book; she had appraised him, judged him, and she was curious—he was almost certain. Something about him screamed, "Danger, stay out!" But that was the thing about attraction; the allure of exploring forbidden territory overrode all sense of reason. Wasn't that the rush of excitement that youth latched onto? She was drawn in, and he edged away, beckoning her like a spider to a fly.

"It's not the seventies; we have cellphones now." She rolled her eyes and laughed again, like he had said something really dumb.

Kevin smiled. "Sure we do. The question is, will I take your number?"

This time her giggle was that girlish I-am-flirting-with-you laugh.

At that moment, a song came on, and Kevin pulled her up from the tree trunk they had perched on. "Let's dance." The songs flowed from one reggae hit to another, and when Bebe Cool or Chameleon came on, everyone screamed and sang along. The afternoon quickly slipped by, and before they knew it, it was time to get back on the boat. Mercy stayed by Kevin's side. Once on the boat, Kevin held her to him, felt her shiver.

"I like you. You are different," he told her, arresting her gaze with his, and she shied away, not resisting him either.

"I bet you tell every girl that."

Kevin sighed. "Actually, no..."

When she looked at him again , he was convinced he was making some headway. A warm rush of satisfaction filled him. He held her throughout the ride back, and she entertained him with rousing high school escapades. She attended a mixed Muslim school in Kampala called Kibuli Secondary School.

"The boys in my school are way too childish *and* boring," she groaned. She told him of her father and her upcoming vacation plans. She looked forward to joining the university and basking in independence. She was excited and jittery but calm in her delivery. He missed Kenzi's calmness.

The evening brought with it a chill, and he quickly offered his jacket when he noticed her rub her arms discreetly. "So, tell me about you."

"What do you want to know?" he asked lightly.

She shrugged. "Whatever."

He charmed her with the perfect lies: his parents worked abroad; he was currently studying in Johannesburg, but who knows where his parents would be transferred next? *Macko* is what everyone called him.

When the hourlong ride was over and they got to the shore, Kevin politely thanked her friends for hanging out and was ready to leave, but she stopped him.

"Wait, your number?" she asked boldly.

Kevin smiled. "I will call you." He traced a finger on her cheek, and she stared, mesmerized.

"You…don't have it," she said.

"I am waiting for you to give it to me." He lowered his voice, and she scoffed, a smile lurking on her freshly glossed lips, then rapped out the phone number.

Kevin punched it into his phone, saving it under her name. "Thank you for making me less of a loser," he teased.

She raised an eyebrow. "You are welcome." Then she took off his jacket. "I almost forgot…"

He shook his head. "How about you keep it till we meet the next time? It's the one guarantee that I will call you." He studied her. "Besides, I like my designer clothes."

"Fine."

Their eyes locked, Kevin resisting the urge to kiss her. He could tell she would not resist, but the lingering tension worked for him and not against him, so he shook her hand.

"I hope to see you soon," she told him.

Kevin waited a couple of days. There was still no news from Bampa. No one had seen him for a few days now. "I will find out," he told Festo when he called him to report.

He called Mercy at noon on the third day, and she picked up on the first ring.

"Hi." He perceived the expectation in her voice. "Called to collect?"

"You could say that," he drawled. They talked for half an hour before she let him know it was her birthday and she was spending the day shopping with her mother.

"Happy birthday!" he said amiably.

"Thank you."

"Would the birthday girl like to hang out later?" he asked.

She did not hesitate. "Sure. That sounds nice. What do you have in mind?"

Kevin smiled. "It's a surprise. How late can you hang?"

"Hmm, my dad is not in town this week…. I am officially an adult now…eighteen and eager … so, I am good till midnight."

Kevin took her out later to Faze 2 restaurant for dinner. She had opted to meet him in town, away from the prying eyes of her mother, and expressed approval of his car, the expensive smell of his cologne, and his attire. He had bought her a bouquet of white and red roses and handed them to her when she entered the car.

She smiled, visibly enchanted. "Is this a date?"

He shrugged. "What do you want it to be?"

Then they went dancing after dinner. At eleven, she panicked. "Oh gosh! I lost track of time! My mom will kill me!"

"Whoa, relax; you are with me and an adult now, right? Cinderella will get home before the coach turns into a pumpkin," he assured her, making her smile.

When they got to her gate, she scrambled out of the car apologetically. "I am so sorry. I had a great time…" Kevin reached for her and kissed her.

She responded, relaxing instantly. She pressed closer, and he held her, his hands roaming over her back, down to the dip in her waist and the fair swell of her backside. He drew her closer, and she melted into him. Kevin pulled back. "Happy birthday, Mercy."

"Thanks… this was so…cool," she told him. He squeezed her hand lightly.

"Maybe breakfast tomorrow? I will pick you up." He did not give her an option, and she seemed to like that he took control.

"Yeah? That's so grown up." She lingered, curfew forgotten. "Okay."

For the weeks that followed, Kevin met Mercy regularly, studying her, responding to her, and watching her rapidly fall in love with him. They made out in his car, at the movies, and in the club, and when she pressed for more, he expressed reluctance. That alone drew her to him. He lavished on her discreetly, enough for her parents to not question it and yet the right amount to incite envy in her friends. She was telling her parents half-truths about who she was spending time with; it was the girls, a group of friends studying from school or new friends from another school at Kampala Club. Now and again, he ferried her and her friends wherever they wanted to go and surprised them with an occasional high-end outing. The effect was magical.

December and January passed in courtship bliss, and just before school reopened, Kevin rolled out the next phase of his plan. They were on the beach, watching the sunset, a few weeks before the school term.

"So, will you miss me?" he was asking her, gently caressing her fingers.

"Of course!" She rolled her eyes.

He kissed her cheek. "How about one last surprise?"

She leaned away from him. "Seriously? Every day is a surprise with you. What now?"

Kevin pursed his lips. "First say yes to it, and then I will tell you."

"That's unfair."

"Have I ever been fair?"

"True. No. Okay, yes." She snuggled against him.

"Come with me to Queen Elizabeth National Park."

"Two weeks to school? My parents will flip!" she exclaimed, then added wickedly, "Umm… unless the girls come."

Kevin shrugged. "They can come."

Her eyes widened. "What?"

He had looked into her eyes. "Anything for you."

"Isn't it expensive?" Concern crossed her face. Even though they had gone out for almost two months now, he was still a mystery to her. Who were his parents? How come he lived alone? Why did they give him so much money? The questions were never-ending, and he played them off, expertly… a lie here and there or simply shrugging it off with, "We have time; you will know in time."

"Have I ever complained?" he assured her.

And that is how their four-day weekend became a reality. Kevin was careful; he had planned this weekend weeks in advance.

Their suite was magnificent, and he told her if she wasn't comfortable, she could sleep with the girls, but Mercy quickly dismissed his comment. She was ready. The night he took her virginity, he made sure she wanted it more than he did; they had made out exhaustively after dinner, and she asked to see him. He had undressed; his lean body glowed in the light of the wicker-covered bed lamp. She had never seen a full erection, and her eyes widened.

"Can I touch it?"

"Only if you want to go further," he cautioned naughtily.

She hesitated, and he smiled, pulling up his boxer shorts, but she stopped him.

"I want to. I love you, Macko," she blathered.

Kevin paused. The sincerity struck a chord somewhere in him. She stood before him in her silky nightdress, shying away from his penetrative gaze.

He brushed the feeling of sympathy aside and took her hands. "Are you sure?" He kissed them as he drew her to him. She nodded, and he smothered her lips with his.

"Macko…" she gasped when he pulled away briefly, swaying against him…. Kevin silenced her with another kiss and, with slight reluctance, slipped the straps of her gown off her shoulder, sliding it over her arms. He pinned her to him. Her heartbeat sounded like a drum between her youthful breasts, and he caressed her naked body gently, kissing her neck, her shoulders, her hands. When he took her to bed, she was drunk with need. After years of learning how to please a woman, Kevin delved into his art.

It was more a skill he enjoyed now, speaking in hushed whispers, touching lightly here, kissing deeply there, a tiny nip here and there. He enjoyed the tremors that erupted all over her, the muffled moans she emitted, and when she was wet enough, he faltered; this was something he could not undo. He wrestled with his plan. Up to this point, he had been sure it would be an easy plot, but looking at the innocent naked girl lying beneath him, completely enamored with him, pricked at his conscience, then his mother's sickly face loomed over it, and his heart hardened.

Kevin tore open a condom, slipped it on. He kissed her, licked her, until her moans got louder and more urgent, then gently he penetrated her, giving each inch a moment. When she gasped, he stopped and touched her; she urged him on until he was fully inside her.

Kevin enjoyed her. He preferred the experience of older women, but the pleasure of taking a virgin gave him an ultimately different thrill, like the thrill of winning a race… in first place at that, and Mercy was no exception. The next day she was sore, and they snuggled, but on day three she was seducing him, and he took her again. When they were done, she lay in his arms, glowing blissfully. "I have never felt so good."

He drummed his fingers lightly up and down her back. "We aim to please. You will not find anyone as good as me," he assured her confidently, and she laughed. "You are so cocksure."

He nodded. "I know it."

On their last night, it was easier for her, and he was uninhibited; Kevin enjoyed watching her erupt in multiple orgasms. Her ecstatic cries encouraged him, and when it was over, she drifted off to sleep in exhaustion. Kevin gazed at her peaceful, sleeping face for a while. She did not deserve this. The voice of reason nudged at him. She did not deserve his cruel vendetta. *Neither did my mother,* a voice interjected strongly. When they returned, it was obvious: Mercy was deeply in love with him.

Bampa finally returned for a second meeting to negotiate. He realized he was losing more to Kevin, and fast.

Kevin refused. "Full amount," he told him. "When you are ready to sign over everything, I will be waiting."

Mercy messaged him every day, giving him banal, nonchalant school information, which did not interest him—the little girl conversations that always bored him. At first, he responded with as much rapt attention, and slowly his responses got less frequent and hers more urgent till he gradually stopped responding. The first-term holidays came around quickly, and she called him on her way home; her voice shook, demanding an explanation for his silence. What was going on? She loved him. Was there someone else?

Kevin told her he had been busy.

It seemed to ease her mind for the first few days, but the inconsistency continued, and Kevin intentionally set up a meeting with an old lover he'd had an off-and-on-again affair with at a location Mercy frequented. It worked. Jealous and angry, she stormed their table, and Kevin calmed her down, taking her aside. "You just can't do that." He was firm with her.

"What?" Her eyes portrayed her heartbreak. Tears danced on her eyelids. "Didn't our time together mean anything to you? I thought I was your girl."

He sighed. "I never said that at all. We hung out and it was great..."

"What?"

"Look, I am not trying to date anyone… yet." He broke it to her.

Her expression had clawed at his hardened defenses; he was sure if she had been another man's daughter, he would have quickly rephrased his statement that evening. She wept piteously and uncontrollably. Kevin called one of his regular special-hire drivers and offered to pay for her fare home. He silently watched the cab drive off before he returned to his evening.

In another week, it was Bampa calling him in shock and surprise to learn the man who had broken his daughter's heart was Kevin.

"I am going to kill you!" he threatened Kevin, and the sorrow in a father's voice peered through.

Kevin hung up. It was time to switch it up. Within twenty-four hours, Festo and his boys had effectively displayed notices of eviction on all of Bampa's properties; his taxis that had resumed operation after the twenty-eight-day probation were again held back by the KCCA representative whom Livingstone went to with the document showing his debt. Business for Bampa came to a standstill overnight.

Kevin waited.

He considered a despairing man would want to do something desperate, so Kevin made known that the streets needed to be aware of Bampa. He hired bouncers for his restaurants and paid security guards to patrol his properties. Being alert was second nature. Mercy still messaged him, insistently begging him to reconsider, asking to meet with him. Kevin did not reply. There was a war that needed to be finished.

It was 8 a.m. when Kevin walked into the Original Barito to find Bampa waiting for him, withdrawn and crestfallen.

"Let's talk, man to man," he said finally.

Kevin sat and shrugged. "If it's about money, I am all ears."

He seemed too tired to comment and shook his head. "Why are you doing this?"

Kevin guffawed. "How does it feel to lose everything?"

"You broke my daughter's heart." He gritted his teeth.

"Collateral damage. If you had paid up, we would not have gone this far."

"What do you want?"

"I told you, three hundred and seventy-five million shillings."

"I don't have it."

Kevin shrugged. "Then you can sign over your businesses and properties to me. That will cover the amount."

Even though it was the goal, it took Kevin aback to see the big man bow his head and break down. Destitute and resigned, Bampa was pitiful. "*Nsasira,*" he pleaded.

"You are lucky I used condoms," Kevin taunted him.

Bampa sobbed like a child. "Please, how will I tell my wife…?"

"You will find a way like I did," Kevin told him calmly and produced the paperwork for him and a blue Bic pen. "Sign."

It was a cold, cloudy morning, and business was slow. The streets hummed with the clamor of traffic and regular rush hour. The waitresses pretended not to see the two men in the corner, one bowed over, resigned, the other sitting stiffly at the edge of his chair.

Bampa picked up the pen, letting it hover over the A4 paper with important black print on it. "Please…" he started one last time.

Kevin sat still, waiting. Finally, with a resigned sigh, Bampa slowly signed over five businesses to Kevin. When he got to the sixth, Kevin stopped him. "You did not take over my barito place, so I shall give you a starting point. You can keep the taxi business."

Kevin withdrew the paperwork and handed him his license that the taxi association had confiscated for failure to pay his monthly tariffs. "I will keep the rest."

Bampa sniffed, taking the license.

"Also, don't try anything stupid. I have eyes and ears everywhere. I am watching you."

When Bampa put down the pen, a tiny flicker of relief crossed his face. Then it hardened. "Stay away from my daughter."

Kevin raised his arms in a surrender pose. "I was way ahead of you.

We are even."

Later, Kevin told Ssaka about his last six months. Ssaka whistled. "That was risky; he could have harmed you."

"I know. I calculated everything."

"Ah!" Ssaka said harshly, with an edge of admiration in his voice. "So, how do you feel?"

Kevin sighed. "I did not want to hurt Mercy. That was the part I struggled with."

Ssaka agreed. "Well, in a battle, there are casualties. But you are better than me; you are a fighter with a conscience."

Kevin chewed on his words. Hurting Bampa had been pleasurable. "Yes. It wasn't my mother's, either. I was careful with Mercy. I did not want her to suffer any consequences other than heartbreak."

Ssaka laughed. "Clarity gives you control. That was a good move too, and you don't need a pregnancy following you for the rest of your life, moreover one born from revenge. That's always cursed. Enjoy your life. Now turn those businesses into more millions. We have things to do." Ssaka was laughing and allaying the Bampa affair.

"By the way, his people here don't work for him anymore. I wanted to tell you that for months back, he is struggling with debt."

Kevin frowned. "How did you know them?"

Ssaka replied, "I know this gold region better than anyone. Dongawe, that rat of a man, is a double agent. Bampa did not know this. Bampa? I know of him and his dealings. That's why I insisted you wait. It was a necessary time lag needed to win his middlemen over. Call it, me topping up your revenge plan."

Kevin's eyes widened, recalling the peculiar man, Donga, and the initial meeting with him.

"You did not have to. I wanted to do it myself."

"You actually did. They knew about his debt, so it was easy to win them over."

"Did Bampa suspect foul play?"

Ssaka scoffed, "When things go wrong for most in the jungle, the superstition is that I am behind it, which is…mostly true. Don't be surprised if he suspected I was backing you. He is not without some influence, but I'm far more influential and have more resources."

Secretly, Kevin was grateful that he had Ssaka, but this was personal for him. He did not need Ssaka involved no matter how pure the intention.

When Kevin said nothing, he added, "So you can employ these middlemen now to do the work you cannot over here."

Kevin realized what he was saying and for a second felt ashamed for being slighted by Ssaka's move to secure Bampa's contacts.

"Can I trust them?"

"There is no real trust in this game. Pay them better than Bampa, and they will be loyal."

Kevin agreed. "Thank you Ssaka."

Ssaka laughed shortly. "I will see you in a few months."

Chapter 19

2008–2010
Kampala, Uganda

By the end of 2008, Kevin had comfortably secured the properties that had once belonged to Bampa and exonerated him of his debt. He dedicated a chunk of time to completing the Madirisa complex and Bampa Plaza, which he renamed Classic Plaza. Under Ssaka's guidance, he had bought a mine in Congo and accepted shares in the diamond mines in South Africa and Namibia, biding time to buy two more in Tanzania and Sierra Leone.

After putting Boda and Livingstone through managerial training, he promoted them to manage the barito businesses.

"I want to help as many people off the street as much as possible," he told them. "Still keep a lookout for our territory, hire boys to run around, pick up the tax, do the middleman roles, but I need you here."

"Yes, boss." They happily accepted the roles, while Shakira took charge of all the menus in the different locations of the barito restaurants, staying true to changing them up monthly to keep the growth of their clientele.

He spent more time gorging on business classes and books and running his own projects and those entrusted to him by Ssaka. His time was far from limited. His company expanded as he met more entrepreneurs that inspired and challenged him, as well as older sophisticated women who constantly polished off his unrefined dating edges.

Bosco returned for a month with good news; he had been accepted into a specialized business master's program for two years. "I guess we can talk business in 2010, 2011?"

Bosco shook on it. "You bet. I think we can." In his brief stay in Uganda, Bosco met with Ssaka, who, he agreed with Kevin, was larger than life.

On his twentieth birthday, in 2009, Ssaka threw Kevin a plush, intimate birthday party at the Emin Pasha hotel, hired a band, and invited a selected handful of prominent people he knew, some of whom Kevin had met, and others he hoped to introduce him to. Kevin had had quieter, more intimate birthdays where he traveled with either Ssaka or one of his latest girlfriends. But Ssaka was of the view that a larger gathering at his twentieth was suitable.

"It's a group you have met here and there. All together in one room is a unique thing. It's quite something to watch and learn from. Haven't you learned anything in the last five years?"

Kevin grinned. "How to fuck well."

"That and other things…fuck the crème de la crème, not those prostitutes you were with when I found you," Ssaka teased him.

Kevin beamed. "No offense taken, and if I haven't said it enough, I am grateful."

"I know you are. You prove to be a worthy heir to all my wealth, every day." He winked at Kevin, who frowned.

"Where is that coming from?"

"People die someday, n'est-ce pas?" Ssaka said, then laughed like it was the best joke he had cracked.

The birthday party was, as Ssaka liked to call it, a "bar mitzvah of sorts."

"It is your coming-of-age significance, sitting at the table of the five percent in the eastern part of Africa…and the southern…. We are gradually invading north and west. You have worked so hard since we started out, and I am proud of you," he told him as they sat in the back of his sleek black Mercedes, being chauffeured to Nakasero through a tree-lined suburban route.

It was at this gallant affair that he met Vanessa, daughter to one of Kampala's prominent lawyers. There were rumors he represented the president; international banks and a host of other multinational companies were lining up outside his door for representation. He was as ruthless as he was smart, and even though Vanessa was only four years older than he was, an age gap that he considered too young for him, her father's prominence gave her an upper hand, and he played his cards well. Ssaka was finally present for an enormous event in Kampala, a rarity for him.

"I would not miss your birthday. I organized it, didn't I?" Ssaka clapped him on the back.

Kevin was grateful to have Ssaka in his ear, still naming names and telling him of people he needed to know. At these events, Ssaka mingled amiably as a distinguished host. He blended in with everyone, perceptively meeting each at their level; he laughed with the mayor's wife, spoke with the Libyan ambassador about international relations, dazzled the tycoons that owned steel companies, vast cash crop plantations, or multi billion-dollar investments with his knowledge, speckled with wit and charm.

Kevin always watched him; at first, he had been fascinated, swearing he would be him someday, and as he buried himself in study, in listening, and in absorbing his surroundings wherever he went, Kevin learned to be like Ssaka, and this time Ssaka watched him and nodded in satisfaction.

Ssaka introduced Kevin as his nephew "with an acute business sense," whom he was grooming. "That, you have…nephew." He would wink at Kevin, who would nod and play along.

Kevin scanned the cocktail lounge and carefully picked out a tall glass of orange juice that passed by him on the arm of a smartly dressed waiter, his eyes on the caramel-colored girl with wide hips and an ample chest. She was in the company of two other girls and a good-looking Asian man about her age dressed in an expensive designer suit.

Kevin could tell the difference in clothing now; with the exposure he had and his love for finer things, he did a lot of his shopping in South Africa. The bespoke suit he had on, a black and white Ralph Lauren ensemble, had only come in a week earlier, and it fitted to perfection. Ssaka complained he was like a growing child. "Only five years ago, you were about waist-high; suddenly, you are competing with me?" They were standing side by side staring into the mirror of the dressing room Kevin had taken over to get ready for the night's event in Ssaka's house.

Kevin straightened his bow tie and teased, "Unfortunately for you, I am still growing."

Now as he toyed with his glass, his eyes on the girl while she laughed and leaned into one of the other girls to whisper in her ear, her dark curls, which were piled exquisitely on top of her head with wisps of it flowing down the side of her face, fell over her eyes. He watched in fascination, the delicate movement of her subtle manicured hand brush the slight curls behind her ear. Kevin studied her: her slim wrist, embraced by a thin silver chain bracelet. His eyes lustfully danced over her curves, fitted in the deep blue satin dress, lingering at the smooth bareback exposed by the deep V cut of the design. He creatively thought about a hundred and one things he would do with the perfect contoured legs that were exposed through the knee-length slits of the dress. The gorgeous legs were attached to possibly pretty feet in a pair of silver-studded, strappy stilettos. He was determined to find out. He had a weakness for pretty feet.

Before he could go over and snag her attention, he was bombarded by people he had met earlier, and he dallied pleasantly with them, exchanging greetings and engaging in banal banter. Kevin was side-tracked for another twenty minutes, and then dinner was announced.

Just as he was re-strategizing his approach, someone touched his arm. "Hey!"

It was the stunner in the blue dress. Her smile was radiant, her makeup impeccable. Kevin was dazzled once more.

"Hey yourself," he replied charmingly, and her eyes danced.

"So, you are the birthday boy. How do you know Ssaka?" She was straightforward. "Vanessa…. Call me Van, if you like,"

"Vanessa, Kevin…. Call me Kev, if you like." He took the hand she offered him, soft, attractive fingers, then shrugged. "I thought you heard him say, 'that incorrigible nephew,'" he mimicked Ssaka's voice.

"Kev…oh yes." She lightly tapped him and then, without prior warning, slipped her arm into the crook of his arm. "It's almost dinner, and I definitely want to sit next to the incorrigible nephew."

Kevin smiled. "I am flattered."

They spent the evening mostly together. If a guest took him away, she always found him. She was girlish and funny with a sweet charm. They danced together all evening, and she wasted no time introducing him to her father.

"I think he likes you," she said as she led him to the bar to get another drink.

"It's hard to say; he had many people vying for his attention," Kevin told her.

"Ah!" She waved him away, plopping onto a stool and signaling for the bartender. "He is always like that, but he pays attention to whoever I am with." She winked. "I need a martini," she told the bartender, and when it was time to leave, she gave him her number. "I don't believe in men constantly chasing after the girl. I know what I want," she told him.

Kevin played with her. "Well, I am still the man, and I choose what I want."

She responded as charmingly as he: "And you want me."

Kevin looked into her eyes, enjoying their interchange, and replied, "That, I can't deny."

She beamed and said her goodnight.

Kevin held on to her number, thinking of her soft skin, her laughter that sounded like trickling water, her girlish and carefree attitude, such a juxtaposition to his own serious laser-focused disposition. It made him feel old suddenly.

When he finally called her a week later, she spoke as easily as she had when they had met at his birthday party. She invited him out to the golf club to lunch and to watch her play the under-thirties tournament she was taking part in. They spent the afternoon on random topics from her father, her travels, and she curiously probed Kevin about his own life.

While they talked, a dark medium-height player Kevin had seen on the course walked up to them and, smiling at Kevin and Vanessa, said, "That was a good game, Van."

"Oketcho," she chimed in, shaking his hand. "Oh, flatterer! Have a seat; have you met Kevin?"

Oketcho frowned. "No."

"You should. We had a swanky birthday party for him last weekend. Bhanu was there too, representing the old man."

Oketcho was already eyeing Kevin curiously. "Oh okay, happy belated birthday. I am Steve Oketcho, but everyone calls me Oketcho. What's up? You play golf?"

Kevin smiled. "Thanks. Kevin. No, I don't. I came for moral support." He tossed Vanessa a lazy smile.

Vanessa excused herself, leaving the two men to get acquainted. Thirty minutes in, Kevin was impressed with Oketcho, an IT expert and consultant who ran an IT consulting business that was contracted to work with one of the telecom companies in Uganda and was being headhunted by several companies seeking his brilliance. He was also engaged and getting married the following year. "So what are you into?" he finally asked Kevin, sipping his tea.

Kevin stretched. "Many things, food industry, real estate, for one, and trading."

Oketcho wagged his finger at him. "Ah, those barito restaurants? That complex by Makerere University, the commercial complex downtown, yes? I think I heard your name mentioned. Is it...Byamukama?"

Kevin nodded.

"Sweet, so what do you trade?"

Before he could respond, Vanessa was back complaining the boys had had enough time together.

Oketcho shook his head. "This one is a spoiler." He pulled out his wallet and handed Kevin a business card. "Let's talk some more."

Kevin took it. "You read my mind. Let me get back to catering to the beautiful woman."

Oketcho laughed. "Chicks!" He shook his head.

He got together with Oketcho a few days later at a tech business bazaar, and Oketcho introduced him to his close friend Bhanu, a young man of Arabic descent from a prominent Arab family in Zanzibar. He managed several branches of the family businesses spread out on the continent all the way to Turkey, Oman, and Saudi Arabia.

"Did you say Ganem?" Kevin frowned. The name sounded familiar.

"Yes." He smiled. "I was at your birthday party, and Vanessa took over your night, didn't she?"

Kevin's eyes lightened with recognition. "That, she did. Ah, yes! You were the gentleman with her and the two girls. I think another member of your family was around."

Bhanu nodded. "My uncle. He is in Uganda for a few months. We are expanding the dairy and food processing factories here."

Kevin recalled Ssaka telling him of the Ganem house of products that had opened its doors in Uganda almost five years prior, with household products like snacks, fruit juice, and now milk. He had also told him a brief history of the Ganem family, descendants of the Sultan of Zanzibar from as far back as the seventeenth century. "Boukari Ganem believes he has every right to invest in Uganda because apparently his ancestor Bargash bin Said took one of the Buganda queens as a wife," Ssaka had told him with an amused glint in his eyes. "Could be true…who knows? But Boukari is solid, a man of his word, and we have worked well together, chartering a way through Sudan and establishing factories in Dar-es-Salaam. Possibly his history has endeared him to the Tanzanians because…that's not a simple country to penetrate." Ssaka had clued him in on the vast wealth that the Ganems possessed: the Said luxury hotels that stretched from Saudi Arabia, Dubai, Seychelles, Zanzibar, and Mombasa to Uganda; their shipping business; and ports on the gulf of Gibraltar and Mombasa. Bhanu, the only boy child of billionaire businessman Boukari Ganem, had received mentorship concerning the affairs of the family empire from the age of fourteen in order to run his father's territory when he passed on.

"Nice to meet the heir to the Ganem throne." Kevin's eyes twinkled, and then narrowed with curiosity when he turned to Oketcho. "Say, how do you and Bhanu know each other?"

Oketcho scoffed. They had been friends since high school, when Oketcho's father had taken a twelve-year contract in Kenya, forcing the family to move. Kevin listened, impressed, as the men swapped hilarious adolescent tales of adventure from the lively streets of Nairobi to the white sands in Malindi, hot party nights in Mombasa, and holidays in Zanzibar. Oketcho had introduced young Bhanu to Kampala and its cheerful people.

Kevin liked the congenial respect the men accorded each other and laughed when, in appraising Oketcho, Bhanu had proudly said, "He is so damn good; he can even hack the White House."

Kevin insisted on them meeting up more. He invited them to parties only to find they knew the same people. The circle of elites was small, and everyone knew everyone. Bhanu expressed amazement at seeing Ssaka face to face.

"He is a ghost! The thing of legends you hear your father and uncles speak of," Bhanu commented, confessing he had never met him in person, not until the birthday party.

"He has played a big part in expanding our transportation and mineral business to as far as Sierra Leone." Bhanu had a twinkle in his eyes when he looked at Kevin. "He was a big push for us in Congo, too. We might have a continuation of business interests for decades to come."

Kevin smiled knowingly. "I would like that."

The three of them became fast friends, widening Kevin's scope even further as they shared business ideas and spoke of working on a few ventures together.

Kevin kept in touch with Bosco, and they communicated constantly by email. The year was ending, and it was cold and rainy in England; it was all Bosco talked about. Kevin often wondered if there was anything else people in England talked about apart from the weather. He indulged in his rigorous daily school routines and the girls he met; Kevin was amused that Bosco was taking to white girls at one point, then it was Jamaican girls, and now he was into the Indian girls because, he said, they were brainy.

"So, these dudes are cool?" Bosco was asking him as they chatted in messenger.

"Yeah, I like their minds. Oketcho is impressive with technology. He just signed up with TOTAL and Bhanu…. I believe eventually our paths would cross. Ssaka and his father are close associates …. I think fate has sealed our paths."

"How is Vanessa?" Bosco asked, and Kevin could tell he was laughing.

"Bossy! She redefines daddy's girl," he said. "But she is *kawa*. She's a trophy."

Bosco laughed. "Only?"

"I like her, though. She is beautiful. She knows what she wants, and she's got cute feet."

"That's the shallowest I have heard."

Kevin shrugged. "I have been with the brightest, the smartest, the skinniest, the curviest, she is fine…trophy-wise. I like the looks I get when we are together; plus, she reminds me not to take life too seriously. That's a plus."

"Player," Bosco wrote.

"I haven't found the X factor yet."

"And what's that?"

"Connection."

"Like you and Shenzi had?" Bosco was teasing.

Kevin replied, "Something close but for someone, I intend to sleep with…come on, Bosco!"

"Okay, okay," Bosco said.

They talked about business school and how Bosco would graduate soon and return before he went back for his master's. Kevin cheered his friend. "Maybe I can join this gold business of yours?"

Kevin chuckled. "We will put that to the test."

"Don't throw me in a mine."

Two weeks later, Bosco called. It was midnight.

"Whoa, is everything okay?" Kevin asked in hushed whispers. Vanessa lay beside him, and he glanced over to check the ringtone had not woken her up. He swung out of bed.

"Can you talk? Sorry, I called so late, but I just found out something. You will not believe it!"

Kevin walked out of his room, slid the door shut, and headed downstairs to his living room. "Yes, I can talk. What's up?"

"I found Kenzi!"

Kevin paused, speechless. He plopped into an accent chair, his heart racing. "What? Where? How?" He tried not to stumble over his questions.

Bosco laughed excitedly. "First, it's time you got a Facebook account. That is how I got her. It was a picture, and I could have sworn it was her; everyone was talking about it and wondering who she was, so I traced it, curious, and found it on some photographer's page…. Let me see…. His name…Shawn…Shawn Avery; yeah, that is the photographer! And a story by a medical magazine on her, it must be her! I will send you the link by mail, but do us all a favor and get yourself on Facebook."

Kevin heard nothing except Kenzi…

"Wait, what did she look like?" he asked.

"Man, you need to see her for yourself. I think she got her eyes fixed, and she was probably wearing contact lenses, colored ones, 'cause she had blue eyes. She looks damn good! I knew it was her the moment I saw it. I sent you the link and the picture."

There was a pause.

"You there?" Bosco was asking, the excitement in his voice faltering.

"Yeah, yeah, I am here. I…I just cannot believe it. What are the odds?"

"I know, right? But I think this is a big step. Who knows…? Just get on Facebook, man!"

Kevin, flustered, still processing the news, responded: "I will check out my mail in a few and see this picture. It better be her."

Bosco said, "She may be grown, but I know our Shenzi. It is *her*! Didn't you say her name was now Mackenzie Matthews? Yes, that's the name, unless it's a different person who has the same name and the same ebony-smooth skin."

Kevin's face broke into a grin. "You still like her, don't you? Ask me nicely and I will be the best man giving her away to you."

"Naw man, her skin color stood out!" Bosco brushed the teasing aside. "Also, I had been trying to find her online with little success, but this piece of news…it's a start, this picture I saw was taken about a year and a half ago; look at the date there…. And I went to his page, the Avery person, and there were a few more images of her. She might be a model or something, but this picture was the very first he took of her on the beach. The story is *right* there!"

Somewhere in Kevin, it was as if the chips had finally fallen in place, and it was time, time to go searching for her. His businesses were coming together nicely. He was going to the mines by himself now and reporting to Ssaka. He had grown exponentially and learned a lot about being discreet, being careful, and handling money better than he had four years earlier. Haruna set up his bank accounts for his mineral deposits. He had also saved up a few gold bars and diamonds in an offshore account in Switzerland. With advice from reputable businessmen that he sat with for lunch or late tea while traffic in Kampala stalled, Kevin listened and absorbed crucial life lessons, making a note to apply them when the need arose.

He struggled with the time factor; was he ready to find Kenzi, or was he afraid she would not need him? He wanted to make up for lost time as they had dreamed. Things were eventually coming together by themselves, as everyone had told him. *Patience.*

It had been a long time. Kevin hesitated. There was much to do. He needed to find these articles. He needed to see Kenzi and be sure it was not just someone who looked like her.

They spoke a little more about Bosco's plans to return in two months for the holidays before Bosco bid him goodnight. When they hung up, Kevin made a stop in the kitchen for water, then the study he had carved out of his den and turned his laptop on. When his modem was powered, he opened his email, and the first email that popped up was Bosco's. Kevin opened it and clicked on the link; the image loaded fast. His heart stopped when it fully loaded.

He suddenly could understand why Bosco had called. It *was* Kenzi. The girl on Block 4 that he had protected with his life was staring at him with laughing blue-green eyes. Kevin marveled at how beautiful she was; she had always been, but now she bloomed, a fresh flower after a heavy downpour. She was smiling; her teeth sparkled against her dark smooth skin, her cheekbones high; her hair flew about her narrow face in wide curls, and her slim curves enhanced the two-piece multicolored bathing suit that complemented her appearance. Kevin noticed she had a navel piercing with a conspicuous ring attached to it. The shot was perfect as if time and space suspended their functions to accommodate the fluid motion of her arms raised to push her hair out of her face. The shaft of early afternoon beams grazed her face at an exquisite angle, highlighting the color of her eyes.

Kevin sat for a long time staring at the picture, wondering if her eyes were real. It was certain she could see. She looked happy, and she was *his Shenzi*. The familiar longing he felt for her crept up on him like it had when he was in Congo. Memories rushed in, unhinged, and he basked in them, allowing himself to feel. Suddenly, he missed her—missed her terribly.

Kevin looked up the name of the photographer, saw his profile, and her picture showed up in his portfolio. He read the caption that accompanied the picture: *She was the rarest thing I had ever seen, carefree and light. I had to capture her glowing moment for the world to see.*

The article that Bosco sent him the link to was from another lifestyle paper. It talked about Kenzi being a miracle breakthrough in ophthalmology, her eyes being fixed, the name of her adoptive father, and much more. Kevin read, spellbound. His mind raced as much as his heart.

He scanned the internet for her, typing her name into the search engine, but all the Mackenzie Matthews that came up were white girls with blond or brown hair; none was her. Finally, he gave up the search and sat back, pensive.

When Bosco had joined MySpace, he had harped on Kevin to join to no avail, and this time around, Kevin felt it was relevant for him to get on this social site. Maybe if he kept searching, he would find her. So he typed back a message to Bosco: "All right, you win. Let's do this Facebook thing."

Chapter 20

San Diego, California
Summer 2007

"**D**id you already sign up?" It was Malaika looking over Kenzi's shoulder into the computer as Kenzi invited more friends from the yearbook—which lay open on the desk beside her— onto the Facebook account she had just created.

"Yes," she replied for the fifth time. She shook her head in response to her friend's impatience. They had just arrived at the Hilton San Diego Resort and Spa, where Malaika's mom was going to be for a week on a work retreat. "A great way to start summer vacation before you are off to college." Malaika had mimicked her mother's voice on the phone when she told Kenzi weeks earlier about the invitation to go with her to San Diego.

Kenzi excitedly divulged the details to her parents. They had known Malaika since the fourth grade, when Kenzi eventually started regular school with her own age mates. She had enjoyed the solitude of homeschooling while she went in and out of the research center, but joining an entire nation of children her age was even a bigger thrill. At first, she was shy and very conscious because of the inquisition about her eye color against her skin tone. Brent was instructed to watch her till she was comfortable enough to be by herself, but her first weeks of school were a nightmare, and she was in tears daily by the end of her school day. "Everyone stares so much," she had protested as she sat in the back of her mother's Buick, sinking into the seat, willing it to swallow her. Prepubescent and more conscious, Kenzi was taller than the girls in her class. Her skin tone and eye contrast made her a spectacle on the school compound.

On the first day of school when Brent walked in the hallway with her, students stared and whispered until she had disappeared into the principal's office.

Brent protested to the principal about it: "Everyone is staring! We don't like it." She was glad he was with her.

The principal smiled reassuringly. "Don't worry about them, Kenzi. They will get used to you. In the meantime, try to ignore them."

Kenzi recalled diving into the car when Mrs. Matthews came to pick them up that afternoon. She had counted down the hours impatiently till the end-of-day bell rang. Her first day was horrible. She could feel the eyes of her schoolmates follow the Buick to the main road, even though she later gained some courage when random people commented on how pretty she was.

She spent oodles of time browsing through magazines, envying the tall, slim, blond-haired girls, and when she stared at herself in the mirror, she saw a slim-faced girl with high cheekbones, full lips, large blue-green eyes and a halo of big curly hair, which on good days, if her mother took her to the Dominican salon, fell to her waist, straight and thick. She preferred it straightened out, but Mrs. Matthews encouraged her to love it full and curly, to no avail.

"Oh honey, it will get better. It's that you are new; you will see."

And Brent got into trouble for not being a good "scout."

"You ought to watch out for her and make sure she is fine," his mom reprimanded him.

"But..." Brent had protested and tossed Kenzi a withering look. Away from the prying ears of their parents, he would castigate her: "I do look after you, don't I? But I have friends too; they can't see me with my younger sister all the time!" he tried to explain, and Kenzi would pout and look away.

"Kevin never left me alone…" She would guilt trip him and watch him from the corner of her eyes flail his arms and cuss.

"Really? Are we going to do that? Urgh!" and he would storm out of her room.

The standoff usually lasted a couple of days, then he would relent by checking in on her at lunch and break, and then a day later she would apologize for being mean, saying she missed Kevin sometimes, but him not talking to her made it worse; she missed him too.

That always bolstered his ego. "Okay, okay…you are stuck with me anyway. I am the scout here." She would roll her eyes as he squared his shoulders and suppressed a jubilant smile.

After the grueling initial weeks of school, she made her first friends seated at the cafeteria by herself. Brent had not come in to check on her, and she was pouting, chewing on her sliced apples, occasionally dipping a slice in the little tub of peanut butter it came with when she heard a voice.

"Hi, you must be new."

She had looked up and seen the cocoa-colored-skin girl's eyes widen like saucers. "Wow, are those your eyes?" She had started, almost dropping her tray.

Kenzi had looked away quickly, refusing to reply.

"They are gorgeous, for real!" the girl had said, then added, "Can I sit with you? My best friend Kayla is sick, and Xavier is doing some project over there with Ryan…and I am bored honestly. I want to sit with someone."

The girl did not wait for Kenzi to invite her; she scrambled over the bench, plopped her tray laden with food on the cafeteria table, and sat, then beamed, her round baby-doll face brightening up. "I am Malaika. My parents are from Kenya, second-generation Americans; how about you?"

Kenzi had been taken aback by her boldness. She had looked up at her expectant face and gingerly taken the outstretched hand. "Hi, I am

Mackenzie Matthews. I am adopted," she said simply.

"Really?" Malaika suddenly lost interest in her food as she propped her elbow on the table and focused on Kenzi. "From where? You know Ramesh in our class is adopted too? His parents are Jewish, but he says he is Hindu…. I wonder how that's working out, you know." She rolled her eyes, scrunched her nose, and waved her hands about animatedly. Kenzi found her interesting.

"What?" Kenzi did not know what she was talking about.

"You are in our class. I have seen you," Malaika affirmed, then brushed it off. "Anyway, it doesn't matter. Tell me about yourself; how come you have such eyes?"

Malaika had bubbled on till the end of lunch, and Kenzi wondered if the girl ever stopped talking. Every single day from then on, she insisted on them having lunch together, and when Kayla returned, Malaika introduced her immediately. Even though it had been overwhelming for her at first, Kenzi eventually became comfortable after a few more lunch dates with her new friends.

"I hear you have friends," Mrs. Matthews said when she picked her and Brent up after school.

"Yes, she does…. Hallelujah, amen!" Brent raised his arms and closed his eyes as if in worship. "Kevin would surely celebrate with me." He had side-eyed Kenzi, who poked him, and he winced.

"Stop it, you two, and Brent stop being mean to your sister."

Brent's eyes widened in surprise. "I am just making a point."

"Which is?" Mrs. Matthews asked in matriarchal firmness.

"That babysitting time is over."

"Heather did the same for you, you know," Mrs. Matthews reminded him, much to Kenzi's delight. "Beside you and Kenzi get on so well."

"Yeah, at home, but at school? Mom! I am older than her; my friends tease me for babysitting." He groaned.

Kenzi ignored him, picking up a book from her book bag to read. "He tried." She spoke finally.

"Thank you!" Brent tossed his head dramatically. "Someone understands how hard it is to be in junior high."

Kenzi eventually let him off the hook because she was enjoying her new friends more; besides, she was growing more agitated with him checking in on her and mourning about how he could have been with his friends instead. She enjoyed the solitude at lunch more than she enjoyed him always asking her about this and that girl and whether she thought they were cute. "I am twelve; I don't care."

Their rides home from school were forever imbued with rowdy exchanges as they fought and teased each other until Mrs. Matthews' "stop" reverberated over their heads, "Won't you two just...stop?"

They would smile and give each other sidelong glances.

Junior high was fascinating for Kenzi. Her grade-four friends grew with her, and she gradually got independent, taking the bus home so she could go to the pizza place two blocks from school with them.

Before spring break, Kayla mentioned something about Xavier liking Kenzi, and she brushed it off; however, she admitted to herself there was something different in the way he treated her. He paid her extra attention, falling in step with her when they hung out together to engage her in conversation, walking with her when they strolled to the playground or on Saturdays coming over to help her with a project, while everyone else groaned about it all, preferring to catch up later for a movie or softball at her house.

He finally asked her to be his girlfriend a week before prom, when she was sixteen.

"Four years later!" Kayla had said. "What a chicken!" The girls giggled about it as they browsed through the prom pictures in the yearbook.

Kenzi said yes.

And now they were in San Diego, reminiscing about junior high, the crushes they had, the tears they cried, the pizza they ate, all the love notes they passed in class to each other, the bullies they persevered through, the ones that tried to attack Kenzi about her color, and one time, Brent took the fall for it, going to the principal's office for punching a jock who had called Kenzi names. That night, she had made popcorn and sat with him and watched an episode of *The X-Files,* and as the credits rolled, she had turned to him and said, "Thank you, Scout."

And in his way, Brent had brushed it off, a cold compress still on his cheek. "It was nothing. I should have knocked all his teeth out; pity it was only one that he lost." Kenzi had grinned, and even though she had learned not to compare him to Kevin, she thought about how much they were alike and how she hoped one day they would meet.

"Thanks; you are the best." She had reached out to hug him, and he had protested.

"Can't we just watch another episode of…"

"Come here!" she had insisted, and he reluctantly let her hug him. It was just the two of them since Heather had taken a year off "to figure out what she wanted to do with her life" and traveled with a volunteer group for a year throughout South America.

"Well, next year, I won't have you fucking waking me up, bouncing on my bed and shit," he had told her, dramatically coming up for air from the hug.

Kenzi had laughed. "Yeah, I won't have you driving me to my meetups."

Brent had been accepted to college for an advertising and marketing degree. He was the only person Kenzi knew who could sell you a stone for a million dollars and you would be convinced it was the best thing that ever happened to you. She could not help but smile at how many Girl Scout cookies they sold and their lemonade stand being the most frequented in the summer when she was younger. He was a people person, brimming over with enthusiasm, while she was withdrawn with occasional wild eruptions.

"I won't be too far off. New York is not California far." He told her, "I will drive down to be sure you and Xavier aren't making out…having sex. Don't. Do. It!" He had tapped her nose.

But then in another year she was sixteen; Xavier was taking her to prom, and Brent was leaving for college after the summer. He had made sure he started her out on her driving lessons during the summer. "So you can pass the road test." He winked at her.

When she passed her road test six months later, she called him to let him know. Heather had returned, still unsure what she wanted to do, so she worked for a vet because she loved animals. Then high school was almost over, and Kenzi was excitedly thinking about doing fashion design for college. All they could talk about that summer was college.

When Malaika's mom invited them all to the resort for a week, the girls were elated. Xavier had traveled to Colombia to visit family, Ryan was off to Paris, and the girls were going to be stuck in Maryland possibly going to Ocean City for a week with a bunch of their schoolmates. The Matthews had thought it a good idea that Kenzi go since no one would be home that week of summer. They were finally taking the cruise they had desired to take for a long time.

"Good for you!" Heather had cheered her parents on. She had moved away from home but came back often for dinner or lunch and to catch up with Kenzi on a shopping spree, feeling she had missed out on a lot since she was in South America.

Brent had opted to stay in New York to tour with friends, so it was perfect for Kenzi.

She and her friends had jumped on to the new social site, Facebook, and were looking up all their friends from their yearbook, making sure they were on it or messaging them to add themselves to it.

Once they had checked into a room big enough for the three of them, they had crowded around the computer searching for names and browsing through different people's profiles.

Kayla slumped back on the full-size bed that she had claimed and whooped. "I can't believe we are going to college!"

"Right?" Kenzi was beaming excitedly. "Okay, I found Summer and Craig, Wang, Villanueva, Victoria, Delvina…err…was that Ramesh?"

The girls pored over the yearbook for another hour, then decided they would get back to it later.

"We should post something so everyone can see it!" Malaika took over the computer, logged in, and posted a status update: *We are going to college! Hanging with Kenzi and Kayla in San Diego. Rad way to start summer!*

The girls giggled. They spent most of their days by the pool in the morning and at the bay beachfront in the afternoon. When Malaika's mom had a free day, they went to the San Diego Zoo and Balboa Park. They enjoyed the beachfront more, ogling at the boys and discussing the probability of Xavier and Kenzi eventually getting married. Kenzi smiled. "He is going to architecture school; I am going to do fashion and work for some fashion magazine, dealing with a hot-shot fashion editor or something…." She rolled her eyes when the girls insisted they would make a fine couple.

On that sultry afternoon, the beachfront was sparsely populated, as most people had retired and indulged in the hotel activities indoors. The girls waded in the water delightedly, engaged in their own version of beachball, which included throwing the light-colored enormous ball as far out as they could swim, and then lying back lazily, soaking in the sun.

"Going for another dip," Kenzi announced to the girls ten minutes later. She was getting bored with kicking sand and listening to song after song from the tiny player they carried with them. She jogged to the water's edge, and, as the foamy waves rose to lap at her outstretched feet, she noticed the man in the distance.

Kenzi watched him as he made his way toward her, a smile never leaving his face.

"Hi, I am sorry to bother you. I do not mean to intrude; you girls look like you are having a wonderful time. I just…wanted to ask…." He was looking at Kenzi, and she took a step back. That familiar uneasy feeling she got when people stared at her crept up on her again.

Malaika got up, heading toward Kenzi, Kayla in tow. "I am sorry, do we know you?"

Kayla was watching him suspiciously. "We don't talk to strangers." She folded her arms over her chest. They stood on either side of Kenzi like bodyguards.

With the girls beside her, Kenzi relaxed a little. He did not look threatening. He was actually cute, in the pirate sort of way, she thought.

Thick brown hair held in a ponytail and the deepest tan that would make Kayla jealous. He looked like he spent his whole life at a beach resort, probably skimboarding or surfing. He grinned, revealing even white teeth. "Well, the sisterhood that cares for each other." Pirate-looking guy pulled out his wallet and passed out business cards.

"I am Shawn, a photographer and scout for *Modelle*. It's a..."

"*Modelle*, the magazine?" Kayla interrupted, forgetting their stance.

He nodded. "Uh-huh. Was just idling on vacation but..." He homed in on Kenzi. "I have a good eye for rare gems."

The girls beamed. Kenzi glanced at her friends in surprise. "So much for protection..."

"All I am saying is you are beautiful, so beautiful, rare. Are those... excuse me but are those..." He was peering at her.

"No, she does not wear contact lenses," both Kayla and Malaika said in unison, and Kenzi suppressed a giggle. He raised his brows in surprise.

"Don't you read scientific journals? Peer reviews? Kenzi here is the biggest breakthrough in novel cornea repair surgery," Malaika was rapping out in her nerdy way.

"Kenzi!" Shawn pretended to have heard nothing else save her name. "Your name is Kenzi?" he said.

"Nice move, 'Laika." Kenzi shook her head, amused. "Yeah. So?"

"So, can I have a picture, Kenzi? I promise you it's only for professional purposes. Like I said, I am a scout and photographer, and you definitely caught my eye."

The girls looked at Kenzi. Kenzi stared at him searchingly, then shrugged. "Okay."

"Really?" Malaika was saying, her mouth wide-open as if Kenzi had said she was going to do a nude photo shoot. "We should sign some sort of agreement, those ridiculous two-type font pages and pages of nondisclosure...."

Kenzi interrupted. "Yeah, really. This could be the only time I get to pose for anything...." Shawn beamed. When the two girls were shooed out of the way, Shawn gave directions for Kenzi to stand, walk, or twirl;

her hair was gaining its body of curls again; she had come to San Diego with it straightened, but days of heat and sweat had watched the stubborn curls tangle.

A couple of shots later, Shawn asked for her information, anything she could give him.

"I am on Facebook." She grinned.

He smiled. "That can work. How do I get in touch with you better?"

She hesitated, but then gave him her email address.

That evening, the girls chattered excitedly about the ordeal. "Oh, my goodness! You could be the next Naomi Campbell! Did you hear what he said? That you are 'rare.'" Kayla was bubbling excitedly.

"Right!" Malaika agreed. "But he could be a perv who stole the real Shawn the photographer's identity! We needed an agreement, girls!"

Kenzi downplayed it, laughing. "He is probably looking for the science journal right now, as we speak."

Although inside she felt a flutter of excitement, and for the first time in months, she thought of Kevin again, how she would have loved him here at this very moment in San Diego with her; he would probably be impatient with the whole photographer thing, maybe tease her like Brent and then tease her some more after it was done but, in the end, say she struck "okay" poses, which would be his way of saying "you looked amazing." She wondered if she could find him on Facebook at all; maybe now that they were older, they could figure out what went wrong.

She thought about everything he had missed: her first sight, the sight of snow, school, her crushes, her first period, homework, her friends, first kiss. For that moment, as her friends chattered excitedly, she zoned out, thinking of him, aware of a longing for him, an emptiness, like something was missing, and maybe she could be famous and they could take over the world like he said. But she wondered if it would be the same without him there with her. Was he alive? Where was he?

Later that night, as the girls slept, she turned the computer on to search for him with no information apart from his first name and a foggy memory of what his last name could be; neither did she know what he looked like, then or now. She abandoned the project and went to bed, her mind rummaging through the pile of the past, trying to remember anything until sleep took over.

Chapter 21

Bethesda, Maryland
Summer 2007

Her pictures went viral.

Kenzi saw them first when she turned on her computer. She blinked in disbelief at the news article that screamed its headline to her: "Mysterious Beauty Goes Viral."

It was her; her stubborn curls flying about her face, the two-piece she loved because it showed off the piercing she had gotten in the spring, secretly. She cringed at the thought of her conservative parents seeing it. She had gotten it especially because Xavier had mentioned he liked piercings; it was a birthday surprise for him.

Kenzi was speechless as she read the article. Indeed, the writer had dug out the journal, and the article said she was a beauty adopted from East Africa whose adopted father, a scientist, had got her corneas fixed and the scientific trial experiment had resulted in the rare color of her eyes. The writer further mentioned they had found the picture on one of *Modelle's* top photographers and scout's Facebook page with the caption *she was the rarest thing I had ever seen, carefree and light. I had to capture her glowing moment for the world to see.*

Kenzi had squealed then jumped on a three-way conference call with Kayla and Malaika. They had all Googled the article and shrieked animatedly about how she was going to be famous. In her moment of excitement, she raced to her father's study to tell him she was in the papers.

"Dad!" she called happily, bounding into his cool air conditioned study. It had been years since she had last stepped into it. Her eyes swept over the browns and creams that comprised the room, then dashed upstairs to her parent's bedroom and did a double take to glance outside; her father's car wasn't in the driveway. Kenzi giddily cooked up an idea. She hurried back to his study, sat at his computer, and rummaged through his drawers for a notepad.

A pile of files in the lower cabinet caught her eye, especially one with her name on it. Out of curiosity, she pulled the thick file that no doubt, harbored, her adoption papers, and as she flipped it over, a thick, short envelope fell out. Kenzi opened it, and saw the letters, some in braille. They were *her* letters to Kevin. The others were written in pencil, large, rounded letterings…. A few she perused through sounded familiar, and most of them did not. They asked about her; how was she doing? How they would be together soon and signed at the bottom was *Your loving brother, Kevin.*

Kenzi felt her feet grow cold. She immediately grasped the file and papers, her earlier mission forgotten, and ran up to her room poring through the contents of the file. It contained her life story. Her adoption papers, her citizenship paperwork, medical reports, therapy reports, the clinical trial reports about her eyes along with newspaper clippings from scientific journals and peer reviews on the cornea repair research that Mr. Matthews was working on.

Scattered here and there were bills and receipts, government-resource paperwork and funding proposals, all of it based on her as a study. Then *the* letters; they were all written soon after she had left for the US. They were each carefully dated up till March 2001. It was the last letter that broke her heart. It was a printed email from the warden at the orphanage; she was telling them she felt guilty for lying to Kevin about the adoption.

Then in another email almost a month after the first email, she was saying Kevin had left the orphanage, angry. She did not know where he was. He knew everything.

That afternoon, Kenzi locked herself in, soaking in all the information, reading through Kevin's childish handwriting over and over. Tears slid down her checks onto the letters that smelled faintly of mint. Mr. Matthews kept mint candy in all his drawers. She smiled through his description of things, the school lunch, how he'd had to memorize Psalm 23, how he was still a champion in just about every single game, new and old, how he was tired of being at the orphanage and waiting, but most of all, how they would be together soon; he could not wait. Were they treating her well? Were her eyes fixed? Did she miss eating chips and liver and pancakes with him? Kenzi laughed and cried as she read through the newer letters she had only discovered.

She could not believe her own responses were tucked away, never sent to Kevin. What must he have thought? All these years? Was he mad at her, too? The pain she had felt, the anger and heartbreak that he had abandoned them and their plan, shifted. It was not his fault. The Matthews were to blame.

When she was done, she gathered the scattered documents and letters carefully into the file, returned it to her father's drawer, and went back to bed. The Matthews returned later that night. She faintly heard her mother call for her, but she ignored her. In a little less than an hour, sleep dragged her back into its cocoon mapped with dreams, filtered with memories from childhood, a childhood she had spent in the dark except for smells and sounds.

When she woke up the next day, her anger hadn't abated. It was her mother who noticed her sullen look. "Are you okay? You went to bed early…"

Maxine was pouring coffee from the steaming coffee pot. "I got bagels and a load of cream cheese; I figured you might want some." She rambled on and Kenzi interrupted her.

"Why did you really adopt me?"

Mrs. Matthews paused. "What's that, honey?"

"I asked why you adopted me…. Why?" She almost raised her voice trying to keep the tremor out of it.

Mrs. Matthews flushed. "Because we love you and wanted you to have a better opportunity…."

"But you did not take Kevin; you knew he and I were inseparable. Why did you…?" Kenzi felt the tears well up again. She blinked them back rapidly, then sighed. "I read my file in Dad's study…. You never sent my letters and then…and then…the letters." She choked. "From Kevin…the emails f-from the orphanage…. You and Dad lied to me! I have been lied to!" She yelled the last bit out.

Mr. Matthews walked into the kitchen at that moment. "What's going on?"

Mrs. Matthews stood frozen.

Kenzi wiped her eyes and waited, watching the small woman hug her arms. "Honey, we need to tell Kenzi the truth."

Understanding registered in Mr. Matthews' brown eyes.

Kenzi shook her head. "I think I know all the truth there is to know. You broke my heart. You made me believe Kevin did not care for me… made him think I had forgotten him; you wanted a lab rat for your experiments. You *sure* must be happy." She turned around and stormed up to her room, her father's voice echoing in her footsteps.

Thirty minutes later she heard her father knock on her door. "Kenzi, baby, can we talk?" Kenzi ignored him, embracing the blues she felt; she grabbed her headphones, plopped them over her ears, and listened to a muddled playlist of every genre of music from a playlist she had compiled a year ago. Some were songs Xavier had selected for her.

She attempted to drown out the conflicting emotions with the soulful voices that raged and strangely lulled her soul, begging her to react, to smile, or cry or display anger. Music filtered into her and wreaked havoc, but it was better than hearing the knocking on her door, the calling of her name, even the vibration of her phone. She locked the world out.

* * *

Following her outburst with her parents, she went to Malaika's for a week. "We fought," she told Malaika, not sure how to broach the topic. "About…my adoption." She left a note for her parents saying she needed space.

Brent was the first to call. "Mom and Dad are freaking out that you are not talking to them. What's up, Chip?"

"You ask them!" she shot back at him.

"Easy, I am asking you," he replied compassionately. Kenzi had to remind herself it wasn't his fault, and taking it out on him was wrong.

"I…I am sorry; I didn't mean to be…. rude." She was low and then she told him. At first, she tried to sound nonchalant, but halfway through, her lips trembled and her voice shook, but she labored through it, being as detailed as she could. "I am moving out, Scout. They lied to me. I can't…" she concluded heavily.

"Fuck!" Brent cussed, "Damn, I am so sorry, Chippy; that's messed up!" She could feel him simmer and felt a warm rush. She had been suddenly aware, for the first time, how adopted she was. The feeling she was an addition but not exactly a Matthews had stabbed at her, and she wondered if Brent or Heather would understand. She had hesitated to pick up his call, but when he insisted and called a second time, she decided whatever happened, she would deal with it.

"I just need to get away. I can't look at them right now. I am so pissed!" she confided in him. "I know they are more your parents than mine…"

"Don't say that," Brent cut in. "Hey, you are always my sister, and nothing can change that. Always. What *our* parents did wasn't right. I bet it is eating them up now…. I just don't want you homeless." He was warm and caring.

She shrugged, wiping her eyes, "I can…move in with Heather, I guess… I dunno. I will ask her. You know, crash on her couch, get a job at Walmart…"

Brent laughed. "Geez, Walmart? You can't count to one hundred last I checked."

"Shut up." She laughed despite the situation.

"Damn, I am so sorry. I can't imagine for real. That was cold."

"Yeah, right?" she agreed.

"What do you want me to do, hmm?"

Kenzi sighed and sniffed. "Let me run up your credit card." She smiled, and Brent made a sound of dismay.

"You can even take my car, darling, but don't touch my credit." She could feel him grin. "Tell you what, remember that house in the Potomac, that huge-ass-seven-bedroom mansion with a pool? The one I snuck you into so you could swim?"

Kenzi eyes widened. "Their dog almost ate me up—that house? How can I forget?"

"Oops. Come on, I could get you to house-sit for them…"

"Scout!" she shot out in disbelief.

"What? They paid great when I worked the summer there…"

"Yeah, so picking up poop and cleaning out pools? Err no…that dog traumatized me for life!"

"It just wanted you to pet him…" he insisted.

"You know what? You are hopeless, but a brilliant listener. Thanks, but no thanks. I am going to call Heather and apply to Walmart." She shook her head.

"'A' for listener. I will take that," he said. "Seriously, though, I am in your corner. I love you."

"I love you too, Scout. Thanks for listening," she told him.

When she hung up, she waited a few minutes and called Heather. The phone hardly rang before Heather picked up.

"I was just about to call you, K," she immediately blurted. "What the hell happened? I was just talking to Mom," she bellowed out with concern.

Kenzi slumped back on the garden chair on Malaika's front porch and sighed. Her head hurt. "Can I ask you a favor?"

"Yeah, of course…but first, what happened? Mom sounds hysterical. She said I should talk to you to go back home."

"Oh, damn!" Kenzi groaned. "I hate that they are dragging you into their mess."

"Their…what the hell…?"

Kenzi sensed Heather getting anxious.

"Can we do the favor thing first?"

"Okay, shoot." Kenzi shook her head, knowing Heather was tapping her left leg in anticipation. *Impatience, impatience.* She thought.

Kenzi paused a heartbeat, then gulped air. "Can I move in with you for the rest of the summer? Figure out my life?"

"If you don't start talking…"

"Hush, I will tell you over pizza and wings…if you are buying," Kenzi cut in quickly.

Heather sighed exaggeratedly, and Kenzi could almost feel her shake her head. "Why am I not surprised? The typical Brent move. Okay, I get off work in an hour."

Kenzi beamed. "Works every time…I will be there!"

A week after her heartbreaking discovery, Kenzi got a call from *Modelle.* They wanted her to feature in their fall edition of the magazine. The shoot would take place in New York. She agreed to it.

The call from *Modelle* lifted her spirits. She was excited and in awe to hear what the executive editor and design manager thought of her. She placed the phone on speaker while Malaika and she clung to each other, barely suppressing their excitement as both superiors voiced their opinion: "Shawn told us you live in Maryland, and one of our closest studios and offices is in New York. Do you think you could make it out there? We provide travel and accommodation compensation and a per diem for your stay. Keep the receipts of your travel, and we will reimburse you as soon as you arrive, along with your per diem for three days of the shoot."

Kenzi nodded as if they could see her through the phone, hardly trusting her voice. "Yes, I can make it to New York."

"Good. We look forward to seeing you there next week."

When the line went dead, she was screaming. Malaika and she did a little dance, jumping up and down and plopping onto her bed laughing. "Oh my gosh, that was wild!"

"Crazy wild!" Kenzi agreed as they continued to shriek in excitement.

"So how are you going to get the money?" Malaika asked when they were calm enough.

Kenzi smiled. She was ahead of Malaika already. "Don't worry…"

She called Heather and asked her for a loan, as she filled her in on the modeling gig. Heather was elated. "Oh my gosh, so cool! So will you go home?" she asked hopefully.

Kenzi replied, "To pack a travel bag, yes."

She got home the day before her trip. A sinking feeling sat in the pit of her tummy at the thought of facing her parents. She was relieved to find them out. As she stepped in through the front door and took in a deep breath of the sweet jasmine scent that faintly doused the air, she admitted to herself she could not run from them forever, and there was never a "good time" to sort things. It was seven in the evening when she heard her mom's car pull up in the driveway. Not too long after, she heard her name being called. "Kenzi, honey, are you home? I saw your car in the driveway."

Kenzi walked out of the kitchen, a bowl of cereal in hand. *Looks like today is the day to talk*, she told herself.

Her mother kicked the door shut. Her face lit up with hope, and Kenzi felt almost guilty for taking them through the drama of the week. "Oh! So good to see you well, honey." She placed the bag of groceries on the island in the kitchen.

Kenzi raised a brow and looked away. "Hi," she mumbled, telling herself she could not be weak.

"Hon, your dad and I are…. We want to explain…" Maxine started carefully, her palms open before her in an attempt to reach out to Kenzi.

Kenzi placed the bowl on the table and cut in quickly. "I am going to New York tomorrow. Kayla and Malaika are taking me to the airport…."

Maxine frowned, clasping her palms together. "What? We don't know about this. Why are you going to New York? You have been away for the past week or so…"

Kenzi folded her arms over her chest, her eyes averted from Maxine.

"Because, before I found out you and Dad had been lying to me…I came home to show you something…" She paused and breathed in deeply, wondering how to proceed. The convoluted emotions of anger and excitement roared within, competing for her attention, throwing her focus off. "Anyway, it does not matter now. *Modelle* wants me to model for their fall edition."

Mrs. Matthews' eyes widened. "*Modelle*, the fashion magazine? That… that's amazing, Kenzi. How…? When?"

"I got scouted while in San Diego. Did you not see the article a few days ago?" She sighed exasperatedly. "Anyway, after that I am moving out," she added abruptly.

Mrs. Matthews clasped her hands together and pursed her lips, digesting the information like a mother would. "Kenzi, love, we need to consider these things…."

"I have already thought about it…."

"We are your parents, and you are only seventeen. We need to talk about this when your father comes back…."

Kenzi knew this would happen, but she was not sure how to proceed. "Mom…I have made up my mind. I am moving. I can't…I need to process things."

Mrs. Matthew took a few more cautious steps toward Kenzi, bridging the distance between them. "Darling, I can imagine you are mad at us. I would be upset…."

"Mad? Upset?" Kenzi let out a short indignant laugh. "You can't begin to imagine how I feel. You betrayed me! All this time, I am mad at Kevin when I should be mad at you!" The tempered emotions broke from their confines. She was losing the control she had mastered.

"Then let's talk." Mrs. Matthews was firm yet gentle.

"I don't want to talk! I just want to leave and find Kevin."

"Kenzi, honey, we will help you…"

"No thanks, you have done enough helping…and thanks for it all…" She was curt and turned to walk out of the kitchen into the space that opened to the living room.

"Kenzi..." Mrs. Matthews followed her.

At that moment they both heard the key turn in the door, and Mr. Matthews walked in. He stopped and stared at them, sensing something. "What's going on here?" he asked as he took the key out of the lock and shut the door with his leg, his laptop bag on his left shoulder and a box cradled under his right arm.

Mrs. Matthews ground her jaw, and Kenzi's eyes locked with hers. She could see her hazel eyes mist over, glisten and sparkle with the tears that danced in them.

"Kenzi is leaving," she said, her eyes on Kenzi.

Mr. Matthews dumped his load on the sideboard table by the door and turned around with a frown. "You are what?"

"I am leaving...*Dad*," she said with emphasis.

Mr. Matthews put his hands to his waist, sighed and for a second stared at Kenzi like she was mad. "We all need to calm down. Kenzi, baby, look..." he started. "I know what you found upset you. There is nothing we can say to redeem ourselves except we are sorry we hurt you, but reconsider.... We have given you a better life. You can see there are things to be thankful for..."

Her eyes flashed with sapphire fire. "I was just your lab rat, so this lab rat is moving out."

A hurt look crossed Mr. Matthews' face, but that did not deter him. "No, Kenz, that's not true. I am sorry you feel that way, but we love you. You are our own daughter..."

"But not Kevin..." she cut in. "You did not love me enough to take Kevin.... He persuaded me to come with you, he literally begged, and you did him like this!" Hurt seeped into her words.

"Honey..." Mr. Matthew reached for her, but she flinched back. "So much like the slave masters, separating families and lying to them. You did just that!" she spat out.

"That's hitting way below the belt, K." Mr. Matthews' face flinched, and something close to anger and hurt turned his soft light brown eyes into a steel cold flame. She knew it hurt him, which gave her a little satisfaction but not enough to express just how much she grieved for years blaming Kevin, how guilty she felt, all because they would not tell her the truth.

"You hit below the belt first. That was a slavery move. Kevin was my only family!" She walked away throwing her arms up . "I just need to think…. I need space."

The couple sighed.

"Honey, let's talk about this. College is coming up…" Maxine was calling to her. Kenzi stopped momentarily. It was the moment of truth.

"I am not going to college."

"So where do you think you are going?" Mr. Matthews, still simmering from her previous accusation, demanded. "Kenzi, this is madness!"

Maxine touched his arm and called to him, then added loudly enough for Kenzi to hear, "She has a modeling thing in New York tomorrow."

"And you did not tell us?" Richard was saying. His voice boomed, but Kenzi did not care.

"I told Mom," she said. "I have to finish packing."

Mr. Matthews shook his head. "Young lady…"

Kenzi turned around exhausted with the back-and-forth. "I am tired, I don't want to do this anymore. Just leave me alone. Enough already!" she begged, and she looked away so they could not see the lone tear trickle down her cheek.

Mr. Matthews calmed down. "Honey." He was calm again. "We really didn't…look, you are only seventeen…."

Kenzi folded her arms over her chest. "I am going." She was adamant. She shrugged. "I will figure it out."

"Kenzi…" he started.

But Mrs. Matthews stopped him. "Richard…"

"I am going. You lied to me for years. I can't do this."

Mrs. Matthew was reaching for her husband. "Let's be calm. Please… Kenzi, honey, I am going to fix dinner. Can you at least eat with us? Can we do that?"

Kenzi wiped her eyes, her face averted. Her mind swirled with questions. Anger simmered in her belly, a host of conflicting emotions. She felt vulnerable and lost.

"I have to finish packing…" she repeated and headed toward the stairs to her room, avoiding her father's eyes, knowing he was boring a hole through her with his gaze.

While she packed, she caught faint wisps of their conversation; Mr. Matthews' tone agitated Maxine, who was trying to pacify him.

Kenzi stayed up in her room till dinner. She called Brent, telling him she was going to be in New York for a few days. Brent hooted. "Is it all okay on the home front?"

Kenzi shook her head. "I will tell you after dinner."

Dinner was a tense affair. The three of them ate in silence. The clinking of cutlery against plates and dishes became the accompanying sound, with Maxine occasionally trying to pacify everyone, asking if the squash tasted good. How about the steak? Did anyone want more vegetables? She could have baked the potatoes, but she was in a hurry to feed them. Nervous laugh.

After the main course, Maxine served Kenzi's favorite ice cream, coffee cream, and dark chocolate. It was then that Richard spoke. "Your mom said you were in the magazine. I did not see that. She…er…showed it to me." He was calmer.

Then he smiled. "You looked beautiful. I am proud of you."

Kenzi glanced at him. A part of her loved him. He had been the safest man she had known, taught her how to ride a bike, took her camping with Brent, helped her with her driving, and even had that discussion with her about protecting herself from rape and anyone who said racist things to her, but she could not help feeling conflicted with what she now knew. Did he really care, or was she just a rescue to placate his white privilege? She could not tell.

"Thanks." she replied.

After another bout of silence, he asked, "Will you be back?"

"After the shoot…I will go to Heather's for a while."

From the corner of her eyes, she saw the look of relief on his face, and he was just about to say something when Maxine shook her head discreetly. Richard stopped and stared into his empty bowl of ice cream and let out a faint sigh.

"Okay, that sounds great," Maxine responded for them both, and Richard Matthews nodded briefly.

The next day, Kayla and Malaika picked her up. They hung out all midmorning, had lunch, and then dropped her off at Ronald Reagan International Airport in DC. "You are so going to kill it!" Kayla hugged her.

"Look at everything Xavier is missing." Malaika grinned and Kenzi smiled. "He knows all the juicy deets. I am keeping the other stories for when he comes back and we can talk. He thought I looked sexy too." She winked.

Kenzi had never been to New York. Her Delta flight was a short ninety minutes to John. F. Kennedy Airport, and at 6 p.m. she was at the arrival gate. Shawn met her and took her straight to the hotel that would be her home for the next few days.

She worked closely with him and Christie, the design editor, a small, quirky Asian-looking girl who dressed like Pippi Longstocking, and a makeup artist who looked like an anime character, with multicolored hair and tattoos all over every exposed part of his body. She could only tell his original color from his face, which was smooth and hairless.

She loved the transformations she went through with him and enjoyed his *oohs* and *aahs* at every change of makeup. He constantly assured her she was gorgeous and needed only a dash of makeup. "Your skin and eye contrast is your selling point," he told her, and Kenzi paid attention. For the first time, she mulled over all the compliments she had received since the operation and spent longer hours in front of the mirror critically assessing herself. Was she really as gorgeous as people said? she kept asking herself, not sure what she honestly thought. Somewhere in her she wished she was as milky-skinned as Kayla or even a cocoa brown like Malaika. *But you got the gig, not them*, a voice probed her...

"Xavier, why do you like me?" she asked him on a day her mind betrayed her and she did not like what she saw in the mirror.

Xavier chuckled on the other end of the phone. "We are doing this again, huh?"

"Always, I guess." She smiled, loving the fact that he never castigated her for her image hiccups.

"You are smart, you are funny, you are warm, you are easy to be with, and, if I can be frank, you are hot."

She would melt.

"Am I?"

"*Eres tan sexy, preciosa,*" he would drawl sexily, and she would grin, her ego bolstered.

"*Mucho gracias, mi amor,*" she would purr.

And he wasn't the only one. There were those who liked her, those who fetishized her, and those who were curious. Being a teenager was confusing enough; looking like her as a teenager was even more confusing.

She had never felt more beautiful than she did in those three days. Each shoot comprised multiple brief breaks when she switched clothes. Each day was a different story; one was a work story, the whole affair of "A Day in the Life…" then the party with the girl's story and the date-night story. All told in fall tones and ambience. Each frame was diverse and unveiled sides of her she never knew she possessed.

At the end of the last shoot, the editor came to her in her dressing room, a look of pleased satisfaction plastered on her face. "You are a natural!" she told her. "We usually find girls with looks, but it takes a while to get them to fit into the molds we create."

Kenzi grinned happily. "Am I really?"

"Honey, you've been killing each shot; only one or two frames are pulled out, and *that*…is a big deal. It means you have 'supermodel genes'. Great angles, photogenic, great poses, strong presence, everything about you stands out…your eyes! Your skin. Girl!"

Kenzi was so excited, she could have hugged her. She clasped her hands together and beamed instead. "Thank you for the opportunity."

"No, thank you!" Christie grinned. "We might want you on for longer. Let's see how tomorrow goes."

The next day she had the date-night and wedding-theme pictures done. Kenzi finally admitted to herself she looked good. She peered into the mirror every time wondering who that girl was: slender curves, long graceful neck, high cheekbones and full lips, her eyes almond-shaped, large and piercing in their blue-green gaze, enchanting even. She had practiced posing with Shawn and his assistant, noticing fast how he flirted with her. She pretended not to but could not help being flattered.

"You are perfect," he told her as he arranged the gown's hem around an ornate chair she sat on for the wedding shoot.

"Oh, thank you," she replied sweetly. She secretly hugged herself knowing the only way she went through the shoots were the images she painted in her mind. Kevin's voice resonated on those fringes, just like he did when they took a picture on Block 4. She imagined him there, watching her, encouraging her, describing everything about the shoot, making sure it was funny enough to ease her into it. He was her muse.

Her three days felt like a fairy tale come true, the clothes she had worn, the places she was shuttled to for more organic pictures aside from the studio ones. On her last day, she was presented with paperwork from Christie. "*Modelle* is keeping you, love." She squealed. Kenzi's eyes widened jubilantly.

When she signed and saw her hefty take-home, she gasped. It was money she had never seen working for ten dollars an hour at a pizza place for the summer. This was the biggest upgrade of her life. When she saw her pictures, she agreed she would hire herself if given the chance.

Christie congratulated her. "You are so ethereal. We have seen no one like you, and we would love for you to work with us if that is something you are interested in."

Kenzi did not hesitate; her prayers were answered. She would move in with Heather for a brief period and then move to New York at the end of August. They let her know she would spend two weeks in California at the main office going through a brief training and meeting the crew at home base before returning to New York, which would be her base of operations.

When Kenzi told Brent she would be moving to New York, he quickly volunteered to help her find an apartment. They met for dinner on the last two nights and met his friends for a happy hour on the last night. "You had to show me off, did you not?" she told him when she walked into the Raven, a sports bar and restaurant in Harlem. "Of course," he had bragged. "When you have an almost famous little sis, you need to let the world know."

When they were alone, she filled him in. "Say, Chip, I could be your manager."

Kenzi laughed.

"Congrats!" He hugged her, then asked, "That means college is…out the way?"

Kenzi hummed. "For now. I could work and save enough so I don't have to ask Mom and Dad for anything."

Brent nodded. "You know, frankly, I thought you would stop talking to me and Heather…and…"

Kenzi smiled, touched. "It's not your fault. It's your parents who lied."

"*Our* parents," he corrected her, and she nodded, obliging him.

"Okay, *our*…parents." She added, "Right now, they don't feel that way…they feel like Richard and Maxine. I mean…would they have done this to you…or Heather?"

Brent had rubbed her shoulder. "Don't do this. They love you. Heck, they always punished me for your mistakes!" He made a face.

She laughed. "I know, right? I was really mean to you, though."

"Ah, you think?" Brent was dramatic. He gulped his beer while she laughed at him. "Hey, you may be mad. I get it. But…promise me you won't throw me out. I am the only Scout you will ever know…come for Christmas…Thanksgiving. You know how Mom is about holidays…and birthdays."

Kenzi drummed her fingers against the cocktail table they were sitting at. "Er…yeah…I probably won't show up so they can really suffer for it."

Brent funny-pouted, his hand on his chest. "Show up for me, Chip, if anything. We always watched something bizarre on the holidays. You and me."

She loved Brent, and seeing him support her made her miss Kevin. "I can't make promises…. I will try."

Brent screwed up his face. "That's a start. I will take it."

She sat back and slumped into the past, then said, "I miss Kevin. It's like that door I shut on him opened when I found out," she told Brent.

"Ah! The other brother," he said dramatically. "It was bound to open, no?"

She laughed. "I guess. It's probably one of those things I must face. Find him. Closure. I don't know."

"Have you tried Facebook?" Brent asked, like it was the brightest idea.

Kenzi sighed. "Duh, several times, nothing at least…I know his name, but what am I really looking for? I was blind."

He agreed with her. It was a shifty situation.

They talked about old times and her recent move plans.

"When you get here, I will take you around some really swell places."

"Oh, why thank you!"

"Hey, you are about to be famous. I must savor your un-famous moments!" he teased.

Kenzi returned to DC, and Heather met her at the airport. "I needed to be the one to pick you up to be sure you did not throw out the whole Matthews clan. Just Mom and Dad!" She hugged her. "Deets, girl! The deets!"

Kenzi hugged her back, grateful to see her. "You are so not loyal!" Kenzi feigned shock.

Heather grinned. "Between my parents and gorgeous almost-famous you? Who do you think I should pick? By the way, did I tell you, borrowing from me just got steeper. Let's say 10 percent interest?"

Kenzi's jaw dropped. "You did not just try to rip me off, did you?"

Heather shrugged, unlocked the door to her little Ford Focus. "Call it 'collecting for all those times you and Brent mooched off of me, cleverly too!" She winked at Kenzi.

On the thirty-minute ride to Heather's place, Kenzi told her about the shoot, the glamorous places she had been to—Central Park, the Brooklyn Bridge—the beautiful people she had met. "I never knew I would be among the most beautiful models ever. These guys talked about designers whose names you only see on clothes as if they brunch together every freaking weekend." Kenzi was rambling on and on. "I still can't believe I did that photoshoot and they loved me. I can't!"

In the days that followed, she received even more Facebook friend requests from her high school friends and then more from people she did not even know. There were those from Brent's class, some from Heather, and several of them tagged the article in the science journal and the article with Shawn's picture on to her page, asking her if it was really her.

She spoke with Xavier, telling him about the shoot and her move to New York. The difficult part of their conversation was their future. He was going to Montgomery College, and they had talked about her being there as well, and now the plans had changed. "I want to see how things go with this. My contract is great. Almost one hundred thousand a year! For me? Fresh out of high school!" she had bubbled on excitedly.

"My *chica* is famous; dang, I got to upgrade," he had said with a whistle.

"It's all good," she told him sweetly. "I can't wait for you to return. I leave for New York on August twenty-ninth."

"I will be back on the twentieth .We can spend some time before you go. I can visit New York too," he said.

"How about we all go to New York?" Kenzi suggested.

"We who?"

"You know, me, you, Ryan, the girls…you could all come and help set up my apartment?"

"Sounds fab!" he told her.

She excitedly threw herself into her apartment search with Brent, who , once a week, sent her leads until she found one she liked. It was about a mile and a half from the *Modelle* offices, and she could take the bus or the subway to work and home. She took a bus to New York to sign her lease and look at the apartment in person. It was medium-sized in an old-looking apartment building; it had an enchanting feel about it. "It's a start. My own place." She hugged Brent.

"Thank you!"

Her parents offered little resistance when she moved in with Heather. She told them about New York, and as much as they were happy for her, they did not press the reconciliatory discussion that would be for another time when the dust had settled.

On the day she moved her belongings into boxes in the back of her car, Mr. Matthews handed her an A4 envelope, thick and padded. "I think you should have these," he told her. "We love you and we made a mistake…if you decide to come home…we will be here."

Kenzi took the envelope, avoiding her father's eyes, her soul in conflict.

When she settled into Heather's large apartment, in the second room that overlooked the garden behind her, she opened the package. It was all the letters she had read from Kevin. There was a little notebook paper that hadn't been in it previously. On it was scribbled the address of the orphanage.

Kenzi immediately typed a letter and mailed it to Uganda.

"You know how long it will take to get there?" she asked the six-foot-four tattooed mail clerk.

"To Africa? Twenty-one days." He tossed her letter in a pile of letters in a box that was waiting for the next level in their process.

Kenzi waited all summer for a response and never heard back. Frustrated, she had scoured Facebook and searched online for the address, coming up empty. It fueled her anger against her parents, and she wondered again if it was how most of black America felt, furtively searching for their roots after slavery. She hated the situation she was in with her family, and yet her life was magically getting a facelift, and she could not stop it. Moving to New York was the biggest milestone in her life now.

Kenzi told Xavier everything that occurred between her and her parents and why she wasn't home. He had understood and been her strength. When her moving date arrived, Ryan's father let them borrow the minivan, and Kenzi packed a few boxes of things she needed, opting to buy a bed and furniture when she got to New York. She declined any money her parents offered her, saying she had enough to start off with.

She had excitedly told her friends to buy *Modelle* when it graced the store shelves at the beginning of September, on Labor Day. Kenzi was already beside herself with the wait. They spent the weekend window shopping, being tourists, getting train schedules and subways mixed up, and trying to find the best deals on furniture for Kenzi with Brent's help. They brought blow-up beds for their nights at her apartment, enjoying the freedom of being away from home.

Kenzi and Xavier spent alone time figuring out how their future would go, and after talking about it all night on their first night, he kissed her and shook his head. "Enough...let's just see how things go. Okay?"

Kenzi had agreed with him and snuggled close.

On Labor Day, they had their breakfast at a small restaurant in Times Square. They had bought two issues of *Modelle* and gloated over Kenzi's images. "Damn, girl, is that you?" Xavier had looked at it in shock and admiration.

Kenzi had grinned. "You like it?" Xavier smiled, tilted her chin, and kissed her. "I love it."

"Get a room, you two!" Ryan had piped in.

They all chatted, excitedly browsing through the pictures, and when it was time to leave, they hugged and reluctantly set off, promising to keep in touch. "We need a reunion soon. Maybe spring break? Then Thanksgiving?" Malaika said hopefully.

They agreed to it. "Yeah. I mean, Ryan and I are closest to Kenzi. You guys are in Texas and the Midwest?" Xavier pointed out.

"Well, we will make it work," Kayla assured the boys.

"I can't believe this is us. We are out of high school. Freshmen, wow," Ryan was saying.

"Let's just make it annually if we can't do every break," Malaika insisted.

They agreed to that. When they left, Kenzi had never felt so alone. She had dinner with Brent, voicing her fears about their relationship. "If I can't see Xavier every day, how is it going to work…? I mean, he will have school; I have work…. This is all too much." She pouted.

"Chip, if it's meant to be, it will be. And relationships are work. You got to work at it now." He shrugged.

"That doesn't help." She groaned. "Why do I tell you these things?"

"Because I give the best hugs." He grinned lazily. His carefree attitude eased her up most of the time. It would be all right, she figured. Time would test their love.

Chapter 22

New York, 2008–2009

The year 2008 was blissful for Kenzi after *Modelle*'s fall edition. The festive edition followed, and she enjoyed being decked out in bells as Mrs. Santa or a sexy elf. Her ratings climbed exponentially with *Modelle* selling out both issues.

It was not long before Kenzi was being headhunted by *Carinne's, Bella, Black and Beautiful,* and a host of top fashion magazines, clothing and perfume labels, and well-known designers. She featured in *Bone* and graced their cover by telling the story of her life.

In a few months, her nightly dinners with Brent trickled to weekly and then monthly as the pace of her life quickened so much that by the end of 2008, Xavier and she mutually decided it was best they remained friends. The strain in their relationship was showing. They spoke less. He got insecure, and she wondered who he was meeting in the corridors of his college hallway. The girls were sad about the breakup but recovered quickly on hearing about how many famous, gorgeous people Kenzi was meeting. "Well, damn, you might marry that famous designer after all," Malaika had chirped on one of their weekly conference calls.

She asked Brent to help manage her, and his first advice was for her not to date Shawn, who was flirting inordinately with her. Despite Brent's advice, Kenzi dated Shawn anyway in the spring of 2009, but a couple of months into it, she realized she was his trophy girlfriend. Her contract with *Modelle* expired at the right time to break it off with Shawn. She declined a renewal, and she was immediately scooped up by *Victoria's Secret*. She was excited about being an "Angel" on a three-month project for their summer collection. By this time, the demand for her was overwhelming. She had contracts coming in from everywhere. She eventually signed up with a real agency that handled all her bookings. When *Vogue* came calling, Kenzi's face was already being displayed on the billboard advertising in Town Square.

Heather called often, and she resumed her meetups with Brent, making it weekly on Sunday mornings. She needed to hold on to the familiar. She only spoke with her friends on Facebook or their conference calls. Ryan and Xavier visited but not frequently, and the models she worked with were catty and superficial. "I need real friends," she lamented to Brent, who thought the models were amazing. "It's dog-eat-dog here, and I have no friends!"

"Hook me up with one of those girls. I will get you friends," he had joked, but he called her twice as frequently.

"I don't want you to become a Marilyn Monroe. Don't be a stranger," he told her one night they were out dining, and she told him how exhausted she was. "Promise."

It was a pact.

After Shawn, she crushed on Jiao, a model she had partnered with for a *Grass and Grace* shoot. The papers and fashion network called them the perfect couple—a case of ebony and ivory. Jiao was as pale as Kenzi was dark, his eyes a dreamy brown pool of sexiness and hers a fiery aquamarine.

"I think we kind of dated because of the media pressure. It was so everywhere," she would tell Heather later on the phone when she inquired about her new boyfriend. The papers had come out later revealing that Jiao had been seen cozying up with another male model after a project.

"Did you guess at all that he liked guys?" Heather inquired like a reporter.

Kenzi laughed. "Not at first, but yeah, it was awkward that he did not really want to make out with me. I just thought it was the pressure and he wasn't into me, but we made a great camera couple. Our pictures were gorgeous when we were out there hanging at a party or event. He was just gay. We are still good friends."

After him, there had been two more before she met the enigmatic Devon at a fundraising dinner for children with autism hosted by another magazine she was working with. She was the centerpiece. He walked up to her and told her she was as stunning as an Egyptian goddess.

Her eyes had appraised him, his well-toned body encased in the fitting charcoal gray suit. His smile made her think of Michael Ealy, and his amiable nature had her instantly attached to him.

They had lunch a few days later, followed by dinner. He was thoughtful and romantic, almost twenty years her senior, an engineer, totally out of her line of work, divorced with a ten-year-old autistic son, whom she loved immediately.

Three weeks later, he asked her to be his girlfriend, and she agreed.

Devon was the most mature relationship she'd had. He taught her to love herself; she loved his conscious talk of black people, black queens and the power they wield. She absorbed his knowledge on Egypt and black civilization. She learned the history of the Black Panthers and black leaders she had not fully read about. He excited her mind, pushed her mental boundaries, and when he called her queen, she radiated poise; his phrase, "the darker the berry, the sweeter the juice," always had her wowed by him. In the ten months of their romantic affair, she saw her children in his eyes. Their wedding day was closer to her than finding Kevin. She had their life story together all written out in the stars. It seemed like finally she had found a love that felt just right.

The media followed them around. She *tsk-tsk*ed at the headlines, "Nouvelle top model Kenzi with her beau at the Hamptons" or when she attended the Super Bowl and their pictures together splashed most gossip papers, magazines, and culture pages. It was exhilarating when the media adoringly published a dream relationship, but not when it dug for dirt. Kenzi's world came crashing down when she discovered she wasn't the only berry he was picking. The media posted a CCTV picture of Devon leaving a hotel with a woman whose shades partially shielded her facial features. Devon dismissed it as rumors, serenading her back to him after a forty-eight-hour fight, but more dirty linen hit the press, more evidence of his philandering. Kenzi cried her heart out, not wanting to talk to anyone for a week.

Her new personal assistant, Sketch, had his first task cut out for him a week before the breakup and when she had not answered his several phone calls. He went to her apartment and found her passed out from excessive alcohol consumption and sleeping pills. She had a photo shoot in four hours.

He revived her with water and coffee, then listened to her rant about Devon. All professionalism was lost when he held her and let her cry. When she was sober, he waited outside her door while she showered and dressed. "Don't tell anyone, please," she pleaded with him.

"I got you, Kenzi." He nodded.

He hung around while she did her shoot, assuring her she was fine and there was no trace of the unpleasant affair on her. After the shoot, he took her to a block party. "It's not your kind of place, but I think you will like this crowd, my people. Down to earth." Kenzi accepted and did not regret it. She told him about Kevin by the end of the night, her family, and how she could not stand the other models.

It was the beginning of a friendship. A bond formed between them. He became more than her PA. Brent was leaving New York for an internship in Atlanta, and then graduation would bring them all to the same central place. "You can't avoid it, Kenz, unless you won't come for my graduation."

Kenzi had pleaded with Brent, "I will brunch with you the next day?" It was his last day in New York, and Kenzi took him to dinner at a high-end restaurant in Bedford-Stuyvesant.

"I am going to miss you, Scout. Keep in touch. Thank you…. I loved being here with you…well, half the time…" she added, tossing lettuce at him.

"Sketch is here now. I think I was officially fired," Brent told her.

Kenzi grinned. "Nah, I fired you long before him."

They had spoken about her search for Kevin, and still, there was nothing.

"So will you go to Uganda then?"

Kenzi shook her head. "Not until I can trace him, and we figure it out."

About her parents, Kenzi was still hesitant. "I don't want to go there yet. Life has been so fast these last two years; I don't know how to broach the topic now. I need to find Kevin first. I dunno if I can forgive them if I don't or if he died or something horrible happened to him." She shivered.

Brent told her to give it time. "I don't think they intended to hurt you. At least believe that."

Kenzi glanced at him. "I don't know…well. We will see." It was always a sensitive topic, and they tried to skirt around it.

"They ask about you all the time. They buy all the magazines, and I tell them you are fine, busy but all right," he told her.

She nodded. "Thanks for keeping my secrets and drama."

"Hey, I got you." He squeezed her hand. "So, no…Easter egg painting, no turkey carving, no Christmas cheer or birthday dinners until you are good and ready, huh?" he asked with a soulful look.

"I guess," she had said, then added, "I miss us…all of us together…. I just need more time, you know, to find it in me to talk to them without being mad."

Brent waited.

"I get the letters and cards and emails they send. Even the checks. I don't need the money. I got this."

Brent shrugged. "Parents are parents."

She beamed at him. "Sometimes you say such grown-up things, I am not sure you did not get switched."

Chapter 23

New York
November 2010

It was late November, Kenzi had stayed in all week, recovering from a cold. She had languidly browsed her social media, which had grown immensely. Her pictures that Sketch worked with her to upload were receiving a lot of attention, and her fan base was exploding.

"Europe has noticed you, girl." Sketch told her while he nursed her with his grandmother's favorite chicken soup recipe. They had a few clients calling already, and the agency would let her know who she would work with come 2011.

She had typed in Kevin's full name in the search bar on Facebook, recalling them to memory from the letters. She had scoured the many Kevin Byamukamas that came up. Some looked older. She imagined he would be younger. Most profiles she saw she did not browse through simply from the pictures, eventually settling on three. One had a handsome light-skinned young man with a pretty girl on his arm. The other was the headshot of a man two shades darker than the Kevin with a girl. His smile made her think of how she imagined Kevin would look, a teasing glint in his eyes; a lovely smile; square, confident shoulders; and in her mind, he was handsome. The last Kevin profile was blank with a blue cutout shape customary of Facebook's default image for those who did not put up their picture.

She had scanned the profile for more information, and all she saw under "occupation" was "businessman." Their tag line had piqued her interest. "I own the world," something so Kevin-like.

With a deep breath, Kenzi had crossed her fingers. "Here goes nothing." She messaged them all, "*Hi, do you remember Block 4 rooftop? You and me against the world?*" she had typed and sent.

Her watch said 7 p.m., possibly after midnight in Uganda. Kenzi searched for the actual time and decided it would be too late for anyone to respond. They were asleep. She kept her laptop open anyway and cozied up with the heated blanket, remote in hand, and switched to the next episode of *Sex and the City.*

* * *

Kampala, Uganda

Late November 2010

Kevin and Bosco spent all afternoon with Bhanu and Oketcho. Kevin had introduced Bosco to the boys, and they dined at the Serena on Nile Avenue. They talked about their different fields of influence and business, their dreams and plans, and it fascinated Bosco.

At the beginning of December, a youth innovator conference had Kevin speak about wealth creation and financial intelligence. His aim had been to scout out youthful minds who had potential lucrative projects he could invest in.

"That's a great idea," said Oketcho, and the rest of them agreed to come along. It could be an opportunity for all of them.

They were out till late, and when they finally retired, Kevin drove Bosco home, and Bosco brought up Kenzi once more. It always ended up there between them.

"She is taking the modeling world by storm, Kev. I saw an American magazine called *Modelle.* They had her for their autumn issue in 2008 and Christmas, too, and there is a lady's brand called *Victoria's Secret,* yeah; they had her too; there was *Black and Beautiful*.... I really don't follow fashion like that but…. She had an interview in one of them, possibly *Vogue*. It blew me away, boss. Like wow! Is this the girl we knew?"

"I can't find her on your Facebook. I have looked," Kevin assured him.

Bosco shook his head. "You cannot tell me all this time you haven't found her…."

"Have you?" Kevin challenged him.

"I haven't really looked, been getting the magazines."

Kevin laughed. "Liar…. I am this close, B, I am this close." He used his forefinger and thumb to show the slim distance between them.

"Anyway, I know her online name. I want you to find it out yourself, Mister-I-got-skills."

"Is that right?" Kevin grinned. "I have a particular skill: *patience*."

When Kevin got home, the first thing he turned on was his computer and then Facebook. The messenger portion had one unread message. Kevin, curious because he hardly got online and had not gotten back on the social site in weeks after he opened it and searched for her to no avail, now sat down before the computer and opened the message with a click.

"*Hi, do you remember Block 4 rooftop…. You and me against the world?*" Kevin read it twice to be sure he was registering it right. A smile crept up his face, then he laughed shortly despite himself. There was no way anyone knew that line but Kenzi.

"*It's always been you and me against the world…. Hi, Kenzi!*" he had typed back, feeling his heart swell. An overwhelming sense of coming home to roost settled on him. It was a calm he had not had for a long time, and it fluttered slowly, gently down on him, amid his excitement.

His eyes strayed to the name of the sender, and he realized why he had not found her, it was Kenzi Zawadi. He had completely forgotten she had that as her middle name…. When he clicked on the profile picture, it was a side-view photo of her face, her hair a gorgeous curly crown with strings of pearls lining her forehead, her long neck partially hidden by the soft ringlets of curls falling past her bare shoulders. She looked like

Queen Nefertiti, only darker. Kevin clicked the "request friend" button, lingered a while longer, then went to bed.

Sleep eluded him, and at 4 a.m. he was up staring into the delicate crisscrossing lines that etched into his snow-white ceiling. He swung his long legs out of bed, walked back to his study, and turned the computer on. His request had been accepted, and there was another message: *"Kevin? It's really you then! Oh my God! I can't believe I found you! How are you? Where are you...? We have so much to catch up on. So much to tell! Love, Kenzi."*

Kevin chuckled, giddy with excitement, and that sensation of wholeness fondled his heart. It felt so unfamiliar and yet familiar, as if it had been away for a while and only returned, jolting him to remember what it was like to feel complete.

"I was awake, it's 4 a.m. I know we are in different time zones, something I found out about when you left for the States. Wow...this does not feel real...I have thought of this day, Kenzi, and I have thought about you every single day since September 2000. Indeed, we need to catch up. Is there a number I can call you on?"

In another minute, a reply popped up: *"I have thought about you, Kevin! Missed you too much! We have so much catching up to do! I am so excited."*

He had made note of her phone number and email address, a smug grin on his face.

Another message popped up instantly: *"Oh, and put up a damn picture so I can see what you look like!"*

They communicated every day for a week. If he was not emailing her, he was messaging her via Facebook. Soon, email became too archaic, too slow for their instant need for real-time conversation. Then Kevin had to travel, and conversation became scattered greetings on messenger; when he returned, she was busy with fashion events, but they left each other messages, about the past, the present, and a potential future. Eventually, he called her, when they both could afford time to speak and all the scattered messages that littered their computer screens were repeated in a four-hour phone call, even though, Kevin could hear the birds chirp outside and the cock crow, he did not want to get off the phone. Her voice was a delight to hear. He loved the mesh of her accent, more refined, foreign, and yet familiar. It was as if the worlds she had lived in meshed into one and gave her a different intonation, and he loved it.

No matter how often they spoke, the distance between them gaped like an abyss, the yearning within their souls hungrily eating at every opportunity they had to connect. Kevin promised to visit when she said she was not willing to come yet. She asked after her mother dismissively, and the third time they spoke, Kevin told of his mother and Bampa. Several weeks later, he told her of Ssaka with pride.

It became an episode of tales between them, thirty minutes or more of the soap opera that was their lives, stretched across the distance of time and space. They lingered for as long as time allowed them and longed for the day they could see each other face to face and sit down to properly recount everything they had just spoken about all over again. This time slowly, leisurely even, as they embraced the *them* they had become; there was much to see, feel, and hear. So much.

"I will come to you, I promise," Kevin assured her.

BOOK 4

Kevin and Kenzi

2012–2017

"We own the world, Kenz. We always said we would. Remember?"

Chapter 1

Kampala
September 2016

Kevin had been putting off calling Kenzi. This was a big week for her, and today, especially, was her crowning night. He figured he would wait and call her the next day. It was six o'clock in the evening according to his Movado multi-time-zone-faced wristwatch, meaning 4 p.m. in Italy. He shrugged it off.

"Tomorrow." He spoke to the six-foot-two, attractive reflection that gazed back at him through dark brown pools of thoughtful irises. He appraised his lean, contoured self, sideways—a handsome portrait of one who worked out and took care of himself—and raised a brow in approval. He straightened his bowtie, smoothing his freshly shaven chin. He ruminated on the tasks he had accomplished that week, shifting from one bullet point to the next with practiced vigilance, as if to relieve himself of checking off these undertakings; a second more would cost him a diamond mine.

His thoughts anchored themselves on the most important event yet to come, a meeting with the president of Uganda concerning the oil refinery bid, in two days. He dragged himself back to the present reluctantly. Tonight was important; he was an honored guest of the governor, Bank of Uganda, who had smoothed their path to meeting the president. But Kevin could not rule out the intervention of Haruna either. The meticulous middleman still watched over his dealings, now even more than ever.

The news was grim since the elections earlier this year with the president winning a fourth term in office; there were rumors that were no longer rumors but sermons preached on every opposition pulpit, online and on television, that the Leopard—as the president liked to refer to himself—was gunning to be president for life.

The debate he was engaged in earlier that day at the Ssese Patisserie in the Serena Hotel was as fresh as the minty mouthwash he had just spat out. The intimate party of six young aspiring Under 40 Forbes Most Wanted, who preferred to flourish under the radar, met regularly at this spot for banter and coffee.

"How bad can it be? Let the old man die in power," Tisa was saying rather curtly, which was how he often was. Kevin wondered if he was shortsighted or just enjoyed the position of devil's advocate.

Oketcho, clearly irritated, jeered. "*Oli mu kintu*, that's why you speak like that."

These diverse, brilliant young men taught him a little more about life daily, so he ignored Tisa, smirked, and chipped in. "Which one of you isn't in things, heh? I am not even a *mushe*; neither are any of you, but we are making it. So how do you think *you* profit? All these deals you make with Sudhir, minister of Transport and Works, *si jui* Bitature, Mbire. We have dipped our hands in the honey pot because we are in bed with them all…but we have an understanding…I hope…of how we can do better than them. Besides, Museveni is not going anywhere. He has the country on lockdown like an angry girlfriend who won't give you pussy when she catches you sexting with another chick."

It was a topic that always reared its head in their weekly business brunch, and he watched them shift in their garden chairs uncomfortably, sipping their coffee and scanning messages lighting up their multiple phones lined up on the round garden table.

Bosco cut the tension. His light-skinned baby face broke into a smile, and he edged his heavy-set body toward the glass table. "Let's put a pause on that and resume next week, same time, same place…because." He waved a bound planner in midair before setting it on the table again. "We have *proggy*."

"It's Friday night." Oketcho grinned.

Bosco shook his head. "Not that *proggy*. The black-tie Nile Breweries Awards, 7 p.m. tonight." He opened the gray and black bound planner and placed down six black and gold executive black-tie invites creatively designed to look like the outline of a bottle—a black bowtie around the bottle's neck—on the table.

"Proudly sponsored by the governor, Bank of Uganda. It is happening here at Serena, Victoria Hall. Got them early this morning. You are welcome." Bosco was grinning smugly as he waved at the cards dismissively.

Bhanu, a lanky, roguishly handsome Arab with a conspicuous mole between the bridge of his nose and left eye, whistled as he picked up one of them. "So do you know who is on the guest list?"

"Very snobbishly selected. The usual embassy folks, press, foreign investors, your Sudhirs and whatnots, and *us*," Bosco added, that smug grin still plastered on his face.

"Okay, I will be there," said Oketcho, picking up his card. "I need to get going. My secretary won't stop calling me. I think my wife is in the office again." He looked bored.

The others laughed. "That's why we are not married," Kevin jested.

Oketcho threw him a nasty look. "We will see about that. And I will be the best man. Let's bet!"

Abe, the shortest of them all, hooted, "Hear! Hear!"

"Hahaha, you just want to spend bet money to appease your wife. Not on my account, *Ssebo*," Kevin teased.

"We will see." Oketcho smiled, wagging a finger at Kevin.

Slowly, the rest left with their invites, and he was alone with Bosco. A waitress clad in a cream-colored shirt and black slacks approached their table, smiling.

"Is there anything else you would like, sirs?" she asked, looking from Kevin to Bosco.

Kevin shook his head.

"Mineral water for me, and maybe another pot of African coffee," Bosco replied.

The waitress noted it down in the mini notebook she retrieved from her pocket and scurried away to get his order.

"So, have you heard from Kenzi?" Bosco always asked him about her.

Kevin sat back and stretched his legs under the table. "No, not since Tuesday. Fashion Week is hectic. I remember her debut as a runway model with Luz. She was really nervous, but she looked…my goodness…." He had a faraway look as the image of her on the runway in Paris during Fashion Week 2015 steadied into focus in his mind.

Bosco smiled. "Oketcho might win this bet."

Kevin let the image dissolve and laughed. "There is *no* bet to win. If I can help it."

Bosco shrugged. The waitress came with his coffee and water. He thanked her and filled his teacup.

"Meanwhile, my niece is such a fan. She is always showing me her pictures on Facebook and is it *Insta*-something. These young people. They waste so much time admiring other people instead of working hard to be *those* people."

Kevin shook his head, still plagued by thoughts of how the youth could be encouraged to make money off social media. He flicked through Kenzi's pictures stored in his phone—those he alone could collect when visiting her in the States.

"My camera takes better pictures of you than certified photographers." He recalled teasing her when he browsed her airbrushed pictures that littered the internet.

"I tell you, this thing called social media is killing these young chaps. Have you heard the phrase 'slay queen'?" Bosco asked.

Kevin roused from his thoughts, scoffed, and shook his head. "I feel too old. Carissa said Kenzi was 'slaying,'" Kevin responded, amused by the constantly mushrooming phrases and slang flung across the internet by zillennials. At only twenty-seven, he could swear he was going on forty-five, what with a tumultuous history that had doubled his years and forcibly thrust the weighty burden of maturity upon him at an incredibly young age.

He had no time to think about slay queens or swipe through pictures or respond to paragraphs on paragraphs of opinions shared on social media. His argument was always "When did we start sharing our food, our toes…our most trivial banal lives for the world to see?"

"Attention is an asset, and the internet owns it," Bosco replied matter-of-factly. And that is why business was the only way he would get into social media—run by Bosco's niece, Carissa, who was in her second year of journalism school at Makerere University. Her quick-wittedness and social media savviness had gotten Kevin to take up Bosco's suggestion to hire her as an intern to manage their business social media pages. However, six months down the road, he trusted her with his personal page that he seldom visited.

Kevin sat up and picked up the little silver pot, pouring the last cupful of coffee it held. "So how are we looking, with the meeting with the president?"

Bosco clasped his thick hands together. "It's all a go. If there is any delay, it will be because the Leopard is out of the country. I am reliably informed, though, that his calendar is free for that period. Tonight, just make a good impression with the governor, but the deal is ours."

Kevin nodded. "Okay, let me go meet some people. Will see you at the party tonight." He downed the coffee in a gulp, grabbed his black-tie invite, and dished out a couple of fifty-thousand-shilling notes.

"Brunch is on me." He patted Bosco on the back and left.

* * *

Kevin glanced at his wristwatch again: 6:30 p.m. He needed to leave now. Kampala traffic was murder, especially leaving his home in Kisaasi. He was not sure he would be there by 7 p.m. After another quick appraisal of his clean look in a tux he had worn only once before at a gala dinner some months back, he picked up his invite, phone, and wallet and headed for the door.

"Doctor!" he called out to his gateman. "I'm going for an important meeting. If anyone comes to see me, tell them to come back on Monday. Also, double-check the security cameras. Turn them on."

"Yes, sir," the short sturdy man with quick footsteps replied as he sprinted to the gate before Kevin slid into his sleek, deep blue BMW.

As he drove out, he saluted Doctor, who beamed widely.

He resisted the urge to use a different route from his usual Kisaasi-Bukoto Road then through the Lugogo Bypass. The bypass was smooth sailing up until he got to Kololo Terrace, and traffic intensified for what seemed like a five-mile stretch. The fading daylight highlighted with hues of blue painted a breathtaking background to the increasing city lights and the streets. The scenery jolted a long-ago memory, a devastating memory, one that still haunted him, and he quickly shook it off. Tonight was not a night to revisit the ghosts of the past. However, even as he said it to himself, the ghosts of the past never left. They danced about his head like an invisible halo.

Kenzi.

He thought of her again and reached for his phone in the co-driver's seat, swiped the screen open, and clicked on the Facebook icon; his notifications were down to two—thanks to Carissa—and the latest was a reaction from Kenzi on her own picture. He clicked on it and smiled; she *did* look remarkable. So far there were more than a hundred thousand likes. She looked like a delicate ebony Barbie doll with sparkling blue-green eyes in a dress that was the embodiment of water ripples on a calm inky night. The reflection against her eyes and the glitter of diamonds spread on the material lent her an ethereal look. The caption of the picture read, *"Highlight of the spring collection: 'Outbacks' from the House of Luz* hashtag *second last night. Hashtag house of Luz* hashtag *spring,* hashtag *fashionweekMilan."*

He shook his head in wonder and pride. She had always been beautiful to him. Her large blue-green eyes brimmed of the innocence of a child and the stubborn determination of a woman. He was always proud of who she had become. That familiar stab of longing wedged itself in his heart. "I should have been there through it all," he whispered.

He glanced up and traffic was still not moving, so he switched out to his messaging section and texted her.

"You look like a goddess! Just saw your picture on Facebook. Will Luz let you keep the dress?"

Then he thought about it. Of course he had seen it on Facebook; it sounded dumb to repeat oneself, but before he could change it, someone hooted impatiently behind him, and he looked up in time to see traffic loosen up. He hit "send" hastily, and he was finally rolling along.

Victoria Gallery was crowded with about a hundred richly dressed guests in clusters of five or eight at high-top tables and chairs draped in the Nile Breweries gold and black theme colors. Ambient music he could identify as K'ofa—one of Kampala's well-known jazz musicians who played both a xylophone and bass guitar with such luster, it left one misty eyed—completed the tasteful atmosphere.

Kevin strode in easily, like he had always belonged to this crowd of the extravagant rich all his life. When he spoke with the governor or CEOs and billionaires in these settings, they deliberated with ease in banter littered with superficial grace and money. Always money. If it led to the money, they spoke about it. Politics was high on the list of money conversations and he learned the money talk early in life.

"Kevin!" a shrill voice called out to him. Immediately, an arm encircled his free arm and the person who called to him came into his view. A young woman with big breasts that threatened to tear through the low sweetheart neckline of her bright blue ruffle dress reached forward; her neck craned upward for a cheek-to-cheek greeting. He sighed but responded to the gesture.

"Hey, Vanessa." He lightened up like an actor on cue, oozing charm. "Long time no see. How have you been?" She leaned back, pleased; a wide smile touched her deep red lips.

"Oh, you know, nothing much. Missed me? I came with Daddy." She motioned with her head toward the elderly gentleman, who was shaking hands with other elderly, respectable gentlemen. Vanessa's father, Mr. Kakembo, was the co-owner of Kakembo and Joules law firm. He was every prominent person's lawyer, including every government bigshot. He was tall and lean with a shock of silver-gray hair on his head, and Kevin always wondered whether Mr. Kakembo's abundant hair was God given or was the product of some hair-growth supplement or cream. He was a fine-looking man, undefiled by age—if anything, he was enhanced by it, and, of course, money kept him looking as fresh and as pampered as a Hollywood star.

"How is the old fox doing?" he asked with a smile.

She rolled her eyes. "Fine. We just came back from Dubai. Can you imagine he cut our trip short for this meeting? We were guests of that tycoon, Majid Al Futtaim. God! He is allergic to fun, I tell you." She huffed slightly like a spoiled child, tightening her hold on his arm, making her full chest brush up against him. Kevin glanced at it. He lusted after her chest, but that was it.

"So how have you been?" She nudged him, her girlish charm restored, and strolled toward a waiter who stood still like a stone statue at the corner of the room, a tray laden with tall champagne glasses propped over his gloved hand. Reluctantly, he went along. "You don't pick up your calls anymore? I see you are now making your girlfriend your secretary." She picked up a flute of champagne and gingerly brought it to her lips. He watched her sip from it effortlessly. The action had no impact on her impeccably lined lips or the glass's rim.

"It's Carissa, how may I help you?" She mimicked Carissa's voice, batting her eyes comically and moving her neck from side to side as she spoke. "Urgh, where do you get such girls?"

Kevin laughed. "Jealous after all these years?" He deliberately withheld Carissa's identity just to watch her smooth caramel face almost darken with envy.

"Hmp!" She pursed her lips. "I am the best you ever had. Always have. Your loss."

"Ouch, you *did* come to spite me."

She smirked, a phantom of a smile playing on her lips, then she pressed closer to him and half-whispered, "We could go to Equator Bar after this boring meetup."

"Tempting, Van." He smiled, returning her charming, flirtatious poise. "But what shall we do about Carissa, hmm?"

She shrugged. "You were busy, like always."

He spied the yearning in her eyes. There was nothing stopping him from spending a night with her except sheer will. Their relationship had been off and on for several years. Most times, he fought the temptation, but when he needed release, she was on his speed dial. He knew she humored him, hoping one day it would be final. Kevin had thought about it often, but there was more that he wanted from a relationship than what he had with Vanessa; besides, settling down was the last thing on his mind now. Especially now. Vanessa loved him till now, but she was just too superficial for him.

"Van..." he started, carefully thinking up the words he would use to decline the offer, when a voice interrupted. "Ah my son-in-law is still looking as handsome as he always has, many years later."

Mr. Kakembo's voice boomed, causing Kevin to wheel around on his heels gratefully.

"How are you, sir?" He laughed the diplomatic laugh he had mastered over the years as he was groomed from one high-profile party to another. "Yes, Vanessa and I were just talking."

Mr. Kakembo's face, caramel-colored as his daughter's, sprinkled with a few black specks on the upper groove of his drooping cheeks, brightened. "Are we going to have a wedding finally?"

Kevin and Vanessa both laughed. "You never know, Daddy," Vanessa chimed in, looking from Kevin to her father expectantly.

Kevin furrowed his brow, suddenly feeling trapped. "It's been a minute, but we were thinking of catching up after this event."

The older man clapped him on the back. "Oh nice, nice. But before *you* young people slip away from us, Kevin, let's talk."

Kevin was glad to be relieved of Vanessa, and the two men walked away together. Several minutes later, the rest of Kevin's crew trickled in, and the ceremony started almost immediately with announcements and speeches. More cocktail hors d'oeuvres, wine, and champagne circled the hall, and dinner followed with light live band entertainment and the Ngozi dancing troupe. Nile Breweries made a splendid presentation of their next unveiling and profusely thanked the Bank of Uganda's governor for his efforts in working with them on this project.

Congratulatory speeches peppered the first half of the evening, and Kevin did his level best to avoid Vanessa's communicative eyes from across the room where she sat with her father.

Four hours later, the evening's corporate air fizzled as the live band did several covers of local artists' songs. Then, proper mingling began. Kevin and Bosco spent some time speaking with the governor and a few other key guests that Bosco pointed out were extremely important in the deal they had been planning for months now.

"So, the president will be away for a week, and when he returns, I have a meeting with him." The governor sat back in the chair, letting his spilling belly rest comfortably on his lap like a coddled, fat tabby cat.

"You are all such industrious young men. Surely this nation needs youthful men like you with a vision." He labored in his breathing. "But see the young people of today, all they care about is Facebook, Facebook, Facebook, and beer, huh!"

"There is a job creation problem, and our education system needs an overhaul. Besides, Uganda is one of the youngest countries in the world. That, in a nutshell, says a lot about our advantages and disadvantages," Kevin replied matter-of-factly. He was tired of hearing most of these rich people in privileged positions blame poverty on lazy youth. Bosco jabbed him with his elbow and *harrumphed*.

"That's why, this deal, governor, *this deal* could change the face of employment for these youth who are tomorrow's future. Don't you think so?" he added passionately, ignoring Bosco.

A slow smile spread across the governor's chubby face. "I like you, young man. You think just like me!" He let out a raucous laugh, then leaned in confidentially. "You see all these people blaming the government for their problems, hmm! And you, *you* are thinking of solutions!"

Kevin agreed sardonically: "I am sure we will help the Facebooking youth see that, Governor."

Kevin ignored the dirty look Bosco served him. The governor did not catch the sarcasm, full of himself and the fact that he had identified ambitious youthful men.

He looked at his watch and widened his eyes. "Oh dear. I need to be in Ibanda by nine o'clock tomorrow morning. But call me if you need anything, okay? So, give me two…three weeks, give the president three weeks, eh? You know, protocol…." He laughed unconvincingly like he needed to persuade them further.

Bosco jumped in: "It's okay, boss, we understand, and we thank you for taking time to meet with us often and even off your schedule."

"Where money can be made, I am there." The governor grinned, got up slowly, shook each of their hands, and left.

"Kevin, really?" Bosco shook his head.

"I don't like the man. I respect his shrewdness, but I don't like him. He does not get it, just like most of these people in the room. All they care about is themselves, not the helpless starving on the street or those with visions and dreams but no helping hand to realize that vision. I am all about creating as many job opportunities in Uganda because, if going by the Mo Ibrahim Index, Africa is the youngest continent in the world, we need to make great strides in harnessing that potential."

Kevin kept his gaze fixed on the retreating back of the governor as he continued: "When one has not spent chilly nights on the streets of Kampala fending for their lives and their space; when they have not faced the hardships that life thrusts upon people and are in position to help but don't, I don't exactly respect them or their shortsighted viewpoint.

That's all, Bosco." He returned his gaze levelly to his partner and friend. "You understand, don't you?" Bosco looked away uneasily for the briefest of moments.

"Of course I do. Life was difficult for you. You..." He shrugged. "This is the opportunity to help Facebooking youth," he replied lamely.

Kevin did not avert his gaze. As much as they had an almost ten-year gap of lost time, he was still glad that Bosco had picked up like they were eleven again. He only vaguely wrestled with the fact that he would never fully understand the struggle of unemployment, the streets, the reason for violence and survival instincts, or any of that. Still, they were good together, Bosco polished and diplomatic, adept at being deceptively nice with a barbed sting. And him? Well...he completed their art with relentless wit, hard-nosed ambition, and primal street smarts. Opportunities, however small, were meant to be taken. They had paired up and trained each other, eventually becoming sinuously identical in the craft of business. Their passion and ambition had placed them at the helm of wealth that young people in Uganda merely envisioned like a far-off mirage.

Kevin often thought of how Kenzi and he had made a formidable team while in the flats and on the streets under the Kampala streetlamps, dreaming of more and fighting for it. Their bond had come easily, and it felt right. She was always his strength. Bosco was loyal, but his piece of the puzzle of his life always fitted in tight. *Too* tight.

Kevin shrugged at that recurring thought. Maybe they would eventually move on with their lives, but for now, they were a force to be reckoned with.

He blinked the ghosts out of his eyes and nodded. "True. Two days is now bumped up to two weeks...gives us more time to prepare."

"Meeting the president is a gamble sometimes—uh-oh, here comes trouble," Bosco was motioning slightly with his head. Kevin looked over his shoulder in time to catch Vanessa hug him from behind.

"So, are we going?" She pressed up to him, giggling. The mounds on her chest deliberately made to brush up on him, sensually.

Bosco grinned, enjoying his friend's discomfort. "Where are you two off to?"

"Equator!" she piped in.

"It's not decided," Kevin protested.

"Aww come on, *mukwano*." She glided to his side and slid her arm into his.

"Take the woman out, Kev." Bosco grinned wickedly. "Don't forget to text me when you get home." He winked and walked away.

Kevin shook his head. "That's cold betrayal," he whispered under his breath.

"What?" Vanessa was asking.

"Nothing. How long do you want to stay out?" He turned his attention to her.

She rolled and batted her eyes, excited. "Errr, let's close the place down!"

Kevin shook his head, defeated. "Let's go. We only live once, right?"

Three hours later, Kevin was scrolling through his phone book, tempted to call Kenzi. He excused himself and walked out of the club for fresh air. He started to type a message but held back. She had promised to call when it was all over, and today was the last day of the fashion show. He absently went through her feed again and admired her slim curves in the silver and black see-through gown. *"Kenzi, face of Luz spring collection, adorns an exquisite delicate evening see-through gown draped in silver and black watery shimmer, the description of moon on water reflection. Highlight of the spring collection. Outbacks from the House of Luz hashtag aboutlastnight. Hashtag Kenzi, Hashtag houseofLuz hashtag springcollection."* Only posted three hours earlier and it was already at ten thousand likes and hundreds of comments. His chest swelled with pride, thinking of the little blind girl on Block 4. The woman she had become, soft yet strong, independent, fiercely passionate, and what Carissa called, *"An influencer!"*

His eyes glided to the time on the phone; it was almost three in the morning. He needed to sleep and get up in time to hear from Kenzi. As he turned to walk back in, a text lighted his screen. It was Bosco, teasing him about Vanessa. Was he taking her home tonight?

No, that ship is sort of docked. He was dropping her home in a few, and he would proceed to his bed, solo, at about 4 a.m.

Hmm, that's what you said a month ago. Be safe, Bosco wrote.

And Kevin had chuckled. *I am unsafe with this woman,* he jokingly replied, then set out to find Vanessa, so they could retire.

Three forty-five a.m. found him pulling up to his gate. He decided it would be quite sinful to wake Doctor up so late. His head throbbed faintly with the embers of the pounding music, noise and fatigue all coursing through him like an intoxicatingly potent cocktail.

Kevin pulled himself out of the car with effort. He groaned, feeling the ache in his legs as he swung them out of the car. He dragged himself to the gate, jingling the bunch of keys, sifting through the many sets for the gate key.

Then everything happened quickly: At the corner of his sleepy eyes he saw a *boda boda* swiftly approach him. His instincts told him something was wrong, and he immediately rushed back to his car to slam the horn as hard as he could. But one of the men had gotten to the car before him. With one powerful blow, he swung something metallic and heavy into the side window, shattering the glass. Kevin shielded his face with an arm to prevent the sharp shards from entering his eyes.

Another blow followed.

And another, blowing the frame out of the window space.

The door was yanked open, and he was bodily dragged out. He regained his composure and charged at the first man, who had smashed the window, catching his jaw and winced in pain as the cold, heavy bar came down hard against his rib cage. Kevin buckled slightly, swung round, catching the assailant with the bar in midair. He kicked hard into his groin, grabbing the bar simultaneously.

The first man kicked his knees in from behind, and he fell to his face. Kevin rolled over and used his legs and the bar to fight off the advancing man. It did not take long for the second man to recover, and, with a growl, he threw himself at Kevin as he scrambled to his feet, knocking him back down. The first man lunged for the bar. Kevin was not going to let anyone keep him down. He shoved the burly man, who clamped onto him like a leech and reached for Kevin's neck, digging into the hollow below his Adam's apple. Adrenaline spiked through his body, and with a powerful, swift move, Kevin used his free hand to poke into his assailant's eyes. The man yelped, his grip loosening. Then Kevin was rolling him over and taking a vantage point. That was when he felt the bar heavily connect with his head and knock him over.

Kevin saw the light bulb of the world around him dim…Kenzi swam into focus. In the silver and black dress, she smiled and mouthed "Goodnight."

Then she laughed and choked like an animal in pain…and said, "It's done," but the voice was not hers, it was a deep masculine voice with a thick western accent. The dim light faded altogether, even as he struggled against the pain that raged like a wildfire all over his body. He badly wanted to stay awake, but his senses ran into a darkness that frightened him…he tried to focus on Kenzi's smiling face, but it shifted and changed into a dark shadowy figure towering over him accompanied by the faint gasps and curses of what sounded like the hushed moans of a wounded animal.

His body begged for rest…just a little nap…only a little nap, and he finally yielded to the urge.

Chapter 2

Milan, Italy
Fashion Week Spring/Summer Collection
September 2016

Lights, flashing...

Dwele's voice, sexy and ethereal, crooned over the stomping beat of Kanye West's "Flashing Lights." It was a hypnotic loop of the bridge of the song that eased the models onto the glassy shimmery runway. They seemed to float as if suspended by unseen hands as they filed in and out with lithe elegance, showcasing Luzkit's latest collection labeled "Outback," a sensual after-hours couture, a blend of sheer eclectic material barely covering the slim figures of the twelve models. In an interview with the press, when asked why only twelve models and the Outback label, Luzkit had related it to his Catholic upbringing, his reverence for the disciples and their dedication to Jesus.

"Twelve is magical," the petite Latvian designer exclaimed with flair. "And the disciples always met with their leader after hours. Also, I am opening at the end of Lent. That is very key. I dedicate this to my mother who taught me how to pray." Luzkit kissed the diamond-studded crucifix that clung to his neck on a pure white-gold chain and cast his gaze heavenward briefly.

536

Kenzi suppressed her smile at the dramatic display that always accompanied Luzkit. She was sure he got his inspiration wrong. Her Christian upbringing forbade her from extravagantly using biblical imagery in any setting but church. However, it was his collection, not hers, and she was the face of *Luz Spring*.

"*That* was nice, heh?" Luzkit whispered excitedly to Kenzi when they were back in the dressing room, which was secured especially for her.

Kenzi raised her eyebrows, her blue-green eyes sparkling mischievously. "Jesus and the disciples met after hours?"

"But yes!" Luzkit grinned, revealing an all gold-capped upper dental and waved a slim arm dismissively. "No one reads the Bible anymore. They will eat it up, anyway. But what did you think of tonight?" he asked in rapt impatience.

Kenzi got up and took his hands in hers, urging him close for a hug. "Closing night is always great! *So* many fabulous designers and models!"

"I saw Chicca Lualdi eyeing you. And *why* were you speaking to Francesco the other evening at the patio? Don't get scooped away from me!" Luz pulled back and wagged a delicate bejeweled finger in her face.

Kenzi kissed his cheek, charming him, and smiled. "You mean Scognamiglio, every celebrity's dream designer? Aww, come on now! *They* approached *me*."

"Everyone approaches you." He pouted like a privileged, spoiled child. "Why can't you be only mine?"

Her laughter rose from the depth of her soul. "Ask the agency. You have had me twice now, though." Then she added warmly, "Thank you for the opportunity, Luz. This was phenomenal."

"Ah! You speak such big words! But I think it means it was good, yes?" He hugged her back, "You are phe…that word too!"

Kenzi was beaming. Luzkit was comfortable with not being able to harness English to its fullest, and that endeared her to him. He often commented on how limited it was compared to Latvian.

"So, tomorrow afternoon, *Mogul* magazine will do the shoot. You are ready, yes?"

Kenzi nodded. "You don't have to ask me twice."

He harrumphed. "You sexy sexy models are divas! Today you say 'yes', tomorrow, 'no'. Today 'I am too drunk,' tomorrow, 'I am on my period,' *ak man's dievs!*"

Kenzi grinned. "You are still hung up on Sophia for refusing your proposal. When will I hear the last of it?"

Luzkit shrugged. "Maybe after Christmas. So will you stay a little in Milan? After the shoot? I have lunch with Curly. She wants to bitch about Armani!"

"Ooh the new designer Clarencia Sanchez? You are on a nickname basis now?" Kenzi winked at him. "And you will indulge her?"

He swept his bejeweled slim fingers in the air as if conjuring a spell. "Why not? Misery is good company, no?"

She chuckled—Giorgio Armani's collection was being considered as the best for this season—shaking her head as she removed the pins that held her dark hair with chestnut highlights straightened out and coiffed. She shook it loose, and the thick mane tumbled softly to her back in rivulets.

Luzkit stared at her through the mirror, struck again by her beauty. The first time her agency sent him her pictures, he *knew* she had to be the face of his collection. Kenzi was perfection to him; semi-aquiline features on a black person were a rarity. Her incredibly dark skin—jet dark, in fact—and her eyes. *Her eyes!* Rare aquamarine irises. She was as rare and expensive as the Shenzhen Nongke orchid he traveled to China to bid upon for his high-maintenance ex-wife in 2005. She left him when an anonymous bidder outwitted him for a shocking 1.68 million yuan, almost a quarter of a million dollars. The agricultural research corporation told him he would have to wait another four to five years for another orchid.

"So, off to America again, eh? Ah, extend your stay for another few days, *dargais.*" He tried persuasion. "I am here for two more days, and I can take you on a tour of La Città Dei Mille? This is a most charming Italian town, old buildings, super architecture. We go to the Alta for the

Piazza Vecchia, shopping! Yes! Shopping on Via XX Settembre and eat ice cream at Caffé del Tasso, best *gelateria* in Bergamo? Let's do touristy things in that beautiful town. When in Rome, act like Roman."

Kenzi laughed and motioned to him to help her unzip the light see-through silver and black diamond-studded gown she had sashayed in for the last part of Outback.

"Tempting Luz, really is…" She prepared to respond when a knock on the door interrupted her, and, gratefully, she called to them to come in.

Luz handed her a satin green-blue gown that matched her eyes before heading to the door. It was Kenzi's assistant, Sketch Young, a brawny six-foot-four African American who was both her personal assistant and bodyguard. He held up his black iPhone 7, a slim ensemble, a concerned expression on his face. "This is for you. I believe it's important."

"Who?" Kenzi felt her heart lurch. The elusive feeling of a premonition she had experienced hanging over her slowly seemed to take shape and settle somewhere between her breast and stomach.

Sketch sighed. "It's about *your* friend."

Kenzi grabbed the phone from him and breathed a shaky "hello" into the mouthpiece.

"Kenzi!" She recognized the voice: Bosco.

"What? What's going on?" she asked urgently.

Bosco sighed. "It's Kevin, he…er…got attacked…er…by iron-bar-wielding men on his way home."

"Where is he? Is he okay?" she interrupted, almost harshly. Something dropped in the pit of her tummy, yanking painfully at her heart on its way down. She had to sit down from the force of it, her chest heaving visibly. The large dressing room closed in, and the vulgar diamond choker around her slim neck became a disturbingly tight noose digging into skin. She absently yanked it off and heard Luz exclaim in dismay in the background.

"He is in intensive care…"

"I am coming to Uganda now. I—I will get on the next flight…J—Just stay with him till I come," she stammered. Her lips felt thicker than usual.

"No need for that, Kenzi. We are flying him to Aga Khan Hospital in Nairobi tonight. Don't worry, I got this. I am making sure he gets the best care."

"I know. Thanks. But I shall still come." She hurriedly spoke and handed the phone to Sketch.

Her eyes glistened and misted. Her face felt hot. "Sketch, I need you to arrange a flight to Uganda…er…Kenya."

Luz cleared his throat from behind her. *"Dargais,* we still have the most important shoot tomorrow. *Ludzu,* please."

"Kevin is in trouble!" Her chest heaved; her voice trembled. She stood up to pace.

Sketch had her sit down, while Luz paced and flailed his arms, muttering in Latvian.

"Luz! It's all right. Let's be cool," Sketch responded firmly. Then to Kenzi, "Hey, I know, and I am sorry I had to let you know before your shoot tomorrow, but I can assure you I have that all worked out. You are on contract, and it's important to hold up your part of it.…" He paused and glanced at Luz. "Besides, Luz is an old client and, most importantly, a friend. Tomorrow's shoot is important not only for Luz but for the agency and your profile. Unfortunately, considering the schedule, I cannot push the shoot, but you can take off two weeks. I will work with the travel agency to ensure you are catered for while away." He paused. "Are you considering going to Uganda too? "

He rubbed her arms reassuringly.

Kenzi steadied her trembling hands. Her mind had erupted into a million pieces of dark thoughts. Luz brought her a bottle of spring water from the mini fridge in the dressing room, and the two men waited as she sat there, a rigid ebony statue of magnificence, staring into space.

"Kenzi?" Luz bent over, trying to get her attention, then looked at Sketch, confused.

Sketch sighed and tapped the little man on the shoulder. "Let's leave her alone for a minute. She needs it." He walked out of the room with Luz reluctantly at his heel.

They stood outside, Luz pacing and muttering in Latvian. "She must go through with the shoot, Sketch. Oh my God! Oh, Mary, Joseph, and the disciples! Social media is already going crazy with her. Did you see? A minute after the posting of her in *my* gorgeous gown…oh my God, we have over ten thousand likes!"

Sketch smirked. He thought Luz a little over the top, what the millennials termed "extra" and superficial, but Kenzi liked him and had worked for him twice so far, giving him a lead in his seasonal couture collections for two springs. They were still negotiating about her being the face of Luz since higher bidders like Lancôme, Paris, Vogue, Collezioni, and Madame were offering more. After her six-month stint with Lancôme earlier in the year, Kenzi's career was promising bigger returns than he had ever seen in the career of a model. It was as if she was built for the industry and it had waited for her unveiling with open arms.

Somewhere, *Dwele* cooed beneath the noise and chatter of guests as the evening ended.

"She will do the shoot," Sketch assured Luz blandly. He had been Kenzi's personal assistant, bodyguard, and confidant for six years; he knew her even better than all the boyfriends and designers she had interacted with. When the agency told him he would be her assistant and would have to perform additional duties as required, he had not expected to fly as often and get drawn into her intricate world that even the magazines had not accessed to this point.

"Be as discreet as you can be. We like to keep the agency scandal free," he was told during the hiring interview.

"That won't be a problem," he assured them. And he had proven himself over and over, both with the agency and with Kenzi.

Five minutes later, Kenzi emerged with a pinched smile that did not reach her eyes. "Luz, we have a shoot. Don't worry."

Luz sighed with relief and clasped his hands over his chest. "*Paldies*! I am sorry, too, for your friend."

She turned to Sketch. "But I leave immediately for Kenya. Arrange that, please."

"You got it, babe." Sketch was on his mini laptop, his hands flying on the keyboard at expert speed.

"I can't find my phone; can I use your phone again?" she asked. He handed her his phone.

As she turned to the dressing room, she looked back at Sketch, "Maybe it's time for me to make peace with the past....Put Uganda on the itinerary."

She closed the door behind her and redialed Bosco.

Chapter 3

December 2012

"I will come to you," Kevin had promised and barely had any time gone by from then when he came to see her for the first time in the spring of 2012 in New York.

Meeting him again, she was learning things about him. He was different. *Patient* was the elusive word, *hardened* too and yet the charm and humor he possessed always smoothed over his aggressiveness. Nevertheless, his struggle was not lost on her, the painful demons of the past, his insatiable need to be in control that often made her roll her eyes, badgering him to chill out, and then he would be disarming when he loosened up, partying all night three days in a row, fully immersing himself in the moment so decadently, she marveled at the switch. *We only live once,* he often said.

She was searching for the necklace he had given her when he first saw her. It was the closest thing to being near him, especially now. She absently flipped open the pendant. The oval center had their image perfectly embedded in the hollowed-out frame and on the opposite side the inscription "*K&K forever.*"

"Someone would think you are my boyfriend," she teased, with glowing appreciation in her eyes.

"I would probably be the best you ever had," he responded, winking.

"You wish!" She rolled her eyes at his arrogance.

After his spring visit in 2012, Kevin returned for her birthday when she pleaded with him. "I won't spend another birthday without you," she told him.

They dined at a restaurant in Arlington three days before Christmas, meeting up at a little bar in Dupont Circle for happy hour.

"How in the world does anyone get around New York and DC without getting lost?" He had related to her his exasperating trips as he tried to get to their rendezvous spots on multiple occasions. That afternoon when they met in DC, he told her if it wasn't for the directions of a kindly older man, he would not have known how to look out for P Street. "Make a left and Crammers will be right there. Take the stairs to the basement, little cute place. Oh, all the drafts are two dollars till 7 p.m." He winked

"I bet he asked you where you were from." Kenzi grinned into her second glass of wine. He nodded. "How do you know?"

She shook her head. "You look fresh-faced."

"Hi! Welcome to Crammers, what can I get you?" The cheery waitress behind the counter beamed, her blond hair held in a bun, her lips a bright pink, and her round face younger-looking than she probably was.

She recalled him hesitate and instantly intervened, piping up from behind him as she slid into view beside him.

"A coke with ice for the gentleman and a frozen margarita for me." His expression morphed pleasantly before her; the slight agitation melted into a smile.

"Let's hang out here. We have dinner somewhere else," she told him and without warning hugged him. "Oh my goodness, you are here! I keep thinking it's a dream…that we were in New York months ago and now here…"

He had chuckled, hugging her back tightly. "Right…. I figured we would run into each other when we were eighty! It's good to see you again, a lot sooner than eighty."

She reluctantly let go but held his hand as she mounted her stool and did not let go. They were speaking almost at the same time, sometimes catching what they were saying, sometimes not. Words seeped into the noise and music and disappeared but left her with a feeling of warmth and belonging. Time stopped. The noise started to fade, and the distance between them gradually closed.

The drinks came just as she was appraising him. "Look at you!" She laughed. "Did you get taller?"

He was smiling, that Kevin naughty smile, when he leaned against the bar, his trim body angled to her. "Probably!" he shouted above the music, picked up his glass, and she picked up hers too, and they toasted: "To us!" they shouted in unison.

Words were the most basic form of communication between them, Kenzi decided, because in their silences, they spoke volumes, and it was the same that day as they lapsed into a couple of minutes of silence, sipping their drinks and savoring each other's presence. When they talked, they spoke simultaneously, then sniggered and started the "You go first" game.

They had dinner later at an Italian restaurant in Arlington.

Stuck in the never-ending traffic of I-66 at that hour, she nudged him. "What's on your mind?"

"Almost too much. I feel like New York wasn't enough time." He scratched his headful of short hair. "I am here and..." He shook his head.

Kenzi grinned. "Okay then, we can do touristy things in DC and catch up with New York when you are here again."

"I will come back...on one condition.... I meet with your parents."

"Why?"

"They *are* your parents," he stressed somberly. She squirmed when he got matter-of-fact with her, chiding her like she was eight years old again, unveiling how spoiled she was, how privileged.

"I can't forgive them." She could hear her high-pitched, indignant tone, deliberate with Kevin the first time they met in the spring of 2012. They were seated at the rooftop lounge of her luxury apartment in Soho.

"Without them you would not be here." He was plain and rational.

"They did what they did. You can't keep holding it over their heads forever...."

She flared up in anger. "I did not ask them to adopt me! I was perfectly happy running the streets with you." Maybe Kevin did not understand what her loyalty to him meant. What being without him through the years had been like.

He looked at her with those overly wise eyes and shook his head. "How about your *mother*?"

"What about her?"

"Who are you more willing to forgive?"

Kenzi folded her arms over her chest and, after a long silence, shrugged. "I don't know. I do not care. You are here now, and that's all that I need."

"Look, Kenzi, these people did not sell you, abuse you, or keep you hungry for days. They may have had their reasons. I'm over it now. You should think about who you are because of them." He was blunt.

Then he had told her again, that statement that roused feelings of guilt: *Kenzi, you have had it good. Trust me.*

She had guffawed stubbornly. *I lived a lie, Kevin; don't mansplain it.*

Another one of those American words? He pacified her.

He brushed her protests aside about the tension in their relationship. "I would like to see them again," he insisted, and Kenzi had to relent.

He had told her he was proud of her and could not wait for her to meet Ssaka. She could not wait to meet him either. From the stories Kevin had told of him, his influence over Kevin was obvious, not just the financial aspect but the personality aspect. He had polished the emboldened edges around him, drawn out the classic man from within. She anticipated that day.

"Surely meeting your latest boyfriend for approval would be in order too, no?" He had tossed her a mischievous grin. "Or are we still 'spring cleaning' from the last one." He thought her notions of 'pause and breathe' were things out of *Iyanla, Fix My Life* episodes.

"Life is too fast for me to do that, go for yoga and breathing classes to detox or cry into someone's shoulder, then light candles to commemorate…. Jeez, Kenzi, who comes up with these things?"

Kenzi had delighted in his indignant expression. "This is America."

"It sure is." He had shaken his head, then shifted so he was looking straight into her eyes.

"Top-tier model, huh?" It was *how* he had regarded her, that look of pride that soaked her soul with warmth.

"Uh-huh! Who would have thought? *This?* This is my best year so far! We linked up, doors for bigger earnings just opened up, back-to-back assignments, moving to a fly part of town…" she had prattled enthusiastically .

He had cut in, "I saw those photos from the Algeria and France stint." He had nodded in approval and patted her hand. "I think it's in order for me to ask you to pay for my ticket back home."

He grinned, and she played along. "Sure, first class? I don't see you fly less." She beamed at him.

"How about a private jet?"

"Really? I am sure you can manage that all by yourself."

At the restaurant they had deliberated on everything, repeating some stories she could not get enough of, like how *barito* became a famous name for the chapatti wrap with different fillings.

"That name really took off." She had laughed in disbelief as if it was the first time she was hearing this story. "Oh my gosh you are a trendsetter, always been. From day one."

"It was a spin off from burrito, Ugandan style." Kevin smiled proudly. You *know me. Always setting trends.*

They had talked about sights and sounds, haunts of their street days, from Wandegeya to the clock tower to Jinja and Entebbe resort beach.

Kenzi had grinned. "How can I forget the names of places, the smells of pancakes, chips, and liver…" She had floated into fond reverie, her hands clasped firmly in Kevin's as he guided her through the chaos that was Wandegeya, constantly grabbing her out of the way of danger she could not see.

He agreed, *"Fun times, no?"*

She had nodded.

"And I make the best Rolexes and baritos south of anywhere."

She could attest to that when he did so as a birthday surprise. She had spent the day with him at his rented luxury apartment, a mile away from her parents' home in Bethesda, and they had indulged in the dough-wrapped dishes, just the two of them.

While they ate, she had pressed for his stories with Ssaka, places he had been to, the people he had met, and the group that was considered the rich crew.

"Last time it was Bosco, Steve, and Bhanu; now there is Tisa, Abe, and who else?" she had asked.

"That's all. Hey, I told you all that already," he had protested. "My partners and I are taking over the world, one successful step at a time. You will see," he had told Kenzi as she lounged on his couch bloated with copious *barito* choices.

She had believed him.

Chapter 4

September 2016
Milan, Italy

Kenzi shook her head, her eyes glued to the blue ticks in her WhatsApp. She was waiting for Bosco to respond to her inquiries.

How is he doing?

Is he awake?

How bad is it?

She gave up waiting when several minutes passed by and still no response.

"We have about four hours to kill, Kenz," Sketch reminded her. They had left the hotel early because of her anxiety about getting on the plane for Kenya.

"I know, I will feel better being at the airport."

"Don't forget you have to call your sister."

Kenzi sighed. "Right." She had promised to be home for the family traditional get-together that was happening in two days. But with the latest news, she grimaced at having to break her promise. She dialed Heather.

The phone was almost immediately picked up. "Hey, little famous sis? I saw you on the fashion network last night, killing it! How is it going? Are you heading back?"

Kenzi smiled, "Hey, you, fine thank you! I am exhausted, but I can walk. How is it going?"

Heather sighed. "Same old, same old. Making sure humans have healthy pets, shutting down in a few. What time is it over there?"

Kenzi hummed in the affirmative. She could hear the faint bark of dogs in the background.

"It's about nine-ish. My flight is a little after midnight." She paused, bit her lower lip. "But I am not coming home…."

Kenzi waited.

"Why? I thought we were trying to work *this* out, you know." Heather groaned.

"I can't right now; it's…really not about all that. It's Kevin. He was hurt. Badly. I am going to Kenya to see him."

"Oh, Kevin? What happened?" Heather was attentive, and Kenzi could almost see her poised over a sink removing her gloves, phone caught between neck and shoulder, her wavy light brown hair falling over her wide, generous, and cheery face.

Kenzi related to her what Bosco had told her: "They found him beaten almost to death. Bosco drove over when Kevin did not pick up his phone. Yeah…they took him to a clinic, but there was not much they could do for him, so they transferred him to the ICU in Aga Khan Hospital in Kenya. He could have a concussion and internal bleeding…he is in a coma." Her voice trembled, and she had to breathe in deeply to steady herself.

"I am so sorry, Kenzi. You know what? I will tell Mom and Dad you could not make it. Do you know how long you will be away?"

"The agency has let me off for two weeks. Maybe you can try teaching me how to feed those dogs again when I return?" She steered the conversation away from Kevin to avoid the overthinking spiral she had fought earlier.

Heather chuckled. "You best come with short clean nails without nail polish."

"Aye-aye captain."

"Kevin is lucky to have you care for him. How are you holding up, though?"

Kenzi exhaled slowly. "Meh. Still shell-shocked. Really, it has not sunk in yet."

Heather sympathized, then added, "We will miss you…again. Brent would have been super glad to see you…his homecoming. He is finally getting engaged!"

Kenzi whooped. "Yes! I knew that little bugger would give in, eventually. Kat got his tongue, huh?"

"You bet. The Kat bit hard! The first family wedding…yes! At least make the wedding. Oh gosh, I can't get over it."

"Do we have a date already?" Kenzi asked, trying to push Kevin out of her mind.

Heather scoffed. "You know me, putting the cart before the horse, but he says first months of the New Year. Talk about rushing 2017 in nuptials."

They laughed and deliberated on the goings-on in their lives. Heather was planning to enroll in college for her master's degree in vet school finally and seriously planning out her own vet practice. She had received acceptance from one of the best vet schools in Ohio, but she was waiting to hear from her number-one-choice school, University of Pennsylvania.

"I don't know if I can be so far from home, Kenz." She was giving her reason for not being able to choose anywhere over two hundred miles from Washington, DC.

"It's okay, I understand. You never flew out of the nest like Brent and me."

"Yeah, you two just up and went."

Kenzi agreed. "I guess Thanksgiving will find me coming home."

Heather whooped in excitement. "Well, that will be something! After how long?"

Kenzi hummed. "Three years, I guess. I was home for Christmas when Kevin first came, remember?"

"Feels longer. Geez! If it weren't that you'd been gracing several magazine covers and popping up on just about every hair and clothes commercial, I would think you dropped off the face of the earth."

"I know…Kayla, Malaika, and the guys haven't seen me since that Christmas too. I miss the crew. It just gets so busy too."

"Oh yeah, Xavier has baby number two on the way, you know?"

Kenzi grinned. "Yes, I saw the pictures…"

"That could have been you but…"

"…I chose to be an international model!" they said in unison and laughed.

Even as they casually teased and caught up on the details of each other's lives that they had missed out on in the last several months, Kenzi felt that the reasons for her leaving home always hung over them like an uncomfortable damp draft. It was not something they talked about anymore. It was as if everyone was waiting for the balloon to pop on its own. Her parents sent her postcards, gifts, and tons of messages.

At first, she ignored them, but after she and Kevin spoke about it, she gradually brought herself to respond occasionally, short and abrupt messages, still holding it over their heads for keeping secrets and lying to her.

She said her goodbyes to Heather and immediately texted Brent via WhatsApp.

Congs, Scout! Who woudda thunk it? She added a ring and wink emoji to the message, then hit send.

She eased back against the comfortable leather seats of the Benz and inhaled deeply the cool, fresh cinnamon air-conditioned scent. The phone in her lap vibrated, and she flipped it over to its face.

It was a message from Brent: *Chippy! LMAO, famous little sister. Make a note of the 'little.' We will continue this conversation when I see you! Heather told you, yeah? You coming home for family week?*

Kenzi smiled at the Chippy reference. She could almost see him, hunched over his phone, typing in rapt concentration, his dark wavy hair falling into his narrow, attractive face.

What! You miss me? She grinned as she hit send, and he replied instantly.

You missed me more; see who texted first, he replied with a purple grinning devil emoji.

You did not answer the question. Typical! How did you snag a woman when you can't answer questions? She was giggling.

His name lit up her screen and his WhatsApp profile, a dark-haired, lean-faced man toasting a glass of whiskey, a wicked glint in his eyes and roguish ghost of a smile playing on his lips, filled her phone screen. Kenzi waited a few rings before hitting the "yes" button.

"I must have hit a raw nerve." She laughed into the mouthpiece.

"You have gotten good since last year. Only a little." He was always so upbeat and she welcomed it. *God,* she needed it. "How is it going?"

"Okay, just leaving Milan."

"Oh yes, I saw the pictures, and you looked *gurrreat* in that sea-green dress, and oh! The black netty mesh one. Damn, can that designer dress my fiancée?"

"Can you afford him?"

"You are my bargaining chip, *Chip.*"

"I charge by the hour, so, brother dearest, it will cost you."

"Now is that any way to treat a brother that beat up bullies for you, saved your apple pie from Heather's grabby hands…?"

"Wait, wait…bullies? I remember beating them up myself…except for one…."

"That was after I taught you a few tai-chi moves."

"You *or* Mr. Ling."

"My memory is foggy, but it must have been me."

Kenzi shook her head. "I sure missed you, Scout!"

"*Booyah!* There we go…answer to your previous question."

"Ugh!"

"I knew it would eventually come out, *little* sis."

"Take that win for now, but we are not finished."

"When are we ever?" He was chuckling. "So, Italy?"

"Not enough time to explore. Fiancée?"

"Not enough time to explore either." They both laughed.

"Will you be coming home, then?" he asked haltingly, like he already knew the answer.

Kenzi hummed in response. "Er…no, I am headed to Kenya."

"Another shoot?" he asked. "I used to know all this stuff until Sketch just took over…."

"I fired you, remember? No, it's Kevin. He got into an accident."

"Oh shit! What happened?"

Kenzi filled him in.

"That's fucked up!" He breathed when she finished. "Did they find who did it?"

"I don't know. I haven't even asked Bosco all that, but when I get to Kenya, I hope to know more…"

Brent replied, "Wow, sorry, Chip."

"No, I am sorry I won't be there to send you off." She beamed through the phone.

She heard him sigh on the other end. "I would not be able to stand it!"

"Oh yeah? I shall be back to hound you. Watch!"

When Kenzi hung up, that aching throb in her chest mounted and grew. Her eyes welled up with tears, and when she looked up in the rear-view mirror, Sketch caught her eye, and she smiled. "Hey, remember the first time Kevin came to the US?"

Sketch nodded, smiling faintly. "Can't forget it, can I, your excitement; you stayed up late…. You did not even let me take you to the airport."

Kenzi blinked back the tears rapidly. "I couldn't bother you so early in the morning. Every time I get to JFK, I think of that morning."

Memories rolled out in overlapping waves— between Kevin and her parents— and she hugged them close. They kept her company when New York threatened to swallow her up.

There were broken promises, and some even delayed. Kenzi wiped a stray tear quickly and swiped open her phone screen. The picture of her young self seated between Richard and Maxine had graced her screen wallpaper for the last few months. It interchanged between her and Kevin, a memory snapshot he had held on to from when she was eight and him, eleven.

She held on to that picture dearly because Kevin had held on to it too and presented it to her in its original wrinkled form delicately embedded in a locket with a chain she barely ever took off from around her neck.

The memory of a voice—raspy, husky, and impatient—floated into the peripheral focus of her mind, with it a laughter that rang out distinct and clear. It refused to remain silent this time.

"Are we almost there?" she asked Sketch again, trying to downplay her impatience.

Sketch smiled from the corner of his mouth. "Just arrived."

"Oh good," she mouthed, relieved, glad for a moment of distraction from the past, but the three-hour wait ahead would taunt her, she thought helplessly.

When Sketch had gotten her luggage through customs at Malpensa airport, he double-checked her flight and hotel bookings as well as everything she would need while in East Africa.

"If anything changes, I will be emailing you, keeping you up to date."

Kenzi nodded and hugged him. "Thanks, Sketch, you are always the best," she told him, a slight pout on her lightly glossed lips.

He chuckled, hugging her back. "I got you, babe. You know I always got you."

"I know."

"Kevin will be fine." The strength in his words lent assurance, and she nodded.

"Now, I will go to the VIP lounge and wallow in suicidal thoughts," she added with an edge of melodrama.

His eyes narrowed. "We are not doing that."

"I was kidding. Have a safe flight home. See you in two."

"You bet." He smiled fondly, watching her leave with her plum-colored Lipault carry-on trailing behind her.

Kenzi made her way to the first terminal to Montale lounge. She loved its spacious, airy seating. She strode into the silent room and threw her emotional exhaustion onto the beige chaise lounge. Her wristwatch said 7:30 p.m., and her flight would be at 12:30 a.m. Lights, like raindrops, bounced and danced on the vast glass windows, enhancing her already magnificent view of the Monte Rosa. Something about it held a strange significance for her, the peeling away of old things and the rebirth of new life.

She settled down and soaked in the classical elevator music that bathed the lounge with instrumental charm, tugging her through a labyrinth of time and memory. Since her first flight experience, flying had become a part of her lifestyle. She toyed with the gold teardrop-shaped pendant on her neck attached to a slim white-gold chain. The picture of her young self—slightly faded now with wear and tear—alongside Kevin stirred memories that never putrefied, of a time when they knew for sure nothing would keep them apart…not even a coma of a Monte Rosa magnitude. She could see his face, daring and roguishly attractive, laughing at her. "We can't just die now, not until we conquer the world, Kenz!" She could still feel his energy, his exuberance and burst of life and oh! *How* she had admired him then. Loved him for it and still did.

Looking out into the distance past the tarmac and hangar, the icy caped peak stood elevated against the sunset. Kenzi bathed in its beauty. The Monte Rosa was truly magnificent, she thought, a force of nature that no matter how still it lay exerted its conspicuous relevance. *Like Kevin…*she thought. Her mind traveled unhinged, unraveling memories. Time felt so short, as if Kevin had just returned to her life. Only yesterday he had responded to her Facebook message.

Thinking of him lying in a hospital bed somewhere seemed most unnatural, like a big joke. Something had gone wrong in the script of his life, but it would not stay wrong. She did not know why she believed he would be all right despite her anxiety. She just knew he would be.

The sun had sunk over the Monte Rosa leaving shadows in its wake, and Kenzi glanced at the clock; it was after eight. She got up and went to the bar; a drink would help perhaps, accompany her on her phantom journey.

She stared out the window to the white snowcapped mountains, gently swirling the margarita in her glass. Kevin would wake up. He *just* had to….

It was an hour to boarding time when Kenzi finally turned away from the window. She placed the empty margarita glass on the side table by the chaise lounge. Like a woman who had communed with ghosts of the past, made peace with memories, and gathered courage to face an impending uncertainty, she shouldered her designer tote bag, clasped her carry-on, and strolled out of the lounge.

Chapter 5

Nairobi, Kenya
September 2016

Kenya was nothing close to anything she had imagined, Kenzi observed as she emerged, making her way down the escalator from the plane to a waiting car and chauffeur that flagged first-class passengers to the VIP lounge as they waited for clearance. Her tall, dark chauffeur smiled and nodded stiffly.

"Miss Matthews? I shall be at your service tonight. *Karibu!*" he told her and promptly took her hand luggage.

"Thank you." She smiled.

It was 9:15 p.m. Sunday evening, and the fairly lit airport droned with sounds of busyness and people. The giant propellers on the other planes mounted majestically adorning the Kenyan flag colors—black, red, green, and white—offered her a sense of belonging. It was not Uganda but close. Very close. With her head pressed to the glass of the car, she stared out as the other passengers on the plane she was on alighted in a line…. It was a quick drop-off, where her chauffeur led her to the VIP lounge. "If you need anything, please feel free. Someone shall attend to you." He bowed briefly and left her in the spacious air-conditioned lounge.

She did not have to wait long. Her passport and baggage tickets were brought to her, and she was free to leave at any time. Kenzi messaged Bosco on WhatsApp to let him know she was at the Swiss Aspire Lounge.

Her phone vibrated, and a message popped up on her WhatsApp.

Bosco was two minutes out. Kenzi got her single checked luggage and hand luggage together. Declining help, she proceeded to the exit, out the double doors, and took in a gulp of warm air like she had been suffocating. It was not hard to spot Bosco. He had a manila paper above his head with her name splashed on it in a bold black marker *"Karibu Kenzi!"*

She grinned in spite of herself, dragging her roller travel case, and, adjusting the bag on her shoulder and jacket, she quickly made her way to the chunky man with a shiny bald head.

"Karibu bwana, Kenzi," he mouthed politely. Kenzi hugged him.

"Asante! Good to see you, Bosco!" Her eyes welled up with tears, which she blinked back hastily. "How has it been?"

Bosco sighed. "Pushing on. He is steady but still unconscious. The doctor says there is hope he will recover consciousness."

Kenzi took in a deep sharp breath. "He will be okay. I am here now," she replied, quelling the anxiety that knotted her insides.

Bosco patted her arm. "We are praying for the best too." He reached out to take her bag. "Let me help you with that. The car is over there in the parking, and you might need to be weightless. You look like you could use some sleep."

Kenzi agreed, "It's been a long trip, but…. Can I still see Kevin tonight?"

Bosco bundled her coat and bag together with swift ease. "No." He shook his head. "Visiting hours are done. We can see him as early as nine tomorrow morning." After a quick appraisal, he decided it was too early. "Maybe ten? Or even a little later? Jet lag can be a pain."

"Nine is fine. I shall be up early."

"Are you sure?"

"Positive," Kenzi replied. On the drive to the Villa Rosa Kempinski, where Sketch had booked her stay, Kenzi asked Bosco to relate to her again what had happened and what leads they had on the case.

Bosco shook his head. "No leads, but we might have a suspect."

"Who?" she asked, suddenly more awake than before.

"We are led to believe Kevin's bodyguard and gateman, Doctor, might have had something to do with this. Unfortunately, he is nowhere to be seen. The police are mounting a search as we speak, and they shall notify me if they receive any news."

Kenzi nodded, taking it all in.

"Who calls their child 'Doctor'?" She said out loud after mulling over what Bosco had told her. Then she scoffed. "Who calls their daughter Shenzi?"

Bosco did not reply for a while. "Do you want to go to Uganda at some point?"

Kenzi furrowed her brows. "I don't know. Yesterday I thought it would be a good idea. Now…I don't know. I will see. Kevin is here anyway."

Bosco went silent.

Then, "You know, the flats we grew up in have been remodeled. There is a touch to them that would make America look like a Third World country."

Kenzi chuckled. "Is it now?"

Bosco was pleased she had laughed. "Oh yes. If you change your mind, I can take you on a tour." He hesitated. "Maybe after Kevin improves and wakes up."

Kenzi made a face. The knot in her belly tightened. "Is…is my mother still there?" Her defenses seemed to slip away and that laughter—loud, husky, deep, and full—played like a hypnotic melody in her mind.

Bosco paused. The delicacy of this topic had shifted the atmosphere. "Yes. She is. She actually owns a second apartment in the same estate. Low housing rates were given to the reigning tenants, sort of a subsidized fee if they wanted to own them."

Kenzi was quiet. She thought of Aunty Dina and her unfortunate death. Kevin had never gotten over that. *How could anyone ever?*

As they turned onto Uhuru highway, Bosco seized the moment. "I think it's a good time to see her. You know, she worried when you and Kevin disappeared."

Kenzi stared out into the night. A short, bitter laugh escaped her. "She did not, Bosco. If she told you that, she lied. She never *even* looked for us." *And every day I wished she would come for us!* she wanted to add, but thinking about it drained her more, and the old familiar sensation of emptiness hit her: a pull between the present and the past, a gaping hole in the puzzle of her life. Suddenly the hole had a stronger pull, begging to be heeded to.

"Kenzi, you don't…"

"Why are we even talking about her? Why is she important now when my best friend, *your* friend and business partner, is lying in a coma because some thugs beat him up for God knows what!" she interrupted him.

"Kenzi…" Bosco's face glazed over with embarrassment, wishing he had not broached the subject.

"Bosco!" She was sharp. "I am here to see my best friend who I lost for a big part of my life, and I won't lose him again. That is all I care about now."

"Kenzi…I meant to say, I am sorry. I did not mean it that way."

She tossed her bulky curls to one side and glared at him. "Uh-huh, how else did you mean it? Please…not now." She had her hand in his face.

"Sorry…we are almost there." He withdrew from the conversation.

They pulled up to the wide courtyard of the grand Villa Rosa Kempinski in another five minutes, and a doorman, sharply dressed in a beige waistcoat and white dress shirt beneath it, opened the car door for her, pleasantly greeting them both and aiding with the luggage.

Kenzi was impressed. She took in the deep pink structure that towered before her, the brightly lit entrance sporting architecture from a different time. It lent the hotel an inimitable, exquisite appearance.

Bosco caught her smile and joked, ashamed by his contribution to the outburst they had had on the way from the airport. "Not bad for a Third World country, eh?"

Kenzi laughed. "You got me!"

He shrugged. "If you need to take your shots before walking the streets of Nairobi, we can do that before you even go to see Kevin."

She narrowed her eyes and pursed her lips. "Oh com'n, I am not that fragile. Besides, I get that taken care of all the time."

Bosco smiled. "Of course, how can I forget? You are a celebrity, after all. Do we need to hire bodyguards while you are here? You know these Nairobi youth will be all over you when they make the connection."

Kenzi said, "I am here on a private visit. I am sure I shall pass as a regular…somewhat."

"Is that right? When you came on the scene, all these *jamaas* were crazy about you! They still are!" he added emphatically. "But with some disguise we can make it work."

She grinned.

The night staff at the hotel were cordial and swift in making sure she was settled in her executive suite well.

"So, nine in the morning, for sure?" he confirmed with her for the third time.

Kenzi nodded. "Yup. And my phone is on. Sketch made sure I was on roaming, so you can reach me whenever."

"*Sawa sawa.*" Bosco flipped a thumbs-up sign. "And breakfast?"

She shook her head. "Will grab something on the way. Bosco, I will be fine."

"I am just looking out for you. Don't want two of my friends in hospital, you know."

Kenzi smiled and touched his arm reassuringly. "See you tomorrow."

He nodded, patting her arm briefly. "It's really good to see you on this side of the universe."

She wasn't sure how she felt about that, but she was sure of one thing: she was glad she would see Kevin in a few hours. "I am glad to see you…and Kevin soon."

There was a sea of people, gliding in one direction toward something. Kenzi instinctively knew what it was, and the urgency to get to it before anyone else did was suffocating her. She pushed through the thick crowd of bodies that reluctantly gave her leeway. She pounded against their backs and arms, begging them to let her through, telling them she knew how to help. If only they let her through.

No one paid her any attention. She was on her hands and knees, clawing past legs until those legs started to trample over her, and she fought to get up...but the legs held her down and she clawed viciously—

"No!" Kenzi bolted upright, drenched in sweat. It took her a few seconds to recognize her surroundings and that she was on the ground beside her hotel bed, wrapped up in her sheets like a mummy.

She groaned, yanking sleeves of the sheets from around her neck and getting up off the floor. The clock by the bedside said 8:15 a.m. The dream forgotten, Kenzi made a dash to the bathroom for a quick splash, and in twenty minutes, she was ready, in a pair of khaki shorts with embroidery on the hem and a cold-shoulder halter blouse.

She was in the lobby waiting for Bosco at eight-thirty, a cup of coffee in one hand and a tiny croissant in another. The lobby was draped in warm pinks, cream, browns, and a splash of regal elegance. She told herself she would make time to acquaint herself with it when she returned from Aga Khan Hospital.

The Villa Rosa was one of the closest hotels to the Aga Khan Hospital. The drive was only a few minutes. The foyer of the hospital was crisp, clean, doused over with cleaning detergent, which clung to the heavy Nairobi air that met them as far as the driveway.

The sanitized scents reminded her of the several visits to the research center when her eyes were being worked on. The sterile smell became an unforgettable fixture. This one was different, though, as if in Africa they used different cleaning detergent than those in America.

The semicircular reception desk, complete in the prime colors of white, earthy brown, and green, had two receptionists seated behind it, both covered in hijab. They looked up and acknowledged Bosco and Kenzi as they approached.

Bosco said they were family of the patient, Kevin......and they instantly seemed to know who they were talking about.

"How is his condition?" Kenzi asked.

The younger of the two women responded. "We are calling the head of the medical staff for accident and emergency to give you a report and take you to his room. So far he is steady."

The word *steady* sounded so much more threatening than *terrible shape* or *good shape*. Kenzi let out her breath shakily, hating how anxiety crept up her spine, sparked by that one word…*steady*. Her eyes hovered over the other receptionist, who mumbled into a phone, then slid past the reception desk to the lobby that was sparsely populated, dotted with a couple of people, possibly because it was early. The cleaning staff, in pressed-clean uniforms, filed in and out long corridors on either side of the reception foyer with cleaning gear.

Nurses in white and blue pushed trolleys and drip stands along the same corridors. Once or twice she spied a few people in wheelchairs ferried from one corridor to the next or out the door into the warm, sunny morning. She felt giddy, being back in Africa and only a few miles close to home.

Home.

The elusive place she had been searching for all her life. Since she had heard of Kevin's attack, her life seemed to have been thrown into a whirlwind of fate. The past was calling, loose ends untied. Questions unanswered were all caving in on her.

Finally, a tall, lean, dark gentleman dressed in a blue dress shirt and slacks and a white doctor's overcoat came up to them.

"Dr. Abuya." Bosco lit up. The two men shook hands like long-lost relatives. The doctor smiled a wide, emphatic smile.

"Bosco, good to see you again. I am sure that Kevin appreciates you being here the last couple of days."

He turned to Kenzi, and she quickly shot out her hand to greet him. "Kenzi, I am family." She spoke confidently.

"Nice to meet you, Kenzi." The doctor was looking at her curiously, a look she often got, but said nothing more. "Family is good. Yes, Bosco told me you would come in from overseas."

They were ushered down a winding corridor. Dr. Abuya wasted no time in explaining Kevin's conditions.

"*Mizz* Kenzi, Kevin suffered a traumatic brain injury. They hit him over the head more than twice with a metallic bar. His coma scale is about a nine, and we are hopeful he will wake up in a week's time. The CT scan we did shows he had tissue swelling because of the brain injury, and we needed to perform surgery immediately to remove clotted blood and relieve the pressure…because of this tissue swelling from his brain. That was thirty-six hours ago."

Dr. Abuya paused, looked from Kenzi to Bosco, who both stared at him in anticipation. "We are monitoring him closely for clots that may occur and for the tissue swelling to reduce. We gave him diuretics to reduce the amount of pressure in the head."

He paused again, jabbing his left hand into his pocket and added, "The good news is he will survive with no loss of memory. His memory of the last forty-eight hours might be foggy, but it shall clear as he exercises his brain. Also, he was incredibly lucky they did not hit the base of his neck or else he would have been paralyzed for life."

Kenzi took in a sharp breath. Her legs felt weak; her heart faltered. She reached for Bosco's hand and squeezed, wordlessly.

The ride to the third floor was short, but Kenzi counted the minutes like each precious second brought her closer to Kevin.

They went past the A&E section to the VIP suites.

"Dr. Abuya." Kenzi cleared her throat. "How safe is it to move him when he wakes up?" Her heart pounded almost audibly as each step led them closer to his room.

"We may need to monitor him closely for a few days and verify he has no relapses; brain tissue damage is a very serious matter." He looked at her solemnly.

"It is." She shook her head. "Will the hospital agree to a transfer when he awakes? He will awaken, yes?" She tried not to sound frantic. The gravity of Kevin's condition became more apparent now that she was here, only a few steps away from the room he lay in.

The doctor stopped at the door and furrowed his brow, as if in contemplation. "Let's wait and see what happens, shall we?"

His eyes softened with empathy. Kenzi felt the knot in her belly loosen. His reassuring voice was a breeze blowing away the chaos in her mind.

"I can assure you, he is in the best medical hands possible, *Mizz* Kenzi." Dr Abuya placed a reassuring hand on her slim shoulder briefly and opened the door. "So far, Kevin is stable, and we have a team of nurses monitoring him twenty-four hours, just like you asked, Bosco."

The room was pearly white with lime green trimmings. The floor was sparkling, marble white with specks of green and cream patterns. There was a vase filled with fresh cream and pale blue roses and hydrangea finished with dusty miller, resting atop the bedside drawer, where a dark brown leather-bound Bible sat. The room was deathly quiet, only interrupted by the whirring sound of the monitor and a drip stand with a blood pouch attached to it.

"He lost *quite* some blood," Dr. Abuya explained

Kevin lay in the center of this system, comprising wires and cables going in and out of him. A massive bandage swathed his head, and his neck was propped with neck braces. Kenzi felt a shiver go through her. This was familiar territory. She slid into the chair by his bed and stared at his face. A shudder of emotion whirred and ticked like the machines in the room inside of her. Seeing Kevin helpless in this state was the last thing she had ever imagined. He was always intense and fiery, the one who fought for her and with her. This was not him.

"You have to fight, Kevin. You must. We still have..." She choked. "We still have so much to do...together. Remember...it's always been you...you..." She blinked back the tears; her lips quivered.

"Kenzi..." Bosco had a reassuring hand on her shoulder. She shrunk from it.

"Leave me with him," she half-whispered.

When the door closed behind the doctor and Bosco, the delicate vault encasing her tears burst open. She threw off her strong facade and sobbed into his hand that she clasped like it would fade away unless she held on.

And while she cried, she prayed that he would wake up sooner than later, that he would not leave yet. She cursed his assailants and wished upon them death more excruciating than crucifixion, and she begged him to wake up, promised him she would not leave him again, her body wracked with agonized sobs.

"We must find those who did this!" she sobbed. "We must!"

"Just don't leave me yet. Please don't," she begged.

She sat dazed for a long time, staring at him, caressing his hand, squeezing it as if to be sure he was still alive. While she did, she talked to him like he was right there awake.

"Remember our spot, hmm?" She wiped her eyes. "We talk about that spot a lot. It was...*special;* it was our place." She remembered Bosco mentioning how Block 4 had been renovated. Visiting suddenly seemed like a good idea. *For Kevin.*

She picked up the Kleenex in the box by the bedside, blowing her nose into it. "The balcony in my apartment does not compare to...Block 4 rooftops, does it?" She managed a tiny laugh amid sniffling.

She laced her fingers in his. "I was so so looking forward to speaking with you after the show. Luz—love him to death—was getting on my nerves at one point. He was doing the most!" She rolled her watery eyes. "You've got to wake up, though. We just have a lot to do, Kevin."

She ran a hand over his bandaged head and flinched, unable to fathom what sort of pain he was in. "What was this about?" She sighed. "What do you know...? The cruel joke is...I came here. When you begged me to, I said no. Now I have no excuse."

Her mind vacillated, like a broken pendulum, from the present to the past, everything crammed in a few moments of thought. It did not make sense; life did not make sense, and trying to dissect the meaning of events wearied her.

A faint knock on the door roused her. She did not stand up or look to see who it was.

"Kenzi, Dr. Abuya says Kevin needs to have his head redressed. We can wait in the lobby or cafeteria and return..."

"A few minutes, please." She almost barked. "Give me a few minutes."

"Sure." Bosco retreated quickly.

Kenzi looked him over one more time, caressed his arm, and lightly ran a finger along his jawline. His face begged for a shave. She recalled how she had always envisaged what he looked like when she could not see, and when she saw him eventually, he had exceeded her expectations.

She recalled Bigz's words to her. "You two are good together. Think about dating."

She had met Bigz at the beginning of 2014 in Sandton, South Africa, where she had gone for a shoot. The buoyant South African told her about his upcoming wedding. He was getting married in 2015, and they wanted to throw a Las Vegas wedding.

It had been a hard time for Kevin, especially since Ssaka had gone silent.

It's as if he isn't planning to return…this time. Haruna is to make me a cosigner of all the accounts for the next three years, then roll it over if there is no word from him. Even though he joked and acted strong about it, she could see the troubled glint in his eyes.

The dreams were persistent during this period, and often she stayed on the phone with him till late while he talked… about anything and everything.

However, something about what Bigz had said settled on her, like the scent of smoke after the firewood is long burned out. She dragged it back into the recesses of her mind, where she locked it up as the joke it was.

"You will wake up, and together we will find those who hurt you and why," she whispered as she leaned over to kiss his cheek. With one last hand squeeze, she walked out, turning at the door to appraise him: a curiously imposing figure amid the whirring and ticking machines. She was sure he would wake up. She was determined to whisk him away with her to the US, where he would remain under the supervision of doctors she knew and of her. She would be less worried if she were there for every step of his recovery.

CHAPTER 5

* * *

He was back there, the sound of the machines whirring, the ticking at regular intervals...then voices

"EEG?"

"Stable."

"We need to do another MRI."

A shuffling of papers and then silence. He could feel something on his arm, but try as he might, it was too comfortable to wake up.... Maybe a little more rest. He told himself there was nowhere he had to be. He tried to think of where he needed to be, what he was to do, but it was all dark in that place.

"More electrolytes, we need him consistent."

"Yes, Doctor."

Then something pricked him. He panicked. Maybe it wasn't safe, but the comfort lulled him back.... He needn't move. It was a small prick.... Whatever it was, it was nothing. Had to be nothing.

But why did it hurt? He was confused. What was going on? The pain sliced through him again. This time it stung like someone had crushed his jaw in.

Where was Kenzi? He thought desperately.

Time pulled him in all directions. He floated like an inflated balloon cast off into the sea, going with the current against his will, unable to control the urgency in which it bumped him through his timeline.... He was back there in 2015 at the airport as she got ready to leave for Paris. Her face was all excitement. Expectation. He could taste the sumptuous meal they'd had, matooke mashed to perfection, the savory smoothness of the groundnut stew, the meaty chunks that lacked the smoky aroma, but they tried to roast it as well as the one he always had back home when he lunched with Haruna. He was watching the city crawl by on their way to the airport, the wipers frantically brushing away the flakes that hit the windshield and dissolved.... He could still smell the coffee cream and dark chocolate ice cream he had stopped to get her for dessert.

She mmm-ed all the way to J. F. Kennedy...until she was scrapping the bottom of the cup for any bits of ice cream left. He remembered marveling at

569

her appetite for a girl so slender....

He was tired. Bigz's bachelor party...the wedding only hours away, but it was nothing in her presence. Her voice faded in and out as she spoke to Sketch on the phone. He watched how she smiled sweetly, the way her accent, not fully American, not fully African, just a polished and beautiful mix, delivered in its slightly husky tone. She laughed easily, gracefully. And even as he watched her, she was still Shenzi in so many ways, her calm aura, and her tenderness. It still projected through the different layers of auras. Womanhood, sophistication, and foreignness had supplemented her.

He was hugging her goodbye, and he smelled her. The scent of Lancôme's La Vie Est Belle mingled with her hair shampoo, lingered on the tip of his nose.

He still could not believe she was all grown up. He battled with her being independent of him but gloried because she needed him to be there, and he indulged her.

Then time tugged at him again and weightlessly immersed him in another memory frame.... It was another intense night, his soul stung from the assault of verbal artillery hurtled at him from Taata Bob. Shenzi lay next to him, small and warm. Their fingers intertwined. It was another opportune sleepover. Ameena was out of town on business. It was comforting to lie there and whisper about a better life, a life they could have. They could be together always. Shenzi said, "We should get married."

He thought it a ridiculous idea then, but he rationalized it. If the only way to take care of her was through marriage, then it was all right, but there was a catch: "We need to be grown up for that," he told her.

"What if we don't grow up?" she insisted.

It made sense. Taata Bob might beat him to death one day, or Shenzi's mother might starve her to death. Anything could happen. He shuddered. They might as well. The past echoed in his head like a ghostly replay: "Will you marry me, Shenz?"

"Yes, Kevin, and will you marry me, Kevin?" he heard her whisper back.

"Of course, Shenzi." There was a brief pause, then he heard himself say, "Now we are married Shenzi. Go to sleep. I will take care of you."

Chapter 6

They sat at Coffee Casa on Parklands Avenue waiting for the afternoon session for when they could go into the hospital and monitor Kevin. "He could wake up anytime," Kenzi constantly reminded Bosco when he suggested taking her on a tour of Nairobi.

"I don't have time for that now," she said. "Let's wait for Kev to wake up."

Bosco watched her and sighed. "Look, you will need to take a break for a little just to breathe."

Kenzi looked up from her plate of caprese olive salad. "Bosco, I am fine. If you have things to do, drop me off at the hospital, and I will see you later."

"That's not entirely what I meant…"

"What did you mean?" She folded her arms over her chest, salad abandoned.

Bosco met her gaze. Her eyes flickered a fire he had never seen, but something about it and her posture reminded him of Ameena…

"I meant…" his phone ringing broke his explanation off. He flipped it over and immediately scrambled up from the table, relieved. "I will be back," he said nervously and walked out swiftly to pick up the call. Kenzi shook her head and resumed stabbing at the lettuce leaves on her plate dispassionately.

Her mind raced back and forth over Kevin and why nothing was in the papers about the motive of this accident. She glanced at the New Vision paper—that the restaurant carried, possibly because it was a popular Ugandan paper—they had taken it apart leaf by leaf, each browsing through different sections; and the story of a young businessman who had been attacked forty-eight hours ago was in the section of regional news. A single column, it gave no leads, just his name, no motives. It was just a story of another mugging in Kampala, reflecting the prevailing condition of the growing rate of inflation and unemployment.

Bosco had nothing to say except that he was also trying to find out what had happened.

"Sorry, that was one of our business associates. I must go to Uganda briefly; we had a meeting with the president before all this happened. I represent Kevin, so…"

"When do you have to go?" she asked.

"In a day or two. But…." He hesitated. "I can put that on hold since my associates, the governor, and the minister know what happened."

Kenzi thought a while and shook her head. "Maybe you should not."

"Also, I don't want to leave you in Nairobi alone. It can be dire for a woman like you."

She laughed. "I can take care of myself. I carry pepper spray."

"Ha!" he exclaimed. "Your purse might need more protection than pepper spray, my dear."

Kenzi thought. "How long will you be gone for?"

He lolled his head from side to side in thoughtful gesticulation. "Possibly two days."

Kenzi put down her fork and picked up the coffee mug with coffee that had almost gone cold.

"Okay, I shall come with you."

Bosco inhaled sharply. A huge grin spread across his face, and he sighed with relief. "Phew! Now I can rest easy. I don't need two of my best friends in hospital. Seeing Kevin there is unsettling enough."

Kenzi shrugged. "I would like to meet the other guys. I think I only know you, Kevin, Bo, and…" she trailed off. "I haven't been to Uganda since I was eight."

Bosco nodded. "A lot has changed."

Kenzi smirked. "I bet, but…not *some* people."

Kenzi paused, lanced a single olive in her salad, and gingerly brought it to her lips. "You know, it took me almost ten years to realize my mother never loved me. No, I mean, it took me ten years to *accept* it. There were too many telltale signs, and I wanted her to want me so much…*so much*…" Her fork mercilessly wounded the salad on her plate.

Bosco did not look at her.

"I understand," he finally managed.

She shrugged. "I will come to Uganda with you. Sometimes, I guess to make peace with the past, we should face it."

Bosco nodded in agreement. "True."

"I need to stop hearing her voice and her words in my head." She paused, her gaze far away.

Then, with a sigh, she snapped out of it and smiled briefly. "Is the doctor back from lunch, you think?"

Bosco was mulling over what she had said. "Huh? Errr yes." He glanced at his wristwatch. "Whenever you are ready."

Back at the hospital, Kenzi insisted on Dr. Abuya informing them of any changes in Kevin's condition through Bosco while they were away, and he obliged her.

"By the way, my daughter wants to be like you. She follows you on that social media page young kids are obsessed with," Dr. Abuya said uncertainly as Kenzi turned to leave his office. Kenzi smiled, touched by the gesture.

"Doctor, when I return, I shall like to meet your daughter."

Dr. Abuya laughed and clapped his hands. "*Kweli?* Are you serious?"

Kenzi grinned. "No kidding!"

"Wow, she will be so, so excited!"

"But don't tell her. I want it to be a surprise. "

"I will try to contain it. Haaaa! Oh, this is so good! Thank you, *Mizz* Kenzi,"

"Stop." She waved him off. "Just Kenzi. Thank you for taking care of my brother. I shall see you in a couple of days. We can do lunch with you and your family if that is okay?"

"Okay? I should be asking you if that is okay, Mizz…sorry, Kenzi!" His lean face was lit, elated. "Thank you!"

Kenzi reached out and hugged him, ignoring the hand he had brought to her. "No, thank *you*. I can't thank you enough for being very attentive to Kevin."

The tall doctor blushed, the huge grin on his face never receding. "Oh thank you!"

As they were leaving, Bosco laughed. "I bet you a hundred *bob* he will tell his daughter."

"A hundred what? Tell you what, I bet you two hundred dollars he will shut up. You know I play hard. Don't forget, I was the gatekeeper of all the goodies during your hide-and-seek game back at the flats."

Bosco groaned. "And you and Kevin cheated us all out of our trinkets. How can I forget?"

"So, are you still betting?"

Their Uber arrived, and Bosco got the door for her.

"I don't back down from a challenge," Bosco replied, getting in the back seat beside her.

Kenzi laughed. "I will be smiling, two hundred dollars richer in two days."

"Huh! We shall see."

Later that night, as she lay on her bed, bags packed, ready for an early morning flight to Uganda, she spoke with Heather, letting her know where she was and what was going on so far, lest Heather called the American Embassy. She also called Sketch, letting him know about Kevin's condition as well as to add a two-day itinerary in Uganda. *It was a last-minute decision,* she told him. *I made reservations for that decision,* he assured her.

Kenzi smiled. *You have always been two steps ahead of me, Sketch!*

He replied *I got you.*

"So, you have two nights at the Serena Hotel on Nile Avenue in Kampala, and your flight leaves at 6 a.m. You return to Kenya on a 4 p.m. flight. Good? You and Bosco, right?" he confirmed with her. Kenzi had discussed booking the flight for them both, and Bosco had agreed to it.

"Are you ready for this?' Sketch asked as he verified the bookings with her.

Kenzi sighed. "I don't know."

He grunted in agreement. "You have come this far, you know."

"Yup, demons need to be faced."

Then she went through her calendar for when she returned. A two-day shoot for Lancôme and a meeting with Jimmy Choo. Luz had also been calling, asking after her, Sketch told her.

"Do you think the agency will extend our contract?" she asked Sketch.

"If he can match *Madame*. It looks like *Lancôme* and *Jimmy Choo* are showing an interest, so these short gigs with them might be good for your résumé. I tell you, Kenz, you are heading up the supermodel scale with the legendaries."

She whooped. "It's scary, and it's been much hard work…"

"And your rare looks, girl. Let's just put it out there."

Kenzi grinned. "First time you saw me, you were like…"

"Holy shit, what universe did you crawl out from?" they both said loudly and laughed. Kenzi reminisced.

"Right, I had seen no one quite like you. Still haven't. Remember what I said when you were so nervous about the Paris deal? There are gorgeous dark girls like you. Alek Wek, broke through the industry in the nineties for her skin color. You are 'the new black' in the industry now. Again, there are no dark-skin girls with eyes like yours. Best believe it, the world is yours, baby."

His words stirred her, knowing he meant more than her showstopper looks. "Well, you are an amazing personal assistant and friend. I could use a booster daily!"

"You bet." He chuckled. "I know it gets daunting out there, but you have held your own through it, and I got you, girl. I got you," he said, concentrating on typing. She could hear the rhythmic rattle of fingers flying across the keyboard. "You have been through quite an interesting life. I give you that, and you are still sane and strong."

"Thank you, Sketch, for everything."

"No worries, babe," he boomed.

She said her good mornings to Sketch, and he bid her goodnight.

Brent had messaged her, letting her know their parents were aware. She called him later to chat.

"Sorry, Chip. Mom asked, and…I said Kevin had an accident and you had to go."

She groaned. "Oh all right. I cannot hide everything from them, anyway. My life is out there now and again, no?"

"Unfortunately," Brent agreed. "But they won't get in touch unless you get in touch first."

Kenzi relaxed. "I am glad they respect that."

She told him how Kenya was so far…about the doctor and his daughter. She also told him how she was going to Uganda and hopefully seeing her birth mother.

Their conversation made a turn to the planned wedding in 2017, and Kenzi promised to be there, especially as she was part of the bridal team.

"When you get back, let us know. We might be in New York in October; we can stop by." Brent was saying.

"Fabulous!" Kenzi sang out. "I can't wait! We can paint the town red."

"Like we used to." Brent laughed.

Kenzi grinned, her mind rummaging through catalogues of their escapades in New York City when she had first moved there as a fresh-faced model. Happy hour, brunch till lunch, dinners that evolved into parties that tarried well into the wee hours of the morning. She jogged further back in time to high school house parties. Brent took her to those, got them both in trouble, the most memorable one being Byrd's birthday party, the school's rugby jock that every girl crushed on secretly, except Brent was privy to Kenzi's and got her to go with him to the party. Byrd lived in the posh Potomac area in a six-bedroom single-family house enshrouded by a tree-lined driveway, well-groomed lawns with a fountain in the middle jutting out water from an exquisite stone mermaid. His parents were known for their charity work in the DC area, and he drove all the newest car models advertised annually. Byrd was a showman with no brains, but his charismatic charm and athletic build had the girls all swooning over him. Brent had a way of making friends with the coolest guys in school, no matter what year they were in. He had made his mark as the fearless guy who knew all the hookups for anything, so he was cool.

"Byrd *liked* you, I swear!" Brent was choking with laughter.

"Yeah, right! You pawned your sister for a makeout session with Byrd's *real* crush!"

"Ooh, that's harsh," Brent was saying.

Kenzi shook her head.

"We kinda both got what we wanted."

Kenzi huffed. "Er…yeah, you a black eye, and *we* both got grounded for life!"

"Don't be so harsh, Chip. Byrd kissed you."

Kenzi was rolling over laughing. "He was drunk too! I can't with you."

"But they grounded us all summer," Brent agreed as he drifted off into memory lane.

"Worst summer of my entire life."

They both agreed.

"Where is Byrd now?" Kenzi asked absently.

"Who knows, probably working with the family business, boning some hot blonde with big boobs."

Kenzi rolled her eyes. "Oh my God, after that summer, I was legit over him."

They switched up the conversation, swinging between present and past until Kenzi realized she would not get enough sleep at all if they kept on talking. When he hung up, she set her alarm.

Chapter 7

The plane touched down as the sun rose, like a reborn golden orb peeking through the fast-fading dark clouds, which dissipated with the tiny fingernail-like crescent shape of the moon, painting the sky on the eastern side in bright hues of orange and purple.

Kenzi wrapped her jacket around her tightly as a gust of wind blew into her face, Entebbe airport looked deserted.

"Wow, it's dead here," she told Bosco. The mechanical sounds of engines and propellers gathered and hummed in and out of the wide-open space of the runway.

"Yeah!" he replied. "Are you okay?"

"Yeah," she responded.

It was seven-thirty on the plain-faced wall clock that graced the arrival area wall. A cleaning crew swept up and down the corridors of the lounge. The overnight crew, stooped and tired, were switching over with a new shift, walking in bright-eyed and cheery. They were cleared quickly, Bosco watching that Kenzi was not hustled.

"That was fast," Kenzi said as they walked out with their single bags.

"It's as if there are no planes coming in today. Hmm," Bosco responded more conversationally. Not that he cared.

In the waiting area, Bosco dialed a number and spoke to someone in Luganda, then turned to Kenzi. "Abe will be here in ten minutes."

"The young, rich crew, huh?" Kenzi teased.

Bosco chuckled. "If you like."

"I am excited to meet them all anyhow. I really am. I always wanted to."

Bosco nodded. "I must warn you too that my niece might overwhelm you."

"No worries, perks of being me." She batted her eyelashes at him. Her eye color was more defined, almost sea green, and Bosco stared at her.

"You know, you really were pretty when you were younger, but now…" He shook his head in awe.

Kenzi waved him off, flattered. "Aww, stop."

They were standing outside the airport building when a silver E-class pulled up right in front of them.

The driver rolled down the window and propped his sunglasses over his eyes.

"*Karibu!*" he piped, put the car in park, and slid out of his seat.

"Thanks for picking us up," Bosco said. He turned to Kenzi and made the introductions.

"Abe, Kenzi; Kevin and I grew up with Kenzi in Bugolobi flats."

Abe smiled. Kenzi decided there and then she liked him. His eyes had an inquiring glow, and though she could not call him handsome, the aura about him was magnetic. He gently took her hand in his and gave it a slight squeeze. "My pleasure. I have heard so much about you. It was just slackness on my part for not making those plush trips to the US, but I heard the stories." His eyes twinkled teasingly.

Kenzi flushed. She laughed, flustered. "Is he always like this?" she asked Bosco.

"Oh, believe me, he is just getting started." Bosco walked to the car and shoved their bags in the boot.

Kenzi beamed. "I can't wait."

Even though Abe drove, he asked all the questions, especially about Kevin and his condition. He then entertained Kenzi with stories about their little "rich crew."

"Make no mistake, Kenz—can I call you *Kenz*?"

"Sure."

"Okay, Kenz. We work hard. *Real* hard. But when we party, fuck yeah, we light it up!"

"I agree," Bosco replied.

Forty-five minutes later, they were merging into the rush-hour traffic of downtown Kampala. Kenzi kept her eyes glued to the window. She absorbed the sights and sounds of a city she could not remember except from Kevin's descriptions that had been exaggerated, and yet the occasional taxi calls for passengers to get in to one destination or another brought back memories of the months she and Kevin had traversed the streets, swinging from one taxi to the next to get to the farthest destination.

She marveled thinking of it now, Kevin's wit, how he had easily subdued the gang, then took over, and he always told her, "I can't do this without you." It only made sense to her later that because he had assigned himself to be her arch protector, he had creatively devised every ammunition his young mind could fathom to keep her safe.

She gazed at the streets and buildings as they rolled by; a familiarity hinged on them like old faded photographs with a sliver of their glory hanging precariously, peeking through and jolting memories of a time that this existence was all she knew. She closed her eyes, fading out as the boys talked. The ghost of the past whispered memories. They filtered through the cracks of her relaxed thoughts, picking at the scars. Her mother's voice faded in and out, and she tried to paint an image of her...but all she came up with was the face of Iman. If anyone looked like her mother, she was sure it was Iman.

She had met Iman with her husband, David Bowie, at a gala and had been struck by how stunning she looked. She had adored her immediately and got tongue-tied when her agent made introductions, proudly confirming their shared ethnicity. Not much had been said, but a few pleasantries and the memory of her had remained etched in her mind. She had decided her mother must look like Iman.

They finally got to the Serena; their welcome was stellar as a bellboy waiting in the courtyard opened her car door. Kenzi followed Bosco into the lobby and reception area. She took in the warm colors of gold and a rich brown with afro-centric décor gallantly displayed in the wide lobby.

She had not imagined it would be this pretty.

The lady at the desk beamed when she saw them. She checked Kenzi in after confirming it was her booking by viewing her passport and confirmation email.

Kenzi insisted on having breakfast together with both Bosco and Abe. "No nap?"

She shook her head. "I am napped out. There is much to do."

"We can make it three days."

Kenzi frowned. "Kevin?"

"The doctor said he would let us know, and I think Kevin would like you to breathe a little. Come on."

Kenzi bit her lower lip. "He has no one…" She shook her head. "Maybe I will come back when Kevin is better."

Bosco frowned slightly. Abe nodded. "That's noble, Kenz. I am up for breakfast when you are ready."

They met in the Lakes Brasserie restaurant, where breakfast was served buffet style. Kenzi met them in thirty minutes. She had changed into a pair of skinny distressed jeans and a long semi-sheer gray-blue blouse with a matching midriff cami insert. She had her hair pulled back in an untidy ponytail since the stubborn curls would not lie still.

The two men were sipping tea. They had hijacked a silver carafe from which they refilled their tiny teacups. Abe saw her first and whistled. Bosco turned, his jaw dropping indiscreetly.

"Why don't you catwalk for us," Abe was calling shamelessly. The restaurant was thankfully empty except for a handful of people at a table engrossed in what seemed like a business meeting. Kenzi wanted the floor beneath her to give way, but with every stride, she thought up a smart retort.

"Close your mouth, Bosco, you've known me longer than Abe." She waved a hand in his face when she got to the table, then turned to Abe, who had an amused twinkle in his eye. "Is that how you treat your guests?"

Abe, who had leaned back, one leg over his knee, was enjoying his moment of triumph. He tapped the chair next to him. "Can I make it up to the lady? Have a seat."

She shook her head, the smile never leaving her face.

Bosco, who had slightly recovered himself, nodded slowly. "They say short men make up for lack of stature with lots of other things."

Abe seemed unfazed by the comment and nodded. "Lots…lots of other things."

Kenzi picked it up and raised an eyebrow. "I hope it's worth *it.*" She stressed the *it*, her eyes traveling below his belt.

"Whoa!" He sat up with a short laugh. "Easy, let's all have breakfast."

Kenzi laughed. "I thought we were having a good time."

"Well, You just hurt my feelings." He put his hand on his heart.

Bosco was watching them, amused.

Kenzi paused, her face falling. "I…did not mean…"

Both men burst out laughing. "It's a joke!"

She decided not to take anything seriously with them after that. They left Serena shortly after to Bosco's home, where Abe dropped them. The plan was to meet later that night.

Bosco was going to take Kenzi around, show her Kevin's barito restaurants, and get her to meet his niece, Carissa. They picked up drinks from Javas on Kira Road as she rode in his dark blue hybrid Lexus.

A faint orange-lemon scent lent the car a clean smell, and she commented on it. Kenzi basked in the different melodies playing off his car stereo. She loved how the music changed from one genre to another, unlike the niche-centered stations back home. The mix-up felt more authentic to her the more she listened. They drove around for about an hour from upscale Kololo, Kamwokya, Wandegeya, onto Bombo Road and into the heart of the suburb turned business center, Nakasero. She asked Bosco over and over to tell her the different places and landmarks, and as he did, she pieced together her past slowly, pointing out to him the part of the streets they must have lived on. She excitedly gawked in awe. "I cannot believe I am seeing all this. Literally seeing all this!" she kept exclaiming.

Bosco nodded. "Kevin pointed out a lot to me too," he told her, and as they passed the entrance way to Watoto church, he pointed it out to her. "That is where you met your adopted parents. It was called Kampala Pentecostal church back then."

Kenzi stared, not sure if she should tell him to stop so she could go in or not. *It was so long ago,* she thought. Would anyone recall? She decided against it. Another *time,* she told herself.

"I want to go to the flats, Bosco, if you please."

"Certainly," he replied, and they were making their way out of the city center, past Jinja Road to the industrial area, and in another ten minutes, Bosco was making a turn into Bugolobi. The taxi stage had not changed. Kenzi did not have to see it to recall it. "We took the taxi here that night," she said quietly, her eyes not leaving the activity of the stage as they turned into the wide lane through the shops that lined either side of the dusty lane. They made another turn and drove farther away from the vibrant shopping center.

"The flats have been remodeled, repainted, some restructured."

Kenzi's eyes dropped. "Oh."

She paused, and Bosco noticed she was withdrawn. "Are you sure...?"

She shook it off. "Yeah, yeah, I am okay. I really just want to go up to the rooftop. Is anyone here from our childhood?"

Bosco shook his head. "Most people moved when the government did the renovations. Others sold their flats and bought single houses in other parts of the city. My parents moved too, a year after Kevin's father passed. His death shook the entire block..."

Kenzi listened quietly. She knew the story and ached because she did not know how to help Kevin deal with it.

"I know, I know," she gently spoke, an indicator that he should stop, then sighed. "Kevin cannot forgive himself for it."

"It's been hard, but he is doing better—about it all," Bosco replied just as gently. They both relived the night of her birthday party, each lost in thought. Bosco only found out what had happened the next day when the body was taken out in a mortuary van. Kevin's mother, Aunty Dina, had sat up all night in the same spot; blood stained her *lesu*, her cheeks streaked with dried tears, her eyes a glassy faraway look like somewhere in her she had snapped.

He recalled being horrified like everyone else when the police came and took her away. She limped painfully and did not resist. The story did not make it to the papers somehow, so the missing children did not become an issue until much later—a huge fault in the system. All he could recall was Block 4 was never the same without the Byamukamas or Kenzi. He had cried silent tears, his little heart broken with the sadness of a ten-year-old whose beloved puppy goes missing.

His parents talked in hushed whispers about what had happened. Kenzi and Kevin were somewhere in Bwaise. Aunty Dina was in Luzira prison. She had admitted to murdering her husband. Her sentence was light, life imprisonment, no death penalty because of the marks of abuse her body bore and also the fact that she had said it was an accident. He was drunk and he fell when she pushed him away from her in self-defense. He remembered having nightmares about it. On the weekends, he sat by the stone plank Kenzi used to sit on and watch them play hide-and-seek and miss his friends.

Even as a child he had a feeling any parent would be devastated by the loss of their child, but Ameena seemed to have returned—after the initial shock of the death of Taata Bob and Aunty Dinah's incarceration— to her life like nothing had happened.

She had inquired after Kevin and Kenzi and was told they were at Kevin's uncle's place. That was the end. Although everyone noticed her calm, even cheerful demeanor in surprise, no one said anything further. They pitied Kenzi from the conversations he got a whiff of...

Bambi, if I had a mother like Ameena, I would be a street child...
What sort of mother doesn't look for her child?
Bambi Shenzi...at least Kevin is with her...
The Byamukamas were her proper family.

Bosco did not want to believe these whispered conversations. He wanted to understand what was going on. A month after the tragic death of Taata Bob, he watched Ameena leave the flat with a customer. She looked as happy and elegant as she always did, which baffled him, as if Kenzi being away from her life made no difference. He was seated on the plank Kenzi used to sit on. It was a sunny afternoon, and the rest of the children played hide-and-seek.

"Don't you want her back?" he had called out bravely to Ameena.

Ameena stopped in her tracks, and Bosco had felt his heart pound wildly, suddenly not so brave. His parents would be mortified that he had spoken to an adult like that. He regretted asking, but curiosity had gotten the better of him.

She turned to him, her beautiful face flawless, a brown lipstick coating her lips and thick mascara lining her almond eyes; her hair was straightened and curled at the ends falling down past her shoulders. *"Macaan,"* she said sweetly, "she is happier where she is."

He stared at her, dazed. Her presence was intoxicating, even to him. She was so stunning, and suddenly he was not sure his parents were right about her. She *did* love Shenzi.

"But where?" he had insisted as she started to walk to the car where the gentleman waited.

She stopped and turned again. This time she paused and stared at him, then a small smile touched her lips. Bosco was not sure it was a smile then...she had *known*.

She came back to him, dropping on her haunches, opened her purse, and took out two gold five-hundred-shilling coins. "I hope you can forget about her. *Huku*, go buy yourself biscuits," she had told him. "Don't worry about Shenzi." She winked at him, and he was enthralled. The spell she cast had him tongue-tied. He nodded, his chubby fingers closing over the coins.

"But if she stays in your mind *and* heart." She pointed to his forehead and chest. "When you grow up, find her. Also…let me know." Like a possessed boy, he had nodded in promise. She smiled, got up, and left with the man who waited patiently for her in his Land Rover.

He never talked about Shenzi again. But he never forgot.

"You coming?" he asked finally, heaving out of the reverie like an awakening sleepwalker. He glanced around furtively. There were hardly any cars. It was a weekday and at the peak productive hour of the day, too.

Kenzi hesitated. "Is…my mother here, you think?"

Bosco shook his head.

"No, she isn't."

"How would you know?" she asked curiously.

"I have seen her in town. She likes to hang out at the Sheraton… sometimes Javas on Kisementi." He looked away from Kenzi.

"What is it, Bosco?"

He shifted. "She wants to see you." He heaved out the words like it was a burden he carried.

Kenzi raised a brow. "Oh." She turned and walked to the flat, like she was where she belonged. It surprised her how she effortlessly did so. Even with her eyes closed, she knew how to get up and down those floors, not with all those years of counting steps and paces and feeling her way with a stick.

"I can still count these steps accurately with my eyes closed," she called out to Bosco.

"Maybe you should not try it since you have dulled those senses with the gift of sight." He tried to be light.

"Huh! Watch me!" Kenzi called out, and with her eyes closed, she slowly made her way up the stairs, stumbling once or twice, and Bosco would reach out to hold her in case she fell. She waved his hands away, insisting she could do it.

"Stubborn," he said finally when they got to the roof after a painful, slow trek.

She had her hands to her hips, laughing. "Maybe you are right. I lost the skill. Thanks to sight."

Bosco watched her, a spitting image of her mother, just darker. She did not hold her surroundings captive to an intoxicating sultry presence like Ameena, but she did emit an air of grace and sensual mystery. It was what made her an attention grabber, he wanted to tell her, but he held back. He told himself, *Not yet.*

She caught him staring at her and frowned. "What?"

Bosco shrugged. "It's hard to believe you are back here. And you are…you know." He waved a hand like a wand towards her. "All grown."

Kenzi nodded. "Right."

As she took his hand and pulled him closer to the ledge, Bosco resisted. "Whoa. Acrophobia!"

Kenzi laughed. "Acro-what?"

"Fear of heights. I don't do heights." Kenzi laughed again. "No wonder you never came up with me and Kevin." She let his hand go and went to the ledge, sitting on the hard-baked ground, her legs dangling.

She leaned far back in a slouching position and held her face to the sun. Bosco marveled at her exquisite long neck, the way the wisps of curls blew gently around her narrow face.

He cleared his throat. "Actually, we never came up here. This was Kevin's unspoken rule."

Kenzi shook her head. "Kevin and his rules…."

"Yeah. This was your spot. Him and you."

Kenzi smiled, feeling special. "Hmm. I like that rule."

"I bet you do." He grunted.

"He had special places for you guys, too, that I did not go to, right?"

"Er yeah, but for crying out loud, this is the rooftop. It's no-man's-land!" He held out his hands in protest.

"Not true. It was *our* land. Kevin and me," Kenzi retorted.

"Even the stone slab down by the wash line where you sat when we played hide-and-seek was your land, remember? Kevin fought and terrorized anyone who sat there."

Kenzi threw her head back and laughed. "Bosco, I was the blind girl. I needed someone to treat me special."

Bosco pursed his lips, amused. "Special, like take all our toys and pancakes and money…."

"Oh, don't blame us for that. You guys lost the games always. By the way, where is Marjorie?" She was giggling.

"Ooh, last I heard, she had gone to India to study."

"I cannot forget her voice."

They lapsed into childhood memory, Kenzi laughing at some stories she had missed out on.

"How come you never told me you liked me?" She looked at him through lowered lashes, and Bosco for a second saw the sultry seduction of her mother peek through—for a second and then it was gone.

He huffed. "You knew. Everyone teased me. My friends at least."

She kept her eyes on him, noticing his discomfort and enjoying the moment. "Yeah, and the extra perks," she added. "You know what I mean. Extra gum, extra gifts. Extra *stuff.*"

He brushed it off uneasily. "Get over yourself."

Kenzi laughed aloud and Bosco exclaimed. "Gosh, you do sound exactly like when you were eight."

They stayed for a few more minutes, staring out over the trees and into the town center. The view was not as enthralling as it was in the evening, but being here was enough for Kenzi. It was the doorway to her past, and in those minutes, she relived every moment she had spent with Kevin: the several evenings they had sat together in silence or eating or arguing about nothing only to burst into laughter or slump into more silence. The shared pains and joys, mostly the pains. Silent tears and rage and, oh, the promises and dreams! So many dreams, she could almost feel the ghosts whisper and speak. The memories were so vivid and what she felt then she felt now…pain, admiration, and an irrevocable love for Kevin.

She allowed herself to travel through the thin film of time and feel everything she had felt up to that point. It was strange; she realized nothing had changed…well, a little. She still adored Kevin, but it had grown as she had grown. Anger and pain may have tried to stifle it in the years they were apart, but she knew it was there…sturdy, solid, unmoving but almost oblivious to her growing steadily like an age-old oak tree, digging its roots deeper into her so she could not escape it.

She could justify it. They had been through so much together. When life had thrown them a dirty bargain, Kevin had helped them survive. He had protected her with his life so many times. For being the only one who ever did, she loved him deeply, and now she had the chance to give back, if even half of his sacrifice for her.

"Ready?"

It was Bosco. He was pocketing his phone when he walked up to her. Carissa will meet us at Javas for dinner at seven. She is stoked to see you. She used that word, *stoked*."

Kenzi smiled broadly. "Hey, millennials rock; what can you say? Is she old enough to drink? She should party with us tonight."

Bosco sighed. "Er…we will see about that."

He helped her up, and they left the flat just as the residents started to trickle home from work and school.

Kenzi was glad she had not seen her mother. "Can we pass by the Original Barito place on Kampala Road? I want to get one."

Bosco nodded. "Sure thing."

Her thoughts strayed to her mother again, and she pondered seeing her. It was part of why she had come to Kampala, she told herself.

When they eventually got to Serena, Kenzi asked Bosco, "Can you get my mother to contact me?"

Bosco looked at her searchingly. "Yeah, why?"

"I did not come to Kampala to leave without seeing her…at least if I am making rounds to see my past life, she is a catalyst of a lot of where I am today."

Bosco agreed, "You bet. I will give her your number. She can WhatsApp you, right?"

"Yeah, or regular message, my roaming data is activated. I have Wi-Fi in my room too."

"Okay."

"*Just* messaging." She was firm. She wanted to see her and not be haunted by her voice the day before they met.

"Cool. Cool," Bosco replied. "So, pick you up at six-ish?"

Kenzi nodded. "I need a shower, get the dust out of my hair." She shook her curls free from the little elastic band that held it.

Bosco smiled. "Welcome to Kampala."

"I don't recall it being this dusty."

"It was a long time ago."

She nodded. "You're telling me!" She combed her hair with her fingers.

"So, I guess we are meeting the guys too?"

Bosco nodded. "We shall meet them at the club. It's ladies' night at Boda Boda lounge, then we will hit the Wink and finish the night at Gecko Lounge unless you are looking for something different."

Kenzi shrugged. "I am open tonight."

Chapter 8

Kenzi slept till noon the next day, only waking up to Bosco calling and asking if he should pick her up for her two o'clock with her mother.

"Yeah, of course." She groaned.

"Hangover?"

"Tired. Last night was so much fun!" she raved. "All you guys are cool as shit! And Carissa? She is the bomb! I love her!"

Bosco was laughing.

"Seriously. If we did not have to leave so soon, I would want to hang out with her again."

"I believe you exchanged numbers?"

Kenzi laughed, clearing her throat. She had mixed a lot of cocktails, and though she did not have a pounding headache, she felt tired and thirsty.

"I don't remember. Was it at the end of the night?"

Bosco laughed. "Oh my goodness. You were that drunk?"

"No, I just don't remember." She smiled into the phone, embarrassed.

"Check your phone. I am sure she is there somewhere. I will come by at one-thirty."

Kenzi hung up and went through her phone book, trying to figure out what she had called Carissa. In the *C* section, several Carissas came up, and she scrolled past, till she got to one she did not recognize. "Carl-G?"

She checked the personal info, and it was a Ugandan number.

Kenzi grinned and immediately texted: *"Hey, you are so lit. I had a fab night with you!"* Then made a dash to the bathroom. The last thing she wanted was for her mother to think she was following in her footsteps, reeking of alcohol.

She chose her clothing carefully: a colorful tribal-patterned wrap skirt she had bought at an African American "Back to my roots" bazaar in Brooklyn. She had swooned at the colorful décor, clothing, jewelry and, particularly, at the all-natural vegan spread of bites that a lady called Aquia prepared. It was the first time Kenzi understood the phrase "holistic healing." The bazaar had affected her, and though she had never felt she ever belonged unless she was with Kevin, she felt she could embrace the African American experience. They thought she was beautiful, and like her, they had experienced a loss of roots, taken away from where they belonged. Kenzi identified. Kevin was home for her. Home ceased to be a place when they took the taxi to nowhere on the night of her birthday.

She pulled on a russet-colored tank top and the single necklace that Kevin had given her. Her fingers closed around it like she was channeling power from it.

Her mind constantly went back to Kevin in the hospital bed, strapped to whirring machines. *You've got to come back; you've got to*, she repeated to herself. Tomorrow she would be back by his bedside, waiting for him to wake up. She wondered if she should speak with Sketch in case Kevin did not wake up, to have her stay extended.

At one o'clock, Kenzi was picking a soup cup with cream of mushroom soup and a banana from the buffet table. The smell wafting from the restaurant was irresistible, and her stomach complained.

She munched on the banana with zest; besides, food would be in her periphery soon enough. Why waste an appetite or a time to bond with Mother dearest? Even to her it sounded alien, *Mother dearest*. The closer the time to the meeting drew, the more she talked herself into positivity.

Her WhatsApp chimed. She flicked open her phone and read the message twice, then scrolled back to the short conversation she had had the previous day.

Maybe things would work out. Maybe the answers she had been looking for would surface.

The wind blew open her wrap skirt, parting it as she stepped out of Bosco's dark blue Lexus. The plan was to meet at Javas in Kisementi at 2 p.m. that hot afternoon. As Kenzi flicked the folds of her wrap skirt over her exposed thigh, she sighed, feeling suddenly like years and distance could not dispel the fact that she was a child again. Little, skinny blind girl with a head full of matted hair yearning for approval from the only connection to her history—her *hooyo.*

The Café Javas sign greeted her warmly. From where she stood, it looked busy already. Lunchtime madness.

She lingered. Could this be a mistake, after all? What was she supposed to say to the woman who had never bothered to look for her?

"You, okay?" Bosco was asking from the driver's seat.

"Yeah," she replied and decidedly closed the car door behind her.

"Are you sure you don't want me to come in with you?"

"Fly on the wall much?" she tried to tease. "I am good."

"Okay." Bosco smiled. "Will pick you up in like an hour?"

Kenzi shook her head. "I will take an Uber back to the hotel."

"I dunno…" Bosco started, but she peered at him and smirked.

"I am a big girl, Bosco. I will be fine. I will call you later."

Something in her voice told him insisting would be futile. "Fine."

"Thanks," she added then swiped open her phone to find the WhatsApp message. It was the last message her mother had sent only an hour earlier.

"I will be seated outside on the patio at the far end. When you walk in, I will raise my hand." A smiley face accompanied the message.

Kenzi straightened her tote and adjusted the huge Gucci shades over her eyes, then marched like a woman on a mission toward the glass doors of the restaurant into the warm, bright interior. For a moment, she glanced around, impressed by the décor. The lighting, warm brown, yellows, and oranges mingled together with the succulent smells of meat and strong coffee igniting her appetite.

I could eat, despite the meetup, she told herself. She kept her head down as she walked past the tables and booths, hoping not to draw much attention to herself. She was oddly aware of everyone looking her way and hastily took her shades off.

Bad idea, she thought to herself. Her eyes averted. It seemed forever before she got to the opening that led to the patio. At the entrance, she looked up and caught the smiling eyes of a hostess.

"Are you looking for a seat?"

Kenzi smiled. "No, not really, I am here to meet someone..." she informed the tall slim light-skinned hostess, clad in a beige shirt, *Café Javas* embroidered on it.

"Oh okay," the hostess started to add something when Kenzi heard her name.

"Kenzi!" The voice was deep and husky. Kenzi wheeled around to her right and saw the arm, smooth and elegant. One gold bracelet hung loosely on it. Kenzi stopped for a moment as she looked at the woman who waved at her. She wore her shades over her head. Her hair was wrapped back away from her face in a multicolored headband. It bounced in healthy thick curls to her shoulders. Her smile was enchanting. Her coal-dark eyes and pale pink lip gloss gave off the air of a sophisticated, well-kept woman. Exotic *and* erotic. The sultry magnetic aura about her beckoned to Kenzi.

Kenzi had not expected to stare. She had known her mother was beautiful all the years growing up. She heard her beauty in her voice, the deep husky voice that was both rich when she laughed and cutting when she cursed.

"Is that who you are here to see?" the hostess was asking. She, too, had her eyes trained on Ameena. Kenzi could not blame her.

Kenzi nodded. "Yes, thank you."

"She is a regular," the hostess said, smiling.

"Oh," Kenzi replied politely.

She approached Ameena, who was seated at the far end of the patio, in a corner area under a bright orange parasol on an outdoor chaise sectional.

Meeting her mother like this was suddenly confusing. Kevin had shown her pictures, but she looked so much better in person and…so young. She was more beautiful than Iman, Kenzi concluded.

Ameena was out of her seat waiting for her, her arms raised to gather her in an embrace. Like a child once more, Kenzi was enchanted, unable to resist the charm of the woman she had adored and then resented.

She let Ameena hug her. Her perfume floated past her nose. *J'adore.*

The same perfume she remembered her wear when she was a child. She wore it on special occasions when she was visiting her clients or "uncles."

"Look at you, *macanto*, all grown up and so beautiful." She held her back at arm's length. Then laughed shortly. "*Aad ayaad u qurux badan tahay* . You look so beautiful! Your looks were always promising." She spoke gracefully. Kenzi was enthralled and disturbed by the effect this woman had on her.

"Hmm, maybe I would have been better-looking if I was not blind." She was guarded nonetheless; she was not going to give in unless she could believe her mother.

Ameena frowned. "You look even better now, *macaankayga*. Those eyes! *Tsk-tsk*. Sit, sit," she urged. Kenzi sat across from her, and her mother inched closer, a smile plastered on her flawless face.

"That was the past, *gabadh*. A lot has changed. I *have* changed." She flicked a hand and picked up the menu on the table before her. "Back then, I was young and bitter. Angry at the world for where I was in life." Her eyes scanned the items on the menu, then glanced at Kenzi,

"You must be hungry."

Kenzi was staring at her. Try as she might, she couldn't figure her out yet. She scanned her own menu.

"Kenzi, there are things women go through that change them. I went through things that changed me. I hope we can get past it." She looked at Kenzi, hopefully.

Kenzi shifted, not sure what to think. Being so close to her mother brought up emotions she had not wanted to feel for a long time: a medley of pain and awe, relief and anger, joy, love and, above all, hope. Hope that the fragile bond that tethered them biologically could be stronger.

"So, how have you been? I know you are doing very well. But…you know, how *are* you?" Kenzi could not tell if it was genuine or not. She desperately wanted to believe her.

"I have been fine," she replied shortly. "Maybe I should order a drink?" she added.

"Oh yes, yes." Ameena smiled. "Don't worry; let me signal the waitress."

While the waitress came, Ameena turned to Kenzi like she had forgotten something. "How is your Somali, by the way? I remember you always wanted to show me you knew all I taught you."

"Nonexistent. You were not there for me to please," Kenzi replied tightly.

"Hmm." Ameena put her hand to her cheek and slowly caressed it with meticulously done French manicured nails. "Hmm, I understand. Your English is surely better than mine. We can work at pleasing each other now, huh?" A light laugh escaped her lips.

Kenzi frowned slightly but did not respond. Watching this woman she had known as mother—beautiful and still so youthful—flick her nails lightly and almost absently like a French duchess at tea with her betrothed bothered a part of her that was vulnerable still. She looked so regal and proud. Kenzi admitted to herself then that she still adored her. Even more now that she could see her and was meeting her face to face. It took all her willpower to not reach out and touch her, to feel if she was real.

"We should take a selfie, don't you think?"

Kenzi was not sure she was ready for that commitment so early in their relationship.

"We have more important things to do than take selfies," she retorted.

Ameena shrugged and put her iPhone back at the corner of the table where she had picked it up from.

"No problem, whatever you say, *macanto*," she said with a smile.

The service was quick. Ameena had a mixed tropical juice; Kenzi got herself Earl Grey tea. They were once more left alone, staring at each other. Ameena purred and cooed as she spoke, asking if her tea was right and saying if she did not like it, they could change the order.

"The service here is superb," she told her reassuringly. "Maybe your Starbucks is better?"

Kenzi shrugged and sipped her tea.

"Why did you ask to see me?" Kenzi finally got the courage to ask, breaking the spell of her charm again.

Ameena's eyes widened in innocent surprise. "But why not? You are my daughter."

"You were not too keen on that when I was younger. You called me stupid! *Shenzi!* Neither were you keen on me being your daughter when Kevin and I…left. You did not come for me." The words rushed out from a broken place in her that had been buried deep for years. "I hoped you would come. Every day. I hoped." She choked and gulped some air, looking away as she did.

She hated being weak before this woman she called mother. She wanted Ameena to say she was sorry and that she was wrong, that she looked for her and just did not find her.

Ameena sighed. "I know that hurt you…and a lot of other things. I don't think you can understand. I did not mean to hurt you, but I felt also you were safe."

"Safe? Kevin had to do so much to make sure we survived the streets!" Kenzi hissed in disbelief. "Didn't you care to know where we were?"

"I was told you were in Bwaise, *macanto*. If there was anyone I trusted, it was Dina…"

Kenzi felt a twinge of pain shoot through her. "Don't say her name. She was ten times the mother you were or will ever be."

"You can't understand…" Ameena's eyes registered slight hurt for a second. When she blinked, it was gone.

"Understand what? That you let me go blind? That you named me stupid? That you starved me? Did not protect me from all those uncles? That you were never really there? What do you want me to understand?"

"That I was not a good *hooyo* to you?" Ameena cut in. "I wasn't, I know, and when I came back and heard what happened, I felt…sure that you would be better off with Kevin and his family than with me. I did not know you two had run off and were scavenging on the streets of Kampala till we were told you had not arrived in Bwaise much later. I did not know where to start. I don't know, Kenzi, you would not understand." She paused and stared out into space. "Kevin…hmm. That boy took better care of you than I did. He loved you and always protected you."

"You don't deserve to say his name, *Ameena!*" Kenzi hissed back. "If it were not for him, I would not be here today."

"And here you are. You came all the way from America to see him. I heard about what happened to him. *Pole sana.*" Ameena sipped her tall glass of cocktail fruit juice. "He is your family indeed," she said after a moment's thought. "Mackenzie Matthews, I understand the pain. You think I don't know pain? Hmm!"

Kenzi watched her, puzzled for a second. Her heart crushed within her as she felt rejection seep in again.

Then Ameena continued: "But that does not change the fact that you are my child. I bore you. I went through hell because of you. I lost…I lost your father three times because of you. I lost so many people and my own dreams. And I blamed you…"

"Really?" Kenzi stared at her mother in shock.

"Wait…listen. I blamed you for all my misfortune, but it was not all fair…."

"Who is my father?" Kenzi asked.

Ameena waved her hand dismissively. "Trust me, you don't want to know."

"Why?"

"Because he abandoned us both. *Istiraatiiji.* The bastard." She spat the words out like it was bile.

The Ameena Kenzi had grown up with reared its head.

"…and then you abandoned me." Kenzi half-whispered her response. Her heart plummeted at the realization that she was being fooled. Ameena had not changed. "Looks like you deserve each other."

Ameena ah-haaed. "Is that any way to talk to your mother? You scorn my pain." She shook her head dramatically and sighed like a woman with deep sorrow huddled in her breast.

A familiar weight descended on Kenzi, reminding her of the times her mother was nothing but sweetness to her. She had the eerie feeling the cycle was repeating itself and she suddenly felt exhausted.

"What do you want? I don't think I came here to nurse the past and make up. What do you really want?"

Ameena faced her squarely, caressing the delicate curve of her chin with her well-manicured hand. "I simply want my daughter to call me *hooyo* and forgive me."

Kenzi shrugged. "I forgave you a long time ago. I just did not want to see you. But…like you said, *here we are*. Ghosts of the past need to be appeased."

"Mmh…and don't you want me to be your mother? To try again?"

"It's too late for that."

Ameena picked up the spoon on the side of her plate and stirred her juice, disturbing the separated layers.

"I knew it would be hard, but I did not think you would be this stubborn. You do take after me."

Kenzi felt a fresh wave of anger rise in her, her eyes darkening to a deeper hue of green-blue. "I am nothing like you!"

She immediately composed herself. Lunch in public was a deliberate restraining arrangement; Kenzi could do no more than hiss at the woman seated across from her. Her heart hurt, beating desperately, needing to tear free from her chest. Her mother was breaking her heart again. She would not let it happen. Suddenly, the space between them was suffocating.

"If that is all, I think I should leave."

"Uh-uh. Not yet." Ameena was sharp. "Do you honestly think you can walk out of here without giving me what *I* deserve?"

Kenzi frowned, her tea long forgotten and cold. "What do you want?"

Ameena smiled. "Well then, let's make a deal. You clearly don't want me in your life. I have tried." She shrugged in dramatic resignation.

Kenzi scoffed, indignant at how her mother was backing her up against the wall, guilt-tripping her as she had always done. "Just get to the point."

"I need a refund for the years I had to take care of you." The older woman folded her arms on the table before her, her eyes never leaving Kenzi's, a bold daring stare.

Kenzi froze in her seat, not sure if she was hearing her right. "A… refund?"

Ameena clasped her hands together. "Yes. A refund. I am sure with your swanky career and your face all over the internet you get a handsome check. *Lacag.* Money."

Kenzi felt dizzy. *This was it.*

"So," Ameena continued. "I won't ask for much. Twenty thousand US dollars wired to my account is all I ask for. I am sure you can make that happen. Remember what I went through with you. I had to be a prostitute to put food on the table for us. I did a lot. You should understand, you are a big girl now, and you come from a culture where parents need to be taken care of."

Kenzi felt her insides shatter. A cold dark cloud rained hailstones over her. They pelted madly on her soul, crushing and bruising it as they fell fast and hard. The realization that her mother had planned to meet her to extort money out of her was the last thing she had expected or even dreamed of. But did she really know Ameena? True, what was twenty thousand dollars to her? She was one of the highest-paid models now, with a promising future. Her chest heaved and fell for a good sixty seconds before she responded almost mechanically: "I shall get the money wired to you…and then you are dead to me." She spoke with finality.

Their eyes met and for a moment she thought she saw something flicker in her mother's eyes. Was it shock? Pain? Surprise. It was something, *something* that lingered for a few seconds and made Ameena vulnerable, and for those seconds Kenzi dangled in the uncertainty of her choice. The moment passed, and she was resolute again.

"Okay. How soon?" her mother asked. She picked up the napkin absently and folded it.

"Tonight."

Ameena smiled sweetly, and reached for her bag, pulling out a notebook where she scribbled. "Here are my bank details, Bank of Africa."

Kenzi did not care to ask the reason for the urgency. All she wanted to do was leave. Every second she spent in the presence of the woman she called mother, she loathed her more, and the intensity of her feelings scared her.

"Don't contact me ever again. We are even. From here on out, you are dead to me." She said it slowly, like she was speaking to a two-year-old. Her eyes flashed more green than blue.

Ameena looked away briefly. "Sure." She smiled with her lips. "You turned out to be stronger than I thought. Beautiful. Your *ayeeyo* would have been proud. I think you are more like her."

Kenzi stood up. Her slim frame trembled. Her world dithered, and she felt lightheaded. She dug out a fifty-thousand-shilling note from her purse and left it on the table. "Pay for the drinks…keep the change." Then she hastily returned the shades atop her head to cover her blue-green eyes that glistened with tears and walked away briskly.

Ameena stared after her, knowing full well she had lost her daughter forever this time. She had screwed up, but she needed the money.

It was the devil's deal. She exhaled. A whirlwind of thoughts grazed her mind, stormed through her heart. Echoes of pain meshed with ecstasy and fear…love, love never carried on to anyone but Hassan. Even now, when she blamed herself for his death, she still loved him. Loved and missed him terribly. Their relationship had been as torrid as it had been destructive.

The bitter conversation that ended her relationship with Manga played out like a haunting melody, those off-key tunes that never stop playing. She recalled being so happy to see him when he first came to see her after the birth of Shenzi. They had made passionate love every day, and he doted on Shenzi.

Then he had told her about Hassan.

"Hassan came to Klub Malta drunk. I was at the bar like always. It was a good night for clients. He was making a mess. Being a nuisance. He was looking for his Araweelo, his *precious* Araweelo."

"Then what happened?" she had urged him on impatiently.

"He was going crazy. Breaking bottles. Cussing the sisterhood. I could not let that happen. I tried to stop him. He said he knew we recruited you against your will and soiled you. He could not forgive that."

He had told her he tried to persuade Hassan to leave, but he was baying for a fight. He threw the first punch. After the second punch, Manga lost it.

"So, I told him about us. That I had had you. In all the ways a man could." Manga smirked bitterly. "He tried to cut me with a broken bottle."

Manga had knocked him out cold and dragged his unconscious body into his car.

"I intended to take him home. I did."

But he had not. He burned to finish the fight. She recalled the mad glint in his eyes as he relished in retelling it.

"I stripped him naked, tied him up, and waited for him to wake up. When he did, I beat him, then cut him...tiny slits all over his body."

She had frozen, shaking in horror at how calmly he relayed the events.

"He bled. He begged me for his life. He begged!" His voice was steely and alien. She had never seen him like this. It was as if the monster she had seen subdued repeatedly was unleashed, and it terrified her. "He begged for forgiveness." Manga went on, that bitter chuckle coating his story. When he looked at her, she saw nothing there. No remorse, no fear. Nothing.

"It was unfortunate. I let him bleed out," he told her. He reached for her hand. "I did it for you. So he could never hurt you again."

Manga had knelt by her chair and put his head on her lap, muttering, "I would do it again. I take care of those I love; I always have. I would do it all over again."

Then he had told her, "Soonam wants you back. She would do anything to have…you back. She will kill for you."

Everything had fallen in place then: Soonam's *pretend* discouragement of their affair, Manga's fits of rage, the cruelty he exhibited, especially at the club. And Soonam, *how could she be so evil?* It was why she had let them be together. She had wanted them to fall in love because then…Ameena would *never* leave. Soonam had orchestrated this whole situation. She wanted him vulnerable and erratic…*in love!* She wanted to get rid of Hassan because if he was alive, she would keep losing Ameena to him.

She knew how to turn his madness on. He had cried and laughed simultaneously. *That's why he kept away from the sisters, but he could not keep away from her. Soonam used them both!*

In that moment, her bright and perfect world had rapidly darkened like nimbus clouds quickly invading a clear blue sky. Hayira's cryptic confessions of Manga being crazy had resurfaced from her confined memories. Hayira assuring her Soonam liked her and that it was a good thing. *What if she had not liked her?*

He had then told her he had come on Soonam's instructions to bring her home or *kill her or die in her stead.* But he could not. He loved her. He would rather die than harm her. He would disobey Soonam for her. Could they run away together?

"We take care of those we love," Manga kept telling her as she morphed from numb to frantic to blinding rage.

Later, one of the neighbors would tell her of the commotion she had caused when she erupted, screamed at Manga, cursed him and the sisterhood, threatened him, and threw him out unceremoniously.

It was the last time she ever saw him, but the last memory of him haunted her still, the surprise and confusion in his eyes. The tortured expression of a man who had done everything for a woman he loved… and the pleading eyes of a distressed lover glimmered with immoral weakness.

Ameena heaved.

In Kenzi she saw herself, the her who could have done better if she had made better choices. She saw her mother; she saw Hassan. She saw history, and for twenty thousand dollars she had bartered the only archive of her life.

Was it worth it?

She sipped the last of the fruit cocktail and called for the check. When it was cleared, she walked to the bathroom to refresh her makeup.

The face that stared back at her was haunted and yet still beautiful, a seductress. Today, she had done her best to look like a mother. The act was over. She pulled out the plum matte lipstick and spread it on thick, lightly brushed her long lashes with mascara, dabbed on powder from her little compact powder case, and smiled at herself.

Her eyes told her the truth about her. She could never be a mother. Not to Kenzi, not to anyone. She cared too much for her own comforts.

Hariya's words resounded in her head again: *"You will do well here because you don't care about anyone but yourself."*

Somewhere in her, she doubted it. Had she become that person because life had thrown heavy chunks of disfavor her way? Was it always underneath the covers of tradition? At first, she fought change like the werewolf dilemma on the night of a full moon, but it became easier, after Hassan, Manga, after all the men, after the pain. It *just* got easier.

She leaned closer and appraised herself, massaging the wrinkle at the corner of her eye, conscious of it.

My Araweelo, she could hear both her mother and Hassan say, like an acappella with two voices merged at once in song. The old phantoms plucked on her sore heartstrings that reverberated sad notes through her. Then the moment faded, and it was just her staring back at herself.

Was it worth it?

She smiled, satisfaction creasing the corner of her plum lips, and the question lingered, begging for an answer.

Chapter 9

Kenzi curled up in bed and wept.

The waves of anger and pain swept up to the surface like a wild tide on a troubled ocean: reckless and unstoppable. She cried because there had been a small flicker of hope for a rekindled relationship. A flame that begged to be fanned further was snuffed out. She cried because she was angry that once more her mother had wielded power over her and humiliated her and then unceremoniously rejected her. The pangs of rejection clawed at the candle of hope that still felt warm in her soul and shredded it mercilessly. Scar tissue ripped open and bled afresh. She cried because, after all these years, she had lost the mother she never had.

Sleep stealthily crept upon her like a sly thief, finding its nook between her heavy, tired eyelids. Her dreams were disturbing. They were about her mother, a time before Kenzi, and then it shifted to a father she never knew, and finally to Kevin, and he was making a promise to her.

"Kevin!" She sat up abruptly, realizing suddenly it had been over twelve hours since she had last checked in with the hospital. Flinging the sheets aside, she turned her phone on and dialed Bosco's number.

He answered on the first ring.

"Hey, I was worried about you. Your phone has been off. Are you okay?"

Kenzi sighed. She tapped the lamp switch, splashing the dark interior of her room in a warm glow then unhurriedly dragged herself to the dresser and slumped into the accent chair before the mirror. "I don't know." She stared at her reflection. Her eyes were puffy, her hair tangled.

"You did not tell me how it went with your mother."

A sob rose from her broken, exhausted soul. "She…she is dead to me." A whimper escaped her, and she moaned unhinged.

"Kenzi! I am coming over now!" Bosco panicked. "I will be there in a few."

She sniffed noisily. "Okay." She bit down on her lower lip to trap the fresh wave of grief that threatened to spill from her lips in another set of sobs.

The conversation with her mother hummed continuously in her mind. Her phone rang again. This time it was Sketch.

After a couple of rings, she answered it. "Hey, Kenz."

"Hey," she croaked. "I need you to do something for me today."

"Sure, it's almost 11 a.m. over here," Sketch told her then asked, "Are you okay? You don't sound okay."

"Oh, Sketch. " Kenzi sighed. "Long story."

"Is Kevin all right?"

"It's not him. He is stable from what the doctor said earlier. Still in a coma."

"Where are you?"

"My hotel room," she told him, and heard him exhale in relief.

"What's wrong then?"

"I saw my…" She tried hard not to sob, but the tears flowed freely. Sketch said nothing as he waited.

"I need you to do something for me." She sniffed, reaching for the tissue pack by the mirror.

"Shoot."

"I am going to send you an account information via WhatsApp. Please wire twenty thousand dollars from my savings account to it."

Sketch whistled. "That's quite a chunk, K. Are you in any trouble?"

"No!" She was sharp. "Sorry…. Just do it. It's to…her."

"Okay." Sketch sensed she needed time before she could divulge the details. "Okay, so…"

"Let me know when you do it."

"Sure thing. You need anything else? Adjust the date of your flight?"

Kenzi heaved. "Maybe I will need something later."

"Got it. You sure you will be all right?"

Kenzi closed her eyes. "Yeah. Thank you, Sketch. I wish you were here, though…but thank you."

"You got it, girl. Whatever it is, it will be fine."

She smiled. "Yeah?"

"Yeah. You are a tough cookie."

Her battered esteem lapped at the confidence boost he so liberally dished out.

"Thanks, Sketch, I needed that. I don't feel very tough right now."

"We all have those moments. Doesn't make you less of a tough cookie."

"You can be so corny, sometimes." She giggled.

"Shoo, cheered you up a tad bit, eh?"

"Yeah."

She suddenly missed home and her life. Away from the ugly confrontation with her past.

"Okay, I got to go. I need to find out what's happening to Kevin. It's almost 8 p.m. and…"

"Whoa! Whoa! Slow down; take it one step at a time. You sound upset already. So, relax tonight, go out, and clear your mind. Something. Just don't be by yourself."

"You know me too well."

"You bet I do."

They both paused. She recalled him dragging her out of bed into the shower after her breakup with Devon. She had locked herself in her apartment for days, not speaking to anyone, drugged on sleeping pills and wine.

"I won't. Bosco is coming to see me now."

"You got to go out, okay? I will call in and check on you." He was firm and protective. He was suddenly both her bodyguard and friend.

She nodded. There was a knock on the door.

"Speak of the devil…"

"Good. Just be fine and don't be alone," he told her again.

"I won't," she promised, and hung up as she headed to the door.

Bosco was leaning against the wall, a frown of concern on his face.

"You look like you got into a huge fight…." He appraised her with concern.

"It's okay; come in." She stood back, inviting him in. "Want a drink?"

"Actually, the fellows wanted to have dinner. I told them we leave tomorrow. Maybe a stiff drink could do you some good? Better put: a night out on the town."

The frown of concern never leaving his face, he retrieved a bottle of *waragi* from behind his back. "Grabbed this from the bar for a little Ugandan cheer?" He shook it, gauging her.

She sat back at the dresser table. "One shot. Yeah. Sounds good. I feel like I have been to every club out there since we came." She shook her head, recalling their roller-coaster night of barhopping.

He smiled. "You know, Kampala is a hub for parties. The party doesn't stop. Monday to Monday."

She smiled. Bosco walked straight to her mini living room and opened the gold and black elegant glass cabinet, pulled out two shot glasses and poured out the colorless potent liquid in each glass, measuredly.

"So how was…the meeting?" he asked cautiously. And in his mind, he replayed the conversation he had just had with Ameena on his way to the hotel.

"What did you do to her? She was a mess when I called today!" he was frantically spewing when he called Ameena.

Ameena laughed on the other end. "You young people are too soft these days."

"What happened? I can't keep doing you these favors…."

"Doing me favors? Like you don't benefit? You are in love with the girl, no?" She mocked him.

He bit his lips.

*"So, what is stopping you now from being her knight in shining armor?"
She jeered, "and do I even have to tell you the fat opportunity you have now
with her? She is alone in Uganda with you! No Kevin, no bodyguards, no
what...there! And I, I, Ameena, did it! Don't talk to me about favors! We are
partners!"*

*She hissed at him, and he buckled both regretfully and with dread. For a
minute, he was sure he had made a deal with the devil.*

*"So, she is broken and vulnerable. She will be fine. Go get your prize; fix
her. Maybe get her pregnant. Who knows? It's up to you." She was callous
and dismissive.*

*Then, like a switch had been turned off, she was gentle again. "You are doing
so well, macaan...We are still working things out."*

"I can't...I can't hurt anyone anymore...I can't." He spoke helplessly.

*"Who is going to get hurt? No one.... Everything is as it should be. Just let
me know your moves on the oil deal."*

He was silent.

"Okay?" she pushed.

He paused, thinking. "Okay."

Kenzi picked up the hairbrush and brushed her hair. "I don't think it
was a good idea."

"I am sorry. I...I just thought maybe it would help. You know..."

Kenzi sighed. "I know. If I were you, I would have done the same thing.
It's not your fault."

Bosco felt shards of guilt pierce through him. After all he had done, he
did not understand how he still maintained his stance. He believed he
was just as bad a person as Ameena. He battled with that still. Ameena
was worse than him. He comforted himself that he was in love. People
do strange things for love. He was a victim, and he needed this prize. It
hurt him that she was hurt.

"I am sorry, Kenz. I will make it up to you. How about we do dinner
with the guys, go out on the town, and it's all on me."

She laughed. "You are too kind. It's been 'all on you' since I got here! I
can't let you spend like that...."

"Kenzi, please. I am sure Kevin would have wanted that. He would be glad you were taken care of."

"Thanks. You are a good friend."

"I am only your friend because all those selfies on my Instagram have garnered me followers I never thought I would have." He laughed, trying to disguise his nervousness.

She threw her head back and laughed. And he saw Shenzi again. Laughing hard at something Kevin said as they huddled in their little spot, wherever they chose it to be, and giggled and ate pancakes or *mandazis*. There was always a curious air about them. Like it was just the two of them in the universe, and no one, nothing else mattered. He had craved to be a part of it, but Kevin had his unspoken rule: none of the boys could hang out with him and Kenzi, but the boys could hang out with the boys.

He was always too respectful, and slightly afraid of Kevin, to barge in on their little world. Now he wondered if that unspoken rule had all been in his head. Would Kevin have objected to them hanging out all together even though he fiercely guarded Kenzi like a hawk? Anyway, for the moment, he was in *that* special spot. He was making her happy. The guilt he had felt instantly evaporated, and he gazed at her, enjoying her.

"You just made it to my top ten most hysterical people," she was telling him as she took the shot glass from him.

Bosco shrugged, feigning nonchalance. "To your smile." He raised the glass.

Kenzi shook her head but did not object to the gesture, and they toasted and drank.

"So? Dinner? And a night out?"

"Wooh!" she made a face as the *waragi* invaded her mouth and throat, then replied, "Sketch will send the whole US Army here if I don't. So yes."

"Wait! This decision rests upon Sketch's demeanor?"

She tossed the brush in her hand at him. "Precisely...not! He said I should not be alone, and you came in with the solution. Hand and glove? Perfect fit. Me thinks."

Bosco grinned. "I like that." He got up, paced uncertainly. "I can go down to the lobby and wait if you need to freshen up."

She nodded. "Sure. Anything on Kevin?"

He scrunched his nose. "Same as yesterday, stable. There is a high chance he will wake up."

"I know he will. Kevin is a fighter." There was determination and hope in her tone.

A silence fell between them like a gray cloud, and the light air was suppressed by a fast-gathering forlorn energy.

"Right. We will see him tomorrow," Bosco said uncomfortably, toying with his phone.

Kenzi rested her face on her balled palms, her lower lip protruding in a pout. "It's been a long day, Bosco. I need to feel happy. It's been so long."

"Let's do that. Let's make you happy," he assured her warmly.

Thirty minutes later, Kenzi emerged from her room dressed in a pair of tiny sequin metallic shorts and a sheer blouse with an insert. Bosco whistled. "Is it your plan to wear something more and more revealing each evening?"

She shrugged. "If we are going to a hot club, I need to minimize perspiration. The girls there don't shy away from nakedness either."

"I am glad the guys are coming. We will need an entire army to protect you from these Ugandan men."

She grinned. "I am glad there are…five of you?"

"Yup."

Before the guys showed up, she told him the decision she had come to concerning her mother. "It's a lot." She had waved absently, still sore over it, but she conclusively told him of the agreement over twenty thousand dollars.

"You what?" Bosco asked, shocked.

Kenzi shook her head. "I made my decision. I don't want her in my life. She's not changed, and she does not want or love me. She proved it."

"Kenz…"

"I think we both are happier with our decisions. It hurt to realize that…I had adored someone who did not give a fuck about me!" Her voice quivered, and her fingers shook. Recounting the day's events made her feel sick. She desperately wanted to forget it all.

"I am fine," she added, forcing a smile. "Let's got out and get wasted."

* * *

First stop was dinner at the Kampala Hilton.

Oketcho came in first, talking about being held back by his wife asking numerous questions about this *"summer* model."

"Oh, my *Gaad."* He groaned. "'Who is she? Why are you going to see her? These *summers* steal our men….'" He mimicked his wife as he got into his seat. "I tell you, women!"

Kenzi laughed. "I hung out with you guys only last night and tonight."

"What did you tell her?" Bosco was chuckling.

"*Man,* I simply said Kevin's girlfriend."

Kenzi giggled, flattered. "You said what?"

"Only way to save my skin from men-snatching *summers* who are also famous models. She would have bound me indoors with chains. I tell you, that woman!"

Kenzi played with her earlobe. *Kevin's girlfriend?*

Something about the way he said it…sounded right…natural.

"I hope you are not offended, but that was the expensive ticket to a night out."

Kenzi shook her head. "Oh no. It's fine. If Kevin wasn't such a brother to me, I think he would be the first man I would not mind being a girlfriend to." She grinned.

Bosco tried to smile. "Yeah, we tease him about you a lot. At least I do."

"Tease who; what are we missing?" It was the Arabic-laced accented tone of tall, lithe Bhanu followed by Abe and Tisa.

"You guys came together?" Bosco asked as the men got into their seats around the round cocktail table.

"Yeah, figured driving separately would just be impractical." Abe, the shortest of the three with what Kenzi had called inquiring eyes, pulled the chair to her left side and warmly beamed. "How is our superstar doing?" He reached for her hand and took it in both his hands, holding her gaze as he did.

Kenzi grinned, forcing herself not to shy away from his "inquiring eyes."

"Never better. Especially now that you are here." She flirted with him, enjoying the attention.

"*Anhaaa…*I was hoping for such a response."

She was charmed by him, enjoying the seamless flow their conversations always took and his attentiveness to every detail. He came off as a warm social animal. When they went out, she noticed a lot of the girls took to him. His personality oozed through effortlessly.

"*Mulimutya?*" He turned to Bosco and Oketcho. "The wife threw another tantrum, no?"

"You know how it is. It's a soap opera in that house, worse now with the baby on the way."

"Oh, your wife is pregnant? Congrats, Oketcho." Kenzi piped in, "How come you never mentioned it?"

"I did not?" He frowned. "I think it skipped me to tell you. These boys have known for months."

Tisa laughed. "Kenzi, that chap is a computer guy. They don't have proper social skills. Forgive him. I am starved, ready to eat."

"So, who was being teased?" Bhanu dragged the issue back. Kenzi found him curiously intense and yet private. Apart from a few inquiries into her past connection with Kevin, they had spoken little. She felt he was one that would take a lifetime of breaking into. He was polite and attentive, missing nothing. A quiet, serious-looking man with a common-sense approach to everything.

Bosco waved his hand dismissively. "We were just talking about Kevin."

Oketcho butted in: "My ticket to coming out all these nights has been the lie I have pedaled that Kenzi here is dating Kevin."

Tisa made a clicking sound with his tongue. "That will be the day!"

"What happened to Vanessa?" Bhanu asked, almost as if he had been out of the loop of the social intel.

"I thought you and Vanessa were close," Abe asserted.

Bhanu shrugged. "I can bet you all know more than me." Bhanu traveled more frequently than any of them. Sometimes he was called away on impromptu business, which lasted weeks.

"Vanessa? The same?" Kenzi asked.

Bhanu was not sure how to proceed, so Bosco helped him out. "Yeah. The same..."

"Oh, the...er...lawyer's daughter?" She vaguely recalled seeing several phone calls come in from a Vanessa when Kevin visited her in the US.

"Yeah," Abe replied. "But you know...that lie could become true. What do you think, Bosco? Kevin and Kenzi have known each other forever. You are a witness."

Bosco shook his head, slowly. "Kevin is not the marrying type...."

Tisa groaned. "I remember a few years ago, that was Oketcho's tagline till the Mutooro lilt of that woman of his floored him. Or was it her figure?"

The guys laughed. Kenzi watched them, enjoying their light banter. She wondered what it was like when the whole gang was here. *Kevin.*

She watched them switch easily from serious current affairs to light cordial topics, often drawing her in with questions about the modeling world, America, Obama, and the looming presidential elections, which she cared nothing for.

After their four-course meal, Abe made a few calls for VIP table reservations at Guvnor.

"First stop," he announced. "Then the rest of you can take over. I would suggest Oketcho does us the second honors considering he might leave us at 2 a.m."

The others laughed. "Thankfully, I won't be the one dropping off everyone at home after a night out because we drove in one car."

Tisa whistled. "Shots fired."

Kenzi was laughing, sipping her wine leisurely.

"We might just crash at someone's pad. Whoever is closest by the end of the night," Abe responded, unbothered. "We do it all the time. Don't you miss the bachelor life?" He grinned, side-eyeing Oketcho.

"Nah, free pussy every day if I wanted." Oketcho would not let him win.

The rest whooped and laughed. "And curfew," Abe added with a short, mocking laugh. "Oh, come on, let me just win this. Come on now!" And everyone laughed.

Kevin should be here, Kenzi thought as she watched them. Although she was enjoying herself, she dreaded the thought of spending the night alone in her hotel room until their flight back to Kenya, wrestling her demons, pain, and the empty spaces filled with loss, sadness, and confusion. She envied them all. They seemed so light, so free, and all she could do was soak in their energy, allow it even for the moment to illuminate the dimness in her.

The ache she recognized was a longing to speak to Kevin about her mother—to rant and rave and know he would be there like a rock, steadying her.

Abe charmingly won the argument of who should ride with Kenzi. His argument was she had ridden with everyone else the previous night but him. The retort was he had driven alone. The final decision fell to Bosco, who reluctantly agreed to her going with Abe while Tisa and Bhanu rode with him. Oketcho was already en route to Guvnor.

Abe eased into their flow of conversation, teasing lightly and flirting throughout the short drive from the Hilton to Guvnor. "I call first dibs on the first dance tonight."

She raised her brow humorously. "You are too cute."

"Ah, that breaks my heart." He dramatically stabbed at his chest as his S-class smoothly made a turn at the roundabout on Jinja Road.

She giggled. "You can't help yourself, can you?"

"I do well for myself, don't I?"

"Evidently."

Then more somberly, "You leave tomorrow for Kenya, right?"

"Yeah." She breathed in, clasping her fingers over the little metallic purse on her lap.

"You know I don't say much, but it would be such a blow to us if Kevin, you know…if he…"

"He will wake up," she interjected firmly. "He just has to!" she asserted. "Sorry, I just…I just…"

Abe glanced at her. "Don't be sorry. I feel you. Kevin is our man, and he is the core of us. Smart as hell. Sharpest dude I know. But for you, it's…harder. He is like your brother."

"He is the *only* family I have."

Abe reached out and placed a warm hand over her fingers. "You got more family now. No matter what."

Kenzi felt the lump rise in her throat, and she wrestled with maintaining her composure and keeping the tears that danced on her eyelids from staining her cheeks.

"That's…that's so sweet, Abe…."

He winked. "Anything for a beautiful lady…." He squeezed her hand before steering the car into the lane where the huge luminous Guvnor sign hung and parallel parked in the only available spot. "Parking in this place is a beast!" He threw fists up animatedly.

Kenzi shook her head.

The rest of the crew was already inside when they got in. The dull thump of beats swelled exponentially, rushing out through the doors the moment the bouncer ushered them in. Kenzi whooped as the telltale Nigerian afro beat vibrations from Yemi Alade's "Johnny" thrummed through her, and she was vibrating along with it.

She joined them, sitting next to Bosco, who handed her a shot glass topped with vodka. "We are toasting…. To Kevin."

Kenzi whooped again.

As their glasses met midair with inaudible clinks amid the deafening hum of music, Kenzi saw their lips mouth "Kevin" in unison, and down went one shot.

Then another.

And a final one.

"Three cheers to…" Bosco was literally shouting in her ear. The vodka coursed through her body, numbing her senses till all she could feel was the vibration of the music, the pulse of the beats, and her feet moved of their own volition. "Let's dance!" That lightness and freedom she had craved all day rippled through her. *Finally!*

Abe was the first one up. "First dibs!" he shouted in competition with the music. Kenzi swayed a little but happily took his hand and skipped off to a clearer dance floor space. The rest joined them one by one.

The night seemed to pass like a hazy dream, dancing from one song to the next. Drinks flowed, and the music did not let up, nor did the crowds.

Kenzi did not recall a lot of it except for waking up in her hotel room with a headache and nausea. She stumbled out of bed groaning. Hardly able to find the switch for the bedside lamp, she zigzagged to the bathroom and threw up in the toilet bowl before her legs gave way, and she crumpled to the floor, her hand resting over the toilet seat.

She did not recall someone coming in and picking her up off the floor and putting her back in bed. She did not feel them pull the covers over her and watch her a while and go back to the chair in the corner and try to find a more comfortable angle in which to sleep.

Chapter 10

The aromatic smell of coffee roused her.

"Rise and shine, Sleeping Beauty." The coffee had a voice.

Kenzi jerked up with a deep intake of breath as if she had been drowning and scrambled to the surface for air.

"Easy! Slow. You will spill!" It was Bosco, still dressed in the slacks and blue shirt from the day before.

Kenzi relaxed, slumped back on the pillow, and groaned. "Urghhh, I blacked out, didn't I? I had too much to drink."

"Umm…"

Kenzi groaned louder. "What else, what?"

"The unedited version?" Bosco was laughing.

"Urgh, just give me whichever version."

"You danced like you were on steroids at Guvnor, took more drinks but insisted on going to Sheraton, and we went there. Halfway through the partying, you burst into tears…"

"Urgh! Get out! I just made a fucking mess of myself. Urghhh."

"Nah, the guys figured you were just drunk."

"Did I say anything I shouldn't say?"

"Not really, just that you hated your mom, and then I decided it was best to bring you back."

"What time was it?"

"Three."

"Urgh."

"Then…I got you here, and you threatened to hurt me if I left you alone, and you barricaded the door with your body; you literally sunk to the floor and would not get up…. You clung to me, refused to let me go unless I stayed. So, I stayed. You were asleep the moment you got into bed, then an hour later, you got up, went to the bathroom and threw up."

"Oh lawd." She covered her face with her hands, half-embarrassed, half-relieved. "I threatened you? Oh, my goodness!"

"Yeah, and I got you back into bed and made myself comfy on that there chair." He pointed to the chair. "And now it's…almost noon. Our flight is in three and a half hours." He handed her the little coffee cup.

"Black and sweet as you like it." He smiled.

She shook her head, taking it. "You are so good to me, Bosco."

Bosco felt a warm rush within him. *Because I love you,* he wanted to say, but a wise person once told him that to court a woman who did not know your true intentions, you had to make it her idea to fall in love with you without pressuring her. *"Kill her with goodness,"* was what they had told him. He intended on doing that to Kenzi, slowly gaining her confidence.

"Kevin is my brother, and you are his sister, so you are my sister too," he added for good measure.

"Aww." She put the coffee cup on the side table. "Come here."

He sat by her bed, and she hugged him. "Thank you so much. So, *so* much for everything. I don't think I would have handled it here without you."

"It has been a pleasure. You are always welcome here, you know." He could feel the small of her back. Her spine protruded slightly through the see-through black top. She was slender and small yet shapely. Just like her mother. They carried themselves with patrician grace, and he loved that about her.

She pulled back, and, holding his face in her slender fingers, she kissed his cheek. "Thank you."

Bosco felt his heart stop and his groin grow. Their eyes locked and the smell of coffee mingled with a cocktail of alcohol on her breath fanning his face. The words of the wise man he had once known became a distant mumble in his brain. Before he could stop himself, he was reaching for her, his thick fingers cupping the nape of her neck. He was pressing his lips over hers, feeling their softness against his. He urged her on for a kiss, searching for her mouth with his tongue.

Kenzi drew back, her eyes wide, and he snapped out of it, the spell broken. He realized what he had done.

"I am sorry, Kenz. I…I am sorry." He quickly got up from the bed and walked to the door, trying to hide the bulge in his trousers.

"I…er, will go home and change. See you in an hour?" He had his back to her.

"Y-yes." Kenzi swallowed, slightly embarrassed. "I am sorry, Bosco. I…"

"It's fine. I got carried away." He waved it off, and then cudgeled himself inside. It was obvious she did not see him the same way.

He tried to smile and glanced at her. "No more puking, okay? And eat something."

She nodded. The air had shifted, and the room felt smaller than it was. "I will be fine. I shall see you later then."

He nodded, then turned to the door, mumbling something about checking out, and he was gone.

When the door clicked shut, Kenzi flopped back on the pillow. "Oh, fuck!" She groaned. "Fuck fuck fuck fuck fuck fuck!" she hissed out, slamming the bed with balled fists.

Maybe it was just a moment, she told herself. She could not imagine either of them telling Kevin when he woke up.

Why did it matter? The jarring question asked by a little voice in her head piped up.

"Because he is Kevin's best friend and right hand, stupid!" She shouted out the response.

Frustrated, she got out of bed.

"Just go home, Kenzi," she mumbled to herself stomping to the bathroom while peeling the clothes off herself. Time was of the essence, and there wasn't a moment to think of the drama of the last twenty-four hours.

She needed to focus.

***

The flight to Kenya seemed long. Kenzi tried to dispel their previous awkward moment with conversation. She had hardly had time to bid farewell to the guys and had spoken only to Abe, who had promised he would come to the US next time around.

"I miss the guys already," she said.

"They miss you too, I bet," Bosco responded with as much civility as he could manage. "We never really talked about what happened…"

"Bosco…"

She cut him short, and he raised his hand up, momentarily motioning her to stop. "…between you and your mother."

"Oh." There was tangible relief.

"She chose money over me. I think we talked about it?"

He raised a brow, then shook his head. "Uh-hm, we did not. You said you guys agreed to a sort of payout. As if that solves the biological problem."

Kenzi sighed. Talking about it was still raw, but she could handle it better today. "All she wanted was for me to bankroll her really, like I said, and she was manipulative and…and…." She told him pieces of the conversation they had had.

"And?"

Kenzi shrugged. "So, money is on the way as we speak. I asked Sketch to wire it, and then she is dead to me."

Silence.

"Wow, Kenzi. I am sorry. I really am." He was truly sorry and hated to think of the part he had played in this.

Kenzi shrugged it off. "It's nothing. I have family. Right?" She turned her green-blue gaze on him fully, almost as if she was searching for something.

Bosco dropped his gaze uncomfortably. "Yeah. Of course."

Kenzi frowned. "What?"

Bosco rubbed his hands together. "I guess I haven't been honest with you, Kenzi. I…" He paused, knowing whatever he told her after that would change a lot of things in their relationship, so he paused long enough to regroup his thoughts. "I reached out to your mother and told her you were coming."

Kenzi shrugged. "It's fine, really. It was the inevitable waiting to happen, you know. My mother will always be what she is…a manipulative, selfish bitch." Kenzi shook her head. "I wish I knew what happened to her. Maybe she wasn't always that way." She paused. A part of her felt sorry for her mother, then it closed up. "But we make choices."

Bosco agreed, *choices.* The word felt heavy.

Kenzi was still rumbling on. "Isn't it funny? How you can resent someone so much for what they made you go through but still adore them?"

Bosco scoffed. "Tell me about it." It was a feeling he could understand. He envied Kevin, even resented him at times, yet deeply respected him.

"It's complicated," they said in unison…and laughed, finally breaking the awkward ice between them.

Chapter 11

Aga Khan Hospital
Kenya
October 2016
3 p.m.

The lean figure lay on the hospital bed, tubes and wires connecting him to a monitor whose screen flickered and jumped, registering scribbles in a consistent pattern. They had wrapped his head in bandages. The nurse studied him, adjusted a tube here and there, and inspected a translucent bag of liquid in the drip that trickled ever so slowly through one tube attached to his arm. She rearranged the green hospital sheets to cover his partially exposed chest and glanced at him sympathetically. *So young and attractive.*

She hoped he would survive the coma; his injuries were serious. It was a miracle his spine was intact despite the impact of the blows to his body. Her eyes suddenly caught the monitor screen. The scribbles jerked slowly at first, then wildly. Her eyes widened, as she looked from the monitor to the man in the bed. His eyelids moved rapidly. The nurse pressed the emergency button by his bedside and held him down. Spasms rippled through his body.

"What's going on?" A male doctor ran in, followed closely by another nurse, who rushed to the side of the comatose patient on the bed. His eyes took in the scenario, and the beeping on the EEG monitor alerted him.

"He just started convulsing, but he is still comatose." The nurse spoke with urgency.

"His brain waves are overly active." The doctor inspected the monitor, while the pen in his hand flew rapidly along with an accompanying thin notepad. As suddenly as it had started, the convulsing stopped, but the EEG monitor remained relatively erratic.

"Strange," the doctor finally noted with a frown.

The nurse agreed. "I always thought no one in a coma has any brain activity at all."

The doctor didn't reply immediately. "Maybe it is a good sign. Maybe he is fighting his way back. Or maybe memories are too powerful to let him rest." He spoke more to himself than to her. They watched the monitor for a minute more, still registering brain activity and puzzled over this new scientific slip, while the young man in the deep state of sleep traveled through time unhinged, visiting chapters of a life he would rather keep stowed away in his nightmares.

"So?" the nurse asked.

The doctor lifted a gloved finger, signaling for silence as they watched Kevin.

"Wait," he said. "Let's wait."

* * *

Itombwe Mission Hospital sits at the end of the dusty makeshift road that leads to South Kivu gold mines, only a mile away, a twenty-minute walk, if you are fit but almost an hour if you have a raging fever and a chest-breaking cough.

Kevin sits on the wooden benches outside the waiting room because it is full. The sun burns into his bare swollen feet, but for that moment, he does not think of it. He only sees the crumpled photo in his hand. He has been keeping it with him since he left Kampala three months ago and followed Bampa into the depth of the Congo in search of wealth enough for him to find Shenzi and fulfill his promise to give them the life they always dreamed of. Now all he has are memories and a photo. He remembers that day like it was yesterday. He hears the cameras.

Click!

"Let's take a picture, Shenzi."

Kevin hesitates as the words emit themselves almost involuntarily. He knows this part of his life. He looks around confused but goes on with the script. "Please, I thought maybe we should take a photo together. You and I don't have pictures at all. Together, I mean."

He gazes at the young girl before him: Shenzi at eight years old, and she shakes her head.

As if on cue, he persists, "Let's do this; we take it, and I will describe it to you, and when you finally get to see, you will see I did not lie. It will be that picture that holds me to my promise of you seeing; don't you want to know what you looked like?"

Shenzi sighs. He would not give up. "Okay, okay. Promise me if I look horrid you will tear it."

He smiles jubilantly. "Yes...I promise."

From the look on her face, she is unconvinced of his intentions, but she lets him get away with it.

He beams. "You will not regret it, and when we are out of here and in... Canada or Spain or America, we will always look at it and remember today, not so?"

Shenzi nods.

"So, are you ready?" He knows that she always believes him even though some part of him tells him he lets her down.

She sighs, stands up, and brushes her hand over her dress. A blue, pink, and yellow floral dress. "Am I okay?"

Images flash and merge, an older Kenzi, a younger Shenzi. He nods; he had never known her to not look fine.

"Yeah." He shrugs.

He realizes he is playing out his life, almost like he is there, visiting the past, but little Kevin is not there. It's just him. I must wake up, *he thinks.*

But instead he is up on his feet, throwing an arm carelessly over her shoulder and dragging her along to where the cameraman stands and shouts out to him, "Eh, Abdu! We are ready! I have five hundred shillings."

Abdu follows the money. Kevin nudges Shenzi. "Should we take the picture here?"

"Anywhere, as long as our faces are clear," it was barely a whisper.

Kevin nods at Abdu, the cameraman. "Here is okay," he indicates.

"Kale," Abdu responds, adjusting his Nikon camera. Kevin links his arm over Shenzi, and she leans into him, her lips twisting slowly to form a cynical curve, and right before the smile could form, the camera goes...

Click!

"Byamukama!" His name is called from within the waiting room. Kevin stirs and tucks the photo back in the back pocket of his jeans. He takes in a deep, painful gulp of air only to wheeze and cough hysterically into his hands. He is back somewhere else, and it hurts to be in this place of memory. Kevin shakes the slimy blob to the ground and wipes his hands on the back of his jeans. His eyes blur and clear gradually. The thick bloody sputum has increased; so has the pain. He gets up slowly and stumbles into the waiting room, as he follows the dark-skinned nurse into the room she is walking toward.

There is a bald-headed doctor scribbling something in a long notebook. He looks up briefly when Kevin walks in and sits. "Mr. Byamukama, your results are not good," the doctor promptly opens the conversation.

Kevin sighs, a little anxious. "What...?" He swallows. "What is wrong, Doctor?"

The doctor stops scribbling and looks at him. "Do you have family here?"

Kevin thinks. His mother. Shenzi. That was his family since they left home, and she was taken from him. He shakes his head. "Not here."

The doctor studies him. "I think you need to quit mining. The mercury is making you sick, and you might die in your sleep. Nurse says your bloody cough is worsening; it is not good, baba."

Kevin stares at the floor. The doctor is right; he has seen men die in their sleep abruptly. He has not eaten for three days, as food does not stay down long enough. The women by the mining center have started to whisper that he is going the way of the miners. He can smell death like the first drizzle that hits a dry, thirsty ground. It lingers in the air. He reaches out absently to his pocket for the photo again.

"I promised...I made a promise to Shenzi. That I would be rich enough to take her to a doctor so she would get her eyes back. I promised." He speaks absently, feeling the fever rise.

The doctor shakes his head, convinced Kevin is having an onset of brain fever, and piteously asks, "Is it worth your life, this mining?"

Kevin stares at the photo long and hard, his need to find Shenzi and keep his promise stronger than the looming death the doctor speaks of.

Finally, with renewed resolve, he says, "Yes."

The doctor stares at him and shakes his head. Maybe he thinks he is mad, that he will die, or that he is stupid. Kevin can't tell.

Finally, he calls out to a nurse in Lingala: "Get him a bed. He needs to rest a couple of days. We shall see how he is after that."

The nurse who comes in, skinny and tall, takes notes, then stops. "Doctor, there is only one bed left...."

"Well." The doctor pauses, scribbles something on a notepad, tears it out, and gives it to the nurse.

The nurse hesitates for a split second, then goes out, calling on another nurse to come help her lift Kevin, who has slumped sideways in the chair, unconscious, a silvery line of saliva forming on his parted lips, dripping slowly toward his hand. The doctor reaches for the crumpled picture that looks like it has been through as much as the young man has. He peers at the image of the boy and girl for a long time, then slips it within the pages of his heavy diary.

He hears the young man slur. "I must wake up...I must wake up..."

* * *

Kevin gasped. A claustrophobic feeling gained on him, and he frantically groped at the ventilator over his mouth and the tube to his nose. "Kenzi!" he yelled...suddenly terrified. His brain fuzzy and yet the only name that impressed on his memory was Kenzi.

He must see her…the blurry image of young Shenzi merged with an older Kenzi. The images scrambled in a disturbing miasma before it settled like a dune fading, and he could see her face, bright smile off a distinct smooth ebony face and piercing twinkling blue-green eyes. The monitors whirred, and an alarm went off. Kevin jerked as about three people ran into his room, two women wearing green scrubs and a man with a stethoscope around his neck in a white coat. Kevin stared at them in confusion.

"Check his heart rate," the man in white boomed, and one woman obediently leaned over him. The man in white continued barking out more commands, and the women in scrubs scrambled around busily.

Eventually, he turned to Kevin and said, "I am going to check your eyes, okay? It won't hurt."

Kevin frowned but did not resist as the man in a white coat, who was slipping on transparent latex gloves, reached for his left eye, prying it open gently, then with a tiny torch examined it.

He did the same to the other eye. The door opened, and another person came in wearing green scrubs.

The man in white turned to this newcomer and said something in Kiswahili, then turned back to Kevin. A huge smile of relief cast a light on his chocolate face. "You are at Aga Khan Hospital. You have been in a coma. Your friends will be so happy to see you awake."

Chapter 12

Nairobi, Kenya

The familiar sounds at the Jomo Kenyatta International Airport greeted them like old friends. Bosco called a cab as soon as they were past Customs toward the exit to the airport, and in less than ten minutes, the white Toyota Camry with a yellow stripe along its body, a bright yellow car topper sign with the word *Taxi* written in bold black font, pulled out of the winding driveway of Jomo Kenyatta airport, bound for the Villa Rosa Kempinski Hotel on Chiromo Road once more.

"Let's see how our man is doing," Bosco muttered partly to himself and to Kenzi. As soon as he swiped the screen open to punch in the numbers, the phone lit up with the caller ID, Dr. Abuya.

They glanced at each other, and Bosco clicked *answer*, putting it on speaker simultaneously.

"Yes, Doctor."

"Hello Bosco, how are you? Are you still in Uganda?"

"We are fine. Kenzi and I just got into Nairobi. We are on our way to the hotel. Is everything okay?"

The doctor let out an enormous sigh, and Kenzi's heart faltered. "Yes, everything is okay. In fact...everything is great!" He sounded more jovial than when they had last seen him.

"How is Kevin?" Kenzi interrupted, mouthing a *sorry* to Bosco.

"Oh hello, *Mizz* Kenzi. It's good to hear from you as well. If you can come to the hospital in maybe the next thirty minutes, that would be very good."

"What's going on?"

The doctor paused. "Kevin woke up, but he is in evaluation right now. He has said little except calling out for you when he woke...."

Kenzi interrupted in excitement and relief. "Oh, my God! We are on our way!"

Bosco nodded. "That's great news, Doctor. That's good news. We will be there any moment now."

The doctor chuckled. "I am glad to be the bearer of good news. See you then."

Bosco instructed the driver to change route to Aga Khan Hospital.

Kenzi squealed again. "I told you he would wake up!" She clasped her hands together gleefully.

Bosco couldn't help the dizziness that washed over him. *Kevin awake! What now?* And he asked for Kenzi.

Kenzi could hardly sit still. Absently, she picked up her little makeup mirror, powdered the puffy eyes away, and dabbed a dash of gloss on her lips to look presentable for Kevin.

Traffic was heavy at 4 p.m., and the streets' busyness reminded her of New York. Kenzi drifted off. Her mind danced between her meeting with her mother and seeing Kevin. The message her mother had sent her when she initiated a meeting remained etched in her mind: "I thank God you are here, *qalbi.*'

Qalbi. Sweetheart.

She scoffed. She doled out such sweet salutations at a hefty price. Praise was a reward, an offering of an apology, or just the result of those rare good moods.

Sweetheart.

She reacted to it almost subconsciously, as she had when she was younger. It pacified her, giving her a reason to meet with Ameena. The *God* part too. Her mother mentioning God in anything sounded strange.

Ameena never talked about God; neither did she care. She loathed the idea of God as she loathed humans, so it seemed.

So maybe she had changed. *God?* Ameena abhorred the notion that every religion possibly classified God as a man. She would spit and jeer: "Does what is between our legs classify us on who has more authority?"

She had been the blind spectator to Ameena's dramatics as she slammed doors and chased away many preachers with kitchen ladles, her high-heeled shoes coupled with a colorful touch of magnanimous insults hurled in all the languages she spoke, her somewhat good spoken English, fluent Somali, Kiswahili, and sometimes Luganda. When she did not want them to know how deep her blasphemy was, she spoke sweetly and jovially while cursing them in Somali.

It was funny. Kenzi had stifled laughter while listening to the scenario playing out at the door: her mother unrelentingly quizzing these disciples to exhaustion. They usually left defeated. As blasphemous as she thought Ameena was, she could not help feeling proud of her mother's insightful brilliance. She was always thinking, always questioning, and never relenting unless the facts were presented. If she had finished school, maybe she would have been a lawyer.

Kenzi recalled one day Ameena had just returned from a late lunch with her newest client, a diplomat from Sri Lanka. Hardly had she flopped onto the black leather sofa when there was a knock at the door.

"Shenzi, go check who is there!" she had called out to her in Somali.

Kenzi slowly inched her way to the door, stick in one hand, the other hand against the wall, feeling the corridor that led to the front door. She stood there, feeling for the keyhole before pressing her lips to it and asking as loudly as she could, "Who is it?"

There was no response, just knocking.

She could hear her mother curse from the living room. "Ah! Who are these bothering me?" Her mother had stomped to the door, shoving her aside and flinging the door open.

"We are sorry to bother you and the young girl. I can see you just got home. Please. This is Marcus and I am John. We greet you in the name of Jehovah. Can we ask you a question , just one and we will be on our way?"

Shenzi waited. She knew this dialogue too well. She had heard it many times.

"We are not believers here; we are atheists." She heard her mother scoff. "But…ask."

"Madam, how are you? You have a lovely daughter…." Ameena let her know there were always two men , one black, another *Mzungu,* to which she would frown and ask what a mzungu was.

"Ah! Those white people in films you and your boyfriend Kevin like to watch. Do those people speak like you or me?"

That was Ameena's definition of *mzungu.* She learned to listen to their enunciation, and anyone with an accent she was not familiar with became mzungu to her. Right then, the greeter sounded like the Black man to Shenzi.

Ameena shook her head impatiently. "Ah-ah, we are past the pleas-antries; get on with it."

There was silence. Then she heard the mzungu voice: *"Jambo!* Um…we don't want to take too much of your time, but we thought we could sit down and share our faith with you. You see God *loves* you…."

Ameena interjected quickly, "Ah-ah! You told my daughter and me one question. What is it? Because I have one for you."

The Black man spoke. Shenzi admired his confidence. "Ladies first."

Silence again and then Ameena said slowly, "This…God of yours, is he man or woman?"

The mzungu launched into a recital of a practiced response: "God is an uncreated person with a spiritual body; he also…"

"*He?*" Ameena interrupted.

"Well…"

Ameena was closing the door. "When God can be a *she*, I shall listen to you." And with that she slammed the door in their protesting faces.

"When you see those men, one Black, one mzungu, in a black suit and tie and white shirt, *aad u dhaqso badan!* Run for your life, okay?" she had told her for the umpteenth time and walked away to her room. "Lock that door! I don't want any more disturbances!"

"*Haa hooyo,*" she had replied in Somali then, eager to please. She wondered if her mother noticed her blindness or had hopes she would see again soon. A tiny light flickered inside her. *Maybe.* She heard the door of her mother's room click shut and the key turn. Maybe she had not heard her. Kenzi had vowed to speak louder the next time she tried to speak in Somali like her mother had taught her from time to time.

Chapter 13

Finally, the traffic eased up as they turned from Airport Road to Outer Ring Road. Their taxi driver chatted animatedly about traffic in the city. Kenzi gasped now and again when he squeezed between a *matatu* and tiny Corolla, then somehow snaked around them to get ahead. "This is crazy," she whispered to Bosco, and he exclaimed. "Welcome to Nairobi."

Fifteen minutes later, they were weaving on Embu-Nairobi highway past a busy road crammed with buses and taxis and commercial buildings lining dusty pavements and freeways. Eventually, the white sign post with Third Ave., Parklands, and Aga Khan Hospital loomed into view, and Kenzi spied the green, cream, and redbrick structure of the hospital embellished with scattered floral shrubbery and trees. Her heart beat wildly in her chest.

When they pulled up to the front of the hospital by the visitors-only entrance area, Bosco took out their small travel bags and rolled them to the front doors. Kenzi held them open for him.

"Let me get one," she offered.

Bosco shook his head. "And let Kevin see you lug luggage behind you? He will kill me."

She felt herself get hot in the face, glad she could not blush. "Aww. But I insist."

Bosco was adamant. "You want to fight about bags?"

"Hmm, maybe not. We will finish this later."

"I think so."

She thought he was a little curt but brushed it off. *I am overthinking things,* she chided herself. It had been a rather dramatic thirty-six hours after all.

They let the receptionist know who they were there to see, and Dr. Abuya was with them promptly. He had the look of a man who had solved a most diabolical equation, a curious problem none of the experts that preceded him could. He pumped Bosco's hands emphatically and beamed at Kenzi.

"Yes, at 3:30 p.m. Mr. Kevin Byamukama woke up from the coma he has been in for the past week. His vitals are fine. He is still being diagnosed, so we can tell what level of recovery he will have. His injuries were getting better through the time he was in the coma, and he seems to be cognitively sound. It shall take a little time for him to fully gain all his faculties because…well…in the plainest civilian way I can say it, he is a little scattered and will need time to adjust." The doctor was relating to them Kevin's condition once he had them seated in his office.

"How…how long will that take, Doctor?" Kenzi tried not to sound alarmed by the word *scattered*.

Dr. Abuya shrugged. "Usually it depends on the determination of the patient and surroundings to familiar things."

Bosco nodded, then excused himself from the office.

"I would like to take him back with me to recover in peace. I don't know if he will be safe back home, Doctor. The hit on his life was very devastating for me. I think he will be better away from here while investigations go on."

Dr. Abuya nodded contemplatively. "You are probably right, but we can only authorize his release after three days at least. He should be able to show signs of stability after we check his vitals, making sure he has no clots and other standard procedure. You don't want him on the plane suddenly going into any type of seizure."

"No, of course not."

Kenzi sighed. "That's fine. I shall arrange for him to have medical attention while he is with me."

Her mind raced, poring over the details of the last two days, from heart-gutting pain to being drunk, kissing Bosco and now Kevin waking up. She needed to consult with Sketch about an extra ticket for Kevin, and confirm the validity of his visa, or else it would be another process.

Dr. Abuya smiled. "Great."

"Can I see him now?"

He flicked his wrist to check his watch and shook his head side to side, his lower lip a little drawn out. "Maybe five minutes?" he indicated with a balled fist.

"Sounds good."

"Do you want anything from the vending machine? Water? Chips?" He was heading to the door, and Kenzi started to get up.

"No, please, you can stay here, it's *sawa*...fine."

Kenzi sat back down. "Thanks, and no thanks, I am fine." Five minutes seemed like a long time now that she was so close, so close to seeing him on the mend.

Bosco came back in, informing her that he had called the gang, and they were planning to drive in the next day.

"That's a long drive, right?"

Bosco shrugged and sat on the chair next to hers. "With four pairs of hands, fourteen hours is a breeze."

She agreed.

After a moment's pause, Bosco broke the silence, "Er...it would be good, umm, helpful if what happened today stayed between us. It was an awkward moment." His voice was low.

Kenzi smiled. "It's all good really. It's just..." She shook her head. "Bosco, it's okay. Not a problem. No one has to know."

A short while later, they were walking down an unfamiliar hallway to another room.

"We transferred him from the high-risk department in the ICU to the recovery and outpatient department," Dr. Abuya was explaining. He walked briskly and calculatedly like he was counting every step. They made a sharp left into a wider, shorter hallway with a plaque labeled *outpatient* in green.

The hinged double doors swung open revealing a nurse with a clipboard in her hand and a turgid IV fluid bag in the other hand. Dr. Abuya and she exchanged a quick greeting in Swahili, and she smiled at both Bosco and Kenzi.

The hallway was dull with ivory walls, void of any personality. Hospital smells: Detergent, bleach, and medicine greeted them. She shuddered. The thought of being in hospital again for anything was paralyzing.

"We are here," she heard Dr. Abuya announce. They came to a halt at a door marked *2D*.

"Now I shall let you see him, and if at all you notice anything, if he stops talking, freezes, convulses…anything, please alert us immediately. There is a panic button by his bedside for any emergencies. It alerts my department, and a nurse will be in immediately."

They nodded.

Kevin had his gaze averted to the window a few paces away. Monitors were attached to his chest, and his head was still wrapped in gauze. A bouquet of bright red, white, and yellow roses sat on the table by his bedside.

"You have your first visitors for the day, Kevin," Dr. Abuya announced cheerfully. Kevin turned his head slowly, his eyes fixed on Kenzi and Bosco.

A slow smile crept up his lips. "Doc, where did you pick up these lost children from?"

There was a momentary pause, then Kevin grinned. "Has my sense of humor deteriorated that much?"

Kenzi sighed audibly with relief. "Oh! You gave me such a scare! I thought your memory was scrambled." Her eyes glistened with tears. "I am so glad to see you up and talking." She hugged him as best she could.

"Aww, woman, watch these tubes and things, will you?"

She laughed, relieved; he sounded like there was no heartbeat missed.

"I am fine. Although, I must stay on these pain pills for a while, but I am good. How are you?" Their gaze met and time paused. She searched his soul for pain pulses, for anything amiss, and he absently did the same, worrying she worried too much. He reassured her with the warmth of his gaze. Things he could not put words to, his eyes conveyed.

She nodded. "Good. Worried sick about you." She furrowed her brows.

"Don't start crying now. I was the crier, remember?"

She punched him playfully. "Oh, my goodness you gave me such a scare. Don't do this to me again."

"Come here." He opened his arms wide, and she fell into them, holding him. The faint medicinal odor on him hit her nostrils, but beneath it she smelled him, felt him. Kevin held her. "I am here, boo. I am not going anywhere. Not anywhere without you again."

"No more scares." She choked as she tried to hold back her tears.

He raised his brows, and his eyes held a naughty glint. "We can arrange that."

She pulled back from him, sniffing. "No worries, I already did…. Dr. Abuya said I can take you back to the US for continued monitoring. Also, I want to keep an eye on you." She stressed this.

"*Hmm*, sounds like house arrest…. Do I get to have strippers entertain me?"

Kenzi pursed her lips. "We will see about that…"

The spell was broken with Bosco clearing his throat exaggeratedly.

"That's a bad case of ear, throat, and mouth infection, my friend. Don't swallow," Kevin joked.

"You are full of jokes today, my man." Bosco was walking up to his bed. They clasped hands. "The afterlife must have had an effect."

"The wonders of a near-death experience," Kevin responded.

Bosco nodded, looking away briefly.

"So, flowers?" He was asking as he surveyed the bouquet by the bedside.

"Vanessa had them specially delivered. A note from her and her father." Kevin nodded at them, and Kenzi picked up the little card that was attached to them, reading.

"Ooh, your girlfriend is really sweet." She winked at him.

Kevin grinned. "Did you meet her?"

Bosco shook his head. "We did not have a chance to, but she was blowing up my phone asking about you since she found out."

Kevin nodded briefly.

"It's good to see you conscious, man. The boys will be here tomorrow. They are driving in."

Kevin whistled. "Man that stretch is deadly, but once you are over the border, it's a breeze."

"Not too much for four men."

Kenzi held his hand, quietly massaging it while he spoke with Bosco. Her heart felt full. She wanted to tell him so much, but…not yet. It would be selfish. Now he was awake. Nothing else really mattered. She longed to have him to herself so they could spend time together, figure out what had happened, and follow through with the investigation. She also wanted to ascertain he was fine.

One time, when they were younger, Kevin was sick with malaria and could not go to school for a week. Kenzi went by herself, dropped off by Taata Bob. Her mother had traveled with a client, some rich Swede she only heard about in whispered gossip along the staircases of the flats. They had seen him once or twice pick her up and drop her off. So she was staying at Kevin's home. Every afternoon she got home, she changed out of her uniform, got into bed beside him and almost always exclaimed loudly about his temperature and how she would be baked to a crisp in no time.

She would lie next to him and tell him everything she could about school while trying to feed him her leftover snacks.

Bitter, he would turn his nose at them, grimacing; he never had an appetite, and he complained that everything tasted bitter. The only way she knew how to comfort him was to hold his hand and caress it. In her mind it eased his aches and pains. Kevin would still make her laugh, even in sickness.

Then she would attempt to tell him a story, but it was never quite as riveting as when he told stories. Most times she fell asleep in his bed. Sometimes his mother moved her; other times she whimpered, refusing to leave his side, so they let her stay. When his fever would finally break, they would both be drenched in his sweat.

Kenzi absently raised his hand to her cheek; it was warm and rough. A man's hands. A man who had had his fair share of pain and loss in life.

Bosco and Kevin were still speaking. She vaguely drifted in and out of their conversation, and all of it was business: the oil deal, concern from Haruna and their lawyers, how his attack had caused such a flurry.

"How is Carissa? I hope she has been updating my social media," Kevin was saying.

"Oh, she has been asking about you every day. Kenzi met her."

Kenzi smiled. "A cute girl...."

"They took selfies until her phone memory was done." Bosco shook his head. "In fact, her Instagram for the day was awash with every little thing Kenzi did."

"And you indulged her?" Kevin frowned. "That girl lives in the cloud."

Kenzi grinned. "Why not? It's an iCloud generation. I was glad I made her day."

"Poser." Kevin grinned at Kenzi, and she shrugged, pursing her lips.

Bosco's phone vibrated, and he excused himself.

Kevin turned to Kenzi, appraising her. "You look nice...a little thinner than the last time I saw you," he added with a frown.

She made a face. "You say that all the time. But thanks. You don't look too shabby either. The swelling is down. Do you hurt?"

"I can't feel a thing. Honestly, if I did not know any better, I would say I lost my sense of feeling. Those painkillers in this IV thing are strong as fuck."

"Ooh, what do they have you on?" she asked.

He shrugged. "Whatever it is, I should have reduced amounts of it in another twelve hours." He tried to sit up, and she helped him adjust the bed.

As she did, he watched her, and she caught his gaze. "What?"

"You hate hospitals…. I'd understand if you never came."

"Pssh. It's you, Kevin. Remember, between us there are no phobias."

He laughed. "True. I brave the snow, don't I?

"You hold up pretty well too," she grinned.

"I try … So you were in Uganda?"

"Yeah."

He waited. "And?"

She sat down and ran a hand over her thick ponytail.

"I met Ameena."

"Does not sound like that went well," he noted.

She shook her head. "We can talk about it when you are better."

"I want to know now…. I am better."

"Kevin…" she trailed off, hesitating for a fraction to compose her sentence carefully. "Um, let's just say I won't be seeing her again. She's a closed chapter of my life."

Kevin pursed his lips. "That sounds like a conversation for ten thousand miles away."

She nodded. Then her eyes twinkled. "So, did you get to see the light at the end of the tunnel?"

"Light?" Kevin asked, puzzled, then the familiarity of the phrase dawned on him, and his attractive features softened in amusement. "You watch too much sci-fi. No, I did not leave my body or hear or see anything. But I had peculiar dreams, if that's what they were."

"It does not hurt to ask, does it?" She grinned sheepishly. "The dreams?"

"Just pieces of the past." He gave a short laugh. "And no, it doesn't."

"I am just so glad you are back. What a shame if you…did not wake up." Her lips quivered.

"I am not going anywhere, Kenz, not yet. I decide when it's time to go. We still have an entire world to conquer. Like always…and this just proves further, life is short, no regrets, live it." She liked it when he spoke like that. He called it, *commanding his universe.*

"You and me." She nodded, and they were there again, on the rooftop, staring out into the city, the streetlights and car lights, merging and dazzling, held them captive in a trancelike spell.

"I am sorry I did not bring you pancakes…the hot peppered ones." They both laughed at that.

"I am sure the hospital would find it *non grata,* but thanks for the memories," he teased.

Bosco returned, and they had more deliberations on retrieving his passport and packing a travel bag.

After much insistence, Kevin agreed to travel to the US for a few weeks to recuperate. They largely ignored his ten thousand reasons to stay in Uganda. "You need to get away, big head." Kenzi was firm.

She rolled her eyes at him, watching him trying to coordinate his travel details.

"Kevin, let Bosco and the guys handle it. You need to get well, and we need to find the scumbags who did this to you. I am sorry, but I ain't letting you return before that's sorted." She had her finger in his face.

Kevin shook his head. "American women!" He turned to Bosco. "Just keep me posted."

It was decided that Tisa would put together his travel bag because of his knack for meticulous essential travel packing and keen skill in finding things, no matter where they were concealed. Kevin would coordinate with him via phone to help him locate his passport and a few other work-related files, much to Kenzi's objection.

"We've got to make a deal, Kenz," Kevin was enjoying this part of the negotiation that favored him. "I shall…what do you people call it? Work from home."

With a sigh, she agreed. "Fine!" She cast him a sidelong glare as he triumphantly winked at her.

"And we are traveling private… can you get a refund for your ticket?" He added with a small smile waiting for her to protest. Kenzi glowered at him. "Fine."
Travel arrangements were completed, and they joked and conversed till

the nurse they had seen in the corridor came back in to take his vitals and shooed them out. Kevin needed to rest, but they were free to return for a brief period much later in the night if he was awake or the next morning.

Kenzi agreed to check in later.

She leaned over and hugged him, kissing his cheek. "Who's been giving you alcohol?" he asked.

"Your boys are the best, baddest company a girl can have."

He smiled. "I am glad you did not sit at my bedside day and night like a forlorn widow."

"But…"

He shook his head. "I would never want that. It's selfish. I would want you to enjoy yourself. You have not been home in more than a decade, Kenz."

She nodded slowly. "You are telling me not to see you tonight, right?"

He furrowed his brows. "You are smart."

She hugged him again. "I will see you tomorrow, then. That's only 'cause I know you are awake, and I have Doc Abuya's number on speed dial."

He held her lightly.

"See to it this woman sleeps, Bosco. I don't know what sinful part of Kampala you took her to spoil her, but phew! It's all over her."

She lightly pinched his lean, muscled arm, hardly grabbing any flesh.

"Ouch!"

"I thought the pain meds numbed you." She raised her brow, walking to the door followed by an amused Bosco.

"There is no antidote to your pinches."

Kenzi laughed. "Goodnight, Kev!"

"Sweet dreams, princess," he replied.

* * *

The ringing of the phone by her bed woke her. Kenzi fumbled for it and mumbled a sleepy "hello" into the mouthpiece.

"Hey, did not want to wake you but er...good afternoon...the guys just got here. They are at Bhanu's place and will head to the hospital, letting you know. Text me when you are ready."

"Afternoon? What time is it?"

Bosco hesitated. "Noon-ish?"

Kenzi gasped. "Oh shit!"

"Relax, chill. No one is going anywhere until later. Catch your beauty sleep."

Bosco chuckled, but Kenzi was rolling out of bed in a frenzy.

"It's noon, Bosco. I never sleep in that late!"

"You probably needed it."

"The hell I did! I am awake now. I shall be ready in thirty."

"All right."

* * *

Bigz called Kevin on Skype.

"*Bwana*, I was concerned. Thabiso and I heard from Bosco and kept in touch. We were worried sick. Good to see you back in form."

"Thanks, Bigz," Kevin responded warmly. They talked about the ongoing investigations and the business of the mines.

"*Baba* Ssaka would be proud, Kevin, real proud," the light-skinned man on the other end of the laptop said with conviction. As they spoke of Ssaka, they both seemed to drift off in reverie and pay respects to a man they both loved and respected, a man they were more than convinced could be dead or in graver danger than he had let on. No one had heard from him in three years.

Kevin nodded. "He would."

There was momentary silence as the ghost of a man so influential hovered over them in digital space.

"Good to see you breathing and awake. Please let me know if you need anything. We are meeting with the board on Monday. I shall deliver the news and send you reports," Bigz told him.

"Thanks, man. My regards to Thabiso." Bigz smiled widely and shared his final words before signing out.

The next two days in Kenya, Kenzi enjoyed the boys' company immensely. Now she saw how much they connected, so much that in the absence of one, there was a perceptible gap.

"*Wewe*," Kevin warned Abe who was furiously flirting with Kenzi. "If you are trying to be smooth with Kenzi, you might need to scale this wall." He pointed to himself.

"I think I can manage it…in its current state," Abe responded, sending the whole crew into laughter, save for Bosco, whose short laugh seemed forced.

She found herself increasingly uneasy around Bosco. She was more and more aware of his unspoken body language, his comments, and his energy around her.

She wanted to believe she had imagined it, but her conscience told her what she was seeing could be it; Bosco did like her…*still!* It had been a joke when they were growing up…at least she thought so. He was always shy around her, and Kevin teased him relentlessly. She recalled how he would always let her have extra bubblegum when Kevin sent him to buy some for their group of troublemakers on Block 4. He would secretly slip it into her pocket and whisper in her ear, "More gum for you…because you are the youngest."

She recalled him being at her last birthday party on Block 4 and how reluctant he was to leave when it was time to go home. Kevin had mercilessly assailed his friend with jokes about his feelings for Kenzi until Bosco got sharp and Aunty Dina had to put a stop to it before a fight broke out.

Kevin.

She smiled and shook her head, always fighting, always making someone cry, the Block 4 terrorist who prided himself on not having silly feelings and liking girls, the arch-protector of *Shenzi*.

Shenzi.

The name brought back sad memories of her childhood. At least what she could remember. Words. Smells. Sensations. The most intense being Kevin.

The crew spent the whole day discussing the oil deal and the way forward before Kevin and Kenzi's flight. Kevin entrusted Bosco to oversee it and send him information after meeting with the president.

Chapter 14

October 2016

The flight back to the United States was long and uneventful. Kevin slept a lot, much to Kenzi's relief. The doctor had told her he needed to stay on painkillers for at least two weeks until the swelling reduced. He also would need a lot of bed rest and light movement until he felt able to move faster and for longer distances.

Kenzi watched him sleep and smiled. The joy of finding him again and realizing that her adoration of him had never faltered. Maybe suppressed, but it always lurked. Brent had been a good substitute. He was the best she had for a time, still did. Now they were leveled up. She loved them both. Her brothers.

Do you? A voice inside asked her, prying at the secrets of her mind. Those that she kept hidden away from the light of truth.

She balled her fingers into a small fist and pounded on her thigh, lightly. The voice nudged her. *Do you?*

She looked at him again, his chin smooth and freshly shaved. The hospital had covered the cut he had gotten from the recent accident in a small bandage at the side of his head. He still had the gauze over his head, and there was much teasing about getting him a wig to conceal his bald head. But the almost forgotten scar that etched his forehead got her attention—a long thin line, so subtle and easy to miss. It looked a lot more like crease marks when he frowned, blending in perfectly with the furrows. She reached out and lightly traced it with one long acrylic nail, then gasped as his hand shot up and captured her wrist in midair.

"Fuck! You scared me!" she hissed.

He drawled. "What you get for staring at a sleeping man, *then* almost touching him."

Her mouth flew open. "I did not! Besides, how did you know? You were asleep!" she responded, more surprised than shocked.

"Developed instincts, my dear. And… I am a light sleeper." He put a finger to his lips, his eyes dancing. "Also, you sold yourself out."

She shook her head. "Funny, I never seem to fully grasp it."

"Since you have decided to kidnap me and keep me…against my will in New York, you might ship me home after two nights of strange and curious events."

Kenzi *harrumph*ed out loud.

"I might sign you up for Broadway while you are here. I think."

"I might like that." He winked at her then asked, "Do you know how long we are off?"

"Another eight hours," she said.

"Hmm." He shifted. "Did you nap?"

"Umm…Mr. I-am-a-light-sleeper-who-is-alert-in-his-sleep…what do you think?"

He patted her arm. "Aww, it's pretty obvious you were rather enjoying the view."

She grinned.

"Hmm, it's not all that. But…that scar…that scar." She pointed at his forehead.

"How did I miss that? It has…character."

"Yeah?"

"Yeah." She grinned.

"Unlike your flawless skin." He traced a finger lightly against her cheek. "Well kept." The smile was content.

"Oh you know, new cosmetic lines and a beautician, what can I say?"

She fluttered her eyelashes.

His eyes flickered. The past played in his dark brown irises. "I am glad you got away. You would be a Lil Wayne look-alike by now." He teased.

She nudged him playfully. "There can only be one Lil Wayne look-alike between us, no?"

He inhaled deeply. "Spot's been taken indeed."

She drew her knees in and leaned into him. "So, *Lil Wayne*, care to indulge…this scar I missed…"

His hand smoothed over his brow like rubbing it would conjure up his thoughts. "There is a lot *we* missed. *This* is one of them. Although I am glad you missed this one."

"Yeah? Tell me."

He had dropped out of time, spiralling into the past. "That street fight I told you about. Almost took out my eye, but it got me my street."

There was a hollowness in his voice every time they spoke about the past, like he was dragging around old rags whose threads were stuck to his shoe with stray chewing gum.

"And there were the other places, scars…South Africa, Sierra Leone… Ssaka," she trailed off.

Kevin drummed his fist lightly on the seat arm.

"Congo was the wildest. Ssaka…God knows where the heck he is…. It's…been three years." He stopped talking, and they drifted into a heavy silence.

He told her about different facets of Congo, like a series with multiple layers and plots. There was always a new scene he had not told her in the past, and when he spoke, it was not indulgent like a woman but like a man who had seen death and sworn an oath not to talk about it.

Sometimes memories embraced him and pulled him away from her, no matter how close they sat. She could understand why, but she could not get used to how it crept up so suddenly, like now.

She cleared her throat. "I never told you of the time I tried to scrub the black off of me?"

Kevin shifted in his seat to look at her, and she kept her gaze straight ahead. It was something she never talked about easily, but…

"This flawless skin…" She half-chuckled. "I hated it. I hated being stared at in school. One time this white boy called me…well, he was straight out offensive. In school. I was only thirteen and super self-conscious. I got home and tried to scrub the black off me. My mother… Maxine came into the bathroom because I was taking forever in there. Everyone was concerned. I was in tears. I told her I wanted to be like her, like all of them…that I hated being this black. I wanted to scrub it right off." She took in a deep, shaky breath and looked at him. She could read the compassion in his eyes.

"What did she say?"

Kenzi scoffed, shaking her head. "She cried with me. She told me I was beautiful, that I was so damn beautiful God would not have me any other way. I was enough."

Kevin reached for her hand and squeezed it. "Damn right she was. What happened to the boy?"

"Actually, Brent beat him up. He was the first of about three that Brent beat up. But my parents caused a stir when the principal suggested Brent get punished; instead, they made sure that other kid was suspended. His parents came to school. *Urgh*. Shit storm for a week!"

Kevin 's face lit up. "Big up to Brent! That bully deserved that." Then in a more concerned tone: "I hope you know you are beautiful."

Kenzi shrugged. "Because I make billboards and strut catwalks? I am just rare." She tried to be light, but he was staring at her gravely. "No, because you are beautiful." She searched his eyes. They meant every word he said. Kevin would not lie to her. It was just that…sometimes she wavered. She was better than when she was twelve or sixteen. Still…she wavered.

She nodded instead.

They were inseparable fifteen years back, and with a nudge they understood each other's thoughts and even healed each other, but now, the connection was interrupted by scars, walls, and pain. The people they were and the scars they carried made them strangers to each other sometimes.

It will take time.

Give it time, she told herself.

Maybe now was the time to properly get past it. "We haven't lived normal lives," Kenzi said.

"Pray, tell, what is normal?" he inquired.

"I guess the definition differs from person to person."

"Exactly! As abnormal as it may have been, there is a probability that more than half a billion people on this planet are saying the same thing."

"Living their own abnormal lives." Kenzi said.

"Yet here we are. " He smiled at her. "Making the best of it."

She scoffed. "That's sweet."

"When did you become a cynic?" He frowned.

"When you became so optimistic." She folded her arms across her chest, leaning back.

He hummed. "We swapped places somewhere along the course of this decade, eh? How does it feel walking on the dark side?" he teased.

She laughed. "You are so dumb, you know?"

He smiled. "You've got to get back to work as soon as we get to New York, right?" He was asking instead.

"Sort of. I have a photo shoot for Luz in two days and a new project my agent has assigned me starting in about a week or so. Will get the details."

He nodded. "Have you ever thought about starting your own modeling line…cosmetics, maybe?"

"I did, especially for the dark-skinned girl who can't seem to find any foundation to coat her color. Yes, that's somewhere in the back of my mind, but right now…." She shrugged. "I was thinking of a foundation that supports blind girls in Africa. I want to explore my heritage."

Kevin raised a brow, impressed. "That's a great idea."

"Yeah, you know how fucked up it is to really figure out who you are from many miles away?"

Kevin shook his head. "I can't imagine."

"Yeah, so I found Somali communities and connected with a few people making a difference starting organizations that supported women and children who had been dealt a heavy hand by the political instability, early marriages and Female Genital Mutilation." She spoke and he listened.

"I found out about all these things here, Kevin!" it made her angry thinking about how little she knew about her heritage. "That woman did nothing for me. I never want to see her again."

Kevin took her hand in his and pressed it reassuringly. "I really like the idea. Forget Ameena; she is her own destruction. You are better off and about to make a difference. I want to support you, so I will give a donation, get you connected…."

She made a face. "So now you can just rise from the dead and dictate things?" she joked.

"It's resurrection energy, my dear. A foundation is so you…. And I can help any way I can."

Kenzi shook her head. "How about we get to that when you are better?"

"Is that a yes?" he stubbornly insisted.

"I am not answering that now." She shook her head.

"So, will you leave me hanging? What would you rather?" He coaxed her, mischief playing in his eyes.

She lit up. "Er…you getting better?"

Kevin shook his head and smiled. The smile touched his eyes, and they glowed with a warmth that nudged at her soul, and she could feel that familiar connection they had on the streets. "Maybe we can look after each other for a few weeks, no?"

She smiled back. "Agreed…. We can do the foundation thing after all this."

Kevin sighed. "I tried."

∗ ∗ ∗

J.F Kennedy Airport was abuzz when they landed. Kenzi insisted on pushing Kevin in his wheelchair.

"You know I can do it myself."

"I know," she replied. "But I want to." She stubbornly held on to the handlebars.

"My God, I am not going anywhere, not far enough."

"Don't play with me, Kevin Byamukama!" she fake-scolded him.

"My, are we in a mood!" He leaned back.

Sketch met them at the executive terminal sounding a warning about the dropping temperatures. "It is October after all," he said and greeted Kevin. The two men quickly delved into conversation like they were the best of childhood friends. Kevin told him the highlights of the attack and how the investigations were being handled by his friends back home.

"That must have been a defining moment for you," Sketch said.

"Yeah. One of many. It was," Kevin agreed.

"I remember a time I got into a fight. You know I am from Chicago: South Side, born and raised, the worst neighborhood ever. We slept with our eyes open. You don't miss a beat 'cause some thug will sneak up on you, and before you know it, you are making chalk for the cops, man," Sketch told him.

Kevin nodded. "Oh, I hear you. I tell Kenzi here she is very pampered." He grinned and patted her hand.

"Don't forget I am pushing the wheelchair."

Both men laughed.

* * *

With the traffic, it took them almost an hour to get to her two-bedroom apartment in the West Village, making a left on Tenth Street and pulling up on a lane Kevin remembered too well: happy hour afternoons and walking by cobble-stoned streets to get to FAERS cosmetic boutique; it was quaint, fashionable, and artsy. The sort of atmosphere he grew to realize was up Kenzi's alley. After being in New York several times over the years since they had reunited, he much preferred the financial district.

"That's where the money is at," he would tell Kenzi. He enjoyed New York, the smells, the fact that downtown Manhattan and Times Square were hubs of human traffic and activity, quite like Kampala streets.

He was shocked at how dirty and littered it was and yet how much it bubbled with artistry and hustle; he figured if he could survive Congo, Sierra Leone, Jo'burg , Namibia and Kampala, New York would be a breeze. His pleasant surprise was when he finally met Kenzi's adoptive parents in DC. They were to him a reasonable bunch, as were her adopted siblings. DC was a pleasant surprise, a lot tamer and cleaner than New York. He anticipated seeing President Barack Obama, proudly calling him, "Our man! The African in the White House."

Kenzi made a face. "He ain't all that. Totally American!"

Given the choice, though, he would live in Los Angeles. "It's all in the weather, Kenz. I can't stand this east side's temperamental climate. One season is hot and muggy, with abnormal rain showers. Then the next, it's freezing with a side of flakes and icy rain to top it all off. I can't do it," he had told her when he first visited her in New York.

The sun had long set, casting lonely shadows on the streets. They could hear distant laughter from a bar a block away.

"Home, sweet home," Sketch was saying.

"Thanks, Sketch."

They got Kevin through the door. The bellman helped with their luggage to the elevator. Kenzi lived on the top floor because she liked to have a rooftop and balcony. It always reminded her of Kevin.

When Kevin settled in the living room, remote in hand, Kenzi went over her schedule with Sketch.

"Appointment with Dr. Sangeeta tomorrow, Luz shoot Thursday all day and half-day Friday, oh and the wire for the money was completed this morning."

Kenzi nodded gratefully. "Thanks. I am exhausted."

"Everything is set. I got the second room set up, and as you can see… your study and living room are refurbished."

Kenzi let her eyes appraise her once minimal living room that looked wider with the addition of a bookshelf framing a plush study corner. She liked it. "Did Maria do this?"

Sketch nodded. "Yup! She was up for the task."

Maria, Sketch's special friend, was an art and interior decorating student whom Kenzi had hired on and off to help upgrade her apartment. After the first few re-dos she made to her living spaces, Kenzi agreed her intuition for her client's needs was remarkable.

"Oh my goodness, she kept it minimal, gold and bone with a dash of burgundy, like I like it. I would say she reads minds if I did not know better."

She turned to Sketch, touched. "I just told you to help get the room ready."

"I am supposed to do my job, above and beyond, right?"

Kenzi squeezed his arm. "Thank you so much. What would I do without you?"

"Prolly nothing." He scrunched his nose, and she guffawed.

"If you are all good, I will leave now."

Kenzi nodded. "Yes, we are. I will take care of this big head here."

"Ah, I heard that!" Kevin responded.

"You listen to things you shouldn't hear!" She called back to him as she walked Sketch to the door.

"Feel better soon, Kevin," Sketch called. He nodded briskly to Kenzi and left. Kenzi leaned back against the door and kicked her shoes off. The heat was on, and she basked in the 74-degree warmth.

"You hungry? I can't stand airline food. I am starved."

"I can eat," Kevin replied.

She ordered Chinese takeout and sweet tea and vowed to buy food, make real home-cooked meals or learn to for as long as Kevin was there.

"Don't stress; we can use an occasional chef, like the last time," he assured her.

"Now, I like that," she agreed.

They dined in front of the TV in silence, each lost in thought.

"What are you thinking of?" Kevin asked first thirty minutes into an

Iraq documentary.

Kenzi stretched, placing her bowl and chopsticks on the place mat on the coffee table.

"I don't know…stuff." She shrugged. "You?"

He picked up the remote and switched the channel to ESPN, volume low. Halftime commentary of a rugby match was on. "That I need to fix you breakfast soon."

She laughed. "If I recall, breakfast disasters that have traumatized me have all come from your well-meaning hands, burnt toast, burnt bacon, and then there was warm cereal. Eww, who does that!"

"You forget your spiked orange juice."

"Kevin, you are mess. I had a shoot that day too!" She shook her head. "For one who makes amazing rolexes and baritos, I can't quite figure out how you can bungle the most basic meals of the day."

Kevin smiled, hardly bothered. "I did not think there would be a day when you would take care of me. It never occurred to me."

She looked at him, and in that moment, they felt closer since their reunion. "That you would need me?"

"That the roles would be reversed." He looked uncomfortable with the word *need*. "Oh, and I would not expect you to pay for anything."

"Oh hush." Kenzi frowned. "I can handle this."

"No, I am serious." He looked at her.

"Oh wow, can't I take care of you for once, in my house?"

Kevin protested, then stopped, flipped the channel one more time, and with a better organization of his words, glanced at Kenzi and responded, "If I am going to have a visiting nurse checking in on me, I want to go in with you on the bill, if that makes it easier for you. I don't like it. I should pay for all my expenses. I am a man, and I am older than you."

"That's sexist…and ageist!" she retorted, then mimicked him: "I am a man, blah-blah-blah."

He laughed. "Ageist? What did America do to you? Do you know a girl back home would bask in that?"

Kenzi tossed her thick curly hair back. "Good for them."

"Ouch, that hurts."

They did not pursue the topic further, but in an unspoken way, it felt settled.

"You did not tell me about the meeting with your mother." Kevin broached the subject.

She drew her legs in, folding them under her on the sofa, hugged a burgundy-covered pillow throw, and told him, detached from it all like it was someone else's story.

"I gather the money you gave her got to her. Kale "

"Sketch said it was completed. I did not hear from her. No 'thank you,' nothing."

"Why would you expect a 'thank you'?" Kevin switched channels again and dallied on what looked like an episode of *Law and Order: SVU*.

"You did not have to give it to her, you know."

The lingering, hollow, dull ache threatened to resurface. "But I did. To fucking get rid of her!" She knew she had spoken a little too harshly, but it was all she could do not to cry again.

After the first commercial break, he took her hand and squeezed it. "I am sorry. I hoped after all these years maybe she would be different. It was a slim hope. I wish I had known Bosco was trying to get you to see her…." He shook his head. " It's done."

Kenzi nodded slowly. "I…wanted to see…home, too. The flat is so different now. It did not feel the same on the roof. But yeah…it is done." She had learned to detach from memories and people, a mechanism that she had developed after her separation from Kevin. It was easier to let go and not return.

"It is done." She repeated it, more to herself.

* * *

There was a sea of people gliding in one direction toward something. Kenzi knew what it was, and the urgency to get to it before anyone else did was suffocating her. She pushed through the thick crowd of bodies that reluctantly gave her leeway. She pounded against their backs and arms, begging them to let her through, telling them she knew how to help. If only they let her through.

No one paid her any attention. She was on her hands and knees, clawing past legs until those legs started to trample over her, and she fought to get up...but the legs held her down, and she clawed viciously, then suddenly someone propelled her forward into a clearing, and there she saw him...Kevin. Lying on the ground. There was blood all around him. She screamed.

Kenzi woke up sweating, her heart pounding wildly in her chest. She threw the covers aside and rushed to Kevin's room, tiptoed to his bedside and stared at his sleeping form.

The dream puzzled her. This was the same dream possibly concluded. She had the uncanny feeling it meant something; the blood was frightening. The only thing she could think of was Kevin dying if he went back to Uganda. She dropped to a squat, staring closely, making sure he was breathing. He could not go back. Not until they had found who was behind his attack.

The next day she called Bosco; he picked up on the first ring.

"Hey." He breathed. "Charmed to hear from you."

"Oh you know, it's been busy, wanted to check on you guys." Something in his tone reminded her of what had happened between them in Uganda.

"We are good."

"Anything about Kevin's attackers?" she asked.

Bosco hummed. "No, not really. We are still looking for the gateman, Doctor, and we might need to get forensics in for fingerprints."

"Well, do it. I think Kevin would like that."

"Yeah, I spoke to Kevin about it; we are on it." He sounded bored.

"Okay."

"But how are you?" He brightened on that note. "I hope Kev isn't a lot to deal with."

Something in his tone annoyed her, so she was plain. "When isn't he? We are good. He is doing much better. Maybe he will be in Uganda soon, unless I stop him."

"Ha, who can stop Kevin?"

"I think I can," she replied possessively, as if Kevin was only hers, and she alone had some secret power to wield over him.

"Okay," he replied flatly. "Hope to see you soon, though. You are missed."

That *thing* in his tone again.

"Oh." Kenzi did not know what to say. Suddenly, it was awkward. "Sure. Okay, got to go. Call me if you know anything. I bet you will call Kevin first, but keep in touch."

Bosco agreed. "I definitely will. Bye."

When he hung up, the feeling something was off sat in her gut. She could not help thinking about their accidental kiss.

The dream hovered, fresh as the daylight that streamed in through the window of her room. She made a note to look up the meaning of dreams later but more still figure out how to keep Kevin away from Uganda at least until they found his assailants.

<h1 style="text-align:center">Chapter 15</h1>

The weeks rolled on by like the leaves that turned golden and fell off the branches littering the streets and lanes in gold, russet, and brown. The coffee shops along walkways scented the air between them with delectable aromas of peppermint, marshmallows, and pumpkin as New Yorkers ushered fall in with Thanksgiving and Halloween.

Presidential elections were underway, and the talk of town was Hillary would be "Madame President" without a doubt. The Democratic Party was already rejoicing for a landmark sweep in the votes as the Republican candidate Donald Trump seemed to fail miserably as a presidential candidate on all fronts. Literally most Americans were practicing how to address the new female presidential hopeful, from the news anchors to the bank teller to the salesgirl at Bergdorf Goodman's men's store.

"Can't wait to say, 'Madame President,'" the short, chubby Hispanic girl with bleached hair and thick mascara on her fake lashes said to Kenzi as she carefully packed the gray and white cashmere scarf she had picked out for Kevin.

Kenzi smiled. "We can't wait for real." She watched the news with Kevin and was aghast that they had to choose between Hillary and Donald Trump.

"What if Donald Trump wins?" Kevin asked her, always playing devil's advocate.

"Don't jinx the elections!" She threw a mini slice of bread at him, which he expertly caught midair and plopped into his mouth.

"I kind of like him," he had told Kenzi. "Breath of fresh air. He is definitely different."

"Yeah, in a retarded sort of way," she replied with a scowl on her face, and Kevin grinned impishly as he watched her spread Nutella on toast with extra effort.

On her way out, the girl, whose name tag read "Graciela," cleared her throat and said, "By the way, I think you are the most gorgeous model on the cover of *Vogue*. Yeah." She was nodding, her full purple-colored lips spreading into a smile. Her eyes, now that Kenzi was looking at her fully, danced excitedly.

"Thank you!" Kenzi smiled, then added, "Adore the lip color!"

Kevin was tired of the news, hungry for anything other than American press and occasionally Googled *The Daily Monitor* and *The East African* for any information on eastern Africa. He perused papers from other African countries that harbored his business interests, lingering on the economy pages and stock market. When he wasn't checking his emails or skyping Bosco or Bigz, he flipped channels, bored with the exhausting commercials that pushed the season in your face and gut.

"No wonder Americans are crazy spenders," he once commented to Kenzi over a past Christmas shopping spree. "Look at all these billboards. If it isn't food advertised, it's a new mall."

"We are slaves to consumerism," she had belted out dramatically.

He was walking more steadily, and Dr. Sangeeta ruled out any unforeseen danger, letting him know that in another couple of weeks, he could even return to the gym if he so wished.

"Return home, too?" he asked the doctor, who agreed that in a couple of weeks, he would be free to go home.

Kenzi protested. "You can't just go; the criminals are still at large! Also...you have only been here three weeks, and then it will be only a month and some..."

"I've got business to take care of."

"I know, but…I thought we could do some things together for a little while longer."

"Ah, that's why the kidnapping," he joked to Kenzi who was drinking her coffee in gulps. She had an appointment with a hair product line for a shoot in an hour in Brooklyn.

"I don't think I am willing to see you go back in there when we don't have any information yet…. Besides, I wanted you to get fine, and you are…except for the hair…but that's growing." She motioned with her hand, then paused, her eyes on her coffee; her long French manicured nails tapped the sides of the mug absently. "Kevin, this is serious…."

Kevin folded his arms over his chest. "I know, but I am also on the brink of a life-changing deal."

Kenzi looked at him helplessly. She did not know how to explain the dream.

"yeah, I know…anyway…I heard you speak with Bosco earlier…. Anything new?"

Kevin shifted with her. "Yeah, meeting is set with the president end of next week. I could go for it. "

"And any word on the motherfuckers who tried to kill you?"

He shook his head. "Language, Miss! And nope, but that's Uganda for the most part."

"So, you simply want to waltz in and have them come at you to finish it?" she asked, aghast.

"You worry too much. I am going to find those sons of bitches, Kenzi, and nothing is going to happen to me, not ever. I promise."

She pressed her lips together. "Promise me you will not go until it's cleared."

"Kenzi…"

"Promise me that at least!" She was firm and her blue-green eyes sparkled. She hissed the words at him half-whispered, and the little girl he had known on Block 4 reared her head. Solid, calm *Shenzi,* and something in Kevin snapped. She meant well. Looking into her eyes as they glinted with both fear and something else he could not place, he reevaluated himself.

"Okay, I got to go."

Kenzi put the coffee mug on the marble island and realized her hands were shaking. "See you later."

"How about lunch?" Kevin nudged her gently, needing to appease her.

"Sure." She had her eyes averted. "Sounds good."

"I will call you," he told her.

Kenzi left, still shaken. Sketch was waiting for her in the Mazda 5 she refused to drive. She saw no need to drive in New York; it was just a way of keeping the press out of her life. Since her return, there had been nothing mentioned about her, and she was glad there were so many other people to gossip about. Besides, everyone was talking about the elections, the primaries, Hilary being a most promising candidate, and there was Trump. He would never win.

"Everything okay?" Sketch asked her after they had gone a mile.

"Yeah. Why?"

"You seem out of sorts."

Kenzi took in a deep breath. "Kevin won't stop. I get it. We did not have money, and he has worked hard to be where he is, but he won't stop and breathe and take care of himself. He is up half the night on the phone or on email or something…."

"A man's got to work."

"Right. But…he won't stop for a second…." She felt helpless. "And I am concerned. Does that make sense?"

Sketch nodded slowly, as if in contemplation. "Is that really what's bothering you?"

She glanced out the window. The bustle of the city could be dizzying. Was it? she asked herself.

"Let him be. When he needs to relax, he will. I get it, a man and his money, especially when he never had it, *shoo*." Sketch was matter-of-fact.

"Sketch, I know, but I am afraid for him."

They pulled up to the tall building that housed Leila's, the name and owner of the new hair product for women of color. Leila had been quite taken with Kenzi after seeing her pictures in magazines. The contract with her was better than Kenzi's agency had thought it would be for an up-and-coming business, but Leila was not just anyone; she was best friends with top designers and married to a reality show star. She often took those gigs since their remuneration was hefty and it was great exposure, especially now since her agency was still in negotiations with House of Luz to match the offer of their highest bidder, Closet. Her agency so far considered her their highest-paid and most sought-after model, for her type of black, was rare and in demand.

"You doin' too much. Relax. Kevin has survived till today." Sketch smiled at her as she got ready to enter the building. "He a'ight."

"Yeah, okay." She rolled her eyes and pursed her lips.

* * *

Kevin replayed their conversation over and over like a tape set on rewind and play. After several minutes, he realized it was not so much what she said alone but the way she said it.

She was scared, and rightly so. But there was *more;* it was that more he wasn't sure he wanted to decipher. His mind told him he wasn't ready. He got out of the apartment, and, heading downstairs to the gym with headphones on, he drowned the echo of her voice, but her eyes burned through him.

At noon, he was calling her about lunch.

They had a late lunch at Bryant Park since Kevin was feeling touristy. They sat under a parasol at Fever Tree porch, taking in the view. It was not the most private place to dine, and Kevin made note of the glances they constantly got from the customers seated near them. Recognition would light their eyes when they caught sight of Kenzi, who was digging into her fries, oblivious.

"Okay Miss Famous, if this isn't a spot to get onto social media, I don't know where then." He bit into his beef burger.

Kenzi grinned. "Oh, you know…" she trailed off with a shrug, chewing delicately, then meeting his eyes. "So, Brent is coming down for a few days to New York. I thought it would be great to hang out with him and Kat, his fiancée."

Kevin furrowed his brows, as if trying to recall something. "Brent? The other brother? Okay."

Kenzi eyed him mischievously. "You still tripping?"

Kevin smiled from the corner of his mouth, a teasing glint in his eyes. "It's hard to have been someone's world once, and now you are only their…Australia. "

Kenzi smiled wickedly. "Aww, throw all of Asia and Russia in there too."

"So, what's the plan?" he asked.

"So…" She was still smiling. "I thought we would have dinner with them on Saturday night, then go out, paint the town red. We haven't done that in a while."

"With me or Brent?" He feigned seriousness.

Kenzi giggled, enjoying his displeasure. Something in her belly fluttered. "Both. I get to have my cake and eat it!"

Kevin chewed deliberately, taking his time to savor the smoked beef and caramelized onion flavor in his burger. "Okay, Can I make suggestions for where we can go?"

Kenzi laughed. The last time they had gone out to a very high-end club on the east side that played EDM all night till Kevin was irate.

* * *

Kenzi did not know why she jolted upright in bed. It wasn't the dream this time. She stared around the dark room; a pale sliver of light pierced through the slight parting of curtain draping her window onto the chaise…then she heard it…a sound of a struggle and grunting…

"Kevin!"

She rushed out of her room to his, only a few feet away along the corridor. Her eyes widened as she saw him struggle before sitting up with a strangled gasp and shout.

"Kevin!" she called out, frightened for a second, then flicked the switch, flooding the room with warm pearlescent light.

Kevin was panting, his head bowed.

She rushed to him and touched him gently. A slight film of sweat coated his naked chest. His heartbeat pounded ferociously through her fingers.

"Kevin…night terrors," she whispered gently. His nightmares never subsided. When they met again, a couple of nights out on the town, and he crashed at her house, she had witnessed him fight, cry, beg, and shake in his sleep. Sometimes she woke him; other times she soothingly spoke to him till he relaxed and slept. Some nights, they sat up and ate ice cream. Most times, he stayed awake after that and worked. Occasionally, he would ask her to stay with him, and the ghost of the boy that he once was would surface. She would curl up beside him, and they would chat till sleep crept up on them.

It was happening again.

He raised his eyes to meet hers, and the haunting pain she saw in them rippled through her own soul. Kenzi edged closer; her heart pulsated in response to his pain. "Just dreams, Kevin, just dreams." She caressed his hand.

He shook his head. He struggled to speak. "The past doesn't forgive."

She nodded, wanting to tell him he needed to forgive himself, but it did not seem appropriate now, so she placed her head on his chest and held him.

"It wasn't your fault. It wasn't your fault, Kevin." She spoke of his torment.

He heaved. She did not move. The night of her birthday flashed before her. The night everything had happened. The night Taata Bob died. Kevin punished himself for his death…for Aunt Dina's demise. He could not stop.

When his breathing normalized, she straightened up. "How about some tea or ice cream?"

"Ah, that breakup ice cream, huh?" He was grown-up Kevin again, cocksure and full of smart retorts.

She smiled. Her hands lingered on his arm, tracing the veiny lines. She enjoyed touching him, she admitted to herself. Something within her stirred, and she dropped her hand. "I don't know, breaking up with the past?"

He reached and rubbed her bare arms, and the smile waned a little. "It does not want to go away," he told her, gazing past her toward the door.

His palms were just as hot as his whole body, almost feverish. "I think if you can let it go…"

Kevin shook his head. "I don't know how."

She nodded understandingly. "I wish I knew how to…but I can sit here with you."

She reached for his hand again, gently caressing it. She opened his palm and placed her hand over his. She stared at it, his bigger than hers, his fingers longer by a crown. "Maybe in time, you shall know how."

He was staring at their hands melded together, then folded his over hers. "You are the only one who hasn't been freaked out by them."

She shrugged. "It's our history. I was the first to witness it, remember? It's you and I together always, through whatever. Besides, if even Vanessa can't handle it, how can she handle all of you?"

His eyes narrowed; their gaze locked. "It's funny how the years of absence do not change how much you…complete me."

Kenzi felt her throat catch; the stirring she had felt mounted. All week, she was growing increasingly aware of another feeling creeping up on her. She stifled it again. It was confusing.

They were close, too close. The tip of their heads touched as if drawn together by an unseen force. She absently caressed his arm, trailing her fingers to his shoulder blade and back down to their clasped hands.

Time seemed to stop and, in this moment, all confusion melted. She *knew* this feeling. She felt no need to hide. The never-ending crush she had always had for him boiled to the surface, erupting from a place that she had locked and thrown the key away. It burst forth and she let it.

Unbridled, it peered through the blue-green irises.

"Kevin." Her voice did not seem to belong to her. It sounded strange even to her ears. Her eyes traveled to his lips. "Ice cream…then?" she managed raising her head to meet his eyes.

Her soul floated, realizing he was looking at her, too. Their eyes locked and words lost their potency. Time spoke for them.

She did not realize she was inching closer or that her lips parted, making her breathing sound raspy.

Kevin was watching her, for a moment taken aback, not registering the emotions that charged and sparked the air and swirled around them subtly.

He broke the spell first, inching away from her. Kenzi dropped her gaze, looking away hurriedly, feeling almost stupid, for now she could feel it, the wedge between them. Kevin had put it up. "You have to work, right? I…have Bigz conference call, emails and the guys…. It's going to be crazy tomorrow." He was babbling, suddenly awake.

There was an awkward moment of silence before Kenzi got up from his bed and turned her back to him. "Yeah sure."

He could tell she was hurt, but it was overwhelming. Everything had escalated too fast, and he hated to be ambushed.

"Kenzi," he called out to her.

She stopped at the doorway but did not turn around.

"Thank you," he said after a beat.

Kenzi felt her heart latch on to the words. She hesitated as if to add something but mumbled her goodnights, turned off the light, and closed the door behind her.

In her room, she drew the covers to her chin and sighed, feeling raw and vulnerable. A part of her carefully concealed was out of containment, and she did not know how to put it back, did not *want* to put it back. She could not sleep. Her mind became an ocean of memories washing up into the present scattered moments of her life with him, where she had secretly harbored a realization that he was more than a brother to her. She had not understood the feelings until later in her teenage years.

A lot of it was anger and what she thought was hate for him abandoning her, only it felt like heartbreak. Alarmed, she had boxed the feelings, convincing herself it was an error of perception. After all, life after him was an emotional roller coaster. But from the moment they reconnected online, something buried subtly resurrected. As they collected the pieces of the past, explained the hard parts, put together the missing pieces…the anger melted, the pain healed, and the feelings were reignited. There was so much going on with her life, and she could not make sense of it, except that he was back, and there was no way she would lose him again.

She felt that her trip to Kenya had cemented something in her for him. The feelings she had so well packaged away were grown and were begging to be let out. Bosco kissing her had further ascertained that she wished for more from Kevin.

Kenzi breathed in deeply, rolling over to her left side; the slow unraveling of what was clear and had always been there was unnerving. *I need a moment, I need a moment.*

* * *

Kevin stared at the dark ceiling, a slight frown on his face. He scoffed slightly. For the first time, he allowed himself to feel Kenzi. He *really saw* her… delicate, grounded, and beautiful.

He was shocked at how a violent need to hold her and not just hold her like he always did enveloped him. It surpassed that; it was a gnawing need to belong with her, a familiar feeling that hovered all his life like a guardian angel, a sentiment he had never acknowledged that deeply, fleeting, out of reach but always there, a yearning that displaced his emotions for everyone he had been with. They were never enough; they never quite fitted. At first, he chucked it to restlessness, wrestling his demons, working hard, obsessed with ambition for more, but this *thing*—it seemed to be a need buried behind a wall he had unconsciously placed.

When he had said she completed him, he meant it. In so many ways.

He let his guard down around her; it was a familiarity born from platonic intimacy and shared lives. They had walked the same path in the most precarious time of their lives and forged a bond so strong not even decades could destroy it. Just seeing her brought him a peace that no one else could, or ever had. He had convinced himself it was because they had gone through so much together. For almost fifteen years of their life, he was a raging lion devoid of his peace and light; he lost sight of it and sought it in everything else…ambition, revenge, money, women and more money, but the nightmares reminded him he was locked behind a wall of pain, and no one seemed to have the key.

Kenzi did.

He knew she did, and all this while he was too busy to let her in because…he was afraid of his demons, afraid to be vulnerable like he had been with her on Block 4. Afraid she could not handle it.

Sleep stayed at bay, allowing him to visit the deep secret places in his mind and soul, unlock forbidden doors and archways veiled in pain and rage but mostly regret and fear. His inner house needed a spring cleaning.

When he finally got up, it was almost ten and Kenzi was gone. She had left him a note telling him the maid service would come by to clean and that there was enough breakfast food he could fix. She did that now and again when she left for work, letting him know he could order food from the menus she had stuck to her fridge door or that she would be late.

He was a little relieved they did not have to have an uncomfortable morning dealing with the previous night.

He lingered around in the archways and closets of his soul, knowing even to himself admittedly, it was overtime. His mother had always told him, "Everything happens for a reason." He had thought she had become overly religious, faced with a life sentence for a murder she did not commit. The memory of his final dialogue with her stayed etched in his fondest mind's room: her hair plaited in three cornrows all the way to the back. She was clad in the yellow prisoner attire, and he wanted to run seeing her there, knowing it was his fault. He had never gotten used to it, no matter how much she assured him it was all right.

She had smiled at him, and he could not believe she was at peace, and yet she exuded it, and she told him, "I am proud of you Kevin, my son. When you find Shenzi—because you will; I see it—just know that you were always destined to be together."

He had not interpreted it any way then than what he had always recited: she was his sister, and they would rule the world together. But that memory jarring its way through a dust-clogged door of his mind suddenly made more sense; *did his mother know something he did not?* By three o'clock, he was sure about a few things, just unsure about how to proceed.

He picked up the phone and dialed a number he always reverted to. Bosco.

The phone was picked up in less than a second. "What's up, man?" Bosco's upbeat energy flooded his ears. The background was loud, and he could hear familiar afro beat music.

"A party out there?" Kevin laughed.

"Sorry, hang on; let me get somewhere quiet…."

Kevin waited on the line as the music gradually faded out.

"Is this how you roll? Without me?" Kevin teased.

Bosco laughed. "Boys night out as usual. What's up?"

"Cool. I am cool. I probably should be coming back soon."

Bosco paused. "Cool. Cool. I think you should find us all set here."

"Thanks, man, for all the work. Thanks. I owe you big time." Kevin meant every word and laughed when the other man seemed to hesitate and express embarrassment.

"It's business. We do this." Bosco tried to be light.

Kevin grinned; they deliberated banally, not entirely getting to the gist of the call. "Say, man, if you wanted to take a girl you liked out. You know *out*. Date, romance…."

"Aaaah…" Bosco was saying, "You already met a new someone you like?"

Kevin raked his fingers over the thin layer of hair sprouting over his scalp. "Something like that…."

"But why ask me, Kev? You are a master at this!"

Kevin groaned. "Help a brother out. For the first time I am sort of stuck."

Bosco laughed. "That's a first from you. I would say don't sleep with her on the first night."

Both men laughed. "Damn, you know me too well."

"Right?…it's been some years. You take 'em down like Tiger Woods knocking that ball into the hole, man."

Kevin laughed, realizing this wasn't helping much.

"Thanks for the tip."

"And wear protection if you do."

"You know me, bro."

"Does Kenzi know?" Bosco suddenly asked, and Kevin felt a little knot tighten around his heart.

"Um…no. not yet." He cleared his throat.

They steered the topic to something else. Finally, Bosco had to go back to his night out and Kevin to trying to figure out his next move.

Kenzi *is* special, he told himself and was not sure how all he was already doing to make up for lost time could be any different from what he wanted to do; besides, he had never been lost for romantic ideas, even with the women he had been with. He picked up the remote control and browsed channels. *Relax….* He breathed. They still had dinner with Brent to focus on.

Maybe it was best to let nature take its course.

* * *

Saturday was a couple of days off, and Kenzi was grateful she had downtime before the meetup with Brent and Kat.

"How about before brother dearest takes up all the time, we have ourselves some nights and days of wild fun. I'm better and I could really

672

use it, " Kevin suggested as they left the gym, taking the elevator back to her apartment.

Kenzi narrowed her eyes suspiciously. "What's this about?"

Kevin laughed. "Really? How about you leave that to me…no catch." He searched her soul with his gaze, allowing himself a shard of vulnerability, letting her see he wanted them to spend some time together.

He took her hand. "Like old times." He put pressure on them. She felt hot and slowly let her eyes stray to the back of the elevator. Then shrugged. "Okay."

"We will start tonight…." He cast her a wicked glance as the elevator doors opened.

"Uh-oh."

* * *

Kenzi groaned as white light flooded into her eyes. She turned away from the light and whined, "*Ugh*, too bright!"

In the fog of her mind, she deciphered a distant muffled throat clearing. Then silence, then the delicious smell of coffee, bacon, and eggs wafted into the room, getting stronger by the minute, and her stomach growled. She reluctantly opened her eyes just as Kevin walked into her room.

"Wakey-wakey, sleepyhead!" he bellowed. She hated the fact that he sounded louder than necessary.

"Oh my, what time is it?" She dragged herself into a sitting position. "Aren't we staying in today? Binge-watching something? You promised to make *fulas*…."

"Okay, first, it's time to get up. Second, it's a little warmer today than the days before, and third, I took up the breakfast challenge…to redeem myself. I. made. Breakfast." Kenzi rubbed her eyes and grinned when she saw Kevin balance the ceramic bone-colored tray in his right hand.

"We can make fulas later. You like?"

The fula was the newest addition to the menu at the Original Barito restaurant. Kevin had told her the story of how it came to be with such dramatic flair, it had gotten her laughing to tears.

"Desire should have stopped being your girlfriend that day!" she told him.

"Hey! That's harsh. She revolutionized barito…because of her, we made fulas." He said good-naturedly.

"Wow!" she whispered, watching him shirtless, and she drank in the view hungrily. Memories of their night out replaced all the groggy sleep. When Kevin proposed a night out, he went all out. This was for him as well, a recovered Kevin in need of excitement. He took over planning it, suggesting a play to watch, unfamiliar territory for them both. The play left them hungrier for a wilder evening, and their itchy feet sauntered into a club because the song that played as they passed by was one they both liked, and the randomness of the evening escalated to a wild night trip around Manhattan. Kevin had to support her when she got drunk, and by four in the morning, a yellow cab was dropping them off at her apartment.

Kevin placed the tray on the stand by her bed. "Nothing's burnt and your coffee is as you like it…black and sweet." Kenzi beamed. Her head throbbed with a dull ache.

He had brought her to bed, and she had mumbled drunkenly for him to sleep with her. Kevin's eyes softened as he watched her. She had held on to him when they slept, her arms flung over his body, her hair an enormous distraction in his face, and she muttered his name in her sleep.

"Gosh, I need it." She groaned then turned to look at him, her eyes amused. "My goodness, I hate it when I drink like this and can't remember much."

He grinned. "Just like when we were young…. I could not sleep. Your arms and legs were all over me."

"Oh no!" Kenzi made a face. " I must have been a mess out there last night, right?"

He laughed. "Quite!"

She bit into the buttered toast. "Goodness, how much did I eat and smoke? The kabobs on that stand were to die for…wait, the honey nuts!

God, Kevin!"

"Err, a lot! No more weed for you." He wagged a finger in her face.

Kenzi ran a hand through her disheveled hair. "That was wild, though! And you got me into bed too…aww."

"Yup. Right next to me, in the night shirt I like, and you wound up on me like a snake. You never outgrew that, you know?" he told her, reaching for her coffee, sipping it, then handing it back to her.

Kenzi smiled, taking a gulp of her coffee, enjoying every moment of the attention he was lavishing on her. Her lashes lowered, and she appraised him almost accusingly.

"You are being extra sweet…what's going on?" She took another gulp and the semi-bitter liquid rushed through her with invigorating force. "Umm, and while you are figuring out that answer, what's the plan for today?"

"Can't I be sweet? I have a surprise for you." He feigned surprise.

"Hmm…." She narrowed her eyes, her mouth full of bacon and eggs.

The day proved to be warmer than most, a perfect day to enjoy the outdoors, if even for a few hours before the temperatures dropped. These surprise warm days in the middle of fall were gems. "It's colder over here than it is in DC," she was telling Kevin as she pulled on her tan boots and jacket. They were getting ready to leave for a day out, savor what little warmth a fall sun could offer.

Kevin shook his head. "It's all the same to me." He looked at his wristwatch and pursed his lips. "It says 68 degrees. And then again, Fahrenheit messes with my brain."

Kenzi laughed at him. "Stop complaining!"

She held back her hair in a ponytail and leaned in. "Where are we going?"

"I would have to kill you if I told you. I am sure you will like it."

And he was not wrong. Kenzi had lived in New York for five years and had passed up numerous opportunities to wander the streets of the cosmopolitan city like a tourist, except for the week that he had come by to see her in 2012. Kevin, armed with information from Sketch, took her on a skyline tour of New York and relished in her enjoyment of seeing the five boroughs from an aerial point.

"Oh my goodness! I am legit surprised!" She squealed amid the loud hum of the helicopter propellers.

Kevin grinned. "I can see!"

He waltzed her off to a rooftop luncheon close to Central Park and then got her onto a horse and carriage ride.

"I can't believe I am doing this for fun." Kenzi laughed, recounting her photo shoots that involved the horse-and-carriage theme. Kevin recalled seeing them.

"Being a tourist in your own city?"

"Yes! And to think I avoided it 'cause I thought it was boring."

"Because it wasn't with me." He winked at her.

"Turn that ego a notch down." She rolled her eyes at him playfully

"I thought you loved it." He feigned shock.

At four in the afternoon, they headed out to the One World Observatory. Kevin, more than Kenzi, was in awe. "This is what Uganda should emulate. This is fine architectural design, hi-tech and a perfect attraction."

Kenzi grinned. "I know. I came here once, a long time ago. It's still breathtaking. Now this is one of the touristy places I have seen at least. What else is in the bag?"

Kevin smiled. "Three guesses."

They hopped out of the elevator to the 101st floor heading for a snack and jumped back in to the hundredth floor for a view of the See Forever Theater.

"Lady Liberty?" Kenzi asked.

Kevin scrunched his nose. "Nope."

"Brooklyn Bridge? I love that one."

Kevin smiled. "Aah, not today...so no."

Kenzi grinned..."Empire State Building?"

"Surprises don't work for you, do they?"

"Huh!" Kenzi did a little dance. "Is it that?"

Kevin sighed. "You got two wrong."

Kenzi threw her head back and laughed. They were looking out from the hundredth floor at the surrounding city. Kevin watched her and she caught his eye. "What?"

He tilted his head to one side. "That look, that laugh, it took me back."

She smiled and looked away briefly. "And we seem to love heights."

Kevin grinned. "We do, don't we?"

When they finally caught up with Sketch, as evening drew nigh, they were glad for the ride to the Empire State Building where, on Fifth Avenue, they could see its tall looming top.

"Perfect timing too," Sketch was saying. It was almost seven, and the sun was slowly setting.

When they got to the eighty-sixth floor, tourists filed in to gaze through the binoculars, lounged by the windows overlooking the panoramic view of the city, and Kevin and Kenzi walked each corner, glimpsing the different perspectives.

"Must take pictures," she told him. He obediently took her pictures and posed for selfies now and again with her.

"Don't you tire of doing that?" he asked finally.

"Goodness no!" she huffed. "This is Instagram- Snapchat-worthy!"

They scaled the heights, sixteen floors more to the 102nd floor, where the crowd dwindled to a handful, and it was just them staring out at the magnificent expanse of streets, the Hudson River, Brooklyn Bridge, Central Park, and all of New York with its high-rise buildings and lights.

"My God, it's beautiful," she told him. "From up here, the density and pollution is a myth."

"It is," Kevin agreed, and for a moment they were lost in time, traveling between time zones and places that reminded them what they were to each other.

"I never thought I would see the world from up any place that was not Block 4," Kevin said.

"I know. I never thought, I would see," Kenzi replied, tearing her eyes from the view and planting them squarely on him.

Kevin pulled her to him, and they both stared out nostalgically. "You and me against the world, right?"

Kenzi smiled. "Right." He whispered into her hair, resisting the urge to kiss her. The feeling had been mounting all day.

Satisfied with his surprise package, seeing New York this way with her would forever be embalmed in his mind.

Kenzi was saying, "I loved today. I really did."

He smiled. "I am glad you did. I could have flown you anywhere else, but you've got Brent tomorrow and work…"

She grinned. "We always fly too close to the sun, don't we? Why wouldn't you do it?"

"Oh, don't remind me…that time we took a private jet to Miami for a boat cruise with those Moroccan business fellows? That was a kinky business meeting, I daresay. Then we had to get back in sixteen hours and you had to work in an hour?"

She giggled. "I would do it again."

Kevin grinned. "Wild boat cruise, no? Don't give me ideas. I was really trying to be tame."

"Tame does not look good on you." She dared him.

Kevin winked. "Neither does daring me…but…we have one more thing…."

"You spoil me…."

He shushed her. "I haven't even started."

They had dinner at a high-end phantom-night-themed restaurant with outstanding ratings at the edge of Harlem, which was a suggestion from Sketch, who assured them it would be a fun experience, and they both agreed.

They retired to Kenzi's living room, and Kenzi snuggled on the couch as they watched a movie. No one seemed to say it, but something between them was changing.

"I loved today, Kevin." Kenzi breathed out again, then added, "And I love you."

Kevin was massaging her foot. He tickled it and she squealed, kicking him spontaneously, and they both laughed.

"Now we can take over the world," Kevin said absently, not sure how to respond to her "I love you."

"Sounds like a plan!"

Chapter 16

It was gloomy and cold when Kevin and Kenzi called for a taxi, their destination, The Khazan, a lavish French-influenced Moroccan restaurant in Midtown Manhattan.

"Look who's early!" Kenzi hooted once they were led to the table, where a roguishly handsome dark-haired Caucasian accompanied by a slim blond girl sat.

The Caucasian man, in a fitted shirt and corduroy jacket against a pair of fitted dark-wash jeans, stood up, arms wide-open. "Bring it in, Chippy. Bring it in…."

Kenzi shrieked, reaching for Brent.

"I know, I know." He embraced her. "I know you missed me…*hard!*"

Kenzi squeezed him. "Scout! Drop the act."

"I just need to hear those words, 'you are awesome,'" he mouthed.

Kenzi nudged his rib cage. "You wish! That ended when I was thirteen!"

He pulled back, grinning, and kissed her cheek. "You look well!"

She twirled. "Don't I always?"

Brent threw his head back. "Ahh, she eats up compliments, I tell you." He spoke to everyone, his eyes darting from Kevin to Kat, before he quickly introduced Kat and emphatically greeted Kevin.

"I heard about the attack, man. Good to see you well," he told him as he pumped his hand. A firm handshake.

Kevin smiled. "Nine lives!"

Brent grinned. "Looks like. But yeah, Kenzi was really shook. Did they find who?" he was saying, his brown eyes assessing Kevin as if for an affirmative answer.

Kevin shook his head. "Ongoing investigations, but my fellows are on it, so we should have that sorted soon."

"Cool. Cool." He clapped Kevin on the back. "It's good to see you again. It's been what? Two years? Three?"

Kenzi cut in: "Oh my gosh, are you being Dad now?"

"It's been a while," was his defense with a shrug.

"2012…then briefly in 2015…so I would say maybe a year?" Kevin squinted, as if jogging his mind for that memory.

"Ah, no wonder it seems long. Good to see you, man, really is. Maybe Kat and I will come to Uganda." He moved into the booth next to the blond girl, whose big blue eyes scanned both Kevin and Kenzi in awe. "Won't we, Kat?" Brent had his arm around blond blue eyes.

"Sure," she drawled out in her high-pitched schoolgirl voice. "I am so glad to meet you! I have heard so much about you!" she was saying as she extended her hand to Kevin.

Kevin smiled. "Only the good parts, I hope."

She giggled. "I guess that's everything then, but I hear there is a story, and Brent won't tell me."

Kenzi sipped her water and eyed her brother. "I have not seen Scout in months; he probably has a bigger story to tell."

They all laughed, and light haggling began on who should tell what story. While they waited for their dinner orders, they ordered more drinks. Brent insisted Kenzi and Kevin go first.

"So, you haven't filled us in," Brent was saying as he sipped his second Manhattan.

"Brother dearest, I have only met Kat, and you are diving into the details of other things. Excuse him, Kat. I have failed to train him right."

"Ooh, you came with guns blazing…" Brent winked. His quick wit, just like Kevin's, was what had drawn her to him first when they were growing up.

"I never lose, you know." She winked back. Kat was star struck by

Kenzi, constantly telling her how beautiful she was.

"You know you are nothing like your pictures; you are so much more beautiful in real life. Oh my God," she sang out every so often.

Kevin grinned, always amused by both American fanfare and fans. No matter where they had gone in the last few years, people were constantly star struck by Kenzi.

Eventually Kenzi had to tell the story of her adoption, and Kevin chipped in now and again. Kenzi tactfully left out a lot of the gory details and sped it up to Kevin's attack in Uganda and his eventual recovery in the States.

"Oh my God!" Kat purred, her hand on her heart. "That is so amazing, you guys! Sounds almost unreal." She looked from Kevin to Kenzi.

"Except that it is true. All of it." Kevin replied.

They deliberated on the investigations that were still ongoing but with not much to report.

Then Brent filled them in on how Kat and he had met. Kenzi watched them dreamily. Even though she thought Kat a little shallow, Brent looked happy, and that was all that mattered.

"I am so happy for both of you," Kenzi said at the end of the 'how we met,' tale.

"I hope you will catch the bouquet at my wedding. I can't leave you on the shelf all by yourself, *famous sister*," Brent boomed, giving Kenzi a mischievous look, then glancing at Kevin. "What do you think?"

Kevin caught the teasing tone and replied, "She might die an old maid."

And Kenzi gasped in horror. "I know you did not team up with Brent!"

"They sure did." Kat was giggling. "I hope you can be a bridesmaid at my wedding?"

Kenzi smiled. "Of course!"

Kat shrieked. "Oh my God, I am so excited! Oh, my gosh!"

They talked about Christmas with the family before the wedding, which was confirmed in late January. A small, intimate gathering was what they had agreed to.

"I shall expect both of you there." Brent was pointing from Kenzi to

Kevin.

Kevin laughed. "I shall be here, don't worry. Besides, I will need to be here for Christmas and Kenzi's birthday, or I won't hear the last of it." He rubbed Kenzi's back gently.

His touch was doing things to her, and she stiffened. Kevin felt it and a small smile touched his eyes.

"Okay then, great! You are coming home for Christmas, right?" He looked at Kenzi almost pleadingly.

"Scout…yes. I spoke with Heather, and…I will!"

Brent tossed his head back in triumph. "Aah yes! You have no idea how that makes me feel."

"Slow down." Kenzi giggled. "You might not like it much."

He made a face at her. Kevin watched them, and he admitted he was glad Kenzi had had someone like Brent with her. Brent reminded him a little of himself: daredevil, humorous, and above all, he cared for Kenzi. However, Kenzi was always his. He would always be her first brother, he told himself, and now maybe more than her brother because he accepted that what he felt surpassed brotherly affection.

Dinner all done, the four of them went to a lounge of Kevin's choice, an upscale bar with music that one could do more than bob their head to.

They got a VIP table and danced periodically between drink breaks. The dance floor swelled with revelers, and Kenzi danced a handful of times with Brent first and then as a group. She was more aware of Kevin when he slightly touched her, his eyes darting to her occasionally. When their eyes met, he winked. Kat and Brent waltzed to every song, lost in their little romantic island. At almost three, the club making its last call eased into sultry soul tracks. Kat and Brent were wrapped up in each other's arms, swaying gently to the music. Kenzi watched them absently, her brain slightly muddled with alcohol. She let her hand fall on Kevin's thigh, sipping her punched vodka while bobbing her head. Kevin caressed her hand lightly. The hairs on the back of her neck prickled, and she looked at him, their eyes meeting. He was staring at her. She smiled, suddenly shy and disarmed.

"What?" She made a face at him.

Kevin took the glass from her hand, placing it on the table in front of them. "Dance with me…. It's the final call."

She shrugged, took his hand, and let him lead her to the near empty dance floor. Kevin's hands glided to her waist, gathering her closer, and Kenzi held her breath, her eyes meeting his. "It's lovers' rock." He was amused and glad he had an obvious effect on her. Her feelings wreaked havoc in her and she felt vulnerable.

"Okay," she responded, then to dispel the effect he was having on her, she leaned in and whispered in his ear, "It's funny how the short boy I grew up with is now a little taller than me."

He laughed. "Funny…how the little girl on Block 4 got a smarter mouth than me."

They both laughed…lightly, delicately, like if they were any louder, the intimacy of the moment would be lost.

Then he looked at her with solemn eyes. "You know what else is funny?"

"What?" The song merged into another lovers' rock tune.

"It's funny how…" Kevin started, his hand caressing the small of her waist and sending shivers down her back, and then he stopped. The feelings he had worked out seemed so fragile now that he was fully aware of them. He did not like how almost out of control he felt. This was not how it happened. He was always in control.

Not with Kenzi. Not without Kenzi. A voice in his mind confirmed.

"What?" She poked him, feeling her heartbeat quicken.

"How about I tell you when we get out of here?" he charmingly told her, and she could feel his touch change. It was wholesome and possessive. She melted into him.

The lights came on conveniently, and the few revelers let out sad "Aws!" all around them.

Kat was squealing. "We closed the club down!"

Brent was lifting her up and stumbling, tipsy. Kenzi halfheartedly pulled away from Kevin. "Whoa, watch it!" she called to Brent.

Brent was laughing. "We good. Wow, sis!" He reached out and pulled her in for a hug, kissing her cheek. "I love you, sis," he was saying.

"I love you Brent," she replied.

"I miss you; come home soon!" he slurred.

Kenzi half-groaned, hugging him back. "I will, Scout."

Kat hugged and kissed her too. "I love you too!" She burst into tears. Kenzi side-eyed Kevin, who, entertained by the scene, helped them back to their VIP corner, and then together with Kenzi called them a cab.

"I think we should go with them." Kenzi watched them uneasily as they kissed and fondled outside the club's door while the taxi pulled up. Kevin agreed and cussed, for it was bitingly cold for fall, and all he cared for was getting into the warm interior of a car.

The drunk couple made out all the way to their hotel.

When they were safely delivered to their hotel room, Kenzi collapsed against Kevin in the backseat breathing heavily. "Gosh! I am kinda tipsy too."

Kevin agreed. "I know you are…. We might have to put you to bed like the last night."

Kenzi grinned. "Would you sleep with me too?" They were close, and she was fingering the button on his shirt. He closed his hand over hers.

"Do you want that?" he asked her in a half-whisper.

Kenzi looked up at him and did not stop him when he leaned in and lightly brushed his lips over hers. Time buckled.

Kevin drew back…carefully pacing himself, controlling the moment. He was aware of her vulnerable state, and he never took a woman inebriated. She needed to *want* him sober.

"You know I am just a *little* tipsy," she told him, not budging, wanting him to kiss her. It felt so natural. "Don't stop."

"That's what every drunk person says," Kevin replied.

Kenzi shrugged. "We still have some weed from the other night…. I got the vape pen too."

Kevin settled back, and she lay back against him. "You don't want to go down that route, do you?"

She threw her head back. "Try me. I want to be out of control…. One of us ought to be."

He laughed. The alcohol coursed through her veins with a mellowing effect. She reached for his hand and laced it in hers. He did not resist.

When they got into her apartment, Kenzi dropped the pair of stilettos she had taken off while in the elevator and skipped off to her room, while Kevin turned the sound system on, and a slow R&B prearranged playlist embraced the living room.

She emerged in a billow of smoke she blew from the vape pen and handed it to him.

He took the pen from her and dragged on it, blew out the smoke, and nodded in satisfaction. "I told you how I smoked this a lot after you…after Congo…. I did crazy things after Congo."

"Yeah, you did. No matter how much I try, I can't imagine what it was like."

He shrugged it off. "That was then, and Ssaka…" He watched her drag on the pen and sway to the music.

"Yes…Ssaka. I wish I had met him," she said slowly. All she had from him were gifts of jewelry he had specifically made for her.

Kevin smiled slightly, lost in thought, then said, "You never cease to amaze me."

"Uhm-hmm." Kenzi closed her eyes, her head tilted as she hummed faintly to Yuna's "Crush." Kevin was dazzled by her, a slim, curvy frame in a blue low-neckline minidress, her neck long and gracefully draped with the single necklace of their shared history, her delicate aquiline features accentuated further by the hairstyle she wore. She looked a lot like Ameena in that moment. He took the pen and dragged on it, closing his eyes as the effect of marijuana reached into his core, his blood, calming him instantly.

"…I think I got a crush…a little crush on you," Yuna crooned over the soulful beat.

Kenzi opened her eyes, fixing him with her blue-green gaze. This time she reached for him, and he held her.

"I love this song." Her voice dropped.

"Why?" he asked, swaying with her to the song.

She took another drag. "Because it's about having a crush…."

He arched his brow. "Really? And all this time I thought it was about dinosaurs."

She sniggered, throwing her arms around his neck and curling her fingers at its base. "Don't be silly."

He smiled. "You were saying?"

"And I have a crush on you." The words filtered through the cloud of smoke she blew.

"Umm…" Kevin's gaze traveled over her smooth, ebony face. His finger traced her cheek and jawline. "Funny how…all these years, I have been running from the one thing…that saves me from me. *You.*"

The song faded out, and Musiq Soul Child's "One Thing" started.

"That's unfortunate…." her voice broke. They stopped moving.

He put a finger to her lips. "I can't keep running."

She nipped at his finger seductively, then leaned into him, listening to his heartbeat beneath the crisp shirt he wore. "I think I love you, Kevin." She spoke effortlessly and with relief as if her confession freed her. "I have loved you since we were kids. Donno when it happened…. It never went away."

She heard him take in a deep gulp of air and let it out slowly. Then he was lifting her off her feet, and she clung to him. That moment was a blur. The weed was clouding her mind. She felt the couch beneath her dip, and Kevin hovered over her.

"It's funny how you are the only one that eases my mind." He kissed her hand, pressing it close to his chest, fighting to keep his intensity in check.

"Do I?" She was eight again, her eyes lighting up with adoration.

He nodded, holding her gaze, and time lost its effect on them, the music in the background a montage of unspoken feelings.

He kissed her cheek, her nose, her forehead. "I can't do life without you, Kenz. Fifteen years was enough proof. I need you."

"Me neither," she replied. Her fingers played with the upper button on his dress shirt.

He brushed her lips with his, and the vibration of desire that shot through her melded into him.

"I want to be more than your brother." He had never been surer.

Kenzi choked with emotion. "Me too."

"I think I am okay with Brent holding that position," he added easily, and she threw her head back, laughing.

He kissed her, and she let him in, his tongue searching the crevices of her mouth. He could taste the weed, smell the alcohol, and he searched for the true taste of her. She urged him on, responding to his kiss. Their bodies resonated with decades of pent-up need. The kiss became urgent, fervent, and with a groan, Kevin pulled away. She looked so intoxicated and as much as he wanted her, he did not think it would be fair to take her half-sober.

"Maybe you should go to bed, get this alcohol and weed out of your system...."

"No..." she whimpered, holding on to his half-undone shirt.

Her eyes pleaded and his heart lurched; she was everything he had left. It was taking all the control he could muster not to take her. He would not spoil that.

He kissed her palm and shook his head. Kenzi pleaded weakly, but Kevin was adamant. "I want to do this right."

"This *is* right," she told him, her hand on his cheek, turning his face to her.

He smiled at her. She was beautiful and almost fragile. His heart melted. "Kenzi, I have had any woman I wanted. *Easily.*" He took her hand from his cheek and planted a kiss on it. "It's been more than a decade trying to find you. And..."

She waited.

He caressed her arms. "I want this to be special. I want to do it right. Let me."

She wanted to protest, but he was kissing her again. "Let me," he whispered, his lips trailing to her ear, and she shivered.

"I am taking you to bed." It was final.

* * *

Kevin opened his eyes; he thought he heard something. He propped up on an elbow, his eyes sweeping through the room and resting on the illumined clock face by his bedside; *6:37 a.m.* Two and a half hours ago he was kissing Kenzi, putting her to bed….

Kenzi.

Then he heard the faint shuffle outside his door and sat up; his bedroom door opened, and in the dim light he made out the figure in a flimsy night gown. It was sheer and light enough for him to make out the outline of her curves. She had on a bikini; her round, heavy-looking breasts jiggled as she glided to the foot of his bed.

"Kenzi?" he was asking.

"Shh," she replied.

"You okay?" His heartbeat quickened; his loins pulsated.

Kenzi climbed atop his bed, crawling toward him; she hoisted herself over him and sat, her hair a huge halo about her face.

"I could not sleep, and it's cold…" she said huskily and peeled the flimsy gown off, her breasts bounced enticingly.

Kevin swallowed hard, his eyes glued to the perfect mounds on her chest. "Wait, aren't you cold?"

"I am fine, Kevin. I just don't want to be alone…" she was saying. "Can I sleep here…like we used to?"

"Kenzi, we can't…" He started to protest, to tell her it wasn't the same anymore, but she was throwing the covers aside, crawling into the crook of his arm, and drawing her knees in.

Kevin felt his breath catch. They had shared beds before, on drunken wild nights out, but something had changed, and his resolve was failing.

Her naked skin was smooth and cool against his own heated mass. She slid in even closer. "Hold me," she whispered.

Kevin obediently trailed his hands down the length of her arm before draping them over her breasts, then pulling her back against his chest. "Is this better?"

She responded in the affirmative. His palm lightly grazed over her nipples; they teased him. She was not making it easy. He started to caress her gently. "Kenzi..."

Kenzi rolled over, facing him, she slid a slim, cool leg between his legs and raised it inch by inch, her eyes wide and intense. "When we were apart, I wanted to die. When I thought you had abandoned me, it hurt so, so bad...." The child on Block 4 and the woman in his bed melded and separated creating a blurry effect of past and present before him. She tugged at his heart.

Kevin propped up on an elbow and peered at her; the morning light danced over her lean face against the dusty blue pillow framed with a mass of hair. She looked like a porcelain ebony doll. "I know." He was gentle. "And I found you. You will never be alone again. Not without me. It was not the same without you."

"You love me...I mean...*really* love me?" Her hand snaked up his bare waist. Her bright gaze danced with liquid fire, and for a moment he was looking at Shenzi, the little, blind, innocent angel who had adored him.

"Kenz..." He looked at her in the pale light of morning seeping into his room. "More than you can imagine. I have always loved you. I just..." He shrugged limply.

She let out a laugh of relief. "I thought you did not see me; it was always a Vanessa or a Carina or...who was that in California a year ago?"

"Ssh...they were just...sex.... That's why they did not last."

He was undone. His hand absently traced the contours of her hips, aware of how her knee was only a smidgen away from his erect penis trapped in his boxers.

"But..." She felt tears first, as they danced on her lower lid before sliding out of the pockets of her eyes down her cheek.

Kevin kissed them. "No, no, no. I just did not want to see you *any other way…*. But I always did…. I just wasn't sure…. I thought we had enough." He wiped the tears away with his other hand. "You know it always has been you and me."

She sniffed, clinging to him. "Uh-huh."

"Let me show you how much I love you; let me prove myself. Let me do it my way."

She was clinging to him, whispering. The pressure of her knee in his groin teased his senses. "Show me now. It's been too long."

Kevin groaned; his body vibrated with heightened need. He could hold off, life had taught him, but did he want to?

"Kenzi…" He attempted to reason with her one more time.

Her nipples brushed up on his bare chest; her thighs grinded seductively against him.

Reason evaporated as the frangible threads of restraint snapped.

He cupped her face in his hands and kissed her lips. She parted them, and he accepted the invitation, gently caressing her mouth with his tongue, and she urged him on, her hands trailing down his toned arms and back. She could feel him hard, pulsating against her.

His kiss deepened, and his hands tangled in her hair. "You are so beautiful," he whispered breaking away from her mouth.

He flipped her onto her back and impatiently pulled the sheets away, tossing them aside. Kenzi gasped audibly. Her mind swam with tangled emotions, his voice, his touch…. Seamlessly the past and present consummated their estranged existence in a most natural way, closing the emptiness, the wedge dissipating, and a sequence of predestined normalcy seemed to start to flow again.

"Kenz," he whispered as he dipped, possessing her lips again.

"Yes," she was responding. The emptiness, the yearning, and the ache filled up with something warm and healing.

This is it, she thought happily. *This is the missing link.*

Kevin slid a hand over her breasts, cupping and kneading tenderly as his tongue trailed down to her navel, where it played with the loop piercing. His hands awoke her senses gently traveling over every curve, swell, and valley, rubbing, caressing, and feeling every inch of her body unhurriedly. She moaned. He retraced his trail back up to a hardened nipple and gently sucked on it, watching her writhe. His lips found hers again, and he teased them. "Are you sure?" he asked.

"Yes," she whispered urgently back to him.

He reached down, slipping off the tiny satin thong from her firm hips. Kenzi tugged at his boxer shorts, revealing his stiff thickness. She reached for it, massaging him in her hand and relishing his deep sighs of satisfaction.

He took his time teasing, licking, and biting her, touching her in places that caused her to moan with unbridled pleasure. When his tongue stroked her clitoris, she shivered and shrieked.

"Let me taste you," he mumbled, and she invited him in, surrendering to him, and he tasted every bit of her, devouring her with the expert appreciation of a man who had mastered the art of pleasure and was dishing his stellar performance to the woman he loved more than life itself. He consumed her.

He exhausted her with his foreplay until she was pleading with him to take her. He chuckled at her craving, and when he mock-hesitated, she took over, rolling over on top and guiding him into her. The sensation of him filling her made her clench her teeth; she came almost instantly. He held her as she writhed, moaning with her, steadying her as she moved over him, rocking gently, jerking, and crying. He gently took over, pinning her beneath him; her thighs lifted, gyrating against him; her legs encircled his waist, and he crushed deeper into her, rocking gently at first, and she came, gushing against him; he could feel her warmth on his balls. He moaned with her steadily rising to meet her frenzied need. She dug her nails into him, and he choked her …. She begged him to go harder and faster and came again, not getting enough of him. And when he felt ready to come, he readied himself to pull out of her, but she bound him to her with her legs. "No," she pleaded. Overwhelmed with desire and the need to release, he allowed himself to flow his essence into her, growling and shuddering. He crushed her to him, and their souls meshed as their bodies clung to each other, absorbing each subsiding passionate wave.

They lay in each other's arms, their breathing normalizing. Kevin gathered Kenzi into his arms. "Was that too much?" he asked.

She snuggled against him. "No. It was perfect," she mumbled. "I love you, Kev." And she was asleep.

Kevin smiled. "I love you, Kenz." It was perfect. This moment was perfect.

He drifted off into sleep and for the first time in fifteen years; he slept deeply.

* * *

It was Sunday, and they spent the day inside perfectly happy with cuddling, loving, and ordering in. The feeling that something had instantly rejoined their lives, like the absent years were nothing more than a memory of an alternate reality, gripped them both. The elusive pieces of their lives simply fell into place, erasing the thin wall between them. Destiny finally clicked.

They savored the comfortable silence that draped them sporadically, where they relished the depth of their souls only to bare them out in intimate expressions.

The phone rang, rousing Kenzi from her early afternoon nap; it was Kevin's. She reached for it, flipping it over. The caller ID registered "private number."

Kenzi slid out of bed and walked to the kitchen, where Kevin hovered over the kitchen counter scooping teaspoons of sugar and emptying them into two mugs.

"Phone call." She planted a kiss on his bare back and wrapped her arms about him, taking in the scent of citrus and musk that coated his skin from the body wash he loved.

Kevin took the phone. "*Hmm?* Do I want to answer it?" he said, glancing at the caller ID.

He glanced her way over his shoulder almost like he sought permission. She made a face and shook her head.

He placed it on the kitchen island and spun her to face him. "Today is our day off."

"I agree," she drawled lazily.

He took a second to stare at her. There was an exquisiteness to her fresh-out-of-bed appearance: her hair was disheveled and her eyes dreamy; his heart skipped a beat. "I can't believe it."

"What?" She bit her lower lip, the intensity in his eyes burned into her, melting her heart.

"That you are mine," he murmured truthfully.

"I was always yours…." She breathed the words delicately. "Always."

"There was er…Xavier…."

Kenzi jabbed him. "Stop!"

"And the bastard, Shawn…Devon…Jorgio, Jiao? And that creep…"

She jabbed him again.

"Ouch, you are fierce." He took in her lovely nakedness and breathed out. "Yes, mine always. Not even Brent's. "

"Oh?" She pressed closer to him. "Tell me?"

Kevin winked and caressed her cheek with the back of his hand. "Aaah, where to start? I will do anything for you, you know."

Within her, a warm rush flooded her veins. She could not recall how special anyone had ever made her feel the way Kevin did.

"But first, let me fix you a cup of tea, and then we can…" He kissed her forehead, letting the words hang in midair. "Do something later tonight, unless you want to stay in, Netflix and chill?"

"We have been Netflix and chilling all day." She laughed, and her eyes flickered with a mischievous grin.

"I am not opposed to more Netflix and chilling; are you?" He returned to the electric kettle that had shut off automatically when the water boiled. "Coffee? Tea?"

"Coffee, black, strong, sweet…like you." She flirted with him, batting her eyes. "I am not opposed…. And maybe late-night craziness?"

"Umm, I like that." And he was kissing her, cupping her buttocks, possessively.

* * *

"Try again!" she hissed.

The woman holding the phone huffed in exasperation at the customer who was getting on her nerves.

"He is not picking up!" This was the third time they were calling.

"Just try one more time!" The customer hurled the words cruelly at her and cussed under her breath.

The woman with the phone glared back defiantly; she had had enough of her, and, with raised brows, responded just as cruelly: "Hm, excuse me, madam; it's not my fault the person isn't picking up. You can try elsewhere if you like!"

The customer made a noise of contemplation and simmered down. "Ah pole, I did not mean to be rude, but...tsk, I really need to speak with my son, tsk. Anyway, it's okay, let's give it two days and try again. Maybe he is busy."

The customer slipped the woman with the phone a twenty-thousand-shilling note. "Asante."

The woman with the phone, still smarting from their exchange, smirked. "Okay." And turned to her stall, where a customer waited patiently for her to return to selling airtime.

The other woman walked away muttering to herself. Time was running out. She needed to do something fast.

* * *

It was 6:00 a.m. when Kevin heard the phone vibrate. He fumbled for it on the side table and flipped it over.

The same "private number" call.

He frowned; this was the fifth in seventy-two hours.

Initially, he had thought it was Bosco, but Bosco said he hadn't called when they texted on WhatsApp. His phone continued to vibrate. Kevin slowly disentangled himself from Kenzi's legs and arms, kissing her when she stirred and protested in her sleep, then he strolled out of the room to the bathroom in the corridor.

He stood over the toilet bowl naked and peed.

"Hello," he drawled into the phone, his eyes closed, savoring the sheer ecstasy of his bladder emptying.

"Hi, I know you don't know me, but it's not important. I have information concerning your attack. I know who attacked you. I can send you pictures of this person by email, a person close to you."

Kevin's brows creased. "Who is this?"

It was a clear feminine voice with a slight central Ugandan accent. She ignored his question and continued: "If you want evidence, I will send you pictures; just tell me your email address. They are planning to steal from you, by the way. That deal you have...be careful."

"Who...?"

"Email." The voice was abrupt.

Kevin contemplated it for a moment. What was there to lose? He gave his unofficial email, wary that it could be a hacker.

"Thank me later," said the voice on the other end and hung up.

Kevin shook his dick, which had long since gone limp, and placed the phone on the vanity before turning on the tap. As the water cascaded between his fingers, he replayed the conversation, trying to place the voice. Unfamiliar.

Hands washed and dried off, Kevin lingered by the vanity, waiting for the pictures. He calculated his next moves; alert Haruna and seek Oketcho's expert tech skills in unraveling unavailable number identifications.

Chapter 17

Kampala

The sun was merciless that day.

Kampala streets seemed to catch on to the fever heat and drain pedestrians of every ounce of motivation. Traffic stalled. The fat man cursed, unbuttoning the second button on his dress shirt. Sweat beads glistened at the nape of his neck, and he dabbed at it surreptitiously. He leaned against the roughly painted wall of the little take-away to get a draft of the adulterated cool air blowing from the overhead fan. The plastic laminated placemat with a picture of a bouquet of roses and hydrangea embedded in it on the table before him was curling at the corners with slight splits, worn from overuse. There was a circular ring of water made by the sweating glass of passion fruit juice in his hand.

Radio and Weasel's *nakudata* meshed with the erratic conversations carried on by half a dozen people in Zoe's Take-Away. The fat man glanced at his watch again. It was almost five o'clock. He reached for his phone, then hesitated and put it back on the placemat, tapping it absently. He drained the glass of juice and called out to the waitress.

"Another one. Add water in it; this one was too sweet," he told her.

She scoffed like he had cracked a joke she was afraid to laugh at. *"Kale, ssebo."* Yes, sir.

"Eh!" He summoned her as she walked away. She wheeled around on her heel, not attempting to go back to him. "Can you turn down the music? I can't hear myself think!"

She scoffed again, her lips twisted in amusement, then she called out to someone and told them in Luganda to turn down the music.

The fat man shook his head. This was the most inconspicuous place he could find where no one he knew would see him or question why he had fallen so low from the lofty heights of Parliament Avenue to downtown Nasser Road.

His juice came, and this time the girl also brought him a bottle of mineral water. "The juice is already mixed. So…you can just *steer* for yourself." She told him, gesticulating with her fingers to imitate a spoon stirring liquid in a cup.

The fat man glared at her receding back in exasperation. He decided to treat himself to high tea at The Serena after this ordeal.

Two men walked in at fifteen minutes after five. One walked with a limp; the other was stocky and eagle-eyed. They swept the place with their furtive glances, then saw the fat man and came over to his table in the corner. The stocky one had a grin on his face. He reached out, swinging his hand to greet the fat man. *"Ki bossi, wange!"*

The fat man inched back, folded his arms over his chest, and gave him a withering look, and the toothy smile disappeared as fast as it had come on. The newcomers took their seats, meekly.

The fat man sighed loudly. "It's about time!" He glowered at them.

The stocky one recovered the grin. "Ah, boss, you know how it is…" he started casually, slumping back into the wooden chair as if he belonged.

"Yeah?" The fat man was curt. "That's ten *k* off for being late. *You know how it is….*" He mimicked the stocky man, who immediately sat up on hearing ten thousand Uganda shillings was being deducted for tardiness.

"Nawe, boss, didn't we do a good job? I even got scratched by that *ka* guy." He sucked his teeth as he bent to roll up his faded jeans and pointed to the scar just above his ankles. Deep scars evidently from fingernails, perforated and still slightly swollen.

"You were careless." The fat man did not bother looking. "You did not finish the job. He was supposed to be dead. So..." He pulled out two sealed brown letter envelopes. "Each of you gets four hundred and ninety thousand shillings...instead of five hundred k."

"*Iiyii!*" The shorter guy complained. "You said a million each!"

"Didn't you hear me? You were late *and then* he is alive, and police are crawling all over the place trying to find you two. I am here attempting to cover your half-assed job and not get us put in jail! So, you take the money, or you leave it."

The men looked angry. The taller one started to open the envelope, but the fat man snapped at him. He shot the fat man a sulky look.

"Now, I have the video recording of you two at the scene, in case you decide you are unhappy with the payment. I know how to end you," he assured them, his voice low and severe.

"We won't tell, *walahi*," the stocky one replied quickly, nudging the taller one, who agreed with a severe nod.

The fat man looked from one man to the other, instilling the fear of God in them with his eyes. Then he sat back.

"Okay, you can go. I have your numbers. This business is not finished... . That is if you want full payment."

The men got up, saluted the fat man, and left.

The fat man stared out the dusty window; the noise from the street was deafening, and now *Love You Every Day* by Bebe Cool blared in competitive pitch with the noises all around. The fat man cursed. He spotted the waitress who had served him and started, "I told you to turn down the volume..." then stopped. It did not matter; his business was done here. He needed an English coffee from Serena and those little round shortbread cookies he often got on the side.

As he picked up his jacket, his phone rang. He saw the caller ID and rolled his eyes.

"So...when do we talk business?" the husky feminine voice on the other end asked sultrily when he answered the phone. The fat man looked at his wristwatch, a titanium Richard Mille.

5:50 p.m. High tea would have to be postponed.

"How about Sheraton 7:00 p.m. Dinner?"

The voice on the other end gushed appreciation. "Of course, my sweet. I will see you then."

Chapter 18

Kenzi walked into her apartment, pushing the door open with her elbow. Her eyes lit up as they fell on Kevin, his gaze intent on the computer screen, headphones on. She dumped the brown paper bag laden with pastries and bread onto the kitchen counter, threw her heavy coat off, and tiptoed to the back of the couch. She hugged him and planted a kiss on the back of his neck.

Kevin roused, kissing her back while pulling off the headphones.

"Hey, beautiful." He smiled at her.

"Hey." She tapped his nose.

"You know what…?" His eyes registered mischief.

Kenzi furrowed her brows. "What?" She followed his finger that motioned to the screen of his laptop. It was the "rich crew" on Skype. Kevin unplugged the headphone so she could hear them cheering.

"We did not see that coming!" Tisa was saying, a surprised look camped on his face.

"Hold up! You guys are an item now?" It was Abe pointing from Kevin to Kenzi. "I feel so betrayed, Kenzi!"

Oketcho was shaking his head. "*Ah-haaa,* women! That's how they trap you."

"So, should we order a tux already?" Bhanu was asking. A slight smile touched the corner of his well-defined lips.

Tisa *tsk*ed. "Don't rush them!"

"Well, granted, they have known each other forever. Why wait?" Oketcho was saying in Bhanu's defense.

"Wait a whole damn minute! *Pause*! I still have to have an affair with Kenzi," Abe was saying, his "inquiring" eyes flashing naughtily. "Kenzi, you are free to leave me for Kev, but...come on!"

The boys booed.

Kenzi was laughing. She sat next to Kevin, who threw a protective arm around her. "You had your chance when she was in Uganda, Abe. I bet you came close. I think you should settle for groomsman now."

The boys groaned and whooped. "That's harsh, man." Abe put up his best dramatics. "I did not have a chance, I swear. Bosco was hoarding her from all of us." He turned to the guys for support. "Right?"

They jeered, waving him off. Kenzi noticed the crew wasn't complete. "Where *is* Bosco?"

The guys recovered their composure. "We had a minor setback in the case and the oil deal, so he is out handling it. But we are definitely going to bring him up to speed," Oketcho was saying.

"Yeah, that's what we were talking about until you waltzed in and kissed our man. You guys are sneaky. So how long has this been going on?" Abe would not let it go.

The others waited intently. They were already in November. Kenzi filled them in as best as a woman could.

"Congrats are in order! I am happy for you. I don't know about the rest. Abe..." Oketcho trailed off, grinning.

"There could be no better fit, seriously," Bhanu said.

"Yeah, finally!" Tisa agreed.

"Kev, my man, can we talk...?" Abe started, his head poised dramatically in his hands; everyone was snickering.

"Can't wait to see you guys!" Kenzi chimed in. "I am sorry I hijacked your meeting."

"No, please. We needed this break," Oketcho was saying, then rubbed his hands gleefully. "Welcome to the club!"

The boys booed. "Like it's all swanky."

"No curfew, though, Kenzi. I doubt Kevin would handle bars," Abe was saying.

Kevin took her hand and squeezed it reassuringly. "No need to. I will impose it myself." His eyes spoke a promise to her, and she felt that vow fuse with her soul. He was truly hers.

"Urgh, get a room already!" Abe sighed as Kevin teased him.

Since Bosco was not yet back from his meetings, they decided it was best to adjourn until they had heard from him.

"So, now the boys know," Kenzi said when the call was over.

"You are okay with that?"

"Of course!" She beamed. "I can't wait for everyone else to, though."

Kevin agreed, then got silent.

Kenzi frowned. "Everything okay?"

He did not respond right away.

"I am not sure. It's what I want to find out." He pulled her in his arms, rubbing her cold fingers in his. "I need to tell you something."

"Okay…." She waited, tucking her leg beneath her. He was warm from staying indoors.

He took in a deep breath, let it out slowly. "I have to go to Uganda as soon as this week."

Kenzi sat up. "What? This week?"

"Yeah. We hit a snag with the oil deal. The guys did not meet with the president as scheduled. Bosco was a no-show today. I need to find out what's really going on."

Kenzi was quiet. "Is everything okay? That's not like Bosco."

Kevin nodded. "Yup. Something doesn't feel right." He turned to her. "Hey, just a month or so to figure things out. I pulled this deal, and I should finish it."

"And your life?" she asked quietly.

Kevin shrugged. "I got that covered. I will be back for Christmas, I promise. Christmas, your birthday, the family get-together. *I promise.*"

She smiled, missing him already. "Gosh, I don't want you to go, but…I understand."

He smiled. "I don't want to leave either, but once this is sorted, I shall take off a month. This deal is very lucrative. It's more than just the money; it's how it places us strategically in several seats of influence on the whole economy. I saw how coordinated street activities could be; I always imagined training those as ambitious and smart as Festo and Boda and Livingstone, how much it could change their lives. My number one project has been to create centers of vocation and skills training for street people. There is a lot of talent out there."

"I know," she responded.

"And Bigz and I have some projects for southern Africa, something Ssaka initiated. The board Ssaka placed there has given me the backing to go ahead with it." His eyes were soulful when they rested on her. "I never said this, but...it's scary filling his shoes."

Kenzi hugged him. They sat in silence.

Kevin had worked so hard to be where he was, and Kenzi marveled at how generous his heart still was despite everything. His ambition inspired her. When they first talked about all he was involved in, he told her, *every half an inch of opportunity brings me closer to owning the world, no matter how small.* The oil deal was that half-inch.

"Okay. Call me every day. I just want to be sure you are okay."

He kissed her palm. "Tell you what, I will call you more than once a day." He was serious, too.

She narrowed her eyes as she said, "Okay. And I will save up pinches for every time you miss."

"Ouch." He made a pained expression.

Kevin booked his ticket for Uganda, and in the few days before his flight, they spent every moment they could find together, planning out Christmas at her parents. Kevin was of the view that he would find a hotel until they could tell her parents what was really going on. But Kenzi would not have it. She had grown up in a charming, spacious colonial home in Woodhaven, Bethesda, and she was sure there was room for them both.

The final messages he was waiting for came in at 2:00 a.m.

"Check your mail," it read.

He could hear the whistling wind outside the window. The weather update had called for rain for the next twelve hours, and it was promising to pour resoundingly from the sound of the wind and the branches tapping against the windows. Kenzi had never been a proper sleeper; she was half-sprawled over him, and like he did most nights now that they shared the same bed and he had switched rooms, he gently took each limb aside, trying not to wake her up, and slipped out of bed. He made it to the living room, where his Apple laptop sat on the coffee table, flipped it open, and clicked the Safari browser on before typing in his email address.

The pictures he had been waiting for were the ultimate proof of things. He checked his messages from time to time; he was waiting for correlating information from Boda and Livingstone.

After Oketcho had located the caller, he had had Livingstone approach them.

"She sells airtime at the Kisementi stage," Livingstone told him. "A woman…she thinks *mukyotara* asked her to call you."

"And the emails?"

"Ah-ah. That one wasn't her," he confirmed with Kevin, who mulled over the evidence. He hesitated, asking Oketcho to track the IP address. It could have been sent from a café. The mystery caller said it was someone close. Ssaka always said betrayal came from within, never without. Could it be happening to him? He kept most of the information to himself, simply asking Livingstone and Boda to check on different things without divulging much information. Both men hardly questioned him; they naturally obeyed.

His email opened, and three unread messages popped up. Kevin sucked in air, not sure what to expect, partly not wanting to know. He had come too far already to ignore it, so he opened them. And there it was…all the evidence he needed. The last piece of the puzzle that had eluded him.

He stared at the images and the message from username *123pixy* that had remained anonymous but had fed him information.

Kevin downloaded the images into the zip folder he had named "mystery" on his desktop then sat pensively staring into space. He felt nothing. Perhaps, he thought, it came from dealing with a lot of traumas in the past. The darkness he had experienced and seen, the cold harshness of humanity and greed had hardened his resolve. If it wasn't for Kenzi, he was sure he would have remained in the seductive clutches of the darkness that had dragged him down often through the years. Kevin was not sure anything more could hurt him unless it was Kenzi.

His phone vibrated, tearing him from the somber thoughts that reached into his sunny bay with dark shadows. Kevin answered it.

"*Sitori kyi.*" He kept his voice low, and yet it bounced off the walls of the study and carried. His laptop clock said 2:00 a.m., nine o'clock in the morning in Uganda.

"*Ah-ah,* boss," the male voice on the other end said cordially, then continued in Luganda. "Boda followed him to the Sheraton. He was there meeting a woman."

Kevin frowned. "A woman? Describe her."

The male voice on the other end did and added, "We can send you pictures. Boda managed to get three. It wasn't easy."

"That will do. Did you see anything?"

The man on the other side *harrumph*ed. "He gave her an envelope. Those ones with *money* in it."

Kevin absorbed the information with technical grace. *Maybe this was a mistake?*

"When was that?" he asked.

"Yesterday," the male voice replied.

Kevin was silent for a moment, then asked, "Did Boda stay till they left?"

The male voice replied, "Yes. I am here seeing the woman now. I think she is going somewhere."

"Where are you?"

"Bugolobi. She is entering a *special* with a suitcase. Do you want me to follow? I am on a *boda.* I can..."

He pondered it, his mind unraveling pieces from his life to the present.

"No," he finally told Livingstone. "Don't follow. Just find out where the man is, and keep me in the know. I am coming back day after tomorrow. I will call you when I land. Thanks a lot."

"*Kawa*, no problem," the other man replied, promising to keep him updated.

Kevin stared into space for a long time, piecing this puzzle together. Whoever the mystery mailer was, they had not mentioned the woman, who was surely an accomplice.

His WhatsApp lit up as Livingstone did his due diligence, sending the pictures he had promised to send. Kevin saved them. It amazed him how composed he was. It frightened him. The last time he had been this calm was when he carried out his calculated revenge upon Bampa.

The feeble patter of rain on the windowsill dragged him back to the present. Kevin's gaze strayed into the dimly lit night. Through the bay windows, he could see the lights of the different apartment blocks shaped like Legos flicker on or off. He was motionless until it was pouring increasingly, then sauntered back to bed. Kenzi was sprawled all over his side of the bed. The sight of her calmed him. It engulfed him and relegated the past minutes of his treacherous discovery into a little dark box in the corner of his mind. She took center stage.

He shook his head and gently tugged the sheets that were now jammed between her legs and wrapped over her. He marveled at how anyone could get so tied up in their own sheets and sleep comfortably. Fortunately for him, she stirred and moved, allowing him to unravel the sheets and then slide in next to her while lifting her arms out of the way.

Almost instantly she was nuzzling up to him, sighing his name. Her leg draped over his groin, her arm over his chest. *Now* he considered it adorable. When they slept on the street, she would hold on to his shirt and sleep that way till morning. Sometimes he would wake up with a start because her arm would drop heavily onto his face or tummy; her little skinny legs would kick him.

Some things don't change, he mused, the back of his hand brushing against her cheek while he watched her sleep. Then he thought about the pictures of the woman Livingstone had sent him. Neither *do some people*.

On the night he was leaving, they made love like it was the first time, discovering each other again, awakening pieces of their buried desires and shoving aside their fears. It was all right to love and be loved. They basked in a medley of convoluting emotions like buried treasure being carefully unearthed from its grave of forgottenness: passion and pain, sentiments they could not dictate with their lips, a language that surpassed the mind and eclipsed the soul, melded together, healing and soothing the chasm of past and present. The future looked bright. They made gestured commitments to uphold the bond that had increasingly deepened, establishing its unshakable roots in the grounds of their love.

Sketch took them to the airport, and at the final call, Kenzi could not hold back the tears as Kevin hugged her. He promised her with every pulsating nerve in his body that he would be back on the day before Christmas Eve.

"Baby *wange*," he whispered, their foreheads touching.

Kenzi giggled, sniffing. "I like the sound of that.

"I will see you soon."

She nodded and kissed him lingeringly.

He shook hands with Sketch. "Take care of her like you do, my man."

Sketch grinned. "You got it." And then he was gone.

They rode back in silence, Kenzi lost in disquieting thoughts. The investigation was slow. Only Doctor had been apprehended.

Sketch dropped her off, reminding her that her next few weeks would be busy, a new call in Florida. She was going to work with an acclaimed Arabian photographer who was trying to replicate a tropical forest theme for a top magazine in Dubai. Occasionally, they got clients out of the regular range of clientele pools, and usually the agency negotiated viciously for those top-dollar contracts.

She was to go through the contract in the next few days and arrange to fly to Florida for a week.

"Sun and water. Best combination for a getaway. You are lucky it wasn't to Chicago," Sketch was saying.

Kenzi agreed: "Yes lawd!"

Back in the silence of her apartment, she missed Kevin. His conspicuous presence still filled it. The air smelled faintly of his Creed cologne. The plates they had had dinner on sat in the sink, unwashed, and their crumpled sheets remained, pillows on the floor, telltale signs of their lovemaking. She grabbed one pillow and hurdled up on the bed. The smell of citrus shampoo filled her nose. The bedside digital alarm clock said 1:00 a.m. Kevin would board soon.

She flipped her phone open to WhatsApp and typed him a message. *"I miss you."*

Her phone rang instantly. It was Bosco, and she frowned. They had not heard from him since the conference Skype call with the guys a couple of days ago.

"Hey." She tried to smile as she greeted him. "Is everything okay?"

Bosco was light as he responded. "Yeah. Yeah, I am fine. It's just been crazy."

"Yeah, I heard…."

Bosco got quiet. "Oh?"

"Yeah, I kinda walked in on a conference call Kevin was having with the guys, and…you were not there."

"Oh, that. Yeah, they told me." He sounded slightly off. "Is Kevin around?"

Kenzi shook her head. "No, he isn't. I just dropped him off. He is coming home."

Bosco mouthed a silent "Oh."

Kenzi probed. Something seemed off about him and had seemed off for a while now. She was not sure if it had anything to do with what had happened between them or more. "Is everything okay, Bosco? You just seem out of sorts."

Bosco laughed uncomfortably. "You know, I was not really surprised when I heard you and Kevin hooked up…. *Finally*, by the way." His words dripped with sullenness.

Kenzi shifted. "Bosco, I am sorry." She suddenly felt she needed to explain. "I…I love Kevin…."

"No need for apologies. I think I missed my chance when you were here. I could have been more…."

"Bosco!" she cut in. "Stop. Don't do this. We all had crushes when we were younger…."

"Apparently you scored yours. I did not." He was annoying her with his attitude.

"I am sorry we cannot be or could not be."

"Yeah…well…we could have, if you had paid me some mind, you know. It was always Kevin. Always Kevin! Do you know how many girls he has been through? Changing them like diapers? Do you honestly think he will be true to you? Do you? Just because you went through a lot together? I grew up with you guys. I always loved you!" He lost control; he was raving.

"Stop, Bosco. What the fuck?" Kenzi was sitting up, her mind reeling, listening to Bosco rant.

"I have done so much for you, you have no idea, Kenzi. So much! Only Kevin stood in my way. I was afraid he would get to you before me…."

"Bosco, nobody got to anybody. We love each other! Always have! This is crazy!"

Bosco would not stop. "Kenzi, he is not good for you; mark my words. I know Kevin. I know him!"

Kenzi felt anger rise in her. "That's *your* friend too, Bosco, and if you are going to go off on us like that, forget you!" She hung up on him. Kenzi stared at the phone in her lap, frozen. Bosco called again. She cleared it. When he called a third time, she turned her phone off altogether, flopped back on the bed, and lay in the dark.

Her mind reeled. "What the fuck?" she mouthed, not sure how to feel or think. She thought about telling Kevin but decided against it. The last thing she wanted was to come between them. She had thought the kiss was a weak moment and his alleged crush on her when they were younger was Kevin being a bully. Now she could see it wasn't. His voice raged in her mind.

"I have done so much for you, so much!"

Something loaded with a strain of toil in his voice when he said that made her revisit it in her mind over and over. She wondered what he meant. If it was what he paid for while she was in Uganda and partly in Kenya, she was willing to reimburse that. However, the way he had stressed it seemed like he had done more. What was she missing? Suddenly, the dream projected into her mind—Kevin lying in a pool of blood—and fear gripped her. Kenzi turned her phone back on. Her message notifications lighted her screen, a message from Kevin.

"I miss you more. Can't wait for the 23rd. Take care."

She smiled; the message dissipated the paranoia she was feeling. Maybe there was nothing to fear and Bosco would be all right. He was upset, and she could understand the disappointment he felt, but she would talk to him when he could be reasonable with her.

Her phone vibrated and two messages swiftly popped up in her notifications. It was Bosco.

"I am sorry. I lost myself. Please don't tell Kevin."

* * *

Kevin adjusted his seat and fastened his seat belt. The intimacy of first class allowed him enough privacy for his undertaking. The plane was still grounded, and passengers slowly filed in. The sunny voice of the hostess welcomed them and reconfirmed their flight and told them to double check their surroundings and ticket to be sure they had the right seats. Kevin smiled as he responded to Kenzi's message. He missed her, but there was a peace that settled in him, a calm so reminiscent of their time on Block 4 and the streets that she was there. She was *his for good*. And that was final. He settled back, relishing in that knowledge and in the way it made him feel.

Complete.

That old familiar feeling that they could conquer anything together. It was back, and it was how he was going to solve the complex problem ahead.

His phone chimed and he flicked open the message. He scrolled through pictures slowly, his jaws clenching and unclenching as he expanded some for a clearer view. He saved them and responded to the sender.

Kevin eased back and sighed, wondering how they had gotten to this place.

His phone lit up again, and it was a message from Bosco.

"Hey, boss, how are you?"

Kevin mouthed a "wow" as he responded: *"Fine. You?"*

"Good. Good," the message popped up.

"I am on my way home. Should arrive by 2:00 p.m. tomorrow." He lingered over the message, hovering over the send button…then clicked send.

"Oh good! We need you here. Should I pick you up?"

Kevin read the message again. He hated to play the game of the streets on a man he had trusted for the last six years.

"No, no need, I am covered."

He waited. The blue tick confirmed Bosco had read the message, but he hesitated to respond.

After a minute or two. *"Okay. See you then, boss. Sorry, I have been so busy trying to save our asses."*

"Hmm." Kevin smirked and sent a thumbs-up emoji.

The call for them to switch their phones off boomed through the speakers, and Kevin swiped right, turning the phone off.

He leaned back, adjusting the seat farther back and closed his eyes.

Chapter 19

Kevin took his time. He called Kenzi late on the second night of his arrival, letting her know he was home safe. She was nervous, but he warded off her fears.

"It's all right, Kenz. Will let you know what happens."

After that he had kept his ringer off, poring through the emails and evidence he had collected over a two-week period while in the US. He pondered everything, trying to trace what he may have missed, what could have caused this.

At 4:00 p.m., he finally picked up his phone. There were missed calls from Bosco, Carissa, and his secretary from the office. Everyone knew he was back because Bosco had announced it. It was customary for him to walk into the office the next day, asking to see everything and calling for a meeting. He had been back for over sixteen hours and had not said a thing to anyone. He finally called Bosco, who picked up on the first ring.

"Everything okay?" He could hear the nervous twinge in Bosco's voice that only raised more questions. Until that point, he believed there had to be an explanation for the photos.

Kevin smiled. "Yeah, everything is fine." He waited, then added, "I needed a day to get over being in love."

Bosco replied, almost relieved. "Ah, yes. Congs by the way. It was about time." He seemed to falter, then added searchingly, "How is Kenzi?"

"She is great," Kevin responded. A part of him warmed up thinking about her. "We haven't caught up concerning business." He steered the conversation away from her.

Bosco let out a slow sigh. "Yeah, man. I am glad you are back. I missed the meeting the last time. The guys conveyed my apologies, but apparently our bid was pending. I don't know what changed the president's mind."

"Did you speak to the governor?"

"Yes, yes. He is the one who said it was delayed and hoped to catch up with you when you returned. I was trying to iron that out before you came."

Kevin took in the information, alert, listening for any clues. "Good. Good. What are you doing tonight, around seven?" Kevin was asking, his other hand thumbing the pictures he had printed out.

"Er…" Bosco hesitated. "Nothing much. What's up?"

"I was thinking you can bring me up to speed over dinner. Our usual place," he said easily.

"Sure. With the guys?"

"Oh no, you and me first. Then when we figure things out, we can talk to the guys."

Bosco agreed: "Sure."

* * *

Kevin swung his long legs off the couch he was lying on and made for the shower. He felt a little fatigued from the flight, but his mind was working overtime, calculating the possibilities of everything.

Ten minutes later, he alighted from the shower, a white towel around his lean waist. He stared at his reflection in the mirror as he shaved and slapped on aftershave lotion and deodorant. He took out a pair of gray stonewashed jeans and a fitted bone-colored T-shirt with an interesting exclamation mark printed on it he had gotten from an H & M store in Times Square.

His rather unique and quality fashion sense had impressed all the women he had dated—that worldly-wise stylish bunch. They had been good markers on how well his outer appearance impressed on the most important people that he had to meet on his path to success. He had scanned magazines every day religiously and mentally, put together outfits he knew would work for him. When he recreated those looks, he got stares; he got the women, and he got his foot in the door in any place he needed something. Kenzi had been impressed by his fashion sense as well, and he could satisfactorily claim her view as the most important in the end.

He spoke with Kenzi again; she was leaving for Florida on an early flight. Since it was late, he kept it short, leaving out the details of his evening plans so far. He wanted to be sure he had the proper information before he filled her in on what was going on.

He took his messenger bag carefully, placing the pictures he had printed out alongside his laptop. His phone clock showed 5:30 p.m. As he picked up his elbow-patched jacket that was hanging on the armless accent chair in his room, he got another call. This time, it was Vanessa. Kevin sighed. He had not responded to her much while in New York, and, although she had been very frugal with her communication, she was still persistent.

"Hey, lover," she breathed into his ear when he picked up the phone. "So, you are back, I heard. How are you?"

Kevin smiled. "I am fine, Van. What's going on?"

She sighed. "I'm just glad you are fine. When we heard about what happened, I really blamed myself for keeping you out late that night."

"Van, that was months ago."

"I know. I can't help thinking about it. I really can't, *mukwano*. I almost died, thinking I had lost you."

Kevin pushed up the jacket sleeves, chuckling. "Who, me? Gone? Impossible."

"Yes, you, Mr. all that and a bag of chips, eh?" she flirted lightly. "I was afraid your nine lives had run out. I wanted to visit you but…hmm…your girlfriend from the US was around, so I decided to wait till you were back."

Kevin laughed. "Kenzi?"

"Yeah. I was seeing her pictures on social media on Bosco's feed and all your group of boys. Your 'rich clique.'" She added the last bit with a scoff. "So. I see she kept you well."

Kevin, still laughing, noted the twinge of jealousy in Vanessa's voice. "Mmm…she did. She always does," he replied.

"Aha! Don't I take care of you?"

Kevin smiled. "Yes, you have," he replied sincerely.

"Maybe I can make it up to you tomorrow night? I can come over. Cook? Music? And you can show me how much you have missed me?"

Kevin cocked his head to one side, Kenzi on his mind. Her offer felt like chaff in the wind. It was time to end this game. "Tell you what, how about I treat you to lunch tomorrow?"

She paused. They *never* did lunch. It was always dinners. "Oh?" She sounded surprised.

"Yeah. Let's do lunch, around noon at the Seven Hills in Kololo?"

She quickly regained her composure. "Okay, if it's what you want, *mukwano*."

He smiled and, with as much charm as he could muster, replied, "It would make me happy to see you there."

He was relieved he had left an effect; she was giggly and light, suddenly her gushing, pampered self again. He needed to break it to her easily enough, without her feeling he had robbed her of her self-esteem.

After he hung up with her, he made one more call.

Chapter 20

Kevin found Bosco waiting for him on the terrace of Pearl restaurant at an intimate table detached from the other diners serenaded by the trickling sound of water from the fountains on the patio. Kevin and Bosco had made it a habit to meet and speak about business when there were kinks and knots that needed resolving before presenting it to the rest of the guys. As the biggest shareholder of the oil deal, Kevin knew a lot rested on their decision following the delay so far.

Bosco had a distracted, faraway look on his face. His glass of Coca-Cola was still full. The bottle beside it was almost empty. Kevin called from a few paces away, "One would think you got stood up. It's only six forty-five!"

Bosco looked toward the sound of the voice, and Kevin spied the visual relief that washed over it. Bosco's smooth, plump face broke into a smile. "Boss!" he said as Kevin came over, and they clasped arms in greeting. "Good to see you on your feet. Hard to believe you were almost gone months ago. Kenzi kept you well." He looked his friend over.

Kevin shrugged. "Thanks. You don't look too shabby yourself. Been going to the gym?" He appraised Bosco in his beige suit, with the jacket draped over his chair, the charcoal dress shirt, and striped tie. They hung a little loose on him.

"I am laying off milk for a while," Bosco said with a short, nervous laugh.

Kevin raised a brow. "I think it's working. But the Coke, though?" When they sat, a waitress came to take their order. Kevin ordered a pot of freshly brewed tea, claiming he needed to taste some Ugandan tea before he dove into the menu.

"Cheat day," Bosco said and sipped the dark brown liquid that danced and fizzed in his glass.

They spoke about banal things as Kevin asked after Bosco's family and what Carissa was thinking of doing during her semester break over Christmas.

When the tea came, Kevin steered the conversation toward what he had been mulling over the last few weeks. "So Kenzi told me she met her mother." He paused, sipping his tea.

Bosco clasped his hands together. "Yeah." He cleared his throat. "I thought maybe it would be a good idea since it's been so long. Maybe they could talk or something. It apparently did not turn out well."

"Hmm." Kevin stroked his chin. "It did not. I am just curious...we have known each other so long, Bosco. You know how I feel about Ameena. You never told me you were in touch with her."

Bosco opened his mouth and closed it soundlessly. Clearly trapped.

"So, imagine my surprise when Kenzi told me. I figured you two were in touch much longer than that."

Bosco kept his eyes on the table. "Kevin, I thought it was in Kenzi's best interests to meet her mother."

Kevin scoffed, pouring more of the hot caramel-colored tea into his cup and sipping unhurriedly. "*Everyone,* you inclusive, knew what Ameena did to Kenzi. That was cold."

Bosco shrugged. "She agreed to meet with her, Kevin, and Kenzi is a grown woman. She is not eight!" He ended on a sharp note.

Kevin raised an eyebrow. The man seated across from him shifted his gaze to the fountain. "You are right. However, why do I feel there is more to all this?"

"What are you saying?" Bosco's gaze returned to Kevin.

Kevin flipped open the bag beside him, pulled out his planner, and opened it to where he had placed the photographs. He spread them on the table before Bosco.

"This is you, no?" He pointed at the man in the neatly lined photos: five or six images that showed Bosco with a beautiful caramel-colored woman in a restaurant at five different times. Kevin had handpicked these pictures from several that Boda and Livingstone had sent him. "This is Sheraton…. Café Javas, Africana…ummm even here Serena… yeah." He held Bosco's gaze. The chunky man's eyes widened.

"Where did you get these…?" he stammered. It was then that all benefit of the doubt in Kevin's mind dissipated, and a feeling of betrayal lodged itself deep in the pit of his tummy.

"What were you doing with her?" Kevin asked coolly. He kept his voice low.

Bosco's eyes flashed with anger. "What is this? What are you accusing me of? You are the one having me followed! Are you serious? I won't deal with this!" He scrambled to his feet, adding, "This is ridiculous!"

"What's ridiculous is this!" Kevin pointed at the pictures.

"What do you want?"

"The truth! What's really going on?" Kevin replied, knowing that the only thing that kept him in his seat was the fact that they were in a public setting.

Bosco shook his head. "I have nothing to say. You are the one who has to answer to my lawyer."

Kevin guffawed dispassionately. "Sit the *fuck* down. One move from you and the chief inspector of police will be in here in minutes."

Bosco's mouth fell open.

"I am one step ahead of you. You forgot who I am, Bosco. You forgot. I got a tip and followed the breadcrumbs. You don't have a lawyer, at least not our lawyer. So, I suggest you start talking…."

Bosco shook his head. "Un-fucking-believable."

"You best believe it."

Beads of sweat erupted on his brow, and with the back of his plump hand, he wiped it off. "I have nothing to say." He shrugged in defiance, but Kevin knew Bosco. He was terrified.

Kevin went on: "Okay…" He dug into his messenger bag again. "My bag isn't empty." A cool smile touched his lips. He pulled out a brown A4 envelope and emptied its contents on the table. More pictures of Bosco, this time meeting with two men in a take-away, handing them envelopes, a few photos placed him at Luzira prison, a couple more outside Bank of Uganda, shaking hands with the governor, at the bank in line, leaving with a briefcase.

Kevin downed his tea in a gulp, poured a second cup, and eased back on the lawn chair. Somewhere at a distant table a woman laughed, and the fountain trickled on in a calculated pattern that if he had paid attention, he would have heard the song in its liquid notes.

"What is going on? I am made to believe you are behind this deal, stalling. Also, I am made to believe you had something to do with my accident as you have something to do with Kenzi meeting her mother. So, I will ask again… What. Is. Going. On?"

Bosco sat stoic like a statue; terror emanated from his pores. Kevin studied him. The pain of his betrayal grew and hardened like a kidney stone in the pit of his belly. He still wanted to understand …why?

Bosco broke. "Okay…. Okay. I stalled the deal because…I doctored the books…." He paused, his mouth opening and closing. "I… I…"

Kevin knew that even if he reached across the table and punched Bosco repeatedly, he would not retrieve the pleasure of watching him squirm uncomfortably in his own hell. So, he watched him.

"Go on." His voice was hard and low.

"Ameena threatened to…tell you…to come to you if I did not give her money. She bloody turned on me."

"Tell me what?"

Bosco was heaving. "That…I did…We did it. She made me arrange the hit on you."

Kevin felt the air lock in his lungs. He had known there was something dark, but he had not imagined it would be this dark. "Why?" he demanded

Bosco was almost wheezing. "Kevin, I am so sorry," he whined.

"Why?"

"She said it was the only way we could get what we wanted. She needed money from Kenzi…and…"

"What did you get?" Kevin could feel his face get hot.

Bosco took in a huge gulp of air, then let it out slowly like a deflating balloon, his head drooped, "You got her."

Suddenly, the one piece of the puzzle he had pondered for days fitted. The motive.

"*Kenzi?*" It was rhetoric.

Bosco nodded, a defeated man. "She was never going to be mine. She almost was…almost."

Kevin listened.

"After she met her mother, she was wounded, vulnerable. I made a move…but it was always you. Always!" Bosco hurled out the *always* with disdain, much to Kevin's surprise.

"I thought it was a childhood crush," he told Bosco coldly. "All this time…"

"I did nothing about it until Ameena approached me, got close."

The information came fast, and Kevin let it sit before it sunk in. It was unbelievable that he had known this man for years and had not realized he was in love with Kenzi, nursing the infatuation he had had from when they were children.

"You just cost yourself your freedom, Bosco."

"But it was her! Ameena planned *everything*. She wanted the oil deal; she wanted more money; she just wants more and more."

"Fuck you, man! You knew better than to deal with her!" Kevin felt the words ricochet off him like a cannonball. He did not stir or look over his shoulder to see that one or two diners had glanced their way.

He pointed at the pictures. "Who are these? What is all this? Tell me now," he demanded in a steely tone.

Bosco faltered, his armpits sweating, spreading wet, ugly maps on his shirt.

"The men…I got to beat you up. You were not supposed to live."

Kevin looked at the man he had called a close associate for years, a man he had trusted with a lot of the company's details, a man he considered intelligent and focused, bring himself low because he was in love with a woman he could never have.

"And you came to Aga Khan Hospital with Kenzi and acted like you cared."

"I was guilty. And because it hurt Kenzi…I…" he trailed off.

"How much did you pay them?"

Bosco cleared his throat. "Half a million. Each." He squeezed his eyes shut.

"Where is Ameena? Where did she go?"

Bosco did not hesitate. Helplessly, he replied, "Dubai."

"When is she coming back?"

Bosco chuckled bitterly. "She isn't."

Kevin sat back; a bitter laugh emanated from his throat. More pieces fell into place. Suddenly the caller who had whistle-blown on Bosco and sent pictures as evidence came back to him. It all made sense. Ameena had double-crossed Bosco, taken his money and Kenzi's money and fled the country, leaving him to pick up the pieces in jail. He would not have known Ameena was behind it if he had not asked Boda and Livingstone to do some sleuthing.

"What happened to the oil deal?"

Bosco sighed. "Nothing. I met the president myself. I told him you were not in the country and…I would handle it. We got the tender and an advance. I…" He paused. "I gave Ameena the advance…so she could shut up. The deal was…she leaves the country and not come back. Not for some years until all this had blown over. So, I told the guys the deal had stalled. I…needed time to figure things out."

Kevin cursed under his breath. "My God…Bosco." He buried his face in his hands, still unable to believe what he was hearing. "Well, I guess Ameena was smarter than us both…because that's how I knew. And she screwed you over."

Bosco did not have the strength to ask how.

Kevin processed everything slowly. He ordered a second pot of tea and mulled over the information while Bosco sat, head bowed, stoic.

"Where did she go?" he asked again, wanting to verify he had heard right.

"Dubai."

"Was she alone?"

Bosco shook his head. "She has an Arab lover."

Kevin sipped his tea. The anger at the betrayal clumped into an icy block in his chest.

When he was done thinking and the teapot was empty, Kevin sat up.

"Call your lawyer if you like. But I have your confession, and tomorrow first thing I shall meet with the chief inspector of police who I am sending this confession to right now." Kevin held his phone up, and for the first time, Bosco realized he was being recorded. "He will take care of this. I also need the names of the men you paid to kill me. You had my gateman accosted for a crime he did not commit? God, Bosco…you could have told me you wanted Kenzi!"

Bosco kept his eyes averted. "Would that have changed anything?"

Kevin thought for a second. The night breeze was cool, and it caressed the two men as if in pacification. "No."

Bosco shrugged, despondent.

"You were my brother," Kevin told him, bitterly. "But tonight, I lost him." His eyes dropped to the table, the little teacup with a drop of golden brown, a fusion of milk and black tea at the bottom, gone cold and drying out.

It took all the effort he could muster to leave the terrace, all appetite vanished. Kevin walked away, leaving Bosco, head bowed, at the table.

Kevin felt numb, a familiar feeling. He had naively thought this was something he would not have to do again. Not after so many years. But life on the street and after had taught him to watch his back, be closed off, and not let anyone close. With Bosco he had opened a door because he was a link to his past and some of the best times they had shared in school and on Block 4. The betrayal from Bosco was a blow on so many levels; it knocked the air out of his lungs recounting their meeting; all he had wanted was the truth, but he had not prepared for *this*. He hoped it was all a misunderstanding. The memories of childhood flashed before him: Bosco following him and Kenzi around, wanting to be the third wheel, which Kevin would not agree to. He pretended not to see the extra perks he gave Kenzi, and only later in life did he bring it up teasingly, the teasing he meted upon him for being puppy-eyed around her. He had never thought his infatuation had grown with him as well. And then again, he kept everyone else at bay when it came to Kenzi, and in his own childish way, he knew that Kenzi and he would always be together no matter what happened to them. He just knew. It was what he told the doctor in Itombwe hospital when he started to recover from the mercury poisoning.

"What if you never find her?"

He had shaken his head vigorously, "Impossible! How? I will. We are going to always be together."

Kevin got home drained and hollow; his mind had been replaying the conversation over and over. How could he tell Kenzi? The biggest task of all was telling the rest of the crew and dealing with the money; they would have to find a way to freeze Ameena's account if she had put it in a bank. But Ameena had proved smarter than that; she had taken the money in cash. Bosco would have to hand over all the paperwork he was dealing with. Police would be in his home gathering everything as evidence. He had requested to meet with Doctor, who was still being held at Luzira, and with this new evidence, he would use it to have him released. Kevin lay back between his cool grey sheets. He stared at the circular pattern in his ceiling that converged in the center where the semi-curved light holder with the encased bulb glowed from within, his mind occupied.

Chapter 21

He fell into a restless sleep, waking up periodically through the night until at 6 a.m. he decided it was pointless trying. He sauntered into the living room and flicked on the channel to NTV. It was a habit to switch between NTV and NBS every morning for an hour before getting ready for work, simply to catch up on what was happening. Kevin watched it distractedly, reading messages from his WhatsApp, then texted Kenzi.

Hey beautiful, how are you?

Kenzi responded instantly, smiley kissy-face emoji.

Miss you plenty! Is everything okay? Did you see Bosco?

The memory of the conversation on the terrace washed over him like a high tide on troubled water, chilling his bones.

Yes, I did, he told her. *I will call you later.*

Okay, I love you. Be safe. Tell me everything. I am worried.

He smiled, warmed. *I will. I love you too.*

He averted his eyes to the screen in time to catch a breaking news item. Kevin froze in his seat as the presenter played a recorded phone video of a bulky man zigzagging drunkenly on the top of the Garden City rooftop, then, amid screams from a few onlookers, scrambled over the railing and tittered as if unsure of his next move, slipped and fell off the ledge.

"...at four this morning, an unidentified young man was seen leaving Boda

Boda Restaurant. Onlookers allege he was in a distressed state and very inebriated. He was shouting as most drunk people would, drawing attention of the clientele until he took to the railing and threw himself over. He was unconscious at the time police arrived. More details on this story...."

Kevin quickly flipped the channel from NBS to NTV, and there it was again. This time the breaking news headline read *"Young man falls to his death,"* and the NTV story had his name and a mug shot of him. He was confirmed dead soon after the police arrived. Kevin felt his whole body convulse in shock, and he buried his head in his hands as the news reporter's voice on the television became white noise, a humming chaos of static in his head, as images in his mind merged, blurred, and taunted him. He saw Bosco, and then his father, both heavy, drunk, slurring, angry, and dying.

Kevin groaned in agony. This was not supposed to happen. The voices mocked him...told him it was his fault. He had killed again.

"No!" Kevin fought back. "No!"

The phone was ringing. The TV was humming. It was suddenly too loud. The past that he thought he had exorcised crowded the living room: his father lay in a corner sprawled with blood draining out of him from the stake that jutted through his body, his mother cold and pale, death calling to her, waiting on her, and Bosco falling. Falling. Kevin gasped for breath, begging, pleading with the ghosts of the past with the voice that accused him.

"No!" he cried. He cried just as hard as when Taata Bob beat him. He cried as hard as when Kenzi was taken away. He cried as hard now for all the pain that jutted out of the graves. He cried because agony and pain whipped him senseless. Then the moment was over. The frenzied tears subsided, and he noticed his phone ringing somewhere. Kevin sat up, wiped his face with the back of his hand, and got up, sat on the couch, and stared at the number calling...Oketcho.

"Yeah." He cleared his throat.

"Did you see the news? God! What happened?" Oketcho sounded horrified.

"I did," Kevin said as calmly as he could muster, feeling slightly disconnected, like a spectator watching the world burning, unable to do anything about it. The shock and helplessness engulfed him, and he fought back. He had to keep it together for the guys. For himself.

He could hear another call coming in. "I will see you all later today. Can we have a 4 p.m.? Usual place. Gather the guys."

Oketcho agreed.

Kevin answered the next caller. Abe. "I saw the news," he was saying without waiting for Abe to say a word.

"What the fuck!" Abe blurted out.

"I asked Oketcho to convene a meeting. I will see you all later."

"What the hell happened?"

Kevin shook his head. "I...can't talk now. I will see you later."

He dropped the phone in his lap, inhaling deeply. Waves of anguish washed over him; it was unbelievable. The story was playing again. He could hear it faintly in the background, not sure if he wanted to hear it again, yet not wanting to leave the living room either. It had become his only connection to Bosco. The only lifeline to seeing his last minutes alive. He could see him again, on the terrace at Serena, as he dragged the truth out of him, shards of betrayal slicing him with every revelation and the sad question that drowned the pain he felt then was why? Even after it was answered, he still wondered why.

The phone vibrated in his lap. It was Kenzi. Nothing mattered.

He picked it up, and she chirped happily into his ear: "Hey, I am between shoots. I can't get enough of the sun, ummm. And I wanted to hear your voice, sexy."

Kevin felt his throat close, not sure what to say. He inhaled sharply, leaned his forehead into his hand, and closed his eyes, conflicting emotions riding over the calm that seeped in by talking to her. "Kenzi... um...something horrible has happened. I don't want to..."

"Are you, okay? What...what's wrong?" Kenzi cut him off. "Please tell me you are all right. Please...."

He breathed. "I am okay. I am good. I am...but...Bosco..." He paused, shifting the sleek iPhone to his left hand. He took in another gulp of air.

"What?"

Kevin shook his head, his hand rubbing his head. "Bosco is dead." The words rolled off his tongue like sandpaper, dry and tasteless. "I did not expect him to..." he trailed off, waiting.

The silence that reigned seemed not to break for more than half a minute.

"No...what?" Kenzi whispered in shock. "No. No. Kevin! What happened?"

Kevin shook his head, his free hand rubbed his eyes. "Kenzi, I don't want you to..."

"Tell me! I have a whole freaking hour!" She was frantic. "Oh my gosh! It's my fault, right?"

"No! No babe, it's not your fault," Kevin asserted into the phone. The last thing he wanted was for Kenzi to get sucked into mindless guilt. He felt the pain soar, rise up to his head. "I forced him to confess. He...was behind my accident and more."

He heard Kenzi gasp. "Oh my God, Kevin, What! Why?"

He blinked back the tears. Talking about it made it true, and his stomach churned; his head pounded an empty dull thudding like his head wasn't his.

"He loved you.... He made a dirty deal with your mother."

Kenzi was silent.

"He killed himself...this morning..." Kevin went on. His voice shook, and he cleared his throat often to stabilize it. "It's on the news...now."

Silence reigned between them for another minute. Kevin had to call her name to find out if she was still on the line.

"Oh God.... What can I do, Kevin...? I feel..." Kenzi groaned, finally trailing off, not knowing what to say, her chest constricted with sorrow.

"I am so so sorry," she whispered, choking from emotion that clumped her throat.

He shook his head. "I am sorry too. This is so tragic." He spoke more to himself.

"I don't know…I did this…."

"It's not your fault." Kenzi was firmly interrupting him. "It isn't!"

Kevin blinked to clear the misting over his eyes. What he was seeing on the news was the only way he could believe it had just happened. "Kenz, he was drunk and raving, threw himself off the fourth floor of Garden City. I can't…I can't believe this."

Kenzi gasped. "Goodness, Kevin…I wish I was there now."

"Would be nice," he agreed. "I don't know who would understand…."

Kenzi squeezed her eyes tight, the face of her mother swimming into focus. She allowed herself to focus on it, and from deep within her spewed all the anger she could at the image in her mind and screamed hateful words at her. She clawed at the image, she spat at it, and she destroyed it inch by inch.

"Kevin, it's all her. It's all Ameena," she vented. "She did *this* to us. To you, to me, to Bosco. Because…" Her voice broke. Inside she wept. "Because she is not a good person or a happy person. She. Did. This! And I hate her for this!"

Kevin could hear her sob silently: angry, painful sobs. And just like that, they were children again, stuck in an unforgiving world of adults, helpless to change the fate of events. He comforted her, and she spoke to his torment. They gently tugged at the scabs torn over healing wounds, reaching deep, and cleaning the sore regions, embracing the loss they had experienced, and he let her love him. She loved him with her voice, her comfort, her words. That strength that seemed specially stored for him flowed like a healing balm, renewing him, empowering him, reminding him he was not alone. "It's always been you and me against the world, remember? It's always been us." She repeated over and over in his ear.

Kevin sighed again, wiped his eyes, and sniffed the last of his hot tears, and when she felt him relax, she waited for him to say something.

After what felt like an eternity, he spoke. "Kenz, we have lost so much… too much." His voice carried sorrow she had not heard in a long time. "I can't do life without you. I *need* you."

A volley of volcanic emotion erupted within her, bringing fresh tears to her eyes. "Me neither."

Their silence over the RF waves was a cascade of unspoken words; their thoughts deliberated on another shocking loss, on pain that seemed to hound them, even though they ran from it. They hung on their phones, silently savoring their distant presence, not wanting to let go because for that moment, they were holding each other through a shattering experience with roots dredged in their past. It was their world, and no one else would be able to understand it.

In their own thoughts, they imagined themselves seated on a roof, feet dangling over the ledge, watching the world below them and the setting sun on the horizon, city lights stretched for miles flickering on and off against a half dark sky.

"So, what now?" Kenzi finally asked.

"I will be meeting with my lawyers and Haruna. They will handle the recording from the chief inspector. And...I am meeting with the boys later.... I will have to speak to Carissa; Bosco's parents will hear of it or already have. There is that, too." He paused and took in a deep breath, gathering himself together, then added, "I told Vanessa I would meet her for lunch."

"Okay...."

"You know me, Kenz. Before you, I roamed around. Vanessa and I were on and off, and she was always there, hoping that...maybe...I would settle down with her. I just need to break it to her that you are the only one I have eyes for now. Always have. And forever."

Kenzi glowed like a newly born firefly, his declaration easing the shock they both shared given the circumstances.

"I understand. I should have told you about...Bosco. It was before all this."

"He told me. It's all right. It does not matter."

Kenzi continued anyway. "He called me the night you left, and he was upset I chose you."

Kevin nodded.

"We can't help who we want, can we?" he said sadly.

Kenzi agreed: "No, we can't. We can't help who we are meant to be with too."

Kevin closed his eyes. He saw her face, her smile. "No, we can't."

Her break was soon over, and they were both comforted. "Please let me know what happens," she told him as she said her farewell.

"I will. Thank you. I was going crazy."

Kenzi smiled. The dream she had had twice came back to her, and it all made sense. She was here. She *needed* to be here with him. That was what it meant.

"Not while I am here, you won't. I love you."

"Love you more."

* * *

The rich crew tried to squash the story in the press as best as they could, and bits and pieces of it ran loose with some media houses claiming it was a money deal gone wrong; others, a love triangle. However, they had been exposed as Uganda's best-kept secret, rising young billionaires.

"The papers will try to make money off this." Kevin was meeting with Haruna and Mike Bangirana. He had spent endless days following Bosco's death and investigations in their company, seeking counsel.

"When do you travel?" Mike asked him.

"Before Christmas...the twenty-second."

"It will be good to get away for a few weeks. We will handle everything here," Mike assured him.

"How about Ameena?" he asked quietly.

Haruna harrumphed . "She won't get away with it. Give it time."

Kevin smiled weakly, "Ssaka would say that."

* * *

"Shit!" Tisa cursed when he read the paper that morning, a week after the burial.

They met at the Ssese Patisserie as usual, catching up on stock market figures, and each of them openly expressed how not having Bosco was so tangible. Bosco was numbers smart, book smart.

"It was unfortunate his heart robbed him of sense," Bhanu had said in one of those meetings.

The power of love, Tisa had said, and Oketcho agreed. The meeting morphed into a memorial for their friend, and it bonded them further.

"They need to leave it alone." Oketcho was bothered by the press as well. "My wife is getting a lot of press calls at her workplace, and this is not good."

Abe shrugged. "We would have been outed, anyway. Someday soon. Especially after the oil deal." He was spearheading the PR efforts that absorbed a lot of the media attention they were getting.

Kevin labored to tell the crew the whole truth of the ordeal between him and Bosco. As much as they had known a lot of their history, the twist in the story was Kenzi's mother, which stunned the boys.

He offered Carissa the choice to move on or keep working for him and understood when she chose to distance herself from him. He knew that he carried the weight of blame for now and possibly would for a while until Ameena was brought to book. He asked the chief inspector how they would be able to go about this.

"The case is still open, but Dubai is big, and it would require resources to get her, resources we don't have. If she took the money. Huh. I don't know if we can track her," the inspector told him. "I am so sorry, but our hands are tied. Maybe if she returns, we will get her." That sounded more like an admission of resignation.

"I can fund the department that takes on this case, Inspector. Just name the price," Kevin told him. The inspector hesitated. Kevin understood how the system worked, possibly best to find her himself, he thought. The case as it stood was pending and would be closed without Ameena facing the trial she deserved for the pain she had caused.

The rich crew was somber, reeling from the loss of two hundred thousand dollars. For the next few weeks, they had meetings with the governor and then the president, the conclusion being they needed to work with what was left, which was still frozen in Bosco's account as probes into the case continued.

Kevin spoke to Kenzi every day, filling her in, and once more she was there, holding him up, keeping him strong. "Babe, you took harder hits. Congo for one, that crazy issue with the diamonds in South Africa, and then the housing deal, remember? You got this."

He sighed. "This feels like one you cannot recover from."

"I bet they all felt that way," she told him, and she was right. Each of the obstacles he had faced had felt like there was no coming back from it, and yet he had made it out alive.

"True," he agreed, so grateful he could bounce things off her. "Ssaka would be so necessary right now."

Kenzi agreed.

The crew would wait till the investigations were over and the bank had given its go-ahead, then the rest of the advance, still in Bosco's account, would be released to the rich crew's business account. After everything that had happened, they agreed to a partnership for the oil deal, and Ochola and Bangirana Advocates were working tirelessly to draw up their papers and protect them from the backlash of Bosco's death, extortion of money and the unwarranted publicity. Kevin still wanted to know how far Ameena had gotten to; however, she had simply vanished, somewhere in Dubai.

"That might be something you will need to leave alone for now," Kenzi had told him.

Kevin smirked. "I will find her, and she will pay."

Chapter 22

New York
December 21, 2016

Kenzi checked the calendar again and frowned. Her period was either late, or she was not counting her days right. The agency gave her a break for the Christmas holidays, and she decided there would be no better time to clean up and put up the decorations and tree than now. Kevin needed to come back to Christmas cheer in a clean house. She liked to call him OCD with his knack for spotlessness.

November and the earlier part of December had been busy with photo shoots, the Victoria's Secret annual fashion show, and a charity ball organized by Graciella Nueva, a Venezuelan model in Atlanta who was championing a cause against child trafficking, springing from her own horrifying experience as a child. It was a charming fundraiser filled with models from across the world; some upcoming, others so long in the game they hardly stopped to chat except for muttered superficial hi's, and air kisses dusted off with empty promises to keep in touch. She had gotten used to the superficiality of the modeling world. Kenzi figured she would get to that status soon and thought how funny her own superficial greeting would be. She decided she would practice a fresh one that would be an internet breaker. She could almost hear Kevin guffaw at her for that.

In between gigs and checking on Kevin, Kenzi had not been in touch with Heather until she called that morning as Kenzi scanned her calendar, counting her days, trying to figure out if she was getting irregular or if the stress of the past month had taken its toll on her.

"Kenz? Where are you? My goodness, did you throw me out too? Like Mom and Dad?" Heather teased.

Kenzi laughed. "No, I saw your calls and would forget to call back. It's been…busy." She sighed.

"Oh? Tell me?"

"Oof! all over; first Florida, then California, then back here, and only last week was in Atlanta for a gala. Got back last night, and I have ten days to while away and ruminate on the presidential elections. Urgh!" she half-shrieked.

"Girl, you are so popular!" Heather whooped. "And yes, America sucks! Obama should have had an extended-term…but you can't tell Mom and Dad that!"

They groaned together as they discussed the recent results of the elections that had placed Republican hopeful Donald Trump almost sixty points ahead in the presidential lead against his Democratic opponent. "Kevin is going to tease me for saying he could never be president!" she told Heather lightheartedly.

"Hey, it's America; you can be one thing today and president tomorrow. Say, Kenzi, the model today, Madame President 2020, whoop!" They both laughed.

Kenzi said, "I am tired, so, so tired. I have been the most tired this month. Like my body just can't hold up."

"Have you seen a doctor?" Heather sounded concerned. "You are like a lava of energy always. What's up?"

Kenzi sighed. "No, maybe I will go after the holidays; probably just fatigue. How are you, though?" She had abandoned counting her days on the calendar and plopped on the sofa to speak with Heather.

"Pretty good, pretty good. Did I tell you I got in? Vet school? Yeah, I got the response. It was a yes!"

Kenzi whooped with her. "Oh, my word! Good for you, girl! So many glad tidings at the holiday party."

"So many?" Heather always had her ears up for gossip. "You have some glad tidings?"

Kenzi giggled. "Oh, Brent did not tell you?"

"Brent?" Heather grunted. "Kat got him, remember? He talks to no one! So what's the big secret? You know I live through you guys; my life is boring as fuck!" She nudged.

Kenzi dillydallied, riling Heather up. "But…you have to promise not to tell Mom and Dad."

"Really!" Kenzi could see Heather shake her left leg, an interesting habit she had had since she had known her, an indication she was getting impatient.

"Yes." She dangled the carrot.

"You know I won't," Heather blurted out. "Now spill."

She told her about Kevin, about their relationship, about how happy she was.

Heather's jaw dropped. "Pick that up off the floor." Kenzi laughed into the phone, knowing her expressions all too well.

"No way."

"Yes way!"

"And Brent knew this before me, why?"

Kenzi made a face. "Umm, yes. He kinda figured it out."

"Oh, wow! Glad tidings indeed." Heather squealed with her. "I hope we have two weddings soon."

Kenzi laughed. "Not too fast. We still need to be engaged."

"Right, there is that. Wow, okay. Whoa, I need a moment to woosah. You and I need girl time to talk about this…in great, *great* detail!"

Kenzi smiled; a hint of sadness lingered over the more recent loss of Bosco. "Oh, there is a whole lot to tell."

They talked about Brent and his proposed wedding date, and then Heather had to go. Kenzi lay back on the couch, smiling to herself. The year had been busy and great for her career, but it had also been great gaining strides with Kevin after four years.

She marveled at how everything had fallen into place as if by an unseen force or hand guiding them, bringing them to each other, like it was letting her know the universe approved of their love.

She did not know how long she lay there but started when the doorbell rang and realized with a glance at her phone clock she had dozed off for an hour. Sketch was at the door. He had an armful of decorations he had told her he would bring by later that day. It was while she was placing the fourth crystal ornament on the tree that a strong wave of nausea passed through her. She wobbled on the stepladder, and Sketch reached out to steady her.

"You okay?"

She nodded and excused herself to the bathroom to spit the thickening saliva that formed fast in her mouth the more she spat. When the wave passed, she sat on the toilet seat, leaning back, feeling tired. Her eyes fell on the calendar again in her bathroom by the mirror. She was four days late.

Kenzi suddenly sat up. "Sketch. I need to go to the CVS. I will be back!" she called out to him.

"It's snowing out there, girl. Are you sure?"

"Yeah, yeah, there is one two blocks away. I will be back soon." She forced a smile, grabbing her coat, scarf and an oversize thick woolen beanie that covered most of her head to her ears, something she was grateful for since her big curly hair always got in the way. The snowflakes were not coming down as hard or as fast as she had thought, but it had snowed two days before, and it covered the streets and lanes in patches of white, erasing the beauty of the cobblestones and sunny buildings along her five-minute walk. Lights flickered on from apartments to bars; the streetlamps cast charming shadows against the walls and snowy lanes. In the distance, she could hear sirens, laughter, and faint music fade in and out.

The sights and sounds reminded her of her first Christmas with eyesight. Brent had volunteered to take her out in the snow. She had been starry-eyed, gazing around her, gawking as the flakes came down fast on her face and tangled in her hair. Brent had taught her how to stick her tongue out and catch a flake, and from then on, they competed for who would catch the most snowflakes until their tongues were blue. He had taught her about snow angels, weaving some tale about guardian angels in the snow and how they could bring them to life. Her first image of the world was cold and white and dazzlingly beautiful. That was a Christmas and birthday she had spent truly happy without Kevin. She made a wish for Kevin as she lay on the snow, waving her arms and legs, staring out at the dull sky laden with snowflakes. She wished he would be with them soon and she, too, would teach him to make snow angels.

Kenzi smiled to herself; she was at the CVS sooner than she expected. "Silent Night" played soothingly over the speaker. A handful of people were out tonight. Nobody wanted to deal with the cold. Almost all the Christmas shopping got done weeks earlier. Kenzi was sure if she had had the time, she would have shopped in November. She scanned the aisles for what she was looking for, and in minutes she was out of the CVS.

* * *

Kevin loved Christmas. It always reminded him of how his mother busied herself cooking and rushing around the house preparing Christmas dinner. Taata Bob stayed out longer during the holiday season, and Kevin was glad of it. Usually, he came home and slept it off and was out again. They always decorated the tree on the twenty-fourth, and his mother was meticulous about how she wanted it done. Kevin decided he had picked up that meticulous neatness perk from her. As he thought of her, he missed her. *Some ghosts never go away; they are happier, but they linger*, he thought.

"Oh, holy night" caressed his living room into life as he walked between bedroom and bathroom, picking items he needed for the trip. His flight was at two o'clock in the morning. Abe as usual, loving to drive, chose to drop Kevin off at the airport. They agreed the pickup time would be

11:00 p.m., and Kevin was packing a small hand luggage bag and one carry-on.

He neatly placed the clothes in separate piles, toiletry in a sac on the side, and his laptop on top along with a book on investing he had just bought from Aristoc. He was already chartering new investment courses. Since the publicity of the rich crew, more people were open to doing business with them, seeing their portfolio was not small. They also realized they could do a lot more together, although working independently of one another would still be honored. Among some of his projects, Kevin decided to invest in setting up a self-sustaining community in Entebbe. It was going to be a multimillion-dollar project, and he had proposed the idea to the Ministry of Urban Planning. The crew were thinking it would be a good idea to invest in creating a pleasure destination on one of the islands in Lake Victoria. Kevin, always ahead of his time with his visionary instincts, had smiled and thrown a bone amid them all: "I say let's venture out. I am grateful I knew and was mentored by someone as ambitious as Ssaka. He showed me how to fly. Borders are only a political paper trail; we can go beyond them. Maybe a plan for next year and beyond. But let's grow our influence much, much further. The world is our oyster."

"I will bite," Tisa had agreed. "I like Seychelles, personally."

Oketcho and Bhanu had argued it was best to start from home and spread abroad.

"We literally have tea with the governor of BOU and the president. Let's explore our opportunities and use them to the max," Oketcho prompted, and they mapped out the yearly plan at their end-of-year in the weeks that followed. Kevin reflected on his childhood and on his relationship with Bosco. His betrayal had become so minuscule in the light of his death because Kevin believed in honor among friends.

The items strewn on his bed diminished as he quickly put them away. It was half-past ten already. He rolled the bags to the front door and decided on a quick shower. Twenty minutes later, he was ready. His gaze swept the bedroom for anything he could have forgotten and fell on the little velvet box on the dresser.

"Ooh." He walked to the dresser to retrieve it. His phone vibrated in his pocket, and he was sure it was Abe. Kenzi's name and picture in the gown he had liked on Facebook for the outback couture for House of Luz lit up on his screen. He smiled.

"Babe, it's pretty early." His voice was low and loving.

"Um-hmm. I could not sleep. It's snowing hard. I hope JFK won't have any landing delays."

"I am glad I am dressed for it."

He picked up the velvet box, opening it. A smile touched his eyes as he stared at the ring, a simple, elegant band with a turquoise stone, the color of a clear ocean.

"Are you bringing me pancakes?" She giggled.

He replied, "I would not hold that back from you for the world. Abe is bringing tons of them. The mild and the hot ones with pepper."

"Hmm, yum, I can't wait to see you again. I don't know if we will leave here for home. Maybe we should skip it and just stay here, in bed, all Christmas," she suggested seductively.

"I am tempted. Can we still cancel?" He flirted back. "I got a surprise for you, though. A huge surprise."

She squealed and the Shenzi, with matted braids from Block 4, loomed in his mind's eye. "Really? What?"

"Didn't I say it's a surprise?"

She groaned. "Urgh. How long do I have to wait?"

"Twenty-four, maybe forty-eight hours?" He was enjoying her agony. He flipped the box closed. "Is that too long?"

Kenzi, who had been sitting on the toilet seat all this time looked up at the time on her phone quickly before returning it to her ear, got up, and walked to her vanity sink. "Umm… if you are okay with waiting on a surprise, I have one for you as well."

"Ouch, touché!" he replied. "How long do I have to wait?"

Kenzi picked up the pregnancy test results. The two pink bars screamed their confirmation in her face. She almost screamed with excitement but suppressed it and cleared her throat instead. "Twenty-four, maybe forty-eight hours?"

He laughed. His doorbell going off interrupted them. "Abe is here, love."

"Tell him I can't wait to see him here."

"Will do. Can't wait to see you and do bad things with you."

"Umm, I agree!" She giggled. "I love you. Be safe."

She placed the pregnancy test stick against two more beside it all with screaming pink double bars.

Kenzi placed the phone on the vanity and hugged her belly. She was going to be a mother. And not just anyone's mother, but to Kevin's child. She could not think of anything she wanted more than that. In the past few weeks, she had thought about her relationship with her adoptive parents and her real mother. After a conversation with Brent, she decided no one was more evil than Ameena, and the Matthews had been nothing but good to her. They had made a mistake, and maybe she could accept the olive branch they had extended to her every year since she had left home, waiting for her to pick it up.

They never gave up.

Maybe she needed to let it all go.

Too much had happened in the past months for her to ignore the growth she had experienced. She never got to know her *hooyo* and *awoowe*, she wanted her child to have both, and the Matthews would make amazing grandparents. Even as she basked in that decision, she thought about her mother, wondered where she was, what she was doing and if she would ever show up in her life again. Kenzi shuddered at the thought. She looked at the three confirmation sticks, turned the light out, and went back to bed.

Epilogue

January 2017
Emirates Hills, Dubai
11:00 a.m.

The villa stands elegant and exquisite, daring the sun on a hot January morning. Its smooth bone-colored walls have a just polished look to them. The gate is remote control operated, and a shiny black Mercedes S class eases out of an equally remote-operated garage- into the pristine neighborhood's narrow, empty byway. It glides through the intersecting lanes, turning left at a roundabout before joining traffic along a palmed driveway. The sleek Benz skims by well-manicured lawns as it heads toward an unknown destination, past the prestigious Emirates Hill golf course.

The streets hum with traffic and life, so different from the serene, picturesque gated community where the rich humor each other behind great oak doors and marble floors, in villas with tall ceilings and extravagant décor and furnishings. In this tall sunbaked villa with huge black lion sculptures gracing the front entrance lies a woman on the cream-colored marble floor in a wide, decadently furnished bedroom suite. In the center is a grand king-size bed anchored on poles made of expensive mahogany with Arabic inscriptions detailing its trunks. The bed is rumpled; silken navy sheets lie sprawled on the floor, a pillow here, a bedsheet there. A heavy wooden sculpture of a deity of sorts, lies broken, its head severed from its body and a tall, brown and white porcelain swirl vase lies shattered by the door.

On the floor, next to the king-size bed, lies a woman with long curly dark hair streaked with gold and light brown highlights. She has one sheet wrapped around her half-naked body, caramel-colored, smooth, and glowing, inviting to touch, except for her back that's ridged with deep slash marks as if slashed with a whip. She shudders and groans in obvious pain. Under her breath, she mumbles measuredly as if in meditation, "*Kow...laaba...saddex...afar...shan...lix...toddoba...siddeed...sagaal...toban...*"

A girl comes into the room cautiously, about fifteen years old, although she is so petite, she looks eleven. Her hair is hidden behind a black hijab. She stops by the door, a magazine in her hand.

"*Sayyida,*" she whispers. She looks around to guarantee no one is coming and edges in closer.

The woman, groaning the words she mumbles over and over on the ground, has her back to the girl.

"*Sayyida,* please get dressed. He has gone. But he comes soon. He comes," the girl pleads urgently, dropping lightly to her haunches. She winces as her eyes take in the deep red gashes on the woman's back. The woman turns her head slowly and looks at the girl. One eye is swollen shut, and her lips are bruised, but she is still beautiful, enchantingly so, and the young girl's heart breaks to see her so battered.

"You must stop. Please, *Sayyida.* Stop. Do as he says."

The woman chuckles. "I don't do what men tell me to do; haven't I told you…. I am Araweelo. No one tells Araweelo what to do!" She groans and, with effort, rolls to her side so she can look at the girl. The girl looks away as the sheet peels off the woman's body.

"Where did he put it?" she asks the girl, her voice coarse, impatient even.

The girl shakes her head, knowingly. "I don't know."

The woman's face falls slightly. She curses under her breath. *This should be my better life, a new start. Why did she pick all the violent men only!*

"I get you an *abaya,*" the girl says, hoping it will help. She gets up, and the beautiful, battered woman stops her. "Wait! What is that?"

The girl smiles faintly, glad she has been asked something she can answer. "American magazine, *Classy*." She stresses *American* with her Arabian accent. The woman beckons for her to hand it over, and the young girl obediently does so as the woman props up on an elbow and yelps in pain, gritting her teeth. "Oh, *wiilka eey!*" she cusses. The girl does not understand but likes the sound of it.

"What's that?"

The woman laughs dispassionately. "Son of a dog," she spits out her response.

The girl is quiet. She watches the woman thumb through the magazine as if searching for something. She gets frantic. The magazine is almost two hundred pages. She goes back and forth, picks it up with a groan, and tries to flip it fast but skips pages. The girl is getting antsy, glancing from her to the wide-open door in case someone she does not want to see walks in. Then, after flipping through twice, the woman exclaims, "Huh!"

The young girl peers at the page the woman is looking at. It's a woman with the darkest, smoothest ebony skin she has ever seen and eyes the color of a gemstone held up to the light of the sun. The girl gasps. "*Jamila....* Is she real?" she asks in wonder.

The woman nods. The girl sees that the woman in the magazine has a ring, a stone the color of her peculiar eyes, and it seems the story is about the ring. She can't read it well, but there are smaller pictures that only focus on the ring, and there is a man with her. He is dark but not as dark as her—much lighter, a young man with intense eyes, attractive and lean, but there is something behind the intensity in his eyes, like he has seen a lot of pain. The girl feels sorry for him. The woman flips the page, and there is another picture of them together, staring at each other. They look like they love each other very much. Their love feels like an old love that will last forever because it has been tested by time and trials.

The woman on the floor with a whipped, bleeding back is reading the story. The young girl wonders why she is interested in them.

"Who are they?"

The woman laughs hysterically, then gasps because she is in pain. She laughs and laughs. Tears roll from her eyes. She howls in pain and laughs again. The girl frowns, wondering what has gotten into her, and gets up, slowly backing away, puzzled. Could it be her question? Or was it the story she is reading? She glances into the long, winding corridor and panics; no one should find her here. She finally turns and flees down the winding corridor.

The beautiful, battered woman's hysterical laughter simmers to a sob. Her finger traces the face in the magazine…the story headline screams, "Engaged!"

She lies back on the polished cold marble floor pushing the magazine aside and groans, recalling her mother's words and counts again, "*Kow… laaba…saddex…afar…shan…lix…toddoba…siddeed…sagaal…toban…*"

"You are not afraid are you, my Araweelo?"

Ghosts dance before her, play a dizzying tune. She shakes her head, "No."

"Good," she hears her mother's soothing response, and she knows what she needs to do. Find the safe where he put *her* money. She will not be his prisoner. She must get out…*maybe* kill him. Find that plastic surgeon. No one will recognize her ever again. She will make certain of it.

* * *

New York
January 2017

The phone rings twice.

Kevin's reflexes are swift from force of habit. The number is a series of zeroes and ones. That's *new*, he frowns. "Hello?"

"Did not think you would hear this voice again, did you?" The voice that responds is familiar.

Kevin sits up; Kenzi stirs beside him. "What? Is it…?" His heartbeat quickens.

"Don't get too excited." The voice interrupts with patriarchal congeniality.

Kevin steps out of the bedroom and makes his way to the living room. The snowflakes are falling more rapidly than before they turned in for the night. The clock on the mantelpiece reads 3:26 a.m.

He half-chuckles in surprise. His hand absently brushes over his low-cut head of hair. "Where are you? Where have you been?" A renewed sense of joy fills him.

"Right now, I am at a gate to a villa in Emirates Hills in Dubai. Paying a small visit. There is too much to tell but not now."

"Dubai…why?"

Kevin is curious. He keeps shaking his head in wonder, still grappling with his disbelief. *Could it really be?*

"I found out an old friend, incidentally, had something I am very interested in. So I am here to collect. Settle a score. I spoke with Haruna a few days ago, and he told me of your troubles that ended last year. And that's why I am here in Dubai."

"Wait? Is this about…Ameena?"

The other man says nothing, then, "Unfortunate what happened to your dear friend, Bosco."

Kevin sighs, taken back to the previous year's events. "I was wrong…." He feels a need to explain, but the other voice is impatient.

"Betrayal is inevitable. I can forgive it, given the circumstances." There is understanding in his tone. "But malice…I cannot. I think I can solve the mystery and close that pending case police in Uganda could not."

Kevin furrows his brow, still puzzled. "But how…. I don't understand…. When…?"

"Kevin, too many questions," the voice chides him. "I will see you in a few days. I will find you."

Kevin shakes his head in awe. "I...don't believe it...."

"How is your sister who is *not* your sister anymore? I have the magazine with me now. Congratulations," the other voice continues, benevolently.

Kevin guffaws. "She is fine. Thank you. We *do* have a lot of catching up to do."

"Till then. It is good to know you're safe and happy. Got to go."

"Okay."

The phone line goes dead, and he stands in the living room staring at the snowflakes dust against the bay windows. His mind fills with questions and streaks of hope. That part of him that ached for a loss so great throbs in a new way. When Kevin returns to bed, Kenzi is awake. "Who was it?" she whispers as she snuggles into his arms.

"Ssaka." Kevin cannot wipe the smile off his face. "And he found Ameena."

END

About the Author

Lucie Chihandae is a writer, an award-winning podcaster, and co-founder of the media company 2Sistars Media, LLC.

Having started writing at the age of nine, Lucie, throughout her career, has worked in various media, as a writer, radio host and journalist, where she honed her storytelling skills.

She has dabbled in poetry, novels and short story, writing young adult fiction, horror, romance, and fantasy genres.

She is also the author of her debut adult saga *The World Is Ours*, which is a work that combines the romance, saga, and adventure genres.

At the heart of Lucie is storytelling, which she indulges in, given any form of media, because she believes life is one giant storybook waiting to be written.

She lives in Maryland, in the United States, where she hosts a literary podcast exploring the lives and works of Black and African authors.

You can connect with me on:

- https://www.chihandae.com
- https://www.facebook.com/TheWorldisOursLC
- https://www.goodreads.com/lchihandae